THE CAXTON LIBRARY
of the World's Greatest Literature

SELECTED NOVELS OF

HENRY JAMES

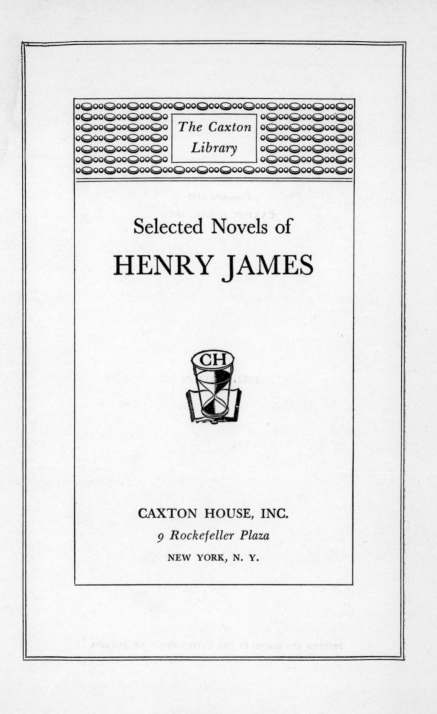

The Caxton Library

Selected Novels of
HENRY JAMES

CAXTON HOUSE, INC.

9 Rockefeller Plaza

NEW YORK, N. Y.

Contents

Contents

HENRY JAMES

(1843-1916)

THE MIGRATORY CHILDHOOD of Henry and William James was the result of their father's attempt to keep them from taking premature root. He succeeded perhaps too well with Henry, for the latter remained rootless all his days. Even though he permanently settled in England in 1875, he became, as he confessed to Hamlin Garland a quarter of a century afterward, "a man who is neither American nor European." In 1915, unhappy over America's neutrality,* he severed the last formal tie binding him to the country of his birth, and adopted British citizenship. His death in 1916 left the matter of his preferences as to nationality still inconclusive. He directed that after cremation his ashes be taken to Mount Auburn Cemetery in Cambridge, Massachusetts.

James's life was self-dedicated to the ideal of artistry. Any but its intellectual events are unimportant. There is, it may be, an exception to this last generalization: James, in early youth, sustained an "obscure hurt" which kept him out of the Civil War, and which, it was rumored, kept him from marrying. It is unfortunate for the Freudians that Frank Harris never quite got around to asking him the question direct.

Much has been made of the "problem of Henry James," since it is so fundamentally the problem of the American writer. Alfred Kazin, one of the best of the younger critics, has summed up for the defense. Perhaps, he writes, the only problem for the American writer to solve is how to be himself "and thus find a more deeply human and perceptive self to be." But some thoroughly intelligent critics—Parrington and Van Wyck Brooks lead the list—have assailed James for his desertion of America.

* Edna Kenton has, however, conjectured "that if the Great War had not made simple trips from Rye (where, from 1897 on, James had established his residence) to London highly irritating, James would never have surrendered his American citizenship."

vii

James, however, had his reasons. American life, he affirmed was "provincial and uninteresting." He held that "it takes an old civilization to set a novelist in motion—a proposition that seems to me so true as to be a truism. It is on manners, customs, usages, habits, forms, upon all of these things matured and established, that a novelist lives—they are the very stuff his work is made of. . . ." At any rate, they are the stuff of which James's work was made. His rationalization is hardly a sufficient statement applied to Twain, or Melville, or even his own favorite, Hawthorne. Eventually James regretted his decision to abandon America. In 1900 he told Hamlin Garland: "If I were to live my live over again I would be an American. I would steep myself in America. I would know no other land. . . . The mixture of Europe and America which you see in me has proved disastrous."

To explore the variations of a cosmopolitan theme in such fashion that his own nationality could not be determined from internal evidence was his dominating ambition. Why did he emphasize the international contrast? Because, it struck him, there existed "no possibility of contrast in the human lot so great as that encountered as we turn back and forth between the distinctively American and the distinctively European outlook." And why choose "the greater extravagance when the less would serve"? Because it was the "course of greater amusement"—the difficult intrigued James above all else (and finally, he admitted, became his only interest).

Here are collected four of the "international novels," all of them difficult to procure. They exhibit representatively James's early work in the field of his special interest. In them, James pretty well exhausts the possibilities of the bicontinental contrast. We have portrayed Americans in Europe, Europeans in America, and Americans and Europeans both at home and abroad.

The texts employed are those of the original editions, rather those of the revised New York edition which James undertook in 1905. This procedure has seemed advisable because, though James's later style is beautifully wrought and of a surpassing subtlety, its superimposition upon a novel conceived along essentially simple lines, sets up a faintly absurd stylistic antimony. Rebecca West holds that in several novels (notably *Daisy Miller*), the revision amounted to their ruin. Our objection is not William James's, who complained of the "complication of innuendo and associative reference" of his brother's later style. But we do believe that these novels, at any rate, are crafts too slight to be freighted with the ponderous paraphernalia of their maker's perceptivity, to say nothing of his punctuation.

The American was begun in Paris in the winter of 1875-1876, and printed serially in the *Atlantic Monthly* from June, 1876 to May, 1877, in which latter year it was published in book form by James R. Osgood and Company of Boston. James's recount of the genesis of *The American* is instructive, both for the light it sheds on his methods of composition and as an instance of his developed style:

It had come to me this happy, halting view of the interesting case some years before: I recall sharply the felicity of the first glimpse, though I forget the accident of thought that produced it—I recall that I was seated in an American "horse-car" when I found myself, of a sudden, considering with enthusiasm, as the theme of a "story", the situation in another country and an aristocratic society, of some robust but insidiously beguiled and betrayed, some cruelly wronged, compatriot: the point being that he should suffer at the hands of persons pretending to represent the highest possible civilsation and to be of an order in every way superior to his own. What would he "do" in that predicament, how would he right himself, or how, failing a remedy, would he conduct himself under his wrong.

James, some thirty years after the conception of *The American,* wrote that the "outrage" against his hero, Newman was performed in a "manner more showy than sound"; that, in reality, the Belle-gardes would have accepted Newman and adjusted their pretensions. Accordingly, he termed *The American* a "romance," since the generic quality of romance, what distinguishes it from realism, is the free play of fancy disengaged from fact. But, though romantic, he considered it "consistently, consummately—and I would really make bold to say charmingly—romantic."

The Europeans appeared in the *Atlantic Monthly* from July to October of 1878 and was published by Macmillan and Co. of London in the same year. It was, unfortunately, excluded from the canonical New York Edition—unfortunately, because it is plainly a companion-piece to *The Americans.* One of James's prefaces, which illumine his methods and purposes, would be eminently welcome. It is patent that he wished to examine the obverse of the social situation which was the real theme of *The American.* But his attitudes toward his characters remains dubious. Mr. Wentworth, who treats his European visitors as if he regarded their entertainment as an extension of duty,—is he admired as an exemplar of the cultured and controlled New Englander, or satirized as a specimen of the dehydrated Puritan? Similarly—is Felix merely a light-weight intellect or a clever and charming young man? The portraiture lacks firmness and consistency; perhaps, as Thomas H. Higginson alleged, because James was a stranger in his own country and unsure. Moreover, C. H. Grattan points out, there is a certain thinness about the novel. Yet, he further reminds us, "comedy is the medium and great depth would be an impertinence." That cues the reader; for read not as social analysis, but as high comedy involving the clash of contrary types, the novel succeeds.

An anecdote frequently supplied the germ of a subsequent James novel. His interest, though, centered only on that fraction of it which was grist, and he must have maddened his friends by interrupting before the point of the story could be realized: too much, he was afraid, might influence his approach. A young lady, vaguely prototypical of Daisy Miller, was casually described to James. He pencilled a notation which enjoined him to "Dramatise, dramatise!" He heeded the injunction, and submitted the novel to a magazine in Philadelphia. The editor returned it without comment, a circumstance James thought "rather grim." He learned that the "Philadelphian critic" had taken his "study" (as it was subtitled) for an attack on sacrosanct American girlhood. The editor of *Cornhill Magazine*, apparently not as reverent of American girlhood, accepted *Daisy Miller*. It appeared in the June-July issues of 1878, and was published by Harper & Brothers of New York the next year. James insisted that Daisy was meant "to no degree whatever in critical but, quite inordinately and extravagantly, in poetical terms." He was amazed to discover that she was considered—and actually was—a typical figure, though of a somewhat different social level.

The virulence of the attacks on *Daisy Miller*, the "most prosperous child" of his invention, moved James to extend his analysis by changing the locus of his observation. *An International Episode* followed *Daisy Miller* in the *Cornhill Magazine* and was put out by Harper & Brothers in 1879. Bessie Alden's behavior, and its direct and implied criticism of the English nobility, was resented by English readers quite as Daisy Miller's unreflecting behavior, which allegedly reflected on American girlhood, was resented by Daisy's compatriots. James wrote his mother from England: "It seems to me myself that I have been very delicate; but I shall keep off dangerous ground in the future. It is an entirely new sensation for them (the people here) to be (at all delicately) ironized or satirized, from the American point of view." The Preface is not explicit as to his motivation in writing *An International Episode*, but it may be conjectured from the circumstances preceding the writing. First, there was the rudeness of the London social leaders, concerning which James complained in several conversations. Second, there was the irritating acceptance on their part that the eastward movement of young American ladies was matrimonial in purpose. Incidentally, the switch from direct exposition—here as in *Daisy Miller*—is noteworthy. It enables James to express a succinct viewpoint without personal involvement.

Not long ago most critics agreed that James was "feathers" (Whitman's term). And most historians of American Literature discussed him as if they were not really sure that he fell within their scope. The balance has been righted. In fact, overcompensation is the danger now. Philip Rahv states quite confidently that James "is generally regarded by discriminating critics as America's greatest novelist and a master of modern prose belonging in the company of Proust and Joyce." Edmund Wilson agrees as to the nature of the company: "His work is incomplete as his experience was; but it is in no respect second rate, and he can be judged only in the company of the very greatest." T. S. Eliot, whose expatriate career gives him a special insight relative to James, affirms that as a creative critic of living beings "no novelist in our language can approach James." And William Troy, analyzing the cause of the James Renaissance, declares: "At a moment when loss of continuity is our gravest threat, when personality is everywhere at a discount, when all consequent values dissolve in the general terror, it is probably no great wonder that more and more people are turning to Henry James."

ARTHUR ZEIGER

THE AMERICAN

CHAPTER I

ON A brilliant day in May, in the year 1868, a gentleman was reclining at his ease on the great circular divan which at that period occupied the centre of the Salon Carré, in the Museum of the Louvre. This commodious ottoman has since been removed, to the extreme regret of all weak-kneed lovers of the fine arts, but the gentleman in question had taken serene possession of its softest spot, and, with his head thrown back and his legs outstretched, was staring at Murillo's beautiful moon-borne Madonna in profound enjoyment of his posture. He had removed his hat, and flung down beside him a little red guide-book and an opera-glass. The day was warm; he was heated with walking, and he repeatedly passed his handkerchief over his forehead, with a somewhat wearied gesture. And yet he was evidently not a man to whom fatigue was familiar; long, lean, and muscular, he suggested the sort of vigor that is commonly known as "toughness." But his exertions on this particular day had been of an unwonted sort, and he had performed great physical feats which left him less jaded than his tranquil stroll through the Louvre. He had looked out all the pictures to which an asterisk was affixed in those formidable pages of fine print in his Bädeker; his attention had been strained and his eyes dazzled, and he had sat down with an æsthetic headache. He had looked, moreover, not only at all the pictures, but at all the copies that were going forward around them, in the hands of those innumerable young women in irreproachable toilets who devote themselves, in France, to the propagation of masterpieces, and if the truth must be told, he had often admired the copy much more than the original. His physiognomy would have sufficiently indicated that he was a shrewd and capable fellow, and in truth he had often sat up all night over a bristling bundle of accounts, and heard the cock crow without a yawn. But Raphael and Titian and Rubens were a new kind of arithmetic, and they inspired our friend, for the first time in his life, with a vague self-mistrust.

An observer with anything of an eye for national types would have had no difficulty in determining the local origin of this undeveloped connoisseur, and indeed such an observer might have felt a certain humorous relish of the almost ideal completeness with which he filled out the national mould. The gentleman on the divan was a powerful specimen of an American. But he was not only a fine American; he was in the first place, physically, a fine man. He appeared to possess that kind of health and strength which, when found in perfection, are the most impressive—the physical capital which the owner does nothing to "keep up." If he was a muscular Christian, it was quite without knowing it. If it was necessary to walk to a remote spot, he walked, but he had never known himself to "exercise." He had no theory with regard to cold bathing or the use of Indian clubs; he was neither an oarsman, a rifleman, nor a fencer—he had never had time for these amusements—and he was quite unaware that the saddle is recommended for certain forms of indigestion. He was by inclination a temperate man; but he had supped the night before his visit to the Louvre at the Café Anglais —some one had told him it was an experience not to be omitted—and he had slept none the less the sleep of the just. His usual attitude and carriage were of a rather relaxed and lounging kind, but when, under a special inspiration, he straightened himself, he looked like a grenadier on parade. He never smoked. He had been assured—such things are said—that cigars were excellent for the health, and he was quite capable of believing it; but he knew as little about tobacco as about homœopathy. He had a very well-formed head, with a shapely, symmetrical balance of the frontal and the occipital development, and a good deal of straight, rather dry brown hair. His complexion was brown, and his nose had a bold, well-marked arch. His eye was of a clear, cold gray, and save for a rather abundant mustache he was clean-shaved. He had the flat jaw and sinewy neck which are frequent in the American type; but the traces of national origin are a matter of expression even more than of feature, and it was in this respect that our friend's countenance was supremely eloquent. The discriminating observer we have been supposing might, however, perfectly have measured its expressiveness, and yet have been at a loss to describe it. It had that typical vagueness which is not vacuity, that blankness which is not simplicity, that look of being committed to nothing in particular, of standing in an attitude of general hospitality to the chances of life, of being very much at one's own disposal, so characteristic of many American faces. It was our friend's eye that chiefly told his story; an eye in which innocence and experience were singularly blended. It was full of contradictory suggestions, and though it was by no means the glowing orb of a hero of romance, you could find in it almost anything you looked for. Frigid and yet friendly, frank yet cautious, shrewd yet credulous, positive yet skeptical, confident yet shy, extremely intelligent and extremely good-humored, there was something vaguely defiant in its concessions, and something profoundly reassuring in its reserve. The cut of this gentleman's mustache, with the two premature wrinkles in the cheek above it, and the fashion of his garments, in which an exposed shirt-front and a cerulean cravat played perhaps an obtrusive part, completed the conditions of his identity. We have approached him, perhaps, at a not especially favorable moment; he is by no means sitting for his portrait. But listless as he lounges there, rather baffled on the æsthetic question, and guilty of the damning fault (as we have lately discovered it to be) of confounding the merit of the artist with that of his work (for he admires the squinting Madonna of the young lady with the boyish coiffure, because he thinks the young lady herself uncommonly taking), he is a sufficiently promising acquaintance. Decision, salubrity, jocosity, prosperity, seem to hover within his call; he is evidently a practical man, but the idea, in his case, has undefined and mysterious boundaries, which invite the imagination to bestir itself on his behalf.

As the little copyist proceeded with her work, she sent every now and then a responsive glance toward her admirer. The cultivation of the fine arts appeared to necessitate, to her mind, a great deal of by-play, a great standing off with folded arms and head drooping from side to side, stroking of a dimpled chin with a dimpled hand, sighing and frowning and patting of the foot, fumbling in disordered tresses for wandering hair-pins. These performances were accompanied by a restless glance, which lingered longer than elsewhere upon the gentleman we have described. At last he rose abruptly, put on his hat, and approached the young lady. He placed himself before her picture and looked at it for some moments, during which she pretended to be quite unconscious of his inspection. Then, addressing her with the single word which constituted the strength of his French vocabulary, and holding up one finger in a manner which appeared to him to illuminate his meaning, "*Combien?*" he abruptly demanded.

The artist stared a moment, gave a little pout, shrugged her shoulders, put down her palette and brushes, and stood rubbing her hands.

"How much?" said our friend, in English. "Combien?"

"Monsieur wishes to buy it?" asked the young lady in French.

"Very pretty, *splendide*. Combien?" repeated the American.

"It pleases monsieur, my little picture? It's a very beautiful subject," said the young lady.

"The Madonna, yes; I am not a Catholic, but I want to buy it. Combien? Write it here." And he took a pencil from his pocket and showed her the fly-leaf of his guide-book. She stood looking at him and scratching her chin with the pencil. "Is it not for sale?" he asked. And as she still stood reflecting, and looking at him with an eye which, in spite of her desire to treat this avidity of patronage as a very old story, betrayed an almost touching incredulity, he was afraid he had offended her. She simply trying to look indifferent, and wondering how far she might go. "I haven't made a mistake—*pas insulté*, no?" her interlocutor continued. "Don't you understand a little English?"

The young lady's aptitude for playing a part at short notice was remarkable. She fixed him with her conscious, perceptive eye and asked him if he spoke no French. Then, "*Donnez!*" she said briefly, and took the open guide-book. In the upper corner of the fly-leaf she traced a number, in a minute and extremely neat hand. Then she handed back the book and took up her palette again.

Our friend read the number: "2,000 francs." He said nothing for a time, but stood looking at the picture, while the copyist began actively to dabble with her paint. "For a copy, isn't that a good deal?" he asked at last. "*Pas beaucoup?*"

The young lady raised her eyes from her palette, scanned him from head to foot, and alighted with admirable sagacity upon exactly the right answer. "Yes, it's a good deal. But my copy has remarkable qualities, it is worth nothing less."

The gentleman in whom we are interested understood no French, but I have said he was intelligent, and here is a good chance to prove it. He apprehended, by a natural instinct, the meaning of the young woman's phrase, and it gratified him to think that she was so honest. Beauty, talent, virtue; she combined everything! "But you must finish it," he said. "*Finish*, you know;" and he pointed to the unpainted hand of the figure.

"Oh, it shall be finished in perfection; in the perfection of perfections!" cried mademoiselle; and to confirm her promise, she deposited a rosy blotch in the middle of the Madonna's cheek.

But the American frowned. "Ah, too red, too red!" he rejoined. "Her complexion," pointing to the Murillo, "is more delicate."

"Delicate? Oh, it shall be delicate, monsieur; delicate as Sèvres *biscuit.* I am going to tone that down; I know all the secrets of my art. And where will you allow us to send it to you? Your address?"

"My address? Oh yes!" And the gentleman drew a card from his pocket-book and wrote something upon it. Then hesitating a moment he said, "If I don't like it when it is finished, you know, I shall not be obliged to take it."

The young lady seemed as good a guesser as himself. "Oh, I am very sure that monsieur is not capricious," she said with a roguish smile.

"Capricious?" And at this monsieur began to laugh. "Oh no, I'm not capricious. I am very faithful. I am very constant. *Comprenez?*"

"Monsieur is constant; I understand perfectly. It's a rare virtue. To recompense you, you shall have your picture on the first possible day; next week—as soon as it is dry. I will take the card of monsieur." And she took it and read his name: "Christopher Newman." Then she tried to repeat it aloud, and laughed at her bad accent. "Your English names are so droll!"

"Droll?" said Mr. Newman, laughing too. "Did you ever hear of Christopher Columbus?"

"*Bien sûr!* He invented America; a very great man. And is he your patron?"

"My patron?"

"Your patron-saint, in the calendar."

"Oh, exactly; my parents named me for him."

"Monsieur is American?"

"Don't you see it?" monsieur inquired.

"And you mean to carry my little picture away over there?" and she explained her phrase with a gesture.

"Oh, I mean to buy a great many pictures—*beaucoup, beaucoup,*" said Christopher Newman.

"The honor is not less for me," the young lady answered, "for I am sure monsieur has a great deal of taste."

"But you must give me your card," Newman said; "your card, you know."

The young lady looked severe for an instant, and then said, "My father will wait upon you."

But this time Mr. Newman's powers of divination were at fault. "Your card, your address," he simply repeated.

"My address?" said mademoiselle. Then with a little shrug, "Happily for you, you are an American! It is the first time I ever gave my card to a gentleman." And, taking from her pocket a rather greasy porte-monnaie, she extracted from it a small glazed visiting card, and presented the latter to her patron. It was neatly inscribed in pencil, with a great many flourishes, "Mlle. Noémie Nioche." But Mr. Newman, unlike his companion, read the name with perfect gravity; all French names to him were equally droll.

"And precisely, here is my father, who has come to escort me home," said Mademoiselle Noémie. "He speaks English. He will arrange with you." And she turned to welcome a little old gentleman who came shuffling up, peering over his spectacles at Newman.

M. Nioche wore a glossy wig, of an unnatural color which overhung his little meek, white, vacant face and left it hardly more expressive than the unfeatured block upon which these articles are displayed in the barber's window. He was an exquisite image of shabby gentility. His scant ill-made coat, desperately brushed, his darned gloves, his highly polished boots, his rusty, shapely hat, told the story of a person who had "had losses" and who clung to the spirit of nice habits even though the letter had been hopelessly effaced. Among other things M. Nioche had lost courage. Adversity had not only ruined him, it had frightened him, and he was evidently going through his remnant of life on tiptoe, for fear of waking up the hostile fates. If this strange gentleman was saying anything improper to his daughter, M. Nioche would entreat him huskily, as a particular favor, to forbear; but he would admit at the same time that he was very presumptious to ask for particular favors.

"Monsieur has bought my picture," said Mademoiselle Noémie. "When it's finished you'll carry it to him in a cab."

"In a cab!' cried M. Nioche; and he stared, in a bewildered way, as if he had seen the sun rising at midnight.

"Are you the young lady's father?" said Newman. "I think she said you speak English."

"Speak English—yes," said the old man slowly rubbing his hands. "I will bring it in a cab."

"Say something, then," cried his daughter. "Thank him a little—not too much."

"A little, my daughter, a little?" said M. Nioche perplexed. "How much?"

"Two thousand!" said Mademoiselle Noémie. "Don't make a fuss or he'll take back his word."

"Two thousand!" cried the old man, and he began to fumble for his snuff-box. He looked at Newman from head to foot; he looked at his daughter and then at the picture. "Take care you don't spoil it!" he cried almost sublimely.

"We must go home," said Mademoiselle Noémie. "This is a good day's work. Take care how you carry it!" And she began to put up her utensils.

"How can I thank you?" said M. Noiche. "My English does not suffice."

"I wish I spoke French as well," said Newman, good-naturedly. "Your daughter is very clever."

"Oh, sir!" and M. Nioche looked over his spectacles with tearful eyes and nodded several times with a world of sadness. "She has had an education—*tres-supérieure!* Nothing was spared. Lessons in pastel at ten francs the lesson, lessons in oil at twelve francs. I didn't look at the francs then. She's an *artiste*, ah!"

"Do I understand you to say that you have had reverses?" asked Newman.

"Reverses? Oh, sir, misfortunes—terrible."

"Unsuccessful in business, eh?"

"Very unsuccessful, sir."

"Oh, never fear, you'll get on your legs again," said Newman cheerily.

The old man drooped his head on one side and looked at him with an expression of pain, as if this were an unfeeling jest.

"What does he say? demanded Mademoiselle Noémie.

M. Nioche took a pinch of snuff. "He says I will make my fortune again."

"Perhaps he will help you. And what else?"

"He says thou art very clever."

"It is very possible. You believe it yourself, my father?"

"Believe it, my daughter? With this evidence!" And the old man turned afresh, with a staring, wondering homage, to the audacious daub on the easel.

"Ask him, then, if he would not like to learn French."

"To learn French?"

"To take lessons."

"To take lessons, my daughter? From thee?"

"From you!"

"From me, my child? How should I give lessons?"

"*Pas de raisons!* Ask him immediately!" said Mademoiselle Noémie, with soft brevity.

M. Nioche stood aghast, but under his daughter's eye he collected his wits, and, doing his best to assume an agreeable smile, he executed her commands. "Would it please you to receive instruction in our beautiful language?" he inquired, with an appealing quaver.

"To study French?" asked Newman, staring.

M. Nioche pressed his finger-tips together and slowly raised his shoulders. "A little conversation!"

"Conversation—that's it!" murmured Mademoiselle Noémie, who had caught the word. "The conversation of the best society."

"Our French conversation is famous, you know," M. Nioche ventured to continue. "It's a great talent."

"But isn't it awfully difficult?" asked Newman, very simply.

"Not to a man of *esprit*, like monsieur, an admirer of beauty in every form!" and M. Nioche cast a significant glance at his daughter's Madonna.

"I can't fancy myself chattering French!" said Newman with a laugh. "And yet, I suppose that the more a man knows the better."

"Monsieur expresses that very happily. *Hélas, oui!*"

"I suppose it would help me a great deal, knocking about Paris, to know the language."

"Ah, there are so many things monsieur must want to say: difficult things!"

"Everything I want to say is difficult. But you give lessons?"

Poor M. Nioche was embarrassed; he smiled more appealingly. "I am not a regular professor," he admitted. "I can't nevertheless tell him that I'm a professor," he said to his daughter.

"Tell him it's a very exceptional chance," answered Mademoiselle Noémie; "an *homme du monde*—one gentleman conversing with another! Remember what you are—what you have been!"

"A teacher of languages in neither case! Much more formerly and much less to-day! And if he asks the price of the lessons?"

"He won't ask it," said Mademoiselle Noémie.

"What he pleases, I may say?"

"Never! That's bad style."

"If he asks, then?"

Mademoiselle Noémie had put on her bonnet and was tying the ribbons. She smoothed them out, with her soft little chin thrust forward. "Ten francs," she said quickly.

"Oh, my daughter! I shall never dare."

"Don't dare, then! He won't ask till the end of the lessons, and then I will make out the bill."

M. Nioche turned to the confiding foreigner again, and stood rubbing his hands, with an air of seeming to plead guilty which was not intenser only because it was habitually so striking. It never occurred to Newman to ask him for a guarantee of his skill in imparting instruction; he supposed of course M. Nioche knew his own language, and his appealing forlornness was quite the perfection of what the American, for vague reasons, had always associated with all elderly foreigners of the lesson-giving class. Newman had never reflected upon philological processes. His chief impression with regard to ascertaining those mysterious correlatives of his familiar English vocables which were current in this extraordinary city of Paris was, that it was simply a matter of a good deal of unwonted and rather ridiculous muscular effort on his own part. "How did you learn English?" he asked of the old man.

"When I was young, before my miseries. Oh, I was wide awake, then. My father was a great *commerçant;* he placed me for a year in a counting-house in England. Some of it stuck to me; but I have forgotten!"

"How much French can I learn in a month?"

"What does he say?" asked Mademoiselle Noémie.

M. Nioche explained.

"He will speak like an angel!" said his daughter.

But the native integrity which had been vainly exerted to secure M. Nioche's commercial prosperity flickered up again. "*Dame,* monsieur!" he answered. "All I can teach you!" And then, recovering himself at a sign from his daughter, "I will wait upon you at your hotel."

"Oh yes, I should like to learn French," Newman went on, with democratic confidingness. "Hang me if I should ever have thought of it! I took for granted it was impossible. But if you learned my language, why shouldn't I learn yours?" and his frank, friendly laugh drew the sting from the jest. "Only, if we are going to converse, you know, you must think of something cheerful to converse about."

"You are very good, sir; I am overcome!" said M. Nioche, throwing out his hands. "But you have cheerfulness and happiness for two!"

"Oh no," said Newman more seriously. "You must be bright and lively; that's part of the bargain."

M. Nioche bowed, with his hand on his heart. "Very well, sir; you have already made me lively."

"Come and bring me my picture then; I will pay you for it, and we will talk about that. That will be a cheerful subject!"

Mademoiselle Noémie had collected her accessories, and she gave the precious Madonna in charge to her father, who retreated backwards out of sight, holding it at arm's-length and reiterating his obeisance. The young lady gathered her shawl about her like a perfect Parisienne, and it was with the smile of a Parisienne that she took leave of her patron.

Chapter II

HE WANDERED back to the divan and seated himself on the other side, in view of the great canvas on which Paul Veronese had depicted the marriage-feast of Cana. Wearied as he was he found the picture entertaining; it had an illusion for him; it satisfied his conception, which was ambitious, of what a splendid banquet should be. In the left-hand corner of the picture is a young woman with yellow tresses confined in a golden head-dress; she is bending forward and listening, with the smile of a charming woman at a dinner-party, to her neighbor. Newman detected her in the crowd, admired her, and perceived that she too had her votive copyist—a young man with his hair standing on end. Suddenly he became conscious of the germ of the mania of the "collector;" he had taken the first step; why should he not go on? It was only twenty minutes before that he had bought the first picture of his life, and now he was already thinking of art-patronage as a fascinating pursuit. His reflections quickened his good-humor, and he was on the point of approaching the young man with another "*Combien?*" Two or three facts in this relation are noticeable, although the logical chain which connects them may seem imperfect. He knew Mademoiselle Nioche had asked too much; he bore her no grudge for doing so, and he was determined to pay the young man exactly the proper sum. At this moment, however, his attention was attracted by a gentleman who had come from another part of the room and whose manner was that of a stranger to the gallery, although he was equipped with neither guide-book nor opera-glass. He carried a white sun-umbrella, lined with blue silk, and he strolled in front of the Paul Veronese, vaguely looking at it, but much too near to see anything but the grain of the canvas. Opposite to Christopher Newman he paused and turned, and then our friend, who had been observing him, had a chance to verify a suspicion aroused by an imperfect view of his face. The result of this larger scrutiny was that he presently sprang to his feet, strode across the room, and, with an outstretched hand, arrested the gentleman with the blue-lined umbrella. The latter stared, but put out his hand at a venture. He was corpulent and rosy, and though his countenance, which was ornamented with a beautiful flaxen beard, carefully divided in the middle and brushed outward at the sides, was not remarkable for intensity of expression, he looked like a person who would willingly shake hands with any one. I know not what Newman thought of his face, but he found a want of response in his grasp.

"Oh, come, come," he said, laughing; "don't say, now, you don't know me—if I have *not* got a white parasol!"

The sound of his voice quickened the other's memory, his face expanded to its fullest capacity, and he also broke into a laugh. "Why, Newman—I'll be blowed! Where in the world—I declare—who would have thought? You know you have changed."

"You haven't!" said Newman.

"Not for the better, no doubt. When did you get here?"

"Three days ago."

"Why didn't you let me know?"

"I had no idea *you* were here."

"I have been here these six years."

"It must be eight or nine since we met."

"Something of that sort. We were very young."

"It was in St. Louis, during the war. You were in the army."

"Oh no, not I! But you were."

"I believe I was."

"You came out all right?"

"I came out with my legs and arms—and with satisfaction. All that seems very far away."

"And how long have you been in Europe?"

"Seventeen days."

"First time?"

"Yes, very much so."

"Made your everlasting fortune?"

Christopher Newman was silent a moment, and then with a tranquil smile he answered, "Yes."

"And come to Paris to spend it, eh?"

"Well, we shall see. So they carry those parasols here—the men-folk?"

"Of course they do. They're great things. They understand comfort out here."

"Where do you buy them?"

"Anywhere, everywhere."

"Well, Tristram, I'm glad to get hold of you. You can show me the ropes. I suppose you know Paris inside out."

Mr. Tristram gave a mellow smile of self-gratulation. "Well, I guess there are not many men that can show me much. I'll take care of you."

"It's a pity you were not here a few minutes ago. I have just bought a picture. You might have put the thing through for me."

"Bought a picture?" said Mr. Tristram, looking vaguely round at the walls. "Why, do they sell them?"

"I mean a copy."

"Oh, I see. These," said Mr. Tristram, nodding at the Titians and Vandykes, "these, I suppose, are originals."

"I hope so," cried Newman. "I don't want a copy of a copy."

"Ah," said Mr. Tristram, mysteriously, "you can never tell. They imitate, you know, so deucedly well. It's like the jewelers, with their false stones. Go into the Palais Royal, there; you see 'Imitation' on half the windows. The law obliges them to stick it on, you know; but you can't tell the things apart. To tell the truth," Mr. Tristram continued, with a wry face, "I don't do much in pictures. I leave that to my wife."

"Ah, you have got a wife?"

"Didn't I mention it? She's a very nice woman; you must know her. She's up there in the Avenue d'Iéna."

"So you are regularly fixed—house and children and all."

"Yes, a tip-top house and a couple of youngsters."

"Well," said Christopher Newman, stretching his arms a little, with a sigh, "I envy you."

"Oh no! you don't!" answered Mr. Tristram, giving him a little poke with his parasol!

"I beg your pardon; I do!"

"Well, you won't, then, when—when—"

"You don't certainly mean when I have seen your establishment?"

"When you have seen Paris, my boy. You want to be your own master here."

"Oh, I have been my own master all my life, and I'm tired of it."

"Well, try Paris. How old are you?"

"Thirty-six."

"*C'est le bel âge*, as they say here."

"What does that mean?"

"It means that a man shouldn't send away his plate till he has eaten his fill."

"All that? I have just made arrangements to take French lessons."

"Oh, you don't want any lessons. You'll pick it up. I never took any."

"I suppose you speak French as well as English?"

"Better!" said Mr. Tristram, roundly. "It's a splendid language. You can say all sorts of bright things in it."

"But I suppose," said Christopher Newman, with an earnest desire for information, "that you must be bright to begin with."

"Not a bit; that's just the beauty of it."

The two friends, as they exchanged these remarks, had remained standing where they met, and leaning against the rail which protected the pictures. Mr. Tristram at last declared that he was overcome with fatigue and should be happy to sit down. Newman recommended in the highest terms the great divan on which he had been lounging, and they prepared to seat themselves. "This is a great place; isn't it?" said Newman, with ardor.

"Great place, great place. Finest thing in the world." And then, suddenly, Mr. Tristram hesitated and looked about him. "I suppose they won't let you smoke here."

Newman stared. "Smoke? I'm sure I don't know. You know the regulations better than I."

"I? I never was here before!"

"Never! in six years?"

"I believe my wife dragged me here once when we first came to Paris, but I never found my way back."

"But you say you know Paris so well!"

"I don't call this Paris!" cried Mr. Tristram, with assurance. "Come; let's go over to the Palais Royal and have a smoke."

"I don't smoke," said Newman.

"A drink, then."

And Mr. Tristram led his companion away. Then passed through the glorious halls of the Louvre, down the staircases, along the cool, dim galleries of sculpture, and out into the enormous court. Newman looked about him as he went, but he made no comments, and it was only when they at last emerged into the open air that he said to his friend, "It seems to me that in your place I should have come here once a week."

"Oh, no you wouldn't!" said Mr. Tristram. "You think so, but you wouldn't. You wouldn't have had time. You would always mean to go, but you never would go. There's better fun than that, here in Paris. Italy's the place to see pictures; wait till you get there. There you have to go; you can't do anything else. It's an awful country; you can't get a decent cigar. I don't know why I went in there, to-day; I was strolling along, rather hard up for amusement. I sort of noticed the Louvre as I passed, and I thought I would go in and see what was going on. But if I hadn't found you there I should have felt rather sold. Hang it, I don't care for pictures; I prefer the reality!" And Mr. Tristram tossed off this happy formula with an assurance which the numerous class of persons suffering from an overdose of "culture" might have envied him.

The two gentlemen proceeded along the Rue de Rivoli and into the Palais Royal, where they seated themselves at one of the little tables stationed at the door of the café which projects into the great open quadrangle. The place was filled with people, the fountains were spouting, a band was playing, clusters of chairs were gathered beneath all the lime-trees, and buxom, white-capped nurses, seated along the benches, were offering to their infant charges the amplest facilities for nutrition. There was an easy, homely gayety ir. the whole scene, and Christopher Newman felt that it was most characteristically Parisian.

"And now," began Mr. Tristram, when they had tested the decoction which he had caused to be served to them, "now just give an account of yourself. What are your ideas, what are your plans, where have you come from and where are you going? In the first place, where are you staying?"

"At the Grand Hotel," said Newman.

Mr. Tristram puckered his plump visage. "That won't do! You must change."

"Change?" demanded Newman. "Why, it's the finest hotel I ever was in."

"You don't want a 'fine' hotel; you want something small and quiet and elegant, where your bell is answered and you—your person is recognized."

"They keep running to see if I have rung before I have touched the bell," said Newman, "and as for my person, they are always bowing and scraping to it."

"I suppose you are always tipping them. That's very bad style."

"Always? By no means. A man brought me something yesterday, and then stood loafing about in a beggarly manner. I offered him a chair and asked him if he wouldn't sit down. Was that bad style?"

"Very!"

"But he bolted, instantly. At any rate, the place amuses me. Hang your elegance, if it bores me. I sat in the court of the Grand Hotel last night until two o'clock in the morning, watching the coming and going, and the people knocking about."

"You're easily pleased. But you can do as you choose—a man in your shoes. You have made a pile of money, eh?"

"I have made enough."

"Happy the man who can say that! Enough for what?"

"Enough to rest awhile, to forget the confounded thing, to look about me, to see the world, to have a good time, to improve my mind, and, if the fancy takes me, to marry a wife." Newman spoke slowly, with a certain dryness of accent and with frequent pauses. This was his habitual mode of utterance, but it was especially marked in the words I have just quoted.

"Jupiter! There's a programme!" cried Mr. Tristram. "Certainly, all that takes money, especially the wife; unless indeed she gives it, as mine did. And what's the story? How have you done it?"

Newman had pushed his hat back from his forehead, folded his arms, and stretched his legs. He listened to the music, he looked about him at the bustling crowd, at the plashing fountains, at the nurses and the babies. "I have worked!" he answered at last.

Tristram looked at him for some moments, and allowed his placid eyes to measure his friend's generous longitude and rest upon his comfortably contemplative face. "What have you worked at?" he asked.

"Oh, at several things."

"I suppose you're a smart fellow, eh?"

Newman continued to look at the nurses and babies; they imparted to the scene a kind of primordial, pastoral simplicity. "Yes," he said at last, "I suppose I am." And then, in answer to his companion's inquiries, he related briefly his history since their last meeting. It was an intensely Western story, and it dealt with enterprises which it will be needless to introduce to the reader in detail. Newman had come out of the war with a brevet of brigadier-general, an honor which in this case—without invidious comparisons—had lighted upon shoulders amply competent to bear it. But though he could manage a fight, when need was, Newman heartily disliked the business; his four years in the army had left him with an angry, bitter sense of the waste of precious things—life and time and money and "smartness" and the early freshness of purpose; and he had addressed himself to the pursuits of peace with passionate zest and energy. He was of course as penniless when he plucked off his shoulder-straps as when he put them on, and the only capital at his disposal was his dogged resolution and his lively perception of ends and means. Exertion and action were as natural to him as respiration; a more completely healthy mortal had never trod the elastic soil of the West. His experience, moreover, was as wide as his capacity; when he was fourteen years old, necessity had taken him by his slim young shoulders and pushed him into the street, to earn that night's supper. He had not earned it, but he had earned the next night's, and afterwards, whenever he had had none, it was because he had gone without it to use the money for something else, a keener pleasure or a finer profit. He had turned his hand, with his brain in it, to many things; he had been enterprising, in an eminent sense of the term; he had been adventurous and even reckless, and he had known bitter failure as well as brilliant success; but he was a born experimentalist, and he had always found something to enjoy in the pressure of necessity, even when it was as irritating as the haircloth shirt of the mediæval monk. At one time failure seemed inexorably his portion; ill-luck became his bed-fellow, and whatever he touched he turned, not to gold, but to ashes. His most vivid conception of a supernatural element in the world's affairs had come to him once when this pertinacity of misfortune was at its climax; there seemed to him something stronger in life than his own will. But the mysterious something could only be the devil, and he was accordingly seized with an intense personal enmity to this impertinent force. He had known what it was to have utterly exhausted his credit, to be unable to raise a dollar, and to find himself at nightfall in a strange city, without a penny to mitigate its strangeness. It was under these circumstances that he made his entrance into San Francisco, the scene, subsequently, of his happiest strokes of fortune. If he did not, like Dr. Franklin in Philadelphia, march along the street munching a penny-loaf, it was only because he had not the penny-loaf necessary to the performance. In his darkest days he had had but one simple, practical impulse—the desire, as he would have phrased it, to see the thing through. He did so at last, buffeted his way into smooth waters, and made money largely. It must be admitted, rather nakedly, that Christopher Newman's sole aim in life had been to make money; what he had been placed in the world for was, to his own perception, simply to wrest a fortune, the bigger the better, from defiant opportunity. This idea completely

filled his horizon and satisfied his imagination. Upon the uses of money, upon what one might do with a life into which one had succeeded in injecting the golden stream, he had up to his thirty-fifth year very scantily reflected. Life had been for him an open game, and he had played for high stakes. He had won at last and carried off his winnings; and now what was he to do with them? He was a man to whom, sooner or later, the question was sure to present itself, and the answer to it belongs to our story. A vague sense that more answers were possible than his philosophy had hitherto dreamt of had already taken possession of him, and it seemed softly and agreeably to deepen as he lounged in this brilliant corner of Paris with his friend.

"I must confess," he presently went on, "that here I don't feel at all smart. My remarkable talents seem of no use. I feel as simple as a little child, and a little child might take me by the hand and lead me about."

"Oh, I'll be your little child," said Tristram, jovially; "I'll take you by the hand. Trust yourself to me."

"I am a good worker," Newman continued, "but I rather think I am a poor loafer. I have come abroad to amuse myself, but I doubt whether I know how."

"Oh, that's easily learned."

"Well, I may perhaps learn it, but I am afraid I shall never do it by rote. I have the best will in the world about it, but my genius doesn't lie in that direction. As a loafer I shall never be original, as I take it that you are."

"Yes," said Tristram, "I suppose I am original; like all those immoral pictures in the Louvre."

"Besides," Newman continued, "I don't want to work at pleasure, any more than I played at work. I want to take it easily. I feel deliciously lazy, and I should like to spend six months as I am now, sitting under a tree and listening to a band. There's only one thing; I want to hear some good music."

"Music and pictures! Lord, what refined tastes! You are what my wife calls intellectual. I an't, a bit. But we can find something better for you to do than to sit under a tree. To begin with, you must come to the club."

"What club?"

"The Occidental. You will see all the Americans there; all the best of them, at least. Of course you play poker?"

"Oh, I say," cried Newman, with energy, "you are not going to

lock me up in a club and stick me down at a card-table! I haven't come all this way for that."

"What the deuce *have* you come for! You were glad enough to play poker in St. Louis, I recollect, when you cleaned me out."

"I have come to see Europe, to get the best out of it I can. I want to see all the great things, and do what the clever people do."

"The clever people? Much obliged. You set me down as a blockhead, then?"

Newman was sitting sidewise in his chair, with his elbow on the back and his head leaning on his hand. Without moving he looked a while at his companion with his dry, guarded, half-inscrutable, and yet altogether good-natured smile. "Introduce me to your wife!" he said at last.

Tristram bounced about in his chair. "Upon my word, I won't. She doesn't want any help to turn up her nose at me, nor do you, either!"

"I don't turn up my nose at you, my dear fellow; nor at any one, or anything. I'm not proud, I assure you I'm not proud. That's why I am willing to take example by the clever people."

"Well, if I'm not the rose, as they say here, I have lived near it. I can show you some clever people, too. Do you know General Packard? Do you know C. P. Hatch? Do you know Miss Kitty Upjohn?"

"I shall be happy to make their acquaintance; I want to cultivate society."

Tristram seemed restless and suspicious; he eyed his friend askance, and then, "What are you up to, any way?" he demanded. "Are you going to write a book?"

Christopher Newman twisted one end of his mustache a while, in silence, and at last he made answer. "One day, a couple of months ago, something very curious happened to me. I had come on to New York on some important business; it was rather a long story—a question of getting ahead of another party, in a certain particular way, in the stock-market. This other party had once played me a very mean trick. I owed him a grudge, I felt awfully savage at the time, and I vowed that, when I got a chance, I would, figuratively speaking, put his nose out of joint. There was a matter of some sixty thousand dollars at stake. If I put it out of his way, it was a blow the fellow would feel, and he really deserved no quarter. I jumped into a hack and went about my business, and it was in this hack—this immortal, historical hack—that the curious thing I speak of occurred.

It was a hack like any other, only a trifle dirtier, with a greasy line along the top of the drab cushions, as if it had been used for a great many Irish funerals. It is possible I took a nap; I had been traveling all night, and though I was excited with my errand, I felt the want of sleep. At all events I woke up suddenly, from a sleep or from a kind of a reverie, with the most extraordinary feeling in the world— a mortal disgust for the thing I was going to do. It came upon me like *that!*"—and he snapped his fingers—"as abruptly as an old wound that begins to ache. I couldn't tell the meaning of it; I only felt that I loathed the whole business and wanted to wash my hands of it. The idea of losing that sixty thousand dollars, of letting it utterly slide and scuttle and never hearing of it again, seemed the sweetest thing in the world. And all this took place quite independently of my will, and I sat watching it as if it were a play at the theatre. I could feel it going on inside of me. You may depend upon it that there are things going on inside of us that we understand mighty little about."

"Jupiter! you make my flesh creep!" cried Tristram. "And while you sat in your hack, watching the play, as you call it, the other man marched in and bagged your sixty thousand dollars?"

"I have not the least idea. I hope so, poor devil! but I never found out. We pulled up in front of the place I was going to in Wall Street, but I sat still in the carriage, and at last the driver scrambled down off his seat to see whether his carriage had not turned into a hearse. I couldn't have got out, any more than if I had been a corpse. What was the matter with me? Momentary idiocy, you'll say. What I wanted to get out of was Wall Street. I told the man to drive down to the Brooklyn ferry and to cross over. When we were over, I told him to drive me out into the country. As I had told him originally to drive for dear life down town, I suppose he thought me insane. Perhaps I was, but in that case I am insane still. I spent the morning looking at the first green leaves on Long Island. I was sick of business; I wanted to throw it all up and break off short; I had money enough, or if I hadn't I ought to have. I seemed to feel a new man inside my old skin, and I longed for a new world. When you want a thing so very badly you had better treat yourself to it. I didn't understand the matter, not in the least; but I gave the old horse the bridle and let him find his way. As soon as I could get out of the game I sailed for Europe. That is how I come to be sitting here."

"You ought to have bought up that hack," said Tristram; "it isn't a safe vehicle to have about. And you have really sold out, then; you have retired from business?"

"I have made over my hand to a friend; when I feel disposed, I can take up the cards again. I dare say that a twelvemonth hence the operation will be reversed. The pendulum will swing back again. I shall be sitting in a gondola or on a dromedary, and all of a sudden I shall want to clear out. But for the present I am perfectly free. I have even bargained that I am to receive no business letters."

"Oh, it's a real *caprice de prince*," said Tristram. "I back out; a poor devil like me can't help you to spend such very magnificent leisure as that. You should get introduced to the crowned heads."

Newman looked at him a moment, and then, with his easy smile, "How does one do it?" he asked.

"Come, I like that!" cried Tristram. "It shows you are in earnest."

"Of course I am in earnest. Didn't I say I wanted the best? I know the best can't be had for mere money, but I rather think money will do a good deal. In addition, I am willing to take a good deal of trouble."

"You are not bashful, eh?"

"I haven't the least idea. I want the biggest kind of entertainment a man can get. People, places, art, nature, everything! I want to see the tallest mountains, and the bluest lakes, and the finest pictures, and the handsomest churches, and the most celebrated men, and the most beautiful women."

"Settle down in Paris, then. There are no mountains that I know of, and the only lake is in the Bois du Boulogne, and not particularly blue. But there is everything else: plenty of pictures and churches, no end of celebrated men, and several beautiful women."

"But I can't settle down in Paris at this season, just as summer is coming on."

"Oh, for the summer go up to Trouville."

"What is Trouville?"

"The French Newport. Half the Americans go."

"It it anywhere near the Alps?"

"About as near as Newport is to the Rocky Mountains."

"Oh, I want to see Mont Blanc," said Newman, "and Amsterdam, and the Rhine, and a lot of places. Venice in particular. I have great ideas about Venice."

"Ah," said Mr. Tristram, rising, "I see I shall have to introduce you to **my** wife!"

Chapter III

He performed this ceremony on the following day, when, by appointment, Christopher Newman went to dine with him. Mr. and Mrs. Tristram lived behind one of those chalk-colored façades which decorate with their pompous sameness the broad avenues manufactured by Baron Haussmann in the neighborhood of the Arc de Triomphe. Their apartment was rich in the modern conveniences, and Tristram lost no time in calling his visitor's attention to their principal household treasures, the gas-lamps and the furnace-holes. "Whenever you feel homesick," he said, "you must come up here. We'll stick you down before a register, under a good big burner, and—"

"And you will soon get over your homesickness," said Mrs. Tristram.

Her husband stared; his wife often had a tone which he found inscrutable; he could not tell for his life whether she was in jest or in earnest. The truth is that circumstances had done much to cultivate in Mrs. Tristram a marked tendency to irony. Her taste on many points differed from that of her husband, and though she made frequent concessions it must be confessed that her concessions were not always graceful. They were founded upon a vague project she had of some day doing something very positive, something a trifle passionate. What she meant to do she could by no means have told you; but meanwhile, nevertheless, she was buying a good conscience, by installments.

It should be added, without delay, to anticipate misconception, that her little scheme of independence did not definitely involve the assistance of another person, of the opposite sex; she was not saving up virtue to cover the expenses of a flirtation. For this there were various reasons. To begin with, she had a very plain face and she was entirely without illusions as to her appearance. She had taken its measure to a hair's breadth, she knew the worst and the best, she had accepted herself. It had not been, indeed, without a struggle. As a young girl she had spent hours with her back to her mirror, crying her eyes out; and later she had from desperation and bravado adopted the habit of proclaiming herself the most ill-favored of women, in order that she might—as in common politeness was inevitable—be contradicted and reassured. It was since she had come to live in Europe that she had begun to take the matter philosophically. Her

observation, acutely exercised here, had suggested to her that a
woman's first duty is not to be beautiful, but to be pleasing, and she
encountered so many women who pleased without beauty that she
began to feel that she had discovered her mission. She had once
heard an enthusiastic musician, out of patience with a gifted bungler,
declare that a fine voice is really an obstacle to singing properly;
and it occurred to her that it might perhaps be equally true that a
beautiful face is an obstacle to the acquisition of charming manners.
Mrs. Tristram, then, undertook to be exquisitely agreeable, and she
brought to the task a really touching devotion. How well she would
have succeeded I am unable to say; unfortunately she broke off
in the middle. Her own excuse was the want of encouragement in
her immediate circle. But I am inclined to think that she had not a
real genius for the matter, or she would have pursued the charming
art for itself. The poor lady was very incomplete. She fell back upon
the harmonies of the toilet, which she thoroughly understood, and
contented herself with dressing in perfection. She lived in Paris,
which she pretended to detest, because it was only in Paris that
one could find things to exactly suit one's complexion. Besides out
of Paris it was always more or less of a trouble to get ten-button
gloves. When she railed at this serviceable city and you asked her
where she would prefer to reside, she returned some very unexpected
answer. She would say in Copenhagen, or in Barcelona; having, while
making the tour of Europe, spent a couple of days at each of these
places. On the whole, with her poetic furbelows and her misshapen,
intelligent little face, she was, when you knew her, a decidedly
interesting woman. She was naturally shy, and if she had been born
a beauty, she would (having no vanity) probably have remained
shy. Now, she was both diffident and importunate; extremely
reserved sometimes with her friends, and strangely expansive with
strangers. She despised her husband; despised him too much, for
she had been perfectly at liberty not to marry him. She had been
in love with a clever man who had slighted her, and she had married
a fool in the hope that this thankless wit, reflecting on it, would
conclude that she had no appreciation of merit, and that he had
flattered himself in supposing that she cared for his own. Restless,
discontented, visionary, without personal ambitions, but with a
certain avidity of imagination, she was, as I have said before,
eminently incomplete. She was full—both for good and for ill—of
beginnings that came to nothing; but she had nevertheless, morally,
a spark of the sacred fire.

Newman was fond, under all circumstances, of the society of women, and now that he was out of his native element and deprived of his habitual interests, he turned to it for compensation. He took a great fancy to Mrs. Tristram; she frankly repaid it, and after their first meeting he passed a great many hours in her drawing-room. After two or three talks they were fast friends. Newman's manner with women was peculiar, and it required some ingenuity on a lady's part to discover that he admired her. He had no gallantry, in the usual sense of the term; no compliments, no graces, no speeches. Very fond of what is called chaffing, in his dealings with men, he never found himself on a sofa beside a member of the softer sex without feeling extremely serious. He was not shy, and so far as awkwardness proceeds from a struggle with shyness, he was not awkward; grave, attentive, submissive, often silent, he was simply swimming in a sort of rapture of respect. This emotion was not at all theoretic, it was not even in a high degree sentimental; he had thought very little about the "position" of women, and he was not familiar either sympathetically or otherwise, with the image of a President in petticoats. His attitude was simply the flower of his general good-nature, and a part of his instinctive and genuinely democratic assumption of every one's right to lead an easy life. If a shaggy pauper had a right to bed and board and wages and a vote, women, of course, who were weaker than paupers, and whose physical tissue was in itself an appeal, should be maintained, sentimentally, at the public expense. Newman was willing to be taxed for this purpose, largely, in proportion to his means. Moreover, many of the common traditions with regard to women were with him fresh personal impressions; he had never read a novel! He had been struck with their acuteness, their subtlety, their tact, their felicity of judgment. They seemed to him exquisitely organized. If it is true that one must always have in one's work here below a religion, or at least an ideal, of some sort, Newman found his metaphysical inspiration in a vague acceptance of final responsibility to some illumined feminine brow.

He spent a great deal of time in listening to advice from Mrs. Tristram; advice, it must be added, for which he had never asked. He would have been incapable of asking for it, for he had no perception of difficulties, and consequently no curiosity about remedies. The complex Parisian world about him seemed a very simple affair; it was an immense, amazing spectacle, but it neither inflamed his imagination nor irritated his curiosity. He kept his hands in his pockets, looked on good-humoredly, desired to miss nothing important, observed a great many things narrowly, and never reverted to himself. Mrs. Tristram's "advice" was a part of the show, and a more entertaining element, in her abundant gossip, than the others. He enjoyed her talking about himself; it seemed a part of her beautiful ingenuity; but he never made an application of anything she said, or remembered it when he was away from her. For herself, she appropriated him; he was the most interesting thing she had had to think about in many a month. She wished to do something with him—she hardly knew what. There was so much of him; he was so rich and robust, so easy, friendly, well-disposed, that he kept her fancy constantly on the alert. For the present, the only thing she could do was to like him. She told him that he was "horribly Western," but in this compliment the adverb was tinged with insincerity. She led him about with her, introduced him to fifty people, and took extreme satisfaction in her conquest. Newman accepted every proposal, shook hands universally and promiscuously, and seemed equally unfamiliar with trepidation or with elation. Tom Tristram complained of his wife's avidity, and declared that he could never have a clear five minutes with his friend. If he had known how thing were going to turn out, he never would have brought him to the Avenue d'Iéna. The two men, formerly, had not been intimate, but Newman remembered his earlier impression of his host, and did Mrs. Tristram, who had by no means taken him into her confidence, but whose secret he presently discovered, the justice to admit that her husband was a rather degenerate mortal. At twenty-five he had been a good fellow, and in this respect he was unchanged; but of a man of his age one expected something more. People said he was sociable, but this was as much a matter of course as for a dipped sponge to expand; and it was not a high order of sociability. He was a great gossip and tattler, and to produce a laugh would hardly have spared the reputation of his aged mother. Newman had a kindness for old memories, but he found it impossible not to perceive that Tristram was nowadays a very light weight. His only aspirations were to hold out at poker, at his club, to know the names of all the *cocottes*, to shake hands all round, to ply his rosy gullet with truffles and champagne, and to create uncomfortable eddies and obstructions among the constituent atoms of the American colony. He was shamefully idle, spiritless, sensual, snobbish. He irritated our friend by the tone of his allusions to their native country, and Newman was at a loss to understand why the United

States were not good enough for Mr. Tristram. He had never been a very conscious patriot, but it vexed him to see them treated as little better than a vulgar smell in his friend's nostrils, and he finally broke out and swore that they were the greatest country in the world, that they could put all Europe into their breeches' pockets, and that an American who spoke ill of them ought to be carried home in irons and compelled to live in Boston. (This, for Newman, was putting it very vindictively.) Tristram was a comfortable man to snub, he bore no malice, and he continued to insist on Newman's finishing his evenings at the Occidental Club.

Christopher Newman dined several times in the Avenue d'Iéna, and his host always proposed an early adjournment to this institution. Mrs. Tristram protested, and declared that her husband exhausted his ingenuity in trying to displease her.

"Oh no, I never try, my love," he answered. "I know you loathe me quite enough when I take my chance."

Newman hated to see a husband and wife on these terms, and he was sure one or other of them must be very unhappy. He knew it was not Tristram. Mrs. Tristram had a balcony before her windows, upon which, during the June evenings, she was fond of sitting, and Newman used frankly to say that he preferred the balcony to the club. It had a fringe of perfumed plants in tubs, and enabled you to look up the broad street and see the Arch of Triumph vaguely massing its heroic sculptures in the summer starlight. Sometimes Newman kept his promise of following Mr. Tristram, in half an hour, to the Occidental, and sometimes he forgot it. His hostess asked him a great many questions about himself, but on this subject he was an indifferent talker. He was not what is called subjective, though when he felt that her interest was sincere, he made an almost heroic attempt to be. He told her a great many things he had done, and regaled her with anecdotes of Western life; she was from Philadelphia, and with her eight years in Paris, talked of herself as a languid Oriental. But some other person was always the hero of the tale, by no means always to his advantage; and Newman's own emotions were but scantily chronicled. She had an especial wish to know whether he had ever been in love—seriously, passionately— and, failing to gather any satisfaction from his allusions, she at last directly inquired. He hesitated a while, and at last he said, "No!" She declared that she was delighted to hear it, as it confirmed her private conviction that he was a man of no feeling.

"Really?" he asked, very gravely. "Do you think so? How do

you recognize a man of feeling?"

"I can't make out," said Mrs. Tristram, "whether you are very simple or very deep."

"I'm very deep. That's a fact."

"I believe that if I were to tell you with a certain air that you have no feeling, you would implicitly believe me."

"A certain air?" said Newman. "Try it and see."

"You would believe me, but you would not care," said Mrs. Tristram.

"You have got it all wrong. I should care immensely, but I shouldn't believe you. The fact is I have never had time to feel things. I have had to *do* them, to make myself felt."

"I can imagine that you may have done that tremendously, sometimes."

"Yes, there's no mistake about that."

"When you are in a fury it can't be pleasant."

"I am never in a fury."

"Angry, then, or displeased."

"I am never angry, and it is so long since I have been displeased that I have quite forgotten it."

"I don't believe," said Mrs. Tristram, "that you are never angry. A man ought to be angry sometimes, and you are neither good enough nor bad enough always to keep your temper."

"I lose it perhaps once in five years."

"The time is coming round, then," said his hostess. "Before I have known you six months I shall see you in a fine fury."

"Do you mean to put me into one?"

"I should not be sorry. You take things too coolly. It exasperates me. And then you are too happy. You have what must be the most agreeable thing in the world, the consciousness of having bought your pleasure beforehand and paid for it. You have not a day of reckoning staring you in the face. Your reckonings are over."

"Well, I suppose I am happy," said Newman, meditatively.

"You have been odiously successful."

"Successful in copper," said Newman, "only so-so in railroads, and a hopeless fizzle in oil."

"It is very disagreeable to know how Americans have made their money. Now you have the world before you. You have only to enjoy."

"Oh, I suppose I am very well off," said Newman. "Only I am

tired of having it thrown up at me. Besides, there are several draw-backs. I am not intellectual."

"One doesn't expect it of you," Mrs. Tristram answered. Then in a moment, "Besides, you are!"

"Well, I mean to have a good time, whether or no," said Newman. "I am not cultivated, I am not even educated; I know nothing about history, or art, or foreign tongues, or any other learned matters. But I am not a fool, either, and I shall undertake to know something about Europe by the time I have done with it. I feel something under my ribs here," he added in a moment, "that I can't explain—a sort of a mighty hankering, a desire to stretch out and haul in."

"Bravo!" said Mrs. Tristram, "that is very fine. You are the great Western Barbarian, stepping forth in his innocence and might, gazing a while at this poor effete Old World, and then swooping down on it."

"Oh, come," said Newman. "I am not a barbarian, by a good deal. I am very much the reverse. I have seen barbarians; I know what they are."

"I don't mean that you are a Comanche chief, or that you wear a blanket and feathers. There are different shades."

"I am a highly civilized man," said Newman. "I stick to that. If you don't believe it, I should like to prove it to you."

Mrs. Tristram was silent a while. "I should like to make you prove it," she said, at last. "I should like to put you in a difficult place."

"Pray do," said Newman.

"That has a little conceited sound!' his companion rejoined.

"Oh," said Newman, "I have a very good opinion of myself."

"I wish I could put it to the test. Give me time and I will." And Mrs. Tristram remained silent for some time afterwards, as if she was trying to keep her pledge. It did not appear that evening that she succeeded; but as he was rising to take his leave she passed suddenly, as she was very apt to do, from the tone of unsparing persiflage to that of almost tremulous sympathy. "Speaking seriously," she said, "I believe in you, Mr. Newman. You flatter my patriotism."

"Your patriotism?" Christopher demanded.

"Even so. It would take too long to explain, and you probably would not understand. Besides, you might take it—really, you might take it for a declaration. But it has nothing to do with you personally; it's what you represent. Fortunately you don't know all that, or your conceit would increase insufferably."

Newman stood staring and wondering what under the sun he "represented."

"Forgive all my meddlesome chatter and forget my advice. It is very silly in me to undertake to tell you what to do. When you are embarrassed, do as you think best, and you will do very well. When you are in a difficulty, judge for yourself."

"I shall remember everything you have told me," said Newman. "There are so many forms and ceremonies over here——"

"Forms and ceremonies are what I mean, of course."

"Ah, but I want to observe them," said Newman. "Haven't I as good a right as another? They don't scare me, and you needn't give me leave to violate them. I won't take it."

"That is not what I mean. I mean, observe them in your own way. Settle nice questions for yourself. Cut the knot or untie it, as you choose."

"Oh, I am sure I shall never fumble over it!" said Newman.

The next time that he dined in the Avenue d'Iéna was a Sunday, a day on which Mr. Tristram left the cards unshuffled, so that there was a trio in the evening on the balcony. The talk was of many things, and at last Mrs. Tristram suddenly observed to Christopher Newman that it was high time he should take a wife.

"Listen to her; she has the audacity!" said Tristram, who on Sunday evenings was always rather acrimonious.

"I don't suppose you have made up your mind not to marry?" Mrs. Tristram continued.

"Heaven forbid!" cried Newman. "I am sternly resolved on it."

"It's very easy," said Tristram; "fatally easy!"

"Well, then, I suppose you do not mean to wait till you are fifty."

"On the contrary, I am in a great hurry."

"One would never suppose it. Do you expect a lady to come and propose to you?"

"No; I am willing to propose. I think a great deal about it."

"Tell me some of your thoughts."

"Well," said Newman, slowly, "I want to marry very well."

"Marry a woman of sixty, then," said Tristram.

" 'Well' in what sense?"

"In every sense. I shall be hard to please."

"You must remember that, as the French proverb says, the most beautiful girl in the world can give but what she has."

"Since you ask me," said Newman, "I will say frankly that I want extremely to marry. It is time to begin with; before I know it I shall be forty. And then I'm lonely and helpless and dull. But if I marry now, so long as I didn't do it in hot haste when I was twenty, I must do it with my eyes open. I want to do the thing in handsome style. I do not only want to make no mistakes, but I want to make a great hit. I want to take my pick. My wife must be a magnificent woman."

"*Voilà ce qui s'appelle parler!*" cried Mrs. Tristram.

"Oh, I have thought an immense deal about it."

"Perhaps you think too much. The best thing is simply to fall in love."

"When I find the woman who pleases me, I shall love her enough. My wife shall be very comfortable."

"You are superb! There's a chance for the magnificent women."

"You are not fair," Newman rejoined. "You draw a fellow out and put him off guard, and then you laugh at him."

"I assure you," said Mrs. Tristram, "that I am very serious. To prove it, I will make you a proposal. Should you like me, as they say here, to marry you?"

"To hunt up a wife for me?"

"She is already found. I will bring you together."

"Oh, come," said Tristram, "we don't keep a matrimonial bureau. He will think you want your commission."

"Present me to a woman who comes up to my notions," said Newman, "and I will marry her to-morrow."

"You have a strange tone about it, and I don't quite understand you. I didn't suppose you would be so cold-blooded and calculating."

Newman was silent a while. "Well," he said, at last, "I want a great woman. I stick to that. That's one thing I *can* treat myself to, and if it is to be had I mean to have it. What else have I toiled and struggled for, all these years? I have succeeded, and now what am I to do with my success? To make it perfect, as I see it, there must be a beautiful woman perched on the pile, like a statue on a monument. She must be as good as she is beautiful, and as clever as she is good. I can give my wife a good deal, so I am not afraid to ask a good deal myself. She shall have everything a woman can desire; I shall not even object to her being too good for me; she may be cleverer and wiser than I can understand, and I shall only be the better pleased. I want to possess, in a word, the best article in the market."

"Why didn't you tell a fellow all this at the outset?" Tristram demanded. "I have been trying so to make you fond of *me!*"

"This is very interesting," said Mrs. Tristram. "I like to see a man know his own mind."

"I have known mine for a long time," Newman went on. "I made up my mind tolerably early in life that a beautiful wife was the thing best worth having, here below. It is the greatest victory over circumstances. When I say beautiful, I mean beautiful in mind and in manners, as well as in person. It is a thing every man has an equal right to; he may get it if he can. He doesn't have to be born with certain faculties, on purpose; he needs only to be a man. Then he needs only to use his will, and such wits as he has, and to try."

"It strikes me that your marriage is to be rather a matter of vanity."

"Well, it is certain," said Newman, "that if people notice my wife and admire her, I shall be mightily tickled."

"After this," cried Mrs. Tristram, "call any man modest!"

"But none of them will admire her so much as I."

"I see you have a taste for splendor."

Newman hesitated a little; and then, "I honestly believe I have!" he said.

"And I suppose you have already looked about you a good deal."

"A good deal, according to opportunity."

"And you have seen nothing that satisfied you?"

"No," said Newman, half reluctantly, "I am bound to say in honesty that I have seen nothing that really satisfied me."

"You remind me of the heroes of the French romantic poets, Rolla and Fortunio and all those other insatiable gentlemen for whom nothing in this world was handsome enough. But I see you are in earnest, and I should like to help you."

"Who the deuce is it, darling, that you are going to put upon him?" Tristram cried. "We know a good many pretty girls, thank Heaven, but magnificent women are not so common."

"Have you any objections to a foreigner?" his wife continued, addressing Newman, who had tilted back his chair, and, with his feet on a bar of the balcony railing and his hands in his pockets, was looking at the stars.

"No Irish need apply," said Tristram.

Newman meditated a while. "As a foreigner, no," he said at last; "I have no prejudices."

"My dear fellow, you have no suspicions!" cried Tristram. "You don't know what terrible customers these foreign women are; especially the 'magnificent' ones. How should you like a fair Circassian, with a dagger in her belt?"

Newman administered a vigorous slap to his knee. "I would marry a Japanese, if she pleased me," he affirmed.

"We had better confine ourselves to Europe," said Mrs. Tristram. "The only thing is, then, that the person be in herself to your taste?"

"She is going to offer you an unappreciated governess!" Tristram groaned.

"Assuredly. I won't deny that, other things being equal, I should prefer one of my own countrywomen. We should speak the same language, and that would be a comfort. But I am not afraid of a foreigner. Besides, I rather like the idea of taking in Europe, too. It enlarges the field of selection. When you choose from a greater number, you can bring your choice to a finer point!"

"You talk like Sardanapalus!" exclaimed Tristram.

"You say all this to the right person," said Newman's hostess. "I happen to number among my friends the loveliest woman in the world. Neither more nor less. I don't say a very charming person or a very estimable woman or a very great beauty; I say simply the loveliest woman in the world."

"The deuce!" cried Tristram, "you have kept very quiet about her. Were you afraid of me?"

"You have seen her," said his wife, "but you have no perception of such merit as Claire's."

"Ah, her name is Claire? I give it up."

"Does your friend wish to marry?" asked Newman.

"Not in the least. It is for you to make her change her mind. It will not be easy; she has had one husband, and he gave her a low opinion of the species."

"Oh, she is a widow, then?" said Newman.

"Are you already afraid? She was married at eighteen, by her parents, in the French fashion, to a disagreeable old man. But he had the good taste to die a couple of years afterward, and she is now twenty-five."

"So she is French?"

"French by her father, English by her mother. She is really more English than French, and she speaks English as well as you or I—or rather much better. She belongs to the very top of the basket, as they say here. Her family, on each side, is of fabulous antiquity; her mother is the daughter of an English Catholic earl. Her father is dead, and since her widowhood she has lived with her mother and a married brother. There is another brother, younger, who I believe is wild. They have an old hotel in the Rue de l'Université, but their fortune is small, and they make a common household, for economy's sake. When I was a girl I was put into a convent here for my education, while my father made the tour of Europe. It was a silly thing to do with me, but it had the advantage that it made me acquainted with Claire de Bellegarde. She was younger than I but we became fast friends. I took a tremendous fancy to her, and she returned my passion as far as she could. They kept such a tight rein on her that she could do very little, and when I left the convent she had to give me up. I was not of her *monde;* I am not now, either, but we sometimes meet. They are terrible people—her monde; all mounted upon stilts a mile high, and with pedigrees long in proportion. It is the skim of the milk of the old noblesse. Do you know what a Legitimist is, or an Ultramontane? Go into Madame de Cintré's drawing-room some afternoon, at five o'clock, and you will see the best-preserved specimens. I say go, but no one is admitted who can't show his fifty quarterings."

"And this is the lady you propose to me to marry?" asked Newman. "A lady I can't even approach?"

"But you said just now that you recognized no obstacles."

Newman looked at Mrs. Tristram a while, stroking his mustache. "Is she a beauty?" he demanded.

"No."

"Oh, then it's no use—"

"She is not a beauty, but she is beautiful, two very different things. A beauty has no faults in her face, the face of a beautiful woman may have faults that only deepen its charm."

"I remember Madame de Cintré, now," said Tristram. "She is as plain as a pike-staff. A man wouldn't look at her twice."

"In saying that *he* would not look at her twice, my husband sufficiently describes her," Mrs. Tristram rejoined.

"Is she good; is she clever?" Newman asked.

"She is perfect! I won't say more than that. When you are praising a person to another who is to know her, it is bad policy to go into details. I won't exaggerate. I simply recommend her. Among all women I have known she stands alone; she is of a different clay."

"I should like to see her," said Newman, simply.

"I will try to manage it. The only way will be to invite her to dinner. I have never invited her before, and I don't know that she will come. Her old feudal countess of a mother rules the family with an iron hand, and allows her to have no friends but of her own choosing, and to visit only in a certain sacred circle. But I can at least ask her."

At this moment Mrs. Tristram was interrupted; a servant stepped out upon the balcony and announced that there were visitors in the drawing-room. When Newman's hostess had gone in to receive her friends, Tom Tristram approached his guest.

"Don't put your foot into *this*, my boy," he said, puffing the last whiffs of his cigar. "There's nothing in it!"

Newman looked askance at him, inquisitive. "You tell another story, eh?"

"I say simply that Madame de Cintré is a great white doll of a woman, who cultivates quiet haughtiness."

"Ah, she's haughty, eh?"

"She looks at you as if you were so much thin air, and cares for you about as much."

"She is very proud, eh?"

"Proud? As proud as I'm humble."

"And not good-looking?"

Tristram shrugged his shoulders: "It's a kind of beauty you must be *intellectual* to understand. But I must go in and amuse the company."

Some time elapsed before Newman followed his friends into the drawing-room. When he at last made his appearance there he remained but a short time, and during this period sat perfectly silent, listening to a lady to whom Mrs. Tristram had straightway introduced him and who chattered, without a pause, with the full force of an extraordinarily high-pitched voice. Newman gazed and attended. Presently he came to bid good-night to Mrs. Tristram.

"Who is that lady?" he asked.

"Miss Dora Finch. How do you like her?"

"She's too noisy."

"She is thought so bright! Certainly, you are fastidious," said Mrs. Tristram.

Newman stood a moment, hesitating. Then at last, "Don't forget about your friend," he said; "Madame What's-her-name? the proud beauty. Ask her to dinner, and give me good notice." And with this he departed.

Some days later he came back; it was in the afternoon. He found Mrs. Tristram in her drawing-room; with her was a visitor, a woman young and pretty, dressed in white. The two ladies had risen and the visitor was apparently taking her leave. As Newman approached, he received from Mrs. Tristram a glance of the most vivid significance, which he was not immediately able to interpret.

"This is a good friend of ours," she said, turning to her companion, "Mr. Christopher Newman. I have spoken of you to him and he has an extreme desire to make your acquaintance. If you had consented to come and dine, I should have offered him an opportunity."

The stranger turned her face toward Newman, with a smile. He was not embarrassed, for his unconscious *sang-froid* was boundless; but as he became aware that this was the proud and beautiful Madame de Cintré, the loveliest woman in the world, the promised perfection, the proposed ideal, he made an instinctive movement to gather his wits together. Through the slight preoccupation that it produced he had a sense of a long, fair face, and of two eyes that were both brilliant and mild.

"I should have been most happy," said Madame de Cintré. "Unfortunately, as I have been telling Mrs. Tristram, I go on Monday to the country."

Newman had made a solemn bow. "I am very sorry," he said.

"Paris is getting too warm," Madame de Cintré added, taking her friend's hand again in farewell.

Mrs. Tristram seemed to have formed a sudden and somewhat venturesome resolution, and she smiled more intensely, as women do when they take such resolution. "I want Mr. Newman to know you," she said, dropping her head on one side and looking at Madame de Cintré's bonnet ribbons.

Christopher Newman stood gravely silent, while his native penetration admonished him. Mrs. Tristram was determined to force her friend to address him a word of encouragement which should be more than one of the common formulas of politeness; and if she was prompted by charity, it was by the charity that begins at home. Madame de Cintré was her dearest Claire, and her especial admiration but Madame de Cintré had found it impossible to dine with her, and Madame de Cintré should for once be forced gently to render tribute to Mrs. Tristram.

"It would give me great pleasure," she said, looking at Mrs. Tristram.

"That's a great deal," cried the latter, "for Madame de Cintré to say!"

"I am very much obliged to you," said Newman. "Mrs. Tristram can speak better for me than I can speak for myself."

Madame de Cintré looked at him again, with the same soft

brightness. "Are you to be long in Paris?" she asked.

"We shall keep him," said Mrs. Tristram.

"But you are keeping *me!*" and Madame de Cintré shook her friend's hand.

"A moment longer," said Mrs. Tristram.

Madame de Cintré looked at Newman again; this time without her smile. Her eyes lingered a moment. "Will you come and see me?" she asked.

Mrs. Tristram kissed her. Newman expressed his thanks, and she took her leave. Her hostess went with her to the door, and left Newman alone a moment. Presently she returned, rubbing her hands. "It was a fortunate chance," she said. "She had come to decline my invitation. You triumphed on the spot, making her ask you, at the end of three minutes, to her house."

"It was you who triumphed," said Newman. "You must not be too hard upon her."

Mrs. Tristram stared. "What do you mean?"

"She did not strike me as so proud. I should say she was shy."

"You are very discriminating. And what do you think of her face?"

"It's handsome!" said Newman.

"I should think it was! Of course you will go and see her."

"To-morrow!" cried Newman.

"No, not to-morrow; the next day. That will be Sunday; she leave Paris on Monday. If you don't see her; it will at least be a beginning." And she gave him Madame de Cintré's address.

He walked across the Seine, late in the summer afternoon, and made his way through those gray and silent streets of the Faubourg St. Germain whose houses present to the outer world a face as impassive and as suggestive of the concentration of privacy within as the blank walls of Eastern seraglios. Newman thought it a queer way for rich people to live; his ideal of grandeur was a splendid façade diffusing its brilliancy outward too, irradiating hospitality. The house to which he had been directed had a dark, dusty, painted portal, which swung open in answer to his ring. It admitted him into a wide, graveled court, surrounded on three sides with closed windows, and with a doorway facing the street, approached by three steps and surmounted by a tin canopy. The place was all in the shade; it answered to Newman's conception of a convent. The portress could not tell him whether Madame de Cintré was visible;

he would please to apply at the farther door. He crossed the court; a gentleman was sitting, bare-headed, on the steps of the portico, playing with a beautiful pointer. He rose as Newman approached, and, as he laid his hand upon the bell, said with a smile, in English, that he was afraid Newman would be kept waiting; the servants were scattered, he himself had been ringing, he didn't know what the deuce was in them. He was a young man, his English was excellent, and his smile very frank. Newman pronounced the name of Madame de Cintré.

"I think," said the young man, "that my sister is visible. Come in, and if you will give me your card I will carry it to her myself."

Newman had been accompanied on his present errand by a slight sentiment, I will not say of defiance—a readiness for aggression or defense, as they might prove needful—but of reflection, good-humored suspicion. He took from his pocket, while he stood on the portico, a card upon which, under his name, he had written the words "San Francisco," and while he presented it he looked warily at his interlocutor. His glance was singularly reassuring; he liked the young man's face; it strongly resembled that of Madame de Cintré. He was evidently her brother. The young man, on his side, had made a rapid inspection of Newman's person. He had taken the card and was about to enter the house with it when another figure appeared on the threshold—an older man, of a fine presence, wearing evening dress. He looked hard at Newman, and Newman looked at him. "Madame de Cintré," the younger man repeated, as an introduction of the visitor. The other took the card from his hand, read it in a rapid glance, looked again at Newman from head to foot, hesitated a moment, and then said, gravely but urbanely, "Madame de Cintré is not at home."

The younger man made a gesture, and then, turning to Newman, "I am very sorry, sir," he said.

Newman gave him a friendly nod, to show that he bore him no malice, and retraced his steps. At the porter's lodge he stopped; the two men were still standing on the portico.

"Who is the gentleman with the dog?" he asked of the old woman who reappeared. He had begun to learn French.

"That is Monsieur le Comte."

"And the other?"

"That is Monsieur le Marquis."

"A marquis?" said Christopher in English, which the old woman fortunately did not understand. "Oh, then he's not the butler!"

CHAPTER IV

EARLY ONE morning, before Christopher Newman was dressed, a little old man was ushered into his apartment, followed by a youth in a blouse, bearing a picture in a brilliant frame. Newman, among the distractions of Paris, had forgotten M. Nioche and his accomplished daughter; but this was a effective reminder.

"I am afraid you had given me up, sir," said the old man, after many apologies and salutations. "We have made you wait so many days. You accused us, perhaps, of inconstancy, of bad faith. But behold me at last! And behold also the pretty Madonna. Place it on a chair, my friend, in a good light, so that monsieur may admire it." And M. Nioche, addressing his companion, helped him to dispose the work of art.

It had been endued with a layer of varnish an inch thick, and its frame, of an elaborate pattern, was at least a foot wide. It glittered and twinkled in the morning light, and looked, to Newman's eyes, wonderfully splendid and precious. It seemed to him a very happy purchase, and he felt rich in the possession of it. He stood looking at it complacently, while he proceeded with his toilet, and M. Nioche, who had dismissed his own attendant, hovered near, smiling and rubbing his hands.

"It has wonderful *finesse*," he murmured, caressingly. "And here and there are marvelous touches, you probably perceive them, sir. It attracted great attention on the Boulevard, as we came along. And then a gradation of tones! That's what it is to know how to paint. I don't say it because I am her father, sir; but as one man of taste addressing another I cannot help observing that you have there an exquisite work. It is hard to produce such things and to have to part with them. If our means only allowed us the luxury of keeping it! I really may say, sir—" and M. Nioche gave a little feebly insinuating laugh— "I really may say that I envy you! You see," he added in a moment, "we have taken the liberty of offering you a frame. It increases by a trifle the value of the work, and it will save you the annoyance—so great for a person of your delicacy—of going about to bargain at the shops."

The language spoken by M. Nioche was a singular compound, which I shrink from the attempt to reproduce in its integrity. He had apparently once possessed a certain knowlege of English, and his accent was oddly tinged with the cockneyism of the British metropolis. But his learning had grown rusty with disuse, and his vocabulary was defective and capricious. He had repaired it with large patches of French, with words anglicized by a process of his own, and with native idioms literally translated. The result, in the form in which he in all humility presented it, would be scarcely comprehensible to the reader, so that I have ventured to trim and sift it. Newman only half understood it, but it amused him, and the old man's decent forlornness appealed to his democratic instincts. The assumption of a fatality in misery always irritated his strong good nature—it was almost the only thing that did so; and he felt the impulse to wipe it out, as it were, with the sponge of his own prosperity. The papa of Mademoiselle Noémie, however, had apparently on this occasion been vigorously indoctrinated, and he showed a certain tremulous eagerness to cultivate unexpected opportunities.

"How much do I owe you, then, with the frame?" asked Newman.

"It will make in all three thousand francs," said the old man, smiling agreeably, but folding his hands in instinctive suppliance.

"Can you give me a receipt?"

"I have brought one," said M. Nioche. "I took the liberty of drawing it up, in case monsieur should happen to desire to discharge his debt." And he drew a paper from his pocket-book and presented it to his patron. The document was written in a minute, fantastic hand, and couched in the choicest language.

Newman laid down the money, and M. Nioche dropped the napoleons one by one, solemnly and lovingly, into an old leathern purse.

"And how is your young lady?" asked Newman. "She made a great impression on me."

"An impression? Monsieur is very good. Monsieur admires her appearance?"

"She is very pretty, certainly."

"Alas, yes, she is very pretty!"

"And what is the harm in her being pretty?"

M. Nioche fixed his eyes upon a spot on the carpet and shook his head. Then looking up at Newman with a gaze that seemed to brighten and expand, "Monsieur knows what Paris is. She is dangerous to beauty, when beauty hasn't the sou."

"Ah, but that is not the case with your daughter. She is rich, now."

"Very true; we are rich for six months. But if my daughter were a plain girl I should sleep better all the same."

"You are afraid of the young men?"

"The young and the old!"

"She ought to get a husband."

"Ah, monsieur, one doesn't get a husband for nothing. Her husband must take her as she is: I can't give her a sou. But the young men don't see with that eye."

"Oh," said Newman, "her talent is in itself a dowry."

"Ah, sir, it needs first to be converted into specie!" and M. Nioche slapped his purse tenderly before he stowed it away. "The operation doesn't take place every day."

"Well, your young men are very shabby," said Newman; "that's all I can say. They ought to pay for your daughter, and not ask money themselves."

"Those are very noble ideas, monsieur; but what will you have? They are not the ideas of this country. We want to know what we are about when we marry."

"How big a portion does your daughter want?"

M. Nioche stared, as if he wondered what was coming next; but he promptly recovered himself, at a venture, and replied that he knew a very nice young man, employed by an insurance company, who would content himself with fifteen thousand francs.

"Let your daughter paint half a dozen pictures for me, and she shall have her dowry."

"Half a dozen pictures—her dowry! Monsieur is not speaking inconsiderately?"

"If she will make me six or eight copies in the Louvre as pretty as that Madonna, I will pay her the same price," said Newman.

Poor M. Nioche was speechless a moment, with amazement and gratitude, and then he seized Newman's hand, pressed it between his own ten fingers, and gazed at him with watery eyes. "As pretty as that? They shall be a thousand times prettier—they shall be magnificent, sublime. Ah, if I only knew how to paint, myself, sir, so that I might lend a hand! What can I do to thank you? *Voyons!*" And he pressed his forehead while he tried to think of something.

"Oh, you have thanked me enough," said Newman.

"Ah, here it is, sir!" cried M. Nioche. "To express my gratitude, I will charge you nothing for the lessons in French conversation."

"The lessons? I had quite forgotten them. Listening to your English," added Newman, laughing, "is almost a lesson in French."

"Ah, I don't profess to teach English, certainly," said M. Nioche.

"But for my own admirable tongue I am still at your service."

"Since you are here, then," said Newman, "we will begin. This is a very good hour. I am going to have my coffee; come every morning at half-past nine and have yours with me."

"Monsieur offers me my coffee, also?" cried M. Nioche. "Truly, my *beaux jours* are coming back."

"Come," said Newman, "let us begin. The coffee is almighty hot. How do you say that in French?"

Every day, then, for the following three weeks, the minutely respectable figure of M. Nioche made its appearance, with a series of little inquiring and apologetic obeisances, among the aromatic fumes of Newman's morning beverage. I don't know how much French our friend learned, but, as he himself said, if the attempt did him no good, it could at any rate do him no harm. And it amused him; it gratified that irregularly sociable side of his nature which had always expressed itself in a relish for ungrammatical conversation, and which often, even in his busy and preoccupied days, had made him sit on rail fences in young Western towns, in the twilight, in gossip hardly less than fraternal with humorous loafers and obscure fortune-seekers. He had notions, wherever he went, about talking with the natives; he had been assured, and his judgment approved the advice, that in traveling abroad it was an excellent thing to look into the life of the country. M. Nioche was very much of a native and, though his life might not be particularly worth looking into, he was a palpable and smoothly-rounded unit in that picturesque Parisian civilization which offered our hero so much easy entertainment and propounded so many curious problems to his inquiring and practical mind. Newman was fond of statistics; he liked to know how things were done; it gratified him to learn what taxes were paid, what profits were gathered, what commercial habits prevailed, how the battle of life was fought. M. Nioche, as a reduced capitalist, was familiar with these considerations, and he formulated his information, which he was proud to be able to impart, in the neatest possible terms and with a pinch of snuff between finger and thumb. As a Frenchman—quite apart from Newman's napoleons—M. Nioche loved conversation, and even in his decay his urbanity had not grown rusty. As a Frenchman, too, he could give a clear account of things, and—still as a Frenchman—when his knowledge was at fault he could supply its lapses with the most convenient and ingenious hypotheses. The little shrunken financier was intensely delighted to have questions asked him, and he scraped together information, by frugal processes, and took notes, in his little greasy pocket-book, of incidents which might interest his munificent friend, He read old almanacs at the book-stalls on the quays, and he began to frequent another café, where more newspapers were taken and his post-prandial *demitasse* cost him a penny extra, and where he used to con the tattered sheets for curious anecdotes, freaks of nature, and strange coincidences. He would relate with solemnity the next morning that a child of five years of age had lately died at Bordeaux, whose brain had been found to weigh sixty ounces—the brain of a Napoleon or a Washington! or that Madame P ——, *charcutière* in the Rue de Clichy, had found in the wadding of an old petticoat the sum of three hundred and sixty francs, which she had lost five years before. He pronounced his words with great distinctness and sonority, and Newman assured him that his way of dealing with the French tongue was very superior to the bewildering chatter that he heard in other mouths. Upon this M. Nioche's accent became more finely trenchant than ever; he offered to read extracts from Lamartine, and he protested that, although he did endeavor according to his feeble lights to cultivate refinement of diction, monsieur, if he wanted the real thing, should go to the Théâtre Français.

Newman took an interest in French thriftiness and conceived a lively admiration for Parisian economies. His own economic genius was so entirely for operations on a larger scale, and, to move at his ease, he needed so imperatively the sense of great risks and great prizes, that he found an ungrudging entertainment in the spectacle of fortunes made by the aggregation of copper coins, and in the minute subdivision of labor and profit. He questioned M. Nioche about his own manner of life, and felt a friendly mixture of compassion and respect over the recital of his delicate frugalities. The worthy man told him how, at one period, he and his daughter had supported existence, comfortably, upon the sum of fifteen sous *per diem;* recently, having succeeded in hauling ashore the last floating fragments of the wreck of his fortune, his budget had been a trifle more ample. But they still had to count their sous very narrowly, and M. Nioche intimated with a sigh that Mademoiselle Noémie did not bring to this task that zealous coöperation which might have been desired.

"But what will you have?" he asked, philosophically. "One is young, one is pretty, one needs new dresses and fresh gloves; one can't wear shabby gowns among the splendors of the Louvre."

"But your daughter earns enough to pay for her own clothes," said Newman.

M. Nioche looked at him with weak, uncertain eyes. He would have liked to be able to say that his daughter's talents were appreciated, and that her crooked little daubs commanded a market; but it seemed a scandal to abuse the credulity of this free-handed stranger, who, without a suspicion or a question, had admitted him to equal social rights. He compromised, and declared that while it was obvious that Mademoiselle Noémie's reproductions of the old masters had only to be seen to be coveted, the prices which, in consideration of their altogether peculiar degree of finish, she felt obliged to ask for them had kept purchasers at a respectful distance. "Poor little one!" said M. Nioche, with a sigh; "it is almost a pity that her work is so perfect! It would be in her interest to paint less well."

"But if Mademoiselle Noémie has this devotion to her art, Newman once observed, "why should you have those fears for her that you spoke of the other day?"

M. Nioche meditated: there was an inconsistency in his position; it made him chronically uncomfortable. Though he had no desire to destroy the goose with the golden eggs—Newman's benevolent confidence—he felt a tremulous impulse to speak out all his trouble. "Ah, she is an artist, my dear sir, most assuredly," he declared. "But, to tell you the truth, she is also a *franche coquette*. I am sorry to say," he added in a moment, shaking his head with a world of harmless bitterness, "that she comes honestly by it. Her mother was one before her!"

"You were not happy with your wife?" Newman asked.

M. Nioche gave half a dozen little backward jerks of his head. "She was my purgatory, monsieur!"

"She deceived you?"

"Under my nose, year after year. I was too stupid, and the temptation was too great. But I found her out at last. I have only been once in my life a man to be afraid of; I know it very well; it was in that hour! Nevertheless I don't like to think of it. I loved her—I can't tell you how much. She was a bad woman."

"She is not living?"

"She has gone to her account."

"Her influence on your daughter, then," said Newman encouragingly, "is not to be feared."

"She cared no more for her daughter than for the sole of her shoe! But Noémie has no need of influence. She is sufficient to herself. She is stronger than I."

"She doesn't obey you, eh?"

"She can't obey, monsieur, since I don't command. What would be the use? It would only irritate her and drive her to some *coup de tête*. She is very clever, like her mother; she would waste no time about it. As a child—when I was happy, or supposed I was—she studied drawing and painting with first-class professors, and they assured me she had a talent. I was delighted to believe it, and when I went into society I used to carry her pictures with me in a portfolio and hand them round to the company. I remember, once, a lady thought I was offering them for sale, and I took it very ill. We don't know what we may come to! Then came my dark days, and my explosion with Madame Nioche. Noémie had no more twenty-franc lessons; but in the course of time, when she grew older, and it became highly expedient that she should do something that would help to keep us alive, she bethought herself of her palette and brushes. Some of our friends in the *quartier* pronounced the idea fantastic: they recommended her to try bonnet making, to get a situation in a shop, or—if she was more ambitious—to advertise for a place of *dame de compagnie*. She did advertise, and an old lady wrote her a letter and bade her come and see her. The old lady liked her, and offered her her living and six hundred francs a year; but Noémie discovered that she passed her life in her arm-chair and had only two visitors, her confessor and her nephew: the confessor very strict, and the nephew a man of fifty, with a broken nose and a government clerkship of two thousand francs. She threw her old lady over, bought a paint-box, a canvas, and a new dress, and went and set up her easel in the Louvre. There in one place and another, she has passed the last two years; I can't say it has made us millionaires. But Noémie tells me that Rome was not built in a day, that she is making great progress, that I must leave her to her own devices. The fact is, without prejudice to her genius, that she has no idea of burying herself alive. She likes to see the world, and to be seen. She says, herself, that she can't work in the dark. With her appearance it is very natural. Only, I can't help worrying and trembling and wondering what may happen to her there all alone, day after day, amid all that coming and going of strangers. I can't be always at her side. I go with her in the morning, and I come to fetch her away, but she won't have me near her in the interval; she says I make her nervous. As if it didn't make me nervous

to wander about all day without her! Ah, if anything were to
happen to her!" cried M. Nioche, clenching his two fists and
jerking back his head again, portentously.

"Oh, I guess nothing will happen," said Newman.

"I believe I should shoot her!" said the old man, solemnly.

"Oh, we'll marry her," said Newman, "since that's how you
manage it; and I will go and see her tomorrow at the Louvre and
pick out the pictures she is to copy for me."

M. Nioche had brought Newman a message from his daughter,
in acceptance of his magnificent commission, the young lady declaring herself his most devoted servant, promising her most zealous
endeavor, and regretting that the proprieties forbade her coming
to thank him in person. The morning after the conversation just
narrated, Newman reverted to his intention of meeting Mademoiselle
Noémie at the Louvre. M. Nioche appeared preoccupied, and left
his budget of anecdotes unopened; he took a great deal of snuff, and
sent certain oblique, appealing glances toward his stalwart pupil.
At last, when he was taking his leave, he stood a moment, after he
had polished his hat with his calico pocket-handkerchief, with his
small, pale eyes fixed strangely upon Newman.

"What's the matter?" our hero demanded.

"Excuse the solicitude of a father's heart!" said M. Nioche. "You
inspire me with boundless confidence, but I can't help giving you
a warning. After all, you are a man, you are young and at liberty.
Let me beseech you, then, to respect the innocence of Mademoiselle
Nioche!"

Newman had wondered what was coming, and at this he broke
into a laugh. He was on the point of declaring that his own innocence
struck him as the more exposed, but he contented himself with
promising to treat the young girl with nothing less than veneration.
He found her waiting for him, seated upon the great divan in the
Salon Carré. She was not in her working-day costume, but wore
her bonnet and gloves and carried her parasol, in honor of the
occasion. These articles had been selected with unerring taste, and
a fresher, prettier image of youthful alertness and blooming discretion was not to be conceived. She made Newman a most respectful
curtsey and expressed her gratitude for his liberality in a wonderfully graceful little speech. It annoyed him to have a charming
young girl stand there thanking him, and it made him feel uncomfortable to think that this perfect young lady, with her excellent
manners and her finished intonation, was literally in his pay. He

assured her, in such French as he could muster, that the thing was not worth mentioning, and that he considered her services a great favor.

"Whenever you please, then," said Mademoiselle Noémie, "we will pass the review."

They walked slowly round the room, then passed into the others and strolled about for half an hour. Mademoiselle Noémie evidently relished her situation, and had no desire to bring her public interview with her striking-looking patron to a close. Newman perceived that prosperity agreed with her. The little thin-lipped, peremptory air with which she had addressed her father on the occasion of their former meeting had given place to the most lingering and caressing tones.

"What sort of pictures do you desire?" she asked. "Sacred, or profane?"

"Oh, a few of each," said Newman. "But I want something bright and gay."

"Something gay? There is nothing very gay in this solemn old Louvre. But we will see what we can find. You speak French to-day like a charm. My father had done wonders."

"Oh, I am a bad subject," said Newman. "I am too old to learn a language."

"Too old? *Quelle folie!*" cried Mademoiselle Noémie, with a clear, shrill laugh. "You are a very young man. And how do you like my father?"

"He is a very nice old gentleman. He never laughs at my blunders."

"He is very *comme il faut*, my papa," said Mademoiselle Noémie, "and as honest as the day. Oh, an exceptional probity! You could trust him with millions."

"Do you always obey him?" asked Newman.

"Obey him?"

"Do you do what he bids you?"

The young girl stopped and looked at him; she had a spot of color in either cheek, and in her expressive French eye, which projected too much for perfect beauty, there was a slight gleam of audacity. "Why do you ask me that?" she demanded.

"Because I want to know."

"You think me a bad girl?" And she gave a strange smile.

Newman looked at her a moment; he saw that she was pretty, but he was not in the least dazzled. He remembered poor M. Nioche's solicitude for her "innocence," and he laughed out again as his eyes met hers. Her face was the oddest mixture of youth and maturity, and beneath her candid brow her searching little smile seemed to contain a world of ambiguous intentions. She was pretty enough, certainly, to make her father nervous; but, as regards her innocence, Newman felt ready on the spot to affirm that she had never parted with it. She had simply never had any; she had been looking at the world since she was ten years old, and he would have been a wise man who could tell her any secrets. In her long mornings at the Louvre she had not only studied Madonnas and St. Johns; she had kept an eye upon all the variously embodied human nature around her, and she had formed her conclusions. In a certain sense, it seemed to Newman, M. Nioche might be at rest; his daughter might do something very audacious, but she would never do anything foolish. Newman, with his long-drawn, leisurely smile, and his even, unhurried utterance, was always, mentally, taking his time; and he asked himself, now, what she was looking at him in that way for. He had an idea that she would like him to confess that he did think her a bad girl.

"Oh, no," he said at last; "it would be very bad manners in me to judge you that way. I don't know you."

"But my father has complained to you," said Mademoiselle Noémie.

"He says you are a coquette."

"He shouldn't go about saying such things to gentlemen! But you don't believe it."

"No," said Newman gravely, "I don't believe it."

She looked at him again, gave a shrug and a smile, and then pointed to a small Italian picture, a Marriage of St. Catherine. "How should you like that?" she asked.

"It doesn't please me," said Newman. "The young lady in the yellow dress is not pretty."

"Ah, you are a great connoisseur," murmured Mademoiselle Noémie.

"In pictures? Oh, no; I know very little about them."

"In pretty women, then."

"In that I am hardly better."

"What do you say to that, then?" the young girl asked, indicating a superb Italian portrait of a lady. "I will do it for you on a smaller scale."

"On a smaller scale? Why not as large as the original?"

Mademoiselle Noémie glanced at the glowing splendor of the

Venetian masterpiece and gave a little toss of her head. "I don't like
that woman. She looks stupid."

"I do like her," said Newman. "Decidedly, I must have her, as
large as life. And just as stupid as she is there."

The young girl fixed her eyes on him again, and with her mocking
smile, "It certainly ought to be easy for me to make her look stupid!"
she said.

"What do you mean?" asked Newman, puzzled.

She gave another little shrug. "Seriously, then, you want that
portrait—the golden hair, the purple satin, the pearl necklace, the
two magnificent arms?"

"Everything—just as it is."

"Would nothing else do, instead?"

"Oh, I want some other things, but I want that too."

Mademoiselle Noémie turned away a moment, walked to the
other side of the hall, and stood there, looking vaguely about her.
At last she came back. "It must be charming to be able to order
pictures at such a rate. Venetian portraits, as large as life! You go
at it *en prince*. And you are going to travel about Europe that way?"

"Yes, I intend to travel," said Newman.

"Ordering, buying, spending money?"

"Of course I shall spend some money."

"You are very happy to have it. And you are perfectly free?"

"How do you mean, free?"

"You have nothing to bother you—no family, no wife, no *fiancée*?"

"Yes, I am tolerably free."

"You are very happy," said Mademoiselle Noémie, gravely.

"*Je le veux bien!*" said Newman, proving that he had learned more
French than he admitted.

"And how long shall you stay in Paris?" the young girl went on.

"Only a few days more."

"Why do you go away?"

"It is getting hot, and I must go to Switzerland."

"To Switzerland? That's a fine country. I would give my new
parasol to see it! Lakes and mountains, romantic valleys and icy
peaks! Oh, I congratulate you. Meanwhile, I shall sit here through
all the hot summer, daubing at your pictures."

"Oh, take your time about it," said Newman. "Do them at your
convenience."

They walked farther and looked at a dozen other things. Newman
pointed out what pleased him, and Mademoiselle Noémie generally

criticised it, and proposed something else. Then suddenly she diverged and began to talk about some personal matter.

"What made you speak to me the other day in the Salon Carré?" she abruptly asked.

"I admired your picture."

"But you hesitated a long time."

"Oh, I do nothing rashly," said Newman.

"Yes, I saw you watching me. But I never supposed you were going to speak to me. I never dreamed I should be walking about here with you to-day. It's very curious."

"It is very natural," observed Newman.

"Oh, I beg your pardon; not to me. Coquette as you think me, I have never walked about in public with a gentleman before. What was my father thinking of, when he consented to our interview?"

"He was repenting of his unjust accusations," replied Newman.

Mademoiselle Noémie remained silent; at last she dropped into a seat. "Well then, for those five it is fixed," she said. "Five copies as brilliant and beautiful as I can make them. We have one more to choose. Shouldn't you like one of those great Rubenses—the marriage of Marie de Médicis? Just look at it and see how handsome it is."

"Oh, yes; I should like that," said Newman. "Finish off with that."

"Finish off with that—good!" And she laughed. She sat a moment, looking at him, and then she suddenly rose and stood before him, with her hands hanging and clasped in front of her. "I don't understand you," she said with a smile. "I don't understand how a man can be so ignorant."

"Oh, I am ignorant, certainly," said Newman, putting his hands into his pockets.

"It's ridiculous! I don't know how to paint."

"You don't know how?"

"I paint like a cat; I can't draw a straight line. I never sold a picture until you bought that thing the other day." And as she offered this surprising information she continued to smile.

Newman burst into a laugh. "Why do you tell me this?" he asked.

"Because it irritates me to see a clever man blunder so. My pictures are grotesque."

"And the one I possess—"

"That one is rather worse than usual."

"Well," said Newman, "I like it all the same!"

She looked at him askance. "That is a very pretty thing to say," she answered; "but it is my duty to warn you before you go farther.

This order of yours is impossible, you know. What do you take me for? It is work for ten men. You pick out the six most difficult pictures in the Louvre, and you expect me to go to work as if I were sitting down to hem a dozen pocket handkerchiefs. I wanted to see how far you would go."

Newman looked at the young girl in some perplexity. In spite of the ridiculous blunder of which he stood convicted, he was very far from being a simpleton, and he had a lively suspicion that Mademoiselle Noémie's sudden frankness was not essentially more honest than her leaving him in error would have been. She was playing a game; she was not simply taking pity on his æsthetic verdancy. What was it she expected to win? The stakes were high and the risk was great; the prize therefore must have been commensurate. But even granting that the prize might be great, Newman could not resist a movement of admiration for his companion's intrepidity. She was throwing away with one hand, whatever she might intend to do with the other, a very handsome sum of money.

"Are you joking," he said, "or are you serious?"

"Oh, serious!" cried Mademoiselle Noémie, but with her extraordinary smile.

"I know very little about pictures or how they are painted. If you can't do all that, of course you can't. Do what you can, then."

"It will be very bad," said Mademoiselle Noémie.

"Oh," said Newman, laughing, "if you are determined it shall be bad, of course it will. But why do you go on painting badly?"

"I can do nothing else; I have no real talent."

"You are deceiving your father, then."

The young girl hesitated a moment. "He knows very well!"

"No," Newman declared; "I am sure he believes in you."

"He is afraid of me. I go on painting badly, as you say, because I want to learn. I like it, at any rate. And I like being here; it is a place to come to, every day; it is better than sitting in a little dark, damp room, on a court, or selling buttons and whalebones over a counter."

"Of course it is much more amusing," said Newman. "But for a poor girl isn't it rather an expensive amusement?"

"Oh, I am very wrong, there is no doubt about that," said Mademoiselle Noémie. "But rather than earn my living as some girls do—toiling with a needle, in little black holes, out of the world—I would throw myself into the Seine."

"There is no need of that," Newman answered; "your father told you my offer?"

"Your offer?"

"He wants you to marry, and I told him I would give you a chance to earn your *dot*."

"He told me all about it, and you see the account I make of it! Why should you take such an interest in my marriage?"

"My interest was in your father. I hold to my offer; do what you can, and I will buy what you paint."

She stood for some time, meditating, with her eyes on the ground. At last, looking up, "What sort of a husband can you get for twelve thousand francs?" she asked.

"Your father tells me he knows some very good young men."

"Grocers and butchers and little *maîtres de cafés!* I will not marry at all if I can't marry well."

"I would advise you not to be too fastidious," said Newman. "That's all the advice I can give you."

"I am very much vexed at what I have said!" cried the young girl. "It has done me no good. But I couldn't help it."

"What good did you expect it to do you?"

"I couldn't help it, simply."

Newman looked at her a moment. "Well, your pictures may be bad," he said, "but you are too clever for me, nevertheless. I don't understand you. Good-by!" And he put out his hand.

She made no response, and offered him no farewell. She turned away and seated herself sidewise on a bench, leaning her head on the back of her hand, which clasped the rail in front of the pictures. Newman stood a moment and then turned on his heel and retreated. He had understood her better than he confessed; this singular scene was a practical commentary upon her father's statement that she was a frank coquette.

Chapter V

When Newman related to Mrs. Tristram his fruitless visit to Madame de Cintré, she urged him not to be discouraged, but to carry out his plan of "seeing Europe" during the summer, and return to Paris in the autumn and settle down comfortably for the winter. "Madame de Cintré will keep," she said; "she is not a woman who will marry from one day to another." Newman made no distinct affirmation that he would come back to Paris; he even talked about Rome and the Nile, and abstained from professing any especial interest in Madame de Cintré's continued widowhood. This circumstance was at variance with his habitual frankness, and may perhaps be regarded as characteristic of the incipient stage of that passion which is more particularly known as the mysterious one. The truth is that the expression of a pair of eyes that were at once brilliant and mild had become very familiar to his memory, and he would not easily have resigned himself to the prospect of never looking into them again. He communicated to Mrs. Tristram a number of other facts, of greater or less importance, as you choose; but on this particular point he kept his own counsel. He took a kindly leave of M. Nioche, having assured him that, so far as he was concerned, the blue-cloaked Madonna herself might have been present at his interview with Mademoiselle Noémie; and left the old man nursing his breast-pocket, in an ecstasy which the acutest misfortune might have been defied to dissipate. Newman then started on his travels, with all his usual appearance of slow-strolling leisure, and all his essential directness and intensity of aim. No man seemed less in a hurry, and yet no man achieved more in brief periods. He had certain practical instincts which served him excellently in his trade of tourist. He found his way in foreign cities by divination, his memory was excellent when once his attention had been at all cordially given, and he emerged from dialogues in foreign tongues, of which he had, formally, not understood a word, in full possession of the particular fact he had desired to ascertain. His appetite for facts was capacious, and although many of those which he noted would have seemed woefully dry and colorless to the ordinary sentimental traveler, a careful inspection of the list would have shown that he had a soft spot in his imagination. In the charming city of Brussels—his first stopping-place after leaving Paris—he asked a great many questions about the street-cars, and took extreme satisfaction in the reappearance of this familiar symbol of American civilization; but he was also greatly struck with the beautiful Gothic tower of the Hôtel de Ville, and wondered whether it would not be possible to "get up" something like it in San Francisco. He stood for half an hour in the crowded square before this edifice, in imminent danger from carriage-wheels, listening to a toothless old cicerone mumble in broken English the touching history of Counts Egmont and Horn; and he wrote the names of these gentlemen—for reasons best known to himself—on the back of an old letter.

At the outset, on his leaving Paris, his curiosity had not been intense; passive entertainment, in the Champs Elysées and at the theatres, seemed about as much as he need expect of himself, and although, as he had said to Tristram, he wanted to see the mysterious, satisfying *best*, he had not the Grand Tour in the least on his conscience, and was not given to cross-questioning the amusement of the hour. He believed that Europe was made for him, and not he for Europe. He had said that he wanted to improve his mind, but he would have felt a certain embarrassment, a certain shame, even—a false shame, possibly—if he had caught himself looking intellectually into the mirror. Neither in this nor in any other respect had Newman a high sense of responsibility; it was his prime conviction that a man's life should be easy, and that he should be able to resolve privilege into a matter of course. The world, to his sense, was a great bazaar, where one might stroll about and purchase handsome things; but he was no more conscious, individually, of social pressure than he admitted the existence of such a thing as an obligatory purchase. He had not only a dislike, but a sort of moral mistrust, of uncomfortable thoughts, and it was both uncomfortable and slightly contemptible to feel obliged to square one's self with a standard. One's standard was the ideal of one's own good-humored prosperity, the prosperity which enabled one to give as well as take. To expand, without bothering about it—without shiftless timidity on one side, or loquacious eagerness on the other—to the full compass of what he would have called a "pleasant" experience, was Newman's most definite programme of life. He had always hated to hurry to catch railroad trains, and yet he had always caught them; and just so an undue solicitude for "culture" seemed a sort of silly dawdling at the station, a proceeding properly confined to women, foreigners, and other unpractical persons. All this admitted, Newman enjoyed his journey, when once he had fairly entered the current, as profoundly as the most zealous *dilettante*. One's theories, after all, matter little; it is one's humor that is the great thing. Our friend was intelligent, and he could not help that. He lounged through Belgium and Holland and the Rhineland, through Switzerland and Northern Italy, planning about nothing, but seeing everything. The guides and *valets de place* found him an excellent subject. He was always approachable, for he was much addicted to standing about in the vestibules and porticos of inns, and he availed himself little of the opportunities for impressive seclusion which are so liberally offered in Europe to gentlemen who travel with long purses. When an excursion, a church, a gallery, a ruin, was proposed to him, the first thing Newman usually did, after surveying his postulant in silence, from head to foot, was to sit down at a little table and order something to drink. The cicerone, during this process, usually retreated to a respectful distance; otherwise I am not sure that Newman would not have bidden him sit down and have a glass also, and tell him as an honest fellow whether his church or his gallery was really worth a man's trouble. At last he rose and stretched his long legs, beckoned to the man of monuments, looked at his watch, and fixed his eye on his adversary. "What is it?" he asked. "How far?" And whatever the answer was, although he sometimes seemed to hesitate, he never declined. He stepped into an open cab, made his conductor sit beside him to answer questions, bade the driver go fast (he had a particular aversion to slow driving) and rolled, in all probability through a dusty suburb, to the goal of his pilgrimage. If the goal was a disappointment, if the church was meagre, or the ruin a heap of rubbish, Newman never protested or berated his cicerone; he looked with an impartial eye upon great monuments and small, made the guide recite his lesson, listened to it religiously, asked if there was nothing else to be seen in the neighborhood, and drove back again at a rattling pace. It is to be feared that his perception of the difference between good architecture and bad was not acute, and that he might sometimes have been seen gazing with culpable serenity at inferior productions. Ugly churches were a part of his pastime in Europe, as well as beautiful ones, and his tour was altogether a pastime. But there is sometimes nothing like the imagination of these people who have none, and Newman, now and then, in an unguided stroll in a foreign city, before some lonely, sad-towered church, or some angular image of one who had rendered civic service in an unknown past, had felt a singular inward tremor. It was not an excitement or a perplexity; it was a placid, fathomless sense of diversion.

He encountered by chance in Holland a young American, with whom, for a time, he formed a sort of traveler's partnership. They were men of a very different cast, but each, in his way, was so good a fellow that, for a few weeks at least, it seemed something of a pleasure to share the chances of the road. Newman's comrade, whose name was Babcock, was a young Unitarian minister; a small, spare, neatly-attired man, with a strikingly candid physiognomy. He was a native of Dorchester, Massachusetts, and had spiritual charge of a small congregation in another suburb of the New England metropolis. His digestion was weak, and he lived chiefly on

Graham bread and hominy—a regimen to which he was so much attached that his tour seemed to him destined to be blighted when, on landing on the Continent, he found that these delicacies did not flourish under the table d'hôte system. In Paris he had purchased a bag of hominy at an establishment which called itself an American Agency, and at which the New York illustrated papers were also to be procured, and he had carried it about with him, and shown extreme serenity and fortitude in the somewhat delicate position of having his hominy prepared for him and served at anomalous hours, at the hotels he successively visited. Newman had once spent a morning, in the course of business, at Mr. Babcock's birthplace, and, for reasons too recondite to unfold, his visit there always assumed in his mind a jocular cast. To carry out his joke, which certainly seems poor so long as it is not explained, he used often to address his companion as "Dorchester." Fellow-travelers very soon grow intimate; but it is highly improbable that at home these extremely dissimilar characters would have found any very convenient points of contact. They were, indeed, as different as possible. Newman, who never reflected on such matters, accepted the situation with great equanimity, but Babcock used to meditate over it privately; used often, indeed, to retire to his room early in the evening for the express purpose of considering it conscientiously and impartially. He was not sure that it was a good thing for him to associate with our hero, whose way of taking life was so little his own. Newman was an excellent, generous fellow; Mr. Babcock sometimes said to himself that he was a *noble* fellow, and, certainly, it was impossible not to like him. But would it not be desirable to try to exert an influence upon him, to try to quicken his moral life and sharpen his sense of duty? He liked everything, he accepted everything, he found amusement in everything; he was not discriminating, he had not a high tone. The young man from Dorchester accused Newman of a fault which he considered very grave, and which he did his best to avoid: what he would have called a want of "moral reaction." Poor Mr. Babcock was extremely fond of pictures and churches, and carried Mrs. Jameson's works about in his trunk; he delighted in æsthetic analysis, and received peculiar impressions from everything he saw. But nevertheless in his secret soul he detested Europe, and he felt an irritating need to protest against Newman's gross intellectual hospitality. Mr. Babcock's moral *malaise*, I am afraid, lay deeper than where any definition of mine can reach it. He mistrusted the European temperament, he suffered from the European climate, he hated the European dinner-hour; European life seemed to him unscrupulous and impure. And yet he had an exquisite sense of beauty; and as beauty was often inextricably associated with the above displeasing conditions, as he wished, above all, to be just and dispassionate, and as he was, furthermore, extremely devoted to "culture," he could not bring himself to decide that Europe was utterly bad. But he thought it was very bad indeed, and his quarrel with Newman was that this unregulated epicure had a sadly insufficient perception of the bad. Babcock himself really knew as little about the bad, in any quarter of the world, as a nursing infant; his most vivid realization of evil had been the discovery that one of his college classmates, who was studying architecture in Paris, had a love affair with a young woman who did not expect him to marry her. Babcock had related this incident to Newman, and our hero had applied an epithet of an unflattering sort to the young girl. The next day his companion asked him whether he was very sure he had used exactly the right word to characterize the young architect's mistress. Newman stared and laughed. "There are a great many words to express that idea," he said; "you can take your choice!"

"Oh, I mean," said Babcock, "was she possibly not to be considered in a different light? Don't you think she *really* expected him to marry her?"

"I am sure I don't know," said Newman. "Very likely she did; I have no doubt she is a grand woman." And he began to laugh again.

"I didn't mean that either," said Babcock; "I was only afraid that I might have seemed yesterday not to remember—not to consider; well, I think I will write to Percival about it."

And he had written to Percival (who answered him in a really impudent fashion), and he had reflected that it was, somehow, raw and reckless in Newman to assume in that off-hand manner that the young woman in Paris might be "grand." The brevity of Newman's judgments very often shocked and discomposed him. He had a way of damning people without farther appeal, or of pronouncing them capital company in the face of uncomfortable symptoms, which seemed unworthy of a man whose conscience had been properly cultivated. And yet poor Babcock liked him, and remembered that even if he was sometimes perplexing and painful, this was not a reason for giving him up. Goethe recommended seeing human nature in the most various forms, and Mr. Babcock thought Goethe perfectly splendid. He often tried, in odd half-hours of conversation, to infuse into Newman a little of his own spiritual starch, but Newman's personal texture was too loose to admit of stiffening. His mind could no more hold principles than a sieve can hold water. He admired principles extremely, and thought Babcock a mighty fine little fellow for having so many. He accepted all that his high-strung companion offered him, and put them away in what he supposed to be a very safe place; but poor Babcock never afterwards recognized his gifts among the articles that Newman had in daily use.

They traveled together through Germany and into Switzerland, where for three or four weeks they trudged over passes and lounged upon blue lakes. At last they crossed the Simplon and made their way to Venice. Mr. Babcock had become gloomy and even a trifle irritable; he seemed moody, absent, preoccupied; he got his plans into a tangle, and talked one moment of doing one thing and the next of doing another. Newman led his usual life, made acquaintances, took his ease in the galleries and churches, spent an unconscionable amount of time in strolling in the Piazza San Marco, bought a great many bad pictures, and for a fortnight enjoyed Venice grossly. One evening, coming back to his inn, he found Babcock waiting for him in the little garden beside it. The young man walked up to him, looking very dismal, thrust out his hand, and said with solemnity that he was afraid they must part. Newman expressed his surprise and regret, and asked why a parting had become necessary. "Don't be afraid I'm tired of you," he said.

"You are not tired of me?" demanded Babcock, fixing him with his clear gray eye.

"Why the deuce should I be? You are a very plucky fellow. Besides, I don't grow tired of things."

"We don't understand each other," said the young minister.

"Don't I understand you?" cried Newman. "Why, I hoped I did. But what if I don't; where's the harm?"

"I don't understand *you*," said Babcock. And he sat down and rested his head on his hand, and looked up mournfully at his immeasurable friend.

"Oh Lord, I don't mind that!" cried Newman, with a laugh.

"But it's very distressing to me. It keeps me in a state of unrest. It irritates me; I can't settle anything. I don't think it's good for me."

"You worry too much; that's what's the matter with you," said Newman.

"Of course it must seem so to you. You think I take things too hard, and I think you take things to easily. We can never agree."

"But we have agreed very well all along."

"No, I haven't agreed," said Babcock, shaking his head. "I am very uncomfortable. I ought to have separated from you a month ago."

"Oh, horrors! I'll agree to anything!" cried Newman.

Mr. Babcock buried his head in both hands. At last, looking up, "I don't think you appreciate my position," he said. "I try to arrive at the truth about everything. And then you go too fast. For me, you are too passionate, too extravagant. I feel as if I ought to go over all this ground we have traversed again, by myself, alone. I am afraid I have made a great many mistakes."

"Oh, you needn't give so many reasons," said Newman. "You are simply tired of my company. You have a good right to be."

"No, no, I am not tired!" cried the pestered young divine. "It is very wrong to be tired."

"I give it up!" laughed Newman. "But of course it will never do to go on making mistakes. Go your way, by all means. I shall miss you; but you have seen I make friends very easily. You will be lonely, yourself; but drop me a line, when you feel like it, and I will wait for you anywhere."

"I think I will go back to Milan. I am afraid I didn't do justice to Luini."

"Poor Luini!" said Newman.

"I mean that I am afraid I overestimated him. I don't think that he is a painter of the first rank."

"Luini?" Newman exclaimed; "why, he's enchanting—he's magnificent! There is something in his genius that is like a beautiful woman. It gives one the same feeling."

Mr. Babcock frowned and winced. And it must be added that this was, for Newman, an unusually metaphysical flight; but in passing through Milan he had taken a great fancy to the painter. "There you are again!" said Mr. Babcock. "Yes, we had better separate." And on the morrow he retraced his steps and proceeded to tone down his impressions of the great Lombard artist.

A few days afterwards Newman received a note from his late companion which ran as follows:—

MY DEAR MR. NEWMAN,—I am afraid that my conduct at Venice, a week ago, seemed to you strange and ungrateful, and I wish to explain my position, which, as I said at the time, I do not think you appreciate. I had long had it on my mind to propose that we should part company, and this step was not really so abrupt as it seemed. In the first place, you know, I am traveling in Europe on funds supplied by my congregation, who kindly offered me a vacation and an opportunity to enrich my mind with the treasures of nature and art in the Old World. I feel, therefore, as if I ought to use my time to the very best advantage. I have a high sense of responsibility. You appear to care only for the pleasure of the hour, and you give yourself up to it with a violence which I confess I am not able to emulate. I feel as if I must arrive at some conclusion and fix my belief on certain points. Art and life seem to me intensely serious things, and in our travels in Europe we should especially remember the immense seriousness of Art. You seem to hold that if a thing amuses you for the moment, that is all you need ask for it; and your relish for mere amusement is also much higher than mine. You put, however, a kind of reckless confidence into your pleasure which at times, I confess, has seemed to me—shall I say it?—almost cynical. Your way at any rate is not my way, and it is unwise that we should attempt any longer to pull together. And yet, let me add that I know there is a great deal to be said for your way; I have felt its attraction, in your society, very strongly. But for this I should have left you long ago. But I was so perplexed. I hope I have not done wrong. I feel as if I had a great deal of lost time to make up. I beg you take all this as I mean it, which, Heaven knows, is not invidiously. I have a great personal esteem for you, and hope that some day, when I have recovered my balance, we shall meet again. I hope you will continue to enjoy your travels, only *do* remember that Life and Art *are* extremely serious. Believe me your sincere friend and well-wisher,

BENJAMIN BABCOCK

P. S. I am greatly perplexed by Luini.

This letter produced in Newman's mind a singular mixture of exhilaration and awe. At first, Mr. Babcock's tender conscience seemed to him a capital farce, and his traveling back to Milan only to get into a deeper muddle appeared, as the reward of his pedantry, exquisitely and ludicrously just. Then Newman reflected that these are mighty mysteries; that possibly he himself was indeed that baleful and barely mentionable thing, a cynic, and that his manner of considering the treasures of art and the privileges of life was probably very base and immoral. Newman had a great contempt for immorality, and that evening, for a good half hour, as he sat watching the star-sheen on the warm Adriatic, he felt rebuked and depressed. He was at a loss how to answer Babcock's letter. His good nature checked his resenting the young minister's lofty admonitions, and his tough, inelastic sense of humor forbade his taking them seriously. He wrote no answer at all, but a day or two afterward he found in a curiosity shop a grotesque little statuette in ivory, of the sixteenth century, which he sent off to Babcock without a commentary. It represented a gaunt, ascetic-looking monk, in a tattered gown and cowl, kneeling with clasped hands and pulling a portentously long face. It was a wonderfully delicate piece of carving, and in a moment, through one of the rents of his gown, you espied a fat capon hung round the monk's waist. In Newman's intention what did the figure symbolize? Did it mean that he was going to try to be as "high-toned" as the monk looked at first, but that he feared he should succeed no better than the friar, on a closer inspection, proved to have done? It is not supposable that he intended a satire upon Babcock's own asceticism, for this would have been a truly cynical stroke. He made his late companion, at any rate, a very valuable little present.

Newman, on leaving Venice, went through the Tyrol to Vienna, and then returned westward, through Southern Germany. The autumn found him at Baden-Baden, where he spent several weeks. The place was charming, and he was in no hurry to depart; besides, he was looking about him and deciding what to do for the winter. His summer had been very full, and he sat under the great trees beside the miniature river that trickles past the Baden flower-beds, he slowly rummaged it over. He had seen and done a great deal, enjoyed and observed a great deal; he felt older, and yet he felt younger too. He remembered Mr. Babcock and his desire to form conclusions, and he remembered also that he had profited very little by his friend's exhortation to cultivate the same respectable habit. Could he not scrape together a few conclusions? Baden-Baden was the prettiest place he had seen yet, and orchestral music in the evening, under the stars, was decidedly a great institution. This was one of his conclusions! But he went on to reflect that he had done very wisely to pull up stakes and come abroad; this seeing of the world was a very interesting thing. He had learned a great deal; he couldn't say just what, but he had it there under his hat-band. He had done what he wanted; he had seen the great things, and he had given his mind a chance to "improve," if it would. He cheerfully believed that it had improved. Yes, this seeing of the world was very pleasant, and he would willingly do a little more of it. Thirty-six years old as he was, he had a handsome stretch of life before him yet, and he need not begin to count his weeks. Where should he take the world next? I have said he remembered the eyes of the lady whom he had found standing in Mrs. Tristram's drawing-room; four months had elapsed, and he had not forgotten them yet. He had looked—he had made a point of looking—into a great many other eyes in the interval, but the only ones he thought of now were Madame de Cintré's. If he wanted to see more of the world, should he find it in Madame de Cintré's eyes? He would certainly find something there, call it this world or the next. Throughout these rather formless meditations he sometimes thought of his past life and the long array of years (they had begun so early) during which he had had nothing in his head but "enterprise." They seemed far away now, for his present attitude was more than a holiday, it was almost a rupture. He had told Tristram that the pendulum was swinging back, and it appeared that the backward swing had not yet ended. Still "enterprise," which was over in the other quarter, wore to his mind a different aspect at different hours. In its train a thousand forgotten episodes came trooping back into his memory. Some of them he looked complacently enough in the face; from some he averted his head. They were old efforts, old exploits, antiquated examples of "smartness" and sharpness. Some of them, as he looked at them, he felt decidedly proud of; he admired himself as if he had been looking at another man. And, in fact, many of the qualities that make a great deed were there: the decision, the resolution, the courage, the celerity, the clear eye, and the strong hand. Of certain other achievements it would be going too far to say that he was ashamed of them, for Newman had never had a stomach for dirty work. He was blessed with a natural impluse to disfigure with a direct, unreasoning blow the comely visage of temptation. And certainly, in no man could a want of integrity have been less excusable. Newman knew the crooked from the straight at a glance, and the former had cost him, first and last, a great many moments of lively disgust. But none the less some of his memories seemed to wear at present a rather graceless and sordid mien, and it struck him that if he had never done anything very ugly, he had never, on the other hand, done anything particularly beautiful. He had spent his years in the unremitting effort to add thousands to thousands, and, now that he stood well outside of it, the business of money-getting appeared tolerably dry and sterile. It is very well to sneer at money-getting after you have filled your pockets, and Newman, it may be said, should have begun somewhat earlier to moralize thus delicately. To this it may be answered that he might have made another fortune, if he chose; and we ought to add that he was not exactly moralizing. It had come back to him simply that what he had been looking at all summer was a very rich and beautiful world, and that it had not all been made by sharp railroad men and stock-brokers.

During his stay at Baden-Baden he received a letter from Mrs. Tristram, scolding him for the scanty tidings he had sent to his friends of the Avenue d'Iéna, and begging to be definitely informed that he had not concocted any horrid scheme for wintering in outlying regions, but was coming back sanely and promptly to the most comfortable city in the world. Newman's answer ran as follows:—

"I supposed you knew I was a miserable letter-writer, and didn't expect anything of me. I don't think I have written twenty letters of pure friendship in my whole life; in America I conducted my correspondence altogether by telegrams. This is a letter of pure friendship; you have got hold of a curiosity, and I hope you will value it. You want to know everything that has happened to me these three months. The best way to tell you, I think, would be to sent you my half dozen guide-books, with my pencil-marks in the margin. Wherever you find a scratch, or a cross, or a 'Beautiful!' or a 'So true!' or a 'Too thin!' you may know that I have had a sensation of some sort or other. That has been about my history, ever since I left you. Belgium, Holland, Switzerland, Germany, Italy, I have been through the whole list, and I don't think I am any the worse for it. I know more about Madonnas and church-steeples than I supposed any man could. I have seen some very pretty things, and shall perhaps talk them over this winter, by your fireside. You see, my face is not altogether set against Paris. I have had all kinds of plans and visions, but your letter has blown most of them away. 'L'appétit vient en mangeant,' says the French proverb, and I find that the more I see of the world the more I want to see. Now that I am in the shafts, why shouldn't I trot to the end of the course? Sometimes I think of the far East, and keep rolling the names of Eastern cities under my tongue: Damascus and Bagdad, Medina and Mecca. I spend a week last month in the company of a returned missionary, who told me I ought to be ashamed to be loafing about Europe when there are such big things to be seen out there. I do want to explore, but I think I would rather explore over in the Rue de l'Université. Do you ever hear from that pretty lady? If you can get her to promise she will be at home the next time I call, I will go back to Paris straight. I am more than ever in the state of mind I told you about that evening; I want a first-class wife. I have kept an eye on all the pretty girls I have come across this summer, but none of them came up to my notion, or anywhere near it. I should have enjoyed all this a thousand times more if I had had the lady just mentioned by my side. The nearest approach to her was a Unitarian minister from Boston, who very soon demanded a separation, for incompatibility of temper. He told me I was low-minded, immoral, a devotee of 'art for art'—whatever that is: all of which greatly afflicted me, for he was really a sweet little fellow. But shortly afterwards I met an Englishman, with whom I struck up an acquaintance which at first seemed to promise well—a very bright man, who writes in the London papers and knows Paris nearly as well as Tristram. We knocked about for a week together, but he very soon gave me up in disgust. I was too virtuous by half; I was too stern a moralist. He told me, in a friendly way, that I was cursed with a conscience; that I judged things like a Methodist and talked about them like an old lady. This was rather bewildering. Which of my two critics was I to believe? I didn't worry about it and very soon made up my mind they were both idiots. But there is one thing in which no one will ever have the impudence to pretend I am wrong, that is, in being your faithful friend,   C. N."

Chapter VI

NEWMAN GAVE up Damascus and Bagdad and returned to Paris before the autumn was over. He established himself in some rooms selected for him by Tom Tristram, in accordance with the latter's estimate of what he called his social position. When Newman learned that his social position was to be taken into account, he professed himself utterly incompetent, and begged Tristram to relieve him of the care. "I didn't know I had a social position," he said, "and if I have, I haven't the smallest idea what it is. Isn't a social position knowing some two or three thousand people and inviting them to dinner? I know you and your wife and little old Mr. Nioche, who gave me French lessons last spring. Can I invite you to dinner to meet each other? If I can, you must come to-morrow."

"That is not very grateful to me," said Mrs. Tristram, "who introduced you last year to every creature I know."

"So you did; I had quite forgotten. But I thought you wanted me to forget," said Newman, with that tone of simple deliberateness which frequently marked his utterance, and which an observer would not have known whether to pronounce a somewhat mysteriously humorous affection of ignorance or a modest aspiration to knowledge; "you told me you disliked them all."

"Ah, the way you remember what I say is at least very flattering. But in future," added Mrs. Tristram, "pray forget all the wicked things and remember only the good ones. It will be easily done, and it will not fatigue your memory. But I forewarn you that if you trust my husband to pick out your rooms, you are in for something hideous."

"Hideous, darling?" cried Tristram.

"To-day I must say nothing wicked; otherwise I should use stronger language."

"What do you think she would say, Newman?" asked Tristram. "If she really tried, now? She can express displeasure, volubly, in two or three languages; that's what it is to be intellectual. It gives her the start of me completely, for I can't swear, for the life of me, except in English. When I get mad I have to fall back on our dear old mother tongue. There's nothing like it, after all."

Newman declared that he knew nothing about tables and chairs, and that he would accept, in the way of a lodging, with his eyes shut, anything that Tristram should offer him. This was partly veracity on our hero's part, but it was also partly charity. He knew that to pry about and look at rooms, and make people open windows, and poke into sofas with his cane, and gossip with landladies, and ask who lived above and who below—he knew that this was of all pastimes the dearest to Tristram's heart, and he felt the more disposed to put it in his way as he was conscious that, as regards his obliging friend, he had suffered the warmth of ancient good-fellowship somewhat to abate. Besides, he had no taste for upholstery; he had even no very exquisite sense of comfort or convenience. He had a relish for luxury and splendor, but it was satisfied by rather gross contrivances. He scarcely knew a hard chair from a soft one, and he possessed a talent for stretching his legs which quite dispensed with adventitious facilities. His idea of comfort was to inhabit very large rooms, have a great many of them, and be conscious of their possessing a number of patented mechanical devices—half of which he should never have occasion to use. The apartments should be light and brilliant and lofty; he had once said that he liked rooms in which you wanted to keep your hat on. For the rest, he was satisfied with the assurance of any respectable person that everything was "handsome." Tristram accordingly secured for him an apartment to which this epithet might be lavishly applied. It was situated on the Boulevard Haussmann, on a first floor, and consisted of a series of rooms, gilded from floor to ceiling a foot thick, draped in various light shades of satin, and chiefly furnished with mirrors and clocks. Newman thought them magnificent, thanked Tristram heartily, immediately took possession, and had one of his trunks standing for three months in his drawing-room.

One day Mrs. Tristram told him that her beautiful friend, Madame de Cintré, had returned from the country; that she had met her three days before, coming out of the Church of St. Sulpice; she herself having journeyed to that distant quarter in quest of an obscure lace-mender, of whose skill she had heard high praise.

"And how were those eyes?" Newman asked.

"Those eyes were red with weeping, if you please!" said Mrs. Tristram. "She had been to confession."

"It doesn't tally with your account of her," said Newman, "that she should have sins to confess."

"They were not sins; they were sufferings."

"How do you know that?"

"She asked me to come and see her; I went this morning."

"And what does she suffer from?"

"I didn't ask her. With her, somehow, one is very discreet. But I guessed, easily enough. She suffers from her wicked old mother and her Grand Turk of a brother. They persecute her. But I can almost forgive them, because, as I told you, she is a saint, and a persecution is all that she needs to bring out her saintliness and make her perfect."

"That's a comfortable theory for her. I hope you will never impart it to the old folks. Why does she let them bully her? Is she not her own mistress?"

"Legally, yes, I suppose; but morally, no. In France you must never say nay to your mother, whatever she requires of you. She may be the most abominable old woman in the world, and make your life a purgatory; but, after all, she is *ma mère*, and you have no right to judge her. You have simply to obey. The thing has a fine side to it. Madame de Cintré bows her head and folds her wings."

"Can't she at least make her brother leave off?"

"Her brother is the *chef de la famille*, as they say; he is the head of the clan. With those people the family is everything; you must act, not for your own pleasure, but for the advantage of the family."

"I wonder what *my* family would like me to do!" exclaimed Tristram.

"I wish you had one!" said his wife.

"But what do they want to get out of that poor lady?" Newman asked.

"Another marriage. They are not rich, and they want to bring more money into the family."

"There's your chance, my boy!" said Tristram.

"And Madame de Cintré objects," Newman continued.

"She has been sold once; she naturally objects to being sold again. It appears that the first time they made rather a poor bargain; M. de Cintré left a scanty property."

"And to whom do they want to marry her now?"

"I thought it best not to ask; but you may be sure it is to some horrid old nabob, or to some dissipated little duke."

"There's Mrs. Tristram, as large as life!" cried her husband. "Observe the richness of her imagination. She has not asked a single question—it's vulgar to ask questions—and yet she knows everything. She has the history of Madame de Cintré's marriage at her fingers' ends. She has seen the lovely Claire on her knees, with loosened tresses and streaming eyes, and the rest of them standing over her with spikes and goads and red-hot irons, ready to come down on her if she refuses the tipsy duke. The simple truth is that they made a fuss about her milliner's bill or refused her an opera-box."

Newman looked from Tristram to his wife with a certain mistrust in each direction. "Do you really mean," he asked of Mrs. Tristram, "that your friend is being forced into an unhappy marriage?"

"I think it extremely probable. Those people are very capable of that sort of thing."

"It is like something in a play," said Newman; "that dark old house over there looks as if wicked things had been done in it, and might be done again."

"They have a still darker old house in the country, Madame de Cintré tells me, and there, during the summer, this scheme must have been hatched."

"*Must* have been; mind that!" said Tristram.

"After all," suggested Newman, after a silence, "she may be in trouble about something else."

"If it is something else, then it is something worse," said Mrs. Tristram, with rich decision.

Newman was silent a while, and seemed lost in meditation. "Is it possible," he asked at last, "that they do that sort of thing over here? that helpless women are bullied into marrying men they hate?"

"Helpless women, all over the world, have a hard time of it," said Mrs. Tristram. "There is plenty of bullying everywhere."

"A great deal of that kind of thing goes on in New York," said Tristram. "Girls are bullied or coaxed or bribed, or all three together, into marrying nasty fellows. There is no end of that always going on in the Fifth Avenue, and other bad things besides. The Mysteries of the Fifth Avenue! Some one ought to show them up."

"I don't believe it!" said Newman, very gravely. "I don't believe that, in America, girls are ever subjected to compulsion. I don't believe there have been a dozen cases of it since the country began."

"Listen to the voice of the spread eagle!" cried Tristram.

"The spread eagle ought to use his wings," said Mrs. Tristram. "Fly to the rescue of Madame de Cintré!"

"To her rescue?"

"Pounce down, seize her in your talons, and carry her off. Marry her yourself."

Newman, for some moments, answered nothing; but presently, "I should suppose she had heard enough of marrying," he said. "The kindest way to treat her would be to admire her, and yet never to speak of it. But that sort of thing is infamous," he added; "it makes me feel savage to hear of it."

He heard of it, however, more than once afterward. Mrs. Tristram again saw Madame de Cintré, and again found her looking very sad. But on these occasions there had been no tears; her beautiful eyes were clear and still. "She is cold, calm, and hopeless," Mrs. Tristram declared, and she added that on her mentioning that her friend Mr. Newman was again in Paris and was faithful in his desire to make Madame de Cintré's acquaintance, this lovely woman had found a smile in her despair, and declared that she was sorry to have missed his visit in the spring and that she hoped he had not lost courage. "I told her something about you," said Mrs. Tristram.

"That's a comfort," said Newman, placidly. "I like people to know about me."

A few days after this, one dusky autumn afternoon, he went again to the Rue de l'Université. The early evening had closed in as he applied for admittance at the stoutly guarded Hôtel de Bellegarde. He was told that Madame de Cintré was at home; he crossed the court, entered the farther door, and was conducted through a vestibule, vast, dim, and cold, up a broad stone staircase with an

ancient iron balustrade, to an apartment on the second floor. Announced and ushered in, he found himself in a sort of paneled
boudoir, at one end of which a lady and gentleman were seated
before the fire. The gentleman was smoking a cigarette; there was
no light in the room save that of a couple of candles and the glow
from the hearth. Both persons rose to welcome Newman, who, in
the firelight, recognized Madame de Cintré. She gave him her hand
with a smile which seemed in itself an illumination, and, pointing
to her companion, said softly, "My brother." The gentleman offered
Newman a frank, friendly greeting, and our hero then perceived
him to be the young man who had spoken to him in the court of
the hotel on his former visit and who had struck him as a good
fellow.

"Mrs. Tristram has spoken to me a great deal of you," said Madame
de Cintré gently, as she resumed her former place.

Newman, after he had seated himself, began to consider what,
in truth, was his errand. He had an unusual, unexpected sense of
having wandered into a strange corner of the world. He was not
given, as a general thing, to anticipating danger, or forecasting
disaster, and he had had no social tremors on this particular occasion.
He was not timid and he was not impudent. He felt too kindly
toward himself to be the one, and too good-naturedly toward the
rest of the world to be the other. But his native shrewdness sometimes placed his ease of temper at its mercy; with every disposition
to take things simply, it was obliged to perceive that some things
were not so simple as others. He felt as one does in missing a step,
in an ascent, where one expected to find it. This strange, pretty
woman, sitting in fire-side talk with her brother, in the gray depths
of her inhospitable-looking house—what had he to say to her? She
seemed enveloped in a sort of fantastic privacy; on what grounds
had he pulled away the curtain? For a moment he felt as if he had
plunged into some medium as deep as the ocean, and as if he must
exert himself to keep from sinking. Meanwhile he was looking at
Madame de Cintré, and she was settling herself in her chair and
drawing in her long dress and turning her face towards him. Their
eyes met; a moment afterwards she looked away and motioned to
her brother to put a log on the fire. But the moment, and the glance
which traversed it, had been sufficient to relieve Newman of the
first and the last fit of personal embarrassment he was ever to know.
He performed the movement which was so frequent with him, and
which was always a sort of symbol of his taking mental possession of

a scene—he extended his legs. The impression Madame de Cintré had made upon him on their first meeting came back in an instant; it had been deeper than he knew. She was pleasing, she was interesting; he had opened a book and the first lines held his attention.

She asked him several questions: how lately he had seen Mrs. Tristram, how long he had been in Paris, how long he expected to remain there, how he liked it. She spoke English without an accent, or rather with that distinctively British accent which, on his arrival in Europe, had struck Newman as an altogether foreign tongue, but which, in women, he had come to like extremely. Here and there Madame de Cintré's utterance had a faint shade of strangeness, but at the end of ten minutes Newman found himself waiting for these soft roughnesses. He enjoyed them, and he marveled to see that gross thing, error, brought down to so fine a point.

"You have a beautiful country," said Madame de Cintré, presently.

"Oh, magnificent!" said Newman. "You ought to see it."

"I shall never see it," said Madame de Cintré with a smile.

"Why not?" asked Newman.

"I don't travel; especially so far."

"But you go away sometimes; you are not always here?"

"I go away in summer, a little way, to the country."

Newman wanted to ask her something more, something personal, he hardly knew what. "Don't you find it rather—rather quiet here?" he said; "so far from the street?" Rather "gloomy," he was going to say, but he reflected that that would be impolite.

"Yes, it is very quiet," said Madame de Cintré; "but we like that."

"Ah, you like that," repeated Newman, slowly.

"Besides, I have lived here all my life."

"Lived here all your life," said Newman, in the same way.

"I was born here, and my father was born here before me, and my grandfather, and my great-grandfathers. Were they not, Valentin?" and she appealed to her brother.

"Yes, it's a family habit to be born here!" the young man said with a laugh, and rose and threw the remnant of his cigarette into the fire, and then remained leaning against the chimney-piece. An observer would have perceived that he wished to take a better look at Newman, whom he covetly examined, while he stood stroking his mustache.

"How old is it, brother?" asked Madame de Cintré.

The young man took the two candles from the mantel-shelf, lifted one high in each hand, and looked up toward the cornice of the room, above the chimney-piece. This latter feature of the apartment was of white marble, and in the familiar rococo style of the last century; but above it was a paneling of an earlier date, quaintly carved, painted white, and gilded here and there. The white had turned to yellow, and the gilding was tarnished. On the top, the figures ranged themselves into a sort of shield, on which an armorial device was cut. Above it, in relief, was a date—1627. "There you have it," said the young man. "That is old or new, according to your point of view."

"Well, over here," said Newman, "one's point of view gets shifted round considerably." And he threw back his head and looked about the room. "Your house is of a very curious style of architecture," he said.

"Are you interested in architecture?" asked the young man at the chimney-piece.

"Well, I took the trouble, this summer," said Newman, "to examine—as well as I can calculate—some four hundred and seventy churches. Do you call that interested?"

"Perhaps you are interested in theology," said the young man.

"Not particularly. Are you a Roman Catholic, madam?" And he turned to Madame de Cintré.

"Yes, sir," she answered, gravely.

Newman was struck with the gravity of her tone; he threw back his head and began to look round the room again. "Had you never noticed that number up there?" he presently asked.

She hesitated a moment, and then, "In former years," she said.

Her brother had been watching Newman's movement. "Perhaps you would like to examine the house," he said.

Newman slowly brought down his eyes and looked at him; he had a vague impression that the young man at the chimney-piece was inclined to irony. He was a handsome fellow, his face wore a smile, his mustaches were curled up at the ends, and there was a little dancing gleam in his eye. "Damn his French impudence!" Newman was on the point of saying to himself. "What the deuce is he grinning at?" He glanced at Madame de Cintré; she was sitting with her eyes fixed on the floor. She raised them, they met his, and she looked at her brother. Newman turned again to this young man and observed that he strikingly resembled his sister. This was in his favor, and our hero's first impression of the Count Valentin, moreover, had been agreeable. His mistrust expired, and he said he would be very glad to see the house.

The young man gave a frank laugh, and laid his hand on one of the candlesticks. "Good, good!" he exclaimed. "Come, then."

But Madame de Cintré rose quickly and grasped his arm, "Ah, Valentin!" she said. "What do you mean to do?"

"To show Mr. Newman the house. It will be very amusing."

She kept her hand on his arm, and turned to Newman with a smile. "Don't let him take you," she said; "you will not find it amusing. It is a musty old house, like any other."

"It is full of curious things," said the count, resisting. "Besides, I want to do it; it is a rare chance."

"You are very wicked, brother," Madame de Cintré answered.

"Nothing venture, nothing have!" cried the young man. "Will you come?"

Madame de Cintré stepped toward Newman, gently clasping her hands and smiling softly. "Would you not prefer my society, here, by my fire, to stumbling about dark passages after my brother?"

"A hundred times!" said Newman. "We will see the house some other day."

The young man put down his candlestick with mock solemnity, and, shaking his head, "Ah, you have defeated a great scheme, sir!" he said.

"A scheme? I don't understand," said Newman.

"You would have played your part in it all the better. Perhaps some day I shall have a chance to explain it."

"Be quiet, and ring for the tea," said Madame de Cintré.

The young man obeyed, and presently a servant brought in the tea, placed the tray on a small table, and departed. Madame de Cintré, from her place, busied herself with making it. She had but just begun when the door was thrown open and a lady rushed in, making a loud rustling sound. She stared at Newman, gave a little nod and a "Monsieur!" and then quickly approached Madame de Cintré and presented her forehead to be kissed. Madame de Cintré saluted her, and continued to make tea. The new-comer was young and pretty, it seemed to Newman; she wore her bonnet and cloak, and a train of royal proportions. She began to talk rapidly in French. "Oh, give me some tea, my beautiful one, for the love of God! I'm exhausted, mangled, massacred." Newman found himself quite unable to follow her; she spoke much less distinctly than M. Nioche.

"That is my sister-in-law," said the Count Valentin, leaning towards him.

"She is very pretty," said Newman.

"Exquisite," answered the young man, and this time, again, Newman suspected him of irony.

His sister-in-law came round to the other side of the fire with her cup of tea in her hand, holding it out at arm's-length, so that she might not spill it on her dress, and uttering little cries of alarm. She placed the cup on the mantel-shelf and begun to unpin her veil and pull off her gloves, looking meanwhile at Newman.

"Is there any thing I can do for you, my dear lady?" the Count Valentin asked, in a sort of mock-caressing tone.

"Present monsieur," said his sister-in-law.

The young man answered, "Mr. Newman!"

"I can't courtesy to you, monsieur, or I shall spill my tea," said the lady. "So Claire receives strangers, like that? she added, in a low voice, in French, to her brother-in-law.

"Apparently!" he answered with a smile. Newman stood a moment, and then he approached Madame de Cintré. She looked up at him as if she were thinking of something to say. But she seemed to think of nothing; so she simply smiled. He sat down near her and she handed him a cup of tea. For a few moments they talked about that, and meanwhile he looked at her. He remembered what Mrs. Tristram had told him of her "perfection" and of her having, in combination, all the brilliant things that he dreamed of finding. This made him observe her not only without mistrust, but without uneasy conjectures; the presumption, from the first moment he looked at her, had been in her favor. And yet, if she was beautiful, it was not a dazzling beauty. She was tall and moulded in long lines; she had thick fair hair, a wide forehead, and features with a sort of harmonious irregularity. Her clear gray eyes were strikingly expressive; they were both gentle and intelligent, and Newman liked them immensely; but they had not those depths of splendor—those many-colored rays—which illumine the brows of famous beauties. Madame de Cintré was rather thin, and she looked younger than probably she was. In her whole person there was something both youthful and subdued, slender and yet ample, tranquil yet shy; a mixture of immaturity and repose, of innocence and dignity. What had Tristram meant, Newman wondered, by calling her proud? She was certainly not proud now, to him; or if she was, it was of no use, it was lost upon him; she must pile it up higher if she expected him to mind it. She was a beautiful woman, and it was very easy to get on with her. Was she a countess, a *marquise*, a kind of historical formation? Newman, who had rarely heard these words used, had never been at pains to attach any particular image to them; but they occurred to him now and seemed charged with a sort of melodious meaning. They signified something fair and softly bright, that had easy motions and spoke very agreeably.

"Have you many friends in Paris; do you go out?" asked Madame de Cintré, who had at last thought of something to say.

"Do you mean do I dance, and all that?"

"Do you go *dans le monde*, as we say?"

"I have seen a good many people. Mrs. Tristram has taken me about. I do whatever she tells me."

"By yourself, you are not fond of amusements?"

"Oh yes, of some sorts. I am not fond of dancing, and that sort of thing; I am too old and sober. But I want to be amused; I came to Europe for that."

"But you can be amused in America, too."

"I couldn't; I was always at work. But after all, that was my amusement."

At this moment Madame de Bellegarde came back for another cup of tea, accompanied by the Count Valentin. Madame de Cintré, when she had served her, began to talk again with Newman, and recalling what he had last said, "In your own country you were very much occupied?" she asked.

"I was in business. I have been in business since I was fifteen years old."

"And what was your business?" asked Madame de Bellegarde, who was decidedly not so pretty as Madame de Cintré.

"I have been in everything," said Newman. "At one time I sold leather; at one time I manufactured wash-tubs."

Madame de Bellegarde made a little grimace. "Leather? I don't like that. Wash-tubs are better. I prefer the smell of soap. I hope at least they made your fortune." She rattled this off with the air of a woman who had the reputation of saying everything that came into her head, and with a strong French accent.

Newman had spoken with cheerful seriousness, but Madame de Bellegarde's tone made him go on, after a meditative pause, with a certain light grimness of jocularity. "No, I lost money on wash-tubs, but I came out pretty square on leather."

"I have made up my mind, after all," said Madame de Bellegarde, "that the great point is—how do you call it?—to come out square. I am on my knees to money; I don't deny it. If you have it, I ask no questions. For that I am a real democrat—like you, monsieur.

Madame de Cintré is very proud; but I find that one gets much more pleasure in this sad life if one doesn't look too close."

"Just Heaven, dear madam, how you go at it," said the Count Valentin, lowering his voice.

"He's a man one can speak to, I suppose, since my sister receives him," the lady answered. "Besides, it's very true; those are my ideas."

"Ah, you call them ideas," murmured the young man.

"But Mrs. Tristram told me you had been in the army—in your war," said Madame de Cintré.

"Yes, but that is not business!" said Newman.

"Very true!" said M. de Bellegarde. "Otherwise perhaps I should not be penniless."

"Is it true," asked Newman in a moment, "that you are so proud? I had already heard it."

Madame de Cintré smiled. "Do you find me so?"

"Oh," said Newman, "I am no judge. If you are proud with me, you will have to tell me. Otherwise I shall not know it."

Madame de Cintré began to laugh. "That would be pride in a sad position!" she said.

"It would be partly," Newman went on, "because I shouldn't want to know it. I want you to treat me well."

Madame de Cintré, whose laugh had ceased, looked at him with her head half averted, as if she feared what he was going to say.

"Mrs. Tristram told you the literal truth," he went on; "I want very much to know you. I didn't come here simply to call to-day; I came in the hope that you might ask me to come again."

"Oh, pray come often," said Madame de Cintré.

"But will you be at home?" Newman insisted. Even to himself he seemed a trifle "pushing," but he was, in truth, a trifle excited.

"I hope so!" said Madame de Cintré.

Newman got up. "Well, we shall see," he said smoothing his hat with his coat-cuff.

"Brother," said Madame de Cintré, "invite Mr. Newman to come again."

The Count Valentin looked at our hero from head to foot with his peculiar smile, in which impudence and urbanity seemed perplexingly commingled. "Are you a brave man?" he asked, eying him askance.

"Well, I hope so," said Newman.

"I rather suspect so. In that case, come again."

"Ah, what an invitation!" murmured Madame de Cintré, with

something painful in her smile.

"Oh, I want Mr. Newman to come—particularly," said the young man. "It will give me great pleasure. I shall be desolate if I miss one of his visits. But I maintain he must be brave. A stout heart, sir!" And he offered Newman his hand.

"I shall not come to see you; I shall come to see Madame de Cintré," said Newman.

"You will need all the more courage."

"Ah, Valentin!" said Madame de Cintré, appealingly.

"Decidedly," cried Madame de Bellegarde, "I am the only person here capable of saying something polite! Come to see me; you will need no courage," she said.

Newman gave a laugh which was not altogether an assent, and took his leave. Madame de Cintré did not take up her sister's challenge to be gracious, but she looked with a certain troubled air at the retreating guest.

CHAPTER VII

ONE EVENING, very late, about a week after his visit to Madame de Cintré, Newman's servant brought him a card. It was that of young M. de Bellegarde. When, a few moments later, he went to receive his visitor, he found him standing in the middle of his great gilded parlor and eying it from cornice to carpet. M. de Bellegarde's face, it seemed to Newman, expressed a sense of lively entertainment. "What the devil is he laughing at now?" our hero asked himself. But he put the question without acrimony, for he felt that Madame de Cintré's brother was a good fellow, and he had a presentiment that on this basis of good fellowship they were destined to understand each other. Only, if there was anything to laugh at, he wished to have a glimpse of it too.

"To begin with," said the young man, as he extended his hand, "have I come too late?"

"Too late for what?" asked Newman.

"To smoke a cigar with you."

"You would have to come early to do that," said Newman. "I don't smoke."

"Ah, you are a strong man!"

"But I keep cigars," Newman added. "Sit down.

"Surely, I may not smoke here," said M. de Bellegarde.

"What is the matter? Is the room too small?"

"It is too large. It is like smoking in a ball-room, or a church."

"That is what you were laughing at just now?" Newman asked; "the size of my room?"

"It is not size only," replied M. de Bellegarde, "but splendor, and harmony, and beauty of detail. It was the smile of admiration."

Newman looked at him a moment, and then, "So it *is* very ugly?" he inquired.

"Ugly, my dear sir? It is magnificent."

"That is the same thing, I suppose," said Newman. "Make yourself comfortable. Your coming to see me, I take it, is an act of friendship. You were not obliged to. Therefore, if anything around here amuses you, it will be all in a pleasant way. Laugh as loud as you please; I like to see my visitors cheerful. Only, I must make this request: that you explain the joke to me as soon as you can speak. I don't want to lose anything, myself."

M. de Bellegarde stared, with a look of unresentful perplexity. He laid his hand on Newman's sleeve and seemed on the point of saying something, but he suddenly checked himself, leaned back in his chair, and puffed at his cigar. At last, however, breaking silence,—"Certainly," he said, "my coming to see you is an act of friendship. Nevertheless I was in a measure obliged to do so. My sister asked me to come, and a request from my sister is, for me, a law. I was near you, and I observed lights in what I supposed were your rooms. It was not a ceremonious hour for making a call, but I was not sorry to do something that would show I was not performing a mere ceremony."

"Well, here I am as large as life," said Newman, extending his legs.

"I don't know what you mean," the young man went on, "by giving me unlimited leave to laugh. Certainly I am a great laugher, and it is better to laugh too much than too little. But it is not in order that we may laugh together—or separately—that I have, I may say, sought your acquaintance. To speak with almost impudent frankness, you interest me!" All this was uttered by M. de Bellegarde with the modulated smoothness of the man of the world, and, in spite of his excellent English, of the Frenchman; but Newman, at the same time that he sat noting its harmonious flow, perceived that it was not mere mechanical urbanity. Decidedly, there was something in his visitor that he liked. M. de Bellegarde was a foreigner to his finger-tips, and if Newman had met him on a Western prairie he would have felt it proper to address him with a "How-d'ye-do, Mosseer?" But there was something in his physiognomy which seemed to cast a sort of aerial bridge over the impassable gulf produced by difference of race. He was below the middle height, and robust and agile in figure. Valentin de Bellegarde, Newman afterwards learned, had a mortal dread of the robustness overtaking the agility; he was afraid of growing stout; he was too short, as he said, to afford a belly. He rode and fenced and practiced gymnastics with un-remitting zeal, and if you greeted him with a "How well you are looking!" he started and turned pale. In your *well* he read a grosser monosyllable. He had a round head, high above the ears, a crop of hair at once dense and silky, a broad, low forehead, a short nose, of the ironical and inquiring rather than of the dog-matic or sensitive cast, and a mustache as delicate as that of a page in a romance. He resembled his sister not in feature, but in the expression of his clear, bright eye, completely void of introspection, and in the way he smiled. The great point in his face was that it was intensely alive—frankly, ardently, gallantly alive. The look of it was like a bell, of which the handle might have been in the young man's soul: at a touch of the handle it rang with a loud, silver sound. There was something in his quick, light brown eye which assured you that he was not economizing his consciousness. He was not living in a corner of it to spare the furniture of the rest. He was squarely encamped in the centre and he was keeping open house. When he smiled, it was like the movement of a person who in emptying a cup turns it upside down: he gave you the last drop of his pollity. He inspired Newman with something of the same kindness that our hero used to feel in his earlier years for those of his companions who could perform strange and clever tricks—make their joints crack in queer places or whistle at the back of their mouths.

"My sister told me," M. de Bellegarde continued, "that I ought to come and remove the impression that I had taken such great pains to produce upon you; the impression that I am a lunatic. Did it strike you that I behaved very oddly the other day?"

"Rather so," said Newman.

"So my sister tells me." And M. de Bellegarde watched his host for a moment through his smoke-wreaths. "If that is the case, I think we had better let it stand. I didn't try to make you think I was a lunatic, at all; on the contrary, I wanted to produce a favorable impression. But if, after all, I made a fool of myself, it was the intention of Providence. I should injure myself by protesting too much, for I should seem to set up a claim for wisdom which, in the sequel of our acquaintance, I could by no means justify. Set me down as a lunatic with intervals of sanity."

"Oh, I guess you know what you are about," said Newman.

"When I am sane, I am very sane; that I admit," M. de Bellegarde answered. "But I didn't come here to talk about myself. I should like to ask you a few questions. You allow me?"

"Give me a specimen," said Newman.

"You live here all alone?"

"Absolutely. With whom should I live?"

"For the moment," said M. de Bellegarde with a smile, "I am asking questions, not answering them. You have come to Paris for your pleasure?"

Newman was silent a while. Then, at last, "Every one asks me that!" he said with his mild slowness. "It sounds so awfully foolish."

"But at any rate you had a reason."

"Oh, I came for my pleasure!" said Newman. "Though it is foolish, it is true."

"And you are enjoying it?"

Like any other good American, Newman thought it as well not to truckle to the foreigner. "Oh, so-so," he answered.

M. de Bellegarde puffed his cigar again in silence. "For myself," he said at last, "I am entirely at your service. Anything I can do for you I shall be very happy to do. Call upon me at your convenience. Is there any one you desire to know—anything you wish to see? It is a pity you should not enjoy Paris."

"Oh, I do enjoy it!" said Newman, good-naturedly. "I'm much obliged to you."

"Honestly speaking," M. de Bellegarde went on, "there is something absurd to me in hearing myself make you these offers. They represent a great deal of good-will, but they represent little else. You are a successful man and I am a failure, and it's a turning of the tables to talk as if I could lend you a hand."

"In what way are you a failure?" asked Newman.

"Oh, I'm not a tragical failure!" cried the young man with a laugh. "I have fallen from a height, and my fiasco has made no noise. You, evidently, are a success. You have made a fortune, you have built up an edifice, you are a financial, commercial power, you can travel about the world until you have found a soft spot, and lie down in it with the consciousness of having earned your rest. Is not that true? Well, imagine the exact reverse of all that, and you have me. I have done nothing—I can do nothing!"

"Why not?"

"It's a long story. Some day I will tell you. Meanwhile, I'm right, eh? You are a success? You have made a fortune? It's none of my business, but, in short, you are rich?"

"That's another thing that it sounds foolish to say," said Newman. "Hang it, no man is rich!"

"I have heard philosophers affirm," laughed M. de Bellegarde, "that no man was poor; but your formula strikes me as an improvement. As a general thing, I confess, I don't like successful people, and I find clever men who have made great fortunes very offensive. They tread on my toes; they make me uncomfortable. But as soon as I saw you, I said to myself, 'Ah, there is a man with whom I shall get on. He has the good-nature of success and none of the *morgue;* he has not our confoundedly irritable French vanity.' In short, I took a fancy to you. We are very different, I'm sure; I don't believe there is a subject on which we think or feel alike. But I rather think we shall get on, for there is such a thing, you know, as being too different to quarrel."

"Oh, I never quarrel," said Newman.

"Never? Sometimes it's a duty—or at least it's a pleasure. Oh, I have had two or three delicious quarrels in my day!" and M. de Bellegarde's handsome smile assumed, at the memory of these incidents, an almost voluptuous intensity.

With the preamble embodied in his share of the foregoing fragment of dialogue, he paid our hero a long visit; as the two men sat with their heels on Newman's glowing hearth, they heard the small hours of the morning striking larger from a far-off belfry. Valentin de Bellegarde was, by his own confession, at all times a great chatterer, and on this occasion he was evidently in a particularly loquacious mood. It was a tradition of his race that people of its blood always conferred a favor by their smiles, and as his enthusiasms were as rare as his civility was constant, he had a double reason for not suspecting that his friendship could ever be importunate. Moreover, the flower of an ancient stem as he was, tradition (since I have used the word) had in his temperament nothing of disagreeable rigidity. It was muffled in sociability and urbanity, as an old dowager in her laces and strings of pearls. Valentin was what is called in France a *gentilhomme*, of the purest source, and his rule of life, so far as it was definite, was to play the part of a gentilhomme. This, it seemed to him, was enough to occupy comfortably a young man of ordinary good parts. But all that he was he was by instinct and not by theory, and the amiability of his character was so great that certain of the aristocratic virtues, which in some aspects seem rather brittle and trenchant, acquired in his application of them an extreme geniality. In his younger years he had been suspected of low tastes, and his mother had greatly feared he would make a slip in the mud of the highway and bespatter the family shield. He had been treated, therefore, to more than his share of schooling and drilling, but his instructors had not succeeded in mounting him upon stilts. They could not spoil his safe spontaneity, and he remained the least cautious and the most lucky of young nobles. He had been tied with so short a rope in his youth that he had now a mortal grudge against family discipline. He had been known to say, within the limits of the family, that, light-headed as he was, the honor of the name was safer in his hands than in those of some of its other members, and that if a day ever came to try it, they should see. His talk was an odd mixture of almost boyish garrulity and of the reserve and discretion of the man of the world, and he seemed to Newman, as afterwards young members of the Latin races often seemed to him, now amusingly juvenile and now appallingly mature. In America, Newman reflected, lads of twenty-five and thirty have old heads and young hearts, or at least young morals; here they have young heads and very aged hearts, morals the most grizzled and wrinkled.

"What I envy you is your liberty," observed M. de Bellegarde, "your wide range, your freedom to come and go, your not having a lot of people, who take themselves awfully seriously, expecting something of you. I live," he added with a sigh, "beneath the eyes of my admirable mother."

"It is your own fault; what is to hinder your ranging?" said Newman.

"There is a delightful simplicity in that remark." Everything is to hinder me. To begin with, I have not a penny."

"I had not a penny when I began to range."

"Ah, but your poverty was your capital. Being an American, it was impossible you should remain what you were born, and being born poor—do I understand it?—it was therefore inevitable that you should become rich. You were in a position that makes one's mouth water; you looked round you and saw a world full of things you had only to step up to and take hold of. When I was twenty, I looked around me and saw a world with everything ticketed 'Hands off!' and the deuce of it was that the ticket seemed meant only for me. I couldn't go into business, I couldn't make money, because I was a Bellegarde. I couldn't go into politics, because I was a Bellegarde—the Bellegardes don't recognize the Bonapartes. I couldn't go into literature, because I was a dunce. I couldn't marry a rich girl, because no Bellegarde had ever married a *roturière*, and it was not proper that I should begin. We shall have to come to it, yet. Marriageable heiresses, *de notre jord*, are not to be had for nothing; it must be name for name, and fortune for fortune. The only thing I could do was to go and fight for the Pope. That I did, punctiliously, and received an apostolic flesh-wound at Castlefidardo. It did neither the Holy Father nor me any good, that I could see. Rome was doubtless a very amusing place in the days of Caligula, but it has sadly fallen off since. I passed three years in the Castle of St. Angelo, and then came back to secular life."

"So you have no profession—you do nothing," said Newman.

"I do nothing! I am supposed to amuse myself, and, to tell the truth, I have amused myself. One can, if one knows how. But you can't keep it up forever. I am good for another five years, perhaps, but I foresee that after that I shall lose my appetite. Then what shall I do? I think I shall turn monk. Seriously, I think I shall tie a rope round my waist and go into a monastery. It was an old custom, and the old customs were very good. People understood life quite as well as we do. They kept the pot boiling till it cracked, and then they put it on the shelf altogether."

"Are you very religious?" asked Newman, in a tone which gave the inquiry a grotesque effect.

M. de Bellegarde evidently appreciated the comical element in the question, but he looked at Newman a moment with extreme soberness. "I am a very good Catholic. I respect the Church. I adore the blessed Virgin. I fear the Devil."

"Well, then," said Newman, "you are very well fixed. You have got pleasure in the present and religion in the future; what do you complain of?"

"It's a part of one's pleasure to complain. There is something in your own circumstances that irritates me. You are the first man I have ever envied. It's singular, but so it is. I have known many men who, besides any factitious advantages that I may possess, had money and brains into the bargain; but somehow they have never disturbed my good-humor. But you have got something that I should have liked to have. It is not money, it is not even brains—though no doubt yours are excellent. It is not your six feet of height, though I should have rather liked to be a couple of inches taller. It's a sort of air you have of being thoroughly at home in the world. When I was a boy, my father told me that it was by such an air as that that people recognized a Bellegarde. He called my attention to it. He didn't advise me to cultivate it; he said that as we grew up it always came of itself. I supposed it had come to me, because I think I have always had the feeling. My place in life was made for me, and it seemed easy to occupy it. But you who, as I understand it, have made your own place, you who, as you told us the other day, have manufactured wash-tubs—you strike me, somehow, as a man who stands at his ease, who looks at things from a height. I fancy you going about the world like a man traveling on a railroad in which he owns a large amount of stock. You make me feel as if I had missed something. What is it?"

"It is the proud consciousness of honest toil—of having manufactured a few wash-tubs," said Newman, at once jocose and serious.

"Oh no; I have seen men who had done even more, men who had made not only wash-tubs, but soap—strong-smelling yellow soap, in great bars; and they never made me the least uncomfortable."

"Then it's the privilege of being an American citizen," said Newman. "That sets a man up."

"Possibly," rejoined M. de Bellegarde. "But I am forced to say that I have seen a great many American citizens who didn't seem at all set up or in the least like large stockholders. I never envied them. I rather think the thing is an accomplishment of your own."

"Oh, come," said Newman, "you will make me proud!"

"No, I shall not. You have nothing to do with pride, or with humility—that is a part of this easy manner of yours. People are proud only when they have something to lose, and humble when they have something to gain."

"I don't know what I have to lose," said Newman, "but I certainly have something to gain."

"What is it?" asked his visitor.

Newman hesitated a while. "I will tell you when I know you better."

"I hope that will be soon! Then, if I can help you to gain it, I shall be happy."

"Perhaps you may," said Newman.

"Don't forget, then, that I am your servant," M. de Bellegarde answered; and shortly afterwards he took his departure.

During the next three weeks Newman saw Bellegarde several times, and without formally swearing an eternal friendship the two men established a sort of comradeship. To Newman, Bellegarde was the ideal Frenchman, the Frenchman of tradition and romance, so far as our hero was acquainted with these mystical influences. Gallant, expansive, amusing, more pleased himself with the effect he produced than those (even when they were well pleased) for whom he produced it; a master of all the distinctively social virtues and a votary of all agreeable sensations; a devotee of something mysterious and sacred to which he occasionally alluded in terms more ecstatic even than those in which he spoke of the last pretty woman, and which was simply the beautiful though somewhat superannuated image of *honor;* he was irresistibly entertaining and enlivening, and he formed a character to which Newman was as capable of doing justice when he had once been placed in contact with it, as he was unlikely, in musing upon the possible mixtures of our human ingredients, mentally to have foreshadowed it. Bellegarde did not in the least cause him to modify his needful premise that all Frenchmen are of a frothy and imponderable substance; he simply reminded him that light materials may be beaten up into a most agreeable compound. No two companions could be more different, but their differences made a capital basis for a friendship of which the distinctive characteristic was that it was extremely amusing to each.

Valentin de Bellegarde lived in the basement of an old house in the Rue d'Anjou St. Honoré, and his small apartments lay between the court of the house and an old garden which spread itself behind it—one of those large, sunless, humid gardens into which you look unexpectingly in Paris from back windows, wondering how among the grudging habitations they find their space. When Newman returned Bellegarde's visit, he hinted that *his* lodging was at least as much a laughing matter as his own. But its oddities were of a different cast from those of our hero's gilded saloons on the Boulevard Haussmann: the place was low, dusky, contracted, and crowded with curious bric-à-brac. Bellegarde, penniless patrician as he was,

was an insatiable collector, and his walls were covered with rusty arms and ancient panels and platters, his doorways draped in faded tapestries, his floors muffled in the skins of beasts. Here and there was one of those uncomfortable tributes to elegance in which the upholsterer's art, in France, is so prolific; a curtained recess with a sheet of looking-glass in which, among the shadows, you could see nothing; a divan on which, for its festoons and furbelows, you could not sit: a fireplace draped, flounced, and frilled to the complete exclusion of fire. The young man's possessions were in picturesque disorder, and his apartment was pervaded by the odor of cigars, mingled with perfumes more inscrutable. Newman thought it a damp, gloomy place to live in, and was puzzled by the obstructive and fragmentary character of the furniture.

Bellegarde, according to the custom of his country talked very generously about himself, and unveiled the mysteries of his private history with an unsparing hand. Inevitably, he had a vast deal to say about women, and he used frequently to indulge in sentimental and ironical apostrophes to these authors of his joys and woes. "Oh, the women, the women, and the things they have made me do!" he would exclaim with a lustrous eye. "*C'est égal*, of all the follies and stupidities I have committed for them I would not have missed one!" On this subject Newman maintained an habitual reserve; to expatiate largely upon it had always seemed to him a proceeding vaguely analogous to the cooing of pigeons and the chattering of monkeys, and even inconsistent with a fully developed human character. But Bellegarde's confidences greatly amused him, and rarely displeased him, for the generous young Frenchman was not a cynic. "I really think," he had once said, "that I am not more depraved than most of my contemporaries. They are tolerably depraved, my contemporaries!" He said wonderfully pretty things about his female friends, and, numerous and various as they had been, declared that on the whole there was more good in them than harm. "But you are not to take that as advice," he added. "As an authority I am very untrustworthy. I'm prejudiced in their favor; I'm an *idealist!*" Newman listened to him with his impartial smile, and was glad, for his own sake, that he had fine feelings; but he mentally repudiated the idea of a Frenchman having discovered any merit in the amiable sex which he himself did not suspect. M. de Bellegarde, however, did not confine his conversation to the autobiographical channel; he questioned our hero largely as to the events of his own life, and Newman told him some better stories than any that

Bellegarde carried in his budget. He narrated his career, in fact, from the beginning, through all its variations, and whenever his companion's credulity, or his habits of gentility, appeared to protest, it amused him to heighten the color of the episode. Newman had sat with Western humorists in knots, round cast-iron stoves, and seen "tall" stories grow taller without toppling over, and his own imagination had learned the trick of piling up consistent wonders. Bellegarde's regular attitude at last became that of laughing self-defense; to maintain his reputation as an all-knowing Frenchman, he doubted of everything, wholesale. The result of this was that Newman found it impossible to convince him of certain time-honored verities.

"But the details don't matter," said M. de Bellegarde. "You have evidently had some surprising adventures; you have seen some strange sides of life, you have revolved to and fro over a whole continent as I walked up and down the Boulevard. You are a man of the world with a vengeance! You have spent some deadly dull hours, and you have done some extremely disagreeable things: you have shoveled sand, as a boy, for supper, and you have eaten roast dog in a gold-diggers' camp. You have stood casting up figures for ten hours at a time, and you have sat through Methodist sermons for the sake of looking at a pretty girl in another pew. All that is rather stiff, as we say. But at any rate you have done something and you are something; you have used your will and you have made your fortune. You have not stupefied yourself with debauchery and you have not mortgaged your fortune to social conveniences. You take things easily, and you have fewer prejudices even than I, who pretend to have none, but who in reality have three or four. Happy man, you are strong and you are free. But what the deuce," demanded the young man in conclusion, "do you propose to do with such advantages? Really to use them you need a better world than this. There is nothing worth your while here."

"Oh, I think there is something," said Newman.

"What is it?"

"Well," murmured Newman, "I will tell you some other time!"

In this way our hero delayed from day to day broaching a subject which he had very much at heart. Meanwhile, however, he was growing practically familiar with it; in other words, he had called again, three times, on Madame de Cintré. On only two of these occasions had he found her at home, and on each of them she had other visitors. Her visitors were numerous and extremely loquacious, and they exacted much of their hostess's attention. She found time, however, to bestow a little of it on Newman, in an occasional vague smile, the very vagueness of which pleased him, allowing him as it did to fill it out mentally, both at the time and afterwards, with such meanings as most pleased him. He sat by without speaking, looking at the entrances and exits, the greetings and chatterings, of Madame de Cintré's visitors. He felt as if he were at the play, and as if his own speaking would be an interruption; sometimes he wished he had a book, to follow the dialogue; he half expected to see a woman in a white cap and pink ribbons come and offer him one for two francs. Some of the ladies looked at him very hard—or very soft, as you please; others seemed profoundly unconscious of his presence. The men looked only at Madame de Cintré. This was inevitable; for whether one called her beautiful or not she entirely occupied and filled one's vision, just as an agreeable sound fills one's ear. Newman had but twenty distinct words with her, but he carried away an impression to which solemn promises could not have given a higher value. She was part of the play that he was seeing acted, quite as much as her companions; but how she filled the stage and how much better she did it! Whether she rose or seated herself; whether she went with her departing friends to the door and lifted up the heavy curtain as they passed out, and stood an instant looking after them and giving them the last nod; or whether she leaned back in her chair with her arms crossed and her eyes resting, listening and smiling; she gave Newman the feeling that he should like to have her always before him, moving slowly to and fro along the whole scale of expressive hospitality. If it might be *to* him, it would be well; if it might be *for* him, it would be still better! She was so tall and yet so light, so active and yet so still, so elegant and yet so simple, so frank and yet so mysterious! It was the mystery—it was what she was off the stage, as it were—that interested Newman most of all. He could not have told you what warrant he had for talking about mysteries; if it had been his habit to express himself in poetic figures he might have said that in observing Madame de Cintré he seemed to see the vague circle which sometimes accompanies the partly-filled disk of the moon. It was not that she was reversed; on the contrary, she was as frank as flowing water. But he was sure she had qualities which she herself did not suspect.

He had abstained for several reasons from saying some of these things to Bellegarde. One reason was that before proceeding to any act he was always circumspect, conjectural, contemplative; he had little eagerness, as became a man who felt that whenever he really began to move he walked with long steps. And then, it simply pleased him not to speak—it occupied him, it excited him. But one day Bellegarde had been dining with him, at a restaurant, and they had sat long over their dinner. On rising from it, Bellegarde proposed that, to help them through the rest of the evening, they should go and see Madame Dandelard. Madame Dandelard was a little Italian lady who had married a Frenchman who proved to be a rake and a brute and the torment of her life. Her husband had spent all her money, and then, lacking the means of obtaining more expensive pleasures, had taken, in his duller hours, to beating her. She had a blue spot somewhere, which she showed to several persons, including Bellegarde. She had obtained a separation from her husband, collected the scraps of her fortune (they were very meagre) and come to live in Paris, where she was staying at a *hôtel garni*. She was always looking for an apartment, and visiting, inquiringly, those of other people. She was very pretty, very child-like, and she made very extraordinary remarks. Bellegarde had made her acquaintance, and the source of his interest in her was, according to his own declaration, a curiosity as to what would become of her. "She is poor, she is pretty, and she is silly," he said; "it seems to me she can go only one way. It's a pity, but it can't be helped. I will give her six months. She has nothing to fear from me, but I am watching the process. I am curious to see just how things will go. Yes, I know what you are going to say: this horrible Paris hardens one's heart. But it quickens one's wits, and it ends by teaching one a refinement of observation! To see this little woman's little drama play itself out, now, is, for me, an intellectual pleasure."

"If she is going to throw herself away," Newman had said, "you ought to stop her."

"Stop her? How stop her?"

"Talk to her; give her some good advice."

Bellegarde laughed. "Heaven deliver us both! Imagine the situation! Go and advise her yourself."

It was after this that Newman had gone with Bellegarde to see Madame Dandelard. When they came away, Bellegarde reproached his companion. "Where was your famous advice?" he asked. "I didn't hear a word of it."

"Oh, I give it up," said Newman, simply.

"Then you are as bad as I!" said Bellegarde.

"No, because I don't take an 'intellectual pleasure' in her prospective adventures. I don't in the least want to see her going down hill. I had rather look the other way. But why," he asked, in a moment "don't you get your sister to go and see her?"

Bellegarde stared. "Go and see Madame Dandelard—my sister?"

"She might talk to her to very good purpose."

Bellegarde shook his head with sudden gravity. "My sister can't see that sort of person. Madame Dandelard is nothing at all; they would never meet."

"I should think," said Newman, "that your sister might see whom she pleased." And he privately resolved that after he knew her a little better he would ask Madame de Cintré to go and talk to the foolish little Italian lady.

After his dinner with Bellegarde, on the occasion I have mentioned, he demurred to his companion's proposal that they should go again and listen to Madame Dandelard describe her sorrows and her bruises. "I have something better in mind," he said; "come home with me and finish the evening before my fire."

Bellegarde always welcomed the prospect of a long stretch of conversation, and before long the two men sat watching the great blaze which scattered its scintillations over the high adornments of Newman's ballroom.

CHAPTER VIII

"TELL ME something about your sister," Newman began abruptly.

Bellegarde turned and gave him a quick look. "Now that I think of it, you have never yet asked me a question about her."

"I know that very well."

"If it is because you don't trust me, you are very right," said Bellegarde. "I can't talk of her rationally. I admire her too much."

"Talk of her as you can," rejoined Newman. "Let yourself go."

"Well, we are very good friends; we are such a brother and sister as have not been seen since Orestes and Electra. You have seen her; you know what she is: tall, thin, light, imposing, and gentle, half a *grande dame* and half an angel; a mixture of pride and humility, of the eagle and the dove. She looks like a statue which had failed as stone, resigned itself to its grave defects, and come to life as flesh and blood, to wear white capes and long trains. All I can say is that she really possesses every merit that her face, her glance, her smile, the tone of her voice, lead you to expect; it is saying a great deal. As a general thing, when a woman seems very charming, I should say 'Beware!' But in proportion as Claire seems charming you may fold your arms and let yourself float with the current; you are safe. She is so good! I have never seen a woman half so perfect or so complete. She has everything; that is all I can say about her. There!" Bellegarde concluded; "I told you I should rhapsodize."

Newman was silent a while, as if he were turning over his companion's words. "She is very good, eh?" he repeated at last.

"Divinely good!"

"Kind, charitable, gentle, generous?"

"Generosity itself; kindness double-distilled!"

"Is she clever?"

"She is the most intelligent woman I know. Try her, some day, with something difficult, and you will see."

"Is she fond of admiration?"

"Parbleu!" cried Bellegarde; "what woman is not?"

"Ah, when they are too fond of admiration they commit all kinds of follies to get it."

"I did not say she was too fond!" Bellegarde exclaimed. "Heaven forbid I should say anything so idiotic. She is not *too* anything! If I were to say she was ugly, I should not mean she was too ugly. She is fond of pleasing, and if you are pleased she is grateful. If you are not pleased, she lets it pass and thinks the worse neither of you nor of herself. I imagine, though, she hopes the saints in heaven are, for I am sure she is incapable of trying to please by any means of which they would disapprove."

"Is she grave or gay?" asked Newman.

"She is both; not alternately, for she is always the same. There is gravity in her gayety, and gayety in her gravity. But there is no reason why she should be particularly gay."

"Is she unhappy?"

"I won't say that, for unhappiness is according as one takes things, and Claire takes them according to some receipt communicated to her by the Blessed Virgin in a vision. To be unhappy is to be disagreeable, which, for her, is out of the question. So she has arranged her circumstances so as to be happy in them."

"She is a philosopher," said Newman.

"No, she is simply a very nice woman."

"Her circumstances, at any rate, have been disagreeable?"

Bellegarde hesitated a moment—a thing he very rarely did. "Oh, my dear fellow, if I go into the history of my family I shall give you more than you bargain for."

"No, on the contrary, I bargain for that," said Newman.

"We shall have to appoint a special séance, then, beginning early. Suffice it for the present that Claire has not slept on roses. She made at eighteen a marriage that was expected to be brilliant, but that turned out like a lamp that goes out; all smoke and bad smell. M. de Cintré was sixty years old, and an odious old gentleman. He lived, however, but a short time, and after his death his family pounced upon his money, brought a lawsuit against his widow, and pushed things very hard. Their case was a good one, for M. de Cintré, who had been trustee for some of his relatives, appeared to have been guilty of some very irregular practices. In the course of the suit some revelations were made as to his private history which my sister found so displeasing that she ceased to defend herself and washed her hands of the property. This required some pluck, for she was between two fires, her husband's family opposing her and her own family forcing her. My mother and my brother wished her to cleave to what they regarded as her rights. But she resisted firmly, and at last bought her freedom—obtained my mother's assent to dropping the suit at the price of a promise."

"What was the promise?"

"To do anything else, for the next ten years, that was asked of her—anything, that is, but marry."

"She had disliked her husband very much?"

"No one knows how much!"

"The marriage had been made in your horrible French way." Newman continued, "made by the two families, without her having any voice?"

"It was a chapter for a novel. She saw M. de Cintré for the first time a month before the wedding, after everything, to the minutest detail, had been arranged. She turned white when she looked at him, and white she remained till her wedding-day. The evening before the ceremony she swooned away, and she spent the whole night in sobs. My mother sat holding her two hands, and my brother walked up and down the room. I declared it was revolting and told my sister publicly that if she would refuse, downright, I would stand by her. I was told to go about my business, and she became Comtesse de Cintré."

"Your brother," said Newman, reflectively, "must be a very nice young man."

"He is very nice, though he is not young. He is upward of fifty, fifteen years my senior. He has been a father to my sister and me.

He is a very remarkable man; he has the best manners in France. He is extremely clever; indeed he is very learned. He is writing a history of The Princesses of France Who Never Married." This was said by Bellegarde with extreme gravity, looking straight at Newman, and with an eye that betokened no mental reservation; or that, at least, almost betokened none.

Newman perhaps discovered there what little there was, for he presently said, "You don't love your brother."

"I beg your pardon," said Bellegarde, ceremoniously; "well-bred people always love their brothers."

"Well, I don't love him, then!" Newman answered.

"Wait till you know him!" rejoined Bellegarde, and this time he smiled.

"Is your mother also very remarkable?" Newman asked, after a pause.

"For my mother," said Bellegarde, now with intense gravity, "I have the highest admiration. She is a very extraordinary woman. You cannot approach her without perceiving it."

"She is the daughter, I believe, of an English nobleman."

"Of the Earl of St. Dunstan's."

"Is the Earl of St. Dunstan's a very old family?"

"So-so; the sixteenth century. It is on my father's side that we go back—back, back, back. The family antiquaries themselves lose breath. At last they stop, panting and fanning themselves, somewhere in the ninth century, under Charlemagne. That is where we begin."

"There is no mistake about it?" said Newman.

"I'm sure I hope not. We have been mistaken at least for several centuries."

"And you have always married into old families?"

"As a rule; though in so long a stretch of time there have been some exceptions. Three or four Bellegardes, in the seventeenth and eighteenth centuries, took wives out of the bourgoisie—married lawyers' daughters."

"A lawyer's daughter; that's very bad, is it?" asked Newman.

"Horrible! one of us, in the middle ages, did better: he married a beggar-maid, like King Cophetua. That was really better; it was like marrying a bird or a monkey; one didn't have to think about her family at all. Our women have always done well; they have never even gone into the *petite noblesse*. There is, I believe, not a case on record of a misalliance among the women."

Newman turned this over for a while, and then at last he said,

"You offered, the first time you came to see me, to render me any service you could. I told you that some time I would mention something you might do. Do you remember?"

"Remember? I have been counting the hours."

"Very well; here's your chance. Do what you can to make your sister think well of me."

Bellegarde stared, with a smile. "Why, I'm sure she thinks as well of you as possible, already."

"An opinion founded on seeing me three or four times? That is putting me off with very little. I want something more. I have been thinking of it a good deal, and at last I have decided to tell you. I should like very much to marry Madame de Cintré."

Bellegarde had been looking at him with quickened expectancy, and with the smile with which he had greeted Newman's allusion to his promised request. At this last announcement he continued to gaze; but his smile went through two or three curious phases. It felt, apparently, a momentary impulse to broaden; but this it immediately checked. Then it remained for some instants taking counsel with itself, at the end of which it decreed a retreat. It slowly effaced itself and left a look of seriousness modified by the desire not to be rude. Extreme surprise had come into the Count Valentin's face; but he had reflected that it would be uncivil to leave it there. And yet, what the deuce was he to do with it? He got up, in his agitation, and stood before the chimney-piece, still looking at Newman. He was a longer time thinking what to say than one would have expected.

"If you can't render me the service I ask," said Newman, "say it out!"

"Let me hear it again, distinctly," said Bellegarde. "It's very important, you know. I shall plead your cause with my sister, because you want—you want to marry her? That's it, eh?"

"Oh, I don't say plead my cause, exactly; I shall try and do that myself. But say a good word for me, now and then—let her know that you think well of me."

At this, Bellegarde gave a little light laugh.

"What I want chiefly, after all," Newman went on, "is just to let you know what I have in mind. I suppose that is what you expect, isn't it? I want to do what is customary over here. If there is any thing particular to be done, let me know and I will do it. I wouldn't for the world approach Madame de Cintré without all the proper forms. If I ought to go and tell your mother, why I will go and tell her. I will go and tell your brother, even. I will go and tell any one you please. As I don't know any one else, I begin by telling you. But that, if it is a social obligation, is a pleasure as well."

"Yes, I see—I see," said Bellegarde, lightly stroking his chin. "You have a very right feeling about it, but I'm glad you have begun with me." He paused, hesitated, and then turned away and walked slowly the length of the room. Newman got up and stood leaning against the mantel-shelf, with his hands in his pockets, watching Bellegarde's promenade. The young Frenchman came back and stopped in front of him. "I give it up," he said; "I will not pretend I am not surprised. I am—hugely! *Ouf!* It's a relief."

"That sort of news is always a surprise," said Newman. "No matter what you have done, people are never prepared. But if you are so surprised, I hope at least you are pleased."

"Come!" said Bellegarde. "I am going to be tremendously frank. I don't know whether I am pleased or horrified."

"If you are pleased, I shall be glad," said Newman, "and I shall be—encouraged. If you are horrified, I shall be sorry, but I shall not be discouraged. You must make the best of it."

"That is quite right—that is your only possible attitude. You are perfectly serious?"

"Am I a Frenchman, that I should not be?" asked Newman. "But why is it, by the bye, that you should be horrified?"

Bellegarde raised his hand to the back of his head and rubbed his hair quickly up and down, thrusting out the tip of his tongue as he did so. "Why, you are not noble, for instance," he said.

"The devil I am not!" exclaimed Newman.

"Oh," said Bellegarde a little more seriously, "I did not know you had a title."

"A title? What do you mean by a title?" asked Newman. "A count, a duke, a marquis? I don't know anything about that, I don't know who is and who is not. But I say I am noble. I don't exactly know what you mean by it, but it's a fine word and a fine idea: I put in a claim to it."

"But what have you to show, my dear fellow, what proofs?"

"Anything you please! But you don't suppose I am going to understake to prove that I am noble. It is for you to prove the contrary."

"That's easily done. You have manufactured wash-tubs."

Newman stared a moment. "Therefore I am not noble? I don't

see it. Tell me something I have *not* done—something I cannot do."

"You cannot marry a woman like Madame de Cintré for the asking."

"I believe you mean," said Newman slowly, "that I am not good enough."

"Brutally speaking—yes!"

Bellegarde had hesitated a moment, and while he hesitated Newman's attentive glance had grown somewhat eager. In answer to these last words he for a moment said nothing. He simply blushed a little. Then he raised his eyes to the ceiling and stood looking at one of the rosy cherubs that was painted upon it. "Of course I don't expect to marry any woman for the asking," he said at last; "I expect first to make myself acceptable to her. She must like me, to begin with. But that I am not good enough to make a trial is rather a surprise."

Bellegarde wore a look of mingled perplexity, sympathy, and amusement. "You should not hesitate, then, to go up to-morrow and ask a duchess to marry you?"

"Not if I thought she would suit me. But I am very fastidious; she might not at all."

Bellegarde's amusement began to prevail. "And you should be surprised if she refused you?"

Newman hesitated a moment. "It sounds conceited to say yes, but nevertheless I think I should. For I should make a very handsome offer."

"What would it be?"

"Everything she wishes. If I get hold of a woman that comes up to my standard, I shall think nothing too good for her. I have been a long time looking, and I find such women are rare. To combine the qualities I require seems to be difficult, but when the difficulty is vanquished it deserves a reward. My wife shall have a good position, and I am not afraid to say that I shall be a good husband."

"And these qualities that you require—what are they?"

"Goodness, beauty, intelligence, a fine education, personal elegance —everything, in a word, that makes a splendid woman."

"And noble birth, evidently," said Bellegarde.

"Oh, throw that in, by all means, if it's there. The more the better!"

"And my sister seems to you to have all these things?"

"She is exactly what I have been looking for. She is my dream realized."

"And you would make her a very good husband?"

"That is what I wanted you to tell her."

Bellegarde laid his hand on his companion's arm a moment, looked at him with his head on one side, from head to foot, and then, with a loud laugh, and shaking the other hand in the air, turned away. He walked again the length of the room, and again he came back and stationed himself in front of Newman. "All this is very interesting—it is very curious. In what I said just now I was speaking, not for myself, but for my tradition, my superstitions. For myself, really, your proposal tickles me. It startled me at first, but the more I think of it the more I see in it. It's no use attempting to explain anything; you won't understand me. After all, I don't see why you need; it's no great loss."

"Oh, if there is anything more to explain, try it! I want to proceed with my eyes open. I will do my best to understand."

"No," said Bellegarde, "it's disagreeable to me; I give it up. I liked you the first time I saw you, and I will abide by that. It would be quite odious for me to come talking to you as if I could patronize you. I have told you before that I envy you; *vous m'imposez*, as we say. I didn't know you much until within five minutes. So we will let things go, and I will say nothing to you that, if our positions were reversed, you would not say to me."

I do not know whether, in renouncing the mysterious opportunity to which he alluded, Bellegarde felt that he was doing something very generous. If so, he was not rewarded; his generosity was not appreciated. Newman quite failed to recognize the young Frenchman's power to wound his feelings, and he had now no sense of escaping or coming off easily. He did not thank his companion even with a glance. "My eyes are open, though," he said, "so far as that you have practically told me that your family and your friends will turn up their noses at me. I have never thought much about the reasons that make it proper for people to turn up their noses, and so I can only decide the question off-hand. Looking at it in that way I can't see anything in it. I simply think, if you want to know, that I'm as good as the best. Who the best are, I don't pretend to say. I have never thought much about that either. To tell the truth, I have always had rather a good opinion of myself; a man who is successful can't help it. But I will admit that I was conceited. What I don't say yes to is that I don't stand high—as high as any one else. This is a line of speculation I should not have chosen, but you must remember you began it yourself. I should never have dreamed that I was on the defensive, or that I had to justify myself; but if your people will have it so, I will do my best."

"But you offered, a while ago, to make your court as we say, to my mother and my brother."

"Damn it!" cried Newman, "I want to be polite."

"Good!" rejoined Bellegarde; "this will go far, it will be very entertaining. Excuse my speaking of it in that cold-blooded fashion, but the matter must, of necessity, be for me something of a spectacle. It's positively exciting. But apart from that I sympathize with you, and I shall be actor, so far as I can, as well as spectator. You are a capital fellow; I believe in you and I back you. The simple fact that you appreciate my sister will serve as the proof I was asking for. All men are equal—especially men of taste!"

"Do you think," asked Newman presently, "that Madame de Cintré is determined not to marry?"

"That is my impression. But that is not against you; it's for you to make her change her mind."

"I am afraid it will be hard," said Newman, gravely.

"I don't think it will be easy. In a general way I don't see why a widow should ever marry again. She has gained the benefits of matrimony—freedom and consideration—and she has got rid of the drawbacks. Why should she put her head into the noose again? Her usual motive is ambition: if a man can offer her a great position, make her a princess or an ambassadress she may think the compensation sufficient."

"And—in that way—is Madame de Cintré ambitious?"

"Who knows?" said Bellegarde, with a profound shrug. "I don't pretend to say all that she is or all that she is not. I think she might be touched by the prospect of becoming the wife of a great man. But in a certain way, I believe, whatever she does will be the *improbable*. Don't be too confident, but don't absolutely doubt. Your best chance for success will be precisely in being, to her mind, unusual, unexpected, original. Don't try to be any one else; be simply yourself, out and out. Something or other can't fail to come of it; I am very curious to see what."

"I am much obliged to you for your advice," said Newman. "And," he added with a smile, "I am glad. for vour sake. I am going to be so amusing."

"It will be more than amusing," said Bellegarde; "it will be inspiring. I look at it from my point of view, and you from yours. After all, anything for a change! And only yesterday I was yawning so as to dislocate my jaw, and declaring that there was nothing new under the sun! If it isn't new to see you come into the family as a suitor, I am very much mistaken. Let me say that, my dear fellow; I won't call it anything else, bad or good; I will simply call it *new*." And overcome with a sense of the novelty thus foreshadowed, Valentin de Bellegarde threw himself into a deep arm-chair before the fire, and, with a fixed, intense smile, seemed to read a vision of it in the flame of the logs. After a while he looked up. "Go ahead, my boy; you have my good wishes," he said. "But it is really a pity you don't understand me, that you don't know just what I am doing."

"Oh," said Newman, laughing, "don't do anything wrong. Leave me to myself, rather, or defy me, out and out. I wouldn't lay any load on your conscience."

Bellegarde sprang up again; he was evidently excited; there was a warmer spark even than usual in his eye. "You never will understand—you never will know," he said; "and if you succeed, and I turn out to have helped you, you will never be grateful, not as I shall deserve you should be. You will be an excellent fellow always, but you will not be grateful. But it doesn't matter, for I shall get my own fun out of it." And he broke into an extravagant laugh. "You look puzzled," he added; "you look almost frightened."

"It *is* a pity," said Newman, "that I don't understand you. I shall lose some very good jokes."

"I told you, you remember, that we were very strange people," Bellegarde went on. "I give you warning again. We are! My mother is strange, my brother is strange, and I verily believe that I am stranger than either. You will even find my sister a little strange. Old trees have crooked branches, old houses have queer cracks, old races have odd secrets. Remember that we are eight hundred years old!"

"Very good," said Newman; "that's the sort of thing I came to Europe for. You come into my programme."

"*Touchez-là*, then," said Bellegarde, putting out his hand. "It's a bargain: I accept you; I espouse your cause. It's because I like you, in a great measure; but that is not the only reason!" And he stood holding Newman's hand and looking at him askance.

"What is the other one?"

"I am in the Opposition. I dislike some one else."

"Your brother?" asked Newman, in his unmodulated voice.

Bellegarde laid his fingers upon his lips with a whispered *hush!*

"Old races have strange secrets!" he said. "Put yourself into motion, come and see my sister, and be assured of my sympathy!" And on this he took his leave.

Newman dropped into a chair before his fire, and sat a long time staring into the blaze.

CHAPTER IX

HE WENT to see Madame de Cintré the next day, and was informed by the servant that she was at home. He passed as usual up the large, cold staircase and through a spacious vestibule above, where the walls seemed all composed of small door panels, touched with long-faded gilding; whence he was ushered into the sitting-room in which he had already been received. It was empty, and the servant told him that Madame la Comtesse would presently appear. He had time, while he waited, to wonder whether Bellegarde had seen his sister since the evening before, and whether in this case he had spoken to her of their talk. In this case Madame de Cintré's receiving him was an encouragement. He felt a certain trepidation as he reflected that she might come in with the knowledge of his supreme admiration and of the project he had built upon it in her eyes; but the feeling was not disagreeable. Her face could wear no look that would make it less beautiful, and he was sure beforehand that however she might take the proposal he had in reserve, she would not take it in scorn or in irony. He had a feeling that if she could only read the bottom of his heart and measure the extent of his good will toward her, she would be entirely kind.

She came in at last, after so long an interval that he wondered whether she had been hesitating. She smiled with her usual frankness, and held out her hand; she looked at him straight with her soft and luminous eyes, and said, without a tremor in her voice, that she was glad to see him and that she hoped he was well. He found in her what he had found before—that faint perfume of a personal shyness worn away by contact with the world, but the more perceptible the more closely you approached her. This lingering diffidence seemed to give a peculiar value to what was definite and assured in her manner; it made it seem like an accomplishment, a beautiful talent, something that one might compare to an exquisite touch in a pianist. It was, in fact, Madame de Cintré's "authority," as they say of artists, that especially impressed and fascinated Newman; he always came back to the feeling that when he should complete himself by taking a wife, that was the way he should like his wife to interpret him to the world. The only trouble, indeed, was that when the instrument was so perfect it seemed to interpose too much between you and the genius that used it. Madame de Cintré gave Newman the sense of an elaborate education, of her having passed through mysterious ceremonies and processes of culture in her youth, of her having been fashioned and make flexible to certain exalted social needs. All this, as I have affirmed, made her seem rare and precious—a very exepnsive article, as he would have said, and one which a man with an ambition to have everything about him of the best would find it highly agreeable to possess. But looking at the matter with an eye to private felicity, Newman wondered where, in so exquisite a compound, nature and art showed their dividing line. Where did the special intention separate from the habit of good manners? Where did urbanity end and sincerity begin? Newman asked himself these questions even while he stood ready to accept the admired object in all its complexity; he felt that he could do so in profound security, and examine its mechanism afterwards, at leisure.

"I am very glad to find you alone," he said. "You know I have never had such good luck before."

"But you have seemed before very well contented with your luck," said Madame de Cintré. "You have sat and watched my visitors with an air of quiet amusement. What have you thought of them?"

"Oh, I have thought the ladies were very elegant and very graceful, and wonderfully quick at repartee. But what I have chiefly thought has been that they only helped me to admire you." This was not gallantry on Newman's part—an art in which he was quite unversed. It was simply the instinct of the practical man, who had made up his mind what he wanted, and was now beginning to take active steps to obtain it.

Madame de Cintré started slightly, and raised her eyebrows; she had evidently not expected so fervid a compliment. "Oh, in that case," she said with a laugh, "your finding me alone is not good luck for me. I hope some one will come in quickly."

"I hope not," said Newman. "I have something particular to say to you. Have you seen your brother?"

"Yes; I saw him an hour ago."

"Did he tell you that he had seen me last night?"

"He said so."

"And did he tell you what we had talked about?"

Madame de Cintré hesitated a moment. As Newman asked these questions she had grown a little pale, as if she regarded what was coming as necessary, but not as agreeable. "Did you give him a message to me?" she asked.

"It was not exactly a message—I asked him to render me a service."

"The service was to sing your praises, was it not?" And she accompanied this question with a little smile, as if to make it easier to herself.

"Yes, that is what it really amounts to," said Newman. "Did he sing my praises?"

"He spoke very well of you. But when I know that it was by your special request, of course I must take his eulogy with a grain of salt."

"Oh, that makes no difference," said Newman. "Your brother would not have spoken well of me unless he believed what he was saying. He is too honest for that."

"Are you very deep?" said Madame de Cintré. "Are you trying to please me by praising my brother? I confess it is a good way."

"For me, any way that succeeds will be good. I will praise your brother all day, if that will help me. He is a noble little fellow. He has made me feel, in promising to do what he can to help me, that I can depend upon him."

"Don't make too much of that," said Madame de Cintré. "He can help you very little."

"Of course I must work my way myself. I know that very well; I only want a chance to. In consenting to see me, after what he told you, you almost seem to be giving me a chance."

"I am seeing you," said Madame de Cintré, slowly and gravely, "because I promised my brother I would."

"Blessings on your brother's head!" cried Newman. "What I told him last evening was this: that I admired you more than any woman I had ever seen, and that I should like immensely to make you my wife." He uttered these words with great directness and firmness, and without any sense of confusion. He was full of his idea, he had completely mastered it, and he seemed to look down on Madame de Cintré, with all her gathered elegance, from the height of his bracing good conscience. It is probable that this particlar tone and manner were the very best he could have hit upon. Yet the light, just visibly forced smile with which his companion had listened to him died away, and she sat looking at him with her lips parted and her face as solemn as a tragic mask. There was evidently something very painful to her in the scene to which he was subjecting her, and yet her impatience of it found no angry voice. Newman wondered whether he was hurting her; he could not imagine why the liberal devotion he meant to express should be disagreeable. He got up and stood before her, leaning one hand on the chimney-piece. "I know I have seen you very little to say this," he said, "so little that it may make what I say seem disrespectful. That is my misfortune! I could have said it the first time I saw you. Really, I had seen you before; I had seen you in imagination; you seemed almost an old friend. So what I say is not mere gallantry and compliments and nonsense—I can't talk that way, I don't know how, and I wouldn't, to you, if I could. It's as serious as such words can be. I feel as if I knew you and knew what a beautiful, admirable woman you are. I shall know better, perhaps, some day, but I have a general notion now. You are just the woman I have been looking for, except that you are far more perfect. I won't make any protestations and vows, but you can trust me. It is very soon, I know, to say all this; it is almost offensive. But why not gain time if one can? And if you want time to reflect—of course you do—the sooner you begin, the better for me. I don't know what you think of me; but there is no great mystery about me; you see what I am. Your brother told me that my antecedents and occupations were against me; that your family stands, somehow, on a higher level than I do. That is an idea which of course I don't understand and don't accept. But you don't care anything about that. I can assure you that I am a very solid fellow, and that if I give my mind to it I can arrange things so that in a very few years I shall not need to waste time in explaining who I am and what I am. You will decide for yourself whether you like me or not. What there is you see before you. I honestly believe I have no hidden vices or nasty tricks. I am kind, kind, kind! Everything that a man can give a woman I will give you. I have a large fortune, a very large fortune; some day, if you will allow me, I will go into details. If you want brilliancy, everything in the way of brilliancy that money can give you, you shall have. And as regards anything you may give up, don't take for granted too much that its place cannot be filled. Leave that to me; I'll take care of you; I shall know what you need. Energy and ingenuity can arrange everything. I'm a strong man! There, I have said what I had on my heart! It was better to get it off. I am very sorry if it's disagreeable to you; but think how much better it is that things should be clear. Don't answer me now, if you don't wish it. Think about it, think about it as slowly as you please. Of course I haven't said, I can't say, half I mean, especially about my admiration for you. But take a favorable view of me; it will only be just."

During this speech, the longest that Newman had ever made, Madame de Cintré kept her gaze fixed upon him, and it expanded at the last into a sort of fascinated stare. When he ceased speaking she lowered her eyes and sat for some moments looking down and straight before her. Then she slowly rose to her feet, and a pair of exceptionally keen eyes would have perceived that she was trembling a little in the movement. She still looked extremely serious. "I am very much obliged to you for your offer," she said. "It seems very strange, but I am glad you spoke without waiting any longer. It is better the subject should be dismissed. I appreciate all you say; you do me great honor. But I have decided not to marry."

"Oh, don't say that!" cried Newman, in a tone absolutely *naïf* from its pleading and caressing cadence. She had turned away, and it made her stop a moment with her back to him. "Think better of that. You are too young, too beautiful, too much made to be happy and to make others happy. If you are afraid of losing your freedom, I can assure you that this freedom here, this life you now lead, is a dreary bondage to what I will offer you. You shall do things that I don't think you have ever thought of. I will take you anywhere in the wide world that you propose. Are you unhappy? You give me a feeling that you *are* unhappy. You have no right to be, or to be made so. Let me come in and put an end to it."

Madame de Cintré stood there a moment longer, looking away from him. If she was touched by the way he spoke, the thing was conceivable. His voice, always very mild and interrogative, gradually became as soft and as tenderly argumentative as if he had been talking to a much-loved child. He stood watching her, and she presently turned round again, but this time she did not look at him, and she spoke in a quietness in which there was a visible trace of effort.

"There are a great many reasons why I should not marry," she said, "more than I can explain to you. As for my happiness, I am very happy. Your offer seems strange to me, for more reasons also than I can say. Of course you have a perfect right to make it. But I cannot accept it—it is impossible. Please never speak of this matter again. If you cannot promise me this, I must ask you not to come back."

"Why is it impossible?" Newman demanded. "You may think it

is, at first, without its really being so. I didn't expect you to be
pleased at first, but I do believe that if you will think of it a good
while, you may be satisfied."

"I don't know you," said Madame de Cintré. "Think how little
I know you."

"Very little, of course, and therefore I don't ask for your
ultimatum on the spot. I only ask you not to say no, and to let me
hope. I will wait as long as you desire. Meanwhile you can see more
of me and know me better, look at me as a possible husband—as a
candidate—and make up your mind."

Something was going on, rapidly, in Madame de Cintré's thoughts;
she was weighing a question there, beneath Newman's eyes, weighing
it and deciding it. "From the moment I don't very respectfully beg
you to leave the house and never return," she said, "I listen to you,
I seem to give you hope. I *have* listened to you—against my
judgment. It is because you are eloquent. If I had been told this
morning that I should consent to consider you as a possible husband,
I should have thought my informant a little crazy. I *am* listening to
you, you see!" And she threw her hands out for a moment and let
them drop with a gesture in which there was just the slightest
expression of appealing weakness.

"Well, as far as saying goes, I have said everything," said
Newman. "I believe in you, without restriction, and I think all the
good of you that it is possible to think of a human creature. I firmly
believe that in marrying me you will be *safe*. As I said just now,"
he went on with a smile, "I have no bad ways. I can do *so* much for
you. And if you are afraid that I am not what you have been
accustomed to, not refined and delicate and punctilious, you may
easily carry that too far. I *am* delicate! You shall see!"

Madame de Cintré walked some distance away, and paused before
a great plant, an azalea, which was flourishing in a porcelain tub
before her window. She plucked off one of the flowers and, twisting
it in her fingers, retraced her steps. Then she sat down in silence,
and her attitude seemed to be a consent that Newman should say
more.

"Why should you say it is impossible you should marry?" he
continued. "The only thing that could make it really impossible
would be your being already married. Is it because you have been
unhappy in marriage? That is all the more reason! Is it because your
family exert a pressure upon you, interfere with you, annoy you?
That is still another reason; you ought to be perfectly free, and

marriage will make you so. I don't say anything against your family—understand that!" added Newman, with an eagerness which might have made a perspicacious observer smile. "Whatever way you feel toward them is the right way, and anything that you should wish me to do to make myself agreeable to them I will do as well as I know how. Depend upon that!"

Madame de Cintré rose again and came toward the fire-place, near which Newman was standing. The expression of pain and embarrassment had passed out of her face, and it was illuminated with something which, this time at least, Newman need not have been perplexed whether to attribute to habit or to intention, to art or to nature. She had the air of a woman who has stepped across the frontier of friendship and, looking around her, finds the region vast. A certain checked and controlled exaltation seemed mingled with the usual level radiance of her glance. "I will not refuse to see you again," she said, "because much of what you have said has given me pleasure. But I will see you only on this condition: that you say nothing more in the same way for a long time."

"For how long?"

"For six months. It must be a solemn promise."

"Very well, I promise."

"Good-by, then," she said, and extended her hand.

He held it a moment, as if he were going to say something more. But he only looked at her; then he took his departure.

That evening, on the Boulevard, he met Valentin de Bellegarde. After they had exchanged greetings, Newman told him that he had seen Madame de Cintré a few hours before.

"I know it," said Bellegarde. "I dined in the Rue de l'Université." And then, for some moments, both men were silent. Newman wished to ask Bellegarde what visible impression his visit had made and the Count Valentin had a question of his own. Bellegarde spoke first.

"It's none of my business, but what the deuce did you say to my sister?"

"I am willing to tell you," said Newman, "that I made her an offer of marriage."

"Already!" And the young man gave a whistle. " 'Time is money!' Is that what you say in America? And Madame de Cintré?" he added, with an interrogative inflection.

"She did not accept my offer."

"She couldn't, you know, in that way."

"But I'm to see her again," said Newman.

"Oh, the strangeness of woman!" exclaimed Bellegarde. Then he stopped, and held Newman off at arms'-length. "I look at you with respect!" he exclaimed. "You have achieved what we call a personal success! Immediately, now, I must present you to my brother."

"Whenever you please!" said Newman.

CHAPTER X

NEWMAN CONTINUED to see his friends the Tristrams with a good deal of frequency, though if you had listened to Mrs. Tristram's account of the matter you would have supposed that they had been cynically repudiated for the sake of grander acquaintance. "We were all very well so long as we had no rivals—we were better than nothing. But now that you have become the fashion, and have your pick every day of three invitations to dinner, we are tossed into the corner. I am sure it is very good of you to come and see us once a month; I wonder you don't send us your cards in an envelope. When you do, pray have them with black edges; it will be for the death of my last illusion." It was in this incisive strain that Mrs. Tristram moralized over Newman's so-called neglect, which was in reality a most exemplary constancy. Of course she was joking, but there was always something ironical in her jokes, as there was always something jocular in her gravity.

"I know no better proof that I have treated you very well," Newman had said, "than the fact that you make so free with my character. Familiarity breeds contempt; I have made myself too cheap. If I had a little proper pride I would stay away a while, and when you asked me to dinner say I was going to the Princess Borealska's. But I have not any pride where my pleasure is concerned, and to keep you in the humor to see me—if you must see me only to call me bad names—I will agree to anything you choose; I will admit that I am the biggest snob in Paris." Newman, in fact, had declined an invitation personally given by the Princess Borealska, an inquiring Polish lady to whom he had been presented, on the ground that on that particular day he always dined at Mrs. Tristram's; and it was only a tenderly perverse theory of his hostess of the Avenue d'Iéna that he was faithless to his early friendships. She needed the theory to explain a certain moral irritation by which she was often visited; though, if this explanation was unsound, a

deeper analyst than I must give the right one. Having launched our
hero upon the current which was bearing him so rapidly along, she
appeared but half-pleased at its swiftness. She had succeeded too
well; she had played her game too cleverly and she wished to mix
up the cards. Newman had told her, in due season, that her friend
was "satisfactory." The epithet was not romantic, but Mrs. Tristram
had no difficulty in perceiving that, in essentials, the feeling which
lay beneath it was. Indeed, the mild, expansive brevity with which
it was uttered, and a certain look, at once appealing and inscrutable,
that issued from Newman's half-closed eyes as he leaned his head
against the back of his chair, seemed to her the most eloquent
attestation of a mature sentiment that she had ever encountered.
Newman was, according to the French phrase, only abounding in
her own sense, but his temperate raptures exerted a singular effect
upon that ardor which she herself had so freely manifested a few
months before. She now seemed inclined to take a purely critical
view of Madame de Cintré, and wished to have it understood that
she did not in the least answer for her being a compendium of all
the virtues. "No woman was ever so good as that woman seems,"
she said. "Remember what Shakespeare calls Desdemona; 'a supersubtle Venetian.' Madame de Cintré is a supersubtle Parisian. She is
a charming woman, and she has five hundred merits; but you had
better keep that in mind." Was Mrs. Tristram simply finding out
that she was jealous of her dear friend on the other side of the
Seine, and that in undertaking to provide Newman with an ideal
wife she had counted too much on her own disinterestedness? We
may be permitted to doubt it. The inconsistent little lady of the
Avenue d'Iéna had an insuperable need of changing her place,
intellectually. She had a lively imagination, and she was capable,
at certain times, of imagining the direct reverse of her most cherished
beliefs, with a vividness more intense than that of conviction. She
got tired of thinking aright; but there was no serious harm in it,
as she got equally tired of thinking wrong. In the midst of her
mysterious perversities she had admirable flashes of justice. One of
these occurred when Newman related to her that he had made a
formal proposal to Madame de Cintré. He repeated in a few words
what he had said, and in a great many what she had answered. Mrs.
Tristram listened with extreme interest.

"But after all," said Newman, "there is nothing to congratulate me
upon. It is not a triumph."

"I beg your pardon," said Mrs. Tristram; "it is a great triumph.

It is a great triumph that she did not silence you at the first word, and request you never to speak to her again."

"I don't see that," observed Newman.

"Of course you don't; Heaven forbid you should! When I told you to go on your own way and do what came into your head, I had no idea you would go over the ground so fast. I never dreamed you would offer yourself after five or six morning-calls. As yet, what had you done to make her like you? You had simply sat—not very straight—and stared at her. But she does like you."

"That remains to be seen."

"No, that is proved. What will come of it remains to be seen. That you should propose to marry her, without more ado, could never have come into her head. You can form very little idea of what passed through her mind as you spoke; if she ever really marries you, the affair will be characterized by the usual justice of all human things towards women. You will think you take generous views of her; but you will never begin to know through what a strange sea of feeling she passed before she accepted you. As she stood there in front of you the other day, she plunged into it. She said 'Why not?' to something which, a few hours earlier, had been inconceivable. She turned about on a thousand gathered prejudices and traditions as on a pivot, and looked where she had never looked hitherto. When I think of it—when I think of Claire de Cintré and all that she represents, there seems to me something very fine in it. When I recommended you to try your fortune with her I of course thought well of you, and in spite of your sins I think so still. But I confess I don't see quite what you are and what you have done, to make such a woman do this sort of thing for you."

"Oh, there is something very fine in it!" said Newman with a laugh, repeating her words. He took an extreme satisfaction in hearing that there was something fine in it. He had not the least doubt of it himself, but he had already begun to value the world's admiration of Madame de Cintré, as adding to the prospective glory of possession.

It was immediately after this conversation that Valentin de Belle-garde came to conduct his friend to the Rue de l'Université to present him to the other members of his family. "You are already introduced," he said, "and you have begun to be talked about. My sister has mentioned your successive visits to my mother, and it was an accident that my mother was present at none of them. I have spoken of you as an American of immense wealth, and the best fellow in the world, who is looking for something very superior in the way of a wife."

"Do you suppose," asked Newman, "that Madame de Cintré has related to your mother the last conversation I had with her?"

"I am very certain that she has not; she will keep her own counsel. Meanwhile you must make your way with the rest of the family. Thus much is known about you: you have made a great fortune in trade, you are a little eccentric, and you frankly admire our dear Claire. My sister-in-law, whom you remember seeing in Madame de Cintré's sitting-room, took, it appears, a fancy to you; she has described you as having *beaucoup de cachet*. My mother, therefore, is curious to see you."

"She expects to laugh at me, eh?" said Newman.

"She never laughs. If she does not like you, don't hope to purchase favor by being amusing. Take warning by me!"

This conversation took place in the evening, and half an hour later Valentin ushered his companion into an apartment of the house of the Rue de l'Université into which he had not yet penetrated, the salon of the dowager Marquise de Bellegarde. It was a vast, high room, with elaborate and ponderous mouldings, painted a whitish gray, along the upper portion of the walls and the ceiling; with a great deal of faded and carefully repaired tapestry in the doorways and chair-backs; a Turkey carpet in light colors, still soft and deep, in spite of great antiquity, on the floor, and portraits of each of Madame de Bellegarde's children, at the age of ten, suspended against an old screen of red silk. The room was illumined, exactly enough for conversation, by half a dozen candles, placed in odd corners, at a great distance apart. In a deep arm-chair, near the fire, sat an old lady in black; at the other end of the room another person was seated at the piano, playing a very expressive waltz. In this latter person Newman recognized the young Marquise de Bellegarde.

Valentin presented his friend, and Newman walked up to the old lady by the fire and shook hands with her. He received a rapid impression of a white, delicate, aged face, with a high forehead, a small mouth, and a pair of cold blue eyes which had kept much of the freshness of youth. Madame de Bellegarde looked hard at him, and returned his hand-shake with a sort of British positiveness which reminded him that she was the daughter of the Earl of St. Dunstan's. Her daughter-in-law stopped playing and gave him an agreeable smile. Newman sat down and looked about him, while Valentin went and kissed the hand of the young marquise.

"I ought to have seen you before," said Madame de Bellegarde. "You have paid several visits to my daughter."

"Oh, yes," said Newman, smiling; "Madame de Cintré and I are old friends by this time."

"You have gone fast," said Madame de Bellegarde.

"Not so fast as I should like," said Newman, gravely.

"Oh, you are very ambitious," answered the old lady.

"Yes, I confess I am," said Newman, smiling.

Madame de Bellegarde looked at him with her cold fine eyes, and he returned her gaze, reflecting that she was a possible adversary and trying to take her measure. Their eyes remained in contact for some moments. Then Madame de Bellegarde looked away, and without smiling, "I am very ambitious, too," she said.

Newman felt that taking her measure was not easy; she was a formidable, inscrutable little woman. She resembled her daughter, and yet she was utterly unlike her. The coloring in Madame de Cintré was the same, and the high delicacy of her brow and nose was hereditary. But her face was a larger and freer copy, and her mouth in especial a happy divergence from that conservative orifice, a little pair of lips at once plump and pinched, that looked, when closed, as if they could not open wider than to swallow a gooseberry or to emit an "Oh, dear, no!" which probably had been thought to give the finishing touch to the aristocratic prettiness of the Lady Emmeline Atheling as represented, forty years before, in several Books of Beauty. Madame de Cintré's face had, to Newman's eye, a range of expression as delightfully vast as the wind-streaked, cloud-flecked distance on a Western prairie. But her mother's white, intense, respectable countenance, with its formal gaze, and its circumscribed smile, suggested a document signed and sealed; a thing of parchment, ink, and ruled lines. "She is a woman of conventions and proprieties," he said to himself as he looked at her; "her word is the world of things immutably decreed. But how she is at home in it, and what a paradise she finds it. She walks about in it as if it were a blooming park, a Garden of Eden; and when she sees 'This is genteel,' or 'This is improper,' written on a mile-stone she stops ecstatically, as if she were listening to a nightingale or smelling a rose." Madame de Bellegarde wore a little black velvet hood tied under her chin, and she was wrapped in an old black cashmere shawl.

"You are an American?" she said presently. "I have seen several Americans."

"There are several in Paris," said Newman jocosely.

"Oh, really?" said Madame de Bellegarde. "It was in England I saw these, or somewhere else; not in Paris. I think it must have been in the Pyrenees, many years ago. I am told your ladies are very pretty. One of these ladies was very pretty! such a wonderful complexion! She presented me a note of introduction from some one—I forgot whom—and she sent with it a note of her own. I kept her letter a long time afterwards, it was so strangely expressed. I used to know some of the phrases by heart. But I have forgotten them now, it is so many years ago. Since then I have seen no more Americans. I think my daughter-in-law has; she is a great gad-about, she sees every one."

At this the younger lady came rustling forward, pinching in a very slender waist, and casting idly preoccupied glances over the front of her dress, which was apparently designed for a ball. She was, in a singular way, at once ugly and pretty; she had protuberant eyes, and lips strangely red. She reminded Newman of his friend, Mademoiselle Nioche; this was what that much-obstructed young lady would have liked to be. Valentin de Bellegarde walked behind her at a distance, hopping about to keep off the far-spreading train of her dress.

"You ought to show more of your shoulders behind," he said very gravely. "You might as well wear a standing ruff as such a dress as that."

The young woman turned her back to the mirror over the chimney-piece, and glanced behind her, to verify Valentin's assertion. The mirror descended low, and yet it reflected nothing but a large unclad flesh surface. The young marquise put her hands behind her and gave a downward pull to the waist of her dress. "Like that, you mean?" she asked.

"That is a little better," said Bellegarde in the same tone, "but it leaves a good deal to be desired."

"Oh, I never go to extremes," said his sister-in-law. And then, turning to Madame de Bellegarde, "What were you calling me just now, madame?"

"I called you a gad-about," said the old lady. "But I might call you something else, too."

"A gad-about? What an ugly word! What does it mean?"

"A very beautiful person," Newman ventured to say, seeing that it was in French.

"That is a pretty compliment but a bad translation," said the young marquise. And then, looking at him a moment, "Do you dance?"

"Not a step."

"You are very wrong," she said, simply. And with another look at her back in the mirror she turned away.

"Do you like Paris?" asked the old lady, who was apparently wondering what was the proper way to talk to an American.

"Yes, rather," said Newman. And then he added with a friendly intonation, "Don't you?"

"I can't say I know it. I know my house—I know my friends—I don't know Paris."

"Oh, you lose a great deal," said Newman, sympathetically.

Madame de Bellegarde stared; it was presumably the first time she had been condoled with on her losses. "I am content with what I have," she said with dignity.

Newman's eyes, at this moment, were wandering round the room, which struck him as rather sad and shabby; passing from the high casements, with their small, thickly-framed panes, to the sallow tints of two or three portraits in pastel, of the last century, which hung between them. He ought, obviously, to have answered that the contentment of his hostess was quite natural—she had a great deal; but the idea did not occur to him during the pause of some moments which followed.

"Well, my dear mother," said Valentin, coming and leaning against the chimney-piece, "what do you think of my dear friend Newman? Is he not the excellent fellow I told you?"

"My acquaintance with Mr. Newman has not gone very far," said Madame de Bellegarde. "I can as yet only appreciate his great politeness."

"My mother is a great judge of these matters," said Valentin to Newman. "If you have satisfied her, it is a triumph."

"I hope I shall satisfy you, some day," said Newman, looking at the old lady. "I have done nothing yet."

"You must not listen to my son; he will bring you into trouble. He is a sad scatterbrain."

"Oh, I like him—I like him," said Newman, genially.

"He amuses you, eh?"

"Yes, perfectly."

"Do you hear that, Valentin?" said Madame de Bellegarde. "You amuse Mr. Newman."

"Perhaps we shall all come to that!" Valentin exclaimed.

"You must see my other son," said Madame de Bellegarde. "He is much better than this one. But he will not amuse you."

"I don't know—I don't know!" murmured Valentin, reflectively. "But we shall very soon see. Here comes *Monsieur mon frère*."

The door had just opened to give ingress to a gentleman who stepped forward and whose face Newman remembered. He had been the author of our hero's discomfiture the first time he tried to present himself to Madame de Cintré. Valentin de Bellegarde went to meet his brother, looked at him a moment, and then, taking him by the arm, led him up to Newman.

"This is my excellent friend Mr. Newman," he said very blandly. "You must know him."

"I am delighted to know Mr. Newman," said the marquis with a low bow, but without offering his hand.

"He is the old woman at second-hand," Newman said to himself, as he returned M. de Bellegarde's greeting. And this was the starting-point of a speculative theory, in his mind, that the late marquis had been a very amiable foreigner, with an inclination to take life easily and a sense that it was difficult for the husband of the stilted little lady by the fire to do so. But if he had taken little comfort in his wife he had taken much in his two younger children, who were after his own heart, while Madame de Bellegarde had paired with her eldest-born.

"My brother has spoken to me of you," said M. de Bellegarde; "and as you are also acquainted with my sister, it was time we should meet." He turned to his mother and gallantly bent over her hand, touching it with his lips, and then he assumed an attitude before the chimney-piece. With his long, lean face, his high-bridged nose and his small, opaque eye he looked much like an Englishman. His whiskers were fair and glossy, and he had a large dimple, of unmistakably British origin, in the middle of his handsome chin. He was "distinguished" to the tips of his polished nails, and there was not a movement of his fine, perpendicular person that was not noble and majestic. Newman had never yet been confronted with such an incarnation of the art of taking one's self seriously; he felt a sort of impulse to step backward, as you do to get a view of a great façade.

"Urbain," said young Madame de Bellegarde, who had apparently been waiting for her husband to take her to her ball, "I call your attention to the fact that I am dressed."

"That is a good idea," murmured Valentin.

"I am at your orders, my dear friend," said M. de Bellegarde.

"Only, you must allow me first the pleasure of a little conversation with Mr. Newman."

"Oh, if you are going to a party, don't let me keep you," objected Newman. "I am very sure we shall meet again. Indeed, if you would like to converse with me I will gladly name an hour." He was eager to make it known that would readily answer all questions and satisfy all exactions.

M. de Bellegarde stood in a well-balanced position before the fire, caressing one of his fair whiskers with one of his white hands, and looking at Newman, half askance, with eyes from which a particular ray of observation made its way through a general meaningless smile. "It is very kind of you to make such an offer," he said. "If I am not mistaken, your occupations are such as to make your time precious. You are in—a—as we say, *dans les affaires.*"

"In business, you mean? Oh no, I have thrown business overboard for the present. I am 'loafing,' as *we* say. My time is quite my own."

"Ah, you are taking a holiday," rejoined M. de Bellegarde. " 'Loafing.' Yes, I have heard that expression."

"Mr. Newman is American," said Madame de Bellegarde.

"My brother is a great ethnologist," said Valentin.

"An ethnologist?" said Newman. "Ah, you collect negroes' skulls, and that sort of thing."

The marquis looked hard at his brother, and began to caress his other whisker. Then, turning to Newman, with sustained urbanity, "You are traveling for your pleasure?" he asked.

"Oh, I am knocking about to pick up one thing and another. Of course I get a good deal of pleasure out of it."

"What especially interests you?" inquired the marquis.

"Well, everything interests me," said Newman. "I am not particular. Manufactures are what I care most about."

"That has been your specialty?"

"I can't say I have had any specialty. My specialty has been to make the largest possible fortune in the shortest possible time." Newman made this last remark very deliberately; he wished to open the way, if it were necessary, to an authoritative statement of his means.

M. de Bellegarde laughed agreeably. "I hope you have succeeded," he said.

"Yes, I have made a fortune in a reasonable time. I am not so old, you see."

"Paris is a very good place to spend a fortune. I wish you great enjoyment of yours." And M. de Bellegarde drew forth his gloves and began to put them on.

Newman for a few moments watched him sliding his white hands into the white kid, and as he did so his feelings took a singular turn. M. de Bellegarde's good wishes seemed to descend out of the white expanse of his sublime serenity with the soft, scattered movement of a shower of snow-flakes. Yet Newman was not irritated; he did not feet that he was being patronized; he was conscious of no especial impulse to introduce a discord into so noble a harmony. Only he felt himself suddenly in personal contact with the forces with which his friend Valentin had told him that he would have to contend, and he became sensible of their intensity. He wished to make some answering manifestation, to stretch himself out at his own length, to sound a note at the uttermost end of *his* scale. It must be added that if this impulse was not vicious or malicious, it was by no means void of humorous expectancy. Newman was quite as ready to give play to that loosely-adjusted smile of his, if his hosts should happen to be shocked, as he was far from deliberately planning to shock them.

"Paris is a very good place for idle people," he said, "or it is a very good place if your family has been settled here for a long time, and you have made acquaintances and got your relations round you; or if you have got a good big house like this, and a wife and children and mother and sister, and everything comfortable. I don't like that way of living all in rooms next door to each other. But I am not an idler. I try to be, but I can't manage it; it goes against the grain. My business habits are too deep-seated. Then, I haven't any house to call my own, or anything in the way of a family. My sisters are five thousand miles away, my mother died when I was a youngster, and I haven't any wife; I wish I had! So, you see, I don't exactly know what to do with myself. I am not fond of books, as you are, sir, and I get tired of dining out and going to the opera. I miss my business activity. You see, I began to earn my living when I was almost a baby, and until a few months ago I have never had my hand off the plow. Elegant leisure comes hard."

This speech was followed by a profound silence of some moments, on the part of Newman's entertainers. Valentin stood looking at him fixedly, with his hands in his pockets, and then he slowly, with a half-sidling motion, went out of the room. The marquis continued to draw on his gloves and to smile benignantly.

"You began to earn your living when you were a mere baby?" said the marquise.

"Hardly more—a small boy."

"You say you are not fond of books," said M. de Bellegarde; "but you must do yourself the justice to remember that your studies were interrupted early."

"That is very true; on my tenth birthday I stopped going to school. I thought it was a grand way to keep it. But I picked up some information afterwards," said Newman, reassuringly.

"You have some sisters?" asked old Madame de Bellegarde.

"Yes, two sisters. Splendid women!"

"I hope that for them the hardships of life commenced less early."

"They married very early, if you call that a hardship, as girls do in our Western country. One of them is married to the owner of the largest india-rubber house in the West."

"Ah, you make houses also of india-rubber?" inquired the marquise.

"You can stretch them as your family increases," said young Madame de Bellegarde, who was muffling herself in a long white shawl.

Newman indulged in a burst of hilarity, and explained that the house in which his brother-in-law lived was a large wooden structure, but that he manufactured and sold india-rubber on a colossal scale.

"My children have some little india-rubber shoes which they put on when they go to play in the Tuileries in damp weather," said the young marquise. "I wonder whether your brother-in-law made them."

"Very likely," said Newman; "if he did, you many be very sure they are well made."

"Well, you must not be discouraged," said M. de Bellegarde, with vague urbanity.

"Oh, I don't mean to be. I have a project which gives me plenty to think about, and that is an occupation." And then Newman was silent a moment, hesitating, yet thinking rapidly; he wished to make his point, and yet to do so forced him to speak out in a way that was disagreeable to him. Nevertheless he continued, addressing himself to old Madame de Bellegarde, "I will tell you my project; perhaps you can help me. I want to take a wife."

"It is a very good project, but I am no matchmaker," said the old lady.

Newman looked at her an instant, and then, with perfect sincerity, "I should have thought you were," he declared.

Madame de Bellegarde appeared to think him too sincere. She murmured something sharply in French, and fixed her eyes on her son. At this moment the door of the room was thrown open, and with a rapid step Valentin reappeared.

"I have a message for you," he said to his sister-in-law. "Claire bids me to request you not to start for your ball. She will go with you."

"Claire will go with us!" cried the young marquise. "*En voilà, du nouveau!*"

"She has changed her mind; she decided half an hour ago, and she is sticking the last diamond into her hair," said Valentin.

"What has taken possession of my daughter?" demanded Madame de Bellegarde, sternly. "She has not been into the world these three years. Does she take such a step at half an hour's notice, and without consulting me?"

"She consulted me, dear mother, five minutes since," said Valentin, "and I told her that such a beautiful woman—she is beautiful, you will see—had no right to bury herself alive."

"You should have referred Claire to her mother, my brother," said M. de Bellegarde, in French. "This is very strange."

"I refer her to the whole company!" said Valentin. "Here she comes!" And he went to the open door, met Madame de Cintré on the threshold, took her by the hand, and led her into the room. She was dressed in white; but a long blue cloak, which hung almost to her feet, was fastened across her shoulders by a silver clasp. She had tossed it back, however, and her long white arms were uncovered. In her dense, fair hair there glittered a dozen diamonds. She looked serious and, Newman thought, rather pale; but she glanced round her, and, when she saw him, smiled and put out her hand. He thought her tremendously handsome. He had a chance to look at her full in the face, for she stood a moment in the centre of the room, hesitating, apparently, what she should do, without meeting his eyes. Then she went up to her mother, who sat in her deep chair by the fire, looking at Madame de Cintré almost fiercely. With her back turned to the others, Madame de Cintré held her cloak apart to show her dress.

"What do you think of me?" she asked.

"I think you are audacious," said the marquise. "It was but three days ago, when I asked you, as a particular favor to myself, to go to the Duchess de Lusignan's, that you told me you were going nowhere and that one must be consistent. Is this your consistency? Why should you distinguish Madame Robineau? Who is it you wish to please to-night?"

"I wish to please myself, dear mother," said Madame de Cintré. And she bent over and kissed the old lady.

"I don't like surprises, my sister," said Urbain de Bellegarde; "especially when one is on the point of entering a drawing-room."

Newman at this puncture felt inspired to speak. "Oh, if you are going into a room with Madame de Cintré, you needn't be afraid of being noticed yourself!"

M. de Bellegarde turned to his sister with a smile too intense to be easy. "I hope you appreciate a compliment that is paid you at your brother's expense," he said. "Come, come, madam." And offering Madame de Cintré his arm he led her rapidly out of the room. Valentin rendered the same service to young Madame de Bellegarde, who had apparently been reflecting on the fact that the ball dress of her sister-in-law was much less brilliant than her own, and yet had failed to derive absolute comfort from the reflection. With a farewell smile she sought the complement of her consolation in the eyes of the American visitor, and perceiving in them a certain mysterious brilliancy, it is not improbable that she may have flattered herself she had found it.

Newman, left alone with old Madame de Bellegarde, stood before her a few moments in silence. "Your daughter is very beautiful," he said at last.

"She is very strange," said Madame de Bellegarde.

"I am glad to hear it," Newman rejoined, smiling. "It makes me hope."

"Hope what?"

"That she will consent, some day, to marry me."

The old lady slowly rose to her feet. "That really is your project, then?"

"Yes; will you favor it?"

"Favor it?" Madame de Bellegarde looked at him a moment and then shook her head. "No!" she said, softly.

"Will you suffer it, then? Will you let it pass?"

"You don't know what you ask. I am a very proud and meddlesome old woman."

"Well, I am very rich," said Newman.

Madame de Bellegarde fixed her eyes on the floor, and Newman thought it probable she was weighing the reasons in favor of resenting the brutality of this remark. But at last, looking up, she she said simply, "How rich?"

Newman expressed his income in a round number which had the magnificent sound that large aggregations of dollars put on when they are translated into francs. He added a few remarks of a financial character, which completed a sufficiently striking present-ment of his resources.

Madame de Bellegarde listened in silence. "You are very frank," she said finally. "I will be the same. I would rather favor you, on the whole, than suffer you. It will be easier."

"I am thankful for any terms," said Newman. "But, for the present, you have suffered me long enough. Good night!" And he took his leave.

<h2 align="center">Chapter XI</h2>

Newman, on his return to Paris, had not resumed the study of French conversation with M. Nioche, he found that he had too many other uses for his time. M. Nioche, however, came to see him very promptly, having learned his whereabouts by a mysterious process to which his patron never obtained the key. The shrunken little capitalist repeated his visit more than once. He seemed op-pressed by a humiliating sense of having been overpaid, and wished apparently to redeem his debt by the offer of grammatical and statistical information in small installments. He wore the same decently melancholy aspect as a few months before; a few months more or less of brushing could make little difference in the antique lustre of his coat and hat. But the poor old man's spirit was a trifle more threadbare; it seemed to have received some hard rubs during the summer. Newman inquired with interest about Mademoiselle Noémie; and M. Nioche, at first, for answer, simply looked at him in lachrymose silence.

"Don't ask me, sir," he said at last. "I sit and watch her, but I can do nothing."

"Do you mean that she misconducts herself?"

"I don't know, I am sure. I can't follow her. I don't understand her. She has something in her head; I don't know what she is trying to do. She is too deep for me."

"Does she continue to go to the Louvre? Has she made any of those copies for me?"

"She goes to the Louvre, but I see nothing of the copies. She has something on her easel; I suppose it is one of the pictures you ordered. Such a magnificent order ought to give her fairy-fingers. But she is not in earnest. I can't say anything to her; I am afraid of her. One evening, last summer, when I took her to walk in the Champs Elysées, she said some things to me that frightened me."

"What were they?"

"Excuse an unhappy father from telling you," said M. Nioche, unfolding his calico pocket-handkerchief.

Newman promised himself to pay Mademoiselle Noémie another visit at the Louvre. He was curious about the progress of his copies, but it must be added that he was still more curious about the progress of the young lady herself. He went one afternoon to the great museum, and wandered through several of the rooms in fruitless quest of her. He was bending his steps to the long hall of the Italian masters, when suddenly he found himself face to face with Valentin de Bellegarde. The young Frenchman greeted him with ardor, and assured him that he was a godsend. He himself was in the worst of humors and he wanted some one to contradict.

"In a bad humor among all these beautiful things?" said Newman. "I thought you were so fond of pictures, especially the old black ones. There are two or three here that ought to keep you in spirits."

"Oh, to-day," answered Valentin, "I am not in a mood for pictures, and the more beautiful they are the less I like them. Their great staring eyes and fixed positions irritate me. I feel as if I were at some big, dull party, in a room full of people I shouldn't wish to speak to. What should I care for their beauty? It's a bore, and, worse still, it's a reproach. I have a great many *ennuis;* I feel vicious."

"If the Louvre has so little comfort for you, why in the world did you come here?" Newman asked.

"That is one of my ennuis. I came to meet my cousin—a dreadful English cousin, a member of my mother's family—who is in Paris for a week for her husband, and who wishes me to point out the 'principal beauties.' Imagine a woman who wears a green crape bonnet in December and has straps sticking out of the ankles of her interminable boots! My mother begged I would do something to oblige them. I have undertaken to play *valet de place* this afternoon. They were to have met me here at two o'clock, and I have been waiting for them twenty minutes. Why doesn't she arrive? She has at least a pair of feet to carry her. I don't know whether to be furious at their playing me false, or delighted to have escaped them."

"I think in your place I would be furious," said Newman, "because they may arrive yet, and then your fury will still be of use to you. Whereas if you were delighted and they were afterwards to turn up, you might not know what to do with your delight."

"You give me excellent advice, and I already feel better. I will be furious; I will let them go to the deuce and I myself will go with you—unless by chance you too have a rendezvous."

"It is not exactly a rendezvous," said Newman. "But I have in fact come to see a person, not a picture."

"A woman, presumably?"

"A young lady."

"Well," said Valentin, "I hope for you with all my heart that she is not clothed in green tulle and that her feet are not too much out of focus."

"I don't know much about her feet, but she has very pretty hands."

Valentin gave a sigh. "And on that assurance I must part with you?"

"I am not certain of finding my young lady," said Newman, "and I am not quite prepared to lose your company on the chance. It does not strike me as particularly desirable to introduce you to her, and yet I should rather like to have your opinion of her."

"Is she pretty?"

"I guess you will think so."

Bellegarde passed his arm into that of his companion. "Conduct me to her on the instant! I should be ashamed to make a pretty woman wait for my verdict."

Newman suffered himself to be gently propelled in the direction in which he had been walking, but his step was not rapid. He was turning something over in his mind. The two men passed into the long gallery of the Italian masters, and Newman, after having scanned for a moment its brilliant vista, turned aside into the smaller apartment devoted to the same school, on the left. It contained very few persons, but at the farther end of it sat Mademoiselle Nioche, before her easel. She was not at work; her palette and brushes had been laid down beside her, her hands were folded in her lap, and she was leaning back in her chair and looking intently at two ladies on the other side of the hall, who, with their backs turned to her, had stopped before one of the pictures. These ladies were apparently persons of high fashion; they were dressed with great splendor, and their long silken trains and furbelows were spread over the polished floor. It was at their dresses Mademoiselle Noémie was looking, though what she was thinking of I am unable to say. I hazard the supposition that she was saying to herself that to be able to drag such a train over a polished floor was a felicity worth any price. Her reflections, at any rate, were disturbed by the advent of New-man and his companion. She glanced at them quickly, and then, coloring a little, rose and stood before her easel.

"I came here on purpose to see you," said Newman in his bad French, offering to shake hands. And then, like a good American, he introduced Valentin formally: "Allow me to make you acquainted with the Comte Valentin de Bellegarde."

Valentin made a bow which must have seemed to Mademoiselle Noémie quite in harmony with the impressiveness of his title, but the graceful brevity of her own response made no concession to underbred surprise. She turned to Newman, putting up her hands to her hair and smoothing its delicately-felt roughness. Then, rapidly, she turned the canvas that was on her easel over upon its face. "You have not forgotten me?" she asked.

"I shall never forget you," said Newman. "You may be sure of that."

"Oh," said the young girl, "there are a great many different ways of remembering a person." And she looked straight at Valentin de Bellegarde, who was looking at her as a gentleman may when a "verdict" is expected of him.

"Have you painted anything for me?" said Newman. "Have you been industrious?"

"No, I have done nothing." And taking up her palette, she began to mix her colors at hazard.

"But your father tells me you have come here constantly."

"I have nowhere else to go! Here, all summer, it was cool, at least."

"Being here, then," said Newman, "you might have tried some-thing."

"I told you before," she answered, softly, "that I don't know how to paint."

"But you have something charming on your easel, now," said Valentin, "if you would only let me see it."

She spread out her two hands, with the fingers expanded, over the back of the canvas—those hands which Newman had called pretty, and which, in spite of several paint-stains, Valentin could now admire. "My painting is not charming," she said.

"It is the only thing about you that is not, then, mademoiselle," quoth Valentin, gallantly.

She took up her little canvas and silently passed it to him. He looked at it, and in a moment she said, "I am sure you are a judge."

"Yes," he answered, "I am."

"You know, then, that that is very bad."

"*Mon Dieu*," said Valentin, shrugging his shoulders, "let us distinguish."

"You know that I ought not to attempt to paint," the young girl continued.

"Frankly, then, mademoiselle, I think you ought not."

She began to look at the dresses of the two splendid ladies again—a point on which, having risked one conjecture, I think I may risk another. While she was looking at the ladies she was seeing Valentin de Bellegarde. He, at all events, was seeing her. He put down the roughly-besmeared canvas and addressed a little click with his tongue, accompanied by an elevation of the eyebrows, to Newman.

"Where have you been all these months?" asked Mademoiselle Noémie of our hero. "You took those great journeys, you amused yourself well?"

"Oh, yes," said Newman, "I amused myself well enough."

"I am very glad," said Mademoiselle Noémie with extreme gentleness, and she began to dabble in her colors again. She was singularly pretty, with the look of serious sympathy that she threw into her face.

Valentin took advantage of her downcast eyes to telegraph again to his companion. He renewed his mysterious physiognomical play, making at the same time a rapid tremulous movement in the air with his fingers. He was evidently finding Mademoiselle Noémie extremely interesting; the blue devils had departed, leaving the field clear.

"Tell me something about your travels," murmured the young girl.

"Oh, I went to Switzerland,—to Geneva and Zermatt and Zürich and all those places you know, and down to Venice, and all through Germany, and down the Rhine, and into Holland and Belgium—the regular round. How do you say that, in French—the regular round?" Newman asked of Valentin.

Mademoiselle Nioche fixed her eyes an instant on Bellegarde, and then with a little smile, "I don't understand monsieur," she said, "when he says so much at once. Would you be so good as to translate?"

"I would rather talk to you out of my own head," Valentin declared.

"No," said Newman, gravely, still in his bad French, "you must not talk to Mademoiselle Nioche, because you say discouraging things. You ought to tell her to work, to persevere."

"And we French, mademoiselle," said Valentin, "are accused of being false flatterers!"

"I don't want any flattery, I want only the truth. But I know the truth."

"All I say is that I suspect there are some things that you can do better than paint," said Valentin.

"I know the truth—I know the truth," Mademoiselle Noümie repeated. And, dipping a brush into a clot of red paint, she drew a great horizontal daub across her unfinished picture.

"What is that?" asked Newman.

Without answering, she drew another long crimson daub, in a vertical direction, down the middle of her canvas, and so, in a moment, completed the rough indication of a cross. "It is the sign of the truth," she said at last.

The two men looked at each other, and Valentin indulged in another flash of physiognomical eloquence. "You have spoiled your picture," said Newman.

"I know that very well. It was the only thing to do with it. I had sat looking at it all day without touching it. I had begun to hate it. It seemed to me something was going to happen."

"I like it better that way than as it was before," said Valentin. "Now it is more interesting. It tells a story. Is it for sale, mademoiselle?"

"Everything I have is for sale," said Mademoiselle Noémie.

"How much is this thing?"

"Ten thousand francs," said the young girl, without a smile.

"Everything that Mademoiselle Nioche may do at present is mine in advance," said Newman. "It makes part of an order I gave her some months ago. So you can't have this."

"Monsieur will lose nothing by it," said the young girl, looking at Valentin. And she began to put up her utensils.

"I shall have gained a charming memory," said Valentin. "You are going away? your day is over?"

"My father is coming to fetch me," said Mademoiselle Noémie.

She had hardly spoken when, through the door behind her, which opens on one of the great white stone staircases of the Louvre, M.

Nioche made his appearance. He came in with his usual even, patient shuffle, and he made a low salute to the two gentlemen who were standing before his daughter's easel. Newman shook his hands with muscular friendliness, and Valentin returned his greeting with extreme deference. While the old man stood waiting for Noémie to make a parcel of her implements, he let his mild, oblique gaze hover toward Bellegarde, who was watching Mademoiselle Noémie put on her bonnet and mantle. Valentin was at no pains to disguise his scrutiny. He looked at a pretty girl as he would have listened to a piece of music. Attention, in each case, was simple good manners. M. Nioche at last took his daughter's paint-box in one hand and the bedaubed canvas, after giving it a solemn, puzzled stare, in the other, and led the way to the door. Mademoiselle Noémie made the young men the salute of a duchess, and followed her father.

"Well," said Newman, "what do you think of her?"

"She is very remarkable. *Diable, diable, diable!*" repeated M. de Bellegarde, reflectively; "she is very remarkable."

"I am afraid she is a sad little adventuress," said Newman.

"Not a little one—a great one. She has the material." And Valentin began to walk away slowly looking vaguely at the pictures on the walls, with a thoughtful illumination in his eye. Nothing could have appealed to his imagination more than the possible adventures of a young lady endowed with the "material" of Mademoiselle Nioche. "She is very interesting," he went on. "She is a beautiful type."

"A beautiful type? What the deuce do you mean?" asked Newman.

"I mean from the artistic point of view. She is an artist,—outside of her painting, which obviously is execrable."

"But she is not beautiful. I don't even think her very pretty."

"She is quite pretty enough for her purposes, and it is a face and figure on which everything tells. If she were prettier she would be less intelligent, and her intelligence is half of her charm."

"In what way," asked Newman, who was much amused at his companion's immediate philosophization of Mademoiselle Nioche, "does her intelligence strike you as so remarkable?"

"She has taken the measure of life, and she has determined to *be* something—to succeed at any cost. Her painting, of course, is a mere trick to gain time. She is waiting for her chance; she wishes to launch herself, and to do it well. She knows her Paris. She is one of fifty thousand, so far as the mere ambition goes; but I am very sure that in the way of resolution and capacity she is a rarity. And in one gift—perfect heartlessness—I will warrant she is unsurpassed. She has not as much heart as will go on the point of a needle. That is an immense virtue. Yes, she is one of the celebrities of the future."

"Heaven help us!" said Newman, "how far the artistic point of view may take a man! But in this case I must request that you don't let it take you too far. You have learned a wonderful deal about Mademoiselle Noémie in a quarter of an hour. Let that suffice; don't follow up your researches."

"My dear fellow," cried Bellegarde with warmth, "I hope I have too good manners to intrude."

"You are not intruding. The girl is nothing to me. In fact, I rather dislike her. But I like her poor old father, and for his sake I beg you to abstain from any attempt to verify your theories."

"For the sake of that seedy old gentleman who came to fetch her?" demanded Valentin, stopping short. And on Newman's assenting, "Ah no, ah no," he went on with a smile. "You are quite wrong, my dear fellow; you needn't mind him."

"I verily believe that you are accusing the poor gentleman of being capable of rejoicing in his daughter's dishonor."

"*Voyons*," said Valentin; "who is he? what is he?"

"He is what he looks like: as poor as a rat, but very high-toned."

"Exactly. I noticed him perfectly; be sure I do him justice. He has had losses, *des malheurs*, as we say. He is very low-spirited, and his daughter is too much for him. He is the pink of respectability, and he has sixty years of honesty on his back. All this I perfectly appreciate. But I know my fellow-men and my fellow-Parisians, and I will make a bargain with you." Newman gave ear to his bargain and he went on. "He would rather his daughter were a good girl than a bad one, but if the worst comes to the worst, the old man will not do what Virginius did. Success justifies everything. If Mademoiselle Noémie makes a figure, her papa will feel—well, we will call it relieved. And she will make a figure. The old gentleman's future is assured."

"I don't know what Virginius did, but M. Nioche will shoot Miss Noémie," said Newman. "After that, I suppose his future will be assured in some snug prison."

"I am not a cynic; I am simply an observer," Valentin rejoined. "Mademoiselle Noémie interests me; she is extremely remarkable. If there is a good reason, in honor or decency, for dismissing her from my thoughts forever, I am perfectly willing to do it. Your estimate of the papa's sensibilities is a good reason until it is invalidated. I promise you not to look at the young girl again until you tell me that you have changed your mind about the papa. When he has given distinct proof of being a philosopher, you will raise your interdict. Do you agree to that?"

"Do you mean to bribe him?"

"Oh, you admit, then, that he is bribable? No, he would ask too much, and it would not be exactly fair. I mean simply to wait. You will continue, I suppose, to see this interesting couple, and you will give me the news yourself."

"Well," said Newman, "if the old man turns out a humbug, you may do what you please. I wash my hands of the matter. For the girl herself, you may be at rest. I don't know what harm she may do to me, but I certainly can't hurt her. It seems to me," said Newman, "that you are very well matched. You are both hard cases, and M. Nioche and I, I believe, are the only virtuous men to be found in Paris.

Soon after this M. de Bellegarde, in punishment for his levity, received a stern poke in the back from a pointed instrument. Turning quickly round he found the weapon to be a parasol wielded by a lady in green gauze bonnet. Valentin's English cousins had been drifting about unpiloted, and evidently deemed that they had a grievance. Newman left him to their mercies, but with a boundless faith in his power to plead his cause.

CHAPTER XII

THREE DAYS after his introduction to the family of Madame de Cintré, Newman, coming in toward evening, found upon his table the card of the Marquis de Bellegarde. On the following day he received a note informing him that the Marquise de Bellegarde would be grateful for the honor of his company at dinner.

He went, of course, though he had to break another engagement to do it. He was ushered into the room in which Madame de Bellegarde had received him before, and here he found his venerable hostess, surrounded by her entire family. The room was lighted only by the crackling fire, which illumined the very small pink slippers of a lady who, seated in a low chair, was streching out her toes before it. This lady was the younger Madame de Bellegarde. Madame de Cintré was seated at the other end of the room, holding a little girl against her knee, the child of her brother Urbain, to whom she was apparently relating a wonderful story. Valentin was sitting on a puff, close to his sister-in-law, into whose ear he was certainly distilling the finest nonsense. The marquis was stationed before the fire, with his head erect and his hands behind him, in an attitude of formal expectancy.

Old Madame de Bellegarde stood up to give Newman her greeting, and there was that in the way she did so which seemed to measure narrowly the extent of her condescension. "We are all alone, you see, we have asked no one else," she said, austerely.

"I am very glad you didn't; this is much more sociable," said Newman. "Good evening, sir," and he offered his hand to the marquis.

M. de Bellegarde was affable, but in spite of his dignity he was restless. He began to pace up and down the room, he looked out of the long windows, he took up books and laid them down again. Young Madame de Bellegarde gave Newman her hand without moving and without looking at him.

"You may think that is coldness," exclaimed Valentin; "but it is not, it is warmth. It shows she is treating you as an intimate. Now she detests me, and yet she is always looking at me."

"No wonder I detest you if I am always looking at you!" cried the lady. "If Mr. Newman does not like my way of shaking hands, I will do it again."

But this charming privilege was lost upon our hero, who was already making his way across the room to Madame de Cintré. She looked at him as she shook hands, but she went on with the story she was telling her little niece. She had only two or three phrases to add, but they were apparently of great moment. She deepened hr voice, smiling as she did so, and the little girl gazed at her with round eyes.

"But in the end the young prince married the beautiful Flora-bella," said Madame de Cintré, "and carried her off to live with him in the Land of the Pink Sky. There she was so happy that she forgot all her troubles, and went out to drive every day of her life in an ivory coach drawn by five hundred white mice. Poor Florabella," she exclaimed to Newman, "had suffered terribly."

"She had had nothing to eat for six months," said little Blanche.

"Yes, but when the six months were over, she had a plum-cake as big as that ottoman," said Madame de Cintré. "That quite set her up again."

"What a checkered career!" said Newman. "Are you very fond

of children?" He was certain that she was, but he wished to make her say it.

"I like to talk with them," she answered; "we can talk with them so much more seriously than with grown persons. That is great nonsense that I have been telling Blanche, but it is a great deal more serious than most of what we say in society."

"I wish you would talk to me, then, as if I were Blanche's age," said Newman, laughing. "Were you happy at your ball, the other night?"

"Ecstatically!"

"Now you are talking the nonsense that we talk in society," said Newman. "I don't believe that."

"It was my own fault if I was not happy. The ball was very pretty, and every one very amiable."

"It was on your conscience," said Newman, "that you had annoyed your mother and your brother."

Madame de Cintré looked at him a moment without answering. "That is true," she replied at last. "I had undertaken more than I could carry out. I have very little courage; I am not a heroine." She said this with a certain soft emphasis; but then, changing her tone, "I could never have gone through the sufferings of the beautiful Florabelle," she added, "not even for her prospective rewards."

Dinner was announced, and Newman betook himself to the side of the old Madame de Bellegarde. The dining-room, at the end of a cold corridor, was vast and sombre; the dinner was simple and delicately excellent. Newman wondered whether Madame de Cintré had had something to do with ordering the repast and greatly hoped she had. Once seated at table, with the various members of the ancient house of Bellegarde around him, he asked himself the meaning of his position. Was the old lady responding to his advances? Did the fact that he was a solitary guest augment his credit or diminish it? Were they ashamed to show him to other people, or did they wish to give him a sign of sudden adoption into their last reserve of favor? Newman was on his guard; he was watchful and conjectural; and yet at the same time he was vaguely indifferent. Whether they gave him a long rope or a short one he was there now, and Madame de Cintré was opposite to him. She had a tall candlestick on each side of her; she would sit there for the next hour, and that was enough. The dinner was extremely solemn and measured; he wondered whether this was always the state of things in "old families." Madame de Bellegarde held her head very high, and fixed her eyes, which looked peculiarly sharp in her little, finely-wrinkled white face, very intently upon the table-service. The marquis appeared to have decided that the fine arts offered a safe subject of conversation, as not leading to startling personal revelations. Every now and then, having learned from Newman that he had been through the museums of Europe, he uttered some polished aphorism upon the flesh-tints of Rubens and the good taste of Sansovino. His manners seemed to indicate a fine, nervous dread that something disagreeable might happen if the atmosphere were not purified by allusions of a thoroughly superior cast. "What under the sun is the man afraid of?" Newman asked himself. "Does he think I am going to offer to swap jack-knives with him?" It was useless to shut his eyes to the fact that the marquis was profoundly disagreeable to him. He had never been a man of strong personal aversions; his nerves had not been at the mercy of the mystical qualities of his neighbors. But here was a man towards whom he was irresistibly in opposition; a man of forms and phrases and postures; a man full of possible impertinences and treacheries. M. de Bellegarde made him feel as if he were standing bare-footed on a marble floor; and yet, to gain his desire, Newman felt perfectly able to stand. He wondered what Madame de Cintré thought of his being accepted, if accepted it was. There was no judging from her face, which expressed simply the desire to be gracious in a manner which should require as little explicit recognition as possible. Young Madame de Bellegarde had always the same manners; she was always preoccupied, distracted, listening to everything and hearing nothing, looking at her dress, her rings, her finger-nails, seeming rather bored, and yet puzzling you to decide what was her ideal of social diversion. Newman was enlightened on this point later. Even Valentin did not quite seem master of his wits; his vivacity was fitful and forced, yet Newman observed that in the lapses of his talk he appeared excited. His eyes had an intenser spark than usual. The effect of all this was that Newman for the first time in his life, was not himself; that he measured his movements, and counted his words, and resolved that if the occasion demanded that he should appear to have swallowed a ramrod, he would meet the emergency.

After dinner M. de Bellegarde proposed to his guest that they should go into the smoking-room, and he led the way toward a small, somewhat musty apartment, the walls of which were ornamented with old hangings of stamped leather and trophies of rusty arms. Newman refused a cigar, but he established himself upon one of the divans, while the marquis puffed his own weed before the fire-place, and Valentin sat looking through the light fumes of a cigarette from one to the other.

"I can't keep quiet any longer," said Valentin, at last. "I must tell you the news and congratulate you. My brother seems unable to come to the point; he revolves around his anouncement like the priest around the altar. You are accepted as a candidate for the hand of our sister."

"Valentin, be a little proper!" murmured the marquis, with a look of the most delicate irritation contracting the bridge of his high nose.

"There has been a family council," the young man continued; "my mother and Urbain have put their heads together, and even my testimony has not been altogether excluded. My mother and the marquis sat at a table covered with green cloth; my sister-in-law and I were on a bench against the wall. It was like a committee at the Corps Législatif. We were called up, one after the other, to testify. We spoke of you very handsomely. Madame de Bellegarde said that if she had not been told who you were, she would have taken you for a duke—an American duke, the Duke of California. I said that I could warrant you grateful for the smallest favors—modest, humble, unassuming. I was sure that you would know your own place, always, and never give us occasion to remind you of certain differences. After all, you couldn't help it if you were not a duke. There were none in your country; but if there had been, it was certain that, smart and active as you are, you would have got the pick of the titles. At this point I was ordered to sit down, but I think I made an impression in your favor."

M. de Bellegarde looked at his brother with dangerous coldness, and gave a smile as thin as the edge of a knife. Then he removed a spark of cigar-ash from the sleeve of his coat; he fixed his eyes for a while on the cornice of the room, and at last he inserted one of his white hands into the breast of his waistcoat. "I must apologize to you for the deplorable levity of my brother," he said, "and I must notify you that this is probably not the last time that his want of tact will cause you serious embarrassment."

"No, I confess I have no tact," said Valentin. "Is your embarrassment really painful, Newman? The marquis will put you right again; his own touch is deliciously delicate."

"Valentin, I am sorry to say," the marquis continued, "has never possessed the tone, the manner, that belongs to a young man in his position. It has been a great affliction to his mother, who is very fond of the old traditions. But you must remember that he speaks for no one but himself."

"Oh, I don't mind him, sir," said Newman, good-humoredly. "I know what he amounts to."

"In the good old times," said Valentin, "marquises and counts used to have their appointed fools and jesters, to crack jokes for them. Nowadays we see a great strapping democrat keeping a count about him to play the fool. It's a good situation, but I certainly am very degenerate."

M. de Bellegarde fixed his eyes for some time on the floor. "My mother informed me," he said presently, "of the announcement that you made to her the other evening."

"That I desired to marry your sister?" said Newman.

"That you wished to arrange a marriage," said the marquis, slowly, "with my sister, the Comtesse de Cintré. The proposal was serious, and required, on my mother's part, a great deal of reflection. She naturally took me into her counsels, and I gave my most zealous attention to the subject. There was a great deal to be considered; more than you appear to imagine. We have viewed the question on all its faces, we have weighed one thing against another. Our conclusion has been that we favor your suit. My mother has desired me to inform you of our decision. She will have the honor of saying a few words to you on the subject, herself. Meanwhile, by us, the heads of the family, you are accepted."

Newman got up and came nearer to the marquis. "You will do nothing to hinder me, and all you can to help me, eh?"

"I will recommend my sister to accept you."

Newman passed his hand over his face, and pressed it for a moment upon his eyes. This promise had a great sound, and yet the pleasure he took in it was embittered by his having to stand there so and receive his passport from M. de Bellegarde. The idea of having this gentleman mixed up with his wooing and wedding was more and more disagreeable to him. But Newman had resolved to go though the mill, as he imaged it, and he would not cry out at the first turn of the wheel. He was silent a while, and then he said, with a certain dryness which Valentin told him afterwards had a very grand air, "I am much obliged to you."

"I take note of the promise," said Valentin, "I register the vow."

M. de Bellegarde began to gaze at the cornice again; he apparently had something more to say. "I must do my mother the justice," he resumed, "I must do myself the justice, to say that our decision was not easy. Such an arrangement was not what we had expected. The idea that my sister should marry a gentleman—ah—in business was something of a novelty."

"So I told you, you know," said Valentin raising his finger at Newman.

"The novelty has not quite worn away, I confess," the marquis went on; "perhaps it never will, entirely. But possibly that is not altogether to be regretted," and he gave his thin smile again. "It may be that the time has come when we should make some concession to novelty. There had been no novelties in our house for a great many years. I made the observation to my mother, and she did me the honor to admit that it was worthy of attention."

"My dear brother," interrupted Valentin, "is not your memory just here leading you the least bit astray? Our mother is, I may say, distinguished for her small respect of abstract reasoning. Are you very sure that she replied to your strirking proposition in the gracious manner you describe? You know how terribly incisive she is sometimes. Didn't she, rather, do you the honor to say, 'A fiddlestick for your phrases! There are better reasons than that'?"

"Other reasons were discussed," said the marquis, without looking at Valentin, but with an audible tremor in his voice; "some of them possibly were better. We are conservative, Mr. Newman, but we are not also bigots. We judged the matter liberally. We have no doubt that everything will be comfortable."

Newman had stood listening to these remarks with his arms folded and his eyes fastened upon M. de Bellegarde, "Comfortable?" he said, with a sort of grim flatness of intonation. "Why shouldn't we be comfortable? If you are not, it will be your own fault; I have everything to make *me* so."

"My brother means that with the lapse of time you may get used to the change"— and Valentin paused, to light another cigarette.

"What change?" asked Newman in the same tone.

"Urbain," said Valentin, very gravely, "I am afraid that Mr. Newman does not quite realize the change. We ought to insist upon that."

"My brother goes too far," said M. de Bellegarde. "It is his fatal want of tact again. It is my mother's wish, and mine, that no such allusions should be made. Pray never make them yourself. We prefer to assume that the person accepted as the possible husband of my sister is one of ourselves, and that he should have no explanations to make. With a little discretion on both sides, everything, I think, will be easy. That is exactly what I wished to say—that we quite understand what we have undertaken, and that you may depend upon our adhering to our resolution."

Valentin shook his hands in the air and then buried his face in them. "I have less tact that I might have, no doubt; but oh, my brother, if you knew what you yourself were saying!" And he went off into a long laugh.

M. de Bellegarde's face flushed a little, but he held his head higher, as if to repudiate this concession to vulgar perturbability. "I am sure you understand me," he said to Newman.

"Oh no, I don't understand you at all," said Newman. "But you needn't mind that. I don't care. In fact, I think I had better not understand you. I might not like it. That wouldn't suit me at all, you know. I want to marry your sister, that's all; to do it as quickly as possible, and to find fault with nothing. I don't care how I do it. I am not marrying you, you know, sir. I have got my leave, and that is all I want."

"You had better receive the last word from my mother," said the marquis.

"Very good; I will go and get it," said Newman; and he prepared to return to the drawing-room.

M. de Bellegarde made a motion for him to pass first, and when Newman had gone out he shut himself into the room with Valentin. Newman had been a trifle bewildered by the audacious irony of the younger brother, and he had not needed its aid to point the moral of M. de Bellegarde's transcendent patronage. He had wit enough to appreciate the force of that civility which consists in calling your attention to the impertinences it spares you. But he had felt warmly the delicate sympathy with himself that underlay Valentin's fraternal irreverence, and he was most unwilling that his friend should pay a tax upon it. He paused a moment in the corridor, after he had gone a few steps, expecting to hear the resonance of M. de Bellegarde's displeasure; but he detected only a perfect stillness. The stillness itself seemed a trifle portentous; he reflected however that he had no right to stand listening, and he made his way back to the salon. In his absence several persons had come in. They were scattered about the room in groups, two or three of them having passed into a small boudoir, next to the drawing-room, which had now been lighted and opened. Old Madame de Bellegarde was in her place by the fire, talking to a very old gentleman in a wig and a profuse white neck cloth of the fashion of 1820. Madame de Cintré was bending a listening head to the historic confidences of an old lady who was presumably the wife of the old gentleman in the neckcloth, an old lady in a red satin dress and an ermine cape, who wore across her forehead a band with a topaz set in it. Young Madame de Bellegarde, when Newman came in, left some people among whom she was sitting, and took the place that she had occupied before dinner. Then she gave a little push to the puff that stood near her, and by a glance at Newman seemed to indicate that she had placed it in position for him. He went and took possession of it; the marquis's wife amused and puzzled him.

"I know your secret," she said, in her bad but charming English; "you need make no mystery of it. You wish to marry my sister-in-law. *C'est un beau choix.* A man like you ought to marry a tall, thin woman. You must know that I have spoken in your favor; you owe me a famous taper!"

"You have spoken to Madame de Cintré?" said Newman.

"Oh no, not that. You may think it strange, but my sister-in-law and I are not so intimate as that. No; I spoke to my husband and my mother-in-law; I said I was sure we could do what we chose with you."

"I am much obliged to you," said Newman, laughing; "but you can't."

"I know that very well; I didn't believe a word of it. But I wanted you to come into the house; I thought we should be friends."

"I am very sure of it," said Newman.

"Don't be too sure. If you like Madame de Cintré so much, perhaps you will not like me. We are as different as blue and pink. But you and I have something in common. I have come into this family by marriage; you want to come into it in the same way."

"Oh no, I don't!" interrupted Newman. "I only want to take Madame de Cintré out of it."

"Well, to cast your nets you have to go into the water. Our positions are alike; we shall be able to compare notes. What do you think of my husband? It's a strange question, isn't it? But I shall ask you some stranger ones yet."

"Perhaps a stranger one will be easier to answer," said Newman. "You might try me."

"Oh, you get off very well; the old Comte de la Rochefidèle, yonder, couldn't do it better. I told them that if we only gave you a chance you would be a perfect *talon rouge*. I know something about men. Besides, you and I belong to the same camp. I am a ferocious democrat. By birth I am *vieille roche;* a good little bit of the history of France is the history of my family. Oh, you never heard of us, of course! *Ce que c'est que la gloire!* We are much better than the Bellegardes, at any rate. But I don't care a pin for my pedigree; I want to belong to my time. I'm a revolutionist, a radical, a child of the age! I am sure I go beyond you. I like clever people, wherever they come from, and I take my amusement wherever I find it. I don't pout at the Empire; here all the world pouts at the Empire. Of course I have to mind what I say; but I expect to take my revenge with you." Madame de Bellegarde discoursed for some time longer in this sympathetic strain, with an eager abundance which seemed to indicate that her opportunities for revealing her esoteric philosophy were indeed rare. She hoped that Newman would never be afraid of her, however he might be with the others, for, really, she went very far indeed. "Strong people"—*le gens forts*—were in her opinion equal, all the world over. Newman listened to her with an attention at once beguiled and irritated. He wondered what the deuce she, too, was driving at, with her hope that he would not be afraid of her and her protestations of equality. In so far as he could understand her, she was wrong; a silly, rattling woman was certainly not the equal of a sensible man, preoccupied with an ambitious passion. Madame de Bellegarde stopped suddenly, and looked at him sharply, shaking her fan. "I see you don't believe me," she said, "you are too much on your guard. You will not form an alliance, offensive or defensive? You are very wrong; I could help you."

Newman answered that he was very grateful and that he would certainly ask for help; she should see. "But first of all," he said. "I must help myself." And he went to join Madame de Cintré.

"I have been telling Madame de la Rochefidèle that you are an American," she said, as he came up. "It interests her greatly. Her father went over with the French troops to help you in your battles in the last century, and she has always, in consequence, wanted greatly to see an American. But she has never succeeded till to-night. You are the first—to her knowledge—that she has ever looked at."

Madame de la Rochefidèle had an aged, cadaverous face, with a falling of the lower jaw which prevented her from bringing her lips together, and reduced her conversations to a series of impressive but inarticulate gutturals. She raised an antique eye-glass, elaborately mounted in chased silver, and looked at Newman from head to foot. Then she said something to which he listened deferentially, but which he completely failed to understand.

"Madame de la Rochefidèle says that she is convinced that she must have seen Americans without knowing it," Madame de Cintré explained. Newman thought it probable she had seen a great many things without knowing it; and the old lady, again addressing herself to utterance, declared—as interpreted by Madame de Cintré—that she wished she had known it.

At this moment the old gentleman who had been talking to the elder Madame de Bellegarde drew near, leading the marquise on his arm. His wife pointed out Newman to him, apparently explaining his remarkable origin. M. de la Rochefidèle, whose old age was rosy and rotund, spoke very neatly and clearly, almost as prettily, Newman thought, as M. Nioche. When he had been enlightened, he turned to Newman with an inimitable elderly grace.

"Monsieur is by no means the first American that I have seen," he said. "Almost the first person I ever saw—to notice him—was an American."

"Ah?" said Newman, sympathetically.

"The great Dr. Franklin," said M. de la Rochefidèle. "Of course I was very young. He was received very well in our *monde*."

"Not better than Mr. Newman," said Madame de Bellegarde. "I beg he will offer his arm into the other room. I could have offered no higher privilege to Dr. Franklin."

Newman, complying with Madame de Bellegarde's request, perceived that her two sons had returned to the drawing-room. He scanned their faces an instant for traces of the scene that had followed his separation from them, but the marquis seemed neither more nor less frigidly grand than usual, and Valentin was kissing ladies' hands with at least his habitual air of self-abandonment to the act. Madame de Bellegarde gave a glance at her eldest son, and by the time she had crossed the threshold of her boudoir he was at her side. The room was now empty and offered a sufficient degree of privacy. The old lady disengaged herself from Newman's arm and rested her hand on the arm of the marquis; and in this position she stood a moment, holding her head high and biting her small under-lip. I am afraid the picture was lost upon Newman, but Madame de Bellegarde was, in fact, at this moment a striking image of the dignity which—even in the case of a little time-shrunken old lady—may reside in the habit of unquestioned authority and the absoluteness of a social theory favorable to yourself.

"My son has spoken to you as I desired," she said, "and you understand that we shall not interfere. The rest will lie with yourself."

"M. de Bellegarde told me several thing I didn't understand," said Newman, "but I made out that. You will leave me an open field. I am much obliged."

"I wish to add a word that my son probably did not feel at liberty to say," the marquise rejoined. "I must say it for my own peace of mind. We are stretching a point; we are doing you a great favor."

"Oh, your son said it very well; didn't you?" said Newman.

"Not so well as my mother," declared the marquis.

"I can only repeat—I am much obliged."

"It is proper I should tell you," Madame de Bellegarde went on, "that I am very proud, and that I hold my head very high. I may be wrong, but I am too old to change. At least I know it, and I don't pretend to anything else. Don't flatter yourself that my daughter is not proud. She is proud in her own way—a somewhat different way from mine. You will have to make your terms with that. Even Valentin is proud, if you touch the right spot—or the wrong one. Urbain is proud; that you see for yourself. Sometimes I think he is a little too proud; but I wouldn't change him. He is the best of my children; he cleaves to his old mother. But I have said enough to show you that we are all proud together. It is well that you should know the sort of people you have come among."

"Well," said Newman, "I can only say, in return, that I am *not* proud; I shan't mind you! But you speak as if you intended to be very disagreeable."

"I shall not enjoy having my daughter marry you, and I shall not pretend to enjoy it. If you don't mind that, so much the better."

"If you stick to your own side of the contract we shall not quarrel; that is all I ask of you," said Newman. "Keep your hands off, and give me an open field. I am very much in earnest, and there is not the slightest danger of my getting discouraged or backing out. You will have me constantly before your eyes; if you don't like it, I am sorry for you. I will do for your daughter, if she will accept me, everything that a man can do for a woman. I am happy to tell you that, as a promise—a pledge. I consider that on your side you make me an equal pledge. You will not back out, eh?"

"I don't know what you mean by 'backing out,'" said the marquise.

"It suggests a movement of which I think no Bellegarde has ever been guilty.

"Our word is our word," said Urbain. "We have given it."

"Well, now," said Newman, "I am very glad you are so proud. It makes me believe that you will keep it."

The marquise was silent a moment, and then, suddenly, "I shall always be polite to you, Mr. Newman," she declared, "but, decidedly, I shall never like you."

"Don't be too sure," said Newman, laughing.

"I am so sure that I will ask you to take me back to my arm-chair without the least fear of having my sentiments modified by the service you render me." And Madame de Bellegarde took his arm, and returned to the salon and to her customary place.

M. de la Rochefidèle and his wife were preparing to take their leave, and Madame de Cintré's interview with the mumbling old lady was at an end. She stood looking about her, asking herself, apparently to whom she should next speak, when Newman came up to her.

"Your mother has given me leave—very solemnly—to come here often," he said. "I mean to come often."

"I shall be glad to see you," she answered, simply. And then, in a moment. "You probably think it very strange that there should be such a solemnity—as you say—about your coming."

"Well, yes; I do, rather."

"Do you remember what my brother Valentin said, the first time you came to see me—that we were a strange, strange family?"

"It was not the first time I came, but the second," said Newman.

"Very true. Valentin annoyed me at the time, but now I know you better, I may tell you he was right. If you come often, you will see!" and Madame de Cintré turned away.

Newman watched her a while, talking with other people, and then he took his leave. He shook hands last with Valentin de Bellegarde, who came out with him to the top of the staircase. "Well, you have got your permit," said Valentin. "I hope you liked the process."

"I like your sister, more than ever. But don't worry your brother any more for my sake," Newman added. "I don't mind him. I am afraid he came down on you in the smoking-room, after I went out."

"When my brother comes down on me," said Valentin, "he falls hard. I have a peculiar way of receiving him. I must say," he continued, "that they came up to the mark much sooner than I expected. I don't understand it; they must have had to turn the screw pretty tight. It's a tribute to your millions."

"Well, it's the most precious one they have ever received," said Newman.

He was turning away when Valentin stopped him, looking at him with a brilliant, softly-cynical glance. "I should like to know whether, within a few days, you have seen your venerable friend M. Nioche."

"He was yesterday at my rooms," Newman answered.

"What did he tell you?"

"Nothing particular."

"You didn't see the muzzle of a pistol sticking out of his pocket?"

"What are you driving at?" Newman demanded. "I thought he seemed rather cheerful for him."

Valentin broke into a laugh. "I am delighted to hear it! I win my bet. Mademoiselle Noémie has thrown her cap over the mill, as we say. She has left the paternal domicile. She is launched! And M. Nioche is rather cheerful—*for him!* Don't brandish your tomahawk at that rate; I have not seen her nor communicated with her since that day at the Louvre. Andromeda has found another Perseus than I. My information is exact; on such matters it always is. I suppose that now you will raise your protest."

"My protest be hanged!" murmured Newman, disgustedly.

But his tone found no echo in that in which Valentin, with his hand on the door, to return to his mother's apartment, exclaimed, "But I shall see her now! She is very remarkable—she is very remarkable!"

Chapter XIII

NEWMAN KEPT his promise, or his menace, of going often to the Rue de l'Université, and during the next six weeks he saw Madame de Cintré more times that he could have numbered. He flattered himself that he was not in love, but his biographer may be supposed to know better. He claimed, at least, none of the exemptions and emoluments of the romantic passion. Love, he believed, made a fool of a man, and his present emotion was not folly but wisdom; wisdom sound, serene, well-directed. What he felt was an intense, all-consuming tenderness, which had for its object an extraordinarily graceful and delicate, and at the same time impressive, woman who lived in a large gray house on the left bank of the Seine. This tenderness turned very often into a positive heart-ache; a sign in

which, certainly, Newman ought to have read the appellation which
science has conferred upon his sentiment. When the heart has a
heavy weight upon it, it hardly matters whether the weight be of
gold or of lead; when, at any rate, happiness passes into that place
in which it becomes identical with pain, a man may admit that the
reign of wisdom is temporarily suspended. Newman wished Madame
de Cintré so well that nothing he could think of doing for her in
the future rose to the high standard which his present mood had
set itself. She seemed to him so felicitous a product of nature and
circumstance that his invention, musing on future combinations, was
constantly catching its breath with the fear of stumbling into some
brutal compression or mutilation of her beautiful personal harmony.
This is what I mean by Newman's tenderness: Madame de Cintré
pleased him so, exactly as she was, that his desire to interpose
between her and the troubles of life had the quality of a young
mother's eagerness to protect the sleep of her first-born child.
Newman was simply charmed, and he handled his charm as if it
were a music-box which would stop if one shook it. There can be
no better proof of the hankering epicure that is hidden in every
man's temperament, waiting for a signal from some divine con-
federate that he may safely peep out. Newman at last was enjoying,
purely, freely, deeply. Certain of Madame de Cintré's personal
qualities—the luminous sweetness of her eyes, the delicate mobility
of her face, the deep liquidity of her voice—filled all his consciousness. A rose-crowned Greek of old, gazing at a marble goddess with
his whole bright intellect resting satisfied in the act, could not have
been a more complete embodiment of the wisdom that loses itself
in the enjoyment of quiet harmonies.

He made no violent love to her—no sentimental speeches. He
never trespassed on what she had made him understand was for the
present forbidden ground. But he had, nevertheless, a comfortable
sense that she knew better from day to day how much he admired
her. Though in general he was no great talker, he talked much,
and he succeeded perfectly in making her say many things. He was
not afraid of boring her, either by his discourse or by his silence;
and whether or no he did occasionally bore her, it is probable that
on the whole she liked him only the better for his absence of
embarrassed scruples. Her visitors, coming in often while Newman
sat there, found a tall, lean, silent man in a half-lounging attitude,
who laughed out sometimes when no one had meant to be droll,
and remained grave in the presence of calculated witticisms, for

appreciation of which he had apparently not the proper culture.

It must be confessed that the number of subjects upon which Newman had no ideas was extremely large, and it must be added that as regards those subjects upon which he was without ideas he was also perfectly without words. He had little of the small change of conversation, and his stock of ready-made formulas and phrases was the scantiest. On the other hand he had plenty of attention to bestow, and his estimate of the importance of a topic did not depend upon the number of clever things he could say about it. He himself was almost never bored, and there was no man with whom it would have been a greater mistake to suppose that silence meant displeasure. What it was that entertained him during some of his speechless sessions I must, however, confess myself unable to determine. We know in a general way that a great many things which were old stories to a great many people had the charm of novelty to him, but a complete list of his new impressions would probably contain a number of surprises for us. He told Madame de Cintré a hundred long stories; he explained to her, in talking of the United States, the working of various local institutions and mercantile customs. Judging by the sequel she was interested, but one would not have been sure of it beforehand. As regards her own talk, Newman was very sure himself that she herself enjoyed it: this was as a sort of amendment to the portrait that Mrs. Tristram had drawn of her. He discovered that she had naturally an abundance of gayety. He had been right at first in saying she was shy; her shyness, in a woman whose circumstances and tranquil beauty afforded every facility for well-mannered hardihood, was only a charm the more. For Newman it had lasted some time, and even when it went it left something behind it which for a while performed the same office. Was this the tearful secret of which Mrs. Tristram had had a glimpse, and of which, as of her friend's reserve, her high-breeding, and her profundity, she had given a sketch of which the outlines were, perhaps, rather too heavy? Newman supposed so, but he found himself wondering less every day what Madame de Cintré's secrets might be, and more convinced that secrets were, in themselves, hateful things to her. She was a woman for the light, not for the shade; and her natural line was not picturesque reserve and mysterious melancholy, but frank, joyous, brilliant action, with just so much meditation as was necessary, and not a grain more. To this, apparently, he had succeeded in bringing her back. He felt, himself, that he was an antidote to oppressive secrets; what he offered her was, in fact, above all things a vast, sunny immunity from the need of having any.

He often passed his evenings, when Madame de Cintré had so appointed it, at the chilly fireside of Madame de Bellegarde, contenting himself with looking across the room, through narrowed eyelids, at his mistress, who always made a point, before her family, of talking to some one else. Madame de Bellegarde sat by the fire conversing neatly and coldly with whomsoever approached her, and glancing round the room with her slowly-restless eye, the effect of which, when it lighted upon him, was to Newman's sense identical with that of a sudden spurt of damp air. When he shook hands with her he always asked her with a laugh whether she could "stand him" another evening, and she replied, without a laugh, that thank God she had always been able to do her duty. Newman, talking once of the marquise to Mrs. Tristram, said that after all it was very easy to get on with her; it always was easy to get on with out-and-out rascals.

"And is it by that elegant term," said Mrs. Tristram, "that you designate the Marquise de Bellegarde?"

"Well," said Newman, "she is wicked, she is an old sinner."

"What is her crime?" asked Mrs. Tristram.

"I shouldn't wonder if she had murdered some one—all from a sense of duty, of course."

"How can you be so dreadful?" sighed Mrs. Tristram.

"I am not dreadful. I am speaking of her favorably."

"Pray what will you say when you want to be severe?"

"I shall keep my severity for some one else—for the marquis. There's a man I can't swallow, mix the drink as I will."

"And what has *he* done?"

"I can't quite make out; it is something dreadfully bad, something mean and underhand, and not redeemed by audacity, as his mother's misdemeanors may have been. If he has never committed murder, he has at least turned his back and looked the other way while some one else was committing it."

In spite of this invidious hypothesis, which must be taken for nothing more than an example of the capricious play of "American humor," Newman did his best to maintain an easy and friendly style of communication with M. de Bellegarde. So long as he was in personal contact with people he disliked extremely to have anything to forgive them, and he was capable of a good deal of unsuspected imaginative effort (for the sake of his own personal comfort) to assume for the time that they were good fellows. He did his best to treat the marquis as one; he believed honestly, moreover, that he could not, in reason, be such a confounded fool as he seemed. Newman's familiarity was never importunate; his sense of human equality was not an aggressive taste or an æsthetic theory, but something as natural and organic as a physical appetite which had never been put on a scanty allowance and consequently was innocent of ungraceful eagerness. His tranquil unsuspectingness of the relativity of his own place in the social scale was probably irritating to M. de Bellegarde, who saw himself reflected in the mind of his potential brother-in-law in a crude and colorless form, unpleasantly dissimilar to the impressive image projected upon his own intellectual mirror. He never forgot himself for an instant, and replied to what he must have considered Newman's "advances" with mechanical politeness. Newman, who was constantly forgetting himself, and indulging in an unlimited amount of irresponsible inquiry and conjecture, now and then found himself confronted by the conscious, ironical smile of his host. What the deuce M. de Bellegarde was smiling at he was at a loss to divine. M. de Bellegarde's smile may be supposed to have been, for himself, a compromise between a great many emotions. So long as he smiled he was polite, and it was proper he should be polite. A smile, moreover, committed him to nothing more than politeness, and left the degree of politeness agreeably vague. A smile, too, was neither dissent—which was too serious—nor agreement, which might have brought on terrible complications. And then a smile covered his own personal dignity, which in this critical situation he was resolved to keep immaculate; it was quite enough that the glory of his house should pass into eclipse. Between him and Newman, his whole manner seemed to declare there could be no interchange of opinion; he was holding his breath so as not to inhale the odor of democracy. Newman was far from being versed in European politics, but he liked to have a general idea of what was going on about him, and he accordingly asked M. de Bellegarde several times what he thought of public affairs. M. de Bellegarde answered with suave concision that he thought as ill of them as possible, that they were going from bad to worse, and that the age was rotten to its core. This gave Newman, for the moment, an almost kindly feeling for the marquis; he pitied a man for whom the world was so cheerless a place, and the next time he saw M. de Bellegarde he attempted to call his attention to some of the brilliant features of the time. The marquis presently replied that he had but a single political conviction, which was enough for him: he believed in the divine right of Henry of Bourbon, Fifth of his name, to the throne of France. Newman stared, and after this he ceased to talk politics with M. de Bellegarde. He was not horrified nor scandalized, he was not even amused; he felt as he should have felt if he had discovered in M. de Bellegarde a taste for certain oddities of diet; an appetite, for instance, for fishbones or nutshells. Under these circumstances, of course, he would never have broached dietary questions with him.

One afternoon, on his calling on Madame de Cintré, Newman was requested by the servant to wait a few moments, as his hostess was not at liberty. He walked about the room a while, taking up her books, smelling her flowers, and looking at her prints and photographs (which he thought prodigiously pretty), and at last he heard the opening of a door to which his back was turned. On the threshold stood an old woman whom he remembered to have met several times in entering and leaving the house. She was tall and straight and dressed in black, and she wore a cap which, if Newman had been initiated into such mysteries, would have been a sufficient assurance that she was not a Frenchwoman; a cap of pure British composition. She had a pale, decent, repressed-looking face, and a clear, dull, English eye. She looked at Newman a moment, both intently and timidly, and then she dropped a short, straight English curtsey.

"Madame de Cintré begs you will kindly wait," she said. "She has just come in; she will soon have finished dressing."

"Oh, I will wait as long as she wants," said Newman. "Pray tell her not to hurry."

"Thank you, sir," said the woman, softly; and then, instead of retiring with her message, she advanced into the room. She looked about her for a moment, and presently went to a table and began to arrange certain books and knick-knacks. Newman was struck with the high respectability of her appearance; he was afraid to address her as a servant. She busied herself for some moments with putting the table in order and pulling the curtains straight, while Newman walked slowly to and fro. He perceived at last from her reflection in the mirror, as he was passing that her hands were idle and that she was looking at him intently. She evidently wished to say something, and Newman, perceiving it, helped her to begin.

"You are English?" he asked.

"Yes, sir, please," she answered, quickly and softly; "I was born in Wiltshire."

"And what do you think of Paris?"

"Oh, I don't think of Paris, sir," she said in the same tone. "It is so long since I have been here."

"Ah, you have been here very long?"

"It is more than forty years, sir. I came over with Lady Emmeline."

"You mean with old Madame de Bellegarde?"

"Yes, sir. I came with her when she was married. I was my lady's own woman."

"And you have been with her ever since?"

"I have been in the house ever since. My lady has taken a younger person. You see I am very old. I do nothing regular now. But I keep about."

"You look very strong and well," said Newman, observing the erectness of her figure, and a certain venerable rosiness in her cheek.

"Thank God I am not ill, sir; I hope I know my duty too well to go panting and coughing about the house. But I am an old woman, sir, and it is as an old woman that I venture to speak to you."

"Oh, speak out," said Newman, curiously. "You needn't be afraid of me."

"Yes, sir. I think you are kind. I have seen you before."

"On the stairs, you mean?"

"Yes, sir. When you have been coming to see the countess. I have taken the liberty of noticing that you come often."

"Oh yes; I come very often," said Newman, laughing. "You need not have been wide-awake to notice that."

"I have noticed it with pleasure, sir," said the ancient tirewoman, gravely. And she stood looking at Newman with a strange expression of face. The old instinct of deference and humility was there; the habit of decent self-effacement and knowledge of her "own place." But there mingled with it a certain mild audacity, born of the occasion and of a sense, probably, of Newman's unprecedented approachableness, and, beyond this, a vague indifference to the old proprieties; as if my lady's own woman had at last begun to reflect that, since my lady had taken another person, she had a slight reversionary property in herself.

"You take a great interest in the family?" said Newman.

"A deep interest, sir. Especially in the countess."

"I am glad of that," said Newman. And in a moment he added, smiling, "So do I!"

"So I supposed, sir. We can't help noticing these things and having our ideas; can we, sir?"

"You mean as a servant?" said Newman.

"Ah, there it is, sir. I am afraid that when I let my thoughts meddle with such matters I am no longer a servant. But I am so devoted to the countess; if she were my own child I couldn't love her more. That is how I come to be so bold, sir. They say you want to marry her."

Newman eyed his interlocutress and satisfied himself that she was not a gossip, but a zealot; she looked anxious, appealing, discreet. "It is quite true," he said. "I want to marry Madame de Cintré."

"And to take her away to America?"

"I will take her wherever she wants to go."

"The farther away the better, sir!" exclaimed the old woman, with sudden intensity. But she checked herself, and, taking up a paperweight in mosaic, began to polish it with her black apron. "I don't mean anything against the house or the family, sir. But I think a great change would do the poor countess good. It is very sad here."

"Yes, it's not very lively," said Newman. "But Madame de Cintré is gay herself."

"She is everything that is good. You will not be vexed to hear that she has been gayer for a couple of months past than she had been in many a day before."

Newman was delighted to gather this testimony to the prosperity of his suit, but he repressed all violent marks of elation. "Has Madame de Cintré been in bad spirits before this?" he asked.

"Poor lady, she had good reason. M. de Cintré was no husband for a sweet young lady like that. And then, as I say, it has been a sad house. It is better, in my humble opinion, that she were out of it. So, if you will excuse me for saying so, I hope she will marry you."

"I hope she will!" said Newman.

"But you must not lose courage, sir, if she doesn't make up her mind at once. That is what I wanted to beg of you, sir. Don't give it up, sir. You will not take it ill if I say it's a great risk for any lady at any time; all the more when she has got rid of one bad bargain. But if she can marry a good, kind, respectable gentleman, I think she had better make up her mind to it. They speak very well of you, sir, in the house, and, if you will allow me to say so, I like your face. You have a very different appearance from the late count, he wasn't five feet high. And they say your fortune is beyond everything. There's no harm in that. So I beseech you to be patient, sir, and bide your time. If I don't say this to you, sir, perhaps no one will. Of course it is not for me to make any promises. I can answer for nothing. But I think you chance is not so bad, sir. I am nothing but a weary old woman in my quiet corner, but one woman understands another, and I think I make out the countess. I received her in my arms when she came into the world, and her first wedding day was the saddest of my life. She owes it to me to show me another and a brighter one. If you will hold firm, sir—and you look as if you would—I think we may see it."

"I am much obliged to you for your encouragement," said Newman, heartily. "One can't have too much. I mean to hold firm. And if Madame de Cintré marries me, you must come and live with her."

The old woman looked at him strangely, with her soft, lifeless eyes. "It may seem a heartless thing to say, sir, when one has been forty years in a house, but I may tell you that I should like to leave this place."

"Why, it's just the time to say it," said Newman, fervently. "After forty years one wants a change."

"You are very kind, sir;" and this faithful servant dropped another curtsey and seemed disposed to retire. But she lingered a moment and gave a timid, joyless smile. Newman was disappointed, and his fingers stole half shyly, half irritably into his waistcoat-pocket. His informant noticed the movement. "Thank God I am not a French-woman," she said. "If I were, I would tell you with a brazen simper, old as I am, that if you please, monsieur, my information is worth something. Let me tell you so in my own decent English way. It *is* worth something."

"How much, please?" said Newman.

"Simply this: a promise not to hint to the countess that I have said these things."

"If that is all, you have it," said Newman.

"That is all, sir. Thank you, sir. Good day, sir." And having once more slid down telescope-wise into her scanty petticoats, the old woman departed. At the same moment Madame de Cintré came in by an opposite door. She noticed the movement of the other *portière* and asked Newman who had been entertaining him.

"The British female!" said Newman. "An old lady in a black dress and a cap, who curtsies up and down, and expresses herself ever so well."

"An old lady who curtsies and expresses herself? . . . . Ah, you mean poor Mrs. Bread. I happen to know that you have made a conquest of her."

"Mrs. Cake, she ought to be called," said Newman. "She is very sweet. She is a delicious old woman."

Madame de Cintré looked at him a moment. "What can she have said to you? She is an excellent creature, but we think her rather dismal."

"I suppose," Newman answered presently, "that I like her because she has lived near you so long. Since your birth, she told me."

"Yes," said Madame de Cintré, simply; "she is very faithful; I can trust her."

Newman had never made any reflections to this lady upon her mother and her brother Urbain; had given no hint of the impression they made upon him. But, as if she had guessed his thoughts, she seemed careful to avoid all occasion for making him speak of them. She never alluded to her mother's domestic decrees; she never quoted the opinions of the marquis. They had talked, however, of Valentin, and she had made no secret of her extreme affection for her younger brother. Newman listened sometimes with a certain harmless jealousy; he would have liked to divert some of her tender allusions to his own credit. Once Madame de Cintré told him with a little air of triumph about something that Valentin had done which she thought very much to his honor. It was a service he had rendered to an old friend of the family; something more "serious" than Valentin was usually supposed capable of being. Newman said he was glad to hear of it, and then began to talk about something which lay upon his own heart. Madame de Cintré listened, but after a while she said, "I don't like the way you speak of my brother Valentin." Hereupon Newman, surprised, said that he had never spoken of him but kindly.

"It is too kindly," said Madame de Cintré. "It is a kindness that costs nothing; it is the kindness you show to a child. It is as if you didn't respect him."

"Respect him? Why I think I do."

"You think? If you are not sure, it is no respect."

"Do you respect him?" said Newman. "If you do, I do."

"If one loves a person, that is a question one is not bound to answer," said Madame de Cintré.

"You should not have asked it of me, then. I am very fond of your brother."

"He amuses you. But you would not like to resemble him."

"I shouldn't like to resemble any one. It is hard enough work resembling one's self."

"What do you mean," asked Madame de Cintré, "by resembling one's self?"

"Why, doing what is expected of one. Doing one's duty."

"But that is only when one is very good."

"Well, a great many people are good," said Newman. "Valentin is quite good enough for me."

Madame de Cintré was silent for a short time. "He is not good enough for me," she said at last. "I wish he would do something."

"What can he do?" asked Newman.

"Nothing. Yet he is very clever."

"It is a proof of cleverness," said Newman, "to be happy without doing anything."

"I don't think Valentin is happy, in reality. He is clever, generous, brave; but what is there to show for it? To me there is something sad in his life, and sometimes I have a sort of foreboding about him. I don't know why, but I fancy he will have some great trouble—perhaps an unhappy end."

"Oh, leave him to me," said Newman, jovially. "I will watch over him and keep harm away."

One evening, in Madame de Bellegarde's salon, the conversation had flagged most sensibly. The marquis walked up and down in silence, like a sentinel at the door of some smooth-fronted citadel of the proprieties; his mother sat staring at the fire; young Madame de Bellegarde worked at an enormous band of tapestry. Usually there were three or four visitors, but on this occasion a violent storm sufficiently accounted for the absence of even the most devoted habitués. In the long silences the howling of the wind and the beating of the rain were distinctly audible. Newman sat perfectly still, watching the clock, determined to stay till the stroke of eleven, but not a moment longer. Madame de Cintré had turned her back to the circle, and had been standing for some time within the uplifted curtain of a window, with her forehead against the pane, gazing out into the deluged darkness. Suddenly she turned round toward her sister-in-law.

"For Heaven's sake," she said, with peculiar eagerness, "go to the piano and play something."

Madame de Bellegarde held up her tapestry and pointed to a little white flower. "Don't ask me to leave this. I am in the midst of a masterpiece. My flower is going to smell very sweet; I am putting in the smell with this gold-colored silk. I am holding my breath; I can't leave off. Play something yourself."

"It is absurd for me to play when you are present," said Madame de Cintré. But the next moment she went to the piano and began to strike the keys with vehemence. She played for some time, rapidly and brilliantly; when she stopped, Newman went to the piano and asked her to begin again. She shook her head, and, on his insisting, she said, "I have not been playing for you; I have been playing for myself." She went back to the window again and looked out, and shortly afterwards left the room. When Newman took leave, Urbain de Bellegarde accompanied him, as he always did, just three steps down the staircase. At the bottom stood a servant with his overcoat. He had just put it on when he saw Madame de Cintré coming towards him across the vestibule.

"Shall you be at home on Friday?" Newman asked.

She looked at him a moment before answering his question. "You don't like my mother and my brother," she said.

He hesitated a moment, and then he said softly, "No."

She laid her hand on the balustrade and prepared to ascend the stairs, fixing her eyes on the first step.

"Yes, I shall be at home on Friday," and she passed up the wide dusky staircase.

On the Friday, as soon as he came in, she asked him to please to tell her why he disliked her family.

"Dislike your family?" he exclaimed. "That has a horrid sound. I didn't say so, did I? I didn't mean it, if I did."

"I wish you would tell me what you think of them," said Madame de Cintré.

"I don't think of any of them but you."

"That is because you dislike them. Speak the truth; you can't offend me."

"Well, I don't exactly love your brother," said Newman. "I remember now. But what is the use of my saying so? I had forgotten it."

"You are too good-natured," said Madame de Cintré gravely. Then, as if to avoid the appearance of inviting him to speak ill of the marquis, she turned away, motioning him to sit down.

But he remained standing before her and said presently, "What is of much more importance is that they don't like me."

"No—they don't," she said.

"And don't you think they are wrong?" Newman asked. "I don't believe I am a man to dislike."

"I suppose that a man who may be liked may also be disliked. And my brother—my mother," she added, "have not made you angry?"

"Yes, sometimes."

"You have never shown it."

"So much the better."

"Yes, so much the better. They think they have treated you very well."

"I have no doubt they might have handled me much more roughly," said Newman. "I am much obliged to them. Honestly."

"You are generous," said Madame de Cintré. "It's a disagreeable position."

"For them, you mean. Not for me."

"For me," said Madame de Cintré.

"Not when their sins are forgiven!" said Newman. "They don't think I am as good as they are. I do. But we shan't quarrel about it."

"I can't even agree with you without saying something that has a disagreeable sound. The presumption was against you. That you probably don't understand."

Newman sat down and looked at her for some time. "I don't think I really understand it. But when you say it, I believe it."

"That's a poor reason," said Madame de Cintré, smiling.

"No, it's a very good one. You have a high spirit, a high standard; but with you it's all natural and unaffected; you don't seem to have stuck your head into a vise, as if you were sitting for the photograph of propriety. You think of me as a fellow who has had no idea in life but to make money and drive sharp bargains. That's a fair description of me, but it is not the whole story. A man ought to care for something else, though I don't know exactly what. I cared for money-making, but I never cared particularly for the money. There was nothing else to do, and it was impossible to be idle. I have been very easy to others, and to myself. I have done most of the things that people asked me—I don't mean rascals. As regards your mother and your brother," Newman added, "there is only one point upon which I feel that I might quarrel with them. I don't ask them to sing my praises to you, but I ask them to let you alone.

If I thought they talked ill of me to you, I should come down upon them."

"They have let me alone, as you say. They have not talked ill of you."

"In that case," cried Newman, "I declare they are only too good for this world!"

Madame de Cintré appeared to find something startling in his exclamation. She would, perhaps, have replied, but at this moment the door was thrown open and Urbain de Bellegarde stepped across the threshold. He appeared surprised at finding Newman, but his surprise was but a momentary shadow across the surface of an unwonted joviality. Newman had never seen the marquis so exhilarated; his pale, unlighted countenance had a sort of thin transfiguration. He held open the door for some one else to enter, and presently appeared old Madame de Bellegarde, leaning on the arm of a gentleman whom Newman had not seen before. He had already risen, and Madame de Cintré rose, as she always did before her mother. The marquis, who had greeted Newman almost genially, stood apart, slowly rubbing his hands. His mother came forward with her companion. She gave a majestic little nod at Newman, and then she released the strange gentleman, that he might make his bow to her daughter.

"My daughter," she said, "I have brought you an unknown relative, Lord Deepmere. Lord Deepmere is our cousin, but he has done only to-day what he ought to have done long ago—come to make our acquaintance."

Madame de Cintré smiled, and offered Lord Deepmere her hand. "It is very extraordinary," said this noble laggard, "but this is the first time that I have ever been in Paris for more than three or four weeks."

"And how long have you been here now?" asked Madame de Cintré.

"Oh, for the last two months," said Lord Deepmere.

These two remarks might have constituted an impertinence; but a glance at Lord Deepmere's face would have satisfied you, as it apparently satisfied Madame de Cintré, that they constituted only a naïveté. When his companions were seated, Newman, who was out of the conversation, occupied himself with observing the new-comer. Observation, however, as regards Lord Deepmere's person, had no great range. He was a small, meagre man, of some three and thirty years of age, with a bald head, a short nose, and no front teeth in the upper jaw; he had round, candid, blue eyes, and several pimples on his chin. He was evidently very shy, and he laughed a great deal, catching his breath with an odd, startling sound, as the most convenient imitation of repose. His physiognomy denoted great simplicity, a certain amount of brutality, and probable failure in the past to profit by rare educational advantages. He remarked that Paris was awfully jolly, but that for real, thorough-paced entertainment it was nothing to Dublin. He even preferred Dublin to London. Had Madame de Cintré ever been to Dublin? They must all come over there some day, and he would show them some Irish sport. He always went to Ireland for the fishing, and he came to Paris for the new Offenbach things. They always brought them out in Dublin, but he couldn't wait. He had been nine times to hear La Pomme de Paris. Madame de Cintré, leaning back, with her arms folded, looked at Lord Deepmere with a more visibly puzzled face than she usually showed to society. Madame de Belle-garde, on the other hand, wore a fixed smile. The marquis said that among light operas his favorite was the Gazza Ladra. The marquise then began a series of inquiries about the duke and the cardinal, the old countess and Lady Barbara, after listening to which, and to Lord Deepmere's somewhat irreverent responses, for a quarter of an hour, Newman rose to take his leave. The marquis went with him three steps into the hall.

"Is he Irish?" asked Newman, nodding in the direction of the visitor.

"His mother was the daughter of Lord Finucane," said the marquis; "he has great Irish estates. Lady Bridget, in the complete absence of male heirs, either direct or collateral—a most extraordinary circumstance—came in for everything. But Lord Deepmere's title is English and his English property is immense. He is a charming young man."

Newman answered nothing, but he detained the marquis as the latter was beginning gracefully to recede. "It is a good time for me to thank you," he said, "for sticking so punctiliously to our bargain, for doing so much to help me on with your sister."

The marquis stared. "Really, I have done nothing that I can boast of," he said.

"Oh, don't be modest," Newman answered, laughing. "I can't flatter myself that I am doing so well simply by my own merit. And thank your mother for me, too!" And he turned away, leaving M. de Bellegarde looking after him.

CHAPTER XIV

THE NEXT time Newman came to the Rue de l'Université he had the good fortune to find Madame de Cintré alone. He had come with a definite intention, and he lost no time in executing it. She wore, moreover, a look which he eagerly interpreted as expectancy.

"I have been coming to see you for six months, now," he said, "and I have never spoken to you a second time of marriage. That was what you asked me; I obeyed. Could any man have done better?"

"You have acted with great delicacy," said Madame de Cintré.

"Well, I'm going to change, now," said Newman. "I don't mean that I am going to be indelicate; but I'm going to go back to where I began. I *am* back there. I have been all round the circle. Or rather, I have never been away from here. I have never ceased to want what I wanted then. Only now I am more sure of it, if possible; I am more sure of myself, and more sure of you. I know you better, though I don't know anything I didn't believe three months ago. You are everything—you are beyond everything—I can imagine or desire. You know me now; you *must* know me. I won't say that you have seen the best—but you have seen the worst. I hope you have been thinking all this while. You must have seen that I was only waiting; you can't suppose that I was changing. What will you say to me, now? Say that everything is clear and reasonable, and that I have been very patient and considerate, and deserve my reward. And then give me your hand. Madame de Cintré, do that. Do it."

"I knew you were only waiting," she said; "and I was very sure this day would come. I have thought about it a great deal. At first I was half afraid of it. But I am not afraid of it now." She paused a moment, and then she added, "It's a relief."

She was sitting on a low chair, and Newman was on an ottoman, near her. He leaned a little and took her hand, which for an instant she let him keep. "That means that I have not waited for nothing," he said. She looked at him for a moment, and he saw her eyes fill with tears. "With me," he went on, "you will be as safe—as safe"— and even in his ardor he hesitated a moment for a comparison—"as safe," he said, with a kind of simple solemnity, "as in your father's arms."

Still she looked at him and her tears increased. Then, abruptly, she buried her face on the cushioned arm of the sofa beside her chair, and broke into noiseless sobs. "I am weak—I am weak," he heard her say.

"All the more reason why you should give yourself up to me," he answered. "Why are you troubled? There is nothing but happiness. Is that so hard to believe?"

"To you everything seems so simple," she said, raising her head. "But things are not so. I like you extremely. I liked you six months ago, and now I am sure of it, as you say you are sure. But it is not easy, simply for that, to decide to marry you. There are a great many things to think about."

"There ought to be only one thing to think about—that we love each other," said Newman. And as she remained silent he quickly added, "Very good, if you can't accept that, don't tell me so."

"I should be very glad to think of nothing," she said at last; "not to think at all; only to shut both my eyes and give myself up. But I can't. I'm cold, I'm old, I'm a coward; I never supposed I should marry again, and it seems to me very strange I should ever have listened to you. When I used to think, as a girl, of what I should do if I were to marry freely, by my own choice, I thought of a very different man from you."

"That's nothing against me," said Newman with an immense smile; "your taste was not formed."

His smile made Madame de Cintré smile. "Have you formed it?" she asked. And then she said, in a different tone, "Where do you wish to live?"

"Anywhere in the wide world you like. We can easily settle that."

"I don't know why I ask you," she presently continued. "I care very little. I think if I were to marry you I could live almost anywhere. You have some false ideas about me; you think that I need a great many things—that I must have a brilliant, worldly life. I am sure you are prepared to take a great deal of trouble to give me such things. But that is very arbitrary; I have done nothing to prove that." She paused again, looking at him, and her mingled sound and silence were so sweet to him that he had no wish to hurry her, any more than he would have had a wish to hurry a golden sunrise. "Your being so different, which at first seemed a difficulty, a trouble, began one day to seem to me a pleasure, a great pleasure. I was glad you were different. And yet if I had said so, no one would have understood me; I don't mean simply to my family."

"They would have said I was a queer monster, eh?" said Newman.

"They would have said I could never be happy with you—you

were too different; and I would have said it was just *because* you were so different that I might be happy. But they would have given better reasons than I. My only reason"—and she paused again.

But this time, in the midst of his golden sunrise, Newman felt the impulse to grasp at a rosy cloud. "Your only reason is that you love me!" he murmured with an eloquent gesture, and for want of a better reason Madame de Cintré reconciled herself to this one.

Newman came back the next day, and in the vestibule, as he entered the house, he encountered his friend Mrs. Bread. She was wandering about in honorable idleness, and when his eyes fell upon her she delivered him one of her curtsies. Then turning to the servant who had admitted him, she said, with the combined majesty of her native superiority and of a rugged English accent, "You may retire; I will have the honor of conducting monsieur." In spite of this combination, however, it appeared to Newman that her voice had a slight quaver, as if the tone of command were not habitual to it. The man gave her an impertinent stare, but he walked slowly away, and she led Newman up-stairs. At half its course the staircase gave a bend, forming a little platform. In the angle of the wall stood an indifferent statue of an eighteenth-century nymph, simpering, sallow, and cracked. Here Mrs. Bread stopped and looked with shy kindness at her companion.

"I know the good news, sir," she murmured.

"You have a good right to be first to know it," said Newman. "You have taken such a friendly interest."

Mrs. Bread turned away and began to blow the dust off the statue, as if this might be mockery.

"I suppose you want to congratulate me," said Newman. "I am greatly obliged." And then he added, "You gave me much pleasure the other day."

She turned round, apparently reassured. "You are not to think that I have been told anything," she said; "I have only guessed. But when I looked at you, as you came in, I was sure I had guessed aright."

"You are very sharp," said Newman. "I am sure that in your quiet way you see everything."

"I am not a fool, sir, thank God. I have guessed something else beside," said Mrs. Bread.

"What's that?"

"I needn't tell you that, sir; I don't think you would believe it.

At any rate it wouldn't please you."

"Oh, tell me nothing but what will please me," laughed Newman. "That is the way you began."

"Well, sir, I suppose you won't be vexed to hear that the sooner everything is over the better."

"The sooner we are married, you mean? The better for me, certainly."

"The better for every one."

"The better for you, perhaps. You know you are coming to live with us," said Newman.

"I'm extremely obliged to you, sir, but it is not of myself I was thinking. I only wanted, if I might take the liberty, to recommend you to lose no time."

"Whom are you afraid of?"

Mrs. Bread looked up the staircase and then down and then she looked at the undusted nymph, as if she possibly had sentient ears. "I am afraid of every one," she said.

"What an uncomfortable state of mind!" said Newman. "Does 'every one' wish to prevent my marriage?"

"I am afraid of already having said too much," Mrs. Bread replied. "I won't take it back, but I won't say any more." And she took her way up the staircase again and led him into Madame de Cintré's salon.

Newman indulged in a brief and silent imprecation when he found that Madame de Cintré was not alone. With her sat her mother, and in the middle of the room stood young Madame de Bellegarde, in her bonnet and mantle. The old marquise, who was leaning back in her chair with a hand clasping the knob of each arm, looked at him fixedly, without moving. She seemed barely conscious of his greeting; she appeared to be musing intently. Newman said to himself that her daughter had been announcing her engagement and that the old lady found the morsel hard to swallow. But Madame de Cintré, as she gave him her hand, gave him also a look by which she appeared to mean that he should understand something. Was it a warning or a request? Did she wish to enjoin speech or silence? He was puzzled, and young Madame de Bellegarde's pretty grin gave him no information.

"I have not told my mother," said Madame de Cintré, abruptly, looking at him.

"Told me what?" demanded the marquise. "You tell me too little; you should tell me everything."

"That is what I do," said Madame Urbain, with a little laugh.

"Let *me* tell your mother," said Newman.

The old lady stared at him again, and then turned to her daughter. "You are going to marry him?" she cried, softly.

"*Oui ma mère*," said Madame de Cintré.

"Your daughter has consented, to my great happiness," said Newman.

"And when was this arrangement made?" asked Madame de Bellegarde. "I seem to be picking up the news by chance!"

"My suspense came to an end yesterday," said Newman.

"And how long was mine to have lasted?" said the marquise to her daughter. She spoke without irritation; with a sort of cold, nobie displeasure.

Madame de Cintré stood silent, with her eyes on the ground. "It is over now," she said.

"Where is my son—where is Urbain?" asked the marquise. "Send for your brother and inform him."

Young Madame de Bellegarde laid her hand on the bell-rope. "He was to make some visits with me, and I was to go and knock—very softly, very softly—at the door of his study. But he can come to me!" She pulled the bell, and in a few moments Mrs. Bread appeared, with a face of calm inquiry.

"Send for your brother," said the old lady.

But Newman felt an irresistible impulse to speak, and to speak in a certain way. "Tell the marquis we want him," he said to Mrs. Bread, who quietly retired.

Young Madame de Bellegarde went to her sister-in-law and embraced her. Then she turned to Newman, with an intense smile. "She is charming. I congratulate you."

"I congratulate you, sir," said Madame de Bellegarde, with extreme solemnity. "My daughter is an extraordinarily good woman. She may have faults, but I don't know them."

"My mother does not often make jokes," said Madame de Cintré; "but when she does they are terrible."

"She is ravishing," the Marquise Urbain resumed, looking at her sister-in-law, with her head on one side. "Yes, I congratulate you."

Madame de Cintré turned away, and, taking up a piece of tapestry, began to ply the needle. Some minutes of silence elapsed, which were interrupted by the arrival of M. de Bellegarde. He came in with his hat in his hand, gloved, and was followed by his brother Valentin, who appeared to have just entered the house.

M. de Bellegarde looked around the circle and greeted Newman with his usual finely-measured courtesy. Valentin saluted his mother and his sisters, and, as he shook hands with Newman, gave him a glance of acute interrogation.

"*Arrivez donc, messieurs!*" cried young Madame de Bellegarde. "We have great news for you."

"Speak to your brother, my daughter," said the old lady.

Madame de Cintré had been looking at her tapestry. She raised her eyes to her brother. "I have accepted Mr. Newman."

"Your sister has consented," said Newman. "You see, after all, I knew what I was about."

"I am charmed!" said M. de Bellegarde, with superior benignity.

"So am I," said Valentin to Newman. "The marquis and I are charmed. I can't marry, myself, but I can understand it. I can't stand on my head, but I can applaud a clever acrobat. My dear sister, I bless your union."

The marquis stood looking for a while into the crown of his hat. "We have been prepared," he said at last, "but it is inevitable that in face of the event one should experience a certain emotion." And he gave a most unhilarious smile.

"I feel no emotion that I was not perfectly prepared for," said his mother.

"I can't say that for myself," said Newman, smiling, but differently from the marquis. "I am happier than I expected to be. I suppose it's the sight of your happiness!"

"Don't exaggerate that," said Madame de Bellegarde, getting up and laying her hand upon her daughter's arm. "You can't expect an honest old woman to thank you for taking away her beautiful, only daughter."

"You forgot me, dear madame," said the young marquise demurely.

"Yes, she is very beautiful," said Newman.

"And when is the wedding, pray?" asked young Madame de Bellegarde; "I must have a month to think over a dress."

"That must be discussed," said the marquise.

"Oh, we will discuss it, and let you know!" Newman exclaimed.

"I have no doubt we shall agree," said Urbain.

"If you don't agree with Madame de Cintré, you will be very unreasonable."

"Come, come, Urbain," said young Madame de Bellegarde, "I must go straight to my tailor's."

The old lady had been standing with her hand on her daughter's arm, looking at her fixedly. She gave a little sigh, and murmured, "No, I did *not* expect it! You are a fortunate man," she added, turning to Newman, with an expressive nod.

"Oh, I know that!" he answered. "I feel tremendously proud. I feel like crying it on the housetops,—like stopping people in the street to tell them."

Madame de Bellegarde narrowed her lips. "Pray don't," she said.

"The more people that know it, the better," Newman declared. "I haven't yet announced it here, but I telegraphed it this morning to America."

"Telegraphed it to America?" the old lady murmured.

"To New York, to St. Louis, and to San Francisco; those are the principal cities, you know. To-morrow I shall tell my friends here."

"Have you many?" asked Madame de Bellegarde, in a tone of which I am afraid that Newman but partly measured the impertinence.

"Enough to bring me a great many hand-shakes and congratulations. To say nothing," he added, in a moment, "of those I shall receive from your friends."

"They will not use the telegraph," said the marquise, taking her departure.

M. de Bellegarde, whose wife, her imagination having apparently taken flight to the tailor's, was fluttering her silken wings in emulation, shook hands with Newman, and said with a more persuasive accent than the latter had ever heard him use, "You may count upon me." Then his wife led him away.

Valentin stood looking from his sister to our hero. "I hope you both reflected seriously," he said.

Madame de Cintré smiled. "We have neither your powers of reflection nor your depth of seriousness; but we have done our best."

"Well, I have a great regard for each of you," Valentin continued. "You are charming young people. But I am not satisfied, on the whole, that you belong to that small and superior class—that exquisite group—composed of persons who are worthy to remain unmarried. These are rare souls; they are the salt of the earth. But I don't mean to be invidious; the marrying people are often very nice."

"Valentin holds that women should marry, and that men should not," said Madame de Cintré. "I don't know how he arranges it."

"I arrange it by adoring you, my sister," said Valentin, ardently. "Good-by."

"Adore some one whom you can marry," said Newman. "I will arrange that for you some day. I foresee that I am going to turn apostle."

Valentin was on the threshold; he looked back a moment, with a face that had turned grave. "I adore some one I can't marry!" he said. And he dropped the portière and departed.

"They don't like it," said Newman, standing alone before Madame de Cintré.

"No," she said, after a moment; "they don't like it."

"Well, now, do you mind that?" asked Newman.

"Yes!" she said, after another interval.

"That's a mistake."

"I can't help it. I should prefer that my mother were pleased."

"Why the deuce," demanded Newman, "is she not pleased? She gave you leave to marry me."

"Very true; I don't understand it. And yet I do 'mind it,' as you say. You will call it superstitious."

"That will depend upon how much you let it bother you. Then I shall call it an awful bore."

"I will keep it to myself," said Madame de Cintré, "It shall not bother you." And then they talked of their marriage-day, and Madame de Cintré assented unreservedly to Newman's desire to have it fixed for an early date.

Newman's telegrams were answered with interest. Having dispatched but three electric missives, he received no less than eight gratulatory bulletins in return. He put them into his pocket-book, and the next time he encountered old Madame de Bellegarde drew them forth and displayed them to her. This, it must be confessed, was a slightly malicious stroke; the reader must judge in what degree the offense was venial. Newman knew that the marquise disliked his telegrams, though he could see no sufficient reason for it. Madame de Cintré, on the other hand, liked them, and, most of them being of a humorous cast, laughed at them immoderately, and inquired into the character of their authors. Newman, now that his prize was gained, felt a peculiar desire that his triumph should be manifest. He more than suspected that the Bellegardes were keeping quiet about it, and allowing it, in their select circle, but a limited resonance; and it pleased him to think that if he were to take the trouble he might, as he phrased it, break all the windows. No man likes being repudiated, and yet Newman, if he was not flattered, was not exactly offended. He had not this good excuse for his somewhat aggressive impulse to promulgate his felicity; his sentiment was of another quality. He wanted for once to make the heads of the house of Bellegarde *feel* him; he knew not when he should have another chance. He had had for the past six months a sense of the old lady and her son looking straight over his head, and he was now resolved that they should toe a mark which he would give himself the satisfaction of drawing.

"It is like seeing a bottle emptied when the wine is poured too slowly," he said to Mrs. Tristram. "They make me want to joggle their elbows and force them to spill their wine."

To this Mrs. Tristram answered that he had better leave them alone and let them do things in their own way. "You must make allowances for them," she said. "It is natural enough that they should hang fire a little. They thought they accepted you when you made your application; but they are not people of imagination, they could not project themselves into the future, and now they will have to begin again. But they *are* people of honor, and they will do whatever is necessary."

Newman spent a few moments in narrow-eyed meditation. "I am not hard on them," he presently said, "and to prove it I will invite them all to a festival."

"To a festival?"

"You have been laughing at my great gilded rooms all winter; I will show you that they are good for something. I will give a party. What is the grandest thing one can do here? I will hire all the great singers from the opera, and all the first people from the Théâtre Français, and I will give an entertainment."

"And whom will you invite?"

"You, first of all. And then the old lady and her son. And then every one among her friends whom I have met at her house or elsewhere, every one who has shown me the minimum of politeness, every duke of them and his wife. And then all my friends, without exception: Miss Kitty Upjohn, Miss Dora Finch, General Packard, C. P. Hatch, and all the rest. And every one shall know what it is about, that is, to celebrate my engagement to the Countess de Cintré. What do you think of the idea?"

"I think it is odious!" said Mrs. Tristram. And then in a moment: "I think it is delicious!"

The very next evening Newman repaired to Madame de Belle-garde's salon, where he found her surrounded by her children, and invited her to honor his poor dwelling by her presence on a certain evening a fortnight distant.

The marquise stared a moment. "My dear sir," she cried, "what do you want to do to me?"

"To make you acquainted with a few people, and then to place you in a very easy chair and ask you to listen to Madame Frezzolini's singing."

"You mean to give a concert?"

"Something of that sort."

"And to have a crowd of people?"

"All my friends, and I hope some of yours and your daughter's. I want to celebrate my engagement."

It seemed to Newman that Madame de Bellegarde turned pale. She opened her fan, a fine old painted fan of the last century, and looked at the picture, which represented a *fête champêtre*—a lady with a guitar, singing, and a group of dancers round a garlanded Hermes.

"We go out so little," murmured the marquis, "since my poor father's death."

"But *my* dear father is still alive, my friend," said his wife. "I am only waiting for my invitation to accept it," and she glanced with amiable confidence at Newman. "It will be magnificent; I am very sure of that."

I am sorry to say, to the discredit of Newman's gallantry, that this lady's invitation was not then and there bestowed; he was giving all his attention to the old marquise. She looked up at last, smiling. "I can't think of letting you offer me a fête," she said, "until I have offered you one. We want to present you to our friends; we will invite them all. We have it very much at heart. We must do things in order. Come to me about the 25th; I will let you know the exact day immediately. We shall not have any one so fine as Madame Frezzolini, but we shall have some very good people. After that you may talk of your own fête." The old lady spoke with a certain quick eagerness, smiling more agreeably as she went on.

It seemed to Newman a handsome proposal, and such proposals always touched the sources of his good-nature. He said to Madame de Bellegarde that he should be glad to come on the 25th or any other day, and that it mattered very little whether he met his friends at her house or at his own. I have said that Newman was observant, but it must be admitted that on this occasion he failed to notice a certain delicate glance which passed between Madame de

Bellegarde and the marquis, and which we may presume to have been a commentary upon the innocence displayed in that latter clause of his speech.

Valentin de Bellegarde walked away with Newman that evening, and when they had left the Rue de l'Université some distance behind them he said reflectively, "My mother is very strong—very strong." Then in answer to an interrogative movement of Newman's he continued, "She was driven to the wall, but you would never have thought it. Her fête of the 25th was an invention of the moment. She had no idea whatever of giving a fête, but finding it the only issue from your proposal, she looked straight at the dose—excuse the expression—and bolted it, as you saw, without winking. She is very strong."

"Dear me!" said Newman, divided between relish and compassion. "I don't care a straw for her fête, I am willing to take the will for the deed."

"No, no," said Valentin, with a little inconsequent touch of family pride. "The thing will be done now, and done handsomely."

Chapter XV

Valentin de Bellegarde's announcement of the secession of Madamoiselle Nioche from her father's domicile, and his irreverent reflections upon the attitude of this anxious parent in so grave a catastrophe, received a practical commentary in the fact that M. Nioche was slow to seek another interview with his late pupil. It had cost Newman some disgust to be forced to assent to Valentin's somewhat cynical interpretation of the old man's philosophy, and, though circumstances seemed to indicate that he had not given himself up to a noble despair, Newman thought it very possible he might be suffering more keenly than was apparent. M. Nioche had been in the habit of paying him a respectful little visit every two or three weeks, and his absence might be a proof quite as much of extreme depression as of a desire to conceal the success with which he had patched up his sorrow. Newman presently learned from Valentin several details touching this new phase of Madamoiselle Noémie's career.

"I told you she was remarkable," this unshrinking observer declared, "and the way she has managed this performance proves it. She has had other chances, but she was resolved to take none but the best. She did you the honor to think for a while that you might

be such a chance. You were not; so she gathered up her patience
and waited a while longer. At last her occasion came along, and she
made her move with her eyes wide open. I am very sure she had
no innocence to lose, but she had all her respectability. Dubious little
damsel as you thought her, she had kept a firm hold of that; nothing
could be proved against her, and she was determined not to let her
reputation go till she had got her equivalent. About her equivalent
she had high ideas. Apparently her ideal has been satisfied. It is fifty
years old, bald-headed, and deaf, but it is very easy about money."

"And where in the world," asked Newman, "did you pick up this
valuable information?"

"In conversation. Remember my frivolous habits. In conversation
with a young woman engaged in the humble trade of glove-cleaner,
who keeps a small shop in the Rue St. Roch. M. Nioche lives in the
same house, up six pair of stairs, across the court, in and out of whose
ill-swept doorway Miss Noémie has been flitting for the last five
year. The little glove-cleaner was an old acquaintance; she used to
be the friend of a friend of mine, who has married and dropped such
friends. I often saw her in his society. As soon as I espied her behind
her clear little window-pane, I recollected her. I had on a spotlessly
fresh pair of gloves, but I went in and held up my hands, and said
to her, 'Dear mademoiselle, what will you ask me for cleaning
these?' 'Dear count,' she answered immediately, 'I will clean them
for you for nothing.' She had instantly recognized me, and I had
to hear her history for the last six years. But after that, I put her
upon that of her neighbors. She knows and admires Noémie, and she
told me what I have just repeated."

A month elapsed without M. Nioche reappearing, and Newman,
who every morning read two or three suicides in the "Figaro,"
began to suspect that, mortification proving stubborn, he had sought
a balm for his wounded pride in the waters of the Seine. He had a
note of M. Nioche's address in his pocket-book, and finding himself
one day in the *quartier*, he determined in so far as he might to clear
up his doubts. He repaired to the house in the Rue St. Roch which
bore the recorded number, and observed in a neighboring basement,
behind a dangling row of neatly inflated gloves, the attentive
physiognomy of Bellegarde's informant—a sallow person in a
dressing-gown—peering into the street as if she were expecting that
amiable nobleman to pass again. But it was not to her that Newman
applied; he simply asked of the portress if M. Nioche were at home.
The portress replied, as the portress invariably replies, that her

lodger had gone out barely three minutes before; but then, through the little square hole of her lodge-window taking the measure of Newman's fortunes, and seeing them, by an unspecified process, refresh the dry places of servitude to occupants of fifth floors on courts, she added that M. Nioche would have had just time to reach the Café de la Patrie, round the second corner to the left, at which establishment he regularly spent his afternoons. Newman thanked her for the information, took the second turning to the left, and arrived at the Café de la Patrie. He felt a momentary hesitation to go in; was it not rather mean to "follow up" poor old Nioche at that rate? But there passed across his vision an image of a haggard little septuagenarian taking measured sips of a glass of sugar and water and finding them quite impotent to sweeten his desolation. He opened the door and entered, perceiving nothing at first but a dense cloud of tobacco smoke. Across this, however, in a corner, he presently descried the figure of M. Nioche, stirring the contents of a deep glass, with a lady seated in front of him. The lady's back was turned to Newman, but M. Nioche very soon perceived and recognized his visitor. Newman had gone toward him, and the old man rose slowly, gazing at him with a more blighted expression even than usual.

"If you are drinking hot punch," said Newman, "I suppose you are not dead. That's all right. Don't move."

M. Nioche stood staring, with a fallen jaw, not daring to put out his hand. The lady, who sat facing him, turned round in her place and glanced upward with a spirited toss of her head, displaying the agreeable features of his daughter. She looked at Newman sharply, to see how he was looking at her, then—I don't know what she discovered—she said graciously, "How d' ye do, monsieur? won't you come into our little corner?"

"Did you come—did you come after *me?*" asked M. Nioche, very softly.

"I went to your house to see what had become of you. I thought you might be sick," said Newman.

"It is very good of you, as always," said the old man. "No, I am not well. Yes, I am *seek.*"

"Ask monsieur to sit down," said Mademoiselle Nioche. "Garçon, bring a chair."

"Will you do us the honor to *seat?*" said M. Nioche, timorously, and with a double foreignness of accent.

Newman said to himself that he had better see the thing out, and he took a chair at the end of the table, with Mademoiselle Nioche on his left and her father on the other side. "You will take something, of course," said Miss Noémie, who was sipping a glass of madeira. Newman said that he believed not, and then she turned to her papa with a smile. "What an honor, eh? he has come only for us." M. Nioche drained his pungent glass at a long draught, and looked out from eyes more lachrymose in consequence. "But you didn't come for me, eh?" Mademoiselle Noémie went on. "You didn't expect to find me here?"

Newman observed the change in her appearance. She was very elegant and prettier than before; she looked a year or two older, and it was noticeable that, to the eye, she had only gained in respectability. She looked "lady-like." She was dressed in quiet colors, and wore her expensively unobtrusive toilet with a grace that might have come from years of practice. Her present self-possession and *aplomb* struck Newman as really infernal, and he inclined to agree with Valentin de Bellegarde that the young lady was very remarkable. "No, to tell the truth, I didn't come for you," he said, "and I didn't expect to find you. I was told," he added in a moment, "that you had left your father."

"*Quelle horreur!*" cried Mademoiselle Nioche with a smile. "Does one leave one's father? You have the proof of the contrary."

"Yes, convincing proof," said Newman glancing at M. Nioche. The old man caught his glance obliquely, with his faded, deprecating eye, and then, lifting his empty glass, pretended to drink again.

"Who told you that?" Noémie demanded. "I know very well. It was M. de Bellegarde. Why don't you say yes? You are not polite."

"I am embarrassed," said Newman.

"I set you a better example. I know M. de Bellegarde told you. He knows a great deal about me—or he thinks he does. He has taken a great deal of trouble to find out, but half of it isn't true. In the first place, I haven't left my father; I am much too fond of him. Isn't it so, little father? M. de Bellegarde is a charming young man; it is impossible to be cleverer. I know a good deal about him too; you can tell him that when you next see him."

"No," said Newman, with a sturdy grin; "I won't carry any messages for you."

"Just as you please," said Mademoiselle Nioche. "I don't depend upon you, nor does M. de Bellegarde either. He is very much interested in me; he can be left to his own devices. He is a contrast to you."

"Oh, he is a great contrast to me, I have no doubt," said Newman. "But I don't exactly know how you mean it."

"I mean it in this way. First of all, he never offered to help me to a *dot* and a husband." And Mademoiselle Nioche paused, smiling. "I won't say that is in his favor, for I do you justice. What led you, by the way, to make me such a queer offer? You didn't care for me."

"Oh yes, I did," said Newman.

"How so?"

"It would have given me real pleasure to see you married to a respectable young fellow."

"With six thousand francs of income!" cried Madamoiselle Nioche. "Do you call that caring for me? I'm afraid you know little about women. You were not *galant;* you were not what you might have been."

Newman flushed a trifle fiercely. "Come!" he exclaimed, "that's rather strong. I had no idea I had been so shabby."

Mademoiselle Nioche smiled as she took up her muff. "It is something, at any rate, to have made you angry."

Her father had leaned both his elbows on the table, and his head, bent forward, was supported in his hands, the thin white fingers of which were pressed over his ears. In his position he was staring fixedly at the bottom of his empty glass, and Newman supposed he was not hearing. Mademoiselle Noémie buttoned her furred jacket and pushed back her chair, casting a glance charged with the consciousness of an expensive appearance first down over her flounces and then up at Newman.

"You had better have remained an honest girl," Newman said, quietly.

M. Nioche continued to stare at the bottom of his glass, and his daughter got up, still bravely smiling. "You mean that I look so much like one? That's more than most women do nowadays. Don't judge me yet a while," she added. "I mean to succeed; that's what I mean to do. I leave you; I don't mean to be seen in cafés, for one thing. I can't think what you want of my poor father; he's very comfortable now. It isn't his fault, either. *Au revoir*, little father." And she tapped the old man on the head with her muff. Then she stopped a minute, looking at Newman. "Tell M. de Bellegarde, when he wants news of me, to come and get it from *me!*" And she turned and departed, the white-aproned waiter, with a bow, holding the door wide open for her.

M. Nioche sat motionless, and Newman hardly knew what to

say to him. The old man looked dismally foolish. "So you determined not to shoot her, after all," Newman said, presently.

M. Nioche, without moving, raised his eyes and gave him a long, peculiar look. It seemed to confess everything, and yet not to ask for pity, nor to pretend, on the other hand, to a rugged ability to do without it. It might have expressed the state of mind of an innocuous insect, flat in shape and conscious of the impending pressure of a boot-sole, and reflecting that he was perhaps too flat to be crushed. M. Nioche's gaze was a profession of moral flatness. "You despise me terribly," he said, in the weakest possible voice.

"Oh no," said Newman, "it is none of my business. It's a good plan to take things easily."

"I made you too many fine speeches," M. Nioche added. "I meant them at the time."

"I am sure I am very glad you didn't shoot her," said Newman. "I was afraid you might have shot yourself. That is why I came to look you up." And he began to button his coat.

"Neither," said M. Nioche. "You despise me, and I can't explain to you. I hoped I shouldn't see you again."

"Why, that's rather shabby," said Newman. "You shouldn't drop your friends that way. Besides, the last time you came to see me I thought you particularly jolly."

"Yes, I remember," said M. Nioche, musingly; "I was in a fever. I didn't know what I said, what I did. It was delirium."

"Ah, well, you are quieter now."

M. Nioche was silent a moment. "As quiet as the grave," he whispered softly.

"Are you very unhappy?"

M. Nioche rubbed his forehead slowly, and even pushed back his wig a little, looking askance at his empty glass. "Yes—yes. But that's an old story. I have always been unhappy. My daughter does what she will with me. I take what she gives me, good or bad. I have no spirit, and when you have no spirit you must keep quiet. I shan't trouble you any more."

"Well," said Newman, rather disgusted at the smooth operation of the old man's philosophy, "that's as you please."

M. Nioche seemed to have been prepared to be despised, but nevertheless he made a feeble movement of appeal from Newman's faint praise. "After all," he said, "she is my daughter, and I can still look after her. If she will do wrong, why she will. But there are many different paths, there are degrees. I can give her the benefit

—give her the benefit"—and M. Nioche paused, staring vaguely at Newman, who began to suspect that his brain had softened—"the benefit of my experience," M. Nioche added.

"Your experience?" inquired Newman, both amused and amazed.

"My experience of business," said M. Nioche, gravely.

"Ah, yes," said Newman, laughing, "that will be a great advantage to her!" And then he said good-by, and offered the poor, foolish old man his hand.

M. Nioche took it and leaned back against the wall, holding it a moment and looking up at him. "I suppose you think my wits are going," he said. "Very likely; I have always a pain in my head. That's why I can't explain, I can't tell you. And she's so strong, she makes me walk as she will, anywhere! But there's this—there's this." And he stopped, still staring up at Newman. His little white eyes expanded and glittered for a moment like those of a cat in the dark. "It's not as it seems. I haven't forgiven her. Oh, no!"

"That's right; don't," said Newman. "She's a bad case."

"It's horrible, it's horrible, said M. Nioche; "but do you want to know the truth? I hate her! I take what she gives me, and I hate her more. To-day she brought me three hundred francs; they are here in my waistcoat pocket. Now I hate her almost cruelly. No, I haven't forgiven her."

"Why did you accept the money?" Newman asked.

"If I hadn't," said M. Nioche, "I should have hated her still more. That's what misery is. No, I haven't forgiven her."

"Take care you don't hurt her!" said Newman, laughing again. And with this he took his leave. As he passed along the glazed side of the café, on reaching the street, he saw the old man motioning the waiter, with a melancholy gesture, to replenish his glass.

One day, a week after his visit to the Café de la Patrie, he called upon Valentin de Bellegarde, and by good fortune found him at home. Newman spoke of his interview with M. Nioche and his daughter, and said he was afraid Valentin had judged the old man correctly. He had found the couple hobnobbing together in all amity; the old gentleman's rigor was purely theoretic. Newman confessed that he was disappointed; he should have expected to see M. Nioche take high ground.

"High ground, my dear fellow," said Valentin, laughing; "there is no high ground for him to take. The only perceptible eminence in M. Nioche's horizon is Montmartre, which is not an edifying quarter. You can't go mountaineering in a flat country."

"He remarked, indeed," said Newman, "that he has not forgiven her. But she'll never find it out."

"We must do him the justice to suppose he doesn't like the thing," Valentin rejoined. "Mademoiselle Nioche is like the great artists whose biographies we read, who at the beginning of their career have suffered opposition in the domestic circle. Their vocation has not been recognized by their families, but the world has done it justice. Mademoiselle Nioche has a vocation."

"Oh, come," said Newman, impatiently, "you take the little baggage too seriously."

"I know I do; but when one has nothing to think about, one must think of little baggages. I suppose it is better to be serious about light things than not to be serious at all. This little baggage entertains me."

"Oh, she has discovered that. She knows you have been hunting her up and asking questions about her. She is very much tickled by it. That's rather annoying."

"Annoying, my dear fellow," laughed Valentin; "not the least!"

"Hanged if I should want to have a greedy little adventuress like that know I was giving myself such pains about her!" said Newman.

"A pretty woman is always worth one's pains," objected Valentin. "Mademoiselle Nioche is welcome to be tickled by my curiosity, and to know that I am tickled that she is tickled. She is not so much tickled, by the way."

"You had better go and tell her," Newman rejoined. "She gave me a message for you of some such drift."

"Bless your quiet imagination," said Valentin, "I have been to see her—three times in five days. She is a charming hostess; we talk of Shakespeare and the musical glasses. She is extremely clever and a very curious type; not at all coarse or wanting to be coarse; determined not to be. She means to take very good care of herself. She is extremely perfect; she is as hard and clear-cut as some little figure of a sea-nymph in an antique intaglio, and I will warrant that she has not a grain more of sentiment or heart than if she was scooped out of a big amethyst. You can't scratch her even with a diamond. Extremely pretty,—really, when you know her, she is wonderfully pretty,—intelligent, determined, ambitious, unscrupulous, capable of looking at a man strangled without changing color, she is upon my honor, extremely entertaining."

"It's a fine list of attractions," said Newman; "they would serve as a police-detective's description of a favorite criminal. I should sum them up by another word than 'entertaining.' "

"Why, that is just the word to use. I don't say she is laudable or lovable. I don't want her as my wife or my sister. But she is a very curious and ingenious piece of machinery; I like to see it in operation."

"Well, I have seen some very curious machines too," said Newman; "and once, in a needle factory, I saw a gentleman from the city, who had stepped too near one of them, picked up as neatly as if he had been prodded by a fork, swallowed down straight, and ground into small pieces."

Reëntering his domicile, late in the evening, three days after Madame de Bellegarde had made her bargain with him—the expression is sufficiently correct—touching the entertainment at which she was to present him to the world, he found on his table a card of goodly dimensions bearing an announcement that this lady would be at home on the 27th of the month, at ten o'clock in the evening. He stuck it into the frame of his mirror and eyed it with some complacency; it seemed an agreeable emblem of triumph, documentary evidence that his prize was gained. Stretched out in a chair, he was looking at it lovingly, when Valentin de Bellegarde was shown into the room. Valentin's glance presently followed the direction of Newman's, and he perceived his mother's invitation.

"And what have they put into the corner?" he asked. "Not the customary 'music,' 'dancing,' or 'tabeaux vivants'? They ought at least to put 'An American.' "

"Oh, there are to be several of us," said Newman. "Mrs. Tristram told me to-day that she had received a card and sent an acceptance."

"Ah, then, with Mrs. Tristram and her husband you will have support. My mother might have put on her card 'Three Americans.' But I suspect you will not lack amusement. You will see a great many of the best people in France. I mean the long pedigrees and the high noses, and all that. Some of them are awful idiots; I advise you to take them up cautiously."

"Oh, I guess I shall like them," said Newman. "I am prepared to like every one and everything in these days; I am in high good-humor."

Valentin looked at him a moment in silence and then dropped himself into a chair with an unwonted air of weariness. "Happy man!" he said with a sigh. "Take care you don't become offensive."

"If any one chooses to take offense, he may. I have a good conscience," said Newman.

"So you are really in love with my sister."

"Yes, sir!" said Newman, after a pause.

"And she also?"

"I guess she likes me," said Newman.

"What is the witchcraft you have used?" Valentin asked. "How do *you* make love?"

"Oh, I haven't any general rules," said Newman. "In any way that seems acceptable."

"I suspect that, if one knew it," said Valentin, laughing, "you are a terrible customer. You walk in seven-league boots."

"There is something the matter with you to-night," Newman said in response to this. "You are vicious. Spare me all discordant sounds until after my marriage. Then, when I have settled down for life, I shall be better able to take things as they come."

"And when does your marriage take place?"

"About six weeks hence."

Valentin was silent a while, and then he said, "And you feel very confident about the future?"

"Confident. I knew what I wanted, exactly, and I know what I have got."

"You are sure you are going to be happy?"

"Sure?" said Newman. "So foolish a question deserves a foolish answer. Yes!"

"You are not afraid of anything?"

"What should I be afraid of? You can't hurt me unless you kill me by some violent means. That I should indeed consider a tremendous sell. I want to live and I mean to live. I can't die of illness, I am too ridiculously tough; and the time for dying of old age won't come round yet a while. I can't lose my wife, I shall take too good care of her. I may lose my money, or a large part of it; but that won't matter, for I shall make twice as much again. So what have I to be afraid of?"

"You are not afraid it may be rather a mistake for an American man of business to marry a French countess?"

"For the countess, possibly; but not for the man of business, if you mean me! But my countess shall not be disappointed; I answer for her happiness!" And as if he felt the impulse to celebrate his happy certitude by a bonfire, he got up to throw a couple of logs upon the already blazing hearth. Valentin watched for a few moments the quickened flame, and then, with his head leaning on his hand, gave a melancholy sigh. "Got a headache?" Newman asked.

"*Je suis triste*," said Valentin, with Gallic simplicity.

"You are sad, eh? It is about the lady you said the other night night that you adored and that you couldn't marry?"

"Did I really say that? It seemed to me afterwards that the words had escaped me. Before Claire it was bad taste. But I felt gloomy as I spoke, and I feel gloomy still. Why did you ever introduce me to that girl?"

"Oh, it's Noémie, is it? Lord deliver us! You don't mean to say you are lovesick about her?"

"Lovesick, no; it's not a grand passion. But the cold-blooded little demon sticks in my thoughts; she has bitten me with those even little teeth of hers; I feel as if I might turn rabid and do something crazy in consequence. It's very low, it's disgustingly low. She's the most mercenary little jade in Europe. Yet she really affects my peace of mind; she is always running in my head. It's a striking contrast to your noble and virtuous attachment—a vile contrast! It is rather pitiful that it should be the best I am able to do for myself at my present respectable age. I am a nice young man, eh, *en somme?* You can't warrant my future, as you do your own."

"Drop that girl, short," said Newman; "don't go near her again, and your future will do. Come over to America and I will get you a place in a bank."

"It is easy to say drop her," said Valentin, with a light laugh. "You can't drop a pretty woman like that. One must be polite, even with Noémie. Besides, I'll not have her suppose I am afraid of her."

"So, between politeness and vanity, you will get deeper into the mud? Keep them both for something better. Remember, too, that I didn't want to introduce you to her: you insisted. I had a sort of uneasy feeling about it."

"Oh, I don't reproach you," said Valentin. "Heaven forbid! I wouldn't for the world have missed knowing her. She is really extraordinary. The way she has already spread her wings is amazing. I don't know when a woman has amused me more. But excuse me," he added in an instant; "she doesn't amuse you, at second hand, and the subject is an impure one. Let us talk of something else." Valentin introduced another topic, but within five minutes Newman observed that, by a bold transition, he had reverted to Mademoiselle Nioche, and was giving pictures of her manners and quoting specimens of her *mots*. These were very witty, and, for a young woman who six months before had been painting the most artless madonnas, startlingly cynical. But at last, abruptly, he stopped, became thoughtful, and for some time afterwards said nothing. When he rose to go it was evident that his thoughts were still running upon Mademoiselle Nioche. "Yes, she's a frightful little monster!" he said.

CHAPTER XVI

THE NEXT ten days were the happiest that Newman had ever known. He saw Madame de Cintré every day, and never saw either old Madame de Bellegarde or the elder of his prospective brothers-in-law. Madame de Cintré at last seemed to think it becoming to apologize for their never being present. "They are much taken up," she said, "with doing the honors of Paris to Lord Deepmere." There was a smile in her gravity as she made this declaration, and it deepened as she added, "He is our seventh cousin, you know, and blood is thicker than water. And then, he is so interesting!" And with this she laughed.

Newman met young Madame de Bellegarde two or three times, always roaming about with graceful vagueness, as if in search of an unattainable ideal of amusement. She always reminded him of a painted perfume-bottle with a crack in it; but he had grown to have a kindly feeling for her, based on the fact of her owing conjugal allegiance to Urbain de Bellegarde. He pitied M. de Bellegarde's wife, especially since she was a silly, thirstily-smiling little brunette, with a suggestion of an unregulated heart. The small marquise sometimes looked at him with an intensity too marked not to be innocent, for coquetry is more finely shaded. She apparently wanted to ask him something or tell him something; he wondered what it was. But he was shy of giving her an opportunity, because, if her communication bore upon the aridity of her matrimonial lot, he was at a loss to see how he could help her. He had a fancy, however, of her coming up to him some day and saying (after looking round behind her) with a little passionate hiss, "I know you detest my husband; let me have the pleasure of assuring you for once that you are right. Pity a poor woman who is married to a clock-image in *papier-mâché!*" Possessing, however, in default of a competent knowledge of the principles of etiquette, a very downright sense of the "meanness" of certain actions, it seemed to him to belong to his position to keep on his guard; he was not going to put it into the power of these people to say that in their house he had done anything unpleasant. As it was, Madame de Bellegarde used to give him news of the dress she meant to wear at his wedding, and which had not yet, in her creative imagination, in spite of many interviews with the tailor, resolved itself into its composite totality. "I told you pale blue bows on the sleeves, at the elbows," she said. "But to-day I don't see my blue bows at all. I don't know what has become of them. To-day I see pink—a tender pink. And then I pass through strange, dull phases in which neither blue nor pink says anything to me. And yet I must have the bows."

"Have them green or yellow," said Newman.

"*Malheureux!*" the little marquise would cry. "Green bows would break your marriage—your children would be illegitimate!"

Madame de Cintré was calmly happy before the world, and Newman had the felicity of fancying that before him, when the world was absent, she was almost agitatedly happy. She said very tender things. "I take no pleasure in you. You never give me a chance to scold you, to correct you. I bargained for that, I expected to enjoy it. But you won't do anything dreadful; you are dismally inoffensive. It is very stupid; there is no excitement for me; I might as well be marrying some one else."

"I am afraid it's the worst I can do," Newman would say in answer to this. "Kindly overlook the deficiency." He assured her that he, at least, would never scold her; she was perfectly satisfactory. "If you only knew," he said, "how exactly you are what I coveted! And I am begining to understand why I coveted it; the having it makes all the difference that I expected. Never was a man so pleased with his good fortune. You have been holding your head for a week past just as I wanted my wife to hold hers. You say just the things I want her to say. You walk about the room just as I want her to walk. You have just the taste in dress that I want her to have. In short, you come up to the mark, and, I can tell you, my mark was high."

These observations seemed to make Madame de Cintré rather grave. At last she said, "Depend upon it, I don't come up to the mark; your mark is too high. I am not all that you suppose; I am a much smaller affair. She is a magnificent woman, your ideal. Pray, how did she come to such perfection?"

"She was never anything else," Newman said.

"I really believe," Madame de Cintré went on, "that she is better than my own ideal. Do you know that is a very handsome compliment? Well, sir, I will make her my own!"

Mrs. Tristram came to see her dear Claire after Newman had

announced his engagement, and she told our hero the next day that his good fortune was simply absurd. "For the ridiculous part of it is," she said, "that you are evidently going to be as happy as if you were marrying Miss Smith or Miss Thompson. I call it a brilliant match for you, but you get brilliancy without paying any tax upon it. Those things are usually a compromise, but here you have every-thing, and nothing crowds anything else out. You will be brilliantly happy as well." Newman thanked her for her pleasant, encouraging way of saying things; no woman could encourage or discourage better. Tristram's way of saying things was different; he had been taken by his wife to call upon Madame de Cintré, and he gave an account of the expedition.

"You don't catch me giving an opinion on your countess this time," he said; "I put my foot in it once. That's a d—d underhand thing to do, by the way—coming round to sound a fellow upon the woman you are going to marry. You deserve anything you get. Then of course you rush and tell her, and she takes care to make it pleasant for the poor spiteful wretch the first time he calls. I will do you the justice to say, however, that you don't seem to have told Madame de Cintré; or if you have she's uncommonly mag-nanimous. She was very nice; she was tremendously polite. She and Lizzie sat on the sofa, pressing each other's hands and calling each other *chère belle*, and Madame de Cintré sent me with every third word a magnificent smile, as if to give me to understand that I too was a handsome dear. She quite made up for past neglect, I assure you; she was very pleasant and sociable. Only in an evil hour it came into her head to say that she must present us to her mother—her mother wished to know your friends. I didn't want to know her mother, and I was on the point of telling Lizzie to go in alone and let me wait for her outside. But Lizzie, with her usual infernal ingenuity, guessed my purpose and reduced me by a glance of her eye. So they marched off arm in arm, and I followed as I could. We found the old lady in her arm-chair, twiddling her aristocratic thumbs. She looked at Lizzie from head to foot; but at that game Lizzie, to do her justice, was a match for her. My wife told her we were great friends of Mr. Newman. The marquise started a moment, and then said, 'Oh, Mr. Newman! My daughter has made up her mind to marry a Mr. Newman.' Then Madame de Cintré began to fondle Lizzie again, and said it was this dear lady that had planned the match and brought them together. 'Oh, 'tis you I have to thank for my American son-in-law,' the old lady said to Mrs. Tristram. 'It was a very clever thought of yours. Be sure of my gratitude.' And then she began to look at me and presently said, 'Pray, are you engaged in some species of manufacture?' I wanted to say that I manufactured broom-sticks for old witches to ride on, but Lizzie got in ahead of me. 'My husband, Madame la Marquise,' she said, 'belongs to that unfortunate class of persons who have no profession and no business, and do very little good in the world.' To get her poke at the old woman she didn't care where she shoved me. 'Dear me,' said the marquise, 'we all have our duties.' 'I am sorry mine compel me to take leave of you,' said Lizzie. And we bundled out again. But you have a mother-in-law, in all the force of the term."

"Oh," said Newman, "my mother-in-law desires nothing better than to let me alone."

Betimes, on the evening of the 27th, he went to Madame de Bellegarde's ball. The old house in the Rue de l'Université looked strangely brilliant. In the circle of light projected from the outer gate a detachment of the populace stood watching the carriages roll in; the court was illumined with flaring torches and the portico carpeted with crimson. When Newman arrived there were but a few people present. The marquise and her two daughters were at the top of the staircase, where the sallow old nymph in the angle peeped out from a bower of plants. Madame de Bellegarde, in purple and fine laces, looked like an old lady painted by Vandyke; Madame de Cintré was dressed in white. The old lady greeted Newman with majestic formality, and, looking round her, called several of the persons who were standing near. They were elderly gentlemen, of what Valentin de Bellegarde had designated as the high-nosed category; two or three of them wore cordons and stars. They approached with measured alertness, and the marquise said that she wished to present them to Mr. Newman, who was going to marry her daughter. Then she introduced successively three dukes, three counts, and a baron. These gentlemen bowed and smiled most agreeably, and Newman indulged in a series of impartial hand-shakes, accompanied by a "Happy to make your acquaintance, sir." He looked at Madame de Cintré, but she was not looking at him. If his personal self-consciousness had been of a nature to make him constantly refer to her, as the critic before whom, in company, he played his part, he might have found it a flattering proof of her confidence that he never caught her eyes resting upon him. It is a reflection Newman did not make, but we nevertheless risk it, that in spite of this circumstance she probably saw every movement of his little finger. Young Madame de Bellegarde was dressed in an audacious toilet of crimson crape, bestrewn with huge silver moons —thin crescents and full disks.

"You don't say anything about my dress," she said to Newman.

"I feel," he answered, "as if I were looking at you through a telescope. It is very strange."

"If it is strange it matches the occasion. But I am not a heavenly body."

"I never saw the sky at midnight that particular shade of crimson," said Newman.

"That is my originality; any one could have chosen blue. My sister-in-law would have chosen a lovely shade of blue, with a dozen little delicate moons. But I think crimson is much more amusing. And I give my idea, which is moonshine."

"Moonshine and bloodshed," said Newman.

"A murder by moonlight," laughed Madame de Bellegarde. "What a delicious idea for a toilet! To make it complete, there is the silver dagger, you see, stuck into my hair. But here comes Lord Deepmere," she added in a moment. "I must find out what he thinks of it." Lord Deepmere came up, looking very red in the face, and laughing. "Lord Deepmere can't decide which he prefers, my sister-in-law or me," Madame de Bellegarde. "He likes Claire because she is his cousin, and me because I am not. But he has no right to make love to Claire, whereas I am perfectly *disponible*. It is very wrong to make love to a woman who is engaged, but it is very wrong not to make love to a woman who is married."

"Oh, it's very jolly making love to married women," said Lord Deepmere, "because they can't ask you to marry them."

"Is that what the others do, the spinsters?" Newman inquired.

"Oh dear, yes," said Lord Deepmere; "in England all the girls ask a fellow to marry them."

"And a fellow brutally refuses," said Madame de Bellegarde.

"Why, really, you know, a fellow can't marry any girl that asks him," said his lordship.

"Your cousin won't ask you. She is going to marry Mr. Newman."

"Oh, that's a very different thing!" laughed Lord Deepmere.

"You would have accepted *her*, I suppose. That makes me hope that after all you prefer me."

"Oh, when things are nice I never prefer one to the other," said the young Englishman. "I take them all."

"Ah, what a horror! I won't be taken in that way; I must be kept apart," cried Madame de Bellegarde. "Mr Newman is much better; he knows how to choose. Oh, he chooses as if he were threading a needle. He prefers Madame de Cintré to any conceivable creature or thing."

"Well, you can't help my being her cousin," said Lord Deepmere to Newman, with candid hilarity.

"Oh no, I can't help that," said Newman, laughing back; "neither can she!"

"And you can't help my dancing with her," said Lord Deepmere, with sturdy simplicity.

"I could prevent that only by dancing with her myself," said Newman. "But unfortunately I don't know how to dance."

"Oh, you may dance without knowing how; may you not, milord?" said Madame de Bellegarde. But to this Lord Deepmere replied that a fellow ought to know how to dance if he didn't want to make an ass of himself; and at this moment Urbain de Bellegarde joined the group, slow-stepping and with his hands behind him.

"This is a very splendid entertainment," said Newman, cheerfully. "The old house looks very bright."

"If *you* are pleased, we are content," said the marquis, lifting his shoulders and bending them forward.

"Oh, I suspect every one is pleased," said Newman. "How can they help being pleased when the first thing they see as they come in is your sister, standing there as beautiful as an angel?"

"Yes, she is very beautiful," rejoined the marquis, solemnly. "But that is not so great a source of satisfaction to other people, naturally, as to you."

"Yes, I am satisfied, marquis, I am satisfied," said Newman, with his protracted enunciation. "And now tell me," he added, looking round, "who some of your friends are."

M. de Bellegarde looked about him in silence, with his head bent and his hand raised to his lower lip, which he slowly rubbed. A stream of people had been pouring into the salon in which Newman stood with his host, the rooms were filling up and the spectacle had become brilliant. It borrowed its splendor chiefly from the shining shoulders and profuse jewels of the women, and from the voluminous elegance of their dresses. There was no uniforms, as Madame de Bellegarde's door was inexorably closed against the myrmidons of the upstart power which then ruled the fortunes of France, and the great company of smiling and chattering faces was not graced by any very frequent suggestions of harmonious beauty. It is a pity, nevertheless, that Newman had not been a physiognomist, for a great many of the faces were irregularly agreeable, expressive, and suggestive. If the occasion had been different they would hardly have pleased him; he would have thought the women not pretty enough and the men too smirking; but he was now in a humor to receive none but agreeable impressions, and he looked no more narrowly than to perceive that every one was brilliant, and to feel that the sum of their brilliancy was a part of his credit. "I will present you to some people," said M. de Bellegarde after a while. "I will make a point of it, in fact. You will allow me?"

"Oh, I will shake hands with any one you want," said Newman. "Your mother just introduced me to half a dozen old gentlemen: Take care you don't pick up the same parties again."

"Who are the gentlemen to whom my mother presented you?"

"Upon my word, I forgot them," said Newman, laughing. "The people here look very much alike."

"I suspect they have not forgotten you," said the marquis. And he began to walk through the rooms. Newman, to keep near him in the crowd, took his arm; after which, for some time, the marquis walked straight along, in silence. At last, reaching the farther end of the suite of reception-rooms, Newman found himself in the presence of a lady of monstrous proportions, seated in a very capacious arm-chair, with several persons standing in a semicircle round her. This little group had divided as the marquis came up, and M. de Bellegarde stepped forward and stood for an instant silent and obsequious, with his hat raised to his lips, at Newman had seen some gentlemen stand in churches as soon as they entered their pews. The lady indeed, bore a very fair likeness to a reverend effigy in some idolatrous shrine. She was monumentally stout and imperturbably serene. Her aspect was to Newman almost formidable; he had a troubled consciousness of a triple chin, a small piercing eye, a vast expanse of uncovered bosom, a nodding and twinkling tiara of plumes and gems, and an immense circumference of satin petticoat. With her little circle of beholders this remarkable woman reminded him of the Fat Lady at a fair. She fixed her small, unwinking eyes at the new-comers.

"Dear duchess," said the marquis, "let me present you our good friend Mr. Newman, of whom you have heard us speak. Wishing to make Mr. Newman known to those who are dear to us, I could not possibly fail to begin with you."

"Charmed, dear friend; charmed, monsieur," said the duchess

in a voice which, though small and shrill, was not disagreeable, while Newman executed his obeisance. "I came on purpose to see monsieur. I hope he appreciates the compliment. You have only to look at me to do so, sir," she continued, sweeping her person with a much-encompassing glance. Newman hardly knew what to say, though it seemed that to a duchess who joked about her corpulence one might say almost anything. On hearing that the duchess had come on purpose to see Newman, the gentlemen who surrounded her turned a little and looked at him with sympathetic curiosity. The marquis with supernatural gravity mentioned to him the name of each, while the gentleman who bore it bowed; they were all what are called in France *beaux noms.* "I wanted extremely to see you," the duchess went on. "*C'est positif.* In the first place, I am very fond of the person you are going to marry; she is the most charming creature in France. Mind you treat her well, or you shall hear some news of me. But you look as if you were good. I am told you are very remarkable. I have heard all sorts of extraordinary things about you. *Voyons,* are they true?"

"I don't know what you can have heard," said Newman.

"Oh, you have your *légende.* We have heard that you have had a career the most checkered, the most bizarre. What is that about your having founded a city some ten years ago in the great West, a city which contains to-day half a million of inhabitants? Isn't it half a million, messieurs? You are exclusive proprietor of this flourishing settlement, and are consequently fabulously rich, and you would be richer still if you didn't grant lands and houses free of rent to all new-comers who will pledge themselves never to smoke cigars. At this game, in three years, we are told, you are going to be made president of America."

The duchess recited this amazing "legend" with a smooth self-possession which gave the speech, to Newman's mind, the air of being a bit of amusing dialogue in a play, delivered by a veteran comic actress. Before she had ceased speaking he had burst into loud, irrepressible laughter. "Dear duchess, dear duchess," the marquis began to murmur, soothingly. Two or three persons came to the door of the room to see who was laughing at the duchess. But the lady continued with the soft, serene assurance of a person who, as a duchess, was certain of being listened to, and, as a garrulous woman, was independent of the pulse of her auditors. "But I know you are very remarkable. You must be, to have endeared yourself to this good marquis and to his admirable world. They are very exacting. I myself am not very sure at this hour of really possessing it. Eh, Bellegarde? To please you, I see, one must be an American millionaire. But your real triumph, my dear sir, is pleasing the countess; she is as difficult as a princess in a fairy tale. Your success is a miracle. What is your secret? I don't ask you to reveal it before all these gentlemen, but come and see me some day and give me a specimen of your talents."

"The secret is with Madame de Cintré," said Newman. "You must ask her for it. It consists in her having a great deal of charity."

"Very pretty!" said the duchess. "That's a very nice specimen, to begin with. What, Bellegarde, are you already taking monsieur away?"

"I have a duty to perform, dear friend," said the marquis, pointing to the other groups.

"Ah, for you I know what that means. Well, I have seen monsieur; that is what I wanted. He can't persuade me that he isn't very clever. Farewell."

As Newman passed on with his host, he asked who the duchess was. "The greatest lady in France," said the marquis. M. de Bellegarde then presented his prospective brother-in-law to some twenty other persons of both sexes, selected apparently for their typically august character. In some cases this character was written in good round hand upon the countenance of the wearer; in others Newman was thankful for such help as his companion's impressively brief intimation contributed to the discovery of it. There were large, majestic men, and small demonstrative men; there were ugly ladies in yellow lace and quaint jewels, and pretty ladies with white shoulders from which jewels and everything else were absent. Every one gave Newman extreme attention, every one smiled, every one was charmed to make his acquaintance, every one looked at him with that soft hardness of good society which puts out its hand but keeps its fingers closed over the coin. If the marquis was going about as a bear-leader, if the fiction of Beauty and the Beast was supposed to have found its companion-piece, the general impression appeared to be that the bear was a very fair imitation of humanity. Newman found his reception among the marquis's friends very "pleasant;" he could not have said more for it. It was pleasant to be treated with so much explicit politeness; it was pleasant to hear neatly turned civilities, with a flavor of wit, uttered from beneath carefully-shaped mustaches; it was pleasant to see clever French-women—they all seemed clever—turn their backs to their partners to get a good look at the strange American whom Claire de Cintré was to marry, and reward the object of the exhibition with a charming smile. At last, as he turned away from a battery of smiles and other amenities, Newman caught the eye of the marquis looking at him heavily; and thereupon, for a single instant, he checked himself. "Am I behaving like a d—d fool?" he asked himself. "Am I stepping about like a terrier on his hind legs?" At this moment he perceived Mrs. Tristram at the other side of the room, and he waved his hand in farewell to M. de Bellegarde and made his way toward her.

"Am I holding my head too high?" he asked. "Do I look as if I had the lower end of a pulley fastened to my chin?"

"You look like all happy men, very ridiculous," said Mrs. Tristram. "It's the usual thing, neither better nor worse. I have been watching you for the last ten minutes, and I have been watching M. de Bellegarde. He doesn't like it."

"The more credit to him for putting it through," replied Newman. "But I shall be generous. I shan't trouble him any more. But I am very happy. I can't stand still here. Please to take my arm and we will go for a walk."

He led Mrs. Tristram through all the rooms. There were a great many of them, and, decorated for the occasion and filled with a stately crowd, their somewhat tarnished nobleness recovered its lustre. Mrs. Tristram, looking about her, dropped a series of softly-incisive comments upon her fellow-guests. But Newman made vague answers; he hardly heard her; his thoughts were elsewhere. They were lost in a cheerful sense of success, of attainment and victory. His momentary care as to whether he looked like a fool passed away, leaving him simply with a rich contentment. He had got what he wanted. The savor of success had always been highly agreeable to him, and it had been his fortune to know it often. But it had never before been so sweet, been associated with so much that was brilliant and suggestive and entertaining. The lights, the flowers, the music, the crowd, the splendid women, the jewels, the strangeness even of the universal murmur of a clever foreign tongue, were all a vivid symbol and assurance of his having grasped his purpose and forced along his groove. If Newman's smile was larger than usual, it was not tickled vanity that pulled the strings; he had no wish to be shown with the finger or to achieve a personal success. If he could have looked down at the scene, invisible, from a hole in the roof, he would have enjoyed it quite as much. It would have spoken to him about his own prosperity and deepened that easy feeling about life to which, sooner or later, he made all experience contribute. Just now the cup seemed full.

"It is a very pretty party," said Mrs. Tristram, after they had walked a while. "I have seen nothing objectionable except my husband leaning against the wall and talking to an individual whom I suppose he takes for a duke, but whom I more than suspect to be the functionary who attends to the lamps. Do you think you could separate them? Knock over a lamp!"

I doubt whether Newman, who saw no harm in Tristram's conversing with an ingenious mechanic, would have complied with this request; but at this moment Valentin de Bellegarde drew near. Newman, some weeks previously, had presented Madame de Cintré's youngest brother to Mrs. Tristram, for whose merits Valentin professed a discriminating relish and to whom he had paid several visits.

"Did you ever read Keats's Belle Dame sans Merci?" asked Mrs. Tristram. "You remind me of the hero of the ballad:—

'Oh, what can ail thee, knight-at-arms,
Alone and palely loitering?'"

"If I am alone, it is because I have been deprived of your society," said Valentin. "Besides it is good manners for no man except Newman to look happy. This is all to his address. It is not for you and me to go before the curtain."

"You promised me last spring," said Newman to Mrs. Tristram, "that six months from that time I should get into a monstrous rage. It seems to me the time's up, and yet the nearest I can come to doing anything rough now is to offer you a café glacé."

"I told you we should do things grandly," said Valentin. "I don't allude to the cafés glacés. But every one is here, and my sister told me just now that Urbain had been adorable."

"He's a good fellow, he's a good fellow," said Newman. "I love him as a brother. That reminds me that I ought to go and say something polite to your mother."

"Let it be something very polite indeed," said Valentin. "It may be the last time you will feel so much like it!"

Newman walked away, almost disposed to clasp old Madame de Bellegarde round the waist. He passed through several rooms and at last found the old marquise in the first saloon, seated on a sofa, with her young kinsman, Lord Deepmere, beside her. The young man looked somewhat bored; his hands were thrust into his pockets and his eyes were fixed upon the toes of his shoes, his feet being thrust out in front of him. Madame de Bellegarde appeared to have been talking to him with some intensity and to be waiting for an answer to what she had said, or for some sign of the effect of her words. Her hands were folded in her lap, and she was looking at his lordship's simple physiognomy with an air of politely suppressed irritation.

Lord Deepmere looked up as Newman approached, met his eyes, and changed color.

"I am afraid I disturb an interesting interview," said Newman.

Madame de Bellegarde rose, and her companion rising at the same time, she put her hand into his arm. She answered nothing for an instant, and then, as he remained silent, she said with a smile, "It would be polite for Lord Deepmere to say it was very interesting."

"Oh, I'm not polite!" cried his lordship. "But it *was* interesting."

"Madame de Bellegarde was giving you some good advice, eh?" said Newman; "toning you down a little?"

"I was giving him some excellent advice," said the marquise, fixing her fresh, cold eyes upon our hero. "It's for him to take it."

"Take it, sir—take it," Newman exclaimed. "Any advice the marquise gives you to-night must be good. For to-night, marquise, you must speak from a cheerful, comfortable spirit, and that makes good advice. You see everything going on so brightly and successfully round you. Your party is magnificent; it was a very happy thought. It is much better than that thing of mine would have been."

"If you are pleased I am satisfied," said Madame de Bellegarde. "My desire was to please you."

"Do you want to please me a little more?" said Newman. "Just drop our lordly friend; I am sure he wants to be off and shake his heels a little. Then take my arm and walk through the rooms."

"My desire was to please you," the old lady repeated. And she liberated Lord Deepmere, Newman rather wondering at her docility. "If this young man is wise," she added, "he will go and find my daughter and ask her to dance."

"I have been indorsing your advice," said Newman, bending over her and laughing, "I suppose I must swallow that!"

Lord Deepmere wiped his forehead and departed, and Madame de Bellegarde took Newman's arm. "Yes, it's a very pleasant, sociable entertainment," the latter declared, as they proceeded on their circuit. "Every one seems to know every one and to be glad to see every one. The marquis has made me acquainted with ever so many people, and I feel quite like one of the family. It's an occasion," Newman continued, wanting to say something thoroughly kind and comfortable, "that I shall aways remember, and remember very pleasantly."

"I think it is an occasion that we shall none of us forget," said the marquise, with her pure, neat enunciation.

People made way for her as she passed, others turned round and looked at her, and she received a great many greetings and pressings of the hand, all of which she accepted with the most delicate dignity. But though she smiled upon every one, she said nothing until she reached the last of the rooms, where she found her elder son. Then, "This is enough, sir," she declared with measured softness to Newman, and turned to the marquis. He put out both his hands and took both hers, drawing her to a seat with an air of the tenderest veneration. It was a most harmonious family group, and Newman discreetly retired. He moved through the rooms for some time longer, circulating freely, overtopping most people by his great height, renewing acquaintance with some of the groups to which Urbain de Bellegarde had presented him, and expending generally the surplus of his equanimity. He continued to find it all extremely agreeable; but the most agreeable things have an end, and the revelry on this occasion began to deepen to a close. The music was sounding its ultimate strains and people were looking for the marquise, to make their farewells. There seemed to be some difficulty in finding her, and Newman heard a report that she had left the ball, feeling faint. "She has succumbed to the emotions of the evening," he heard a lady say. "Poor, dear marquise; I can imagine all that they may have been for her!" But he learned immediately afterwards that she had recovered herself and was seated in an armchair near the doorway, receiving parting compliments from great ladies who insisted upon her not rising. He himself set out in quest of Madame de Cintré. He had seen her move past him many times in the rapid circles of a waltz, but in accordance with her explicit instructions he had exchanged no words with her since the beginning of the evening. The whole house having been thrown open, the apartments of the *rez-de-chaussée* were also accessible, though a smaller number of persons had gathered there. Newman wandered through them, observing a few scattered couples to whom this comparative seclusion appeared grateful, and reached a small conservatory which opened into the garden. The end of the conservatory was formed by a clear sheet of glass, unmasked by plants, and admitting the winter starlight so directly that a person standing there would seem to have passed into the open air. Two persons stood there now, a lady and a gentleman; the lady Newman, from within the room and although she had turned her back to it, immediately recognized as Madame de Cintré. He hesitated as to whether he would advance, but as he did so she looked round, feeling apparently that he was there. She rested her eyes on him a moment and then turned again to her companion.

"It is almost a pity not to tell Mr. Newman," she said softly, but in a tone that Newman could hear.

"Tell him if you like!" the gentleman answered, in the voice of Lord Deepmere.

"Oh, tell me by all means!" said Newman advancing.

Lord Deepmere, he observed, was very red in the face, and he had twisted his gloves into a tight cord as if he had been squeezing them dry. These, presumably, were tokens of violent emotion, and it seemed to Newman that the traces of a corresponding agitation were visible in Madame de Cintré's face. The two had been talking with much vivacity. "What I should tell you is only to my lord's credit," said Madame de Cintré, smiling frankly enough.

"He wouldn't like it any better for that!" said my lord, with his awkward laugh.

"Come; what's the mystery?" Newman demanded. "Clear it up. I don't like mysteries."

"We must have some things we don't like, and go without some we do," said the ruddy young nobleman, laughing still.

"It's to Lord Deepmere's credit, but it is not to every one's," said Madame de Cintré. "So I shall say nothing about it. You may be sure," she added; and she put out her hand to the Englishman, who took it half shyly, half impetuously. "And now go and dance!" she said.

"Oh yes, I feel awfully like dancing!" he answered. "I shall go and get tipsy." And he walked away with a gloomy guffaw.

"What has happened between you?" Newman asked.

"I can't tell you—now," said Madame de Cintré. "Nothing that need make you unhappy."

"Has the little Englishman been trying to make love to you?"

She hesitated, and then she uttered a grave "No he's a very honest little fellow."

"But you are agitated. Something is the matter."

"Nothing, I repeat, that need make you unhappy. My agitation is over. Some day I will tell you what it was; not now. I can't now!"

"Well, I confess," remarked Newman, "I don't want to hear anything unpleasant. I am satisfied with everything—most of all with you. I have seen all the ladies and talked with a great many of them; but I am satisfied with you." Madame de Cintré covered him for a moment with her large, soft glance, and then turned her eyes away into the starry night. So they stood silent a moment, side by side. "Say you are satisfied with me," said Newman.

He had to wait a moment for the answer; but it came at last, low yet distinct: "I am very happy."

It was presently followed by a few words from another source, which made them both turn round. "I am sadly afraid Madame de Cintré will take a chill. I have ventured to bring a shawl." Mrs. Bread stood there softly solicitous, holding a white drapery in her hand.

"Thank you," said Madame de Cintré, "the sight of those cold stars gives one a sense of frost. I won't take your shawl, but we will go back into the house."

She passed back and Newman followed her, Mrs. Bread standing respectfully aside to make way for them. Newman paused an instant before the old woman, and she glanced up at him with a silent greeting. "Oh, yes," he said, "you must come and live with us."

"Well then, sir, if you will," she answered, "you have not seen the last of me!"

CHAPTER XVII

NEWMAN WAS fond of music and went often to the opera. A couple of evenings after Madame de Bellegarde's ball he sat listening to "Don Giovanni," having in honor of this work, which he had never yet seen represented, come to occupy his orchestra-chair before the rising of the curtain. Frequently he took a large box and invited a party of his compatriots; this was a mode of recreation to which he was much addicted. He liked making up parties of his friends and conducting them to the theatre, and taking them to drive on high drags or to dine at remote restaurants. He liked doing things which involved his paying for people; the vulgar truth is that he enjoyed "treating" them. This was not because he was what is called purse-proud; handling money in public was on the contrary positively disagreeable to him; he had a sort of personal modesty about it, akin to what he would have felt about making a toilet before spectators. But just as it was a gratification to him to be handsomely dressed, just so it was a private satisfaction to him (he enjoyed it very clandestinely) to have interposed, pecuniarily, in a scheme of pleasure. To set a large group of people in motion and transport them to a distance, to have special conveyances, to charter railway-carriages and steamboats, harmonized with his relish for bold processes, and made hospitality seem more active and more to the purpose. A few evenings before the occasion of which I speak he had invited several ladies and gentlemen to the opera to listen to Madame Alboni—a party which included Miss Dora Finch. It befell, however, that Miss Dora Finch, sitting near Newman in the box, discoursed brilliantly, not only during the entr'actes, but during many of the finest portions of the performance, so that Newman had really come away with an irritated sense that Madame Alboni had a thin, shrill voice, and that her musical phrase was much garnished with a laugh of the giggling order. After this he promised himself to go for a while to the opera alone.

When the curtain had fallen upon the first act of "Don Giovanni" he turned round in his place to observe the house. Presently, in one of the boxes, he perceived Urbain de Bellegarde and his wife. The little marquise was sweeping the house very busily with a glass, and Newman, supposing that she saw him, determined to go and bid her good evening. M. de Bellegarde was leaning against a column, motionless, looking straight in front of him, with one hand in the breast of his white waistcoat and the other resting his hat on his thigh. Newman was about to leave his place when he noticed in that obscure region devoted to the small boxes which in France are called, not inaptly, "bathing-tubs," a face which even the dim light and the distance could not make wholly indistinct. It was the face of a young and pretty woman, and it was surmounted with a coiffure of pink roses and diamonds. This person was looking round the house, and her fan was moving to and fro with the most practiced grace; when she lowered it, Newman perceived a pair of plump white shoulders and the edge of a rose-colored dress. Beside her, very close to the shoulders, and talking, apparently with an earnest-ness which it pleased her scantily to heed, sat a young man with a red face and a very low shirtcollar. A moment's gazing left Newman with no doubts; the pretty young woman was Noémie Nioche. He looked hard into the depths of the box, thinking her father might perhaps be in attendance, but from what he could see the young man's eloquence had no other auditor. Newman at last made his way out, and in doing so he passed beneath the *baignoire* of Mademoiselle Noémie. She saw him as he approached and gave him a nod and smile which seemed meant as an assurance that she was still a good-natured girl, in spite of her enviable rise in the world. Newman passed into the foyer and walked through it. Suddenly he paused in front of a gentleman seated on one of the divans. The gentleman's elbows were on his knees; he was leaning forward and staring at the pavement, lost apparently in meditations of a somewhat gloomy cast. But in spite of his bent head Newman recognized him, and in a moment sat down beside him. Then the gentleman looked up and displayed the expressive countenance of Valentin de Bellegarde.

"What in the world are you thinking of so hard?" asked Newman.

"A subject that requires hard thinking to do it justice," said Valentin. "My immeasurable idiocy."

"What is the matter now?"

"The matter now is that I am a man again, and no more a fool than usual. But I came within an inch of taking that girl *au sérieux*."

"You mean the young lady below stairs, in a baignoire, in a pink dress?" said Newman.

"Did you notice what a brilliant kind of pink it was?" Valentin inquired, by way of answer. "It makes her look as white as new milk."

"White or black, as you please. But you have stopped going to see her?"

"Oh, bless you, no. Why should I stop? I have changed, but she hasn't," said Valentin. "I see she is a vulgar little wretch, after all. But she is as amusing as ever, and one *must* be amused."

"Well, I am glad she strikes you so unpleasantly," Newman rejoined. "I suppose you have swallowed all those fine words you used about her the other night. You compared her to a sapphire, or a topaz, or an amethyst—some precious stone; what was it?"

"I don't remember," said Valentin, "it may have been to a carbuncle! But she won't make a fool of me now. She has no real charm. It's an awfully low thing to make a mistake about a person of that sort."

"I congratulate you," Newman declared, "upon the scales having fallen from your eyes. It's a great triumph; it ought to make you feel better."

"Yes, it makes me _ee. better!" said Valentin, gayly. Then, checking himself, he looked askance at Newman. "I rather think you are laughing at me. If you were not one of the family I would take it up."

"Oh, no, I'm not laughing, any more than I am one of the family. You make me feel badly. You are too clever a fellow, you are made of too good stuff, to spend your time in ups and downs over that class of goods. The idea of splitting hairs about Miss Nioche! It seems to me awfully foolish. You say you have given up taking her seriously; but you take her seriously so long as you take her at all."

Valentin turned round in his place and looked a while at Newman, wrinkling his forehead and rubbing his knees. "*Vous parlez d'or.* But she has wonderfully pretty arms. Would you believe I didn't know it till this evening?"

"But she is a vulgar little wretch, remember, all the same," said Newman.

"Yes; the other day she had the bad taste to begin to abuse her father, to his face, in my presence. I shouldn't have expected it of her; it was a disappointment; heigho!"

"Why, she cares no more for her father than for her door-mat," said Newman. "I discovered that the first time I saw her."

"Oh, that's another affair; she may think of the poor old beggar what she pleases. But it was low in her to call him bad names; it quite threw me off. It was about a frilled petticoat that he was to have fetched from the washer-woman's; he appeared to have neglected this graceful duty. She almost boxed his ears. He stood there staring at her with his little blank eyes and smoothing his old hat with his coattail. At last he turned round and went out without a word. Then I told her it was in very bad taste to speak so to one's papa. She said she should be so thankful to me if I would mention it to her whenever her taste was at fault; she had immense confidence in mine. I told her I couldn't have the bother of forming her manners; I had had an idea they were already formed, after the best models. She had disappointed me. But I shall get over it," said Valentin, gayly.

"Oh, time's a great consoler!" Newman answered with humorous sobriety. He was silent a moment, and then he added, in another tone, "I wish you would think of what I said to you the other day. Come over to America with us, and I will put you in the way of doing some business. You have got a very good head, if you will only use it."

Valentin made a genial grimace. "My head is much obliged to you. Do you mean the place in a bank?"

"There are several places, but I suppose you would consider the bank the most aristocratic."

Valentin burst into a laugh. "My dear fellow, at night all cats are gray! When one derogates there are no degrees."

Newman answered nothing for a minute. Then, "I think you will find there are degrees in success," he said with a certain dryness.

Valentin had leaned froward again, with his elbows on his knees, and he was scratching the pavement with his stick. At last he said, looking up, "Do you really think I ought to do something?"

Newman laid his hand on his companion's arm and looked at him a moment through sagaciously-narrowed eyelids. "Try it and see. You are not good enough for it, but we will stretch a point."

"Do you really think I can make some money? I should like to see how it feels to have a little."

"Do what I tell you, and you shall be rich," said Newman. "Think of it." And he looked at his watch and prepared to resume his way to Madame de Bellegarde's box.

"Upon my word I will think of it," said Valentin. "I will go and listen to Mozart another half hour—I can always think better to music—and profoundly meditate upon it."

The marquis was with his wife when Newman entered their box; he was bland, remote, and correct as usual; or, as it seemed to Newman, even more than usual.

"What do you think of the opera?" asked our hero. "What do you think of the Don?"

"We all know what Mozart is," said the marquis; "our impressions don't date from this evening. Mozart is youth, freshness, brilliancy, facility—a little too great facility, perhaps. But the execution is here and there deplorably rough."

"I am very curious to see how it ends," said Newman.

"You speak as if it were a feuilleton in the 'Fifaro,' " observed the marquis. "You have surely seen the opera before?"

"Never," said Newman. "I am sure I should have remembered it. Donna Elvira reminds me of Madame de Cintré; I don't mean in her circumstances, but in the music she sings."

"It is a very nice distinction," laughed the marquis lightly. "There is no great possibility, I imagine, of Madame de Cintré being forsaken."

"Not much!" said Newman. "But what becomes of the Don?"

"The devil comes down—or comes up," said Madame de Bellegarde, "and carries him off. I suppose Zerlina reminds you of me."

"I will go to the foyer for a few moments," said the marquis, "and give you a chance to say that the commander—the man of stone—resembles me." And he passed out of the box.

The little marquise stared an instant at the velvet ledge of the balcony, and then murmured, "Not a man of stone, a man of wood." Newman had taken her husband's empty chair. She made no protest, and then she turned suddenly and laid her closed fan upon his arm. "I am very glad you came in," she said. "I want to ask you a favor. I wanted to do so on Thursday, at my mother-in-law's ball, but you would give me no chance. You were in such very good spirits that I thought you might grant my little favor then; not that you look particularly doleful now. It is something you must promise me; now is the time to take you; after you are married you will be good for nothing. Come, promise!"

"I never sign a paper without reading it first," said Newman. "Show me your document."

"No, you must sign with your eyes shut; I will hold your hand. Come, before you put your head into the noose. You ought to be thankful to me for giving you a chance to do something amusing."

"If it is so amusing," said Newman, "it will be in even better season after I am married."

"In other words," cried Madame de Bellegarde, "you will not do it at all. You will be afraid of your wife."

"Oh, if the thing is intrinsically improper," said Newman, "I won't go into it. If it is not, I will do it after my marriage."

"You talk like a treatise on logic, and English logic into the bargain!" exclaimed Madame de Bellegarde. "Promise, then, after you are married. After all, I shall enjoy keeping you to it."

"Well, then, after I am married," said Newman serenely.

The little marquise hesitated a moment, looking at him, and he wondered what was coming. "I suppose you know what my life is," she presently said. "I have no pleasure, I see nothing, I do nothing. I live in Paris as I might live at Poitiers. My mother-in-law calls me—what is the pretty word?—a gad-about? accuses me of going to unheard-of places, and thinks it ought to be joy enough for me to sit at home and count over my ancestors on my fingers. But why should I bother about my ancestors? I am sure they never bothered about me. I don't propose to live with a green shade on my eyes; I hold that things were made to look at. My husband, you know, has principles, and the first on the list is that the Tuileries are dreadfully vulgar. If the Tuileries are vulgar, his principles are tiresome. If I chose I might have principles quite as well as he. If they grew on one's family tree I should only have to give mine a shake to bring down a shower of the finest. At any rate, I prefer clever Bonapartes to stupid Bourbons."

"Oh, I see; you want to go to court," said Newman, vaguely conjecturing that she might wish him to appeal to the United States legation to smooth her way to the imperial halls.

The marquise gave a little sharp laugh. "You are a thousand miles away. I will take care of the Tuileries myself; the day I decide to go they will be very glad to have me. Sooner or later I shall dance in an imperial quadrille. I know what you are going to say: 'How will you dare?' But I *shall* dare. I am afraid of my husband; he is soft, smooth, irreproachable; everything that you know; but I am afraid of him—horribly afraid of him. And yet I shall arrive at the Tuileries. But that will not be this winter, nor perhaps next, and meantime I must live. For the moment, I want to go somewhere else; it's my dream. I want to go to the Bal Bullier."

"To the Bal Bullier?" repeated Newman, for whom the words at first meant nothing.

"The ball in the Latin Quarter, where the students dance with their mistresses. Don't tell me you have not heard of it."

"Oh yes," said Newman; "I have heard of it; I remember now. I have even been there. And you want to go there?"

"It is silly, it is low, it is anything you please. But I want to go. Some of my friends have been, and they say it is awfully *drôle*. My friends go everywhere; it is only I who sit moping at home."

"It seems to me you are not at home now," said Newman, "and I shouldn't exactly say you were moping."

"I am bored to death. I have been to the opera twice a week for the last eight years. Whenever I ask for anything my mouth is stopped with that: Pray, madam, haven't you an opera box? Could a woman of taste want more? In the first place, my opera box was down in my *contract;* they have to give it to me. To-night, for instance, I should have preferred a thousand times to go to the Palais Royal. But my husband won't go to the Palais Royal because the ladies of the court go there so much. You may imagine, then,

whether he would take me to Bullier's; he says it is a mere imitation—
and a bad one—of what they do at the Princess Kleinfuss's. But as
I don't go to the Princess Kleinfuss's, the next best thing is to go
to Bullier's. It is my dream, at any rate, it's a fixed idea. All I ask of
you is to give me your arm; you are less compromising than any
one else. I don't know why, but you are. I can arrange it. I shall risk
something, but that is my own affair. Besides, fortune favors the
bold. Don't refuse me; it is my dream!"

Newman gave a loud laugh. It seemed to him hardly worth while
to be the wife of the Marquis de Bellegarde, a daughter of the
crusaders, heiress of six centuries of glories and traditions, to have
centred one's aspirations upon the sight of a couple of hundred
young ladies kicking off young men's hats. It struck him as a theme
for the moralist; but he had no time to moralize upon it. The curtain
rose again; M. de Bellegarde returned, and Newman went back to
his seat.

He observed that Valentin de Bellegarde had taken his place in
the baignoire of Mademoiselle Nioche, behind this young lady and
her companion, where he was visible only if one carefully looked for
him. In the next act Newman met him in the lobby and asked him if
he had reflected upon possible emigration. "If you really meant to
meditate," he said, "you might have chosen a better place for it."

"Oh, the place was not bad," said Valentin. "I was not thinking
of that girl. I listened to the music, and, without thinking of the
play or looking at the stage, I turned over your proposal. At first it
seemed quite fantastic. And then a certain fiddle in the orchestra—I
could distinguish it—began to say as it scraped away, 'Why not,
why not?' And then, in that rapid movement, all the fiddles took
it up and the conductor's stick seemed to beat it in the air: 'Why
not, why not?' I'm sure I can't say! I don't see why not. I don't see
why I shouldn't do something. It appears to me really a very bright
idea. This sort of thing is certainly very stale. And then I could come
back with a trunk full of dollars. Besides, I might possibly find it
amusing. They call me a *raffiné;* who knows but that I might
discover an unsuspected charm in shop-keeping? It would really
have a certain romantic, picturesque side; it would look well in my
biography. It would look as if I were a strong man, a first-rate man,
a man who dominated circumstances."

"Never mind how it would look," said Newman. "It always looks
well to have half a million of dollars. There is no reason why you
shouldn't have them if you will mind what I tell you—I alone—and

not talk to other parties." He passed his arm into that of his companion, and the two walked for some time up and down one of the less frequented corridors. Newman's imagination began to glow with the idea of converting his bright, impracticable friend into a first-class man of business. He felt for the moment a sort of spiritual zeal, the zeal of the propagandist. Its ardor was in part the result of that general discomfort which the sight of all uninvested capital produced in him; so fine an intelligence as Bellegarde's ought to be dedicated to high uses. The highest uses known to Newman's experience were certain transcendent sagacities in the handling of railway stock. And then his zeal was quickened by his personal kindness for Valentin; he had a sort of pity for him which he was well aware he never could have made the Comte de Bellegarde understand. He never lost a sense of its being pitiable that Valentin should think it a large life to revolve in varnished boots between the Rue d'Anjou and the Rue de l'Université, taking the Boulevard des Italiens on the way, when over there in America one's promenade was a continent, and one's Boulevard stretched from New York to San Francisco. It mortified him, moreover, to think that Valentin lacked money; there was a painful grotesqueness in it. It affected him as the ignorance of a companion, otherwise without reproach, touching some rudimentary branch of learning would have done. There were things that one knew about as a matter of course, he would have said in such a case. Just so, if one pretended to be easy in the world, one had money as a matter of course, one had made it! There was something almost ridiculously anomalous to Newman in the sight of lively pretensions unaccompanied by large investments in railroads; though I may add that he would not have maintained that such investments were in themselves a proper ground for pretensions. "I will make you do something," he said to Valentin; "I will put you through. I know half a dozen things in which we can make a place for you. You will see some lively work. It will take you a little while to get used to the life, but you will work in before long, and at the end of six months—after you have done a thing or two on your own account—you will like it. And then it will be very pleasant for you, having your sister over there. It will be pleasant for her to have you, too. Yes, Valentin," continued Newman, pressing his friend's arm genially, "I think I see just the opening for you. Keep quiet and I'll push you right in."

Newman pursued this favoring strain for some time longer. The two men strolled about for a quarter of an hour. Valentin listened and questioned, many of his questions making Newman laugh loud at the naïveté of his ignorance of the vulgar processes of money-getting; smiling himself, too, half ironical and half curious. And yet he was serious; he was fascinated by Newman's plain prose version of the legend of El Dorado. It is true, however, that though to accept an "opening" in an American mercantile house might be a bold, original, and in its consequences extremely agreeable thing to do, he did not quite see himself objectively doing it. So that when the bell rang to indicate the close of the entr'acte, there was a certain mock-heroism in his saying, with his brilliant smile, "Well, then, put me through; push me in! I make myself over to you. Dip me into the pot and turn me into gold."

They had passed into the corridor which encircled the row of baignoires, and Valentin stopped in front of the dusky little box in which Mademoiselle Nioche had bestowed herself, laying his hand on the doorknob. "Oh, come, are you going back there?" asked Newman.

"*Mon Dieu, oui,*" said Valentin.

"Haven't you another place?"

"Yes, I have my usual place, in the stalls."

"You had better go and occupy it, then."

"I see her very well from there, too," added Valentin, serenely; "and to-night she is worth seeing. But," he added in a moment, "I have a particular reason for going back just now."

"Oh, I give you up," said Newman. "You are infatuated!"

"No, it is only this. There is a young man in the box whom I shall annoy by going in, and I want to annoy him."

"I am sorry to hear it," said Newman. "Can't you leave the poor fellow alone?"

"No, he has given me cause. The box is not his. Noémie came in alone and installed herself. I went and spoke to her, and in a few moments she asked me to go and get her fan from the pocket of her cloak, which the *ouvreuse* had carried off. In my absence this gentleman came in and took the chair beside Noémie in which I had been sitting. My reappearance disgusted him, and he had the grossness to show it. He came within an ace of being impertinent. I don't know who he is; he is some vulgar wretch. I can't think where she picks up such acquaintances. He has been drinking, too, but he knows what he is about. Just now, in the second act, he was unmannerly again. I shall put in another appearance for ten minutes—time enough to give him an opportunity to commit himself, if he feels inclined. I really can't let the brute suppose that he is keeping me out of the box."

"My dear fellow," said Newman, remonstrantly, "what child's play! You are not going to pick a quarrel about that girl, I hope."

"That girl has nothing to do with it, and I have no intention of picking a quarrel. I am not a bully nor a fire-eater. I simply wish to make a point that a gentleman must."

"Oh, damn your point!" said Newman. "That is the trouble with you Frenchmen; you must be always making points. Well," he added, "be short. But if you are going in for this kind of thing, we must ship you off to America in advance."

"Very good," Valentin answered, "whenever you please. But if I go to America, I must not let this gentleman suppose that it is to run away from him."

And they separated. At the end of the act Newman observed that Valentin was still in the baignoire. He strolled into the corridor again, expecting to meet him, and when he was within a few yards of Mademoiselle Nioche's box saw his friend pass out, accompanied by the young man who had been seated beside its fair occupant. The two gentlemen walked with some quickness of step to a distant part of the lobby, where Newman perceived them stop and stand talking. The manner of each was perfectly quiet, but the stranger, who looked flushed, had begun to wipe his face very emphatically with his pocket-handkerchief. By this time Newman was abreast of the baignoire; the door had been left ajar, and he could see a pink dress inside. He immediately went in. Mademoiselle Nioche turned and greeted him with a brilliant smile.

"Ah, you have at last decided to come and see me?" she exclaimed. "You just save your politeness. You find me in a fine moment. Sit down." There was a very becoming little flush in her cheek, and her eye had a noticeable spark. You would have said that she had received some very good news.

"Something has happened here!" said Newman, without sitting down.

"You find me in a very fine moment," she repeated. "Two gentlemen—one of them is M. de Bellegarde, the pleasure of whose acquaintance I owe to you—have just had words about your humble servant. Very big words too. They can't come off without crossing swords. A duel—that will give me a push!" cried Mademoiselle Noémie, clapping her little hands. "C'est ça qui pose une femme!"

"You don't mean to say that Bellegarde is going to fight about *you!*" exclaimed Newman, disgustedly.

"Nothing less!" and she looked at him with a hard little smile. "No, no, you are not *galant!* And if you prevent this affair I shall owe you a grudge—and pay my debt!"

Newman uttered an imprecation which, though brief—it consisted simply of the interjection "Oh!" followed by a geographical, or more correctly, perhaps, a theological noun in four letters—had better not be transferred to these pages. He turned his back without more ceremony upon the pink dress and went out of the box. In the corridor he found Valentin and his companion walking towards him. The latter was thrusting a card into his waistcoat pocket. Mademoiselle Noémie's jealous votary was a tall, robust young man with a thick nose, a prominent blue eye, a Germanic physiognomy, and a massive watch-chain. When they reached the box, Valentin with an emphasized bow made way for him to pass in first. Newman touched Valentin's arm as a sign that he wished to speak with him, and Bellegarde answered that he would be with him in an instant. Valentin entered the box after the robust young man, but a couple of minutes afterwards he reappeared, largely smiling.

"She is immensely tickled," he said. "She says we will make her fortune. I don't want to be fatuous, but I think it is very possible."

"So you are going to fight?" said Newman.

"My dear fellow, don't look so mortally disgusted. It was not my choice. The thing is all arranged."

"I told you so!" groaned Newman.

"I told *him* so," said Valentin, smiling.

"What did he do to you?"

"My good friend, it doesn't matter what. He used an expression—I took it up."

"But I insist upon knowing; I can't, as your elder brother, have you rushing into this sort of nonsense."

"I am very much obliged to you," said Valentin. "I have nothing to conceal, but I can't go into particulars now and here."

"We will leave this place, then. You can tell me outside."

"Oh no, I can't leave this place, why should I hurry away? I will go to my orchestra-stall and sit out the opera."

"You will not enjoy it; you will be preoccupied."

Valentin looked at him a moment, colored a little, smiled, and patted him on the arm. "You are delightfully simple! Before an affair a man is quiet. The quietest thing I can do is to go straight to my place."

"Ah," said Newman, "you want her to see you there—you and your quietness. I am not so simple! It is a poor business."

Valentin remained, and the two men, in their respective places, sat out the rest of the performance, which was also enjoyed by Mademoiselle Nioche and her truculent admirer. At the end Newman joined Valentin again, and they went into the street together. Valentin shook his head at his friend's proposal that he should get into Newman's own vehicle, and stopped on the edge of the pavement. "I must go off alone," he said; "I must look up a couple of friends who will take charge of this matter."

"I will take charge of it," Newman declared. "Put it into my hands."

"You are very kind, but that is hardly possible. In the first place, you are, as you said just now, almost my brother; you are about to marry my sister. That alone disqualifies you; it casts doubts on your impartiality. And if it didn't, it would be enough for me that I strongly suspect you of disapproving of the affair. You would try to prevent a meeting."

"Of course I should," said Newman. "Whoever your friends are, I hope they will do that."

"Unquestionably they will. They will urge that excuses be made, proper excuses. But you would be too good-natured. You won't do."

Newman was silent a moment. He was keenly annoyed, but he saw it was useless to attempt interference. "When is this precious performance to come off?" he asked.

"The sooner the better," said Valentin. "The day after to-morrow, I hope."

"Well," said Newman, "I have certainly a claim to know the facts. I can't consent to shut my eyes to the matter."

"I shall be most happy to tell you the facts," said Valentin. "They are very simple, and it will be quickly done. But now everything depends on my putting my hands on my friends without delay. I will jump into a cab; you had better drive to my room and wait for me there. I will turn up at the end of an hour."

Newman assented protestingly, let his friend go, and then betook himself to the picturesque little apartment in the Rue d'Anjou. It was more than an hour before Valentin returned, but when he did so he was able to announce that he had found one of his desired friends, and that this gentleman had taken upon himself the care of securing an associate. Newman had been sitting without lights by Valentin's faded fire, upon which he had thrown a log; the blaze played over the richly-encumbered little sitting-room and produced fantasic gleams and shadows. He listened in silence to Valentin's account of what had passed between him and the gentleman whose card he had in his pocket—M. Stanislas Kapp, of Strasbourg—after his return to Mademoiselle Nioche's box. This hospitable young lady had espied an acquaintance on the other side of the house, and had expressed her displeasure at his not having the civility to come and pay her a visit. "Oh, let him alone!" M. Stanislas Kapp had hereupon exclaimed. "There are too many people in the box already." And he had fixed his eyes with a demonstrative stare upon M. de Bellegarde. Valentin had promptly retorted that if there were too many people in the box it was easy for M. Kapp to diminish the number. "I shall be most happy to open the door for *you!*" M. Kapp exclaimed. "I shall be delighted to fling you into the pit!" Valentin had answered. "Oh, do make a rumpus and get into the papers!" Miss Noémie had gleefully ejaculated. "M. Kapp, turn him out; or, M. de Bellegarde, pitch him into the pit, into the orchestra—anywhere! I don't care who does which, so long as you make a scene." Valentin answered that they would make no scene, but that the gentleman would be so good as to step into the corridor with him. In the corridor, after a brief further exchange of words, there had been an exchange of cards. M. Stanislas Kapp was very stiff. He evidently meant to force his offence home.

"The man, no doubt, was insolent," Newman said; "but if you hadn't gone back into the box the thing wouldn't have happened."

"Why, don't you see," Valentin replied, "that the event proves the extreme propriety of my going back into the box? M. Kapp wished to provoke me; he was awaiting his chance. In such a case—that is, when he has been, so to speak, notified—a man must be on hand to receive the provocation. My not returning would simply have been tantamount to my saying to M. Stanislas Kapp, 'Oh, if you are going to be disagreeable' "—

" 'You must manage it by yourself; damned if I'll help you!' That would have been a thoroughly sensible thing to say. The only attraction for you seems to have been the prospect of M. Kapp's impertinence," Newman went on. "You told me you were not going back for that girl."

"Oh, don't mention that girl any more," murmured Valentin. "She's a bore."

"With all my heart. But if that is the way you feel about her, why couldn't you let her alone?"

Valentin shook his head with a fine smile. "I don't think you quite understand, and I don't believe I can make you. She understood the situation; she knew what was in the air; she was watching us."

"A cat may look at a king! What difference does that make?"

"Why, a man can't back down before a woman."

"I don't call her a woman. You said yourself she was a stone," cried Newman.

"Well," Valentin repoined, "there is no disputing about tastes. It's a matter of feeling; it's measured by one's sense of honor."

"Oh, confound your sense of honor!" cried Newman.

"It is vain talking," said Valentin; "words have passed, and the thing is settled."

Newman turned away, taking his hat. Then pausing with his hand on the door, "What are you going to use?" he asked.

"That is for M. Stanislas Kapp, as the challenged party, to decide. My own choice would be a short, light sword. I handle it well. I'm an indifferent shot."

Newman had put on his hat; he pushed it back, gently scratching his forehead, high up. "I wish it were pistols," he said. "I could show you how to lodge a bullet!"

Valentin broke into a laugh. "What is it some English poet says about consistency? It's a flower or a star, or a jewel. Yours has the beauty of all three!" But he agreed to see Newman again on the morrow, after the details of his meeting with M. Stanislas Kapp should have been arranged.

In the course of the day Newman received three lines from him, saying that it had been decided that he should cross the frontier, with his adversary, and that he was to take the night express to Geneva. He should have time, however, to dine with Newman. In the afternoon Newman called upon Madame de Cintré, but his visit was brief. She was as gracious and sympathetic as he had ever found her, but she was sad, and she confessed, on Newman's charging her with her red eyes, that she had been crying. Valentin had been with her a couple of hours before, and his visit had left her with a painful impression. He had laughed and gossiped, he had brought her no bad news, he had only been, in his manner, rather more affectionate than usual. His fraternal tenderness had touched her, and on his departure she had burst into tears. She had felt as if something strange and sad were going to happen; she had tried to reason away the fancy, and the effort had only given her a headache. Newman, of course, was perforce tongue-tied about Valentin's projected duel, and his dramatic talent was not equal to satirizing Madame de Cintré's presentiment as pointedly as perfect security demanded. Before he went away he asked Madame de Cintré whether Valentin had seen his mother.

"Yes," she said, "but he didn't make her cry."

It was in Newman's own apartment that Valentin dined, having brought his portmanteau, so that he might adjourn directly to the railway. M. Stanislas Kapp had positively declined to make excuses, and he, on his side, obviously, had none to offer. Valentin had found out with whom he was dealing. M. Stanislas Kapp was the son and heir of a rich brewer of Strasbourg, a youth of a sanguineous—and sanguinary—temperament. He was making ducks and drakes of the paternal brewery, and although he passed in a general way for a good fellow, he had already been observed to be quarrelsome after dinner. "*Que voulez-vous?*" said Valentin. "Brought up on beer, he can't stand champagne." He had chosen pistols. Valentin, at dinner, had an excellent appetite; he made a point, in view of his long journey, of eating more than usual. He took the liberty of suggesting to Newman a slight modification in the composition of a certain fish-sauce; he thought it would be worth mentioning to the cook. But Newman had no thoughts for fish-sauce; he felt thoroughly discontented. As he sat and watched his amiable and clever companion going through his excellent repast with the delicate deliberation of hereditary epicurism, the folly of so charming a fellow traveling off to expose his agreeable young life for the sake of M. Stanislas and Mademoiselle Noémie struck him with intolerable force. He had grown fond of Valentin, he felt now how fond; and his sense of helplessness only increased his irritation.

"Well, this sort of thing may be all very well," he cried at last, "but I declare I don't see it. I can't stop you, perhaps, but at least I can protest. I do protest, violently."

"My dear fellow, don't make a scene," said Valentin. "Scenes in these cases are in very bad taste."

"Your duel itself is a scene," said Newman; "that's all it is! It's a wretched theatrical affair. Why don't you take a band of music with you outright? It's d—d barbarous and it's d—d corrupt, both."

"Oh, I can't begin, at this time of day, to defend the theory of dueling," said Valentin. "It is our custom, and I think it is a good thing. Quite apart from the goodness of the cause in which a duel may be fought, it has a kind of picturesque charm which in this age of vile prose seems to me greatly to recommend it. It's a remnant of a higher-tempered time; one ought to cling to it. Depend upon it, a duel is never amiss."

"I don't know what you mean by a higher-tempered time," said Newman. "Because your great-grandfather was an ass, is that any reason why you should be? For my part I think we had better let our temper take care of itself; it generally seems to me quite high enough; I am not afraid of being too meek. If your great-grandfather were to make himself unpleasant to me, I think I could manage him, yet."

"My dear friend," said Valentin, smiling, "you can't invent anything that will take the place of satisfaction for an insult. To demand it and to give it are equally excellent arrangements."

"Do you call this sort of thing satisfaction?" Newman asked. "Does it satisfy you to receive a present of the carcass of that coarse fop? does it gratify you to make him a present of yours? If a man hits you, hit him back; if a man libels you, haul him up."

"Haul him up, into court? Oh, that is very nasty!" said Valentin.

"The nastiness is his—not yours. And for that matter, what you are doing is not particularly nice. You are too good for it. I don't say you are the most useful man in the world, or the cleverest, or the most amiable. But you are too good to go and get your throat cut for a prostitute."

Valentin flushed a little, but he laughed. "I shan't get my throat cut if I can help it. Moreover, one's honor hasn't two different measures. It only knows that it is hurt; it doesn't ask when, or how, or where."

"The more fool it is!" said Newman.

Valentin ceased to laugh; he looked grave. "I beg you not to say any more," he said. "If you do I shall almost fancy you don't care about—about"—and he paused.

"About what?"

"About that matter—about one's honor."

"Fancy what you please," said Newman. "Fancy while you are at it that I care about *you*—though you are not worth it. But come back without damage," he added in a moment, "and I will forgive you. And then," he continued, as Valentin was going, "I will ship you straight off to America."

"Well," answered Valentin, "if I am to turn over a new page, this may figure as a tail-piece to the old." And then he lit another cigar and departed.

"Blast that girl!" said Newman as the door closed upon Valentin.

Chapter XVIII

Newman went the next morning to see Madame de Cintré, timing his visit so as to arrive after the noonday breakfast. In the court of the *hôtel*, before the portico, stood Madame de Bellegarde's old square carriage. The servant who opened the door answered Newman's inquiry with a slightly embarrassed and hesitating murmur, and at the same moment Mrs. Bread appeared in the background, dim-visaged as usual, and wearing a large black bonnet and shawl.

"What is the matter?" asked Newman. "Is Madame la Comtesse at home, or not?"

Mrs. Bread advanced, fixing her eyes upon him: he observed that she held a sealed letter, very delicately, in her fingers. "The countess has left a message for you, sir; she has left this," said Mrs. Bread, holding out the letter, which Newman took.

"Left it? Is she out? Is she gone away?"

"She is going away, sir; she is leaving town," said Mrs. Bread.

"Leaving town!" exclaimed Newman. "What has happened?"

"It is not for me to say, sir," said Mrs. Bread, with her eyes on the ground. "But I thought it would come."

"What would come, pray?" Newman demanded. He had broken the seal of the letter, but he still questioned. "She is in the house? She is visible?"

"I don't think she expected you this morning," the old waiting-woman replied. "She was to leave immediately."

"Where is she going?"

"To Fleurières."

"To Fleurières? But surely I can see her?"

Mrs. Bread hesitated a moment, and then clasping together her two hands, "I will take you!" she said. And she led the way up-stairs. At the top of the staircase she paused and fixed her dry, sad eyes upon Newman. "Be very easy with her," she said; "she is most unhappy!" Then she went on to Madame de Cintré's apartment; Newman, perplexed and alarmed, followed her rapidly. Mrs. Bread threw open the door, and Newman pushed back the curtain at the farther side of its deep embrasure. In the middle of the room stood Madame de Cintré; her face was pale and she was dressed for travel-ing. Behind her, before the fire-place, stood Urbain de Bellegarde, looking at his finger-nails; near the marquis sat his mother, buried in an arm-chair, and with her eyes immediately fixing themselves upon Newman. He felt, as soon as he entered the room, that he was in the presence of something evil; he was startled and pained, as he would have been by a threatening cry in the stillness of the night. He walked straight to Madame de Cintré and seized her by the hand.

"What is the matter?" he asked, commandingly; "what is happening?"

Urbain de Bellegarde stared, then left his place and came and leaned upon his mother's chair, behind. Newman's sudden irruption had evidently discomposed both mother and son. Madame de Cintré stood silent, with her eyes resting upon Newman's. She had often looked at him with all her soul, as it seemed to him; but in this present gaze there was a sort of bottomless depth. She was in distress; it was the most touching thing he had ever seen. His heart rose into his throat, and he was on the point of turning to her companions, with an angry challenge; but she checked him, pressing the hand that held her own.

"Something very grave has happened," she said. "I cannot marry you."

Newman dropped her hand and stood staring, first at her and then at the others. "Why not?" he asked, as quietly as possible.

Madame de Cintré almost smiled, but the attempt was strange. "You must ask my mother, you must ask my brother."

"Why can't she marry me?" said Newman, looking at them.

Madame de Bellegarde did not move in her place, but she was as pale as her daughter. The marquis looked down at her. She said nothing for some moments, but she kept her keen, clear eyes upon Newman, bravely. The marquis drew himself up and looked at the ceiling. "It's impossible!" he said softly.

"It's improper," said Madame de Bellegarde.

Newman began to laugh. "Oh, you are fooling!" he exclaimed.

"My sister, you have no time; you are losing your train," said the marquis.

"Come, is he mad?" asked Newman.

"No; don't think that," said Madame de Cintré. "But I am going away."

"Where are you going?"

"To the country, to Fleurières; to be alone."

"To leave me?" said Newman, slowly.

"I can't see you, now," said Madame de Cintré.

"*Now*—why not?"

"I am ashamed," said Madame de Cintré, simply.

Newman turned toward the marquis. "What have you done to her—what does it mean?" he asked with the same effort at calmness, the fruit of his constant practice in taking things easily. He was excited, but excitement with him was only an intenser deliberateness; it was the swimmer stripped.

"It means that I have given you up," said Madame de Cintré. "It means that."

Her face was too charged with tragic expression not fully to confirm her words. Newman was profoundly shocked, but he felt as yet no resentment against her. He was amazed, bewildered, and the presence of the old marquise and her son seemed to smite his eyes like the glare of a watchman's lantern. "Can't I see you alone?" he asked.

"It would be only more painful. I hoped I should not see you—I should escape. I wrote to you. Good-by." And she put out her hand again.

Newman put both his own into his pockets. "I will go with you," he said.

She laid her two hands on his arm. "Will you grant me a last request?" and as she looked at him, urging this, her eyes filled with tears. "Let me go alone—let me go in peace. I can't call it peace—it's death. But let me bury myself. So—good-by."

Newman passed his hand into his hair and stood slowly rubbing his head and looking through his keenly-narrowed eyes from one to the other of the three persons before him. His lips were compressed, and the two lines which had formed themselves beside his mouth might have made it appear at a first glance that he was smiling. I have said that his excitement was an intenser deliberateness, and now he looked grimly deliberate. "It seems very much as if you had interfered, marquis," he said slowly. "I thought you said you wouldn't interfere. I know you don't like me; but that doesn't make any difference. I thought you promised me you wouldn't interfere. I thought you swore on your honor that you wouldn't interfere. Don't you remember, marquis?"

The marquis lifted his eyebrows; but he was apparently determined to be even more urbane than usual. He rested his two hands upon the back of his mother's chair and bent forward, as if he were leaning over the edge of a pulpit or a lecture-desk. He did not smile, but he looked softly grave. "Excuse me, sir," he said, "I assured you that I would not influence my sister's decision. I adhered, to the letter, to my engagement. Did I not, sister?"

"Don't appeal, my son," said the marquise, "your word is sufficient."

"Yes—she accepted me," said Newman. "That is very true; I can't deny that. At least," he added, in a different tone, turning to Madame de Cintré, "you *did* accept me?"

Something in the tone seemed to move her strongly. She turned away, burying her face in her hands.

"But you have interfered now, haven't you?" inquired Newman of the marquis.

"Neither then nor now have I attempted to influence my sister. I used no persuasion then, I have used no persuasion to-day."

"And what have you used?"

"We have used authority," said Madame de Bellegarde in a rich, bell-like voice.

"Ah, you have used authority," Newman exclaimed. "They have used authority," he went on, turning to Madame de Cintré. "What is it? how did they use it?"

"My mother commanded," said Madame de Cintré.

"Commanded you to give me up—I see. And you obey—I see. But why do you obey?" asked Newman.

Madame de Cintré looked across at the old marquise; her eyes slowly measured her from head to foot. "I am afraid of my mother," she said.

Madame de Bellegarde rose with a certain quickness, crying, "This is a most indecent scene!"

"I have no wish to prolong it," said Madame de Cintré; and turning to the door she put out her hand again. "If you can pity me a little, let me go alone."

Newman shook her hand quietly and firmly. "I'll come down there," he said. The portière dropped behind her, and Newman sank with a long breath into the nearest chair. He leaned back in it, resting his hands on the knobs of the arms and looking at Madame de Bellegarde and Urbain. There was a long silence. They stood side by side, with their heads high and their handsome eyebrows arched.

"So you make a distinction?" Newman said at last. "You make a distinction between persuading and commanding? It's very neat. But the distinction is in favor of commanding. That rather spoils it."

"We have not the least objection to defining our position," said M. de Bellegarde. "We understand that it should not at first appear to you quite clear. We rather expect, indeed, that you should not do us justice."

"Oh, I'll do you justice," said Newman. "Don't be afraid. Please proceed."

The marquise laid her hand on her son's arm, as if to deprecate the attempt to define their position. "It is quite useless," she said, "to try and arrange this matter so as to make it agreeable to you. It can never be agreeable to you. It is a disappointment, and disappointments are unpleasant. I thought it over carefully and tried to arrange it better; but I only gave myself a headache and lost my sleep. Say what we will, you will think yourself ill-treated, and you will publish your wrongs among your friends. But we are not afraid of that. Besides, your friends are not our friends, and it will not matter. Think of us as you please. I only beg you not to be violent. I have never in my life been present at a violent scene of any kind, and at my age I can't be expected to begin."

"Is *that* all you have got to say?" asked Newman, slowly rising out of his chair. "That's a poor show for a clever lady like you, marquise. Come, try again."

"My mother goes to the point, with her usual honesty and intrepidity," said the marquis, toying with his watch-guard. "But it is perhaps well to say a little more. We of course quite repudiate the charge of having broken faith with you. We left you entirely at liberty to make yourself agreeable to my sister. We left her quite at liberty to entertain your proposal. When she accepted you we said nothing. We therefore quite observed our promise. It was only at a later stage of the affair, and on quite a different basis, as it were, that we determined to speak. It would have been better, perhaps, if we had spoken before. But really, you see, nothing has yet been done."

"Nothing has yet been done?" Newman repeated the words, unconscious of their comical effect. He had lost the sense of what the marquis was saying; M. de Bellegarde's superior style was a mere humming in his ears. All that he understood, in his deep and simple indignation, was that the matter was not a violent joke, and that the people before him were perfectly serious. "Do you suppose I can take this?" he asked. "Do you suppose it can matter to me what you say? Do you suppose I can seriously listen to you? You are simply crazy!"

Madame de Bellegarde gave a rap with her fan in the palm of her hand. "If you don't take it you can leave it, sir. It matters very little what you do. My daughter has given you up."

"She doesn't mean it," Newman declared after a moment.

"I think I can assure you that she does," said the marquis.

"Poor woman, what damnable thing have you done to her?" cried Newman.

"Gently, gently!" murmured M. de Bellegarde.

"She told you," said the old lady. "I commanded her."

Newman shook his head, heavily. "This sort of thing can't be, you know," he said. A man can't be used in this fashion. You have got no right; you have got no power."

"My power," said Madame de Bellegarde, "is in my children's obedience."

"In their fear, your daughter said. There is something very strange in it. Why should your daughter be afraid of you?" added Newman, after looking a moment at the old lady. "There is some foul play."

The marquise met his gaze without flinching, and as if she did not hear or heed what he said. "I did my best," she said, quietly. "I could endure it no longer."

"It was a bold experiment!" said the marquis.

Newman felt disposed to walk to him, clutch his neck with his fingers and press his windpipe with his thumb. "I needn't tell you how you strike me," he said; "of course you know that. But I should think you would be afraid of your friends—all those people you introduced me to the other night. There were some very nice people among them; you may depend upon it there were some honest men and women."

"Our friends approve us," said M. de Bellegarde, "there is not a family among them that would have acted otherwise. And however that may be, we take the cue from no one. The Bellegardes have been used to set the example, not to wait for it."

"You would have waited long before any one would have set you such an example as this," exclaimed Newman. "Have I done anything wrong?" he demanded. "Have I given you reason to change your opinion? Have you found out anything against me? I can't imagine."

"Our opinion," said Madame de Bellegarde, "is quite the same as at first—exactly. We have no ill-will towards yourself; we are very far from accusing you of misconduct. Since your relations with us began you have been, I frankly confess, less—less peculiar than I expected. It is not your disposition that we object to, it is your antecedents. We really cannot reconcile ourselves to a commercial person. We fancied in an evil hour that we could; it was a great misfortune. We determined to persevere to the end, and to give you every advantage. I was resolved that you should have no reason to accuse me of want of loyalty. We let the thing certainly go very far; we introduced you to our friends. To tell the truth, it was that, I think, that broke me down. I succumbed to the scene that took place on Thursday night in these rooms. You must excuse me if what I say is disagreeable to you, but we cannot release ourselves without an explanation."

"There can be no better proof of our good faith," said the marquis, "than our committing ourselves to you in the eyes of the world the other evening. We endeavored to bind ourselves—to tie our hands, as it were."

"But it was that," added his mother, "that opened our eyes and broke our bonds. We should have been most uncomfortable! You know," she added in a moment, "that you were forewarned. I told you we were very proud."

Newman took up his hat and began mechanically to smooth it; the very fierceness of his scorn kept him from speaking. "You are not proud enough," he observed at last.

"In all this matter," said the marquis, smiling, "I really see nothing but our humility."

"Let us have no more discussion than is necessary," resumed Madame de Bellegarde. "My daughter told you everything when she said she gave you up."

"I am not satisfied about your daughter," said Newman; "I want to know what you did to her. It is all very easy talking about authority and saying you commanded her. She didn't accept me blindly, and she wouldn't have given me up blindly. Not that I believe yet she has really given me up; she will talk it over with me. But you have frightened her, you have bullied her, you have *hurt* her. What was it you did to her?"

"I did very little!" said Madame de Bellegarde in a tone which gave Newman a chill when he afterwards remembered it.

"Let me remind you that we offered you these explanations," the marquis observed, "with the express understanding that you should abstain from violence of language."

"I am not violent," Newman answered, "it is you who are violent! But I don't know that I have much more to say to you. What you expect of me, apparently, is to go my way, thanking you for favors received, and promising never to trouble you again."

"We expect of you to act like a clever man," said Madame de Bellegarde. "You have shown yourself that already, and what we have done is altogether based upon your being so. When one must submit, one must. Since my daughter absolutely withdraws, what will be the use of your making a noise?"

"It remains to be seen whether your daughter absolutely withdraws. Your daughter and I are still very good friends; nothing is changed in that. As I say, I will talk it over with her."

"That will be of no use," said the old lady. "I know my daughter well enough to know that words spoken as she just now spoke to you are final. Besides, she has promised me."

"I have no doubt her promise is worth a great deal more than your own," said Newman; "nevertheless I don't give her up."

"Just as you please! But if she won't even see you,—and she won't,—your constancy must remain purely Platonic."

Poor Newman was feigning a greater confidence than he felt. Madame de Cintré's strange intensity had in fact struck a chill to his heart; her face, still impressed upon his vision, had been a terribly vivid image of renunciation. He felt sick, and suddenly helpless. He turned away and stood for a moment with his hand on the door; then he faced about and after the briefest hesitation broke out with a different accent. "Come, think of what this must be to me, and let her alone! Why should you object to me so—what's the matter with me? I can't hurt you, I wouldn't if I could. I'm the most unobjectionable fellow in the world. What if I am a commercial person? What under the sun do you mean? A commercial person? I will be any sort of a person you want. I never talked to you about business. Let her go, and I will ask no questions. I will take her away, and you shall never see me or hear of me again. I will stay in America if you like. I'll sign a paper promising never to come back to Europe! All I want is not to lose her!"

Madame de Bellegarde and her son exchanged a glance of lucid irony, and Urbian said, "My dear sir, what you propose is hardly an improvement. We have not the slightest objection to seeing you, as an amiable foreigner, and we have every reason for not wishing to be eternally separated from my sister. We object to the marriage; and in that way," and M. de Bellegarde gave a small, thin laugh, "she would be more married than ever."

"Well, then," said Newman, "where is this place of yours— Fleurières? I know it is near some old city on a hill."

"Precisely. Poitiers is on a hill," said Madame de Bellegarde. "I don't know how old it is. We are not afraid to tell you."

"It is Poitiers, is it? Very good," said Newman. "I shall immediately follow Madame de Cintré."

"The trains after this hour won't serve you," said Urbain.

"I shall hire a special train!"

"That will be a very silly waste of money," said Madame de Bellegarde.

"It will be time enough to talk about waste three days hence," Newman answered; and clapping his hat on his head, he departed.

He did not immediately start for Fleurières; he was too stunned and wounded for consecutive action. He simply walked; he walked straight before him, following the river, till he got out of the *enceinte* of Paris. He had a burning, tingling sense of personal outrage. He had never in his life received so absolute a check; he had never been pulled up, or, as he would have said, "let down," so short; and he found the sensation intolerable; he strode along, tapping the trees and lamp-posts fiercely with his stick and inwardly raging. To lose Madame de Cintré after he had taken such jubilant and triumphant possession of her was as great an affront to his pride as it was an injury to his happiness. And to lose her by the interference and the dictation of others, by an impudent old woman and a pretentious fop stepping in with their "authority"! It was too preposterous, it was too pitiful. Upon what he deemed the unblushing treachery of the Bellegardes Newman wasted little thought; he consigned it, once for all, to eternal perdition. But the treachery of Madame de Cintré herself amazed and confounded him; there was a key to the mystery, of course, but he groped for it in vain. Only three days had elapsed since she stood beside him in the starlight, beautiful and tranquil as the trust with which he had inspired her, and told him that she was happy in the prospect of their marriage. What was the meaning of the change? of what infernal potion had she tasted? Poor Newman had a terrible apprehension that she had really changed. His very admiration for her attached the idea of force and weight to her rupture. But he did not rail at her as false, for he was sure she was unhappy. In his walk he had crossed one of the bridges of the Seine, and he still followed, unheedingly, the long, unbroken quay. He had left Paris behind him, and he was almost in the country; he was in the pleasant suburb of Auteuil. He stopped at last, looked around him without seeing or caring for its pleasantness, and then slowly turned and at a slower pace retraced his steps. When he came abreast of the fantastic embankment known as the Trocadero, he reflected, through his throbbing pain, that he was near Mrs. Tristram's dwelling, and that Mrs. Tristram, on particular occasions, had much of a woman's kindness in her utter-

ance. He felt that he needed to pour out his ire, and he took the road
to her house. Mrs. Tristram was at home and alone, and as soon as
she had looked at him, on his entering the room, she told him that
she knew what he had come for. Newman sat down heavily, in
silence, looking at her.

"They have backed out!" she said. "Well, you may think it
strange, but I felt something the other night in the air." Presently
he told her his story; she listened, with her eyes fixed on him. When
he had finished she said quietly, "They want her to marry Lord
Deepmere." Newman stared. He did not know that she knew anything about Lord Deepmere. "But I don't think she will," Mrs.
Tristram added.

"*She* marry that poor little cub!" cried Newman. "Oh, Lord! And
yet, why did she refuse me?"

"But that isn't the only thing," said Mrs. Tristram. "They really
couldn't endure you any longer. They had overrated their courage.
I must say, to give the devil his due, that there is something rather
fine in that. It was your commercial quality in the abstract they
couldn't swallow. That is really aristocratic. They wanted your
money, but they have given you up for an idea."

Newman frowned most ruefully, and took up his hat again. "I
thought you would encourage me!" he said, with almost childlike
sadness.

"Excuse me," she answered very gently. "I feel none the less
sorry for you, especially as I am at the bottom of your troubles.
I have not forgotten that I suggested the marriage to you. I don't
believe that Madame de Cintré has any intention of marrying Lord
Deepmere. It is true he is not younger than she, as he looks. He is
thirty-three years old; I looked in the Peerage. But no—I can't
believe her so horribly, cruelly false."

"Please say nothing against her," said Newman.

"Poor woman, she *is* cruel. But of course you will go after her
and you will plead powerfully. Do you know that as you are now,"
Mrs. Tristram pursued, with characteristic audacity of comment,
"you are extremely eloquent, even without speaking? To resist you
a woman must have a very fixed idea in her head. I wish I had done
you a wrong, that you might come to me in that fine fashion! But
go to Madame de Cintré at any rate, and tell her that she is a puzzle
even to me. I am very curious to see how far family discipline
will go."

Newman sat a while longer, leaning his elbows on his knees

and his head in his hands, and Mrs. Tristram continued to temper charity with philosophy and compassion with criticism. At last she inquired, "And what does the Count Valentin say to it?" Newman started; he had not thought of Valentin and his errand on the Swiss frontier since the morning. The reflection made him restless again, and he took his leave. He went straight to his apartment, where, upon the table of the vestibule, he found a telegram. It ran (with the date and place) as follows: "I am seriously ill; please to come to me as soon as possible. V. B." Newman groaned at this miserable news, and at the necessity of deferring his journey to the Château de Fleurières. But he wrote to Madame de Cintré these few lines; they were all he had time for:—

"I don't give you up, and I don't really believe you give me up. I don't understand it, but we shall clear it up together. I can't follow you to-day, as I am called to see a friend at a distance who is very ill, perhaps dying. But I shall come to you as soon as I can leave my friend. Why shouldn't I say that he is your brother? C. N."

After this he had only time to catch the night express to Geneva.

CHAPTER XIX

NEWMAN POSSESSED a remarkable talent for sitting still when it was necessary, and he had an opportunity to use it on his journey to Switzerland. The successive hours of the night brought him no sleep, but he sat motionless in his corner of the railway-carriage, with his eyes closed, and the most observant of his fellow-travelers might have envied him his apparent slumber. Toward morning slumber really came, as an effect of mental rather than of physical fatigue. He slept for a couple of hours, and at last, waking, found his eyes resting upon one of the snow-powdered peaks of the Jura, behind which the sky was just reddening with the dawn. But he saw neither the cold mountain nor the warm sky; his consciousness began to throb again, on the very instant, with a sense of his wrong. He got out of the train half an hour before it reached Geneva, in the cold morning twilight, at the station indicated in Valentin's telegram. A drowsy station-master was on the platform with a lantern, and the hood of his overcoat over his head, and near him stood a gentleman who advanced to meet Newman. This personage was a man of forty, with a tall, lean figure, a sallow face, a dark eye, a neat mustache, and a pair of fresh gloves. He took off his hat, looking very grave, and pronounced Newman's name. Our hero assented and said, "You are M. de Bellegarde's friend?"

"I unite with you in claiming that sad honor," said the gentleman. "I had placed myself at M. de Bellegarde's service in this melancholy affair, together with M. de Grosjoyaux, who is now at his bedside. M. de Grosjoyaux, I believe, has had the honor of meeting you in Paris, but as he is a better nurse than I he remained with our poor friend. Bellegarde has been eagerly expecting you."

"And how is Bellegarde?" said Newman. "He was badly hit?"

"The doctor has condemned him; we brought a surgeon with us. But he will die in the best sentiments. I sent last evening for the curé of the nearest French village, who spent an hour with him. The curé was quite satisfied."

"Heaven forgive us!" groaned Newman. "I would rather the doctor were satisfied! And can he see me—shall he know me?"

"When I left him, half an hour ago, he had fallen asleep, after a feverish, wakeful night. But we shall see." And Newman's companion proceeded to lead the way out of the station to the village, explaining as he went that the little party was lodged in the humblest of Swiss inns, where, however, they had succeeded in making M. de Bellegarde much more comfortable than could at first have been expected. "We are old companions in arms," said Valentin's second; "it is not the first time that one of us has helped the other to lie easily. It is a very nasty wound, and the nastiest thing about it is that Bellegarde's adversary was no shot. He put his bullet where he could. It took it into its head to walk straight into Bellegarde's left side, just below the heart."

As they picked their way in the gray, deceptive dawn, between the manure-heaps of the village street, Newman's new acquaintance narrated the particulars of the duel. The conditions of the meeting had been that if the first exchange of shots should fail to satisfy one of the two gentlemen, a second should take place. Valentin's first bullet had done exactly what Newman's companion was convinced he had intended it to do; it had grazed the arm of M. Stanislas Kapp, just scratching the flesh. M. Kapp's own projectile, meanwhile, had passed at ten good inches from the person of Valentin. The representatives of M. Stanislas had demanded another shot, which was granted. Valentin had then fired aside and the young Alsatian had done effective execution. "I saw, when we met him on the ground," said Newman's informant, "that he was not going to be *commode*. It is a kind of bovine temperament." Valentin had immediately been installed at the inn, and M. Stanislas and his friends had withdrawn to regions unknown. The police authorities of the canton had waited upon the party at the inn, had been extremely majestic, and had drawn up a long *procès-verbal;* but it was probable that they would wink at so very gentlemanly a bit of bloodshed. Newman asked whether a message had not been sent to Valentin's family, and learned that up to a late hour on the preceding evening Valentin had opposed it. He had refused to believe his wound was dangerous. But after his interview with the curé he had consented, and a telegram had been dispatched to his mother. "But the marquise had better hurry!" said Newman's conductor.

"Well, it's an abominable affair!" said Newman. "That's all I have to say!" To say this, at least, in a tone of infinite disgust, was an irresistible need.

"Ah, you don't approve?" questioned his conductor, with curious urbanity.

"Approve?" cried Newman. "I wish that when I had him there, night before last, I had locked him up in my *cabinet de toilette!*"

Valentin's late second opened his eyes, and shook his head up and down two or three times, gravely, with a little flute-like whistle. But they had reached the inn, and a stout maid-servant in a night-cap was at the door with a lantern, to take Newman's traveling-bag from the porter who trudged behind him. Valentin was lodged on the ground-floor at the back of the house, and Newman's companion went along a stone-faced passage and softly opened a door. Then he beckoned to Newman, who advanced and looked into the room, which was lighted by a single shaded candle. Beside the fire sat M. de Grosjoyaux asleep in his dressing-gown—a little plump, fair man whom Newman had seen several times in Valentin's company. On the bed lay Valentin, pale and still, with his eyes closed—a figure very shocking to Newman, who had seen it hitherto awake to its finger tips. M. de Grosjoyaux's colleague pointed to an open door beyond, and whispered that the doctor was within, keeping guard. So long as Valentin slept, or seemed to sleep, of course Newman could not approach him; so our hero withdrew for the present, committing himself to the care of the half-waked *bonne.* She took him to a room above-stairs, and introduced him to a bed on which a magnified bolster, in yellow calico, figured as a counterpane. Newman lay down, and, in spite of his counterpane, slept for three or four hours. When he awoke, the morning was advanced and the sun was filling his window, and he heard, outside of it, the clucking

of hens. While he was dressing there came to his door a messenger
from M. de Grosjoyaux and his companion proposing that he should
breakfast with them. Presently he went down-stairs to the little
stone-paved dining-room, where the maid-servant, who had taken
off her night-cap, was serving the repast. M. de Grosjoyaux was
there, surprisingly fresh for a gentleman who had been playing
sick-nurse half the night, rubbing his hands and watching the
breakfast table attentively. Newman renewed acquaintance with
him, and learned that Valentin was still sleeping; the surgeon, who
had had a fairly tranquil night, was at present sitting with him.
Before M. de Grosjoyaux's associate reappeared, Newman learned
that his name was M. Ledoux, and that Bellegarde's acquaintance
with him dated from the days when they served together in the
Pontifical Zouaves. M. Ledoux was the nephew of a distinguished
Ultramontane bishop. At last the bishop's nephew came in with a
toilet in which an ingenious attempt at harmony with the peculiar
situation was visible, and with a gravity tempered by a decent
deference to the best breakfast that the Croix Helvétique had ever
set forth. Valentin's servant, who was allowed only in scanty
measure the honor of watching with his master, had been lending a
light Parisian hand in the kitchen. The two Frenchmen did their
best to prove that if circumstances might overshadow, they could
not really obscure, the national talent for conversation, and M.
Ledoux delivered a neat little eulogy on poor Bellegarde, whom he
pronounced the most charming Englishman he had ever known.

"Do you call him an Englishman?" Newman asked.

M. Ledoux smiled a moment and then made an epigram. "*C'est plus
qu'un Anglais—c'est un Anglomane!*" Newman said soberly that he
had never noticed it; and M. de Grosjoyaux remarked that it was
really too soon to deliver a funeral oration upon poor Bellegarde.
"Evidently," said M. Ledoux. "But I couldn't help observing this
morning to Mr. Newman that when a man has taken such excellent
measures for his salvation as our dear friend did last evening, it seems
almost a pity he should put it in peril again by returning to the
world." M. Ledoux was a great Catholic, and Newman thought
him a queer mixture. His countenance, by daylight, had a sort of
amiably saturnine cast; he had a very large thin nose, and looked
like a Spanish picture. He appeared to think dueling a very perfect
arrangement, provided, if one should get hit, one could promptly
see the priest. He seemed to take a great satisfaction in Valentin's
interview with the curé, and yet his conversation did not at all

indicate a sanctimonious habit of mind. M. Ledoux had evidently a high sense of the becoming, and was prepared to be urbane and tasteful on all points. He was always furnished with a smile (which pushed his mustache up under his nose) and an explanation. *Savoir-vivre*—knowing how to live—was his specialty, in which he included knowing how to die; but, as Newman reflected, with a good deal of dumb irritation, he seemed disposed to delegate to others the application of his learning on this latter point. M. de Grosjoyaux was of quite another complexion, and appeared to regard his friend's theological unction as the sign of an inaccessibly superior mind. He was evidently doing his utmost, with a kind of jovial tenderness, to make life agreeable to Valentin to the last, and help him as little as possible to miss the Boulevard des Italiens; but what chiefly occupied his mind was the mystery of a bungling brewer's son making so neat a shot. He himself could snuff a candle, etc., and yet he confessed that he could not have done better than this. He hastened to add that on the present occasion he would have made a point of not doing so well. It was not an occasion for that sort of murderous work, *que diable!* He would have picked out some quiet fleshy spot and just tapped it with a harmless ball. M. Stanislas Kapp had been deplorably heavy-handed; but really, when the world had come to that pass that one granted a meeting to a brewer's son! . . . This was M. de Grosjoyaux's nearest approach to a generalization. He kept looking through the window, over the shoulder of M. Ledoux, at a slender tree which stood at the end of a lane, opposite to the inn, and seemed to be measuring its distance from his extended arm and secretly wishing that, since the subject had been introduced, propriety did not forbid a little speculative pistol practice.

Newman was in no humor to enjoy good company. He could neither eat nor talk; his soul was sore with grief and anger, and the weight of his double sorrow was intolerable. He sat with his eyes fixed upon his plate, counting the minutes, wishing at one moment that Valentin would see him and leave him free to go in quest of Madame de Cintré and his lost happiness, and mentally calling himself a vile brute the next, for the impatient egotism of the wish. He was very poor company, himself, and even his acute preoccupation and his general lack of the habit of pondering the impression he produced did not prevent him from reflecting that his companions must be puzzled to see how poor Bellegarde came to take such a fancy to this taciturn Yankee that he must needs have him at his

death-bed. After breakfast he strolled forth alone into the village
and looked at the fountain, the geese, the open barn doors, the
brown, bent old women, showing their hugely darned stocking-heels
at the ends of their slowly-clicking sabots, and the beautiful view
of snowy Alp and purple Jura at either end of the little secret. The
day was brilliant; early spring was in the air and the sunshine, and
the winter's damp was trickling out of the cottage eaves. It was
birth and brightness for all nature, even for chirping chickens and
waddling goslings, and it was to be death and burial for poor, foolish,
generous, delightful Bellegarde. Newman walked as far as the
village church, and went into the small grave-yard beside it, where
he sat down and looked at the awkward tablets which were planted
around. They were all sordid and hideous, and Newman could feel
nothing but the hardness and coldness of death. He got up and
came back to the inn, where he found M. Ledoux having coffee and
a cigarette at a little green table which he had caused to be carried
into the small garden. Newman, learning that the doctor was still
sitting with Valentin, asked M. Ledoux if he might not be allowed
to relieve him; he had a great desire to be useful to his poor friend.
This was easily arranged; the doctor was very glad to go to bed.
He was a youthful and rather jaunty practitioner, but he had a
clever face, and the ribbon of the Legion of Honor in his button-
hole; Newman listened attentively to the instructions he gave him
before retiring, and took mechanically from his hand a small volume
which the surgeon recommended as a help to wakefulness, and
which turned out to be an old copy of "Faublas." Valentin was still
lying with his eyes closed, and there was no visible change in his
condition. Newman sat down near him, and for a long time narrowly watched him. Then his eyes wandered away with his thoughts
upon his own situation, and rested upon the chain of the Alps,
disclosed by the drawing of the scant white cotton curtain of the
window, through which the sunshine passed and lay in squares upon
the red-tiled floor. He tried to interweave his reflections with hope,
but he only half succeeded. What had happened to him seemed to
have, in its violence and audacity, the force of a real calamity—the
strength and insolence of Destiny herself. It was unnatural and
monstrous, and he had no arms against it. At last a sound struck upon
the stillness, and he heard Valentin's voice.

"It can't be about *me* you are pulling that long face!" He found,
when he turned, that Valentin was lying in the same position; but
his eyes were open, and he was even trying to smile. It was with a

very slender strength that he returned the pressure of Newman's hand. "I have been watching you for a quarter of an hour," Valentin went on; "you have been looking as black as thunder. You are greatly disgusted with me, I see. Well, of course! So am I!"

"Oh, I shall not scold you," said Newman. "I feel too badly. And how are you getting on?"

"Oh, I'm getting off! They have quite settled that; haven't they?"

"That's for you to settle; you can get well if you try," said Newman, with resolute cheerfulness.

"My dear fellow, how can I try? Trying is violent exercise, and that sort of thing isn't in order for a man with a hole in his side as big as your hat, that begins to bleed if he moves a hair's-breadth. I knew you would come," he continued; "I knew I should wake up and find you here; so I'm not surprised. But last night I was very impatient. I didn't see how I could keep still until you came. It was a matter of keeping still, just like this; as still as a mummy in his case. You talk about trying; I tried that! Well, here I am yet—these twenty hours. It seems like twenty days." Bellegarde talked slowly and feebly, but distinctly enough. It was visible, however, that he was in extreme pain, and at last he closed his eyes. Newman begged him to remain silent and spare himself; the doctor had left urgent orders. "Oh," said Valentin, "let us eat and drink, for to-morrow—to-morrow"—and he paused again. "No, not to-morrow, perhaps, but to-day. I can't eat and drink, but I can talk. What's to be gained, at this pass, by renun—renunciation? I mustn't use such big words. I was always a chatterer; Lord, how I have talked in my day!"

"That's a reason for keeping quiet now," said Newman. "We know how well you talk, you know."

But Valentin, without heeding him, went on in the same weak, dying drawl. "I wanted to see you because you have seen my sister. Does she know—will she come?"

Newman was embarrassed. "Yes, by this time she must know."

"Didn't you tell her?" Valentin asked. And then, in a moment, "Didn't you bring me any message from her?" His eyes rested upon Newman's with a certain soft keenness.

"I didn't see her after I got your telegram," said Newman. "I wrote to her."

"And she sent you no answer?"

Newman was obliged to reply that Madame de Cintré had left Paris. "She went yesterday to Fleurières."

"Yesterday—to Fleurières? Why did she go to Fleurières? What day is this? What day was yesterday? Ah, then I shan't see her," said Valentin, sadly. "Fleurières is too far!" And then he closed his eyes again. Newman sat silent, summoning pious invention to his aid, but he was relieved at finding that Valentin was apparently too weak to reason or to be curious. Bellegarde, however, presently went on. "And my mother—and my brother—will they come? Are they at Fleurières?"

"They were in Paris, but I didn't see them, either," Newman answered. "If they received your telegram in time, they will have started this morning. Otherwise they will be obliged to wait for the night-express, and they will arrive at the same hour as I did."

"They won't thank me—they won't thank me," Valentin murmured. "They will pass an atrocious night, and Urbain doesn't like the early morning air. I don't remember ever in my life to have seen him before noon—before breakfast. No one ever saw him. We don't know how he is then. Perhaps he's different. Who knows? Posterity, perhaps, will know. That's the time he works, in his *cabinet*, at the history of the Princesses. But I had to send for them—hadn't I? And then I want to see my mother sit there where you sit, and say good-by to her. Perhaps, after all, I don't know her, and she will have some surprise for me. Don't think you know her yet, yourself; perhaps she may surprise *you*. But if I can't see Claire, I don't care for anything. I have been thinking of it—and in my dreams, too. Why did she go to Fleurières to-day? She never told me. What has happened? Ah, she ought to have guessed I was here—this way. It is the first time in her life she ever disappointed me. Poor Claire!"

"You know we are not man and wife quite yet,—your sister and I," said Newman. "She doesn't yet account to me for all her actions." And, after a fashion, he smiled.

Valentin looked at him a moment. "Have you quarreled?"

"Never, never, never!" Newman exclaimed.

"How happily you say that!" said Valentin. "You are going to be happy—*va!*" In answer to this stroke of irony, none the less powerful for being so unconscious, all poor Newman could do was to give a helpless and transparent stare. Valentin continued to fix him with his own rather over-bright gaze, and presently he said, "But something *is* the matter with you. I watched you just now; you haven't a bridegroom's face."

"My dear fellow," said Newman, "how can I show *you* a bridegroom's face? If you think I enjoy seeing you lie there and not being able to help you"—

"Why, you are just the man to be cheerful; don't forfeit your rights! I'm a proof of your wisdom. When was a man ever gloomy when he could say, 'I told you so?' You told me so, you know. You did what you could about it. You said some very good things; I have thought them over. But, my dear friend, I was right, all the same. This is the regular way."

"I didn't do what I ought," said Newman. "I ought to have done something else."

"For instance?"

"Oh, something or other. I ought to have treated you as a small boy."

"Well, I'm a very small boy, now," said Valentin. "I'm rather less than an infant. An infant is helpless, but it's generally voted promising. I'm not promising, eh? Society can't lose a less valuable member."

Newman was strongly moved. He got up and turned his back upon his friend and walked away to the window, where he stood looking out, but only vaguely seeing. "No, I don't like the look of your back," Valentin continued. "I have always been an observer of backs; yours is quite out of sorts."

Newman returned to his bedside and begged him to be quiet. "Be quiet and get well," he said. "That's what you must do. Get well and help me."

"I told you you were in trouble! How can I help you?" Valentin asked.

"I'll let you know when you are better. You were always curious; there is something to get well for!" Newman answered, with resolute animation.

Valentin closed his eyes and lay a long time without speaking. He seemed even to have fallen asleep. But at the end of half an hour he began to talk again. "I am rather sorry about that place in the bank. Who knows but that I might have become another Rothschild? But I wasn't meant for a banker; bankers are not so easy to kill. Don't you think I have been very easy to kill? It's not like a serious man. It's really very mortifying. It's like telling your hostess you must go, when you count upon her begging you to stay, and then finding she does no such thing. 'Really—so soon? You've only just come!' Life doesn't make me any such polite little speech."

Newman for some time said nothing, but at last he broke out. "It's a bad case—it's a bad case—it's the worst case I ever met. I don't want to say anything unpleasant, but I can't help it. I've seen men dying before—and I've seen men shot. But it always seemed more natural; they were not so clever as you. Damnation—damnation! You might have done something better than this. It's about the meanest winding-up of a man's affairs that I can imagine!"

Valentin feebly waved his hand to and fro. "Don't insist—don't insist! It is mean—decidedly mean. For you see at the bottom—down at the bottom, in a little place as small as the end of a wine-funnel—I agree with you!"

A few moments after this the doctor put his head through the half-opened door and, perceiving that Valentin was awake, came in and felt his pulse. He shook his head and declared that he had talked too much—ten times too much. "Nonsense!" said Valentin; "a man sentenced to death can never talk too much. Have you never read an account of an execution in a newspaper? Don't they always set a lot of people at the prisoner—lawyers, reporters, priests—to make him talk? But it's not Mr. Newman's fault; he sits there as mum as a death's-head."

The doctor observed that it was time his patient's wound should be dressed again; MM. de Grosjoyaux and Ledoux, who had already witnessed this delicate operation, taking Newman's place as assistants. Newman withdrew and learned from his fellow-watchers that they had received a telegram from Urbain de Bellegarde to the effect that their message had been delivered in the Rue d l'Université too late to allow him to take the morning train, but that he would start with his mother in the evening. Newman wandered away into the village again, and walked about restlessly for two or three hours. The day seemed terribly long. At dusk he came back and dined with the doctor and M. Ledoux. The dressing of Valentin's wound had been a very critical operation; the doctor didn't really see how he was to endure a repetition of it. He then declared that he must beg of Mr. Newman to deny himself for the present the satisfaction of sitting with M. de Belegarde; more than any one else, apparently, he had the flattering but inconvenient privilege of exciting him. M. Ledoux, at this, swallowed a glass of wine in silence; he must have been wondering what the deuce Bellegarde found so exciting in the American.

Newman, after dinner, went up to his room, where he sat for a long time staring at his lighted candle, and thinking that Valentin was dying down-stairs. Late, when the candle had burnt low, there came a soft tap at his door. The doctor stood there with a candlestick and a shrug.

"He must amuse himself, still!" said Valentin's medical adviser.

"He insists upon seeing you, and I am afraid you must come. I think, at this rate, that he will hardly outlast the night."

Newman went back to Valentin's room, which he found lighted by a taper on the hearth. Valentin begged him to light a candle. "I want to see your face," he said. "They say you excite me," he went on, as Newman complied with this request, "and I confess I do feel excited. But it isn't you—it's my own thoughts. I have been thinking—thinking. Sit down there, and let me look at you again." Newman seated himself, folded his arms, and bent a heavy gaze upon his friend. He seemed to be playing a part, mechanically, in a lugubrious comedy. Valentin looked at him for some time. "Yes, this morning I was right; you have something on your mind heavier than Valentin de Bellegarde. Come, I'm a dying man and it's indecent to deceive me. Something happened after I left Paris. It was not for nothing that my sister started off at this season of the year for Fleurières. Why was it? It sticks in my crop. I have been thinking it over, and if you don't tell me I shall guess."

"I had better not tell you," said Newman. "It won't do you any good."

"If you think it will do me any good not to tell me, you are very much mistaken. There is trouble about your marriage."

"Yes," said Newman. "There is trouble about my marriage."

"Good!" And Valentin was silent again. "They have stopped it."

"They have stopped it," said Newman. Now that he had spoken out, he found a satisfaction in it which deepened as he went on. "Your mother and brother have broken faith. They have decided that it can't take place. They have decided that I am not good enough, after all. They have taken back their word. Since you insist, there it is!"

Valentin gave a sort of groan, lifted his hands a moment, and then let them drop.

"I am sorry not to have anything better to tell you about them," Newman pursued. "But it's not my fault. I was, indeed, very unhappy when your telegram reached me; I was quite upside down. You may imagine whether I feel any better now."

Valentin moaned gaspingly, as if his wound were throbbing. "Broken faith, broken faith!" he murmured. "And my sister—my sister?"

"Your sister is very unhappy; she has consented to give me up. I don't know why. I don't know what they have done to her; it must be something pretty bad. In justice to her you ought to know it.

They have made her suffer. I haven't seen her alone, but only before them! We had an interview yesterday morning. They came out, flat, in so many words. They told me to go about my business. It seems to me a very bad case. I'm angry, I'm sore, I'm sick."

Valentin lay there staring, with his eyes more brilliantly lighted, his lips soundlessly parted, and a flush of color in his pale face. Newman had never before uttered so many words in the plaintive key, but now, in speaking to Valentin in the poor fellow's extremity, he had a feeling that he was making his complaint somewhere within the presence of the power that men pray to in trouble; he felt his outgush of resentment as a sort of spiritual privilege.

"And Claire,"—said Bellegarde,—"Claire? She has given you up?"

"I don't really believe it," said Newman.

"No. don't believe it, don't believe it. She is gaining time; excuse her."

"I pity her!" said Newman.

"Poor Claire!" murmured Valentin. "But they—but they"—and he paused again. "You saw them; they dismissed you, face to face?"

"Face to face. They were very explicit."

"What did they say?"

"They said they couldn't stand a commercial person."

Valentin put out his hand and laid it upon Newman's arm. "And about their promise—their engagement with you?"

"They made a distinction. They said it was to hold good only until Madame de Cintré accepted me."

Valentin lay staring a while, and his flush died away. "Don't tell me any more," he said at last. "I'm ashamed."

"You? You are the soul of honor," said Newman simply.

Valentin groaned and turned away his head. For some time nothing more was said. Then Valentin turned back again and found a certain force to press Newman's arm. "It's very bad—very bad. When my people—when my race—come to that, it is time for me to withdraw. I believe in my sister; she will explain. Excuse her. If she can't—if she can't, forgive her. She has suffered. But for the others it is very bad—very bad. You take it very hard? No, it's a shame to make you say so." He closed his eyes and again there was a silence. Newman felt almost awed; he had evoked a more solemn spirit than he expected. Presently Valentin looked at him again, removing his hand from his arm. "I apologize," he said. "Do you understand? Here on my death-bed. I apologize for my family. For my mother. For my brother. For the ancient house of Bellegarde. *Voilà!"* he added, softly.

Newman for all answer took his hand and pressed it with a world of kindness. Valentin remained quiet, and at the end of half an hour the doctor softly came in. Behind him, through the half-open door, Newman saw the two questioning faces of MM. de Grosjoyaux and Ledoux. The doctor laid his hand on Valentin's wrist and sat looking at him. He gave no sign and the two gentlemen came in, M. Ledoux having first beckoned to some one outside. This was M. le curé, who carried in his hand an object unknown to Newman, and covered with a white napkin. M. le curé was short, round, and red: he advanced, pulling off his little black cap to Newman, and deposited his burden on the table; and then he sat down in the best arm-chair, with his hands folded across his person. The other gentlemen had exchanged glances which expressed unanimity as to the timeliness of their presence. But for a long time Valentin neither spoke nor moved. It was Newman's belief, afterwards, that M. le curé went to sleep. At last, abruptly, Valentin pronounced Newman's name. His friend went to him, and he said in French, "You are not alone. I want to speak to you alone." Newman looked at the doctor, and the doctor looked at the curé, who looked back at him; and then the doctor and the curé, together, gave a shrug. "Alone—for five minutes," Valentin repeated. "Please leave us."

The curé took up his burden again and led the way out, followed by his companions. Newman closed the door behind them and came back to Valentin's bedside. Bellegarde had watched all this intently. "It's very bad, it's very bad," he said, after Newman had seated himself close to him. "The more I think of it the worse it is."

"Oh, don't think of it," said Newman.

But Valentin went on, without heeding him. "Even if they should come round again, the shame—the baseness—is there."

"Oh, they won't come round!" said Newman.

"Well, you can make them."

"Make them?"

"I can tell you something—a great secret—an immense secret. You can use it against them—frighten them, force them."

"A secret!" Newman repeated. The idea of letting Valentin, on his death-bed, confide him an "immense secret" shocked him, for the moment, and made him draw back. It seemed an illicit way of arriving at information, and even had a vague analogy with listening at a key-hole. Then, suddenly, the thought of "forcing" Madame de

Bellegarde and her son became attractive, and Newman bent his head closer to Valentin's lips. For some time, however, the dying man said nothing more. He only lay and looked at his friend with his kindled, expanded, troubled eye, and Newman began to believe that he had spoken in delirium. But at last he said,—

"There was something done—something done at Fleurières. It was foul play. My father—something happened to him. I don't know; I have been ashamed—afraid to know. But I know there is something. My mother knows—Urbain knows."

"Something happened to your father?" said Newman, urgently.

Valentin looked at him, still more wide-eyed. "He didn't get well."

"Get well of what?"

But the immense effort which Valentin had made, first to decide to utter these words and then to bring them out, appeared to have taken his last strength. He lapsed again into silence, and Newman sat watching him. "Do you understand?" he began again, presently. "At Fleurières. You can find out. Mrs. Bread knows. Tell her I begged you to ask her. Then tell them that, and see. It may help you. If not, tell every one. It will—it will"—here Valentin's voice sank to the feeblest murmur—"it will avenge you!"

The words died away in a long, soft groan. Newman stood up, deeply impressed, not knowing what to say; his heart was beating violently. "Thank you," he said at last. "I am much obliged." But Valentin seemed not to hear him; he remained silent, and his silence continued. At last Newman went and opened the door. M. le curé reëntered, bearing his sacred vessel and followed by the three gentlemen and by Valentin's servant. It was almost processional.

CHAPTER XX

VALENTIN DE BELLEGARDE died, tranquilly, just as the cold, faint March dawn began to illumine the faces of the little knot of friends gathered about his bedside. An hour afterwards Newman left the inn and drove to Geneva; he was naturally unwilling to be present at the arrival of Madame de Bellegarde and her first-born. At Geneva, for the moment, he remained. He was like a man who has had a fall and wants to sit still and count his bruises. He instantly wrote to Madame de Cintré, relating to her the circumstances of her brother's death— with certain exceptions—and asking her what was the earliest moment at which he might hope that she would consent to see him. M. Ledoux had told him that he had reason to know that Valentin's will—Bellegarde had a great deal of elegant personal property to dispose of—contained a request that he should be buried near his father in the church-yard of Fleurières, and Newman intended that the state of his own relations with the family should not deprive him of the satisfaction of helping to pay the last earthly honors to the best fellow in the world. He reflected that Valentin's friendship was older than Urbain's enmity, and that at a funeral it was easy to escape notice. Madame de Cintré's answer to his letter enabled him to time his arrival at Fleurières. This answer was very brief; it ran as follows:—

"I thank you for your letter, and for your being with Valentin. It is a most inexpressible sorrow to me that I was not. To see you will be nothing but a distress to me; there is no need, therefore, to wait for what you call brighter days. It is all one now, and I shall have no brighter days. Come when you please; only notify me first. My brother is to be buried here on Friday, and my family is to remain here. C. de C."

As soon as he received this letter Newman went straight to Paris and to Poitiers. The journey took him far southward, through green Touraine and across the far-shining Loire, into a country where the early spring deepened about him as he went. But he had never made a journey during which he heeded less what he would have called the lay of the land. He obtained lodging at the inn at Poitiers, and the next morning drove in a couple of hours to the village of Fleurières. But here, preoccupied though he was, he could not fail to notice the picturesqueness of the place. It was what the French call a *petit bourg;* it lay at the base of a sort of huge mound on the summit of which stood the crumbling ruins of a feudal castle, much of whose sturdy material, as well as that of the wall which dropped along the hill to inclose the clustered houses defensively, had been absorbed into the very substance of the village. The church was simply the former chapel of the castle, fronting upon its grass-grown court, which, however, was of generous enough width to have given up its quaintest corner to a little graveyard. Here the very headstones themselves seemed to sleep, as they slanted into the grass; the patient elbow of the rampart held them together on one side, and in front, far beneath their mossy lids, the green plains and blue distances stretched away. The way to church, up the hill, was impracticable to vehicles. It was lined with peasants, two or three rows deep, who stood watching old Madame de Bellegarde slowly ascend it, on the arm of her elder son, behind the pall-bearers of the other. Newman chose to lurk among the common mourners who murmured "Madame la Comtesse" as a tall figure veiled in black passed before them. He stood in the dusky little church while the service was going forward, but at the dismal tomb-side he turned away and walked down the hill. He went back to Poitiers, and spent two days in which patience and impatience were singularly commingled. On the third day he sent Madame de Cintré a note, saying that he would call upon her in the afternoon, and in accordance with this he again took his way to Fleurières. He left his vehicle at the tavern in the village street, and obeyed the simple instructions which were given him for finding the château.

"It is just beyond there," said the landlord, and pointed to the tree-tops of the park, above the opposite houses. Newman followed the first cross-road to the right—it was bordered with mouldy cottages—and in a few moments saw before him the peaked roofs of the towers. Advancing farther, he found himself before a vast iron gate, rusty and closed; here he paused a moment, looking through the bars. The château was near the road; this was at once its merit and its defect; but its aspect was extremely impressive. Newman learned afterwards, from a guide-book of the province, that it dated from the time of Henry IV. It presented to the wide, paved area which preceded it and which was edged with shabby farm-buildings an immense façade of dark time-stained brick, flanked by two low wings, each of which terminated in a little Dutch-looking pavilion capped with a fantastic roof. Two towers rose behind, and behind the towers was a mass of elms and beeches, now just faintly green. But the great feature was a wide, green river which washed the foundations of the château. The building rose from an island in the circling stream, so that this formed a perfect moat spanned by a two-arched bridge without a parapet. The dull brick walls, which here and there made a grand, straight sweep; the ugly little cupolas of the wings, the deep-set windows, the long, steep pinnacles of mossy slate, all mirrored themselves in the tranquil river. Newman rang at the gate, and was almost frightened at the tone with which a big rusty bell above his head replied to him. An old woman came out from the gate-house and opened the creaking portal just wide enough for him to pass, and he went in, across the dry, bare court and the little cracked white slabs of the causeway on the moat. At the door of the château he waited for some moments, and this gave him a chance to reflect that it was a melancholy place of residence. "It looks," said Newman to himself—and I give the comparison for what it is worth —"like a Chinese penitentiary." At last the door was opened by a servant whom he remembered to have seen in the Rue d l'Université. The man's dull face brightened as he perceived our hero, for Newman, for indefinable reasons, enjoyed the confidence of the liveried gentry. The footman led the way across a great central vestibule, with a pyramid of plants in tubs in the middle of glass doors all around, to what appeared to be the principal drawing-room of the château. Newman crossed the threshold of a room of superb proportions, which made him feel at first like a tourist with a guide-book and a cicerone awaiting a fee. But when his guide had left him alone, with the observation that he would call Madame la Comtesse, Newman perceived that the salon contained little that was remarkable save a dark ceiling with curiously carved rafters, some curtains of elaborate, antiquated tapestry, and a dark oaken floor, polished like a mirror. He waited some minutes, walking up and down; but at length, as he turned at the end of the room, he saw that Madame de Cintré had come in by a distant door. She wore a black dress, and she stood looking at him. As the length of the immense room lay between them he had time to look at her before they met in the middle of it.

He was dismayed at the change in her appearance. Pale, heavy-browed, almost haggard, with a sort of monastic rigidity in her dress, she had little but her pure features in common with the woman whose radiant good grace he had hitherto admired. She let her eyes rest on his own, and she let him take her hand; but her eyes looked like two rainy autumn moons, and her touch was portentously lifeless.

"I was at your brother's funeral," Newman said. "Then I waited three days. But I could wait no longer."

"Nothing can be lost or gained by waiting," said Madame de Cintré. "But it was very considerate of you to wait, wronged as you have been."

"I'm glad you think I have been wronged," said Newman, with that oddly humorous accent with which he often uttered words of the gravest meaning.

"Do I need to say so?" she asked. "I don't think I have wronged, seriously, many persons; certainly not consciously. To you, to whom I have done this hard and cruel thing, the only reparation I can make is to say, 'I know it, I feel it!' The reparation is pitifully small!"

"Oh, it's a great step forward!" said Newman, with a gracious smile of encouragement. He pushed a chair towards her and held it, looking at her urgently. She sat down, mechanically, and he seated himself near her; but in a moment he got up, restlessly, and stood before her. She remained seated, like a troubled creature who had passed through the stage of restlessness.

"I say nothing is to be gained by my seeing you," she went on, "and yet I am very glad you came. Now I can tell you what I feel. It is a selfish pleasure, but it is one of the last I shall have." And she paused, with her great misty eyes fixed upon him. "I know how I have deceived and injured you; I know how cruel and cowardly I have been. I see it as vividly as you do—I feel it to the ends of my fingers." And she unclasped her hands, which were locked together in her lap, lifted them, and dropped them at her side. "Anything that you may have said of me in your angriest passion is nothing to what I have said to myself."

"In my angriest passion," said Newman, "I have said nothing hard of you. The very worst thing I have said of you yet is that you are the loveliest of women." And he seated himself before her again, abruptly.

She flushed a little, but even her flush was pale. "That is because you think I will come back. But I will not come back. It is in that hope you have come here, I know; I am very sorry for you. I would do almost anything for you. To say that, after what I have done, seems simply impudent; but what can I say that will not seem impudent? To wrong you and apologize—that is easy enough. I should not have wronged you." She stopped a moment, looking at him, and motioned him to let her go on. "I ought never to have listened to you at first; that was the wrong. No good could come of it. I felt it, and yet I listened; that was your fault. I liked you too much; I believed in you."

"And don't you believe in me now?"

"More than ever. But now it doesn't matter. I have given you up."

Newman gave a powerful thump with his clenched fist upon his knee. "Why, why, why?" he cried. "Give me a reason—a decent reason. You are not a child—you are not a minor, nor an idiot. You are not obliged to drop me because your mother told you to. Such a reason isn't worthy of you."

"I know that; it's not worthy of me. But it's the only one I have to give. After all," said Madame de Cintré, throwing out her hands, "think me an idiot and forget me! That will be the simplest way."

Newman got up and walked away with a crushing sense that his cause was lost, and yet with an equal inability to give up fighting. He went to one of the great windows, and looked out at the stiffly embanked river and the formal gardens which lay beyond it. When he turned round, Madame de Cintré had risen; she stood there silent and passive. "You are not frank," said Newman; "you are not honest. Instead of saying that you are imbecile, you should say that other people are wicked. Your mother and your brother have been false and cruel; they have been so to me, and I am sure they have been so to you. Why do you try to shield them? Why do you sacrifice me to them? I'm not false; I'm not cruel. You don't know what you give up; I can tell you that—you don't. They bully you and plot about you; and I—I"— And he paused, holding out his hands. She turned away and began to leave him. "You told me the other day that you were afraid of your mother," he said, following her. "What did you mean?"

Madame de Cintré shook her head. "I remember; I was sorry afterwards."

"You were sorry when she came down and put on the thumbscrews. In God's name what *is* it she does to you?"

"Nothing. Nothing that you can understand. And now that I have given you up, I must not complain of her to you."

"That's no reasoning!" cried Newman. "Complain of her, on the contrary. Tell me all about it, frankly and trustfully, as you ought, and we will talk it over so satisfactorily that you won't give me up."

Madame de Cintré looked down some moments, fixedly; and then, raising her eyes, she said, "One good at least has come of this: I have made you judge me more fairly. You thought of me in a way that did me great honor; I don't know why you had taken it into your head. But it left me no loop-hole for escape—no chance to be the common, weak creature I am. It was not my fault; I warned you from the first. But I ought to have warned you more. I ought to have convinced you that I was doomed to disappoint you. But I I *was*, in a way, too proud. You see what my superiority amounts to, I hope!" she went on, raising her voice with a tremor which even then and there Newman thought beautiful. "I am too proud to be honest, I am not too proud to be faithless. I am timid and cold and selfish. I am afraid of being uncomfortable."

"And you call marrying me uncomfortable!" said Newman staring.

Madame de Cintré blushed a little and seemed to say that if begging his pardon in words was impudent, she might at least thus mutely express her perfect comprehension of his finding her conduct odious. "It is not marrying you; it is doing all that would go with it. It's the rupture, the defiance, the insisting upon being happy in my own way. What right have I to be happy when—when"— And she paused.

"When what?" said Newman.

"When others have been most unhappy!"

"What others?" Newman asked. "What have you to do with any others but me? Besides you said just now that you wanted happiness, and that you should find it by obeying your mother. You contradict yourself."

"Yes, I contradict myself; that shows you that I am not even intelligent."

"You are laughing at me!" cried Newman. "You are mocking me!"

She looked at him intently, and an observer might have said that she was asking herself whether she might not most quickly end their common pain by confessing that she was mocking him. "No; I am not," she presently said.

"Granting that you are not intelligent," he went on, "that you are weak, that you are common, that you are nothing that I have believed you were—what I ask of you is not a heroic effort, it is a very common effort. There is a great deal on my side to make it easy. The simple truth is that you don't care enough about me to make it."

"I am cold," said Madame de Cintré. "I am as cold as that flowing river."

Newman gave a great rap on the floor with his stick, and a long, grim laugh. "Good, good!" he cried. "You go altogether too far— you overshoot the mark. There isn't a woman in the world as bad as you would make yourself out. I see your game; it's what I said. You are blackening yourself to whiten others. You don't want to give me up, at all; you like me—you like me. I know you do; you have shown it, and I have felt it. After that, you may be as cold as you please! They have bullied you, I say; they have tortured you. It's an outrage, and I insist upon saving you from the extravagance of your own generosity. Would you chop off your hand if your mother requested it?"

Madame de Cintré looked a little frightened. "I spoke of my mother too blindly, the other day. I am my own mistress, by law and by her approval. She can do nothing to me; she has done nothing.

She has never alluded to those hard words I used about her."

"She has made you feel them, I'll promise you!" said Newman.

"It's my conscience that makes me feel them."

"Your conscience seems to me to be rather mixed!" exclaimed Newman, passionately.

"It has been in great trouble, but now it is very clear," said Madame de Cintré. "I don't give you up for any worldly advantage or for any worldly happiness."

"Oh, you don't give me up for Lord Deepmere, I know," said Newman. "I won't pretend, even to provoke you, that I think that. But that's what your mother and your brother wanted, and your mother, at that villainous ball of hers—I liked it at the time, but the very thought of it now makes me rabid—tried to push him on to make up to you."

"Who told you this?" said Madame de Cintré softly.

"Not Valentin. I observed it. I guessed it. I didn't know at the time that I was observing it, but it stuck in my memory. And afterwards, you recollect, I saw Lord Deepmere with you in the conservatory. You said then that you would tell me at another time what he had said to you."

"That was before—before *this*," said Madame de Cintré.

"It doesn't matter," said Newman; "and, besides, I think I know. He's an honest little Englishman. He came and told you what your mother was up to—that she wanted him to supplant me; not being a commercial person. If he would make you an offer she would undertake to bring you over and give me the slip. Lord Deepmore isn't very intellectual, so she had to spell it out to him. He said he admired you 'no end,' and that he wanted you to know it; but he didn't like being mixed up with that sort of underhand work, and he came to you and told tales. That was about the amount of it, wasn't it? And then you said you were perfectly happy."

"I don't see why we should talk of Lord Deepmere," said Madame de Cintré. "It was not for that you came here. And about my mother, it doesn't matter what you suspect and what you know. When once my mind has been made up, as it is now, I should not discuss these things. Discussing anything, now, is very idle. We must try and live each as we can. I believe you will be happy again; even, sometimes, when you think of me. When you do so, think this—that it was not easy, and that I did the best I could. I have things to reckon with that you don't know. I mean I have feelings. I must do as they force me—I must, I must. They would haunt me otherwise," she cried, with vehemence; "they would kill me!"

"I know what your feelings are: they are superstitions! They are the feeling that, after all, though I *am* a good fellow, I have been in business; the feeling that your mother's looks are law and your brother's words are gospel; that you all hang together, and that it's a part of the everlasting proprieties that they should have a hand in everything you do. It makes my blood boil. That *is* cold; you are right. And what I feel here," and Newman struck his heart and became more poetical than he knew, "is a glowing fire!"

A spectator less preoccupied than Madame de Cinté's distracted wooer would have felt sure from the first that her appealing calm of manner was the result of violent effort, in spite of which the tide of agitation was rapidly rising. On these last words of Newman's it overflowed, though at first she spoke low, for fear of her voice betraying her. "No. I was not right—I am not cold! I believe that if I am doing what seems so bad, it is not mere weakness and falseness. Mr. Newman, it's like a religion. I can't tell you—I can't! It's cruel of you to insist. I don't see why I shouldn't ask you to believe me— and pity me. It's like a religion. There's a curse upon the house; I don't know what—I don't know why—don't ask me. We must all bear it. I have been too selfish; I wanted to escape from it. You offered me a great chance—besides my liking you. It seemed good to change completely, to break, to go away. And then I admired you. But I can't—it has overtaken and come back to me." Her self-control had now completely abandoned her, and her words were broken with long sobs. "Why do such dreadful things happen to us —why is my brother Valentin killed, like a beast, in the midst of his youth and his gayety and his brightness and all that we loved him for? Why are there things I can't ask about—that I am afraid to know? Why are there places I can't look at, sounds I can't hear? Why is it given to me to choose, to decide, in a case so hard and so terrible as this? I am not meant for that—I am not made for boldness and defiance. I was made to be happy in a quiet, natural way." At this Newman gave a most expressive groan, but Madame de Cintré went on. "I was made to do gladly and gratefully what is expected of me. My mother has always been very good to me; that's all I can say. I must not judge her; I must not criticise her. If I did, it would come back to me. I can't change!"

"No," said Newman, bitterly; "*I* must change—if I break in two in the effort!"

"You are different. You are a man; you will get over it. You have all kinds of consolation. You were born—you were trained, to changes. Besides—besides, I shall always think of you."

"I don't care for that!" cried Newman. "You are cruel—you are terribly cruel. God forgive you! You may have the best reasons and the finest feelings in the world; that makes no difference. You are a mystery to me; I don't see how such hardness can go with such loveliness."

Madame de Cintré fixed him a moment with her swimming eyes. "You believe I am hard, then?"

Newman answered her look, and then broke out, "You are a perfect, faultless creature! Stay by me!"

"Of course I am hard," she went on. "Whenever we give pain we are hard. And we *must* give pain; that's the world,—the hateful, miserable world! Ah!" and she gave a long, deep sigh, "I can't even say I am glad to have known you—though I am. That too is to wrong you. I can say nothing that is not cruel. Therefore let us part, without more of this. Good-by!" And she put out her hand.

Newman stood and looked at it without taking it, and then raised his eyes to her face. He felt, himself, like shedding tears of rage. "What are you going to do?" he asked. "Where are you going?"

"Where I shall give no more pain and suspect no more evil. I am going out of the world."

"Out of the world?"

"I am going into a convent."

"Into a convent!" Newman repeated the words with the deepest dismay; it was as if she had said she was going into an hospital. "Into a convent—*you!*"

"I told you that it was not for my worldly advantage or pleasure I was leaving you."

But still Newman hardly understood. "You are going to be a nun," he went on, "in a cell—for life—with a gown and white veil?"

"A nun—a Carmelite nun," said Madame de Cintré. "For life, with God's leave."

The idea struck Newman as too dark and horrible for belief, and made him feel as he would have done if she had told him that she was going to mutilate her beautiful face, or drink some potion that would make her mad. He clasped his hands and began to tremble, visibly.

"Madame de Cintré, don't, don't!" he said. "I beseech you! On my knees, if you like, I'll beseech you."

She laid her hand upon his arm, with a tender, pitying, almost reassuring gesture. "You don't understand," she said. "You have wrong ideas. It's nothing horrible. It is only peace and safety. It is to be out of the world, where such troubles as this come to the innocent, to the best. And for life—that's the blessing of it! They can't begin again."

Newman dropped into a chair and sat looking at her with a long, inarticulate murmur. That this superb woman, in whom he had seen all human grace and household force, should turn from him and all the brightness that he offered her—him and his future and his fortune and his fidelity—to muffle herself in ascetic rags and entomb herself in a cell, was a confounding combination of the inexorable and the grotesque. As the image deepened before him the gortesque seemed to expand and overspread it; it was a reduction to the absurd of the trial to which he was subjected. "You—you a nun!" he exclaimed; "you with your beauty defaced—you behind locks and bars! Never, never, if I can prevent it!" And he sprang to his feet with a violent laugh.

"You can't prevent it," said Madame de Cintré, "and it ought—a little—to satisfy you. Do you suppose I will go on living in the world, still beside you, and yet not with you? It is all arranged. Good-by, good-by."

This time he took her hand, took it in both his own. "Forever?" he said. Her lips made an inaudible movement and his own uttered a deep imprecation. She closed her eyes, as if with the pain of hearing it; then he drew her towards him and clasped her to his breast. He kissed her white face; for an instant she resisted and for a moment she submitted; then, with force, she disengaged herself and hurried away over the long shining floor. The next moment the door closed behind her.

Newman made his way out as he could.

CHAPTER XXI

THERE IS a pretty public walk at Poitiers, laid out upon the crest of the high hill around which the little city clusters, planted with thick trees and looking down upon the fertile fields in which the old English princes fought for their right and held it. Newman paced up and down this quiet promenade for the greater part of the next day and let his eyes wander over the historic prospect; but he would have been sadly at a loss to tell you afterwards whether the latter was made up of coal-fields or of vineyards. He was wholly given up to his grievance, of which reflection by no means diminished the weight. He feared that Madame de Cintré was irretrievably lost; and yet, as he would have said himself, he didn't see his way clear to giving her up. He found it impossible to turn his back upon Fleurières and its inhabitants; it seemed to him that some germ of hope or reparation must lurk there somewhere, if he could only stretch his arm out far enough to pluck it. It was as if he had his hand on a door-knob and were closing his clenched fist upon it: he had thumped, he had called, he had pressed the door with his power-ful knee and shaken it with all his strength, and dead, damning si-lence had answered him. And yet something held him there—some-thing hardened the grasp of his fingers. Newman's satisfaction had been too intense, his whole plan too deliberate and mature, his pros-pect of happiness too rich and comprehensive for this fine moral fabric to crumble at a stroke. The very foundation seemed fatally injured, and yet he felt a stubborn desire still to try to save the edi-fice. He was filled with a sorer sense of wrong than he had ever known, or than he had supposed it possible he should know. To accept his injury and walk away without looking behind him was a stretch of good-nature of which he found himself incapable. He looked behind him intently and continually, and what he saw there did not assuage his resentment. He saw himself trustful, generous, liberal, patient, easy, pocketing frequent irritation and furnishing unlimited modesty. To have eaten humble pie, to have been snubbed and patronized and satirized and have consented to take it as one of the conditions of the bargain—to have done this, and done it all for nothing, surely gave one a right to protest. And to be turned off be-cause one was a commercial person! As if he had ever talked or dreamt of the commercial since his connection with the Bellegardes began—as if he had made the least circumstance of the commercial —as if he would not have consented to confound the commercial fifty times a day, if it might have increased by a hair's breadth the chance of the Bellegardes' not playing him a trick! Granted that being commercial was fair ground for having a trick played upon one, how little they knew about the class so designated and its en-terprising way of not standing upon trifles! It was in the light of his injury that the weight of Newman's past endurance seemed so heavy; his actual irritation had not been so great, merged as it was in his vision of the cloudless blue that over-arched his immediate wooing. But now his sense of outrage was deep, rancorous, and ever present; he felt that he was a good fellow wronged. As for Madame de Cintré's conduct, it struck him with a kind of awe, and the fact that he was powerless to understand it or feel the reality of its motives only deepened the force with which he had attached himself to her. He had never let the fact of her Catholicism trouble him; Catholicism to him was nothing but a name, and to express a mistrust of the form in which her religious feelings had moulded themselves would have seemed to him on his own part a rather pretentious affectation of Protestant zeal. If such superb white flowers as that could bloom in Catholic soil, the soil was not insalubrious. But it was one thing to be a Catholic, and another to turn nun—on your hands! There was something lugubriously comical in the way Newman's thoroughly contemporaneous optimism was confronted with this dusky old-world expedient. To see a woman made for him and for motherhood to his children juggled away in this tragic travesty—it was a thing to rub one's eyes over, a nightmare, an illusion, a hoax. But the hours passed away without disproving the thing, and leaving him only the after-sense of the vehemence with which he had embraced Madame de Cintré. He remembered her words and her looks; he turned them over and tried to shake the mystery out of them and to infuse them with an endurable meaning. What had she meant by her feeling being a kind of religion? It was the religion simply of the family laws, the religion of which her implacable little mother was the high priestess. Twist the thing about as her generosity would, the one certain fact was that they had used force against her. Her generosity had tried to screen them, but Newman's heart rose into his throat at the thought that they should go scot-free.

The twenty-four hours wore themselves away, and the next morning Newman sprang to his feet with the resolution to return to Fleurières and demand another interview with Madame de Bellegarde and her son. He lost no time in putting it into practice. As he rolled swiftly over the excellent road in the little calèche furnished him at the inn at Poitiers, he drew forth, as it were, from the very safe place in his mind to which he had consigned it, the last information given him by poor Valentin. Valentin had told him he could do something with it, and Newman thought it would be well to have it at hand. This was of course not the first time, lately, that Newman had given it his attention. It was information in the rough,—it was dark and puzzling; but Newman was neither helpless nor afraid. Valentin had evidently meant to put him in possession of a powerful instrument, though he could not be said to have placed the handle very securely within his grasp. But if he had not really told him the secret, he had at least given him the clew to it—a clew of which that queer old Mrs. Bread held the other end. Mrs. Bread had always looked to Newman as if she knew secrets; and as he apparently enjoyed her esteem, he suspected she might be induced to share her knowledge with him. So long as there was only Mrs. Bread to deal with, he felt easy. As to what there was to find out, he had only one fear—that it might not be bad enough. Then, when the image of the marquise and her son rose before him again, standing side by side, the old woman's hand in Urbain's arm, and the same cold, unsociable fixedness in the eyes of each, he cried out to himself that the fear was groundless. There was blood in the secret at the very last! He arrived at Fleurières almost in a state of elation; he had satisfied himself, logically, that in the presence of his threat of exposure they would, as he mentally phrased it, rattle down like unwound buckets. He remembered indeed that he must first catch his hare—first ascertain what there was to expose; but after that, why shouldn't his happiness be as good as new again? Mother and son would drop their lovely victim in terror and take to hiding, and Madame de Cintré, left to herself, would surely come back to him. Give her a chance and she would rise to the surface, return to the light. How could she fail to perceive that his house would be much the most comfortable sort of convent?

Newman, as he had done before, left his conveyance at the inn and walked the short remaining distance to the château. When he reached the gate, however, a singular feeling took possession of him —a feeling which, strange as it may seem, had its source in its unfathomable good nature. He stood there a while, looking through the bars at the large, time-stained face of the edifice, and wondering to what crime it was that the dark old house, with its flowery name, had given convenient occasion. It had given occasion, first and last, to tyrannies and sufferings enough, Newman said to himself; it was an evil-looking place to live in. Then, suddenly, came the reflection —What a horrible rubbish-heap of iniquity to fumble in! The attitude of inquisitor turned its ignobler face, and with the same movement Newman declared that the Bellegardes should have another chance. He would appeal once more directly to their sense of fairness, and not to their fear, and if they should be accessible to reason, he need know nothing worse about them than what he already knew. That was bad enough.

The gate-keeper let him in through the same stiff crevice as before, and he passed through the court and over the little rustic bridge on the moat. The door was opened before he had reached it, and, as if to put his clemency to rout with the suggestion of a richer opportunity, Mrs. Bread stood there awaiting him. Her face, as usual, looked as hopelessly blank as the tide-smoothed sea-sand, and her black garments seemed of an intenser sable. Newman had already learned that her strange inexpressiveness could be a vehicle for motion, and he was not surprised at the muffled vivacity with which she whispered, "I thought you would try again, sir. I was looking out for you."

"I am glad to see you," said Newman; "I think you are my friend."

Mrs. Bread looked at him opaquely. "I wish you well, sir; but it's vain wishing now."

"You know, then, how they have treated me?"

"Oh, sir," said Mrs. Bread, dryly, "I know everything."

Newman hesitated a moment. "Everything?"

Mrs. Bread gave him a glance somewhat more lucent. "I know at least too much, sir."

"One can never know too much. I congratulate you. I have come to see Madame de Bellegarde and her son," Newman added. "Are they at home? If they are not, I will wait."

"My lady is always at home," Mrs. Bread replied, "and the marquis is mostly with her."

"Please then tell them—one or the other, or both—that I am here and that I desire to see them."

Mrs. Bread hesitated. "May I take a great liberty, sir?"

"You have never taken a liberty but you have justified it," said Newman, with diplomatic urbanity.

Mrs. Bread dropped her wrinkled eyelids as if she were curtseying; but the curtsey stopped there; the occasion was too grave. "You have come to plead with them again, sir? Perhaps you don't know this—that Madame de Cintré returned this morning to Paris."

"Ah, she's gone!" And Newman, groaning, smote the pavement with his stick.

"She has gone straight to the convent—the Carmelites they call it. I see you know, sir. My lady and the marquis take it very ill. It was only last night she told them."

"Ah, she had kept it back, then?" cried Newman. "Good, good! And they are very fierce?"

"They are not pleased," said Mrs. Bread. "But they may well dislike it. They tell me it's most dreadful, sir; of all the nuns in Christendom the Carmelites are the worst. You may say they are really not human, sir; they make you give up everything—forever. And to think of *her* there! If I was one that cried, sir, I could cry."

Newman looked at her an instant. "We mustn't cry, Mrs. Bread; we must act. Go and call them!" And he made a movement to enter farther.

But Mrs. Bread gently checked him. "May I take another liberty? I am told you were with my dearest Mr. Valentin, in his last hours. If you would tell me a word about him! The poor count was my own boy, sir; for the first year of his life he was hardly out of my arms; I taught him to speak. And the count spoke so well, sir! He always spoke well to his poor old Bread. When he grew up and took his pleasure he always had a kind word for me. And to die in that wild way! They have a story that he fought with a wine-merchant. I can't believe that, sir! And was he in great pain?"

"You are a wise, kind old woman, Mrs. Bread," said Newman. "I hoped I might see you with my own children in your arms. Perhaps I shall, yet." And he put out his hand. Mrs. Bread looked for a moment at his open palm, and then, as if fascinated by the novelty of the gesture, extended her own ladylike fingers. Newman held her hand firmly and deliberately, fixing his eyes upon her. "You want to know all about Mr. Valentin?" he said.

"It would be a sad pleasure, sir."

"I can tell you everything. Can you sometimes leave this place?"

"The château, sir? I really don't know. I never tried."

"Try, then; try hard. Try this evening, at dusk. Come to me in the old ruin there on the hill, in the court before the church. I will wait for you there; I have something very important to tell you. An old woman like you can do as she pleases."

Mrs. Bread stared, wondering, with parted lips. "Is it from the count, sir?" she asked.

"From the count—from his death-bed," said Newman.

"I will come, then. I will be bold, for once, for *him*."

She led Newman into the great drawing-room with which he had already made acquaintance, and retired to execute his commands. Newman waited a long time; at last he was on the point of ringing and repeating his request. He was looking round him for a bell when the marquis came in with his mother on his arm. It will be seen that Newman had a logical mind when I say that he declared to himself, in perfect good faith, as a result of Valentin's dark hints, that his adversaries looked grossly wicked. "There is no mistake about it now," he said to himself as they advanced. "They're a bad lot; they have pulled off the mask." Madame de Bellegarde and her son certainly bore in their faces the signs of extreme perturbation; they looked like people who had passed a sleepless night. Confronted, moreover, with an annoyance which they hoped they had disposed of, it was not natural that they should have any very tender glances to bestow upon Newman. He stood before them, and such eye-beams as they found available they leveled at him; Newman feeling as if the door of a sepulchre had suddenly been opened, and the damp darkness were being exhaled.

"You see I have come back," he said. "I have come to try again."

"It would be ridiculous," said M. de Bellegarde, "to pretend that we are glad to see you or that we don't question the taste of your visit."

"Oh, don't talk about taste," said Newman, with a laugh, "or that will bring us round to yours! If I consulted my taste I certainly shouldn't come to see you. Besides, I will make a short work as you please. Promise me to raise the blockade—to set Madame de Cintré at liberty—and I will retire instantly."

"We hesitated as to whether we would see you," said Madame de Bellegarde; "and we were on the point of declining the honor. But it seemed to me that we should act with civility, as we have always done, and I wished to have the satisfaction of informing you that there are certain weaknesses that people of our way of feeling can be guilty of but once."

"You may be weak but once, but you will be audacious many times, madam," Newman answered. "I didn't come, however, for conversational purposes. I came to say this, simply: that if you will write immediately to your daughter that you withdraw your opposition to her marriage, I will take care of the rest. You don't want her to turn nun—you know more about the horrors of it than I do. Marrying a commercial person is better than that. Give me a letter to her, signed and sealed, saying you retract and that she may marry me with your blessing, and I will take it to her at the convent and bring her out. There's your chance—I call those easy terms."

"We look at the matter otherwise, you know. We call them very hard terms," said Urbain de Bellegarde. They had all remained standing rigidly in the middle of the room. "I think my mother will tell you that she would rather her daughter should become Sœur Catherine than Mrs. Newman."

But the old lady, with the serenity of supreme power, let her son make her epigrams for her. She only smiled, almost sweetly, shaking her head and repeating, "But once, Mr. Newman; but once!"

Nothing that Newman had ever seen or heard gave him such a sense of marble hardness as this movement and the tone that accompanied it. "Could anything compel you?" he asked. "Do you know of anything that would force you?"

"This language, sir," said the marquis, "addressed to people in bereavement and grief is beyond all qualification."

"In most cases," Newman answered, "your objection would have some weight, even admitting that Madame de Cintré's present intentions make time precious. But I have thought of what you speak of, and I have come here to-day without scruple simply because I consider your brother and you two very different parties. I see no connection between you. Your brother was ashamed of you. Lying there wounded and dying, the poor fellow apologized to me for your conduct. He apologized to me for that of his mother."

For a moment the effect of these words was as if Newman had struck a physical blow. A quick flush leaped into the faces of Madame de Bellegarde and her son, and they exchanged a glance like a twinkle of steel. Urbain uttered two words which Newman but half heard, but of which the sense came to him as it were in the reverberation of the sound, "Le misérable!"

"You show little respect for the living," said Madame de Belle-garde, "but at least respect the dead. Don't profane—don't insult—the memory of my innocent son."

"I speak the simple truth," Newman declared, "and I speak it for a purpose. I repeat it—distinctly. Your son was utterly disgusted—your son apologized."

Urbain de Bellegarde was frowning portentously, and Newman supposed he was frowning at poor Valentin's invidious image. Taken by surprise, his scant affection for his brother had made a momentary concession to dishonor. But not for an appreciable instant did his mother lower her flag. "You are immensely mistaken, sir," she said. "My son was sometimes light, but he was never indecent. He died faithful to his name."

"You simply misunderstood him," said the marquis, beginning to rally. "You affirm the impossible!"

"Oh, I don't care for poor Valentin's apology," said Newman. "It was far more painful than pleasant to me. This atrocious thing was not his fault; he never hurt me, or any one else; he was the soul of honor. But it shows how he took it."

"If you wish to prove that my poor brother, in his last moments, was out of his head, we can only say that under the melancholy circumstances nothing was more possible. But confine yourself to that."

"He was quite in his right mind," said Newman, with gentle but dangerous doggedness; "I have never seen him so bright and clever. It was terrible to see that witty, capable fellow dying such a death. You know I was very fond of your brother. And I have further proof of his sanity," Newman concluded.

The marquise gathered herself together majestically. "This is too gross!" she cried. "We decline to accept your story, sir—we repudiate it. Urbain, open the door." She turned away, with an imperious motion to her son, and passed rapidly down the length of the room. The marquis went with her and held the door open. Newman was left standing.

He lifted his finger, as a sign to M. de Bellegarde, who closed the door behind his mother and stood waiting. Newman slowly advanced, more silent, for the moment, than life. The two men stood face to face. Then Newman had a singular sensation; he felt his sense of injury almost brimming over into jocularity. "Come," he said, "you don't treat me well; at least admit that."

M. de Bellegarde looked at him from head to foot, and then, in the most delicate, best-bred voice, "I detest you, personally," he said.

"That's the way I feel to you, but for politeness' sake I don't say it," said Newman. "It's singular I should want so much to be your brother-in-law, but I can't give it up. Let me try once more." And he paused a moment. "You have a secret—you have a skeleton in the closet." M. de Bellegarde continued to look at him hard, but Newman could not see whether his eyes betrayed anything; the look of his eyes was always so strange. Newman paused again, and then went on. "You and your mother have committed a crime." At this M. de Bellegarde's eyes certainly did change; they seemed to flicker, like blown candles. Newman could see that he was profoundly startled; but there was something admirable in his self-control.

"Continue," said M. de Bellegarde.

Newman lifted a finger and made it waver a little in the air. "Need I continue? You are trembling."

"Pray where did you obtain this interesting information?" M. de Bellegarde asked, very softly.

"I shall be strictly accurate," said Newman. "I won't pretend to know more than I do. At present that is all I know. You have done something that you must hide, something that would damn you if it were known, something that would disgrace the name you are so proud of. I don't know what it is, but I can find out. Persist in your present course and I *will* find out. Change it, let your sister go in peace, and I will leave you alone. It's a bargain?"

The marquis almost succeeded in looking untroubled; the breaking up of the ice in his handsome countenance was an operation that was necessarily gradual. But Newman's mildly-syllabled argumentation seemed to press, and press, and presently he averted his eyes. He stood some moments, reflecting.

"My brother told you this," he said, looking up.

Newman hesitated a moment. "Yes, your brother told me."

The marquis smiled, handsomely. "Didn't I say that he was out of his mind?"

"He was out of his mind if I don't find out. He was very much in it if I do."

M. de Bellegarde gave a shrug. "Eh, sir, find out or not, as you please."

"I don't frighten you?" demanded Newman.

"That's for you to judge."

"No, it's for you to judge, at your leisure. Think it over, feel yourself all round. I will give you an hour or two. I can't give you more, for how do we know how fast they may be making Madame de Cintré a nun? Talk it over with your mother; let her judge whether she is frightened. I don't believe she is as easily frightened, in general, as you; but you will see. I will go and wait in the village, at the inn, and I beg you to let me know as soon as possible. Say by three o'clock. A simple *yes* or *no* on paper will do. Only, you know, in case of a *yes* I shall expect you, this time, to stick to your bargain." And with this Newman opened the door and let himself out. The marquis did not more, and Newman, retiring, gave him another look. "At the inn, in the village," he repeated. Then he turned away altogether and passed out of the house.

He was extremely excited by what he had been doing, for it was inevitable that there should be a certain emotion in calling up the spectre of dishonor before a family a thousand years old. But he went back to the inn and contrived to wait there, deliberately, for the next two hours. He thought it more than probable that Urbain de Bellegarde would give no sign; for an answer to his challenge, in either sense, would be a confession of guilt. What he most expected was silence—in other words defiance. But he prayed that, as he imaged it, his shot might bring them down. It did bring, by three o'clock, a note, delivered by a footman; a note addressed in Urbain de Bellegarde's handsome English hand. It ran as follows:—

"I cannot deny myself the satisfaction of letting you know that I return to Paris, to-morrow, with my mother, in order that we may see my sister and confirm her in the resolution which is the most effectual reply to your audacious pertinacity.

"HENRI-URBAIN DE BELLEGARDE."

Newman put the letter into his pocket, and continued his walk up and down the inn-parlor. He had spent most of his time, for the past week, in walking up and down. He continued to measure the length of the little *salle* of the Armes de France until the day began to wane, when he went out to keep his rendezvous with Mrs. Bread. The path which led up the hill to the ruin was easy to find, and Newman in a short time had followed it to the top. He passed beneath the rugged arch of the castle wall, and looked about him in the early dusk for an old woman in black. The castle yard was empty, but the door of the church was open. Newman went into the little nave and of course found a deeper dusk than without. A couple of tapers, however, twinkled on the altar and just enabled him to perceive a figure seated by one of the pillars. Closer inspection helped him to recognize Mrs. Bread, in spite of the fact that she was dressed with unwonted splendor. She wore a large black silk bonnet, with imposing bows of crape, and an old black satin dress disposed itself in vaguely lustrous folds about her person. She had judged it proper to the occasion to appear in her stateliest apparel. She had been sitting with her eyes fixed upon the ground, but when Newman passed before her she looked up at him, and then she rose.

"Are you a Catholic, Mrs. Bread?" he asked.

"No, sir; I'm a good Church-of-England woman, very Low," she answered. "But I thought I should be safer in here than outside. I was never out in the evening before, sir."

"We shall be safer," said Newman, "where no one can hear us." And he led the way back into the castle court and then followed a path beside the church, which he was sure must lead into another part of the ruin. He was not deceived. It wandered along the crest of the hill and terminated before a fragment of wall pierced by a rough aperture which had once been a door. Through this aperture Newman passed and found himself in a nook peculiarly favorable to quiet conversation, as probably many an earnest couple, otherwise assorted than our friends, had assured themselves. The hill sloped abruptly away, and on the remnant of its crest were scattered two or three fragments of stone. Beneath, over the plain, lay the gathered twilight, though which, in the near distance, gleamed two or three lights from the château. Mrs. Bread rustled slowly after her guide, and Newman, satisfying himself that one of the fallen stones was steady, proposed to her to sit upon it. She cautiously complied, and he placed himself upon another, near her.

CHAPTER XXII

"I AM very much obliged to you for coming," Newman said. "I hope it won't get you into trouble."

"I don't think I shall be missed. My lady, in these days, is not fond of having me about her." This was said with a certain fluttered eagerness which increased Newman's sense of having inspired the old woman with confidence.

"From the first, you know," he answered, "you took an interest in my prospects. You were on my side. That gratified me, I assure you. And now that you know what they have done to me, I am sure you are with me all the more."

"They have not done well—I must say it," said Mrs. Bread. "But you mustn't blame the poor countess; they pressed her hard."

"I would give a million of dollars to know what they did to her!" cried Newman.

Mrs. Bread sat with a dull, oblique gaze fixed upon the lights of the château. "They worked on her feelings; they knew that was the way. She is a delicate creature. They made her feel wicked. She is only too good."

"Ah, they made her feel wicked," said Newman, slowly; and then he repeated it. "They made her feel wicked,—they made her feel wicked." The words seemed to him for the moment a vivid description of infernal ingenuity.

"It was because she was so good that she gave up—poor sweet lady!" added Mrs. Bread.

"But she was better to them than to me," said Newman.

"She was afraid," said Mrs. Bread, very confidently; "she has always been afraid, or at least for a long time. That was the real trouble, sir. She was like a fair peach, I may say, with just one little speck. She had one little sad spot. You pushed her into the sunshine, sir, and it almost disappeared. Then they pulled her back into the shade and in a moment it began to spread. Before we knew it she was gone. She was a delicate creature."

This singular attestation of Madame de Cintré's delicacy, for all its singularity, set Newman's wound aching afresh. "I see," he presently said; "she knew something bad about her mother."

"No, sir, she knew nothing," said Mrs. Bread, holding her head very stiff and keeping her eyes fixed upon the glimmering windows of the château.

"She guessed something, then, or suspected it."

"She was afraid to know," said Mrs. Bread.

"But *you* know, at any rate," said Newman.

She slowly turned her vague eyes upon Newman, squeezing her hands together in her lap. "You are not quite faithful, sir. I thought it was to tell me about Mr. Valentin you asked me to come here."

"Oh, the more we talk of Mr. Valentin the better," said Newman. "That's exactly what I want. I was with him, as I told you, in his last hour. He was in a great deal of pain, but he was quite himself. You know what that means; he was bright and lively and clever."

"Oh, he would always be clever, sir," said Mrs. Bread. "And did he know of your trouble?"

"Yes, he guessed it of himself."

"And what did he say to it?"

"He said it was a disgrace to his name—but it was not the first."

"Lord, Lord!" murmured Mrs. Bread.

"He said that his mother and his brother had once put their heads together and invented something even worse."

"You shouldn't have listened to that, sir."

"Perhaps not. But I *did* listen, and I don't forget it. Now I want to know what it is they did."

Mrs. Bread gave a soft moan. "And you have enticed me up into this strange place to tell you?"

"Don't be alarmed," said Newman. "I won't say a word that shall be disagreeable to you. Tell me as it suits you, and when it suits you. Only remember that it was Mr. Valentin's last wish that you should."

"Did he say that?"

"He said it with his last breath—'Tell Mrs. Bread I told you to ask her.'"

"Why didn't he tell you himself?"

"It was too long a story for a dying man; he had no breath left in his body. He could only say that he wanted me to know—that, wronged as I was, it was my right to know."

"But how will it help you, sir?" said Mrs. Bread.

"That's for me to decide. Mr. Valentin believed it would, and that's why he told me. Your name was almost the last word he spoke."

Mrs. Bread was evidently awe-struck by this statement; she shook her clasped hands slowly up and down. "Excuse me, sir," she said, "if I take a great liberty. Is it the solemn truth you are speaking? I *must* ask you that; must I not, sir?"

"There's no offense. It *is* the solemn truth; I solemnly swear it. Mr. Valentin himself would certainly have told me more if he had been able."

"Oh, sir, if he knew more!"

"Don't you suppose he did?"

"There's no saying what he knew about anything," said Mrs. Bread, with a mild head-shake. "He was so mightily clever. He could make you believe he knew things that he didn't, and that he didn't know others that he had better not have known."

"I suspect he knew something about his brother that kept the marquis civil to him," Newman propounded; "he made the marquis feel him. What he wanted now was to put me in his place; he wanted to give me a chance to make the marquis feel *me*."

"Mercy on us!" cried the old waiting-woman, "how wicked we all are!"

"I don't know," said Newman; "some of us are wicked, certainly. I am very angry, I am very sore, and I am very bitter, but I don't know that I am wicked. I have been cruelly injured. They have hurt me, and I want to hurt them. I don't deny that; on the contrary, I tell you plainly that that is the use I want to make of your secret."

Mrs. Bread seemed to hold her breath. "You want to publish them —you want to shame them?"

"I want to bring them down,—down, down, down! I want to turn the tables upon them—I want to mortify them as they mortified me. They took me up into a high place and made me stand there for all the world to see me, and then they stole behind me and pushed me into this bottomless pit, where I lie howling and gnashing my teeth! I made a fool of myself before all their friends; but I shall make something worse of them."

This passionate sally, which Newman uttered with the greater fervor that it was the first time he had had a chance to say all this aloud, kindled two small sparks in Mrs. Bread's fixed eyes. "I suppose you have a right to your anger, sir; but think of the dishonor you will draw down on Madame de Cintré."

"Madame de Cintré is buried alive," cried Newman. "What are honor or dishonor to her? The door of the tomb is at this moment closing behind her."

"Yes, it's most awful," moaned Mrs. Bread.

"She has moved off, like her brother Valentin, to give me room to work. It's as if it were done on purpose."

"Surely," said Mrs. Bread, apparently impressed by the ingenuity of this reflection. She was silent for some moments; then she added, "And would you bring my lady before the courts?"

"The courts care nothing for my lady," Newman replied. "If she has committed a crime, she will be nothing for the courts but a wicked old woman."

"And will they hang her, sir?"

"That depends upon what she has done." And Newman eyed Mrs. Bread intently.

"It would break up the family most terribly, sir!"

"It's time such a family should be broken up!" said Newman, with a laugh.

"And me at my age out of place, sir!" sighed Mrs. Bread.

"Oh, I will take care of you! You shall come and live with me. You shall be my housekeeper, or anything you like. I will pension you for life."

"Dear, dear, sir, you think of everything." And she seemed to fall a-brooding.

Newman watched her a while, and then he said suddenly, "Ah, Mrs. Bread, you are too fond of my lady!"

She looked at him as quickly. "I wouldn't have you say that, sir. I don't think it any part of my duty to be fond of my lady. I have served her faithfully this many a year; but if she were to die to-morrow, I believe, before Heaven, I shouldn't shed a tear for her." Then, after a pause, "I have no reason to love her!" Mrs. Bread added. "The most she has done for me has been not to turn me out of the house." Newman felt that decidedly his companion was more and more confidential—that if luxury is corrupting, Mrs. Bread's conservative habits were already relaxed by the spiritual comfort of this preconcerted interview, in a remarkable locality, with a free-spoken millionaire. All his native shrewdness admonished him that his part was simply to let her take her time—let the charm of the occasion work. So he said nothing; he only looked at her kindly. Mrs. Bread sat nursing her lean elbows. "My lady once did me a great wrong," she went on at last. "She has a terrible tongue when she is vexed. It was many a year ago, but I have never forgotten it. I have never mentioned it to a human creature; I have kept my grudge to myself. I dare say I have been wicked, but my grudge has grown old with me. It has grown good for nothing, too, I dare say; but it has lived along, as I have lived. It will die when I die,— not before!"

"And what *is* your grudge?" Newman asked.

Mrs. Bread dropped her eyes and hesitated. "If I were a foreigner, sir, I should make less of telling you; it comes harder to a decent Englishwoman. But I sometimes think I have picked up too many foreign ways. What I was telling you belongs to a time when I was much younger and very different looking to what I am now. I had a very high color, sir, if you can believe it, indeed I was a very smart lass. My lady was younger, too, and the late marquis was youngest of all—I mean in the way he went on, sir; he had a very high spirit; he was a magnificent man. He was fond of his pleasure, like most foreigners, and it must be owned that he sometimes went rather below him to take it. My lady was often jealous, and, if you'll believe it, sir, she did me the honor to be jealous of me. One day I had a red ribbon in my cap, and my lady flew out at me and ordered me to take it off. She accused me of putting it on to make the marquis look at me. I don't know that I was impertinent, but I spoke up like an honest girl and didn't count my words. A red ribbon indeed! As if it was my ribbons the marquis looked at! My lady knew afterwards that I was perfectly respectable, but she never said a word to show that she believed it. But the marquis did!" Mrs. Bread presently added, "I took off my red ribbon and put it away in a drawer, where I have kept it to this day. It's faded now, it's a very pale pink; but there it lies. My grudge has faded, too; the red has all gone out of it; but it lies here yet." And Mrs. Bread stroked her black satin bodice.

Newman listened with interest to this decent narrative, which seemed to have opened up the deeps of memory to his companion. Then, as she remained silent, and seemed to be losing herself in retrospective meditation upon her perfect respectability, he ventured upon a short cut to his goal. "So Madame de Bellegarde was jealous;

I see. And M. de Bellegarde admired pretty women, without distinction of class. I suppose one mustn't be hard upon him, for they probably didn't all behave so properly as you. But years afterwards it could hardly have been jealousy that turned Madame de Bellegarde into a criminal."

Mrs. Bread gave a weary sigh. "We are using dreadful words, sir, but I don't care now. I see you have your idea, and I have no will of my own. My will was the will of my children, as I called them; but I have lost my children now. They are dead—I may say it of both of them; and what should I care for the living? What is any one in the house to me now—what am I to them? My lady objects to me—she has objected to me these thirty years. I should have been glad to be something to young Madame de Bellegarde, though I never was nurse to the present marquis. When he was a baby I was too young; they wouldn't trust me with him. But his wife told her own maid, Mamselle Clarisse, the opinion she had of me. Perhaps you would like to hear it, sir."

"Oh, immensely," said Newman.

"She said that if I would sit in her children's school-room I should do very well for a penwiper! When things have come to that I don't think I need stand upon ceremony."

"Decidedly not," said Newman. "Go on, Mrs. Bread."

Mrs. Bread, however, relapsed again into troubled dumbness, and all Newman could do was to fold his arms and wait. But at last she appeared to have set her memories in order. "It was when the late marquis was an old man and his eldest son had been two years married. It was when the time came on for marrying Mademoiselle Claire; that's the way they talk of it here, you know, sir. The marquis's health was bad; he was very much broken down. My lady had picked out M. de Cintré, for no good reason that I could see. But there are reasons, I very well know, that are beyond me, and you must be high in the world to understand them. Old M. de Cintré was very high, and my lady thought him almost as good as herself; that's saying a good deal. Mr. Urbain took sides with his mother, as he always did. The trouble, I believe, was that my lady would give very little money, and all the other gentlemen asked more. It was only M. de Cintré that was satisfied. The Lord willed it he should have that one soft spot; it was the only one he had. He may have been very grand in his birth, and he certainly was very grand in his bows and speeches; but that was all the grandeur he had. I think he was like what I have heard of comedians; not that

I have ever seen one. But I know he painted his face. He might paint
it all he would; he could never make me like it! The marquis couldn't
abide him, and declared that sooner than take such a husband as that
Mademoiselle Claire should take none at all. He and my lady had
a great scene; it came even to our ears in the servants' hall. It was
not their first quarrel, if the truth must be told. They were not a
loving couple, but they didn't often come to words, because, I
think, neither of them thought the other's doings worth the
trouble. My lady had long ago got over her jealousy, and she had
taken to indifference. In this, I must say, they were well matched.
The marquis was very easy-going; he had a most gentlemanly
temper. He got angry only once a year, but then it was very bad.
He always took to bed directly afterwards. This time I speak of he
took to bed as usual, but he never got up again. I'm afraid the poor
gentleman was paying for his dissipation; isn't it true they mostly
do, sir, when they get old? My lady and Mr. Urbain kept quiet,
but I know my lady wrote letters to M. de Cintré. The marquis
got worse and the doctors gave him up. My lady, she gave him
up too, and if the truth must be told, she gave him up gladly. When
once he was out of the way she could do what she pleased with
her daughter, and it was all arranged that my poor innocent child
should be handed over to M. de Cintré. You don't know what
Mademoiselle was in those days, sir; she was the sweetest young
creature in France, and knew as little of what was going on around
her as the lamb does of the butcher. I used to nurse the marquis, and
I was always in his room. It was here at Fleurières, in the autumn.
We had a doctor from Paris, who came and stayed two or three
weeks in the house. Then there came two others, and there was a
consultation, and these two others, as I said, declared that the
marquis couldn't be saved. After this they went off, pocketing their
fees, but the other one stayed and did what he could. The marquis
himself kept crying out that he wouldn't die, that he didn't want
to die, that he would live and look after his daughter. Mademoiselle
Claire and the viscount—that was Mr. Valentin, you know—were
both in the house. The doctor was a clever man,—that I could see
myself,—and I think he believed that the marquis might get well.
We took good care of him, he and I, between us, and one day, when
my lady had almost ordered her mourning, my patient suddenly
began to mend. He got better and better, till the doctor said he was
out of danger. What was killing him was the dreadful fits of pain in
his stomach. But little by little they stopped, and the poor marquis

began to make his jokes again. The doctor found something that gave him great comfort—some white stuff that we kept in a great bottle on the chimney-piece. I used to give it to the marquis through a glass tube; it always made him easier. Then the doctor went away, after telling me to keep on giving him the mixture whenever he was bad. After that there was a little doctor from Poitiers, who came every day. So we were alone in the house—my lady and her poor husband and their three children. Young Madame de Bellegarde had gone away, with her little girl, to her mother's You know she is very lively, and her maid told me that she didn't like to be where people were dying." Mrs. Bread paused a moment, and then she went on with the same quiet consistency. "I think you have guessed, sir, that when the marquis began to turn my lady was disappointed." And she paused again, bending upon Newman a face which seemed to grow whiter as the darkness settled down upon them.

Newman had listened eagerly—with an eagerness greater even than that with which he had bent his ear to Valentin de Bellegarde's last words. Every now and then, as his companion looked up at him, she reminded him of an ancient tabby cat, protracting the enjoyment of a dish of milk. Even her triumph was measured and decorous; the faculty of exultation had been chilled by disuse. She presently continued. "Late one night I was sitting by the marquis in his room, the great red room in the west tower. He had been complaining a little, and I gave him a spoonful of the doctor's dose. My lady had been there in the early part of the evening; she sat for more than an hour by his bed. Then she went away and left me alone. After midnight she came back, and her eldest son was with her. They went to the bed and looked at the marquis, and my lady took hold of his hand. Then she turned to me and said he was not so well; I remember how the marquis, without saying anything, lay staring at her. I can see his white face, at this moment, in the great black square between the bed-curtains. I said I didn't think he was very bad; and she told me to go to bed—she would sit a while with him. When the marquis saw me going he gave a sort of groan, and called out to me not to leave him; but Mr. Urbain opened the door for me and pointed the way out. The present marquis—perhaps you have noticed, sir—has a very proud way of giving orders, and I was there to take orders. I went to my room, but I wasn't easy; I couldn't tell you why. I didn't undress; I sat there waiting and listening. For what, would you have said, sir? I couldn't have told you; for surely a poor gentleman might be comfortable with his wife and his son. It was as if I expected to hear the marquis moaning after me again. I listened, but I heard nothing. It was a very still night; I never knew a night so still. At last the very stillness itself seemed to frighten me, and I came out of my room and went very softly down-stairs. In the anteroom, outside of the marquis's chamber, I found Mr. Urbain walking up and down. He asked me what I wanted, and I said I came back to relieve my lady. He said *he* would relieve my lady, and ordered me back to bed; but as I stood there, unwilling to turn away, the door of the room opened and my lady came out. I noticed she was very pale; she was very strange. She looked a moment at the count and at me, and then she held out her arms to the count. He went to her, and she fell upon him and hid her face. I went quickly past her into the room and to the marquis's bed. He was lying there, very white, with his eyes shut, like a corpse. I took hold of his hand and spoke to him, and he felt to me like a dead man. Then I turned round; my lady and Mr. Urbain were there. 'My poor Bread,' said my lady, 'M. le Marquis is gone.' Mr. Urbain knelt down by the bed and said softly, 'Mon père, mon père.' I thought it wonderful strange, and asked my lady what in the world had happened, and why she hadn't called me. She said nothing had happened; that she had only been sitting there with the marquis, very quiet. She had closed her eyes, thinking she might sleep, and she had slept, she didn't know how long. When she woke up he was dead. 'It's death, my son, it's death,' she said to the count. Mr. Urbain said they must have the doctor, immediately, from Poitiers, and that he would ride off and fetch him. He kissed his father's face, and then he kissed his mother and went away. My lady and I stood there at the bedside. As I looked at the poor marquis it came into my head that he was not dead, that he was in a kind of swoon. And then my lady repeated, 'My poor Bread, it's death, it's death;' and I said, 'Yes, my lady, it's certainly death.' I said just the opposite to what I believed; it was my notion. Then my lady said we must wait for the doctor, and we sat there and waited. It was a long time; the poor marquis neither stirred nor changed. 'I have seen death before,' said my lady, 'and it's terribly like this.' 'Yes please, my lady,' said I; and I kept thinking. The night wore away without the count's coming back, and my lady began to be frightened. She was afraid he had had an accident in the dark, or met with some wild people. At last she got so restless that she went below to watch in the court for her son's return. I sat there alone and the marquis never stirred."

Here Mrs. Bread paused again, and the most artistic of romancers could not have been more effective. Newman made a movement as if he were turning over the page of a novel. "So he *was* dead!" he exclaimed.

"Three days afterwards he was in his grave," said Mrs. Bread, sententiously. "In a little while I went away to the front of the house and looked out into the court, and there, before long, I saw Mr. Urbain ride in alone. I waited a bit, to hear him come upstairs with his mother, but they stayed below, and I went back to the marquis's room. I went to the bed and held up the light to him, but I don't know why I didn't let the candlestick fall. The marquis's eyes were open—open wide! they were staring at me. I knelt down beside him and took his hands, and begged him to tell me, in the name of wonder, whether he was alive or dead. Still he looked at me a long time, and then he made me a sign to put my ear close to him: 'I am dead,' he said, 'I am dead. The marquise has killed me.' I was all in a tremble; I didn't understand him. He seemed both a man and a corpse, if you can fancy, sir. 'But you'll get well now, sir,' I said. And then he whispered again, ever so weak: 'I wouldn't get well for a kingdom. I wouldn't be that woman's husband again.' And then he said more; he said she had murdered him. I asked him what she had done to him, but he only replied, 'Murder, murder. And she'll kill my daughter,' he said; 'my poor unhappy child.' And he begged me to prevent that, and then he said that he was dying, that he was dead. I was afraid to move or to leave him; I was almost dead myself. All of a sudden he asked me to get a pencil and write for him; and then I had to tell him that I couldn't manage a pencil. He asked me to hold him up in bed while he wrote himself, and I said he could never, never do such a thing. But he seemed to have a kind of terror that gave him strength. I found a pencil in the room and a piece of paper and a book, and I put the paper on the book and the pencil into his hand, and moved the candle near him. You will think all this very strange, sir; and very strange it was. The strangest part of it was that I believed he was dying, and that I was eager to help him to write. I sat on the bed and put my arm round him, and held him up. I felt very strong; I believe I could have lifted him and carried him. It was a wonder how he wrote, but he did write, in a big scratching hand; he almost covered one side of the paper. It seemed a long time; I suppose it was three or four minutes. He was groaning, terribly, all the while. Then he said it was ended, and I let him down upon his pillows, and he gave me

the paper and told me to fold it, and hide it, and give it to those
who would act upon it. 'Whom do you mean?' I said. 'Who are
those who will act upon it?' But he only groaned, for an answer; he
couldn't speak, for weakness. In a few minutes he told me to go and
look at the bottle on the chimney-piece. I knew the bottle he meant;
the white stuff that was good for his stomach. I went and looked at
it, but it was empty. When I came back his eyes were open and he
was staring at me; but soon he closed them and he said no more.
I hid the paper in my dress; I didn't look at what was written upon
it, though I can read very well, sir, if I haven't any handwriting.
I sat down near the bed, but it was nearly half an hour before my
lady and the count came in. The marquis looked as he did when
they left him, and I never said a word about his having been otherwise. Mr. Urbain said that the doctor had been called to a person in
childbirth, but that he promised to set out for Fleurières immediately.
In another half hour he arrived, and as soon as he had examined
the marquis he said that we had had a false alarm. The poor gentleman was very low, but he was still living. I watched my lady and
her son when he said this, to see if they looked at each other,
and I am obliged to admit that they didn't. The doctor said there was
no reason he should die; he had been going on so well. And then
he wanted to know how he had suddenly fallen off; he had left
him so very hearty. My lady told her little story again—what she
had told Mr. Urbain and me—and the doctor looked at her and said
nothing. He stayed all the next day at the château, and hardly
left the marquis. I was always there. Mademoiselle and Mr. Valentin
came and looked at their father, but he never stirred. It was a
strange, deathly stupor. My lady was always about; her face was
as white as her husband's, and she looked very proud, as I had seen
her look when her orders or her wishes had been disobeyed. It was
as if the poor marquis had defied her; and the way she took it
made me afraid of her. The apothecary from Poitiers kept the
marquis along through the day, and we waited for the other doctor
from Paris, who, as I told you, had been staying at Fleurières.
They had telegraphed for him early in the morning, and in the
evening he arrived. He talked a bit outside with the doctor from
Poitiers, and then they came in to see the marquis together. I was
with him, and so was Mr. Urbain. My lady had been to receive
the doctor from Paris, and she didn't come back with him into the
room. He sat down by the marquis; I can see him there now, with his
hand on the marquis's wrist, and Mr. Urbain watching him with a

little looking-glass in his hand. 'I'm sure he's better,' said the little
doctor from Poitiers; 'I'm sure he'll come back.' A few moments
after he had said this the marquis opened his eyes, as if he were
waking up, and looked at us, from one to the other. I saw him look
at me, very softly, as you'd say. At the same moment my lady came
in on tiptoe; she came up to the bed and put in her head between
me and the count. The marquis saw her and gave a long, most
wonderful moan. He said something we couldn't understand, and
he seemed to have a kind of spasm. He shook all over and then
closed his eyes, and the doctor jumped up and took hold of my
lady. He held her for a moment a bit roughly. The marquis was
stone dead! This time there were those there that knew."

Newman felt as if he had been reading by starlight the report
of highly important evidence in a great murder case. "And the
paper—the paper!" he said, excitedly. "What was written upon it?"

"I can't tell you, sir," answered Mrs. Bread. "I couldn't read it;
it was in French."

"But could no one else read it?"

"I never asked a human creature."

"No one has ever seen it?"

"If you see it you'll be the first."

Newman seized the old woman's hand in both his own and pressed
it vigorously. "I thank you ever so much for that," he cried. "I want
to be the first, I want it to be my property and no one else's! You're
the wisest old woman in Europe. And what did you do with the
paper?" This information had made him feel extraordinarily strong.
"Give it to me quick!"

Mrs. Bread got up with a certain majesty. "It is not so easy as
that, sir. If you want the paper, you must wait."

"But waiting is horrible, you know," urged Newman.

"I am sure I have waited; I have waited these many years," said
Mrs. Bread.

"That is very true. You have waited for me. I won't forget it.
And yet, how comes it you didn't do as M. de Bellegarde said, show
the paper to some one?"

"To whom should I show it?" answered Mrs. Bread, mournfully.
"It was not easy to know, and many's the night I have lain awake
thinking of it. Six months afterwards, when they married Mademoiselle to her vicious old husband, I was very near bringing it out.
I thought it was my duty to do something with it, and yet I was
mightily afraid. I didn't know what was written on the paper or

how bad it might be, and there was no one I could trust enough
to ask. And it seemed to me a cruel kindness to do that sweet young
creature, letting her know that her father had written her mother
down so shamefully; for that's what he did, I suppose. I thought she
would rather be unhappy with her husband than be unhappy that
way. It was for her and for my dear Mr. Valentin I kept quiet.
Quiet I call it, but for me it was a weary quietness. It worried me
terribly, and it changed me altogether. But for others I held my
tongue, and no one, to this hour, knows what passed between the
poor marquis and me."

"But evidently there were suspicions," said Newman. "Where did
Mr. Valentin get his ideas?"

"It was the little doctor from Poitiers. He was very ill-satisfied,
and he made a great talk. He was a sharp Frenchman, and coming
to the house, as he did day after day, I suppose he saw more than he
seemed to see. And indeed the way the poor marquis went off as
soon as his eyes fell on my lady was a most shocking sight for any
one. The medical gentleman from Paris was much more accommo-
dating, and he hushed up the other. But for all he could do Mr.
Valentin and Mademoiselle heard something; they knew their
father's death was somehow against nature. Of course they couldn't
accuse their mother, and, as I tell you, I was as dumb as that stone.
Mr. Valentin used to look at me sometimes, and his eyes seemed
to shine, as if he were thinking of asking me something. I was dreadfully afraid he would speak, and I always looked away and went
about my business. If I were to tell him, I was sure he would hate me
afterwards, and that I could never have borne. Once I went up to
him and took a great liberty; I kissed him, as I had kissed him when
he was a child. 'You oughtn't to look so sad, sir,' I said; 'believe your
poor old Bread. Such a gallant, handsome young man can have
nothing to be sad about.' And I think he understood me; he understood that I was begging off, and he made up his mind in his own
way. He went about with his unasked question in his mind, as I did
with my untold tale; we were both afraid of bringing dishonor on
a great house. And it was the same with Mademoiselle. She didn't
know what happened; she wouldn't know. My lady and Mr. Urbain
asked me no questions because they had no reason. I was as still as
a mouse. When I was younger my lady thought me a hussy, and
now she thought me a fool. How should I have any ideas?"

"But you say the little doctor from Poitiers made a talk," said
Newman. "Did no one take it up?"

"I heard nothing of it, sir. They are always talking scandal in these foreign countries—you may have noticed—and I suppose they shook their heads over Madame de Bellegarde. But after all, what could they say? The marquis had been ill, and the marquis had died; he had as good a right to die as any one. The doctor couldn't say he had not come honestly by his cramps. The next year the little doctor left the place and bought a practice in Bordeaux, and if there has been any gossip it died out. And I don't think there could have been much gossip about my lady that any one would listen to. My lady is so very respectable."

Newman, at this last affirmation, broke into an immense, resounding laugh. Mrs. Bread had begun to move away from the spot where they were sitting, and he helped her through the aperture in the wall and along the homeward path. "Yes," he said, "my lady's respectability is delicious; it will be a great crash!" They reached the empty space in front of the church, where they stopped a moment, looking at each other with something of an air of closer fellowship—like two sociable conspirators. "But what was it," said Newman, "what was it she did to her husband? She didn't stab him or poison him."

"I don't know, sir; no one saw it."

"Unless it was Mr. Urbain. You say he was walking up and down, outside the room. Perhaps he looked through the keyhole. But no; I think that with his mother he would take it on trust."

"You may be sure I have often thought of it," said Mrs. Bread. "I am sure she didn't touch him with her hands. I saw nothing on him, anywhere. I believe it was in this way. He had a fit of his great pain, and he asked her for his medicine. Instead of giving it to him she went and poured it away, before his eyes. Then he saw what she meant, and, weak and helpless as he was, he was frightened, he was terrified. 'You want to kill me,' he said. 'Yes, M. le Marquis, I want to kill you,' says my lady, and sits down and fixes her eyes upon him. You know my lady's eyes, I think, sir; it was with them she killed him; it was with the terrible strong will she put into them. It was like a frost on flowers."

"Well, you are a very intelligent woman; you have shown great discretion," said Newman. "I shall value your services as housekeeper extremely."

They had begun to descend the hill, and Mrs. Bread said nothing until they reached the foot. Newman strolled lightly beside her; his head was thrown back and he was gazing at all the stars; he seemed to himself to be riding his vengeance along the Milky Way. "So you are serious, sir, about that?" said Mrs. Bread, softly.

"About your living with me? Why of course I will take care of you to the end of your days. You can't live with those people any longer. And you oughtn't to, you know, after this. You give me the paper, and you move away."

"It seems very flightly in me to be taking a new place at this time of life," observed Mrs. Bread, lugubriously. "But if you are going to turn the house upside down, I would rather be out of it."

"Oh," said Newman, in the cheerful tone of a man who feels rich in alternatives. "I don't think I shall bring in the constables, if that's what you mean. Whatever Madame de Bellegarde did, I am afraid the law can't take hold of it. But I am glad of that; it leaves it altogether to me!"

"You are a mighty bold gentleman, sir," murmured Mrs. Bread, looking at him round the edge of her great bonnet.

He walked with her back to the château; the curfew had tolled for the laborious villagers of Fleurières, and the street was unlighted and empty. She promised him that he should have the marquis's manuscript in half an hour. Mrs. Bread choosing not to go in by the great gate, they passed round by a winding lane to a door in the wall of the park, of which she had the key, and which would enable her to enter the château from behind. Newman arranged with her that he should await outside the wall her return with the coveted document.

She went in, and his half hour in the dusky lane seemed very long. But he had plenty to think about. At last the door in the wall opened and Mrs. Bread stood there, with one hand on the latch and the other holding out a scrap of white paper, folded small. In a moment he was master of it, and it had passed into his waistcoat pocket. "Come and see me in Paris," he said; "we are to settle your future, you know; and I will translate poor M. de Bellegarde's French to you." Never had he felt so grateful as at this moment for M. Nioche's instructions.

Mrs. Bread's dull eyes had followed the disappearance of the paper, and she gave a heavy sigh. "Well, you have done what you would with me, sir, and I suppose you will do it again. You *must* take care of me now. You are a terribly positive gentleman."

"Just now," said Newman, "I'm a terribly impatient gentleman!" And he bade her good-night and walked rapidly back to the inn. He ordered his vehicle to be prepared for his return to Poitiers, and then he shut the door of the common salle and strode toward the solitary lamp on the chimney-piece. He pulled out the paper and quickly unfolded it. It was covered with pencil-marks, which at first, in the feeble light, seemed indistinct. But Newman's fierce curiosity forced a meaning from the tremulous signs. The English of them was as follows:—

"My wife has tried to kill me, and she has done it; I am dying, dying horribly. It is to marry my dear daughter to M. de Cintré. With all my soul I protest,—I forbid it. I am not insane,—ask the doctors, ask Mrs. B——. It was alone with me here, to-night; she attacked me and put me to death. It is murder, if murder ever was. Ask the doctors.

"HENRI-URBAIN DE BELLEGARDE."

CHAPTER XXIII

NEWMAN RETURNED to Paris the second day after his interview with Mrs. Bread. The morrow he had spent at Poitiers, reading over and over again the little document which he had lodged in his pocket-bood, and thinking what he would do in the circumstances and how he would do it. He would not have said that Poitiers was an amusing place; yet the day seemed very short. Domiciled once more in the Boulevard Haussmann, he walked over to the Rue de l'Université and inquired of Madame de Bellegarde's portress whether the marquise had come back. The portress told him that she had arrived, with M. le Marquis, on the preceding day, and further informed him that if he desired to enter, Madame de Bellegarde and her son were both at home. As she said these words the little white-faced old woman who peered out of the dusky gate-house of the Hotel de Bellegarde gave a small wicked smile—a smile which seemed to Newman to mean, "Go in if you dare!" She was evidently versed in the current domestic history; she was placed where she could feel the pulse of the house. Newman stood a moment, twisting his mustache and looking at her; then he abruptly turned away. But this was not because he was afraid to go in—though he doubted whether, if he did so, he should be able to make his way, unchallenged, into the presence of Madame de Cintré's relatives. Confidence—excessive confidence, perhaps—quite as much as timidity prompted his retreat. He was nursing his thunder-bolt; he loved it; he was unwilling to part with it. He seemed to be holding it aloft in the rumbling, vaguely-flashing air, directly over the heads of his victims, and he fancied he could see their pale, upturned faces. Few specimens of the human countenance had ever given him such pleasure as this, lighted in the lurid fashion I have hinted at, and he was disposed to sip the cup of contemplative revenge in a leisurely fashion. It must be added, too, that he was at a loss to see exactly how he could arrange to witness the operation of his thunder. To send in his card to Madame de Bellegarde would be a waste of ceremony; she would certainly decline to receive him. On the other hand he could not force his way into her presence. It annoyed him keenly to think that he might be reduced to the blind satisfaction of writing her a letter; but he consoled himself in a measure with the reflection that a letter might lead to an interview. He went home, and feeling rather tired—nursing a vengeance was, it must be confessed, a rather fatiguing process; it took a good deal out of one—flung himself into one of his brocaded fauteuils, stretched his legs, thrust his hands into his pockets, and, while he watched the reflected sunset fading from the ornate house-tops on the opposite side of the Boulevard, began mentally to compose a cool epistle to Madame de Bellegarde. While he was so occupied his servant threw open the door and announced ceremoniously, "Madame Brett!"

Newman roused himself, expectantly, and in a few moments perceived upon his threshold the worthy woman with whom he had conversed to such good purpose on the starlit hill-top of Fleurières. Mrs. Bread had made for this visit the same toilet as for her former expedition. Newman was struck with her distinguished appearance. His lamp was not lit, and as her large, grave face gazed at him through the light dusk from under the shadow of such a person presenting herself as a servant. He greeted her with high geniality and bade her come in and sit down and make herself comfortable. There was something which might have touched the springs both of mirth and of melancholy in the ancient maidenliness with which Mrs. Bread endeavored to comply with these directions. She was not playing at being fluttered, which would have been simply ridiculous; she was doing her best to carry herself as a person so humble that, that for her, even embarrassment would have been pretentious; but evidently she had never dreamed of its being in her horoscope to pay a visit, at night-fall, to a friendly single gentleman who lived in theatrical-looking rooms on one of the new Boulevards.

"I truly hope I am not forgetting my place, sir," she murmured.

"Forgetting your place?" cried Newman. "Why, you are remembering it. This is your place, you know. You are already in my service; your wages, as housekeeper, began a fortnight ago. I can tel!

you my house wants keeping! Why don't you take off your bonnet and stay?"

"Take off my bonnet?" said Mrs. Bread, with timid literalness. "Oh, sir, I haven't my cap. And with your leave, sir, I couldn't keep house in my best gown."

"Never mind your gown," said Newman, cheerfully. "You shall have a better gown than that."

Mrs. Bread stared solemnly and then stretched her hands over her lustreless satin skirt, as if the perilous side of her situation were defining itself. "Oh, sir, I am fond of my own clothes," she murmured.

"I hope you have left those wicked people, at any rate," said Newman.

"Well, sir, here I am!" said Mrs. Bread. "That's all I can tell you. Here I sit, poor Catherine Bread. It's a strange place for me to be. I don't know myself; I never supposed I was so bold. But indeed, sir, I have gone as far as my own strength will bear me."

"Oh, come, Mrs. Bread," said Newman, almost caressingly, "don't make yourself uncomfortable. Now's the time to feel lively, you know."

She began to speak again with a trembling voice. "I think it would be more respectable if I could—if I could"—and her voice trembled to a pause.

"If you could give up this sort of thing altogether?" said Newman, kindly, trying to anticipate her meaning, which he supposed might be a wish to retire from service.

"If I could give up everything, sir! All I should ask is a decent Protestant burial."

"Burial!" cried Newman, with a burst of laughter. "Why, to bury you now would be a sad piece of extravagance. It's only rascals who have to be buried to get respectable. Honest folks like you and me can live our time out—and live together. Come! did you bring your baggage?"

"My box is locked and corded; but I haven't yet spoken to my lady."

"Speak to her, then, and have done with it. I should like to have your chance!" cried Newman.

"I would gladly give it you, sir. I have passed some weary hours in my lady's dressing-room; but this will be one of the longest. She will tax me with ingratitude."

"Well," said Newman, "so long as you can tax her with murder—"

"Oh, sir, I can't; not I," sighed Mrs. Bread.

"You don't mean to say anything about it? So much the better. Leave that to me."

"If she calls me a thankless old woman," said Mrs. Bread, "I shall have nothing to say. But it is better so," she softly added. "She shall be my lady to the last. That will be more respectable."

"And then you will come to me and I shall be your gentleman," said Newman; "that will be more respectable still!"

Mrs. Bread rose, with lowered eyes, and stood a moment; then, looking up, she rested her eyes upon Newman's face. The disordered proprieties were somehow settling to rest. She looked at Newman so long and so fixedly, with such a dull, intense devotedness, that he himself might have had a pretext for embarrassment. At last she said gently, "You are not looking well, sir."

"That's natural enough," said Newman. "I have nothing to feel well about. To be very indifferent and very fierce, very dull and very jovial, very sick and very lively, all at once,—why, it rather mixes one up."

Mrs. Bread gave a noiseless sigh. "I can tell you something that will make you feel duller still, if you want to feel all one way. About Madame de Cintré."

"What can you tell me?" Newman demanded. "Not that you have seen her?"

She shook her head. "No, indeed, sir, nor ever shall. That's the dullness of it. Nor my lady. Nor M. de Bellegarde."

"You mean that she is kept so close."

"Close, close," said Mrs. Bread, very softly.

These words, for an instant, seemed to check the beating of Newman's heart. He leaned back in his chair, staring up at the old woman. "They have tried to see her, and she wouldn't—she couldn't?"

"She refused—forever! I had it from my lady's own maid," said Mrs. Bread, "who had it from my lady. To speak of it to such a person my lady must have felt the shock. Madame de Cintré won't see them now, and now is her only chance. A while hence she will have no chance."

"You mean the other women—the mothers, the daughters, the sisters; what is it they call them?—won't let her?"

"It is what they call the rule of the house,—or of the order, I believe," said Mrs. Bread. "There is no rule so strict as that of the Carmelites. The bad women in the reformatories are fine ladies to them. They wear old brown cloaks—so the *femme de chambre* told me—

that you wouldn't use for a horse blanket. And the poor countess was so fond of soft-feeling dresses; she would never have anything stiff! They sleep on the ground," Mrs. Bread went on; "they are no better, no better,"—and she hesitated for a comparison,—"they are no better than tinkers' wives. They give up everything, down to the very name their poor old nurses called them by. They give up father and mother, brother and sister,—to say nothing of other persons," Mrs. Bread delicately added. "They wear a shroud under their brown cloaks and a rope round their waists, and they get up on winter nights and go off into cold places to pray to the Virgin Mary. The Virgin Mary is a hard mistress!"

Mrs. Bread, dwelling on these terrible facts, sat dry-eyed and pale, with her hands clasped in her satin lap. Newman gave a melancholy groan and fell forward, leaning his head on his hands. There was a long silence, broken only by the ticking of the great gilded clock on the chimney-piece.

"Where is this place—where is the convent?" Newman asked at last, looking up.

"There are two houses," said Mrs. Bread. "I found out; I thought you would like to know—though it's poor comfort, I think. One is in the Avenue de Messine; they have learned that Madame de Cintré is there. The other is in the Rue d'Enfer. That's a terrible name; I suppose you know what it means."

Newman got up and walked away to the end of his long room. When he came back Mrs. Bread had got up, and stood by the fire with folded hands. "Tell me this," he said. "Can I get near her—even if I don't see her? Can I look through a grating, or some such thing, at the place where she is?"

It is said that all women love a lover, and Mrs. Bread's sense of the preëstablished harmony which kept servants in their "place," even as planets in their orbits (not that Mrs. Bread had ever consciously likened herself to a planet), barely availed to temper the maternal melancholy with which she leaned her head on one side and gazed at her new employer. She probably felt for the moment as if, forty years before, she had held him also in her arms. "That wouldn't help you, sir. It would only make her seem farther away."

"I want to go there, at all events," said Newman. "Avenue de Messine, you say? And what is it they call themselves?"

"Carmelites," said Mrs. Bread.

"I shall remember that."

Mrs. Bread hesitated a moment, and then, "It's my duty to tell you this, sir," she went on. "The convent has a chapel, and some people are admitted on Sunday to the Mass. You don't see the poor creatures that are shut up there, but I am told you can hear them sing. It's a wonder they have any heart for singing! Some Sunday I shall make bold to go. It seems to me I should know *her* voice in fifty."

Newman looked at his visitor very gratefully; then he held out his hand and shook hers. "Thank you," he said. "If any one can get in, I will." A moment later Mrs. Bread proposed, deferentially, to retire, but he checked her and put a lighted candle into her hand. "There are half a dozen rooms there I don't use," he said, pointing through an open door. "Go and look at them and take your choice. You can live in the one you like best." From this bewildering opportunity Mrs. Bread at first recoiled; but finally, yielding to Newman's gentle, reassuring push, she wandered off into the dusk with her tremulous taper. She remained absent a quarter of an hour, during which Newman paced up and down, stopped occasionally to look out of the window at the lights on the Boulevard, and then resumed his walk. Mrs. Bread's relish for her investigation apparently increased as she proceeded; but at last she reappeared and deposited her candlestick on the chimney-piece.

"Well, have you picked one out?" asked Newman.

"A room, sir? They are all to fine for a dingy old body like me. There isn't one that hasn't a bit of gilding."

"It's only tinsel, Mrs. Bread," said Newman. "If you stay there a while it will all peel off of itself." And he gave a dismal smile.

"Oh, sir, there are things enough peeling off already!" rejoined Mrs. Bread, with a head-shake. "Since I was there I thought I would look about me. I don't believe you know, sir. The corners are most dreadful. You do want a housekeeper, that you do; you want a tidy Englishwoman that isn't above taking hold of a broom."

Newman assured her that he suspected, if he had not measured, his domestic abuses, and that to reform them was a mission worthy of her powers. She held her candlestick aloft again and looked around the salon with compassionate glances; then she intimated that she accepted the mission, and that its sacred character would sustain her in her rupture with Madame de Bellegarde. With this she curtsied herself away.

She came back the next day with her worldly goods, and Newman, going into his drawing-room, found her upon her aged knees before a divan, sewing up some detached fringe. He questioned her as to her leave-taking with her late mistress, and she said it had proved easier than she feared. "I was perfectly civil, sir, but the Lord helped me to remember that a good woman has no call to tremble before a bad one."

"I should think so!" cried Newman. "And does she know you have come to me?"

"She asked me where I was going, and I mentioned your name," said Mrs. Bread.

"What did she say to that?"

"She looked at me very hard, and she turned very red. Then she bade me leave her. I was all ready to go, and I had got the coachman, who is an Englishman, to bring down my poor box and to fetch me a cab. But when I went down myself to the gate I found it closed. My lady had sent orders to the porter not to let me pass, and by the same orders the porter's wife—she is a dreadful sly old body—had gone out in a cab to fetch home M. de Bellegarde from his club."

Newman slapped his knee. "She *is* scared! she *is* scared!" he cried, exultantly.

"I was frightened too, sir," said Mrs. Bread, "but I was also mightily vexed. I took it very high with the porter and asked him by what right he used violence to an honorable Englishwoman who had lived in the house for thirty years before he was heard of. Oh, sir, I was very grand, and I brought the man down. He drew his bolts and let me out, and I promised the cabman something handsome if he would drive fast. But he was terribly slow; it seemed as if we should never reach your blessed door. I am all of a tremble still; it took me five minutes, just now, to thread my needle."

Newman told her, with a gleeful laugh, that if she chose she might have a little maid on purpose to thread her needles; and he went away murmuring to himself again that the old woman *was* scared—she *was* scared!

He had not shown Mrs. Tristram the little paper that he carried in his pocket-book, but since his return to Paris he had seen her several times, and she had told him that he seemed to her to be in a strange way—an even stranger way than his sad situation made natural. Had his disappointment gone to his head? He looked like a man who was going to be ill, and yet she had never seen him more restless and active. One day he would sit hanging his head and looking as if he were firmly resolved never to smile again; another he would indulge in laughter that was almost unseemly and make jokes that were bad even for him. If he was trying to carry off his sorrow, he at such times really went too far. She begged him of all things not to be "strange." Feeling in a measure responsible as she did for the affair which had turned out so ill for him, she could endure anything but his strangeness. He might be melancholy if he would, or he might be stoical; he might be cross and cantankerous with her and ask her why she had ever dared to meddle with his destiny: to this she would submit; for this she would make allowances. Only, for Heaven's sake, let him not be incoherent. That would be extremely unpleasant. It was like people talking in their sleep; they always frightened her. And Mrs. Tristram intimated that, taking very high ground as regards the moral obligation which events had laid upon her, she proposed not to rest quiet until she should have confronted him with the least inadequate substitute for Madame de Cintré that the two hemispheres contained.

"Oh," said Newman, "we are even now, and we had better not open a new account! You may bury me some day, but you shall never marry me. It's too rough. I hope, at any rate," he added, "that there is nothing incoherent in this—that I want to go next Sunday to the Carmelite chapel in the Avenue de Messine. You know one of the Catholic ministers—an abbé, is that it?—I have seen him here, you know; that motherly old gentleman with the big waist-band. Please ask him if I need a special leave to go in, and if I do, beg him to obtain it for me."

Mrs. Tristram gave expression to the liveliest joy. "I am so glad you have asked me to do something!" she cried. "You shall get into the chapel if the abbé is disfrocked for his share in it." And two days afterwards she told him that it was all arranged; the abbé was enchanted to serve him, and if he would present himself civilly at the convent gate there would be no difficulty.

Chapter XXIV

SUNDAY WAS as yet two days off; but meanwhile, to beguile his impatience, Newman took his way to the Avenue de Messine and got what comfort he could in staring at the blank outer wall of Madame de Cintré's present residence. The street in question, as some travelers will remember, adjoins the Parc Monceau, which is one of the prettiest corners of Paris. The quarter has an air of modern opulence and convenience which seems at variance with the ascetic institution, and the impression made upon Newman's gloomily-irritated gaze by the fresh-looking, windowless expanse behind which the woman he loved was perhaps even then pledging herself to pass the rest of her days was less exasperating than he had feared. The place suggested a convent with the modern improvements—an asylum in which privacy, though unbroken, might be not quite identical with privation, and meditation, though monotonous, might be of a cheerful cast. And yet he knew the case was otherwise; only at present it was not a reality to him. It was too strange and too mocking to be real; it was like a page torn out of a romance, with no context in his own experience.

On Sunday morning, at the hour which Mrs. Tristram had indicated, he rang at the gate in the blank wall. It instantly opened and admitted him into a clean, cold-looking court, from beyond which a dull, plain edifice looked down upon him. A robust lay sister with a cheerful complexion emerged from a porter's lodge, and, on his stating his errand, pointed to the open door of the chapel, an edifice which occupied the right side of the court and was preceded by a high flight of steps. Newman ascended the steps and immediately entered the open door. Service had not yet begun; the place was dimly lighted, and it was some moments before he could distinguish its features. Then he saw it was divided by a large close iron screen into two unequal portions. The altar was on the hither side of the screen, and between it and the entrance were disposed several benches and chairs. Three or four of these were occupied by vague, motionless figures—figures that he presently perceived to be women, deeply absorbed in their devotion. The place seemed to Newman very cold; the smell of the incense itself was cold. Besides this there was a twinkle of tapers and here and there a glow of colored glass. Newman seated himself; the praying women kept still, with their backs turned. He saw they were visitors like himself and he would have liked to see their faces; for he believed that they were the mourning mothers and sisters of other women who had had the same pitiless courage as Madame de Cintré. But they were better off than he, for they at least shared the faith to which the others had sacrificed themselves. Three or four persons came in; two of them were elderly gentlemen. Every one was very quiet. Newman fastened his eyes upon the screen behind the altar. That was the convent, the real convent, the place where she was. But he could see nothing; no light came through the crevices. He got up and approached the partition very gently, trying to look through. But behind it there was darkness, with nothing stirring. He went back to his place, and after that a priest and two altar boys came in and began to say mass. Newman watched their genuflections and gyrations with a grim, still enmity; they seemed aids and abettors of Madame de Cintré's desertion; they were mouthing and droning out their triumph. The priest's long, dismal intonings acted upon his nerves and deepened his wrath; there was something defiant in his unintelligible drawl; it seemed meant for Newman himself. Suddenly there arose from the depths of the chapel, from behind the inexorable grating, a sound which drew his attention from the altar—the sound of a strange, lugubrious chant, uttered by women's voices. It began softly, but it presently grew louder, and as it increased it became more of a wail and a dirge. It was the chant of the Carmelite nuns, their only human utterance. It was their dirge over their buried affections and over the vanity of earthly desires. At first Newman was bewildered—almost stunned—by the strangeness of the sound; then, as he comprehended its meaning, he listened intently and his heart began to throb. He listened for Madame de Cintré's voice, and in the very heart of the tuneless harmony he imagined he made it out. (We are obliged to believe that he was wrong, inasmuch as she had obviously not yet had time to become a member of the invisible sisterhood.) The chant kept on, mechanical and monotonous, with dismal repetitions and despairing cadences. It was hideous, it was horrible; as it continued, Newman felt that he needed all his self-control. He was growing more agitated; he felt tears in his eyes. At last, as in its full force the thought came over him that this confused, impersonal wail was all that either he or the world she had deserted should ever hear of the voice he had found so sweet, he felt that he could bear it no longer. He rose abruptly and made his way out. On the threshold he paused, listened again to the dreary strain, and then hastily descended into the court. As he did so he saw that the good sister with the high-colored cheeks and the fan-like frill to her coiffure, who had admitted him, was in conference at the gate with two persons who had just come in. A second glance informed him that these persons were Madame de Bellegarde and her son, and that they were about to avail themselves of that method of approach to Madame de Cintré which Newman had found but a mockery of consolation. As he crossed the court M. de Bellegarde recognized him; the marquis was coming to the steps, leading his mother. The old lady also gave Newman a look, and it resembled that of her son. Both faces expressed a franker perturbation, something more akin to the humbleness of dismay, than Newman had yet seen in them. Evidently he startled the Bellegardes, and they had not

their grand behavior immediately in hand. Newman hurried past
them, guided only by the desire to get out of the convent walls and
into the street. The gate opened itself at his approach; he strode over
the threshold and it closed behind him. A carriage which appeared
to have been standing there, was just turning away from the side-
walk. Newman looked at it for a moment, blankly; then he became
conscious, through the dusky mist that swam before his eyes, that a
lady seated in it was bowing to him. The vehicle had turned away
before he recognized her; it was an ancient landau with one half the
cover lowered. The lady's bow was very positive and accompanied
with a smile; a little girl was seated beside her. He raised his hat, and
then the lady bade the coachman stop. The carriage halted again
beside the pavement, and she sat there and beckoned to Newman—
beckoned with the demonstrative grace of Madame Urbain de Bellegarde. Newman hesitated a moment before he obeyed her summons,
during this moment he had time to curse his stupidity for letting the
others escape him. He had been wondering how he could get at
them; fool that he was for not stopping them then and there! What
better place than beneath the very prison walls to which they had
consigned the promise of his joy? He had been too bewildered
to stop them, but now he felt ready to wait for them at the gate. Madame Urbain, with a certain attractive petulance, beckoned to him
again, and this time he went over to the carriage. She leaned out and
gave him her hand, looking at him kindly, and smiling.

"Ah, monsieur," she said, "you don't include me in your wrath? I
had nothing to do with it."

"Oh, I don't suppose *you* could have prevented it!" Newman answered in a tone which was not that of studied gallantry.

"What you say is too true for me to resent the small account it
makes of my influence. I forgive you, at any rate, because you look
as if you had seen a ghost."

"I have!" said Newman.

"I am glad, then, I didn't go in with Madame de Bellegarde and
my husband. You must have seen them, eh? Was the meeting affectionate? Did you hear the chanting? They say it's like the lamenta-
tions of the damned. I wouldn't go in: one is certain to hear that soon
enough. Poor Claire—in a white shroud and a big brown cloak! That's
the *toilette* of the Carmelites, you know. Well, she was always fond
of long, loose things. But I must not speak of her to you; only I must
say that I am very sorry for you, that if I could have helped you I
would, and that I think every one has been very shabby. I was afraid

of it, you know; I felt it in the air for a fortnight before it came. When I saw you at my mother-in-law's ball, taking it all so easily, I felt as if you were dancing on your grave. But what could I do? I wish you all the good I can think of. You will say that isn't much! Yes; they have been very shabby; I am not a bit afraid to say it; I assure you every one thinks so. We are not all like that. I am sorry I am not going to see you again; you know I think you very good company. I would prove it by asking you to get into the carriage and drive with me for a quarter of an hour, while I wait for my mother-in-law. Only if we were seen—considering what has passed, and every one knows you have been turned away—it might be thought I was going a little too far, even for me. But I shall see you sometimes—somewhere, eh? You know"—this was said in English— "we have a plan for a little amusement."

Newman stood there with his hand on the carriage-door, listening to this consolatory murmur with an unlighted eye. He hardly knew what Madame de Bellegarde was saying; he was only conscious that she was chattering ineffectively. But suddenly it occurred to him that, with her pretty professions, there was a way of making her effective; she might help him to get at the old woman and the marquis. "They are coming back soon—your companions?" he said. "You are waiting for them?"

"They will hear the mass out; there is nothing to keep them longer. Claire has refused to see them."

"I want to speak to them," said Newman; "and you can help me, you can do me a favor. Delay your return for five minutes and give me a chance at them. I will wait for them here."

Madame de Bellegarde clasped her hands with a tender grimace. "My poor friend, what do you want to do to them? To beg them to come back to you? It will be wasted words. They will never come back!"

"I want to speak to them, all the same. Pray do what I ask you. Stay away and leave them to me for five minutes; you needn't be afraid; I shall not be violent; I am very quiet."

"Yes, you look very quiet! If they had le cœur tendre you would move them. But they haven't! However, I will do better for you than what you propose. The understanding is not that I shall come back for them. I am going into the Parc Monceau with my little girl to give her a walk, and my mother-in-law, who comes so rarely into this quarter, is to profit by the same opportunity to take the air. We are to wait for her in the park, where my husband is to bring her to us. Follow me now; just within the gates I shall get out of my carriage. Sit down on a chair in some quiet corner and I will bring them near you. There's devotion for you! *Le reste vous regarde.*"

This proposal seemed to Newman extremely felicitous; it revived his drooping spirit, and he reflected that Madame Urbain was not such a goose as she seemed. He promised immediately to overtake her, and the carriage drove away.

The Parc Monceau is a very pretty piece of landscape-gardening, but Newman, passing into it, bestowed little attention upon its elegant vegetation, which was full of the freshness of spring. He found Madame de Bellegarde promptly, seated in one of the quiet corners of which she had spoken, while before her, in the alley, her little girl, attended by the footman and the lap-dog, walked up and down as if she were taking a lesson in deportment. Newman sat down beside the mamma, and she talked a great deal, apparently with the design of convincing him that—if he would only see it—poor dear Claire did not belong to the most fascinating type of woman. She was too tall and thin, too stiff and cold; her mouth was too wide and her nose too narrow. She had no dimples anywhere. And then she was eccentric, eccentric in cold blood; she was an *Anglaise*, after all. Newman was very impatient; he was counting the minutes until his victims should reappear. He sat silent, leaning upon his cane, looking absently and insensibly at the little marquise. At length Madame de Bellegarde said she would walk toward the gate of the park and meet her companions; but before she went she dropped her eyes, and, after playing a moment with the lace of her sleeve, looked up again at Newman.

"Do you remember," she asked, "the promise you made me three weeks ago?" And then, as Newman, vainly consulting his memory, was obliged to confess that the promise had escaped it, she declared that he had made her, at the time, a very queer answer—an answer at which, viewing it in the light of the sequel, she had fair ground for taking offense. "You promised to take me to Bullier's after your marriage. After your marriage—you made a great point of that. Three days after that your marriage was broken off. Do you know, when I heard the news, the first thing I said to myself? 'Oh heaven, now he won't go with me to Bullier's!' And I really began to wonder if you had not been expecting the rupture."

"Oh, my dear lady," murmured Newman, looking down the path to see if the others were not coming.

"I shall be good-natured," said Madame de Bellegarde. "One must not ask too much of a gentleman who is in love with a cloistered nun. Besides, I can't go to Bullier's while we are in mourning. But I haven't given it up for that. The *partie* is arranged; I have my cavalier. Lord Deepmere, if you please! He has gone back to his dear Dublin; but a few months hence I am to name any evening and he will come over from Ireland, on purpose. That's what I call gallantry!"

Shortly after this Madame de Bellegarde walked away with her little girl. Newman sat in his place; the time seemed terribly long. He felt how fiercely his quarter of an hour in the convent chapel had raked over the glowing coals of his resentment. Madame de Bellegarde kept him waiting, but she proved as good as her word. At last she reappeared at the end of the path, with her little girl and her footman; beside her slowly walked her husband, with his mother on his arm. They were a long time advancing, during which Newman sat unmoved. Tingling as he was with passion, it was extremely characteristic of him that he was able to moderate his expression of it, as he would have turned down a flaring gas-burner. His native coolness, shrewdness, and deliberateness, his life-long submissiveness to the sentiment that words were acts and acts were steps in life, and that in this matter of taking steps curveting and prancing were exclusively reserved for quadrupeds and foreigners—all this admonished him that rightful wrath had no connection with being a fool and indulging in spectacular violence. So as he rose, when old Madame de Belegarde and her son were close to him, he only felt very tall and light. He had been sitting beside some shrubbery, in such a way as not to be noticeable at a distance; but M. de Bellegarde had evidently already perceived him. His mother and he were holding their course, but Newman stepped in front of them, and they were obliged to pause. He lifted his hat slightly, and looked at them for a moment; they were pale with amazement and disgust.

"Excuse me for stopping you," he said in a low tone, "but I must profit by the occasion. I have ten words to say to you. Will you listen to them?"

The marquis glared at him and then turned to his mother. "Can Mr. Newman possibly have anything to say that is worth our listening to?"

"I assure you I have something," said Newman, "besides, it is my duty to say it. It's a notification—a warning."

"Your duty?" said old Madame de Bellegarde, her thin lips curving like scorched paper. "That is your affair, not ours."

Madame Urbain meanwhile had seized her little girl by the hand, with a gesture of surprise and impatience which struck Newman, intent as he was upon his own words, with its dramatic effectiveness. "If Mr. Newman is going to make a scene in public," she exclaimed, "I will take my poor child out of the *mêlée*. She is too young to see such naughtiness!" and she instantly resumed her walk.

"You had much better listen to me," Newman went on. "Whether you do or not, things will be disagreeable for you; but at any rate you will be prepared."

"We have already heard something of your threats," said the marquis, "and you know what we think of them."

"You think a good deal more than you admit. A moment," Newman added in reply to an exclamation of the old lady. "I remember perfectly that we are in a public place, and you see I am very quiet. I am not going to tell your secret to the passers-by; I shall keep it, to begin with, for certain picked listeners. Any one who observes us will think that we are having a friendly chat, and that I am complimenting you, madam, on your venerable virtues."

The marquis gave three short sharp raps on the ground with his stick. "I demand of you to step out of our path!" he hissed.

Newman instantly complied, and M. de Bellegarde stepped forward with his mother. Then Newman said, "Half an hour hence Madame de Bellegarde will regret that she didn't learn exactly what I mean."

The marquise had taken a few steps, but at these words she paused, looking at Newman with eyes like two scintillating globules of ice. "You are like a peddler with something to sell," she said, with a little cold laugh which only partially concealed the tremor in her voice.

"Oh, no, not to sell," Newman rejoined; "I give it to you for nothing." And he approached nearer to her, looking her straight in the eyes. "You killed your husband," he said, almost in a whisper. "That is, you tried once and failed, and then, without trying, you succeeded."

Madame de Bellegarde closed her eyes and gave a little cough, which, as a piece of dissimulation, struck Newman as really heroic. "Dear mother," said the marquis, "does this stuff amuse you so much?"

"The rest is more amusing," said Newman. "You had better not lose it."

Madame de Bellegarde opened her eyes; the scintillations had gone out of them; they were fixed and dead. But she smiled superbly with her narrow little lips, and repeated Newman's word. "Amusing? Have I killed some one else?"

"I don't count your daughter," said Newman, "though I might! Your husband knew what you were doing. I have a proof of it whose existence you have never suspected." And he turned to the marquis, who was terribly white—whiter than Newman had ever seen any one out of a picture. "A paper written by the hand, and signed with the name, of Henri-Urbain de Bellegarde. Written after you, madame, had left him for dead, and while you, sir, had gone—not very fast—for the doctor."

The marquis looked at his mother; she turned away, looking vaguely round her. "I must sit down," she said in a low tone, going toward the bench on which Newman had been sitting.

"Couldn't you have spoken to me alone?" said the marquis to Newman, with a strange look.

"Well, yes, if I could have been sure of speaking to your mother alone, too," Newman answered. "But I have had to take you as I could get you."

Madame de Bellegarde, with a movement very eloquent of what he would have called her "grit," her steel-cold pluck and her instinctive appeal to her own personal resources, drew her hand out of her son's arm and went and seated herself upon the bench. There she remained, with her hands folded in her lap, looking straight at Newman. The expression of her face was such that he fancied at first that she was smiling; but he went and stood in front of her and saw that her elegant features were distorted by agitation. He saw, however, equally, that she was resisting her agitation with all the rigor of her inflexible will, and there was nothing like either fear or submission in her stony stare. She had been startled, but she was not terrified. Newman had an exasperating feeling that she would get the better of him still; he would not have believed it possible that he could so utterly fail to be touched by the sight of a woman (criminal or other) in so tight a place. Madame de Bellegarde gave a glance at her son which seemed tantamount to an injunction to be silent and leave her to her own devices. The marquis stood beside her, with his hands behind him, looking at Newman.

"What paper is this you speak of?" asked the old lady, with an imitation of tranquillity which would have been applauded in a veteran actress.

"Exactly what I have told you," said Newman. "A paper written by your husband after you had left him for dead, and during the couple of hours before you returned. You see he had the time; you shouldn't have stayed away so long. It declares distinctly his wife's murderous intent."

"I should like to see it," Madame de Bellegarde observed.

"I thought you might," said Newman, "and I have taken a copy." And he drew from his waist-coat picket a small, folded sheet.

"Give it to my son," said Madame de Bellegarde. Newman handed it to the marquis, whose mother, glancing at him, said simply, "Look at it." M. de Bellegarde's eyes had a pale eagerness which it was useless for him to try to dissimulate; he took the paper in his light-gloved fingers and opened it. There was a silence, during which he read it. He had more than time to read it, but still he said nothing; he stood staring at it. "Where is the original?" asked Madame de Bellegarde, in a voice which was really a consummate negation of impatience.

"In a very safe place. Of course I can't show you that," said Newman. "You might want to take hold of it," he added with conscious quaintness. "But that's a very correct copy—except, of course, the handwriting. I am keeping the original to show some one else."

M. de Bellegarde at last looked up, and his eyes were still very eager. "To whom do you mean to show it?"

"Well, I'm thinking of beginning with the duchess," said Newman; "that stout lady I saw at your ball. She asked me to come and see her, you know. I thought at the moment I shouldn't have much to say to her; but my little document will give us something to talk about."

"You had better keep it, my son," said Madame de Bellegarde.

"By all means," said Newman; "keep it and show it to your mother when you get home."

"And after showing it to the duchess?"—asked the marquis, folding the paper and putting it away.

"Well, I'll take up the dukes," said Newman. "Then the counts and the barons—all the people you had the cruelty to introduce me to in a character of which you meant immediately to deprive me. I have made out a list."

For a moment neither Madame de Bellegarde nor her son said a word; the old lady sat with her eyes upon the ground; M. de Bellegarde's blanched pupils were fixed upon her face. Then, looking at Newman, "Is that all you have to say?" she asked.

"No, I want to say a few words more. I want to say that I hope you quite understand what I'm about. This is my revenge, you know.

You have treated me before the world—convened for the express purpose—as if I were not good enough for you. I mean to show the world that, however bad I may be, you are not quite the people to say it."

Madame de Bellegarde was silent again, and then she broke her silence. Her self-possession continued to be extraordinary. "I needn't ask you who has been your accomplice. Mrs. Bread told me that you had purchased her services."

"Don't accuse Mrs. Bread of venality," said Newman. "She has kept your secret all these years. She has given you a long respite. It was beneath her eyes your husband wrote that paper; he put it into her hands with a solemn injunction that she was to make it public. She was too good-hearted to make use of it."

The old lady appeared for an instant to hesitate, and then, "She was my husband's mistress," she said, softly. This was the only concession to self-defense that she condescended to make.

"I doubt that," said Newman.

Madame de Bellegarde got up from her bench. "It was not to your opinions I undertook to listen, and if you have nothing left but them to tell me I think this remarkable interview may terminate." And turning to the marquis she took his arm again. "My son," she said, "say something!"

M. de Bellegarde looked down at his mother, passing his hand over his forehead, and then, tenderly, caressingly, "What shall I say?" he asked.

"There is only one thing to say," said the marquise. "That it was really not worth while to have interrupted our walk."

But the marquis thought he could improve this. "Your paper's a forgery," he said to Newman.

Newman shook his head a little, with a tranquil smile. "M. de Bellegarde," he said, "your mother does better. She has done better all along, from the first of my knowing you. You're a mighty plucky woman, madam," he continued. "It's a great pity you have made me your enemy. I should have been one of your greatest admirers."

"*Mon pauvre ami*," said Madame de Bellegarde to her son in French, and as if she had not heard these words, "you must take me immediately to my carriage."

Newman stepped back and let them leave him; he watched them a moment and saw Madame Urbain, with her little girl, come out of a by-path to meet them. The old lady stooped and kissed her grandchild. "Damn it, she *is* plucky!" said Newman, and he walked home with a slight sense of being balked. She was so inexpressively defiant! But on reflection he decided that what he had witnessed was no real sense of security, still less a real innocence. It was only a very superior style of brazen assurance. "Wait till she reads the paper!" he said to himself; and he concluded that he should hear from her soon.

He heard sooner than he expected. The next morning, before midday, when he was about to give orders for his breakfast to be served, M. de Bellegarde's card was brought to him. "She has read the paper and she has passed a bad night," said Newman. He instantly admitted his visitor, who came in with the air of the ambassador of a great power meeting the delegate of a barbarous tribe whom an absurd accident had enabled for the moment to be abominably annoying. The ambassador, at all events, had passed a bad night, and his faultlessly careful toilet only threw into relief the frigid rancor in his eyes and the mottled tones of his refined complexion. He stood before Newman a moment, breathing quickly and softly, and shaking his forefinger curtly as his host pointed to a chair.

"What I have come to say is soon said," he declared, "and can only be said without ceremony."

"I am good for as much or for as little as you desire," said Newman.

The marquis looked round the room a moment, and then, "On what terms will you part with your scrap of paper?"

"On none!" And while Newman, with his head on one side and his hands behind him sounded the marquis's turbid gaze with his own, he added, "Certainly, that is not worth sitting down about."

M. de Bellegarde meditated a moment, as if he had not heard Newman's refusal. "My mother and I, last evening," he said, "talked over your story. You will be surprised to learn that we think your little documents is—a"—and he held back his word a moment—"is genuine."

"You forget that with you I am used to surprises!" exclaimed Newman, with a laugh.

"The very smallest amount of respect that we owe to my father's memory," the marquis continued, "makes us desire that he should not be held up to the world as the author of so—so infernal an attack upon the reputation of a wife whose only fault was that she had been submissive to accumulated injury."

"Oh, I see," said Newman. "It's for your father's sake." And he laughed the laugh in which he indulged when he was most amused —a noiseless laugh, with his lips closed.

But M. de Bellegarde's gravity held good. "There are a few of my father's particular friends for whom the knowledge of so—so unfortunate an—inspiration—would be a real grief. Even say we firmly established by medical evidence the presumption of a mind disordered by fever, *il en resterait quelque chose*. At the best it would look ill in him. Very ill!"

"Don't try medical evidence," said Newman. "Don't touch the doctors and they won't touch you. I don't mind your knowing that I have not written to them."

Newman fancied that he saw signs in M. de Bellegarde's discolored mask that this information was extremely pertinent. But it may have been merely fancy; for the marquis remained majestically argumentative. "For instance, Madame d'Outreville," he said, "of whom you spoke yesterday. I can imagine nothing that would shock her more."

"Oh, I am quite prepared to shock Madame d'Outreville, you know. That's on the cards. I expect to shock a great many people."

M. de Bellegarde examined for a moment the stitching on the back of one of his gloves. Then, without looking up, "We don't offer you money," he said. "That we supposed to be useless."

Newman, turning away, took a few turns about the room, and then came back. "What *do* you offer me? By what I can make out, the generosity is all to be on my side."

The marquis dropped his arms at his side and held his head a little higher. "What we offer you is a chance—a chance that a gentleman should appreciate. A chance to abstain from inflicting a terrible blot upon the memory of a man who certainly had his faults, but who, personally, had done you no wrong."

"There are two things to say to that," said Newman. "The first is, as regards appreciating your 'chance,' that you don't consider me a gentleman. That's your great point, you know. It's a poor rule that won't work both ways. The second is that—well, in a word, you are talking great nonsense!"

Newman, who in the midst of his bitterness had, as I have said, kept well before his eyes a certain ideal of saying nothing rude, was immediately somewhat regretfully conscious of the sharpness of these words. But he speedily observed that the marquis took them more quietly than might have been expected. M. de Bellegarde, like the stately ambassador that he was, continued the policy of ignoring what was disagreeable in his adversary's replies. He gazed at the gilded arabesques on the opposite wall, and then presently transferred his glance to Newman, as if he too were a large grotesque in a rather vulgar system of chamber-decoration. "I suppose you know that as regards yourself, it won't do at all."

"How do you mean it won't do?"

"Why, of course you damn yourself. But I suppose that's in your programme. You propose to throw mud at us; you believe, you hope, that some of it may stick. We know, of course, it can't" explained the marquis in a tone of conscious lucidity; "but you take the chance, and are willing at any rate to show that you yourself have dirty hands."

"That's a good comparison; at least half of it is," said Newman. "I take the chance of something sticking. But as regards my hands, they are clean. I have taken the matter up with my finger-tips."

M. de Bellegarde looked a moment into his hat. "All our friends are quite with us," he said. "They would have done exactly as we have done."

"I shall believe that when I hear them say it. Meanwhile I shall think better of human nature."

The marquis looked into his hat again. "Madame de Cintré was extremely fond of her father. If she knew of the existence of the few written words of which you propose to make this scandalous use, she would demand of you proudly for his sake to give it up to her, and she would destroy it without reading it."

"Very possibly," Newman rejoined. "But she will not know. I was in that convent yesterday and I know what *she* is doing. Lord deliver us! You can guess whether it made me feel forgiving!"

M. de Bellegarde appeared to have nothing more to suggest; but he continued to stand there, rigid and elegant, as a man who believed that his mere personal presence had an argumentative value. Newman watched him, and, without yielding an inch on the main issue, felt an incongruously good-natured impulse to help him to retreat in good order.

"Your visit's a failure, you see," he said. "You offer too little."

"Propose something yourself," said the marquis.

"Give me back Madame de Cintré in the same state in which you took her from me."

M. de Bellegarde threw back his head and his pale face flushed. "Never!" he said.

"You can't!"

"We wouldn't if we could! In the sentiment which led us to deprecate her marriage nothing is changed."

" 'Deprecate' is good!" cried Newman. "It was hardly worth

while to come here only to tell me that you are not ashamed of
yourselves. I could have guessed that!"

The marquis slowly walked toward the door, and Newman,
following, opened it for him. "What you propose to do will be
very disagreeable," M. de Bellegarde said. "That is very evident.
But it will be nothing more."

"As I understand it," Newman answered, "that will be quite
enough!"

M. de Bellegarde stood a moment looking on the ground, as if
he were ransacking his ingenuity to see what else he could do to
save his father's reputation. Then, with a little cold sigh, he seemed
to signify that he regretfully surrendered the late marquis to the
penalty of his turpitude. He gave a hardly perceptible shrug, took
his neat umbrella from the servant in the vestibule, and, with his
gentlemanly walk, passed out. Newman stood listening till he heard
the door close; then he slowly exclaimed, "Well, I ought to begin
to be satisfied now!"

CHAPTER XXV

NEWMAN CALLED upon the comical duchess and found her at home.
An old gentleman with a high nose and a gold-headed cane was just
taking leave of her; he made Newman a protracted obeisance as he
retired, and our hero supposed that he was one of the mysterious
grandees with whom he had shaken hands at Madame de Bellegarde's
ball. The duchess, in her arm-chair, from which she did not move,
with a great flower-pot on one side of her, a pile of pink-covered
novels on the other, and a large piece of tapestry depending from
her lap, presented an expansive and imposing front; but her aspect
was in the highest degree gracious, and there was nothing in her
manner to check the effusion of his confidence. She talked to
him about flowers and books, getting launched with marvelous
promptitude; about the theatres, about the peculiar institutions of
his native country, about the humidity of Paris, about the pretty
complexions of the American ladies, about his impressions of France
and his opinion of its female inhabitants. All this was a brilliant
monologue on the part of the duchess, who, like many of her
country-women, was a person of an affirmative rather than an
interrogative cast of mind, who made *mots* and put them herself
into circulation, and who was apt to offer you a present of a convenient little opinion, neatly enveloped in the gilt paper of a happy

Gallicism. Newman had come to her with a grievance, but he found himself in an atmosphere in which apparently no cognizance was taken of grievances; an atmosphere into which the chill of discomfort had never penetrated, and which seemed exclusively made up of mild, sweet, stale intellectual perfumes. The feeling with which he had watched Madame d'Outreville at the treacherous festival of the Bellegardes came back to him; she struck him as a wonderful old lady in a comedy, particularly well up in her part. He observed before long that she asked him no questions about their common friends; she made no allusion to the circumstances under which he had been presented to her. She neither feigned ignorance of a change in these circumstances nor pretended to condole with him upon it; but she smiled and discoursed and compared the tender-tinted wools of her tapestry, as if the Bellegardes and their wicked-ness were not of this world. "She is fighting shy!" said Newman to himself; and, having made the observation, he was prompted to observe, farther, how the duchess would carry off her indifference. She did so in a masterly manner. There was not a gleam of disguised consciousness in those small, clear, demonstrative eyes which con-stituted her nearest claim to personnal loveliness, there was not a symptom of apprehension that Newman would trench upon the ground she proposed to avoid. "Upon my word, she does it very well," he tacitly commented. "They all hold together bravely, and, whether any one else can trust them or not, they can certainly trust each other."

Newman, at this juncture, fell to admiring the duchess for her fine manners. He felt, most accurately, that she was not a grain less urbane than she would have been if his marriage were still in prospect; but he felt also that she was not a particle more urbane. He had come, so reasoned the duchess—Heaven knew why he had come, after what had happened; and for the half hour, therefore, she would be *charmante*. But she would never see him again. Finding no ready-made opportunity to tell his story, Newman pondered these things more dispassionately than might have been expected; he stretched his legs, as usual, and even chuckled a little, appre-ciatively and noiselessly. And then as the duchess went on relating a *mot* with which her mother had snubbed the great Napoleon, it occurred to Newman that her evasion of a chapter of French history more interesting to himself might possibly be the result of an extreme consideration for his feelings. Perhaps it was delicacy on the duchess's part—not policy. He was on the point of saying something himself, to make the chance which he had determined to give her still better, when the servant announced another visitor. The duchess, on hearing the name—it was that of an Italian prince—gave a little imperceptible pout, and said to Newman, rapidly: "I beg you to remain; I desire this visit to be short." Newman said to himself, at this, that Madame d'Outreville intended, after all, that they should discuss the Bellegardes together.

The prince was a short, stout man, with a head disproportionately large. He had a dusky complexion and a bushy eyebrow, beneath which his eye wore a fixed and somewhat defiant expression; he seemed to be challenging you to insinuate that he was top-heavy. The duchess, judging from her charge to Newman, regarded him as a bore; but this was not apparent from the unchecked flow of her conversation. She made a fresh series of *mots*, characterized with great felicity the Italian intellect and the taste of the figs at Sorrento, predicted the ultimate future of the Italian kingdom (disgust with the brutal Sardinian rule and complete reversion, throughout the peninsula, to the sacred sway of the Holy Father), and, finally, gave a history of the love affairs of the Princess X——. This narrative provoked some rectifications on the part of the prince, who, as he said, pretended to know something about that matter; and having satisfied himself that Newman was in no laughing mood, either with regard to the size of his head or anything else, he entered into the controversy with an animation for which the duchess, when she set him down as a bore, could not have been prepared. The sentimental vicissitudes of the Princess X—— led to a discussion of the heart history of Florentine nobility in general; the duchess had spent five weeks in Florence and had gathered much information on the subject. This was merged, in turn, in an examination of the Italian heart *per se*. The duchess took a brilliantly heterodox view—thought it the least susceptible organ of its kind that she had ever encountered, related examples of its want of susceptibility, and at last declared that for her the Italians were a people of ice. The prince became flame to refute her, and his visit really proved charming. Newman was naturally out of the conversation; he sat with his head a little on one side, watching the interlocutors. The duchess, as she talked, frequently loked at him with a smile, as if to intimate, in the charming manner of her nation, that it lay only with him to say something very much to the point. But he said nothing at all, and at last his thoughts began to wander. A singular feeling came over him—a sudden sense of the folly of his errand. What under the sun had he to say to the duchess, after all? Wherein would it profit him to tell her that the Bellegardes were traitors and that the old lady, into the bargain, was a murderess? He seemed morally to have turned a sort of somersault, and to find things looking differently in consequence. He felt a sudden stiffening of his will and quickening of his reserve. What in the world had he been thinking of when he fancied the duchess could help him, and that it would conduce to his comfort to make her think ill of the Bellegardes? What did her opinion of the Bellegardes matter to him? It was only a shade more important than the opinion the Bellegardes entertained of her. The duchess help him—that cold, stout, soft, artificial woman help him?—she who in the last twenty minutes had built up between them a wall of polite conversation in which she evidently flattered herself that he would never find a gate. Had it come to that—that he was asking favors of conceited people, and appealing for sympathy where he had no sympathy to give? He rested his arms on his knees, and sat for some minutes staring into his hat. As he did so his ears tingled—he had come very near being an ass. Whether or no the duchess would hear his story, he wouldn't tell it. Was he to sit there another half hour for the sake of exposing the Bellegardes? The Bellegardes be hanged! He got up abruptly, and advanced to shake hands with his hostess.

"You can't stay longer?" she asked, very graciously.

"I am afraid not," he said.

She hesitated a moment, and then, "I had an idea you had something particular to say to me," she declared.

Newman loked at her; he felt a little dizzy; for the moment he seemed to be turning his somersault again. The little Italian prince came to his help: "Ah, madam, who has not that?" he softly sighed.

"Don't teach Mr. Newman to say *fadaises*," said the duchess. "It is his merit that he doesn't know how."

"Yes, I don't know how to say *fadaises*," said Newman, "and I don't want to say anything unpleasant."

"I am sure you are very considerate," said the duchess with a smile; and she gave him a little nod for good-by, with which he took his departure.

Once in the street, he stood for some time on the pavement, wondering whether, after all, he was not an ass not to have discharged his pistol. And then again he decided that to talk to any one whomsoever about the Bellegardes would be extremely disagreeable to him. The least disagreeable thing, under the circumstances, was to banish them from his mind, and never think of them again. Indecision had not hitherto been one of Newman's weaknesses, and in this case it was not of long duration. For three days after this he did not, or at least he tried not to, think of the Bellegardes. He dined with Mrs. Tristram, and on her mentioning their name, he begged her almost severely to desist. This gave Tom Tristram a much-coveted opportunity to offer his condolences.

He leaned forward, laying his hand on Newman's arm, compressing his lips and shaking his head. "The fact is, my dear fellow, you see, that you ought never to have gone into it. It was not your doing, I know—it was all my wife. If you want to come down on her, I'll stand off; I give you leave to hit her as hard as you like. You know she has never had a word of reproach from me in her life, and I think she is in need of something of the kind. Why didn't you listen to me? You know I didn't believe in the thing. I thought it at the best an amiable delusion. I don't profess to be a Don Juan or a gay Lothario,—that class of man, you know; but I do pretend to know something about the harder sex. I have never disliked a woman in my life that she has not turned out badly. I was not at all deceived in Lizzie, for instance; I always had my doubts about her. Whatever you may think of my present situation, I must at least admit that I got into it with my eyes open. Now suppose you had got into something like this box with Madame de Cintré. You may depend upon it she would have turned out a stiff one. And upon my word I don't see where you could have found your comfort. Not from the marquis, my dear Newman; he wasn't a man you could go and talk things over with in a sociable, common-sense way. Did he ever seem to want to have you on the premises—did he ever try to see you alone? Did he ever ask you to come and smoke a cigar with him of an evening, or step in, when you had been calling on the ladies, and take something? I don't think you would have got much encouragement out of *him*. And as for the old lady, she struck one as an uncommonly strong dose. They have a great expression here, you know; they call it 'sympathetic.' Everything is sympathetic—or ought to be. Now Madame de Bellegarde is about as sympathetic as that mustard-pot. They're a d—d cold-blooded lot, any way; I felt it awfully at that ball of theirs. I felt as if I were walking up and down in the Armory, in the Tower of London! My dear boy, don't think me a vulgar brute for hinting at it, but you may depend upon it, all they wanted was your money. I know something about that; I can tell when people want one's money! Why they stopped wanting yours I don't know; I suppose because they could get some one else's without working so hard for it. It isn't worth finding out. It may be that it was not Madame de Cintré that backed out first; very likely the old woman put her up to it. I suspect she and her mother are really as thick as thieves, eh? You are well out of it, my boy; make up your mind to that. If I express myself strongly it is all because I love you so much; and from that point of view I may say I should as soon have thought of making up to that piece of pale high-mightiness as I should have thought of making up to the Obelisk in the Place de la Concorde."

Newman sat gazing at Tristram during this harangue with a lack-lustre eye; never yet had he seemed to himself to have outgrown so completely the phase of equal comradeship with Tom Tristram. Mrs. Tristram's glance at her husband had more of a spark; she turned to Newman with a slightly lurid smile. "You must at least do justice," she said, "to the felicity with which Mr. Tristram repairs the indiscretions of a too zealous wife."

But even without the aid of Tom Tristram's conversational felicities, Newman would have begun to think of the Bellegardes again. He could cease to think of them only when he ceased to think of his loss and privation, and the days had as yet but scantily lightened the weight of this incommodity. In vain Mrs. Tristram begged him to cheer up; she assured him that the sight of his countenance made her miserable.

"How can I help it?" he demanded with a trembling voice. "I feel like a widower—and a widower who has not even the consolation of going to stand beside the grave of his wife—who has not the right to wear so much mourning as a weed on his hat. I feel," he added in a moment, "as if my wife had been murdered and her assassins were still at large."

Mrs. Tristram made no immediate rejoinder, but at last she said, with a smile which, in so far as it was a forced one, was less successfully simulated than such smiles, on her lips, usually were: "Are you very sure that you would have been happy?"

Newman stared a moment, and then shook his head. "That's weak," he said; "that won't do."

"Well," said Mrs. Tristram with a more triumphant bravery, "I don't believe you would have been happy."

Newman gave a little laugh. "Say I should have been miserable, then; it's a misery I should have preferred to any happiness."

Mrs. Tristram began to muse. "I should have been curious to see; it would have been very strange."

"Was it from curiosity that you urged me to try and marry her?"

"A little," said Mrs. Tristram, growing still more audacious. Newman gave her the one angry look he had been destined ever to give her, turned away and took up his hat. She watched him a moment, and then she said, "That sounds very cruel, but it is less so than it sounds. Curiosity has a share in almost everything I do. I wanted very much to see, first, whether such a marriage could actually take place; second, what would happen if it should take place."

"So you didn't believe," said Newman, resentfully.

"Yes, I believed—I believed that it would take place, and that you would be happy. Otherwise I should have been, among my specu- lations, a very heartless creature. *But*," she continued, laying her hand upon Newman's arm and hazarding a grave smile, "it was the highest flight ever taken by a tolerably bold imagination!"

Shortly after this she recommended him to leave Paris and travel for three months. Change of scene would do him good, and he would forget his misfortune sooner in absence from the objects which had witnessed it. "I really feel," Newman rejoined, "as if to leave *you*, at least, would do me good—and cost me very little effort. You are growing cynical, you shock me and pain me."

"Very good," said Mrs. Tristram, good-naturedly or cynically, as may be thought most probable. "I shall certainly see you again."

Newman was very willing to get away from Paris; the brilliant streets he had walked through in his happier hours, and which then seemed to wear a higher brilliancy in honor of his happiness, appeared now to be in the secret of his defeat and to look down upon it in shining mockery. He would go somewhere; he cared little where; and he made his preparations. Then, one morning, at haphazard, he drove to the train that would transport him to Boulogne and dispatch him thence to the shores of Britain. As he rolled along in the train he asked himself what had become of his revenge, and he was able to say that it was provisionally pigeon- holed in a very safe place; it would keep till called for.

He arrived in London in the midst of what is called "the season," and it seemed to him at first that he might here put himself in the way of being diverted from his heavy-heartedness. He knew no one in all England, but the spectacle of the mighty metropolis roused him somewhat from his apathy. Anything that was enormous usually found favor with Newman, and the multitudinous energies and industries of England stirred within him a dull vivacity of contemplation. It is on record that the weather, at that moment, was of the finest English quality; he took long walks and explored London in every direction; he sat by the hour in Kensington Gardens and beside the adjoining Drive, watching the people and the horses and the carriages; the rosy English beauties, the wonderful English dandies, and the splendid flunkies. He went to the opera and found it better than in Paris; he went to the theatre and found a surprising charm in listening to dialogue the finest points of which came within the range of his comprehension. He made several excursions into the country, recommended by the waiter at his hotel, with whom, on this and similar points, he had established confidential relations. He watched the deer in Windsor Forest and admired the Thames from Richmond Hill; he ate white-bait and brown-bread and butter at Greenwich, and strolled in the grassy shadow of the cathedral of Canterbury. He also visited the Tower of London and Madame Tussaud's exhibition. One day he thought he would go to Sheffield, and then, thinking again, he gave it up. Why should he go to Sheffield? He had a feeling that the link which bound him to a possible interest in the manufacture of cutlery was broken. He had no desire for an "inside view" of any successful enterprise whatever, and he would not have given the smallest sum for the privilege of talking over the details of the most "splendid" business with the shrewdest of overseers.

One afternoon he had walked into Hyde Park, and was slowly threading his way through the human maze which edges the Drive. The stream of carriages was no less dense, and Newman, as usual, marveled at the strange, dingy figures which he saw taking the air in some of the stateliest vehicles. They reminded him of what he had read of eastern and southern countries, in which grotesque idols and fetiches were sometimes taken out of their temples and carried abroad in golden chariots to be displayed to the multitude. He saw a great many pretty cheeks beneath high-plumed hats as he squeezed his way through serried waves of crumpled muslin; and sitting on little chairs at the base of the great serious English trees, he observed a number of quiet-eyed maidens who seemed only to remind him afresh that the magic of beauty had gone out of the world with Madame de Cintré: to say nothing of other damsels, whose eyes were not quiet, and who struck him still more as a satire on possible consolation. He had been walking for some time, when, directly in front of him, borne back by the summer breeze, he heard a few words uttered in that bright Parisian idiom from which his ears had begun to alienate themselves. The voice in which the words were spoken made them seem even more like a thing with which he had once been familiar, and as he bent his eyes it lent an identity to the commonplace elegance of the back hair and shoulders of a young lady walking in the same direction as himself. Mademoiselle Nioche, apparently, had come to seek a more rapid advancement in London, and another glance led Newman to suppose that she had found it. A gentleman was strolling beside her, lending a most attentive ear to her conversation and too entranced to open his lips. Newman did not hear his voice, but perceived that he presented the dorsal expression of a well-dressed Englishman. Mademoiselle Nioche was attracting attention: the ladies who passed her turned round to survey the Parisian perfection of her toilet. A great cataract of flounces rolled down from the young lady's waist to Newman's feet; he had to step aside to avoid treading upon them. He stepped aside, indeed, with a decision of movement which the occasion scarcely demanded; for even this imperfect glimpse of Miss Noémie had excited his displeasure. She seemed an odious blot upon the face of nature; he wanted to put her out of his sight. He thought of Valentin de Bellegarde, still green in the earth of his burial—his young life clipped by this flourishing impudence. The perfume of the young lady's finery sickened him; he turned his head and tried to deflect his course; but the pressure of the crowd kept him near her a few minutes longer, so that he heard what she was saying.

"Ah, I am sure he will miss me," she murmured. "It was very cruel in me to leave him; I am afraid you will think me a very heartless creature. He might perfectly well have come with us. I don't think he is very well," she added; "it seemed to me to-day that he was not very gay."

Newman wondered whom she was talking about, but just then an opening among his neighbors enabled him to turn away, and he said to himself that she was probably paying a tribute to British propriety and playing at tender solicitude about her papa. Was that miserable old man still treading the path of vice in her train? Was he still giving her the benefit of his experience of affairs, and had he crossed the sea to serve as her interpreter? Newman walked some distance farther, and then began to retrace his steps, taking care not to traverse again the orbit of Mademoiselle Nioche. At last he looked for a chair under the trees, but he had some difficulty in finding an empty one. He was about to give up the search when he saw a gentleman rise from the seat he had been occupying, leaving Newman to take it without looking at his neighbors. He sat there for some time without heeding them; his attention was lost in the irritation and bitterness produced by his recent glimpse of Miss Noémie's iniquitous vitality. But at the end of a quarter of an hour, dropping his eyes, he perceived a small pug-dog squatted upon the path near his feet—a diminutive but very perfect specimen of its interesting species. The pug was sniffing at the fashionable world, as it passed him, with his little black muzzle, and was kept from extending his investigation by a large blue ribbon attached to his collar with an enormous rosette and held in the hand of a person seated next to Newman. To this person Newman transferred his attention, and immediately perceived that he was the object of all that of his neighbor, who was staring up at him from a pair of little fixed white eyes. These eyes Newman instantly recognized; he had been sitting for the last quarter of an hour beside M. Nioche. He had vaguely felt that some one was staring at him. M. Nioche continued to stare; he appeared afraid to move, even to the extent of evading Newman's glance.

"Dear me," said Newman; "are you here, too?" And he looked at his neighbor's helplessness more grimly than he knew. M. Nioche had a new hat and a pair of kid gloves; his clothes, too, seemed to belong to a more recent antiquity than of yore. Over his arm was suspended a lady's mantilla—a light and brilliant tissue, fringed with white lace—which had apparently been committed to his keeping; and the little dog's blue ribbon was wound tightly round his hand. There was no expression of recognition in his face—or of anything indeed save a sort of feeble, fascinated dread; Newman looked at the pug and the lace mantilla, and then he met the old man's eyes again. "You know me, I see," he pursued. "You might have spoken to me before." M. Nioche still said nothing, but it seemed to Newman that his eyes began faintly to water. "I didn't expect," our hero went on, "to meet you so far from—from the Café de la Patrie." The old man remained silent, but decidedly Newman had touched the source of tears. His neighbor sat staring and Newman added, "What's the matter, M. Nioche? You used to talk—to talk very prettily. Don't you remmeber you even gave lessons in conversation?"

At this M. Nioche decided to change his attitude. He stooped and picked up the pug, lifted it to his face and wiped his eyes on its little soft back. "I am afraid to speak to you," he presently said, looking over the puppy's shoulder. "I hoped you wouldn't notice me. I should have moved away, but I was afraid that if I moved you would notice me. So I sat very still."

"I suspect you have a bad conscience, sir," said Newman.

The old man put down the little dog and held it carefully in his lap. Then he shook his head, with his eyes still fixed upon his interlocutor. "No, Mr. Newman, I have a good conscience," he murmured.

"Then why should you want to slink away from me?"

"Because—because you don't understand my position."

"Oh, I think you once explained it to me," said Newman. "But it seems improved."

"Improved!" exclaimed M. Nioche, under his breath. "Do you call this improvement?" And he glanced at the treasures in his arms.

"Why, you are on your travels," Newman rejoined. "A visit to London in the season is certainly a sign of prosperity."

M. Nioche, in answer to this cruel piece of irony, lifted the puppy up to his face again, peering at Newman with his small blank eye-holes. There was something almost imbecile in the movement, and Newman hardly knew whether he was taking refuge in a convenient affectation of unreason, or whether he had in fact paid for his dishonor by the loss of his wits. In the latter case, just now, he felt little more tenderly to the foolish old man than in the former. Responsible or not, he was equally an accomplice of his detestably mischievous daughter. Newman was going to leave him abruptly, when a ray of entreaty appeared to disengage itself from the old man's misty gaze. "Are you going away?" he asked.

"Do you want me to stay?" said Newman.

"I should have left you—from consideration. But my dignity suffers at your leaving me—that way."

"Have you got anything particular to say to me?"

M. Nioche looked round him to see that no one was listening, and then he said, very softly but distinctly, "I have *not* forgiven her!"

Newman gave a short laugh, but the old man seemed for the moment not to perceive it; he was gazing away, absently, at some metaphysical image of his implacability. "It doesn't much matter whether you forgive her or not," said Newman. "There are other people who won't, I assure you."

"What has she done?" M. Nioche softly questioned, turning

round again. "I don't know what she does, you know."

"She has done a devilish mischief; it doesn't matter what," said Newman. "She's a nuisance; she ought to be stopped."

M. Nioche stealthily put out his hand and laid it very gently upon Newman's arm. "Stopped, yes," he whispered. "That's it. Stopped short. She is running away—she must be stopped." Then he paused a moment and looked round him. "I mean to stop her," he went on. "I am only waiting for my chance."

"I see," said Newman, laughing briefly again. "She is running away and you are running after her. You have run a long distance!"

But M. Nioche stared insistently: "I shall stop her!" he softly repeated.

He had hardly spoken when the crowd in front of them separated, as if by the impulse to make way for an important personage. Presently, through the opening, advanced Mademoiselle Nioche, attended by the gentleman whom Newman had lately observed. His face being now presented to our hero, the latter recognized the irregular features, the hardly more regular complexion, and the amiable expression of Lord Deepmere. Noémie, on finding herself suddenly confronted with Newman, who, like M. Nioche, had risen from his seat, faltered for a barely perceptible instant. She gave him a little nood, as if she had seen him yesterday, and then, with a good-natured smile, "*Tiens*, how we keep meeting!" she said. She looked consummately pretty, and the front of her dress was a wonderful work of art. She went up to her father, stretching out her hands for the little dog, which he submissively placed in them, and she began to kiss it and murmur over it: "To think of leaving him all alone,—what a wicked, abominable creature he must believe me! He has been very unwell," she added, turning and affecting to explain to Newman, with a spark of infernal impudence, fine as a needle-point, in her eye. "I don't think the English climate agrees with him."

"It seems to agree wonderfully well with his mistress," said Newman.

"Do you mean me? I have never been better, thank you," Miss Noémie declared. "But with *milord*"—and she gave a brilliant glance at her late companion—"how can one help being well?" She seated herself in the chair from which her father had risen, and began to arrange the little dog's rosette.

Lord Deepmere carried off such embarrassment as might be incidental to this unexpected encounter with the inferior grace of a male and a Briton. He blushed a good deal, and greeted the object of his late momentary aspiration to rivalry in the favor of a person other than the mistress of the invalid pug with an awkward nod and a rapid ejaculation—an ejaculation to which Newman, who often found it hard to understand the speech of English people, was able to attach no meaning. Then the young man stood there, with his hand on his hip, and with a conscious grin, staring askance at Miss Noémie. Suddenly an idea seemed to strike him, and he said, turning to Newman, "Oh, you know her?"

"Yes," said Newman, "I know her. I don't believe you do."

"Oh dear, yes, I do!" said Lord Deepmere, with another grin. "I knew her in Paris—by my poor cousin Bellegarde, you know. He knew her, poor fellow, didn't he? It was she, you know, who was at the bottom of his affair. Awfully sad, wasn't it?" continued the young man, talking off his embarrassment as his simple nature permitted. "They got up some story about its being for the Pope; about the other man having said something against the Pope's morals. They always do that, you know. They put it on the Pope because Bellegarde was once in the Zouaves. But it was about *her* morals—*she* was the Pope!" Lord Deepmere pursued, directing an eye illumined by this pleasantry toward Mademoiselle Nioche, who was bending gracefully over her lap-dog, apparently absorbed in conversation with it. "I dare say you think it rather odd that I should—a—keep up the acquaintance," the young man resumed. "But she couldn't help it, you know, and Bellegarde was only my twentieth cousin. I dare say you think it's rather cheeky, by showing with her in Hyde Park. But you see she isn't known yet, and she's in such very good form"— And Lord Deepmere's conclusion was lost in the attesting glance which he again directed toward the young lady.

Newman turned away; he was having more of her than he relished. M. Nioche had stepped aside on his daughter's approach, and he stood there, within a very small compass, looking down hard at the ground. It had never yet, as between him and Newman, been so apposite to place on record the fact that he had not forgiven his daughter. As Newman was moving away he looked up and drew near to him, and Newman, seeing the old man had something particular to say, bent his head for an instant.

"You will see it some day in the papers," murmured M. Nioche.

Our hero departed to hide his smile, and to this day, though the newspapers form his principal reading, his eyes have not been arrested by any paragraph forming a sequel to this announcement.

Chapter XXVI

In that uninitiated observation of the great spectacle of English life upon which I have touched, it might be supposed that Newman passed a great many dull days. But the dullness of his days pleased him; his melancholy, which was settling into a secondary stage, like a healing wound, had in it a certain acrid, palatable sweetness. He had company in his thoughts, and for the present he wanted no other. He had no desire to make acquaintances, and he left untouched a couple of notes of introduction which had been sent him by Tom Tristram. He thought a great deal of Madame de Cintré—sometimes with a dogged tranquillity which might have seemed, for a quarter of an hour at a time, a near neighbor to forgetfulness. He lived over again the happiest hours he had known—that silver chain of numbered days in which his afternoon visits, tending sensibly to the ideal result, had subtilized his good humor to a sort of spiritual intoxication. He came back to reality, after such reveries, with a somewhat muffled shock; he had begun to feel the need of accepting the unchangeable. At other times the reality became an infamy again and the unchangeable an imposture, and he gave himself up to his angry restlessness till he was weary. But on the whole he fell into a rather reflective mood. Without in the least intending it or knowing it, he attempted to read the moral of his strange misadventure. He asked himself, in his quieter hours, whether perhaps, after all, he *was* more commercial than was pleasant. We know that it was in obedience to a strong reaction against questions exclusively commercial that he had come out to pick up æsthetic entertainment in Europe; it may therefore be understood that he was able to conceive that a man might be too commercial. He was very willing to grant it, but the concession, as to his own case, was not made with any very oppressive sense of shame. If he had been too commercial, he was ready to forget it, for in being so he had done no man any wrong that might not be as easily forgotten. He reflected with sober placidity that at least there were no monuments of his "meanness" scattered about the world. If there was any reason in the nature of things why his connection with business should have cast a shadow upon a connection—even a connection broken—with a woman justly proud, he was willing to sponge it out of his life forever. The thing seemed a possibility; he could not feel it, doubtless, as keenly as some people, and it hardly seemed worth while to

flap his wings very hard to rise to the idea; but he could feel it
enough to make any sacrifice that still remained to be made. As to
what such sacrifice was now to be made to, here Newman stopped
short before a blank wall over which there sometimes played a
shadowy imagery. He had a fancy of carrying out his life as he
would have directed it if Madame de Cintré had been left to him—
of making it a religion to do nothing that she would have disliked.
In this, certainly, there was no sacrifice; but there was a pale, oblique
ray of inspiration. It would be lonely entertainment—a good deal
like a man talking to himself in the mirror for want of better
company. Yet the idea yielded Newman several half hours' dumb
exaltation as he sat, with his hands in his pockets and his legs
stretched, over the relics of an expensively poor dinner, in the
undying English twilight. If, however, his commercial imagination
was dead, he felt no contempt for the surviving actualities begotten
by it. He was glad he had been prosperous and had been a great man
of business rather than a small one; he was extremely glad he was
rich. He felt no impulse to sell all he had and give to the poor, or to
retire into meditative economy and asceticism. He was glad he was
rich and tolerably young; if it was possible to think too much about
buying and selling, it was a gain to have a good slice of life left in
which not to think about them. Come, what should he think about
now? Again and again Newman could think only of one thing; his
thoughts always came back to it, and as they did so, with an emo-
tional rush which seemed physically to express itself in a sudden
upward choking, he leaned forward—the waiter having left the room
—and, resting his arms on the table, buried his troubled face.

He remained in England till midsummer, and spent a month in
the country, wandering about among cathedrals, castles, and ruins.
Several times, taking a walk from his inn into meadows and parks,
he stopped by a well-worn stile, looked across through the early
evening at a gray church tower, with its dusky nimbus of thick-
circling swallows, and remembered that this might have been part
of the entertainment of his honeymoon. He had never been so much
alone or indulged so little in accidental dialogue. The period of
recreation appointed by Mrs. Tristram had at last expired, and he
asked himself what he should do now. Mrs. Tristram had written
to him, proposing to him that he should join her in the Pyrenees;
but he was not in the humor to return to France. The simplest thing
was to repair to Liverpool and embark on the first American
steamer. Newman made his way to the great seaport and secured his

berth; and the night before sailing he sat in his room at the hotel, staring down, vacantly and wearily, at an open portmanteau. A number of papers were lying upon it, which he had been meaning to look over; some of them might conveniently be destroyed. But at last he shuffled them roughly together, and pushed them into a corner of the valise; they were business papers, and he was in no humor for sifting them. Then he drew forth his pocket-book and took out a paper of smaller size than those he had dismissed. He did not unfold it; he simply sat looking at the back of it. If he had momentarily entertained the idea of destroying it, the idea quickly expired. What the paper suggested was the feeling that lay in his innermost heart and that no reviving cheerfulness could long quench —the feeling that after all and above all he was a good fellow wronged. With it came a hearty hope that the Bellegardes were enjoying their suspense as to what he would do yet. The more it was prolonged the more they would enjoy it! He had hung fire once, yes; perhaps, in his present queer state of mind, he might hang fire again. But he restored the little paper to his pocket-book very tenderly, and felt better for thinking of the suspense of the Belle-gardes. He felt better every time he thought of it after that, as he sailed the summer seas. He landed in New York and journeyed across the continent to San Francisco, and nothing that he observed by the way contributed to mitigate his sense of being a good fellow wronged.

He saw a great many other good fellows—his old friends—but he told none of them of the trick that had been played him. He said simply that the lady he was to have married had changed her mind, and when he was asked if he had changed his own, he said, "Suppose we change the subject." He told his friends that he had brought home no "new ideas" from Europe, and his conduct probably struck them as an eloquent proof of failing invention. He took no interest in chatting about his affairs and manifested no desire to look over his accounts. He asked half a dozen questions which, like those of an eminent physician inquiring for particular symptoms, showed that he still knew what he was talking about; but he made no comments and gave no directions. He not only puzzled the gentlemen on the stock exchange, but he was himself surprised at the extent of his indifference. As it seemed only to increase, he made an effort to combat it; he tried to interest himself and to take up his old occupations. But they appeared unreal to him; do what he would he some-how could not believe in them. Sometimes he began to fear that there was something the matter with his head; that his brain, perhaps, had softened, and that the end of his strong activities had come. This idea came back to him with an exasperating force. A hopeless, helpless loafer, useful to no one and detestable to himself—this was what the treachery of the Bellegardes had made of him. In his restless idleness he came back from San Francisco to New York, and sat for three days in the lobby of his hotel, looking out through a huge wall of plate-glass at the unceasing stream of pretty girls in Parisian-looking dresses, undulating past with little parcels nursed against their neat figures. At the end of three days he returned to San Francisco, and having arrived there he wished he had stayed away. He had nothing to do, his occupation was gone, and it seemed to him that he should never find it again. He had nothing to do *here*, he sometimes said to himself; but there was something beyond the ocean that he was still to do; something that he had left undone experimentally and speculatively, to see if it could content itself to remain undone. But it was not content: it kept pulling at his heart-strings and thumping at his reason; it murmured in his ears and hovered perpetually before his eyes. It interposed between all new resolutions and their fulfillment; it seemed like a stubborn ghost, dumbly entreating to be laid. Till that was done he should never be able to do anything else.

One day, toward the end of the winter, after a long interval, he received a letter from Mrs. Tristram, who apparently was animated by a charitable desire to amuse and distract her correspondent. She gave him much Paris gossip, talked of General Packard and Miss Kitty Upjohn, enumerated the new plays at the theatre, and inclosed a note from her husband, who had gone down to spend a month at Nice. Then came her signature, and after this her postscript. The latter consisted of these few lines: "I heard three days since from my friend, the Abbé Aubert, that Madame de Cintré last week took the veil at the Carmelites. It was on her twenty-seventh birthday, and she took the name of her patroness, St. Veronica. Sister Veronica has a life-time before her!"

This letter came to Newman in the morning; in the evening he started for Paris. His wound began to ache with its first fierceness, and during his long bleak journey the thought of Madame de Cintré's "life-time," passed within prison walls on whose outer side he might stand, kept him perpetual company. Now he would fix himself in Paris forever; he would extort a sort of happiness from the knowledge that if she was not there, at least the stony sepulchre that held her was. He descended, unannounced, upon Mrs. Bread, whom he found keeping lonely watch in his great empty saloons on the Boulevard Haussmann. They were as neat as a Dutch village; Mrs. Bread's only occupation had been removing individual dust-particles. She made no complaint, however, of her loneliness, for in her philosophy a servant was but a mysteriously projected machine, and it would be as fantastic for a housekeeper to comment upon a gentleman's absences as for a clock to remark upon not being wound up. No particular clock, Mrs. Bread supposed, wept all the time, and no particular servant could enjoy all the sunshine diffused by the career of an exacting master. She ventured, nevertheless, to express a modest hope that Newman meant to remain a while in Paris. Newman laid his hand on hers and shook it gently. "I mean to remain forever," he said.

He went after this to see Mrs. Tristram, to whom he had telegraphed, and who expected him. She looked at him a moment and shook her head. "This won't do," she said; "you have come back too soon." He sat down and asked about her husband and her children, tried even to inquire about Miss Dora Finch. In the midst of this— "Do you know where she is?" he asked, abruptly.

Mrs. Tristram hesitated a moment; of course he couldn't mean Miss Dora Finch. Then she answered, properly: "She has gone to the other house—in the Rue d'Enfer." After Newman had sat a while longer looking very sombre, she went on: "You are not so good a man as I thought. You are more—you are more—"

"More what?" Newman asked.

"More unforgiving."

"Good God!" cried Newman; "do you expect me to forgive?"

"No, not that. I have not forgiven, so of course you can't. But you might forget! You have a worse temper about it than I should have expected. You look wicked—you look dangerous."

"I may be dangerous," he said; "but I am not wicked. No, I am not wicked." And he got up to go. Mrs. Tristram asked him to come back to dinner; but he answered that he did not feel like pledging himself to be present at an entertainment, even as a solitary guest. Later in the evening, if he should be able, he would come.

He walked away through the city, beside the Seine and over it, and took the direction of the Rue d'Enfer. The day had the softness of early spring; but the weather was gray and humid. Newman found himself in a part of Paris which he little knew—a region of convents and prisons, of streets bordered by long dead walls and traversed by few wayfarers. At the intersection of two of these streets stood the house of the Carmelites—a dull, plain edifice, with a high-shouldered blank wall all round it. From without Newman could see its upper windows, its steep roof and its chimneys. But these things revealed no symptoms of human life; the place looked dumb, deaf, inanimate. The pale, dead, discolored wall stretched beneath it, far down the empty side street—a vista without a human figure. Newman stood there a long time; there were no passers; he was free to gaze his fill. This seemed the goal of his journey; it was what he had come for. It was a strange satisfaction, and yet it was a satisfaction; the barren stillness of the place seemed to be his own release from ineffectual longing. It told him that the woman within was lost beyond recall, and that the days and years of the future would pile themselves above her like the huge immovable slab of a tomb. These days and years, in this place, would always be just so gray and silent. Suddenly, from the thought of their seeing him stand there, again the charm utterly departed. He would never stand there again; it was gratuitous dreariness. He turned away with a heavy heart, but with a heart lighter than the one he had brought. Everything was over, and he too at last could rest. He walked down through narrow, winding streets to the edge of the Seine again, and there he saw, close above him, the soft, vast towers of Notre Dame. He crossed one of the bridges and stood a moment in the empty place before the great cathedral; then he went in beneath the grossly-imaged portals. He wandered some distance up the nave and sat down in the splendid dimness. He sat a long time; he heard far-away bells chiming off, at long intervals, to the rest of the world. He was very tired; this was the best place he could be in. He said no prayers; he had no prayers to say. He had nothing to be thankful for, and he had nothing to ask; nothing to ask, because now he must take care of himself. But a great cathedral offers a very various hospitality, and Newman sat in his place, because while he was there he was out of the world. The most unpleasant thing that had ever happened to him had reached its formal conclusion, as it were; he could close the book and put it away. He leaned his head for a long time on the chair in front of him; when he took it up he felt that he was himself again. Somewhere in his mind, a tight knot seemed to have loosened. He thought of the Bellegardes; he had almost forgotten them. He remembered them as people he had meant to do something to. He gave a groan as he remembered what he had meant to do; he was annoyed at having meant to do it; the bottom, suddenly, had fallen out of his

revenge. Whether it was Christian charity or unregenerate good nature—what it was, in the background of his soul—I don't pretend to
say; but Newman's last thought was that of course he would let the
Bellegardes go. If he had spoken it aloud he would have said that he
didn't want to hurt them. He was ashamed of having wanted to hurt
them. They had hurt him, but such things were really not his game.
At last he got up and came out of the darkening church; not with
the elastic step of a man who had won a victory or taken a resolve,
but strolling soberly, like a good-natured man who is still a little
ashamed.

Going home, he said to Mrs. Bread that he must trouble her to
put back his things into the portmanteau she had unpacked the evening before. His gentle stewardess looked at him through eyes a
trifle bedimmed. "Dear me, sir," she exclaimed, "I thought you said
that you were going to stay forever."

"I meant that I was going to stay away forever," said Newman
kindly. And since his departure from Paris on the following day he
has certainly not returned. The gilded apartments I have so often
spoken of stand ready to receive him; but they serve only as a spacious residence for Mrs. Bread, who wanders eternally from room to
room, adjusting the tassels of the curtains, and keeps her wages,
which are regularly brought her by a banker's clerk, in a great pink
Sèvres vase on the drawing-room mantel-shelf.

Late in the evening Newman went to Mrs. Tristram's and found
Tom Tristram by the domestic fireside. "I'm glad to see you back
in Paris," this gentleman declared. "You know it's really the only
place for a white man to live." Mr. Tristram made his friend welcome, according to his own rosy light, and offered him a convenient
résumé of the Franco-American gossip of the last six months. Then
at last he got up and said he would go for half an hour to the club.
"I suppose a man who has been for six months in Colifornia wants a
little intellectual conversation. I'll let my wife have a go at you."

Newman shook hands heartily with his host, but did not ask him
to remain; and then he relapsed into his place on the sofa, opposite
to Mrs. Tristram. She presently asked him what he had done after
leaving her. "Nothing particular," said Newman.

"You struck me," she rejoined, "as a man with a plot in his head.
You looked as if you were bent on some sinister errand, and after
you had left me I wondered whether I ought to have let you go."

"I only went over to the other side of the river—to the Carmelites,"
said Newman.

Mrs. Tristram looked at him a moment and smiled. "What did you do there? Try to scale the wall?"

"I did nothing. I looked at the place for a few minutes and then came away."

Mrs. Tristram gave him a sympathetic glance. "You didn't happen to meet M. de Bellegarde," she asked, "staring hopelessly at the convent wall as well? I am told he takes his sister's conduct very hard."

"No, I didn't meet him, I am happy to say," Newman answered, after a pause.

"They are in the country," Mrs. Tristram went on; "at—what is the name of the place?—Fleurières. They returned there at the time you left Paris and have been spending the year in extreme seclusion. The little marquise must enjoy it; I expect to hear that she has eloped with her daughter's music-master!"

Newman was looking at the light wood-fire; but he listened to this with extreme interest. At last he spoke: "I mean never to mention the name of those people again, and I don't want to hear anything more about them." And then he took out his pocket-book and drew forth a scrap of paper. He looked at it an instant, then got up and stood by the fire. "I am going to burn them up," he said. "I am glad to have you as a witness. There they go!" And he tossed the paper into the flame.

Mrs. Tristram sat with her embroidery needle suspended. "What is that paper?" she asked.

Newman leaning against the fire-place, stretched his arms and drew a longer breath than usual. Then after a moment, "I can tell you now," he said. "It was a paper containing a secret of the Bellegardes—something which would damn them if it were known."

Mrs. Tristram dropped her embroidery with a reproachful moan. "Ah, why didn't you show it to me?"

"I thought of showing it to you—I thought of showing it to every one. I thought of paying my debt to the Bellegardes that way. So I told them, and I frightened them. They have been staying in the country, as you tell me, to keep out of the explosion. But I have given it up."

Mrs. Tristram began to take slow stitches again. "Have you quite given it up?"

"Oh yes."

"Is it very bad, this secret?"

"Yes, very bad."

"For myself," said Mrs. Tristram, "I am sorry you have given it up. I should have liked immensely to see your paper. They have wronged me too, you know, as your sponsor and guarantee, and it would have served for my revenge as well. How did you come into possession of your secret?"

"It's a long story. But honestly, at any rate."

"And they knew you were master of it?"

"Oh, I told them."

"Dear me, how interesting!" cried Mrs. Tristram. "And you humbled them at your feet?"

Newman was silent a moment. "No, not at all. They pretended not to care—not to be afraid. But I know they did care—they were afraid."

"Are you very sure?"

Newman stared a moment. "Yes, I'm sure."

Mrs. Tristram resumed her slow stitches. "They defied you, eh?"

"Yes," said Newman, "it was about that."

"You tried by the threat of exposure to make them retract?" Mrs. Tristram pursued.

"Yes, but they wouldn't. I gave them their choice, and they chose to take their chance of bluffing off the charge and convicting me of fraud. But they *were* frightened," Newman added, "and I have had all the vengeance I want."

"It is most provoking," said Mrs. Tristram, "to hear you talk of the 'charge' when the charge is burnt up. Is it quite consumed?" she asked, glancing at the fire.

Newman assured her that there was nothing left of it.

"Well then," she said, "I suppose there is no harm in saying that you probably did not make them so very uncomfortable. My impression would be that since, as you say, they defied you, it was because they believed that, after all, you would never really come to the point. Their confidence, after counsel taken of each other, was not in their innocence, nor in their talent for bluffing things off; it was in your remarkable good nature! You see they were right."

Newman instinctively turned to see if the little paper was in fact consumed; but there was nothing left of it.

THE EUROPEANS

fifty francs.

"*Voyons*," said the lady, putting out her hand.

He added a touch or two, and then gave her his sketch. She looked at it, but she went on with her idea of a moment before. "If a woman were to ask you to marry her you would say, 'Certainly, my dear, with pleasure!' And you would marry her and be ridiculously happy. Then at the end of three months you would say to her, 'You know that blissful day when I begged you to be mine!'"

The young man had risen from the table, stretching his arms a little; he walked to the window. "That is a description of a charming nature," he said.

"Oh, yes, you have a charming nature; I regard that as our capital. If I had not been convinced of that I should never have taken the risk of bringing you to this dreadful country."

"This comical country, this delightful country!" exclaimed the young man, and he broke into the most animated laughter.

"Is it those women scrambling into the omnibus?" asked his companion. "What do you suppose is the attraction?"

"I suppose there is a very good-looking man inside," said the young man.

"In each of them? They come along in hundreds, and the men in this country don't seem at all handsome. As for the women—I have never seen so many at once since I left the convent."

"The women are very pretty," her brother declared, "and the whole affair is very amusing. I must make a sketch of it." And he came back to the table quickly, and picked up his utensils—a small sketching-board, a sheet of paper, and three or four crayons. He took his place at the window with these things, and stood there glancing out, plying his pencil with an air of easy skill. While he worked he wore a brilliant smile. Brilliant is indeed the word at this moment for his strongly-lighted face. He was eight and twenty years old; he had a short, slight, well-made figure. Though he bore a noticeable resemblance to his sister, he was a better favored person: fair-haired, clear-faced, witty-looking, with a delicate finish of feature and an expression at once urbane and not at all serious, a warm blue eye, an eyebrow finely drawn and excessively arched— an eyebrow which, if ladies wrote sonnets to those of their lovers, might have been made the subject of such a piece of verse—and a light moustache that flourished upwards as if blown that way by the breath of a constant smile. There was something in his physiognomy at once benevolent and picturesque. But, as I have hinted, it was not at all serious. The young man's face was, in this respect, singular; it was not at all serious, and yet it inspired the liveliest confidence.

"Be sure you put in plenty of snow," said his sister. "*Bonté divine, what a climate!*"

"I shall leave the sketch all white, and I shall put in the little figures in black," the young man answered, laughing. "And I shall call it—what is that line in Keats?—Mid-May's Eldest Child!"

"I don't remember," said the lady, "that mamma ever told me it was like this."

"Mamma never told you anything disagreeable. And it's not like this—every day. You will see that to-morrow we shall have a splendid day."

"*Qu'en savez-vous?* To-morrow I shall go away."

"Where shall you go?"

"Anywhere away from here. Back to Silberstadt. I shall write to the Reigning Prince."

The young man turned a little and looked at her, with his crayon poised. "My dear Eugenia," he murmured, "were you so happy at sea?"

Eugenia got up; she still held in her hand the drawing her brother had given her. It was a bold, expressive sketch of a group of miserable people on the deck of a steamer, clinging together and clutching at each other, while the vessel lurched downward, at a terrific angle, into the hollow of a wave. It was extremely clever, and full of a sort of tragi-comical power. Eugenia dropped her eyes upon it and made a sad grimace. "How can you draw such odious scenes?" she asked. "I should like to throw it into the fire!" And she tossed the paper away. Her brother watched, quietly, to see where it went. It fluttered down to the floor, where he let it lie. She came toward the window, pinching in her waist. "Why don't you reproach me—abuse me?" she asked. "I think I should feel better then. Why don't you tell me that you hate me for bringing you here?"

"Because you would not believe it. I adore you, dear sister! I am delighted to be here, and I am charmed with the prospect."

"I don't know what had taken possession of me. I had lost my head," Eugenia went on.

The young man, on his side, went on plying his pencil. "It is evidently a most curious and interesting country. Here we are, and I mean to enjoy it."

His companion turned away with an impatient step, but presently came back. "High spirits are doubtless an excellent thing," she said; "but you give one too much of them, and I can't see that they have done you any good."

The young man stared, with lifted eyebrows, smiling; he tapped his handsome nose with his pencil. "They have made me happy!"

"That was the least they could do; they have made you nothing else. You have gone through life thanking fortune for such very small favors that she has never put herself to any trouble for you."

"She must have put herself to a little, I think, to present me with so admirable a sister."

"Be serious, Felix. You forget that I am your elder."

"With a sister, then, so elderly!" rejoined Felix, laughing. "I hoped we had left seriousness in Europe."

"I fancy you will find it here. Remember that you are nearly thirty years old, and that you are nothing but an obscure Bohemian—a penniless correspondent of an illustrated newspaper."

"Obscure as much as you please, but not so much of a Bohemian as you think. And not at all penniless! I have a hundred pounds in my pocket. I have an engagement to make fifty sketches, and I mean to paint the portraits of all our cousins, and of all *their* cousins, at a hundred dollars a head."

"You are not ambitious," said Eugenia.

"You are, dear Baroness," the young man replied.

The Baroness was silent a moment, looking out at the sleet-darkened grave-yard and the bumping horse-cars. "Yes, I am ambitious," she said at last. "And my ambition has brought me to this dreadful place!" She glanced about her—the room had a certain vulgar nudity; the bed and the window were curtainless—and she gave a little passionate sigh. "Poor old ambition!" she exclaimed. Then she flung herself down upon a sofa which stood near against the wall, and covered her face with her hands.

Her brother went on with his drawing, rapidly and skilfully; after some moments he sat down beside her and showed her his sketch. "Now, don't you think that's pretty good for an obscure Bohemian?" he asked. "I have knocked off another fifty francs."

Eugenia glanced at the little picture as he laid it on her lap. "Yes, it is very clever," she said. And in a moment she added, "Do you suppose our cousins do that?"

"Do what?"

"Get into those things, and look like that."

Felix meditated awhile. "I really can't say. It will be interesting to discover."

"Oh, the rich people can't!" said the Baroness.

"Are you very sure they are rich?" asked Felix, lightly.

His sister slowly turned in her place, looking at him. "Heavenly powers!" she murmured. "You have a way of bringing out things!"

"It will certainly be much pleasanter if they are rich," Felix declared.

"Do you suppose if I had not known they were rich I would ever have come?"

The young man met his sister's somewhat peremptory eye with his bright, contented glance. "Yes, it certainly will be pleasanter," he repeated.

"That is all I expect of them," said the Baroness. "I don't count upon their being clever or friendly—at first—or elegant or interesting. But I assure you I insist upon their being rich."

Felix leaned his head upon the back of the sofa and looked awhile at the oblong patch of sky to which the window served as frame. The snow was ceasing; it seemed to him that the sky had begun to brighten. "I count upon their being rich," he said at last, "and power-ful, and clever, and friendly, and elegant, and interesting, and gen-erally delightful! *Tu vas voir.*" And he bent forward and kissed his sister. "Look there!" he went on. "As a portent, even while I speak, the sky is turning the color of gold; the day is going to be splendid."

And indeed, within five minutes the weather had changed. The sun broke out through the snow-clouds and jumped into the Baron-ess's room. "*Bonté divine,*" exclaimed this lady, "what a climate!"

"We will go out and see the world," said Felix.

And after a while they went out. The air had grown warm as well as brilliant; the sunshine had dried the pavements. They walked about the streets at hazard, looking at the people and the houses, the shops and the vehicles, the blazing blue sky and the muddy crossings, the hurrying men and the slow-strolling maidens, the fresh red bricks and the bright green trees, the extraordinary mixture of smartness and shabbiness. From one hour to another the day had grown ver-nal; even in the bustling streets there was an odor of earth and blos-som. Felix was immensely entertained. He had called it a comical country, and he went about laughing at everything he saw. You would have said that American civilization expressed itself to his sense in a tissue of capital jokes. The jokes were certainly excellent, and the young man's merriment was joyous and genial. He possessed what is called the pictorial sense; and this first glimpse of democratic manners stirred the same sort of attention that he would have given to the movements of a lively young person with a bright complexion. Such attention would have been demonstrative and complimentary; and in the present case Felix might have passed for an undispirited young exile revisiting the haunts of his childhood. He kept looking at the violent blue of the sky, at the scintillating air, at the scattered and multiplied patches of color.

"*Comme c'est bariolé,* eh?" he said to his sister in that foreign tongue which they both appeared to feel a mysterious prompting oc-casionally to use.

"Yes, it is *bariolé* indeed," the Baroness answered. "I don't like the coloring; it hurts my eyes."

"It shows how extremes meet," the young man rejoined. "Instead of coming to the West we seem to have gone to the East. The way the sky touches the house-tops is just like Cairo; and the red and blue sign-boards patched over the face of everything remind one of Mahometan decorations."

"The young women are not Mahometan," said his companion.

"They can't be said to hide their faces. I never saw anything so bold."

"Thank Heaven they don't hide their faces!" cried Felix. "Their faces are uncommonly pretty."

"Yes, their faces are often very pretty," said the Baroness, who was a very clever woman. She was too clever a woman not to be capable of a great deal of just and fine observation. She clung more closely than usual to her brother's arm; she was not exhilarated, as he was; she said very little, but she noted a great many things and made her reflections. She was a little excited; she felt that she had indeed come to a strange country, to make her fortune. Superficially, she was conscious of a good deal of irritation and displeasure; the Baroness was a very delicate and fastidious person. Of old, more than once, she had gone, for entertainment's sake and in brilliant company, to a fair in a provincial town. It seemed to her now that she was at an enormous fair—that the entertainment and the *désagréments* were very much the same. She found herself alternately smiling and shrinking; the show was very curious, but it was probable, from moment to moment, that one would be jostled. The Baroness had never seen so many people walking about before; she had never been so mixed up with people she did not know. But little by little she felt that this fair was a more serious undertaking. She went with her brother into a large public garden, which seemed very pretty, but where she was surprised at seeing no carriages. The afternoon was drawing to a close; the coarse, vivid grass and the slender treeboles were gilded by the level sunbeams—gilded as with gold that was fresh from the mine. It was the hour at which ladies should come out for an airing and roll past a hedge of pedestrians, holding their parasols askance. Here, however, Eugenia observed no indications of this custom, the absence of which was more anomalous as there was a charming avenue of remarkably graceful, arching elms in the most convenient contiguity to a large, cheerful street, in which, evidently, among the more prosperous members of the *bourgeoisie*, a great deal of pedestrianism went forward. Our friends passed out into this well lighted promenade, and Felix noticed a great many more pretty girls and called his sister's attention to them. This latter measure, however, was superfluous; for the Baroness had inspected, narrowly, these charming young ladies.

"I feel an intimate conviction that our cousins are like that," said Felix.

The Baroness hoped so, but this is not what she said. "They are very pretty," she said, "but they are mere little girls. Where are the women—the women of thirty?"

"Of thirty-three, do you mean?" her brother was going to ask; for he understood often both what she said and what she did not say. But he only exclaimed upon the beauty of the sunset, while the Baroness, who had come to seek her fortune, reflected that it would certainly be well for her if the persons against whom she might need to measure herself should all be mere little girls. The sunset was superb; they stopped to look at it; Felix declared that he had never seen such a gorgeous mixture of colors. The Baroness also thought it splendid; and she was perhaps the more easily pleased from the fact that while she stood there she was conscious of much admiring observation on the part of various nice-looking people who passed that way, and to whom a distinguished, strikingly-dressed woman with a foreign air, exclaiming upon the beauties of nature on a Boston street corner in the French tongue, could not be an object of indifference. Eugenia's spirits rose. She surrendered herself to a certain tranquil gayety. If she had come to seek her fortune, it seemed to her that her fortune would be easy to find. There was a promise of it in the gorgeous purity of the western sky; there was an intimation in the mild, unimpertinent gaze of the passers of a certain natural facility in things.

"You will not go back to Silberstadt, eh?" asked Felix.

"Not to-morrow," said the Baroness.

"Nor write to the Reigning Prince?"

"I shall write to him that they evidently know nothing about him over here."

"He will not believe you," said the young man. "I advise you to let him alone."

Felix himself continued to be in high good humor. Brought up among ancient customs and in picturesque cities, he yet found plenty of local color in the little Puritan metropolis. That evening, after dinner, he told his sister that he should go forth early on the morrow to look up their cousins.

"You are very impatient," said Eugenia.

"What can be more natural," he asked, "after seeing all those pretty girls to-day? If one's cousins are of that pattern, the sooner one knows them the better."

"Perhaps they are not," said Eugenia. "We ought to have brought some letters—to some other people."

"The other people would not be our kinsfolk."

"Possibly they would be none the worse for that," she replied.

Her brother looked at her with his eyebrows lifted. "That was not what you said when you first proposed to me that we should come out here and fraternize with our relatives. You said that it was the prompting of natural affection; and when I suggested some reasons against it you declared that the *voix du sang* should go before everything."

"You remember all that?" asked the Baroness.

"Vividly! I was greatly moved by it."

She was walking up and down the room, as she had done in the morning; she stopped in her walk and looked at her brother. She apparently was going to say something, but she checked herself and resumed her walk. Then, in a few moments, she said something different, which had the effect of an explanation of the suppression of her earlier thought. "You will never be anything but a child, dear brother."

"One would suppose that you, madam," answered Felix, laughing, "were a thousand years old."

"I am—sometimes," said the Baroness.

"I will go, then, and announce to our cousins the arrival of a personage so extraordinary. They will immediately come and pay you their respects."

Eugenia paced the length of the room again, and then she stopped before her brother, laying her hand upon his arm. "They are not to come and see me," she said. "You are not to allow that. That is not the way I shall meet them first." And in answer to his interrogative glance she went on. "You will go and examine, and report. You will come back and tell me who they are and what they are; their number, gender, their respective ages—all about them. Be sure you observe everything; be ready to describe to me the locality, the accessories—how shall I say it?—the mise en scène. Then, at my own time, at my own hour, under circumstances of my own choosing, I will go to them. I will present myself—I will appear before them!" said the Baroness, this time phrasing her idea with a certain frankness.

"And what message am I to take to them?" asked Felix, who had a lively faith in the justness of his sister's arrangements.

She looked at him a moment—at his expression of agreeable veracity; and, with that justness that he admired, she replied, "Say what you please. Tell my story in the way that seems to you most —natural." And she bent her forehead for him to kiss.

Chapter II

The next day was splendid, as Felix had prophesied; if the winter had suddenly leaped into spring, the spring had for the moment as quickly leaped into summer. This was an observation made by a young girl who came out of a large square house in the country, and strolled about in the spacious garden which separated it from a muddy road. The flowering shrubs and the neatly-disposed plants were basking in the abundant light and warmth; the transparent shade of the great elms—they were magnificent trees—seemed to thicken by the hour; and the intensely habitual stillness offered a submissive medium to the sound of a distant church-bell. The young girl listened to the church-bell; but she was not dressed for church. She was bare-headed; she wore a white muslin waist, with an embroidered border, and the skirt of her dress was of colored muslin. She was a young lady of some two or three and twenty years of age, and though a young person of her sex walking bare-headed in a garden, of a Sunday morning in spring-time, can, in the nature of things, never be a displeasing object, you would not have pronounced this innocent Sabbath-breaker especially pretty. She was tall and pale, thin and a little awkward; her hair was fair and perfectly straight; her eyes were dark, and they had the singularity of seeming at once dull and restless—differing herein, as you see, fatally from the ideal "fine eyes," which we always imagine to be both brilliant and tranquil. The doors and windows of the large square house were all wide open, to admit the purifying sunshine, which lay in generous patches upon the floor of a wide, high, covered piazza adjusted to two sides of the mansion—a piazza on which several straw-bottomed rocking-chairs and half a dozen of those small cylindrical stools in green and blue porcelain, which suggest an affiliation between the residents and the Eastern trade, were symmetrically disposed. It was an ancient house—ancient in the sense of being eighty years old; it was built of wood, painted a clean, clear, faded gray, and adorned along the front, at intervals, with flat wooden pilasters, painted white. These pilasters appeared to support a kind of classic pediment, which was decorated in the middle by a large triple window in a boldly carved frame, and in each of its smaller angles by a glazed circular aperture. A large white door, furnished with a highly-polished brass knocker, presented itself to the rural-looking road, with which it was connected by a spacious pathway, paved with worn and cracked, but **very clean**, bricks. Behind it there were meadows and orchards, a barn and a pond; and facing it, a short distance along the road, on the opposite side, stood a smaller house, painted white, with external shutters painted green, a little garden on one hand and an orchard on the other. All this was shining in the morning air, through which the simple details of the picture addressed themselves to the eye as distinctly as the items of a "sum" in addition.

A second young lady presently came out of the house, across the piazza, descended into the garden and approached the young girl of whom I have spoken. This second young lady was also thin and pale; but she was older than the other; she was shorter; she had dark, smooth hair. Her eyes, unlike the other's, were quick and bright; but they were not at all restless. She wore a straw bonnet with white ribbons, and a long, red, India scarf, which, on the front of her dress, reached to her feet. In her hand she carried a little key.

"Gertrude," she said, "are you very sure you had better not go to church?"

Gertrude looked at her a moment, plucked a small sprig from a lilac-bush, smelled it and threw it away. "I am not very sure of anything!" she answered.

The other young lady looked straight past her, at the distant pond, which lay shining between the long banks of fir-trees. Then she said in a very soft voice, "This is the key of the dining-room closet. I think you had better have it, if any one should want anything."

"Who is there to want anything?" Gertrude demanded. "I shall be all alone in the house."

"Some one may come," said her companion.

"Do you mean Mr. Brand?"

"Yes, Gertrude. He may like a piece of cake."

"I don't like men that are always eating cake!" Gertrude declared, giving a pull at the lilac-bush.

Her companion glanced at her, and then looked down on the ground. "I think father expected you would come to church," she said. "What shall I say to him?"

"Say I have a bad headache."

"Would that be true?" asked the elder lady, looking straight at the pond again.

"No, Charlotte," said the younger one simply.

Charlotte transferred her quiet eyes to her companion's face. "I am afraid you are feeling restless."

"I am feeling as I always feel," Gertrude replied, in the same tone.

Charlotte turned away; but she stood there a moment. Presently she looked down at the front of her dress. "Doesn't it seem to you, somehow, as if my scarf were too long?" she asked.

Gertrude walked half round her, looking at the scarf. "I don't think you wear it right," she said.

"How should I wear it, dear?"

"I don't know; differently from that. You should draw it differently behind."

"How should I look?" Charlotte inquired.

"I don't think I can tell you," said Gertrude, plucking out the scarf a little behind. "I could do it myself, but I don't think I can explain it."

Charlotte, by a movement of her elbows, corrected the laxity that had come from her companion's touch. "Well, some day you must do it for me. It doesn't matter now. Indeed, I don't think it matters," she added, "how one looks behind."

"I should say it mattered more," said Gertrude. "Then you don't know who may be observing you. You are not on your guard. You can't try to look pretty."

Charlotte received this declaration with extreme gravity. "I don't think one should ever try to look pretty," she rejoined, earnestly.

Her companion was silent. Then she said, "Well, perhaps it's not of much use."

Charlotte looked at her a little, and then kissed her. "I hope you will be better when we come back."

"My dear sister, I am very well!" said Gertrude.

Charlotte went down the large brick walk to the garden gate; her companion strolled slowly toward the house. At the gate Charlotte met a young man, who was coming in—a tall, fair young man, wearing a high hat and a pair of thread gloves. He was handsome, but rather too stout. He had a pleasant smile. "Oh, Mr. Brand!" exclaimed the young lady.

"I came to see whether your sister was not going to church," said the young man.

"She says she is not going; but I am very glad you have come. I think if you were to talk to her a little" . . . . And Charlotte lowered her voice. "It seems as if she were restless."

Mr. Brand smiled down on the young lady from his great height.

"I shall be very glad to talk to her. For that I should be willing to absent myself from almost any occasion of worship, however attractive."

"Well, I suppose you know," said Charlotte, softly, as if positive acceptance of this proposition might be dangerous. "But I am afraid I shall be late."

"I hope you will have a pleasant sermon," said the young man.

"Oh, Mr. Gilman is always pleasant," Charlotte answered. And she went on her way.

Mr. Brand went into the garden, where Gertrude, hearing the gate close behind him, turned and looked at him. For a moment she watched him coming; then she turned away. But almost immediately she corrected this movement, and stood still, facing him. He took off his hat and wiped his forehead as he approached. Then he put on his hat again and held out his hand. His hat being removed, you would have perceived that his forehead was very large and smooth, and his hair abundant but rather colorless. His nose was too large, and his mouth and eyes were too small; but for all this he was, as I have said, a young man of striking appearance. The expression of his little clean-colored blue eyes was irresistibly gentle and serious; he looked, as the phrase is, as good as gold. The young girl, standing in the garden path, glanced, as he came up, at his thread gloves.

"I hoped you were going to church," he said. "I wanted to walk with you."

"I am very much obliged to you," Gertrude answered. "I am not going to church."

She had shaken hands with him; he held her hand a moment. "Have you any special reason for not going?"

"Yes, Mr. Brand," said the young girl.

"May I ask what it is?"

She looked at him smiling; and in her smile, as I have intimated, there was a certain dullness. But mingled with this dullness was something sweet and suggestive. "Because the sky is so blue!" she said.

He looked at the sky, which was magnificent, and then said, smiling too, "I have heard of young ladies staying at home for bad weather, but never for good. Your sister, whom I met at the gate, tells me you are depressed," he added.

"Depressed? I am never depressed."

"Oh, surely, sometimes," replied Mr. Brand, as if he thought this a regrettable account of one's self.

"I am never depressed," Gertrude repeated. "But I am sometimes wicked. When I am wicked I am in high spirits. I was wicked just now to my sister."

"What did you do to her?"

"I said things that puzzled her—on purpose."

"Why did you do that, Miss Gertrude?" asked the young man. She began to smile again. "Because the sky is so blue!"

"You say things that puzzle *me*," Mr. Brand declared.

"I always know when I do it," proceeded Gertrude. "But people puzzle me more, I think. And they don't seem to know!"

"This is very interesting." Mr. Brand observed, smiling.

"You told me to tell you about my—my struggles," the young girl went on.

"Let us talk about them. I have so many things to say."

Gertrude turned away a moment; and then, turning back, "You had better go to church," she said.

"You know," the young man urged, "that I have always one thing to say."

Gertrude looked at him a moment. "Please don't say it now!"

"We are all alone," he continued, taking off his hat; "all alone in this beautiful Sunday stillness."

Gertrude looked around her, at the breaking buds, the shining distance, the blue sky to which she had referred as a pretext for her irregularities. "That's the reason," she said, "why I don't want you to speak. Do me a favor; go to church."

"May I speak when I come back?" asked Mr. Brand.

"If you are still disposed," she answered.

"I don't know whether you are wicked," he said, "but you are certainly puzzling."

She had turned away; she raised her hands to her ears. He looked at her a moment, and then he slowly walked to church.

She wandered for a while about the garden, vaguely and without purpose. The church-bell had stopped ringing; the stillness was complete. This young lady relished highly, on occasion, the sense of being alone—the absence of the whole family and the emptiness of the house. To-day, apparently, the servants had also gone to church; there was never a figure at the open windows; behind the house there was no stout negress in a red turban, lowering the bucket into the great shingle-hooded well. And the front door of the big, un-guarded home stood open, with the trustfulness of the golden age;

or what is more to the purpose, with that of New England's silvery prime. Gertrude slowly passed through it, and went from one of the empty rooms to the other—large, clear-colored rooms, with white wainscots, ornamented with thin-legged mahogany furniture, and, on the walls, with old-fashioned engravings, chiefly of scriptural subjects, hung very high. This agreeable sense of solitude, of having the house to herself, of which I have spoken, always excited Gertrude's imagination; she could not have told you why, and neither can her humble historian. It always seemed to her that she must do something particular—that she must honor the occasion; and while she roamed about, wondering what she could do, the occasion usually came to an end. To-day she wondered more than ever. At last she took down a book; there was no library in the house but there were books in all the rooms. None of them were forbidden books, and Gertrude had not stopped at home for the sake of a chance to climb to the inaccessible shelves. She possessed herself of a very obvious volume—one of the series of the Arabian Nights—and she brought it out into the portico and sat down with it in her lap. There, for a quarter of an hour, she read the history of the loves of the Prince Camaralzaman and the Princess Badoura. At last, looking up, she beheld, as it seemed to her, the Prince Camaralzaman standing before her. A beautiful young man was making her a very low bow—a magnificent bow, such as she had never seen before. He appeared to have dropped from the clouds; he was wonderfully handsome; he smiled—smiled as if he were smiling on purpose. Extreme surprise, for a moment, kept Gertrude sitting still; then she rose, without even keeping her finger in her book. The young man, with his hat in his hand, still looked at her, smiling and smiling. It was very strange.

"Will you kindly tell me," said the mysterious visitor, at last, "whether I have the honor of speaking to Miss Wentworth?"

"My name is Gertrude Wentworth," murmured the young woman.

"Then—then—I have the honor—the pleasure—of being your cousin."

The young man had so much the character of an apparition that this announcement seemed to complete his unreality. "What cousin? Who are you?" said Gertrude.

He stepped back a few paces and looked up at the house; then glanced round him at the garden and the distant view. After this he burst out laughing. "I see it must seem to you very strange," he said.

There was, after all, something substantial in his laughter. Gertrude looked at him from head to foot. Yes, he was remarkably handsome; but his smile was almost a grimace. "It is very still," he went on, coming nearer again. And as she only looked at him, for reply, he added, "Are you all alone?"

"Every one has gone to church," said Gertrude.

"I was afraid of that!" the young man exclaimed. "But I hope you are not afraid of me."

"You ought to tell me who you are," Gertrude answered.

"I am afraid of you!" said the young man. "I had a different plan. I expected the servant would take in my card, and that you would put your heads together, before admitting me, and make out my identity."

Gertrude had been wondering with a quick intensity which brought its result; and the result seemed an answer—a wondrous, delightful answer—to her vague wish that something would befall her. "I know—I know," she said. "You come from Europe."

"We came two days ago. You have heard of us, then—you believe in us?"

"We have known, vaguely," said Gertrude, "that we had relations in France."

"And have you ever wanted to see us?" asked the young man.

Gertrude was silent a moment. "I have wanted to see you."

"I am glad, then, it is you I have found. We wanted to see you, so we came."

"On purpose?" asked Gertrude.

The young man looked round him, smiling still.

"Well, yes; on purpose. Does that sound as if we should bore you?" he added. "I don't think we shall—I really don't think we shall. We are rather fond of wandering, too; and we were glad of a pretext."

"And you have just arrived?"

"In Boston, two days ago. At the inn I asked for Mr. Wentworth. He must be your father. They found out for me where he lived; they seemed often to have heard of him. I determined to come, without ceremony. So, this lovely morning, they set my face in the right direction, and told me to walk straight before me, out of town. I came on foot because I wanted to see the country. I walked and walked, and here I am! It's a good many miles."

"It is seven miles and a half," said Gertrude, softly. Now that this handsome young man was proving himself a reality she found herself vaguely trembling; she was deeply excited. She had never in her life spoken to a foreigner, and she had often thought it would be delightful to do so. Here was one who had suddenly been engendered by the Sabbath stillness for her private use; and such a brilliant, polite, smiling one! She found time and means to compose herself, however: to remind herself that she must exercise a sort of official hospitality. "We are very—very glad to see you," she said. "Won't you come into the house?" And she moved toward the open door.

"You are not afraid of me, then?" asked the young man again, with his light laugh.

She wondered a moment, and then, "We are not afraid—here," she said.

"Ah, *comme vous devez avoir raison!*" cried the young man, looking all round him, appreciatively. It was the first time that Gertrude had heard so many words of French spoken. They gave her something of a sensation. Her companion followed her, watching, with a certain excitement of his own, this tall, interesting-looking girl dressed in her clear, crisp muslin. He paused in the hall, where there was a broad white staircase with a white balustrade. "What a pleasant house!" he said. "It's lighter inside than it is out."

"It's pleasanter here," said Gertrude, and she led the way into the parlor,—a high, clean, rather empty-looking room. Here they stood looking at each other,—the young man smiling more than ever; Gertrude, very serious, trying to smile.

"I don't believe you know my name," he said. "I am called Felix Young. Your father is my uncle. My mother was his half sister, and older than he."

"Yes," said Gertrude, "and she turned Roman Catholic and married in Europe."

"I see you know," said the young man. "She married and she died. Your father's family didn't like her husband. They called him a foreigner; but he was not. My poor father was born in Sicily, but his parents were American."

"In Sicily?" Gertrude murmured.

"It is true," said Felix Young, "that they had spent their lives in Europe. But they were very patriotic. And so are we."

"And you are Sicilian," said Gertrude.

"Sicilian, no! Let's see. I was born at a little place—a dear little place—in France. My sister was born at Vienna."

"So you are French," said Gertrude.

"Heaven forbid!" cried the young man. Gertrude's eyes were fixed upon him almost insistently. He began to laugh again. "I can easily be French, if that will please you."

"You are a foreigner of some sort," said Gertrude.

"Of some sort—yes; I suppose so. But who can say of what sort?
I don't think we have ever had occasion to settle the question. You
know there are people like that. About their country, their religion,
their profession, they can't tell."

Gertrude stood there gazing; she had not asked him to sit down.
She had never heard of people like that; she wanted to hear. "Where
do you live?" she asked.

"They can't tell that, either!" said Felix. "I am afraid you will
think they are little better than vagabonds. I have lived anywhere—
everywhere. I really think I have lived in every city in Europe."
Gertrude gave a little long soft exhalation. It made the young man
smile at her again; and his smile made her blush a little. To take
refuge from blushing she asked him if, after his long walk, he was
not hungry or thirsty. Her hand was in her pocket; she was fumbling
with the little key that her sister had given her. "Ah, my dear young
lady," he said, clasping his hands a little, "if you could give me, in
charity, a glass of wine!"

Gertrude gave a smile and a little nod, and went quickly out of
the room. Presently she came back with a very large decanter in one
hand and a plate in the other, on which was placed a big, round
cake with a frosted top. Gertrude, in taking the cake from the
closet, had had a moment of acute consciousness that it composed
the refection of which her sister had thought that Mr. Brand would
like to partake. Her kinsman from across the seas was looking at the
pale, high-hung engravings. When she came in he turned and smiled
at her, as if they had been old friends meeting after a separation.
"You wait upon me yourself?" he asked. "I am served like the gods!"
She had waited upon a great many people, but none of them had
ever told her that. The observation added a certain lightness to the
step with which she went to a little table where there were some
curious red glasses—glasses covered with little gold sprigs, which
Charlotte used to dust every morning with her own hands. Gertrude
thought the glasses very handsome, and it was a pleasure to her to
know that the wine was good; it was her father's famous madeira.
Felix Young thought it excellent; he wondered why he had been
told that there was no wine in America. She cut him an immense
triangle out of the cake, and again she thought of Mr. Brand. Felix
sat there, with his glass in one hand and his huge morsel of cake in
the other—eating, drinking, smiling, talking. "I am very hungry," he

said. "I am not at all tired; I am never tired. But I am very hungry."

"You must stay to dinner," said Gertrude. "At two o'clock. They will all have come back from church; you will see the others."

"Who are the others?" asked the young man. "Describe them all."

"You will see for yourself. It is you that must tell me; now, about your sister."

"My sister is the Baroness Münster," said Felix.

On hearing that his sister was a Baroness, Gertrude got up and walked about slowly, in front of him. She was silent a moment. She was thinking of it. "Why didn't she come, too?" she asked.

"She did come; she is in Boston, at the hotel."

"We will go and see her," said Gertrude, looking at him.

"She begs you will not!" the young man replied. "She sends you her love; she sent me to announce her. She will come and pay her respects to your father."

Gertrude felt herself trembling again. A Baroness Münster, who sent a brilliant young man to "announce" her; who was coming, as the Queen of Sheba came to Solomon, to pay her "respects" to quiet Mr. Wentworth—such a personage presented herself to Gertrude's vision with a most effective unexpectedness. For a moment she hardly knew what to say. "When will she come?" she asked at last.

"As soon as you will allow her—to-morrow. She is very impatient," answered Felix, who wished to be agreeable.

"To-morrow, yes," said Gertrude. She wished to ask more about her; but she hardly knew what could be predicated of a Baroness Münster. "Is she—is she—married?"

Felix had finished his cake and wine; he got up, fixing upon the young girl his bright, expressive eyes. "She is married to a German prince—Prince Adolf, of Silberstadt-Schreckenstein. He is not the reigning prince; he is a younger brother."

Gertrude gazed at her informant; her lips were slightly parted. "Is she a—a *Princess?*" she asked at last.

"Oh, no," said the young man; "her position is rather a singular one. It's a morganatic marriage."

"Morganatic?" These were new names and new words to poor Gertrude.

"That's what they call a marriage, you know, contracted between a scion of a ruling house and—and a common mortal. They made Eugenia a Baroness, poor woman; but that was all they could do. Now they want to dissolve the marriage. Prince Adolf, between ourselves, is a ninny; but his brother, who is a clever man, has plans for him. Eugenia, naturally enough, makes difficulties; not, however, that I think she cares much—she's a very clever woman; I'm sure you'll like her—but she wants to bother them. Just now everything is *en l'air*."

The cheerful, off-hand tone in which her visitor related this darkly romantic tale seemed to Gertrude very strange; but it seemed also to convey a certain flattery to herself, a recognition of her wisdom and dignity. She felt a dozen impressions stirring within her, and presently the one that was uppermost found words. "They want to dissolve her marriage?" she asked.

"So it appears."

"And against her will?"

"Against her right."

"She must be very unhappy!" said Gertrude.

Her visitor looked at her, smiling; he raised his hand to the back of his head and held it there a moment. "So she says," he answered. "That's her story. She told me to tell it you."

"Tell me more," said Gertrude.

"No, I will leave that to her; she does it better."

Gertrude gave her little excited sigh again. "Well, if she is unhappy," she said, "I am glad she has come to us."

She had been so interested that she failed to notice the sound of a footstep in the portico; and yet it was a footstep that she always recognized. She heard it in the hall, and then she looked out of the window. They were all coming back from church—her father, her sister and brother, and their cousins, who always came to dinner on Sunday. Mr. Brand had come in first; he was in advance of the others, because, apparently, he was still disposed to say what she had not wished him to say an hour before. He came into the parlor, looking for Gertrude. He had two little books in his hand. On seeing Gertrude's companion he slowly stopped, looking at him.

"Is this a cousin?" asked Felix.

Then Gertrude saw that she must introduce him; but her ears, and, by sympathy, her lips, were full of all that he had been telling her. "This is the Prince," she said, "the Prince of Silberstadt-Schreckenstein!"

Felix burst out laughing, and Mr. Brand stood staring, while the others, who had passed into the house, appeared behind him in the open door-way.

Chapter III

THAT EVENING at dinner Felix Young gave his sister, the Baroness Münster, an account of his impressions. She saw that he had come back in the highest possible spirits; but this fact, to her own mind, was not a reason for rejoicing. She had but a limited confidence in her brother's judgment; his capacity for taking rose-colored views was such as to vulgarize one of the prettiest of tints. Still, she supposed he could be trusted to give her the mere facts; and she invited him with some eagerness to communicate them. "I suppose, at least, they didn't turn you out from the door;" she said. "You have been away some ten hours."

"Turn me from the door!" Felix exclaimed. "They took me to their hearts; they killed the fatted calf."

"I know what you want to say: they are a collection of angels."

"Exactly," said Felix. "They are a collection of angels—simply."

"C'est bien vague," remarked the Baroness. "What are they like?"

"Like nothing you ever saw."

"I am sure I am much obliged; but that is hardly more definite. Seriously, they were glad to see you?"

"Enchanted. It has been the proudest day of my life. Never, never have I been so lionized! I assure you, I was cock of the walk. My dear sister," said the young man, "nous n'avons qu'à nous tenir; we shall be great swells!"

Madame Münster looked at him, and her eye exhibited a slight responsive spark. She touched her lips to a glass of wine, and then she said, "Describe them. Give me a picture."

Felix drained his own glass. "Well, it's in the country, among the meadows and woods; a wild sort of place, and yet not far from here. Only, such a road, my dear! Imagine one of the Alpine glaciers reproduced in mud. But you will not spend much time on it, for they want you to come and stay, once for all."

"Ah," said the Baroness, "they want me to come and stay, once for all? Bon."

"It's intensely rural, tremendously natural; and all overhung with this strange white light, this far-away blue sky. There's a big wooden house—a kind of three-story bungalow; it looks like a magnified Nüremberg toy. There was a gentleman there that made a speech to me about it and called it a 'venerable mansion;' but it looks as if it had been built last night."

"Is it handsome—is it elegant?" asked the Baroness.

Felix looked at her a moment, smiling. "It's very clean! No splendors, no gilding, no troops of servants; rather straight-backed chairs. But you might eat off the floors, and you can sit down on the stairs."

"That must be a privilege. And the inhabitants are straight-backed too, of course."

"My dear sister," said Felix, "the inhabitants are charming."

"In what style?"

"In a style of their own. How shall I describe it? It's primitive; it's patriarchal; it's the *ton* of the golden age."

"And have they nothing golden but their ton? Are there no symptoms of wealth?"

"I should say there was wealth without symptoms. A plain, homely way of life: nothing for show, and very little for—what shall I call it?—for the sense: but a great *aisance*, and a lot of money, out of sight, that comes forward very quietly for subscriptions to institutions, for repairing tenements, for paying doctor's bills; perhaps even for portioning daughters."

"And the daughters?" Madame Münster demanded. "How many are there?"

"There are two, Charlotte and Gertrude."

"Are they pretty?"

"One of them," said Felix.

"Which is that?"

The young man was silent, looking at his sister. "Charlotte," he said at last.

She looked at him in return. "I see. You are in love with Gertrude. They must be Puritans to their finger-tips; anything but gay!"

"No, they are not gay," Felix admitted. "They are sober; they are even severe. They are of a pensive cast; they take things hard. I think there is something the matter with them; they have some melancholy memory or some depressing expectation. It's not the epicurean temperament. My uncle, Mr. Wentworth, is a tremendously high-toned old fellow; he looks as if he were undergoing martyrdom, not by fire, but by freezing. But we shall cheer them up; we shall do them good. They will take a good deal of stirring up; but they are wonderfully kind and gentle. And they are appreciative. They think one clever; they think one remarkable!"

"That is very fine, so far as it goes," said the Baroness. "But are we to be shut up to these three people, Mr. Wentworth and the two young women—what did you say their names were—Deborah and

Hephzibah?"

"Oh, no; there is another little girl, a cousin of theirs, a very pretty creature; a thorough little American. And then there is the son of the house."

"Good!" said the Baroness. "We are coming to the gentlemen. What of the son of the house?"

"I am afraid he gets tipsy."

"He, then, has the epicurean temperament! How old is he?"

"He is a boy of twenty; a pretty young fellow, but I am afraid he has vulgar tastes. And then there is Mr. Brand—a very tall young man, a sort of lay-priest. They seem to think a good deal of him, but I don't exactly make him out."

"And is there nothing," asked the Baroness, "between these extremes—this mysterious ecclesiastic and that intemperate youth?"

"Oh, yes, there is Mr. Acton. I think," said the young man, with a nod at his sister, "that you will like Mr. Acton."

"Remember that I am very fastidious," said the Baroness. "Has he very good manners?"

"He will have them with you. He is a man of the world; he has been to China."

Madame Münster gave a little laugh. "A man of the Chinese world! He must be very interesting."

"I have an idea that he brought home a fortune," said Felix.

"That is always interesting. Is he young, good-looking, clever?"

"He is less than forty; he has a baldish head; he says witty things. I rather think," added the young man, "that he will admire the Baroness Münster."

"It is very possible," said this lady. Her brother never knew how she would take things; but shortly afterwards she declared that he had made a very pretty description and that on the morrow she would go and see for herself.

They mounted, accordingly, into a great barouche—a vehicle as to which the Baroness found nothing to criticise but the price that was asked for it and the fact that the coachman wore a straw hat. (At Silberstadt Madame Münster had had liveries of yellow and crimson.) They drove into the country, and the Baroness, leaning far back and swaying her lace-fringed parasol, looked to right and to left and surveyed the way-side objects. After a while she pronounced them "*affreux*." Her brother remarked that it was apparently a country in which the foreground was inferior to the *plans reculés:* and the Baroness rejoined that the landscape seemed to be all foreground. Felix had fixed with his new friends the hour at which he should bring his sister; it was four o'clock in the afternoon. The large, clean-faced house wore, to his eyes, as the barouche drove up to it, a very friendly aspect; the high, slender elms made lengthening shadows in front of it. The Baroness descended; her American kinsfolk were stationed in the portico. Felix waved his hat to them, and a tall, lean gentleman, with a high forehead and a clean shaven face, came forward toward the garden gate. Charlotte Wentworth walked at his side. Gertrude came behind, more slowly. Both of these young ladies wore rustling silk dresses. Felix ushered his sister into the gate. "Be very gracious," he said to her. But he saw the admonition was superfluous. Eugenia was prepared to be gracious as only Eugenia could be. Felix knew no keener pleasure than to be able to admire his sister unrestrictedly; for if the opportunity was frequent, it was not inveterate. When she desired to please she was to him, as to every one else, the most charming woman in the world. Then he forgot that she was ever anything else; that she was sometimes hard and perverse; that he was occasionally afraid of her. Now, as she took his arm to pass into the garden, he felt that she desired, that she proposed, to please, and this situation made him very happy. Eugenia would please.

The tall gentleman came to meet her, looking very rigid and grave. But it was a rigidity that had no illiberal meaning. Mr. Wentworth's manner was pregnant, on the contrary, with a sense of grand responsibility, of the solemnity of the occasion, of its being difficult to show sufficient deference to a lady at once so distinguished and so unhappy. Felix had observed on the day before his characteristic pallor; and now he perceived that there was something almost cadaverous in his uncle's high-featured white face. But so clever were this young man's quick sympathies and perceptions that he already learned that in these semi-mortuary manifestations there was no cause for alarm. His light imagination had gained a glimpse of Mr. Wentworth's spiritual mechanism, and taught him that, the old man being infinitely conscientious, the special operation of conscience within him announced itself by several of the indications of physical faintness.

The Baroness took her uncle's hand, and stood looking at him with her ugly face and her beautiful smile. "Have I done right to come?" she asked.

"Very right, very right," said Mr. Wentworth, solemnly. He had arranged in his mind a little speech; but now it quite faded away.

He felt almost frightened. He had never been looked at in just that way—with just that fixed, intense smile—by any woman; and it perplexed and weighed upon him, now, that the woman who was smiling so and who had instantly given him a vivid sense of her possessing other unprecedented attributes, was his own niece, the child of his own father's daughter. The idea that his niece should be a German Baroness, married "morganatically" to a Prince, had already given him much to think about. Was it right, was it just, was it acceptable? He always slept badly, and the night before he had lain awake much more even than usual, asking himself these questions. The strange word "morganatic" was constantly in his ears; it reminded him of a certain Mrs. Morgan whom he had once known and who had been a bold, unpleasant woman. He had a feeling that it was his duty, so long as the Baroness looked at him, smiling in that way, to meet her glance with his own scrupulously adjusted, consciously frigid organs of vision; but on this occasion he failed to perform his duty to the last. He looked away toward his daughters. "We are very glad to see you," he had said. "Allow me to introduce my daughters—Miss Charlotte Wentworth, Miss Gertrude Wentworth."

The Baroness thought she had never seen people less demonstrative. But Charlotte kissed her and took her hand, looking at her sweetly and solemnly. Gertrude seemed to her almost funereal, though Gertrude might have found a source of gayety in the fact that Felix, with his magnificent smile, had been talking to her; he had greeted her as a very old friend. When she kissed the Baroness she had tears in her eyes. Madame Münster took each of these young women by the hand, and looked at them all over. Charlotte thought her very strange-looking and singularly dressed; she could not have said whether it was well or ill. She was glad, at any rate, that they had put on their silk gowns—especially Gertrude. "My cousins are very pretty," said the Baroness, turning her eyes from one to the other. "Your daughters are very handsome, sir."

Charlotte blushed quickly; she had never yet heard her personal appearance alluded to in a loud, expressive voice. Gertrude looked away—not at Felix; she was extremely pleased. It was not the compliment that pleased her; she did not believe it; she thought herself very plain. She could hardly have told you the source of her satisfaction; it came from something in the way the Baroness spoke, and it was not diminished—it was rather deepened, oddly enough—by the young girl's disbelief. Mr. Wentworth was silent;

and then he asked, formally, "Won't you come into the house?"

"These are not all; you have some other children," said the Baroness.

"I have a son," Mr. Wentworth answered.

"And why doesn't he come to meet me?" Eugenia cried. "I am afraid he is not so charming as his sisters."

"I don't know; I will see about it," the old man declared.

"He is rather afraid of ladies," Charlotte said, softly.

"He is very handsome," said Gertrude, as loud as she could.

"We will go in and find him. We will draw him out of his *cachette*." And the Baroness took Mr. Wentworth's arm, who was not aware that he had offered it to her, and who, as they walked toward the house, wondered whether he ought to have offered it and whether it was proper for her to take it if it had not been offered. "I want to know you well," said the Baroness, interrupting these meditations, "and I want you to know me."

"It seems natural that we should know each other," Mr. Wentworth rejoined. "We are near relatives."

"Ah, there comes a moment in life when one reverts, irresistibly, to one's natural ties—to one's natural affections. You must have found that!" said Eugenia.

Mr. Wentworth had been told the day before by Felix that Eugenia was very clever, very brilliant, and the information had held him in some suspense. This was the cleverness, he supposed; the brilliancy was beginning. "Yes, the natural affections are very strong," he murmured.

"In some people," the Baroness declared. "Not in all." Charlotte was walking beside her; she took hold of her hand again, smiling always. "And you, *cousine*, where did you get that enchanting complexion?" she went on; "such lilies and roses?" The roses in poor Charlotte's countenance began speedily to predominate over the lilies, and she quickened her step and reached the portico. "This is the country of complexions," the Baroness continued, addressing herself to Mr. Wentworth. "I am convinced they are more delicate. There are very good ones in England—in Holland; but they are very apt to be coarse. There is too much red."

"I think you will find," said Mr. Wentworth, "that this country is superior in many respects to those you mention. I have been to England and Holland."

"Ah, you have been to Europe?" cried the Baroness. "Why didn't you come and see me? But it's better, after all, this way," she said.

They were entering the house; she paused and looked round her. "I see you have arranged your house—your beautiful house—in the—in the Dutch taste!"

"The house is very old," remarked Mr. Wentworth. "General Washington once spent a week here."

"Oh, I have heard of Washington," cried the Baroness. "My father used to tell me of him."

Mr. Wentworth was silent a moment, and then, "I found he was very well known in Europe," he said.

Felix had lingered in the garden with Gertrude; he was standing before her and smiling, as he had done the day before. What had happened the day before seemed to her a kind of dream. He had been there and he had changed everything; the others had seen him, they had talked with him; but that he should come again, that he should be part of the future, part of her small, familiar, much-meditating life—this needed, afresh, the evidence of her senses. The evidence had come to her senses now; and her senses seemed to rejoice in it. "What do you think of Eugenia?" Felix asked. "Isn't she charming?"

"She is very brilliant," said Gertrude. "But I can't tell yet. She seems to me like a singer singing an air. You can't tell till the song is done."

"Ah, the song will never be done!" exclaimed the young man, laughing. "Don't you think her handsome?"

Gertrude had been disapointed in the beauty of the Baroness Münster; she had expected her, for mysterious reasons, to resemble a very pretty portrait of the Empress Josephine, of which there hung an engraving in one of the parlors, and which the younger Miss Wentworth had always greatly admired. But the Baroness was not at all like that—not at all. Though different, however, she was very wonderful, and Gertrude felt herself most suggestively corrected. It was strange, nevertheless, that Felix should speak in that positive way about his sister's beauty. "I think I *shall* think her handsome," Gertrude said. "It must be very interesting to know her. I don't feel as if I ever could."

"Ah, you will know her well; you will become great friends," Felix declared, as if this were the easiest thing in the world.

"She is very graceful," said Gertrude, looking after the Baroness, suspended to her father's arm. It was a pleasure to her to say that any one was graceful.

Felix had been looking about him. "And your little cousin, of yesterday," he said, "who was so wonderfully pretty—what has become of her?"

"She is in the parlor," Gertrude answered. "Yes, she is very pretty." She felt as if it were her duty to take him straight into the house, to where he might be near her cousin. But after hesitating a moment she lingered still. "I didn't believe you would come back," she said.

"Not come back!" cried Felix, laughing. "You didn't know, then, the impression made upon this susceptible heart of mine."

She wondered whether he meant the impression her cousin Lizzie had made. "Well," she said, "I didn't think we should ever see you again."

"And pray what did you think would become of me?"

"I don't know. I thought you would melt away."

"That's a compliment to my solidity! I melt very often," said Felix, "but there is always something left of me."

"I came and waited for you by the door, because the others did," Gertrude went on. "But if you had never appeared I should not have been surprised."

"I hope," declared Felix, looking at her, "that you would have been disappointed."

She looked at him a little, and shook her head. "No—no!"

"Ah, *par exemple!*" cried the young man. "You deserve that I should never leave you."

Going into the parlor they found Mr. Wentworth performing introductions. A young man was standing before the Baroness, blushing a good deal, laughing a little, and shifting his weight from one foot to the other—a slim, mild-faced young man, with neatly-arranged features, like those of Mr. Wentworth. Two other gentlemen, behind him, had risen from their seats, and a little apart, near one of the windows, stood a remarkably pretty young girl. The young girl was knitting a stocking; but, while her fingers quickly moved, she looked with wide, brilliant eyes at the Baroness.

"And what is your son's name?" said Eugenia, smiling at the young man.

"My name is Clifford Wentworth, ma'am," he said in a tremulous voice.

"Why didn't you come out to meet me, Mr. Clifford Wentworth?" the Baroness demanded, with her beautiful smile.

"I didn't think you would want me," said the young man, slowly sidling about.

"One always wants a *beau cousin*,—if one has one! But if you are very nice to me in future I won't remember it against you." And Madame Münster transferred her smile to the other persons present. It rested first upon the candid countenance and long-skirted figure of Mr. Brand, whose eyes were intently fixed upon Mr. Wentworth, as if to beg him not to prolong an anomalous situation. Mr. Wentworth pronounced his name. Eugenia gave him a very charming glance, and then looked at the other gentleman.

This latter personage was a man of rather less than the usual stature and the usual weight, with a quick, observant, agreeable dark eye, a small quantity of thin dark hair, and a small mustache. He had been standing with his hands in his pockets; and when Eugenia looked at him he took them out. But he did not, like Mr. Brand, look evasively and urgently at their host. He met Eugenia's eyes; he appeared to appreciate the privilege of meeting them. Madame Münster instantly felt that he was, intrinsically, the most important person present. She was not unconscious that this impression was in some degree manifested in the little sympathetic nod with which she acknowledged Mr. Wentworth's announcement, "My cousin, Mr. Acton!"

"Your cousin—not mine?" said the Baroness.

"It only depends upon you," Mr. Acton declared, laughing.

The Baroness looked at him a moment, and noticed that he had very white teeth. "Let it depend upon your behavior," she said. "I think I had better wait. I have cousins enough. Unless I can also claim relationship," she added, "with that charming young lady," and she pointed to the young girl at the window.

"That's my sister," said Mr. Acton. And Gertrude Wentworth put her arm round the young girl and led her forward. It was not, apparently, that she needed much leading. She came toward the Baroness with a light, quick step, and with perfect self-possession, rolling her stocking round its needles. She had dark blue eyes and dark brown hair; she was wonderfully pretty.

Eugenia kissed her, as she had kissed the other young women, and then held her off a little, looking at her. "Now this is quite another *type*," she said; she pronounced the word in the French manner. "This is a different outline, my uncle, a different character, from that of your own daughters. This, Felix," she went on, "is very much more what we have always thought of as the American type."

The young girl, during this exposition, was smiling askance at every one in turn, and at Felix out of turn. "I find only one type here!" cried Felix, laughing. "The type adorable!"

This sally was received in perfect silence, but Felix, who learned all things quickly, had already learned that the silences frequently observed among his new acquaintances were not necessarily restrictive or resentful. It was, as one might say, the silence of expectation, of modesty. They were all standing round his sister, as if they were expecting her to acquit herself of the exhibition of some peculiar faculty, some brilliant talent. Their attitude seemed to imply that she was a kind of conversational mountebank, attired, intellectually, in gauze and spangles. This attitude gave a certain ironical force to Madame Münster's next words. "Now this is your circle," she said to her uncle. "This is your *salon*. These are your regular habitués, eh? I am so glad to see you all together."

"Oh," said Mr. Wentworth, "they are always dropping in and out. You must do the same."

"Father," interposed Charlotte Wentworth, "they must do something more." And she turned her sweet, serious face, that seemed at once timid and placid, upon their interesting visitor. "What is your name?" she asked.

"Eugenia-Camilla-Dolores," said the Baroness, smiling. "But you needn't say all that."

"I will say Eugenia, if you will let me. You must come and stay with us."

The Baroness laid her hand upon Charlotte's arm very tenderly; but she reserved herself. She was wondering whether it would be possible to "stay" with these people. "It would be very charming—very charming," she said; and her eyes wandered over the company, over the room. She wished to gain time before committing herself. Her glance fell upon young Mr. Brand, who stood there, with his arms folded and his hand on his chin, looking at her. "The gentleman, I suppose, is a sort of ecclesiastic," she said to Mr. Wentworth, lowering her voice a little.

"He is a minister," answered Wentworth.

"A Protestant?" asked Eugenia.

"I am a Unitarian, madam," replied Mr. Brand, impressively.

"Ah, I see," said Eugenia. "Something new." She had never heard of this form of worship.

Mr. Acton began to laugh, and Gertrude looked anxiously at Mr. Brand.

"You have come very far," said Mr. Wentworth.

"Very far—very far," the Baroness replied, with a graceful shake of her head—a shake that might have meant many different things.

"That's a reason why you ought to settle down with us," said Mr. Wentworth, with that dryness of utterance which, as Eugenia was too intelligent not to feel, took nothing from the delicacy of his meaning.

She looked at him, and for an instant, in his cold, still face, she seemed to see a far-away likeness to the vaguely remembered image of her mother. Eugenia was a woman of sudden emotions, and now, unexpectedly, she felt one rising in her heart. She kept looking round the circle; she knew that there was admiration in all the eyes that were fixed upon her. She smiled at them all.

"I came to look—to try—to ask," she said. "It seems to me I have done well. I am very tired; I want to rest." There were tears in her eyes. The luminous interior, the gentle, tranquil people, the simple, serious life—the sense of these things pressed upon her with an overmastering force, and she felt herself yielding to one of the most genuine emotions she had ever known. "I should like to stay here," she said. "Pray take me in."

Though she was smiling, there were tears in her voice as well as in her eyes. "My dear niece," said Mr. Wentworth, softly. And Charlotte put out her arms and drew the Baroness toward her; while Robert Acton turned away, with his hands stealing into his pockets.

CHAPTER IV

A few days after the Baroness Münster had presented herself to her American kinsfolk she came, with her brother, and took up her abode in that small white house adjacent to Mr. Wentworth's own dwelling of which mention has already been made. It was on going with his daughters to return her visit that Mr. Wentworth placed this comfortable cottage at her service; the offer being the result of a domestic colloquy, diffused through the ensuing twenty-four hours, in the course of which the two foreign visitors were discussed and analyzed with a great deal of earnestness and subtlety. The discussion went forward, as I say, in the family circle; but that circle on the evening following Madame Münster's return to town, as on many other occasions, included Robert Acton and his pretty sister. If you had been present, it would probably not have seemed to you that the advent of these brilliant strangers was treated as an exhilarating occurrence, a pleasure the more in this tranquil household, a prospective source of entertainment. This was not Mr.

Wentworth's way of treating any human occurrence. The sudden irruption into the well-ordered consciousness of the Wentworths of an element not allowed for in its scheme of usual obligations required a readjustment of that sense of responsibility which constituted its principal furniture. To consider an event, crudely and baldly, in the light of the pleasure it might bring them was an intellectual exercise with which Felix Young's American cousins were almost wholly unacquainted, and which they scarcely supposed to be largely pursued in any section of human society. The arrival of Felix and his sister was a satisfaction, but it was a singularly joyless and inelastic satisfaction. It was an extension of duty, of the exercise of the more recondite virtues; but neither Mr. Wentworth, nor Charlotte, nor Mr. Brand, who, among these excellent people, was a great promoter of reflection and aspiration, frankly adverted to it as an extension of enjoyment. This function was ultimately assumed by Gertrude Wentworth, who was a peculiar girl, but the full compass of whose peculiarities had not been exhibited before they very ingeniously found their pretext in the presence of these possibly too agreeable foreigners. Gertrude, however, had to struggle with a great accumulation of obstructions, both of the subjective, as the metaphysicians say, and of the objective, order; and indeed it is no small part of the purpose of this little history to set forth her struggle. What seemed paramount in this abrupt enlargement of Mr. Wentworth's sympathies and those of his daughters was an extension of the field of possible mistakes; and the doctrine, as it may almost be called, of the oppressive gravity of mistakes was one of the most cherished traditions of the Wentworth family.

"I don't believe she wants to come and stay in this house," said Gertrude; Madame Münster, from this time forward, receiving no other designation than the personal pronoun. Charlotte and Gertrude acquired considerable facility in addressing her, directly, as "Eugenia;" but in speaking of her to each other they rarely called her anything but "she."

"Doesn't she think it good enough for her?" cried little Lizzie Acton, who was always asking unpractical questions, that required, in strictness, no answer, and to which indeed she expected no other answer than such as she herself invariably furnished in a small, innocently-satirical laugh.

"She certainly expressed a willingness to come," said Mr. Wentworth.

"That was only politeness," Gertrude rejoined.

"Yes, she is very polite—very polite," said Mr. Wentworth.

"She is too polite," his son declared, in a softly growling tone which was habitual to him, but which was an indication of nothing worse than a vaguely humorous intention. "It is very embarrassing."

"That is more than can be said of you, sir," said Lizzie Acton, with her little laugh.

"Well, I don't mean to encourage her," Clifford went on.

"I'm sure I don't care if you do!" cried Lizzie.

"She will not think of you, Clifford," said Gertrude, gravely.

"I hope not!" Clifford exclaimed.

"She will think of Robert," Gertrude continued, in the same tone.

Robert Acton began to blush; but there was no occasion for it, for every one was looking at Gertrude—every one, at least, save Lizzie, who, with her pretty head on one side, contemplated her brother.

"Why do you attribute motives, Gertrude?" asked Mr. Wentworth.

"I don't attribute motives, father," said Gertrude. "I only say she will think of Robert; and she will!"

"Gertrude judges by herself!" Acton exclaimed, laughing. "Don't you, Gertrude? Of course the Baroness will think of me. She will think of me from morning till night."

"She will be very comfortable here," said Charlotte, with something of a housewife's pride. "She can have the large northeast room. And the French bedstead," Charlotte added, with a constant sense of the lady's foreignness.

"She will not like it," said Gertrude; "not even if you pin little tidies all over the chairs."

"Why not, dear?" asked Charlotte, perceiving a touch of irony here, but not resenting it.

Gertrude had left her chair; she was walking about the room; her stiff silk dress, which she had put on in honor of the Baroness, made a sound upon the carpet. "I don't know," she replied. "She will want something more—more private."

"If she wants to be private she can stay in her room," Lizzie Acton remarked.

Gertrude paused in her walk, looking at her. "That would not be pleasant," she answered. "She wants privacy and pleasure together."

Robert Acton began to laugh again. "My dear cousin, what a picture!"

Charlotte had fixed her serious eyes upon her sister; she wondered whence she had suddenly derived these strange notions. Mr. Wentworth also observed his younger daughter.

"I don't know what her manner of life may have been," he said; "but she certainly never can have enjoyed a more refined and salubrious home."

Gertrude stood there looking at them all. "She is the wife of a Prince," she said.

"We are all princes here," said Mr. Wentworth; "and I don't know of any palace in this neighborhood that is to let."

"Cousin William," Robert Acton interposed, "do you want to do something handsome? Make them a present, for three months, of the little house over the way."

"You are very generous with other people's things!" cried his sister.

"Robert is very generous with his own things," Mr. Wentworth observed dispassionately, and looking, in cold meditation, at his kinsman.

"Gertrude," Lizzie went on, "I had an idea you were so fond of your new cousin."

"Which new cousin?" asked Gertrude.

"I don't mean the Baroness!" the young girl rejoined, with her laugh. "I thought you expected to see so much of him."

"Of Felix? I hope to see a great deal of him," said Gertrude, simply.

"Then why do you want to keep him out of the house?"

Gertrude looked at Lizzie Acton, and then looked away.

"Should you want me to live in the house with you, Lizzie?" asked Clifford.

"I hope you never will. I hate you!" Such was this young lady's reply.

"Father," said Gertrude, stopping before Mr. Wentworth and smiling, with a smile the sweeter, as her smile always was, for its rarity; "do let them live in the little house over the way. It will be lovely!"

Robert Acton had been watching her. "Gertrude is right," he said. "Gertrude is the cleverest girl in the world. If I might take the liberty, I should strongly recommend their living there."

"There is nothing there so pretty as the northeast room," Charlotte urged.

"She will make it pretty. Leave her alone!" Acton exclaimed.

Gertrude, at his compliment, had blushed and looked at him: it was as if some one less familiar had complimented her. "I am sure she will make it pretty. It will be very interesting. It will be a place to go to. It will be a foreign house."

"Are we very sure that we need a foreign house?" Mr. Wentworth inquired. "Do you think it desirable to establish a foreign house—in this quiet place?"

"You speak," said Acton, laughing, "as if it were a question of the poor Baroness opening a wine-shop or a gaming-table."

"It would be too lovely!" Gertrude declared again, laying her hand on the back of her father's chair.

"That she should open a gaming-table?" Charlotte asked, with great gravity.

Gertrude looked at her a moment, and then, "Yes, Charlotte," she said, simply.

"Gertrude is growing pert," Clifford Wentworth observed, with his humorous young growl. "That comes of associating with foreigners."

Mr. Wentworth looked up at his daughter, who was standing beside him; he drew her gently forward. "You must be careful," he said. "You must keep watch. Indeed, we must all be careful. This is a great change; we are to be exposed to peculiar influences. I don't say they are bad. I don't judge them in advance. But they may perhaps make it necessary that we should exercise a great deal of wisdom and self-control. It will be a different tone."

Gertrude was silent a moment, in deference to her father's speech; then she spoke in a manner that was not in the least an answer to it. "I want to see how they will live. I am sure they will have different hours. She will do all kinds of little things differently. When we go over there it will be like going to Europe. She will have a boudoir. She will invite us to dinner—very late. She will breakfast in her room."

Charlotte gazed at her sister again. Gertrude's imagination seemed to her to be fairly running riot. She had always known that Gertrude had a great deal of imagination—she had been very proud of it. But at the same time she had always felt that it was a dangerous and irresponsible faculty; and now, to her sense, for the moment, it seemed to threaten to make her sister a strange person who should come in suddenly, as from a journey, talking of the peculiar and possibly unpleasant things she had observed. Charlotte's imagination took no journeys whatever; she kept it, as it were, in her pocket, with the other furniture of this receptacle—a thimble, a little box of peppermint, and a morsel of court-plaster. "I don't believe she would have any dinner—or any breakfast," said Miss Wentworth. "I don't believe she knows how to do anything herself. I should have to get her ever so many servants, and she wouldn't like them."

"She has a maid," said Gertrude; "a French maid. She mentioned her."

"I wonder if the maid has a little fluted cap and red slippers," said Lizzie Acton. "There was a French maid in that play that Robert took me to see. She had pink stockings; she was very wicked."

"She was a *soubrette*," Gertrude announced, who had never seen a play in her life. "They call that a soubrette. It will be a great chance to learn French." Charlotte gave a little soft, helpless groan. She had a vision of a wicked, theatrical person, clad in pink stockings and red shoes, and speaking, with confounding volubility, an incomprehensible tongue, flitting through the sacred penetralia of that large, clean house. "That is one reason in favor of their coming here," Gertrude went on. "But we can make Eugenia speak French to us, and Felix. I mean to begin—the next time."

Mr. Wentworth had kept her standing near him, and he gave her his earnest, thin, unresponsive glance again. "I want you to make me a promise, Gertrude," he said.

"What is it?" she asked, smiling.

"Not to get excited. Not to allow these—these occurrences to be an occasion for excitement."

She looked down at him a moment, and then she shook her head. "I don't think I can promise that, father. I am excited already."

Mr. Wentworth was silent a while; they all were silent, as if in recognition of something audacious and portentous.

"I think they had better go to the other house," said Charlotte, quietly.

"I shall keep them in the other house," Mr. Wentworth subjoined, more pregnantly.

Gertrude turned away; then she looked across at Robert Acton. Her cousin Robert was a great friend of hers; she often looked at him this way instead of saying things. Her glance on this occasion, however, struck him as a substitute for a larger volume of diffident utterance than usual inviting him to observe, among other things, the inefficiency of her father's design—if design it was—for diminishing, in the interest of quiet nerves, their occasions of contact with their foreign relatives. But Acton immediately complimented

Mr. Wentworth upon his liberality. "That's a very nice thing to do," he said, "giving them the little house. You will have treated them handsomely, and, whatever happens, you will be glad of it." Mr. Wentworth was liberal, and he knew he was liberal. It gave him pleasure to know it, to feel it, to see it recorded; and this pleasure is the only palpable form of self-indulgence with which the narrator of these incidents will be able to charge him.

"A three days' visit at most, over there, is all I should have found possible," Madame Münster remarked to her brother, after they had taken possession of the little white house. "It would have been too *intime*—decidedly too intime. Breakfast, dinner, and tea *en famille*—it would have been the end of the world if I could have reached the third day." And she made the same observation to her maid Augustine, an intelligent person, who enjoyed a liberal share of her confidence. Felix declared that he would willingly spend his life in the bosom of the Wentworth family; that they were the kindest, simplest, most amiable people in the world, and that he had taken a prodigious fancy to them all. The Baroness quite agreed with him that they were simple and kind; they were thoroughly nice people, and she liked them extremely. The girls were perfect ladies; it was impossible to be more of a lady than Charlotte Wentworth, in spite of her little village air. "But as for thinking them the best company in the world," said the Baroness, "that is another thing; and as for wishing to live *porte à porte* with them, I should as soon think of wishing myself back in the convent again, to wear a bombazine apron and sleep in a dormitory." And yet the Baroness was in high good humor; she had been very much pleased. With her lively perception and her refined imagination, she was capable of enjoying anything that was characteristic, anything that was good of its kind. The Wentworth household seemed to her very perfect in its kind—wonderfully peaceful and unspotted; pervaded by a sort of dove-colored freshness that had all the quietude and benevolence of what she deemed to be Quakerism, and yet seemed to be founded upon a degree of material abundance for which, in certain matters of detail, one might have looked in vain at the frugal little court of Silberstadt-Schreckenstein. She perceived immediately that her American relatives thought and talked very little about money; and this of itself made an impression upon Eugenia's imagination. She perceived at the same time that if Charlotte or Gertrude should ask their father for a very considerable sum he would at once place it in their hands; and this made a still greater impression. The greatest impression of all, perhaps, was made by another rapid induction. The Baroness had an immediate conviction that Robert Acton would put his hand into his pocket every day in the week if that rattle-pated little sister of his should bid him. The men in this country, said the Baroness, are evidently very obliging. Her declaration that she was looking for rest and retirement had been by no means wholly untrue; nothing that the Baroness said was wholly untrue. It is but fair to add, perhaps, that nothing that she said was wholly true. She wrote to a friend in Germany that it was a return to nature; it was like drinking new milk, and she was very fond of new milk. She said to herself, of course, that it would be a little dull; but there can be no better proof of her good spirits than the fact that she thought she should not mind its being a little dull. It seemed to her, when from the piazza of her eleemosynary cottage she looked out over the soundless fields, the stony pastures, the clear-faced ponds, the rugged little orchards, that she had never been in the midst of so peculiarly intense a stillness; it was almost a delicate sensual pleasure. It was all very good, very innocent and safe, and out of it something good must come. Augustine, indeed, who had an un-bounded faith in her mistress's wisdom and far-sightedness, was a great deal perplexed and depressed. She was always ready to take her cue when she understood it; but she liked to understand it, and on this occasion comprehension failed. What, indeed, was the Baroness doing *dans cette galère?* what fish did she expect to land out of these very stagnant waters? The game was evidently a deep one. Augustine could trust her; but the sense of walking in the dark betrayed itself in the physiognomy of this spare, sober, sallow, middle-aged person, who had nothing in common with Gertrude Wentworth's conception of a soubrette, by the most ironical scowl that had ever rested upon the unpretending tokens of the peace and plenty of the Wentworths. Fortunately, Augustine could quench skepticism in action. She quite agreed with her mistress—or rather she quite outstripped her mistress—in thinking that the little white house was pitifully bare. "*Il faudra,*" said Augustine, "*lui faire un peu de toilette.*" And she began to hang up *portières* in the doorways; to place wax candles, procured after some research, in unexpected situations; to dispose anomalous draperies over the arms of sofas and the backs of chairs. The Baroness had brought with her to the New World a copious provision of the element of costume; and the two Miss Wentworths, when they came over to see her, were somewhat bewildered by the obtrusive distribution of her wardrobe.

There were India shawls suspended, curtain-wise, in the parlor door, and curious fabrics, corresponding to Gertrude's metaphysical vision of an opera-cloak, tumbled about in the sitting-places. There were pink silk blinds in the windows, by which the room was strangely bedimmed; and along the chimney-piece was disposed a remarkable band of velvet, covered with coarse, dirty-looking lace. "I have been making myself a little comfortable," said the Baroness, much to the confusion of Charlotte, who had been on the point of proposing to come and help her put her superfluous draperies away. But what Charlotte mistook for an almost culpably delayed subsidence Gertrude very presently perceived to be the most ingenious, the most interesting, the most romantic intention. "What is life, indeed, without curtains?" she secretly asked herself; and she appeared to herself to have been leading hitherto an existence singularly garish and totally devoid of festoons.

Felix was not a young man who troubled himself greatly about anything—least of all about the conditions of enjoyment. His faculty of enjoyment was so large, so unconsciously eager, that it may be said of it that it had a permanent advance upon embarrassment and sorrow. His sentient faculty was intrinsically joyous, and novelty and change were in themselves a delight to him. As they had come to him with a great deal of frequency, his life had been more agreeable than appeared. Never was a nature more perfectly fortunate. It was not a restless, apprehensive, ambitious spirit, running a race with the tyranny of fate, but a temper so unsuspicious as to put Adversity off her guard, dodging and evading her with the easy, natural motion of a wind-shifted flower. Felix extracted entertainment from all things, and all his faculties—his imagination, his intelligence, his affections, his senses—had a hand in the game. It seemed to him that Eugenia and he had been very well treated; there was something absolutely touching in that combination of paternal liberality and social considerateness which marked Mr. Wentworth's deportment. It was most uncommonly kind of him, for instance, to have given them a house. Felix was positively amused at having a house of his own; for the little white cottage among the apple-trees— the chalet, as Madame Münster always called it—was much more sensibly his own than any domiciliary *quatrième*, looking upon a court, with the rent overdue. Felix had spent a good deal of his life in looking into courts, with a perhaps slightly tattered pair of elbows resting upon the ledge of a high-perched window, and the thin smoke of a cigarette rising into an atmosphere in which street-

cries died away and the vibration of chimes from ancient belfries
became sensible. He had never known anything so infinitely rural
as these New England fields; and he took a great fancy to all their
pastoral roughnesses. He had never had a greater sense of luxurious
security; and at the risk of making him seem a rather sordid adventurer I must declare that he found an irresistible charm in the
fact that he might dine every day at his uncle's. The charm was
irresistible, however, because his fancy flung a rosy light over this
homely privilege. He appreciated highly the fare that was set before
him. There was a kind of fresh-looking abundance about it which
made him think that people must have lived so in the mythological
era, when they spread their tables upon the grass, replenished them
from cornucopias, and had no particular need of kitchen stoves.
But the great thing that Felix enjoyed was having found a family—
sitting in the midst of gentle, generous people whom he might call
by their first names. He had never known anything more charming
than the attention they paid to what he said. It was like a large
sheet of clean, fine-grained drawing-paper, all ready to be washed
over with effective splashes of water-color. He had never had
any cousins, and he had never before found himself in contact so
unrestricted with young unmarried ladies. He was extremely fond
of the society of ladies, and it was new to him that it might be
enjoyed in just this manner. At first he hardly knew what to make
of his state of mind. It seemed to him that he was in love, indis-
criminately, with three girls at once. He saw that Lizzie Acton was
more brilliantly pretty than Charlotte and Gertrude; but this was
scarcely a superiority. His pleasure came from something they had
in common—a part of which was, indeed, that physical delicacy
which seemed to make it proper that they should always dress in
thin materials and clear colors. But they were delicate in other
ways, and it was most agreeable to him to feel that these latter
delicacies were appreciable by contact, as it were. He had known,
fortunately, many virtuous gentlewomen, but it now appeared to
him that in his relations with them (especially when they were
unmarried) he had been looking at pictures under glass. He perceived at present what a nuisance the glass had been—how it per-
verted and interfered, how it caught the reflection of other objects
and kept you walking from side to side. He had no need to ask
himself whether Charlotte and Gertrude, and Lizzie Acton, were
in the right light; they were always in the right light. He liked
everything about them: he was, for instance, not at all above liking

the fact that they had very slender feet and high insteps. He liked their pretty noses; he liked their surprised eyes and their hesitating, not at all positive way of speaking; he liked so much knowing that he was perfectly at liberty to be alone for hours, anywhere, with either of them; that preference for one to the other, as a companion of solitude, remained a minor affair. Charlotte Wentworth's sweetly severe features were as agreeable as Lizzie Acton's wonderfully expressive blue eyes; and Gertrude's air of being always ready to walk about and listen was as charming as anything else, especially as she walked very gracefully. After a while Felix began to distinguish; but even then he would often wish, suddenly, that they were not all so sad. Even Lizzie Acton, in spite of her fine little chatter and laughter, appeared sad. Even Clifford Wentworth, who had extreme youth in his favor, and kept a buggy with enormous wheels and a little sorrel mare with the prettiest legs in the world—even this fortunate lad was apt to have an averted, uncomfortable glance, and to edge away from you at times, in the manner of a person with a bad conscience. The only person in the circle with no sense of oppression of any kind was, to Felix's perception, Robert Acton.

It might perhaps have been feared that after the completion of those graceful domiciliary embellishments which have been mentioned Madame Münster would have found herself confronted with alarming possibilities of *ennui*. But as yet she had not taken the alarm. The Baroness was a restless soul, and she projected her restlessness, as it may be said, into any situation that lay before her. Up to a certain point her restlessness might be counted upon to entertain her. She was always expecting something to happen, and, until it was disappointed, expectancy itself was a delicate pleasure. What the Baroness expected just now it would take some ingenuity to set forth; it is enough that while she looked about her she found something to occupy her imagination. She assured herself that she was enchanted with her new relatives; she professed to herself that, like her brother, she felt it a sacred satisfaction to have found a family. It is certain that she enjoyed to the utmost the gentleness of her kinsfolk's deference. She had, first and last, received a great deal of admiration, and her experience of well-turned compliments was very considerable; but she knew that she had never been so real a power, never counted for so much, as now when, for the first time, the standard of comparison of her little circle was a prey to vagueness. The sense, indeed, that the good people about her had, as regards her remarkable self, no standard of comparison at all gave her a feeling of almost illimitable power. It was true, as she said to herself, that if for this reason they would be able to discover nothing against her, so they would perhaps neglect to perceive some of her superior points; but she always wound up her reflections by declaring that she would take care of that.

Charlotte and Gertrude were in some perplexity between their desire to show all proper attention to Madame Münster and their fear of being importunate. The little house in the orchard had hitherto been occupied during the summer months by intimate friends of the family, or by poor relations who found in Mr. Wentworth a landlord attentive to repairs and oblivious of quarter-day. Under these circumstances the open door of the small house and that of the large one, facing each other across their homely gardens, levied no tax upon hourly visits. But the Misses Wentworth received an impression that Eugenia was no friend to the primitive custom of "dropping in;" she evidently had no idea of living without a doorkeeper. "One goes into your house as into an inn—except that there are no servants rushing forward," she said to Charlotte. And she added that that was very charming. Gertrude explained to her sister that she meant just the reverse; she didn't like it at all. Charlotte inquired why she should tell an untruth, and Gertrude answered that there was probably some very good reason for it which they should discover when they knew her better. "There can surely be no good reason for telling an untruth," said Charlotte. "I hope she does not think so."

They had of course desired, from the first, to do everything in the way of helping her to arrange herself. It had seemed to Charlotte that there would be a great many things to talk about; but the Baroness was apparently inclined to talk about nothing.

"Write her a note, asking her leave to come and see her. I think that is what she will like," said Gertrude.

"Why should I give her the trouble of answering me?" Charlotte asked. "She will have to write a note and send it over."

"I don't think she will take any trouble," said Gertrude, profoundly.

"What then will she do?"

"That is what I am curious to see," said Gertrude, leaving her sister with an impression that her curiosity was morbid.

They went to see the Baroness without preliminary correspondence; and in the little salon which she had already created, with its becoming light and its festoons, they found Robert Acton.

Eugenia was intensely gracious, but she accused them of neglecting her cruelly. "You see Mr. Acton has had to take pity upon me," she said. "My brother goes off sketching, for hours; I can never depend upon him. So I was to send Mr. Acton to beg you to come and give me the benefit of your wisdom."

Gertrude looked at her sister. She wanted to say, "*That* is what she would have done." Charlotte said that they hoped the Baroness would always come and dine with them; it would give them so much pleasure; and, in that case, she would spare herself the trouble of having a cook.

"Ah, but I must have a cook!" cried the Baroness. "An old negress in a yellow turban. I have set my heart upon that. I want to look out of my window and see her sitting there on the grass, against the background of those crooked, dusky little apple-trees, pulling the husks off a lapful of Indian corn. That will be local color, you know. There isn't much of it here—you don't mind my saying that, do you?—so one must make the most of what one can get. I shall be most happy to dine with you whenever you will let me; but I want to be able to ask you sometimes. And I want to be able to ask Mr. Acton," added the Baroness.

"You must come and ask me at home," said Acton. "You must come and see me; you must dine with me first. I want to show you my place; I want to introduce you to my mother." He called again upon Madame Münster, two days later. He was constantly at the other house; he used to walk across the fields from his own place, and he appeared to have fewer scrpules than his cousins with regard to dropping in. On this occasion he found that Mr. Brand had come to pay his respects to the charming stranger; but after Acton's arrival the young theologian said nothing. He sat in his chair with his two hands clasped, fixing upon his hostess a grave, fascinated stare. The Baroness talked to Robert Acton, but, as she talked, she turned and smiled at Mr. Brand, who never took his eyes off her. The two men walked away together; they were going to Mr. Wentworth's. Mr. Brand still said nothing; but after they had passed into Mr. Wentworth's garden he stopped and looked back for some time at the little white house. Then, looking at his companion, with his head bent a little to one side and his eyes somewhat contracted, "Now I suppose that's what is called conversation," he said; "real conversation."

"It's what I call a very clever woman," said Acton laughing

"It is most interesting," Mr. Brand continued. "I only wish she would speak French; it would seem more in keeping. It must be quite the style that we have heard about, that we have read about —the style of conversation of Madame de Staël, of Madame Récamier."

Acton also looked at Madame Münster's residence among its holly-hocks and apple-trees. "What I should like to know," he said, smiling, "is just what has brought Madame Récamier to live in that place!"

CHAPTER V

MR. WENTWORTH, with his cane and his gloves in his hand, went every afternoon to call upon his niece. A couple of hours later she came over to the great house to tea. She had let the proposal that she should regularly dine there fall to the ground; she was in the enjoyment of whatever satisfaction was to be derived from the spectacle of an old negress in a crimson turban shelling peas under the apple-trees. Charlotte, who had provided the ancient negress, thought it must be a strange household, Eugenia having told her that Augustine managed everything, the ancient negress included— Augustine who was naturally devoid of all acquaintance with the expurgatory English tongue. By far the most immoral sentiment which I shall have occasion to attribute to Charlotte Wentworth was a certain emotion of disappointment at finding that, in spite of these irregular conditions, the domestic arrangements at the small house were apparently not—from Eugenia's peculiar point of view—strik-ingly offensive. The Baroness found it amusing to go to tea; she dressed as if for dinner. The tea-table offered an anomalous and picturesque repast; and on leaving it they all sat and talked in the large piazza, or wandered about the garden in the starlight, with their ears full of these sounds of strange insects which, though they are supposed to be, all over the world, a part of the magic of summer nights, seemed to the Baroness to have beneath these western skies an incomparable resonance.

Mr. Wentworth, though, as I say, he went punctiliously to call upon her, was not able to feel that he was getting used to his niece. It taxed his imagination to believe that she was really his half-sister's child. His sister was a figure of his early years; she had been only twenty when she went abroad, never to return, making in foreign parts a willful and undesirable marriage. His aunt, Mrs. Whiteside, who had taken her to Europe for the benefit of the tour, gave, on her return, so lamentable an account of Mr. Adolphus Young, to whom the headstrong girl had united her destiny, that it operated as a chill upon family feeling—especially in the case of the half-brothers. Catherine had done nothing subsequently to propitiate her family; she had not even written to them in a way that indicated a lucid appreciation of their suspended sympathy, so that it had become a tradition in Boston circles that the highest charity, as regards this young lady, was to think it well to forget her, and to abstain from conjecture as to the extent to which her aberrations were reproduced in her descendants. Over these young people—a vague report of their existence had come to his ears—Mr. Wentworth had not, in the course of years, allowed his imagination to hover. It had plenty of occupation nearer home, and though he had many cares upon his conscience the idea that he had been an unnatural uncle was, very properly, never among the number. Now that his nephew and niece had come before him, he perceived that they were the fruit of influences and circumstances very different from those under which his own familiar progeny had reached a vaguely-qualified maturity. He felt no provocation to say that these influences had been exerted for evil; but he was sometimes afraid that he should not be able to like his distinguished, delicate, lady-like niece. He was paralyzed and bewildered by her foreignness. She spoke, somehow, a different language. There was something strange in her words. He had a feeling that another man, in his place, would accommodate himself to her tone; would ask her questions and joke with her, reply to those pleasantries of her own which sometimes seemed startling as addressed to an uncle. But Mr. Wentworth could not do these things. He could not even bring himself to attempt to measure her position in the world. She was the wife of a foreign nobleman who desired to repudiate her. This had a singular sound, but the old man felt himself destitute of the materials for a judgment. It seemed to him that he ought to find them in his own experience, as a man of the world and an almost public character; but they were not there, and he was ashamed to confess to himself—much more to reveal to Eugenia by interrogations possibly too innocent—the un-furnished condition of this repository.

It appeared to him that he could get much nearer, as he would have said, to his nephew; though he was not sure that Felix was altogether safe. He was so bright and handsome and talkative that it was impossible not to think well of him; and yet it seemed as if there were something almost impudent, almost vicious—or as if there ought to be—in a young man being at once so joyous and so positive. It was to be observed that while Felix was not at all a serious young man there was somehow more of him—he had more weight and volume and resonance—than a number of young men who were distinctly serious. While Mr. Wentworth meditated upon this anomaly, his nephew was admiring him unrestrictedly. He thought him a most delicate, generous, high-toned old gentleman, with a very handsome head, of the ascetic type, which he promised himself the profit of sketching. Felix was far from having made a secret of the fact that he wielded the paint-brush, and it was not his own fault if it failed to be generally understood that he was prepared to execute the most striking likenesses on the most reasonable terms. "He is an artist—my cousin is an artist," said Gertrude; and she offered this information to every one who would receive it. She offered it to herself, as it were, by way of admonition and reminder; she repeated to herself at odd moments, in lonely places, that Felix was invested with this sacred character. Gertrude had never seen an artist before; she had only read about such people. They seemed to her a romantic and mysterious class, whose life was made up of those agreeable accidents that never happened to other persons. And it merely quickened her meditations on this point that Felix should declare, as he repeatedly did, that he was really not an artist. "I have never gone into the thing seriously," he said. "I have never studied; I have had no training. I do a little of everything, and nothing well. I am only an amateur."

It pleased Gertrude even more to think that he was an amateur than to think that he was an artist; the former word, to her fancy, had an even subtler connotation. She knew, however, that it was a word to use more soberly. Mr. Wentworth used it freely; for though he had not been exactly familiar with it, he found it convenient as a help toward classifying Felix, who, as a young man extremely clever and active and apparently respectable and yet not engaged in any recognized business, was an importunate anomaly. Of course the Baroness and her brother—she was always spoken of first—were a welcome topic of conversation between Mr. Wentworth and his daughters and their occasional visitors.

"And the young man, your nephew, what is his profession?" asked an old gentleman—Mr. Broderip, of Salem—who had been Mr. Wentworth's classmate at Harvard College in the year 1809, and who came into his office in Devonshire Street. (Mr. Wentworth, in his later years, used to go but three times a week to his office, where he had a large amount of highly confidential trust-business to transact.)

"Well, he's an amateur," said Felix's uncle, with folded hands, and with a certain satisfaction in being able to say it. And Mr. Broderip had gone back to Salem with a feeling that this was probably a "European" expression for a broker or a grain exporter.

"I should like to do your head, sir," said Felix to his uncle one evening, before them all—Mr. Brand and Robert Acton being also present. "I think I should make a very fine thing of it. It's an interesting head; it's very mediæval."

Mr. Wentworth looked grave; he felt awkwardly, as if all the company had come in and found him standing before the looking-glass. "The Lord made it," he said. "I don't think it is for man to make it over again."

"Certainly the Lord made it," replied Felix, laughing, "and he made it very well. But life has been touching up the work. It is a very interesting type of head. It's delightfully wasted and emaciated. The complexion is wonderfully bleached." And Felix looked round at the circle, as if to call their attention to these interesting points. Mr. Wentworth grew visibly paler. "I should like to do you as an old prelate, an old cardinal, or the prior of an order."

"A prelate, a cardinal?" murmured Mr. Wentworth. "Do you refer to the Roman Catholic priesthood?"

"I mean an old ecclesiastic who should have led a very pure, abstinent life. Now I take it that has been the case with you, sir; one sees it in your face," Felix proceeded. "You have been very—a— very moderate. Don't you think one always sees that in a man's face?"

"You see more in a man's face than I should think of looking for," said Mr. Wentworth coldly.

The Baroness rattled her fan, and gave her brilliant laugh. "It is a risk to look so close!" she exclaimed. "My uncle has some peccadilloes on his conscience." Mr. Wentworth looked at her, painfully at a loss; and in so far as the signs of a pure and abstinent life were visible in his face they were then probably peculiarly manifest. "You are a *beau vieillard*, dear uncle," said Madame Münster, smiling with her foreign eyes.

"I think you are paying me a compliment," said the old man.

"Surely, I am not the first woman that ever did so!" cried the Baroness.

"I think you are," said Mr. Wentworth gravely. And turning to

Felix he added, in the same tone, "Please don't take my likeness. My children have my daguerreotype. That is quite satisfactory."

"I won't promise," said Felix, "not to work your head into something!"

Mr. Wentworth looked at him and then at all the others; then he got up and slowly walked away.

"Felix," said Gertrude, in the silence that followed, "I wish you would paint my portrait."

Charlotte wondered whether Gertrude was right in wishing this; and she looked at Mr. Brand as the most legitimate way of ascertaining. Whatever Gertrude did or said, Charlotte always looked at Mr. Brand. It was a standing pretext for looking at Mr. Brand—always, as Charlotte thought, in the interest of Gertrude's welfare. It is true that she felt a tremulous interest in Gertrude being right; for Charlotte, in her small, still way, was an heroic sister.

"We should be glad to have your portrait, Miss Gertrude," said Mr. Brand.

"I should be delighted to paint so charming a model," Felix declared.

"Do you think you are so lovely, my dear?" asked Lizzie Acton, with her little inoffensive pertness, biting off a knot in her knitting.

"It is not because I think I am beautiful," said Gertrude, looking all round. "I don't think I am beautiful, at all." She spoke with a sort of conscious deliberateness; and it seemed very strange to Charlotte to hear her discussing this question so publicly. "It is because I think it would be amusing to sit and be painted. I have always thought that."

"I am sorry you have not had better things to think about, my daughter," said Mr. Wentworth.

"You are very beautiful, cousin Gertrude," Felix declared.

"That's a compliment," said Gertrude. "I put all the compliments I receive into a little money-jug that has a slit in the side. I shake them up and down, and they rattle. There are not many yet—only two or three."

"No, it's not a compliment," Felix rejoined. "See; I am careful not to give it the form of a compliment. I didn't think you were beautiful at first. But you have come to seem so little by little."

"Take care, now, your jug doesn't burst!" exclaimed Lizzie.

"I think sitting for one's portrait is only one of the various forms of idleness," said Mr. Wentworth. "Their name is legion."

"My dear sir," cried Felix, "you can't be said to be idle when you are making a man work so!"

"One might be painted while one is asleep," suggested Mr. Brand, as a contribution to the discussion.

"Ah, do paint me while I am asleep," said Gertrude to Felix, smiling. And she closed her eyes a little. It had by this time become a matter of almost exciting anxiety to Charlotte what Gertrude would say or would do next.

She began to sit for her portrait on the following day—in the open air, on the north side of the piazza. "I wish you would tell me what you think of us—how we seem to you," she said to Felix, as he sat before his easel.

"You seem to me the best people in the world," said Felix.

"You say that," Gertrude resumed, "because it saves you the trouble of saying anything else."

The young man glanced at her over the top of his canvas. "What else should I say? It would certainly be a great deal of trouble to say anything different."

"Well," said Gertrude, "you have seen people before that you have liked, have you not?"

"Indeed I have, thank Heaven!"

"And they have been very different from us," Gertrude went on.

"That only proves," said Felix, "that there are a thousand different ways of being good company."

"Do you think us good company?" asked Gertrude.

"Company for a king!"

Gertrude was silent a moment; and then, "There must be a thousand different ways of being dreary," she said; "and sometimes I think we make use of them all."

Felix stood up quickly, holding up his hand. "If you could only keep that look on your face for half an hour—while I catch it!" he said. "It is uncommonly handsome."

"To look handsome for half an hour—that is a great deal to ask of me," she answered.

"It would be the portrait of a young woman who has taken some vow, some pledge, that she repents of," said Felix, "and who is thinking it over at leisure."

"I have taken no vow, no pledge," said Gertrude, very gravely; "I have nothing to repent of."

"My dear cousin, that was only a figure of speech. I am very sure that no one in your excellent family has anything to repent of."

"And yet we are always repenting!" Gertrude exclaimed. "That is what I mean by our being dreary. You know it perfectly well; you only pretend that you don't."

Felix gave a quick laugh. "The half hour is going on, and yet you are handsomer than ever. One must be careful what one says, you see."

"To me," said Gertrude, "you can say anything."

Felix looked at her, as an artist might, and painted for some time in silence.

"Yes, you seem to me different from you father and sister—from most of the people you have lived with," he observed.

"To say that one's self," Gertrude went on, "is like saying—by implication, at least—that one is better. I am not better; I am much worse. But they say themselves that I am different. It makes them unhappy."

"Since you accuse me of concealing my real impressions, I may admit that I think the tendency—among you generally—is to be made unhappy too easily."

"I wish you would tell that to my father," said Gertrude.

"It might make him more unhappy!" Felix exclaimed, laughing.

"It certainly would. I don't believe you have seen people like that."

"Ah, my dear cousin, how do you know what I have seen?" Felix demanded. "How can I tell you?"

"You might tell me a great many things, if you only would. You have seen people like yourself—people who are bright and gay and fond of amusement. We are not fond of amusement."

"Yes," said Felix, "I confess that rather strikes me. You don't seem to me to get all the pleasure out of life that you might. You don't seem to me to enjoy. . . . Do you mind my saying this?" he said, pausing.

"Please go on," said the girl, earnestly.

"You seem to me very well placed for enjoying. You have money and liberty and what is called in Europe a 'position.' But you take a painful view of life, as one may say."

"One ought to think it bright and charming and delightful, eh?" asked Gertrude.

"I should say so—if one can. It is true it all depends upon that," Felix added.

"You know there is a great deal of misery in the world," said his model.

"I have seen a little of it," the young man rejoined. "But it was all over there—beyond the sea. I don't see any here. This is a paradise."

Gertrude said nothing; she sat looking at the dahlias and the currant bushes in the garden, while Felix went on with his work. "To 'enjoy,'" she began at last, "to take life—not painfully, must one do something wrong?"

Felix gave his long, light laugh again. "Seriously, I think not. And for this reason, among others: you strike me as very capable of enjoying, if the chance were given you, and yet at the same time as incapable of wrong-doing."

"I am sure," said Gertrude, "that you are very wrong in telling a person that she is incapable of that. We are never nearer to evil than when we believe that."

"You are handsomer than ever," observed Felix, irrelevantly.

Gertrude had got used to hearing him say this. There was not so much excitement in it as at first. "What ought one to do?" she continued. "To give parties, to go to the theatre, to read novels, to keep late hours?"

"I don't think it's what one does or one doesn't do that promotes enjoyment," her companion answered. "It is the general way of looking at life."

"They look at it as a discipline—that's what they do here. I have often been told that."

"Well, that's very good. But there is another way," added Felix, smiling: "to look at it as an opportunity."

"An opportunity—yes," said Gertrude. "One would get more pleasure that way."

"I don't attempt to say anything better for it than that it has been my own way—and that is not saying much!" Felix had laid down his palette and brushes; he was leaning back, with his arms folded, to judge the effect of his work. "And you know," he said, "I am a very petty personage."

"You have a great deal of talent," said Gertrude.

"No—no," the young man rejoined, in a tone of cheerful impartiality, "I have not a great deal of talent. It is nothing at all remarkable. I assure you I should know if it were. I shall always be obscure. The world will never hear of me." Gertrude looked at him with a strange feeling. She was thinking of the great world which he knew and which she did not, and how full of brilliant talents it must be, since it could afford to make light of his abilities. "You needn't in general attach much importance to anything I tell you," he pursued; "but you may believe me when I say this,—that I am little better than a good natured feather-head."

"A feather-head?" she repeated.

"I am a species of Bohemian."

"A Bohemian?" Gertrude had never heard this term before, save as a geographical denomination; and she quite failed to understand the figurative meaning which her companion appeared to attach to it. But it gave her pleasure.

Felix had pushed back his chair and risen to his feet; he slowly came toward her, smiling. "I am a sort of adventurer," he said, looking down at her.

She got up, meeting his smile. "An adventurer?" she repeated. "I should like to hear your adventures."

For an instant she believed that he was going to take her hand; but he dropped his own hands suddenly into the pockets of his painting-jacket. "There is no reason why you shouldn't," he said. "I haven't been an adventurer, but my adventures have been very innocent. They have all been happy ones; I don't think there are any I shouldn't tell. They were very pleasant and very pretty; I should like to go over them in memory. Sit down again, and I will begin," he added in a moment, with his naturally persuasive smile.

Gertrude sat down again on that day, and she sat down on several other days. Felix, while he plied his brush, told her a great many stories, and she listened with charmed avidity. Her eyes rested upon his lips; she was very serious; sometimes, from her air of wondering gravity, he thought she was displeased. But Felix never believed for more than a single moment in any displeasure of his own producing. This would have been fatuity if the optimism it expressed had not been much more a hope than a prejudice. It is beside the matter to say that he had a good conscience; for the best conscience is a sort of self-reproach, and this young man's brilliantly healthy nature spent itself in objective good intentions which were ignorant of any test save exactness in hitting their mark. He told Gertrude how he had walked over France and Italy with a painter's knapsack on his back, paying his way often by knocking off a flattering portrait of his host or hostess. He told her how he had played the violin in a little band of musicians—not of high celebrity—who traveled through foreign lands giving provincial concerts. He told her also how he had been a momentary ornament of a troupe of strolling actors, engaged in the arduous task of interpreting Shakespeare to French and German, Polish and Hungarian audiences.

While this periodical recital was going on, Gertrude lived in a fantastic world; she seemed to herself to be reading a romance that came out in daily numbers. She has known nothing so delightful since the perusal of "Nicholas Nickleby." One afternoon she went to see her cousin, Mrs. Acton, Robert's mother, who was a great invalid, never leaving the house. She came back alone, on foot, across the fields—this being a short way which they often used. Felix had gone to Boston with her father, who desired to take the young man to call upon some of his friends, old gentlemen who remembered his mother—remembered her, but said nothing about her—and several of whom, with the gentle ladies their wives, had driven out from town to pay their respects at the little house among the apple-trees, in vehicles which reminded the Baroness, who received her visitors with discriminating civility, of the large, light, rattling barouche in which she herself had made her journey to this neighborhood. The afternoon was waning; in the western sky the great picture of a New England sunset, painted in crimson and silver, was suspended from the zenith; and the stony pastures, as Gertrude traversed them, thinking intently to herself, were covered with a light, clear glow. At the open gate of one of the fields she saw from the distance a man's figure; he stood there as if he were waiting for her, and as she came nearer she recognized Mr. Brand. She had a feeling as of not having seen him for some time; she could not have said for how long, for it yet seemed to her that he had been very lately at the house.

"May I walk back with you?" he asked. And when she had said that he might if he wanted, he observed that he had seen her and recognized her half a mile away.

"You must have very good eyes," said Gertrude.

"Yes, I have very good eyes, Miss Gertrude," said Mr. Brand. She perceived that he meant something; but for a long time past Mr. Brand had constantly meant something, and she had almost got used to it. She felt, however, that what he meant had now a renewed power to distrub her, to perplex and agitate her. He walked beside her in silence for a moment, and then he added, "I have had no trouble in seeing that you are beginning to avoid me. But perhaps," he went on, "one needn't have had very good eyes to see that."

"I have not avoided you," said Gertrude, without looking at him.

"I think you have been unconscious that you were avoiding me," Mr. Brand replied. "You have not even known that I was there."

"Well, you are here now, Mr. Brand!" said Gertrude, with a little laugh. "I know that very well."

He made no rejoinder. He simply walked beside her slowly, as they were obliged to walk over the soft grass. Presently they came to another gate, which was closed. Mr. Brand laid his hand upon, it, but he made no movement to open it; he stood and looked at his companion. "You are very much interested—very much absorbed," he said.

Gertrude glanced at him; she saw that he was pale and that he looked excited. She had never seen Mr. Brand excited before, and she felt that the spectacle, if fully carried out, would be impressive, almost painful. "Absorbed in what?" she asked. Then she looked away at the illuminated sky. She felt guilty and uncomfortable, and yet she was vexed with herself for feeling so. But Mr. Brand, as he stood there looking at her with his small, kind, persistent eyes, represented an immense body of half-obliterated obligations, that were rising again into a certain distinctness.

"You have new interests, new occupations," he went on. "I don't know that I can say that you have new duties. We have always old ones, Gertrude," he added.

"Please open the gate, Mr. Brand," she said; and she felt as if, in saying so, she were cowardly and petulant. But he opened the gate, and allowed her to pass; then he closed it behind himself. Before she had time to turn away he put out his hand and held her an instant by the wrist.

"I want to say something to you," he said.

"I know what you want to say," she answered. And she was on the point of adding, "And I know just how you will say it;" but these words she kept back.

"I love you, Gertrude," he said. "I love you very much; I love you more than ever."

He said the words just as she had known he would; she had heard them before. They had no charm for her; she had said to herself before that it was very strange. It was supposed to be delightful for a woman to listen to such words but these seemed to her flat and mechanical. "I wish you would forget that," she declared.

"How can I—why should I?" he asked.

"I have made you no promise—given you no pledge," she said, looking at him, with her voice trembling a little.

"You have let me feel that I have an influence over you. You have opened your mind to me."

"I never opened my mind to you, Mr. Brand!" Gertrude cried, with some vehemence.

"Then you were not so frank as I thought—as we all thought."

"I don't see what any one else had to do with it!" cried the girl.

"I mean your father and your sister. You know it makes them happy to think you will listen to me."

She gave a little laugh. "It doesn't make them happy," she said. "Nothing makes them happy. No one is happy here."

"I think your cousin is very happy—Mr. Young," rejoined Mr. Brand, in a soft, almost timid tone.

"So much the better for him!" And Gertrude gave her little laugh again.

The young man looked at her a moment. "You are very much changed," he said.

"I am glad to hear it," Gertrude declared.

"I am not. I have known you a long time, and I have loved you as you were."

"I am much obliged to you," said Gertrude. "I must be going home."

He on his side, gave a little laugh.

"You certainly do avoid me—you see!"

"Avoid me, then," said the girl.

He looked at her again; and then, very gently, "No, I will not avoid you," he replied; "but I will leave you, for the present to yourself. I think you will remember—after a while—some of the things you have forgotten. I think you will come back to me; I have great faith in that."

This time his voice was very touching; there was a strong, reproachful force in what he said, and Gertrude could answer nothing. He turned away and stood there, leaning his elbows on the gate and looking at the beautiful sunset. Gertrude left him and took her way home again; but when she reached the middle of the next field she suddenly burst into tears. Her tears seemed to her to have been a long time gathering, and for some moments it was a kind of glee to shed them. But they presently passed away. There was something a little hard about Gertrude; and she never wept again.

Chapter VI

GOING OF an afternoon to call upon his niece, Mr. Wentworth more than once found Robert Acton sitting in her little drawing-room. This was in no degree, to Mr. Wentworth, a perturbing fact, for he had no sense of competing with his young kinsman for Eugenia's good graces. Madame Münster's uncle had the highest opinion of Robert Acton, who, indeed, in the family at large, was the object of a great deal of undemonstrative appreciation. They were all proud of him, in so far as the charge of being proud may be brought against people who were, habitually, distinctly guiltless of the misdemeanor known as "taking credit." They never boasted of Robert Acton, nor indulged in vainglorious reference to him; they never quoted the clever things he had said, nor mentioned the generous things he had done. But a sort of frigidly-tender faith in his unlimited goodness was a part of their personal sense of right; and there can, perhaps, be no better proof of the high esteem in which he was held than the tact that no explicit judgment was ever passed upon his actions. He was no more praised than he was blamed; but he was tacitly felt to be an ornament to his circle. He was the man of the world of the family. He had been to China and brought home a collection of curiosities; he had made a fortune—or rather he had quintupled a fortune already considerable; he was distinguished by that combination of celibacy, "property," and good humor which appeals to even the most subdued imaginations; and it was taken for granted that he would presently place these advantages at the disposal of some well-regulated young woman of his own "set." Mr. Wentworth was not a man to admit to himself that—his paternal duties apart—he liked any individual much better than all other individuals; but he thought Robert Acton extremely judicious; and this was perhaps as near an approach as he was capable of to the eagerness of preference, which his temperament repudiated as it would have disengaged itself from something slightly unchaste. Acton was, in fact, very judicious—and something more beside; and indeed it must be claimed for Mr. Wentworth that in the more illicit parts of his preference there hovered the vague adumbration of a belief that his cousin's final merit was a certain enviable capacity for whistling, rather gallantly, at the sanctions of mere judgment—for showing a larger courage, a finer quality of pluck, than common occasion demanded. Mr. Wentworth would never have risked the intimation that Acton was made, in the smallest degree, of the stuff of a hero; but this is small blame to him, for Robert would certainly never have risked it himself. Acton certainly exercised great discretion in all things—beginning with his estimate of himself. He knew that he was by no means so much of a man of the world as he was supposed to be in local circles; but it must be added that he knew also that his natural shrewdness had a reach of which he had never quite given local circles the measure. He was addicted to taking the humorous view of things, and he had discovered that even in the narrowest circles such a disposition may find frequent opportunities. Such opportunities had formed for some time—that is, since his return from China, a year and a half before—the most active element in this gentleman's life, which had just now a rather indolent air. He was perfectly willing to get married. He was very fond of books, and he had a handsome library; that is, his books, were much more numerous than Mr. Wentworth's. He was also very fond of pictures; but it must be confessed, in the fierce light of contemporary criticism, that his walls were adorned with several rather abortive masterpieces. He had got his learning—and there was more of it than commonly appeared—at Harvard College; and he took a pleasure in old contentment to live so near this institution that he often passed it in driving to Boston. He was extremely interested in the Baroness Münster.

She was very frank with him; or at least she intended to be. "I am sure you find it very strange that I should have settled down in this out-of-the-way part of the world!" she said to him three or four weeks after she had installed herself "I am certain you are wondering about my motives. They are very pure." The Baroness by this time was an old inhabitant; the best society in Boston had called upon her, and Clifford Wentworth had taken her several times to drive in his buggy.

Robert Acton was seated near her, playing with a fan; there were always several fans lying about her drawing-room, with long ribbons of different colors attached to them, and Acton was always playing with one. "No, I don't find it at all strange," he said slowly, smiling. "That a clever woman should turn up in Boston, or its suburbs—that does not require so much explanation. Boston is a very nice place."

"If you wish to make me contradict you," said the Baroness, "*vous vous y prenez mal*. In certain moods there is nothing I am not capable of agreeing to. Boston is a paradise, and we are in the suburbs of Paradise."

"Just now I am not at all in the suburbs; I am in the place itself," rejoined Acton, who was lounging a little in his chair. He was, however, not always lounging; and when he was he was not quite so relaxed as he pretended. To a certain extent, he sought refuge from shyness in this appearance of relaxation; and like many persons in the same circumstances he somewhat exaggerated the ap-

pearance. Beyond this, the air of being much at his ease was a cover
for vigilant observation. He was more than interested in this clever
woman, who, whatever he might say, was clever not at all after the
Boston fashion; she plunged him into a kind of excitement, held
him in vague suspense. He was obliged to admit to himself that he
had never yet seen a woman just like this—not even in China. He
was ashamed, for inscrutable reasons, of the vivacity of his emotion,
and he carried it off, superficially, by taking, still superficially, the
humorous view of Madame Münster. It was not at all true that he
thought it very natural of her to have made this pious pilgrimage.
It might have been said of him in advance that he was too good a
Bostonian to regard in the light of an eccentricity the desire of
even the remotest alien to visit the New England metropolis. This
was an impulse for which, surely, no apology was needed; and
Madame Münster was the fortunate possessor of several New England cousins. In fact, however, Madame Münster struck him as out
of keeping with her little circle; she was at the best a very agreeable, a gracefully mystifying anomaly. He knew very well that it
would not do to address these reflections too crudely to Mr. Wentworth; he would never have remarked to the old gentleman that
he wondered what the Baroness was up to. And indeed he had no
great desire to share his vague mistrust with any one. There was
a personal pleasure in it; the greatest pleasure he had known at least
since he had come from China. He would keep the Baroness, for
better or worse, to himself; he had a feeling that he deserved to
enjoy a monopoly of her, for he was certainly the person who had
most adequately gauged her capacity for social intercourse. Before
long it became apparent to him that the Baroness was disposed to
lay no tax upon such a monopoly.

One day (he was sitting there again and playing with a fan) she
asked him to apologize, should the occasion present itself, to certain
people in Boston for her not having returned their calls. "There are
half a dozen places," she said; "a formidable list. Charlotte Wentworth has written it out for me, in a terrifically distinct hand. There
is no ambiguity on the subject; I know perfectly where I must go.
Mr. Wentworth informs me that the carriage is always at my disposal, and Charlotte offers to go with me, in a pair of tight gloves
and a very stiff petticoat. And yet for three days I have been putting
it off. They must think me horribly vicious."

"You ask me to apologize," said Acton, "but you don't tell me
what excuse I can offer."

"That is more," the Baroness declared, "than I am held to. It would be like my asking you to buy me a bouquet and giving you the money. I have no reason except that—somehow—it's too violent an effort. It is not inspiring. Wouldn't that serve as an excuse, in Boston? I am told they are very sincere; they don't tell fibs. And then Felix ought to go with me, and he is never in readiness. I don't see him. He is always roaming about the fields and sketching old barns, or taking ten-mile walks, or painting some one's portrait, or rowing on the pond, or flirting with Gertrude Wentworth."

"I should think it would amuse you to go and see a few people," said Acton. "You are having a very quiet time of it here. It's a dull life for you."

"Ah, the quiet,—the quiet!" the Baroness exclaimed. "That's what I like. It's rest. That's what I came here for. Amusement? I have had amusement. And as for seeing people—I have already seen a great many in my life. If it didn't sound ungracious I should say that I wish very humbly your people here would leave me alone!"

Acton looked at her a moment, and she looked at him. She was a woman who took being looked at remarkably well. "So you have come here for rest?" he asked.

"So I may say. I came for many of those reasons that are no reasons—don't you know?—and yet that are really the best: to come away, to change, to break with everything. When once one comes away one must arrive somewhere, and I asked myself why I shouldn't arrive here."

"You certainly had time on the way!" said Acton, laughing.

Madame Münster looked at him again; and then, smiling: "And I have certainly had time, since I got here, to ask myself why I came. However, I never ask myself idle questions. Here I am, and it seems to me you ought only to thank me."

"When you go away you will see the difficulties I shall put in your path."

"You mean to put difficulties in my path?" she asked, rearranging the rosebud in her corsage.

"The greatest of all—that of having been so agreeable—"

"That I shall be unable to depart? Don't be too sure. I have left some very agreeable people over there."

"Ah," said Acton, "but it was to come here, where I am!"

"I didn't know of your existence. Excuse me for saying anything so rude; but, honestly speaking, I did not. No," the Baroness pursued, "it was precisely not to see you—such people as you—that I came."

"Such people as me?" cried Acton.

"I had a sort of longing to come into those natural relations which I knew I should find here. Over there I had only, as I may say, artificial relations. Don't you see the difference?"

"The difference tells against me," said Acton. "I suppose I am an artificial relation."

"Conventional," declared the Baroness; "very conventional."

"Well, there is one way in which the relation of a lady and a gentleman may always become natural," said Acton.

"You mean by their becoming lovers? That may be natural or not. And at any rate," rejoined Eugenia, "*nous n'en sommes pas là!*"

They were not, as yet; but a little later, when she began to go with him to drive, it might almost have seemed that they were. He came for her several times, alone, in his "wagon," drawn by a pair of charming light-limbed horses. It was different, her having gone with Clifford Wentworth, who was her cousin, and so much younger. It was not to be imagined that she should have a flirtation with Clifford, who was a mere shamefaced boy, and whom a large section of Boston society supposed to be "engaged" to Lizzie Acton. Not, indeed, that it was to be conceived that the Baroness was a possible party to any flirtation whatever; for she was undoubtedly a married lady. It was generally known that her matrimonial condition was of the "morganatic" order; but in its natural aversion to suppose that this meant anything less than absolute wedlock, the conscience of the community took refuge in the belief that it implied something even more.

Acton wished her to think highly of American scenery, and he drove her to great distances, picking out the prettiest roads and the largest points of view. If we are good when we are contented, Eugenia's virtues should now certainly have been uppermost; for she found a charm in the rapid movement through a wild country, and in a companion who from time to time made the vehicle dip with a motion like a swallow's flight, over roads of primitive construction, and who, as she felt, would do a great many things that she might ask him. Sometimes, for a couple of hours together, there were almost no houses; there were nothing but woods and rivers and lakes and horizons adorned with bright-looking mountains. It seemed to the Baroness very wild, as I have said, and lovely; but the impression added something to that sense of the enlargement of opportunity which had been born of her arrival in the New World.

One day—it was late in the afternoon—Acton pulled up his horses on the crest of a hill which commanded a beautiful prospect. He let them stand a long time to rest, while he sat there and talked with Madame Münster. The prospect was beautiful in spite of there being nothing human within sight. There was a wilderness of woods, and the gleam of a distant river, and a glimpse of half the hill-tops in Massachusetts. The road had a wide, grassy margin, on the further side of which there flowed a deep, clear brook: there were wild flowers in the grass, and beside the brook lay the trunk of a fallen tree. Acton waited a while; at last a rustic wayfarer came trudging along the road. Acton asked him to hold the horses—a service he consented to render, as a friendly turn to a fellow-citizen. Then he invited the Baroness to descend, and the two wandered away, across the grass, and sat down on the log beside the brook.

"I imagine it doesn't remind you of Silberstadt," said Acton. It was the first time that he had mentioned Silberstadt to her, for particular reasons. He knew she had a husband there, and this was disagreeable to him; and, furthermore, it had been repeated to him that this husband wished to put her away—a state of affairs to which even indirect reference was to be deprecated. It was true, nevertheless, that the Baroness herself had often alluded to Silberstadt; and Acton had often wondered why her husband wished to get rid of her. It was a curious position for a lady—this being known as a repudiated wife; and it is worthy of observation that the Baroness carried it off with exceeding grace and dignity. She had made it felt, from the first, that there were two sides to the question, and that her own side, when she should choose to present it, would be replete with touching interest.

"It does not remind me of the town, of course," she said, "of the sculptured gables and the Gothic churches, of the wonderful Schloss, with its moat and its clustering towers. But it has a little look of some other parts of the principality. One might fancy one's self among those grand old German forests, those legendary mountains; the sort of country one sees from the windows at Schreckenstein."

"What is Schreckenstein?" asked Acton.

"It is a great castle,—the summer residence of the Reigning Prince."

"Have you ever lived there?"

"I have stayed there," said the Baroness. Acton was silent; he looked a while at the uncastled landscape before him. "It is the first time you have ever asked me about Silberstadt," she said. "I should think you would want to know about my marriage; it must seem to you very strange."

Acton looked at her a moment. "Now you wouldn't like me to say that!"

"You Americans have such odd ways!" the Baroness declared. "You never ask anything outright; there seem to be so many things you can't talk about."

"We Americans are very polite," said Acton, whose national consciousness had been complicated by a residence in foreign lands, and who yet disliked to hear Americans abused. "We don't like to tread upon people's toes," he said. "But I should like very much to hear about your marriage. Now tell me how it came about."

"The Prince fell in love with me," replied the Baroness simply. "He pressed his suit very hard. At first he didn't wish me to marry him; on the contrary. But on that basis I refused to listen to him. So he offered me marriage—in so far as he might. I was young, and I confess I was rather flattered. But if it were to be done again now, I certainly should not accept him."

"How long ago was this?" asked Acton.

"Oh—several years," said Eugenia. "You should never ask a woman for dates."

"Why, I should think that when a woman was relating history . . ." Acton answered. "And now he wants to break it off?"

"They want him to make a political marriage. It is his brother's idea. His brother is very clever."

"They must be a precious pair!" cried Robert Acton.

The Baroness gave a little philosophic shrug. "*Que voulez-vous?* They are princes. They think they are treating me very well. Silberstadt is a perfectly despotic little state, and the Reigning Prince may annul the marriage by a stroke of his pen. But he has promised me, nevertheless, not to do so without my formal consent."

"And this you have refused?"

"Hitherto. It is an indignity, and I have wished at least to make it difficult for them. But I have a little document in my writing-desk which I have only to sign and send back to the Prince."

"Then it will be all over?"

The Baroness lifted her hand, and dropped it again. "Of course

I shall keep my title; at least, I shall be at liberty to keep it if I choose. And I suppose I shall keep it. One must have a name. And I shall keep my pension. It is very small—it is wretchedly small; but it is what I live on."

"And you have only to sign that paper?" Acton asked.

The Baroness looked at him a moment. "Do you urge it?"

He got up slowly, and stood with his hands in his pockets. "What do you gain by not doing it?"

"I am supposed to gain this advantage—that if I delay, or temporize, the Prince may come back to me, may make a stand against his brother. He is very fond of me, and his brother has pushed him only little by little."

"If he were to come back to you," said Acton, "would you—would you take him back?"

The Baroness met his eyes; she colored just a little. Then she rose. "I should have the satisfaction of saying, 'Now it is my turn. I break with your serene highness!' "

They began to walk toward the carriage. "Well," said Robert Acton, "it's a curious story! How did you make his acquaintance?"

"I was staying with an old lady—an old Countess—in Dresden. She had been a friend of my father's. My father was dead; I was very much alone. My brother was wandering about the world in a theatrical troupe."

"Your brother ought to have stayed with you," Acton observed, "and kept you from putting your trust in princes."

The Baroness was silent a moment, and then, "He did what he could," she said. "He sent me money. The old Countess encouraged the Prince; she was even pressing. It seems to me," Madame Münster added, gently, "that—under the circumstances—I behaved very well."

Acton glanced at her, and made the observation—he had made it before—that a woman looks the prettier for having unfolded her wrongs or her sufferings. "Well," he reflected, audibly, "I should like to see you send his serene highness—somewhere!"

Madame Münster stooped and plucked a daisy from the grass. "And not sign my renunciation?"

"Well, I don't know—I don't know," said Acton.

"In one case I should have my revenge; in another case I should have my liberty."

Acton gave a little laugh as he helped her into the carriage. "At any rate," he said, "take good care of that paper."

A couple of days afterward he asked her to come and see his

house. The visit had already been proposed, but it had been put off in consequence of his mother's illness. She was a constant invalid, and she had passed these recent years, very patiently, in a great flowered arm-chair at her bed-room window. Lately, for some days, she had been unable to see any one; but now she was better, and she sent the Baroness a very civil message. Acton had wished their visitor to come to dinner; but Madame Münster preferred to begin with a simple call. She had reflected that if she should go to dinner Mr. Wentworth and his daughters would also be asked, and it had seemed to her that the peculiar character of the occasion would be best preserved in a *tête-à-tête* with her host. Why the occasion should have a peculiar character she explained to no one. As far as any one could see, it was simply very pleasant. Acton came for her and drove her to his door, an operation which was rapidly performed. His house the Baroness mentally pronounced a very good one; more articulately, she declared that it was enchanting. It was large and square and painted brown; it stood in a well-kept shrubbery, and was approached, from the gate, by a short drive. It was, moreover, a much more modern dwelling than Mr. Wentworth's, and was more redundantly upholstered and expensively ornamented. The Baroness perceived that her entertainer had analyzed material comfort to a sufficiently fine point. And then he possessed the most delightful *chinoiseries*—trophies of his sojourn in the Celestial Empire: pagodas of ebony and cabinets of ivory; sculptured monsters, grinning and jeering on chimney-pieces, in front of beautifully figured hand-screens; porcelain dinner-sets, gleaming behind the glass doors of mahogany buffets; large screens, in corners, covered with tense silk and embroidered with mandarins and dragons. These things were scattered all over the house, and they gave Eugenia a pretext for a complete domiciliary visit. She liked it, she enjoyed it; she thought it a very nice place. It had a mixture of the homely and the liberal, and though it was almost a museum, the large, little-used rooms were as fresh and clean as a well-kept dairy. Lizzie Acton told her that she dusted all the pagodas and other curiosities every day with her own hands; and the Baroness answered that she was evidently a household fairy. Lizzie had not at all the look of a young lady who dusted things; she wore such pretty dresses and had such delicate fingers that it was difficult to imagine her immersed in sordid cares. She came to meet Madame Münster on her arrival, but she said nothing, or almost nothing, and the Baroness again reflected—she had had occasion to do so before

—that American girls had no manners. She disliked this little American girl, and she was quite prepared to learn that she had failed to commend herself to Miss Acton. Lizzie struck her as positive and explicit almost to pertness; and the idea of her combining the apparent incongruities of a taste for housework and the wearing of fresh, Parisian-looking dresses suggested the possession of a dangerous energy. It was a source of irritation to the Baroness that in this country it should seem to matter whether a little girl were a trifle less or a trifle more of a nonentity; for Eugenia had hitherto been conscious of no moral pressure as regards the appreciation of diminutive virgins. It was perhaps an indication of Lizzie's pertness that she very soon retired and left the Baroness on her brother's hands. Acton talked a great deal about his chinoiseries; he knew a good deal about porcelain and bric-a-brac. The Baroness, in her progress through the house, made, as it were, a great many stations. She sat down everywhere, confessed to being a little tired, and asked about the various objects with a curious mixture of alertness and inattention. If there had been any one to say it to she would have declared that she was positively in love with her host; but she could hardly make this declaration—even in the strictest confidence—to Acton himself. It gave her, nevertheless, a pleasure that had some of the charm of unwontedness to feel, with that admirable keenness with which she was capable of feeling things, that he had a disposition without any edges; that even his humorous irony always expanded toward the point. One's impression of his honesty was almost like carrying a bunch of flowers; the perfume was most agreeable, but they were occasionally an inconvenience. One could trust him, at any rate, round all the corners of the world; and, withal, he was not absolutely simple, which would have been excess; he was only relatively simple, which was quite enough for the Baroness.

Lizzie reappeared to say that her mother would now be happy to receive Madame Münster; and the Baroness followed her to Mrs. Acton's apartment. Eugenia reflected, as she went, that it was not the affectation of impertinence that made her dislike this young lady, for on that ground she could easily have beaten her. It was not an aspiration on the girl's part to rivalry, but a kind of laughing, childishly-mocking indifference to the results of comparison. Mrs. Acton was an emaciated, sweet-faced woman of five and fifty, sitting with pillows behind her, and looking out on a clump of hemlocks. She was very modest, very timid, and very ill; she made Eugenie feel grateful that she herself was not like that—neither so ill, nor, possibly, so modest. On a chair, beside her, lay a volume of Emerson's Essays. It was a great occasion for poor Mrs. Acton, in her helpless condition, to be confronted with a clever foreign lady, who had more manner than any lady—any dozen ladies—that she had ever seen.

"I have heard a great deal about you," she said, softly, to the Baroness.

"From your son, eh?" Eugenia asked. "He has talked to me immensely of you. Oh, he talks of you as you would like," the Baroness declared; "as such a son *must* talk of such a mother!"

Mrs. Acton sat gazing; this was part of Madame Münster's "manner." But Robert Acton was gazing too, in vivid consciousness that he had barely mentioned his mother to their brilliant guest. He never talked of this still maternal presence,—a presence refined to such delicacy that it had almost resolved itself, with him, simply into the subjective emotion of gratitude. And Acton rarely talked of his emotions. The Baroness turned her smile toward him, and she instantly felt that she had been observed to be fibbing. She had struck a false note. But who were these people to whom such fibbing was not pleasing? If they were annoyed, the Baroness was equally so; and after the exchange of a few civil inquiries and low-voiced responses she took leave of Mrs. Acton. She begged Robert not to come home with her; she would get into the carriage alone; she preferred that. This was imperious, and she thought he looked disappointed. While she stood before the door with him—the carriage was turning in the gravel-walk—this thought restored her serenity.

When she had given him her hand in farewell she looked at him a moment. "I have almost decided to dispatch that paper," she said.

He knew that she alluded to the document that she had called her renunciation; and he assisted her into the carriage without saying anything. But just before the vehicle began to move he said, "Well, when you have in fact dispatched it, I hope you will let me know!"

Chapter VII

FELIX YOUNG finished Gertrude's portrait, and he afterwards transferred to canvas the features of many members of that circle of which it may be said that he had become for the time the pivot and the center. I am afraid it must be confessed that he was a decidedly flattering painter, and that he imparted to his models a romantic grace which seemed easily and cheaply acquired by the payment of a hundred dollars to a young man who made "sitting" so entertaining. For Felix was paid for his pictures, making, as he did, no secret of the fact that in guiding his steps to the Western world affectionate curiosity had gone hand in hand with a desire to better his condition. He took his uncle's portrait quite as if Mr. Wentworth had never averted himself from the experiment; and as he compassed his end only by the exercise of gentle violence, it is but fair to add that he allowed the old man to give him nothing but his time. He passed his arm into Mr. Wentworth's one summer morning—very few arms indeed had ever passed into Mr. Wentworth's—and led him across the garden and along the road into the studio which he had extemporized in the little house among the apple-trees. The grave gentleman felt himself more and more fascinated by his clever nephew, whose fresh, demonstrative youth seemed a compendium of experiences so strangely numerous. It appeared to him that Felix must know a great deal; he would like to learn what he thought about some of those things as regards which his own conversation had always been formal, but his knowledge vague. Felix had a confident, gayly trenchant way of judging human actions which Mr. Wentworth grew little by little to envy; it seemed like criticism made easy. Forming an opinion—say on a person's conduct—was, with Mr. Wentworth, a good deal like fumbling in a lock with a key chosen at hazard. He seemed to himself to go about the world with a big bunch of these ineffectual instruments at his girdle. His nephew, on the other hand, with a single turn of the wrist, opened any door as adroitly as a horse-thief. He felt obliged to keep up the convention that an uncle is always wiser than a nephew, even if he could keep it up no otherwise than by listening in serious silence to Felix's quick, light, constant discourse. But there came a day when he lapsed from consistency and almost asked his nephew's advice.

"Have you ever entertained the idea of settling in the United States?" he asked one morning, while Felix brilliantly plied his brush.

"My dear uncle," said Felix, "excuse me if your question makes me smile a little. To begin with, I have never entertained an idea. Ideas often entertain *me;* but I am afraid I have never seriously made a plan. I know what you are going to say; or rather, I know what you think, for I don't think you will say it—that this is very frivolous and loose-minded on my part. So it is; but I am made like that; I take things as they come, and somehow there is always some new thing to follow the last. In the second place, I should never propose to *settle*. I can't settle, my dear uncle; I'm not a settler. I know that is what strangers are supposed to do here; they always settle. But I haven't—to answer your question—entertained that idea."

"You intend to return to Europe and resume your irregular manner of life?" Mr. Wentworth inquired.

"I can't say I intend. But it's very likely I shall go back to Europe. I feel that, you know. It will depend a good deal upon my sister. She's even more of a European than I; here, you know, she's a picture out of her setting. And as for 'resuming,' dear uncle, I really have never given up my irregular manner of life. What, for me, could be more irregular than this?"

"Than what?" asked Mr. Wentworth, with his pale gravity.

"Well, than everything! Living in the midst of you, this way; this charming, quiet, serious family life; fraternizing with Charlotte and Gertrude; calling upon twenty young ladies and going out to walk with them; sitting with you in the evening on the piazza and listening to the crickets, and going to bed at ten o'clock."

"Your description is very animated," said Mr. Wentworth; "but I see nothing improper in what you describe."

"Neither do I, dear uncle. It is extremely delightful; I shouldn't like it if it were improper. I assure you I don't like improper things; though I dare say you think I do," Felix went on, painting away.

"I have never accused you of that."

"Pray don't," said Felix, "because, you see, at bottom I am a terrible Philistine."

"A Philistine?" repeated Mr. Wentworth.

"I mean, as one may say, a plain, God-fearing man." Mr. Wentworth looked at him reservedly, like a mystified sage, and Felix continued, "I trust I shall enjoy a venerable and venerated old age. I mean to live long. I can hardly call that a plan, perhaps; but it's a keen desire—a rosy vision. I shall be a lively, perhaps even a frivolous old man!"

"It is natural," said his uncle, sententiously, "that one should desire to prolong an agreeable life. We have perhaps a selfish indisposition to bring our pleasure to a close. But I presume," he added, "that you expect to marry."

"That too, dear uncle, is a hope, a desire, a vision," said Felix. It occurred to him for an instant that this was possibly a preface to the offer of the hand of one of Mr. Wentworth's admirable daughters. But in the name of decent modesty and a proper sense of the hard realities of this world, Felix banished the thought. His uncle was the incarnation of benevolence, certainly; but from that to accepting—much more postulating—the idea of a union between a young lady with a dowry presumptively brilliant and a penniless artist with no prospect of fame, there was a very long way. Felix had lately become conscious of a luxurious preference for the society—if possible unshared with others—of Gertrude Wentworth; but he had relegated this young lady, for the moment, to the coldly brilliant category of unattainable possessions. She was not the first woman for whom he had entertained an unpractical admiration. He had been in love with duchesses and countesses, and he had made, once or twice, a perilously near approach to cynicism in declaring that the disinterestedness of women had been overrated. On the whole, he had tempered audacity with modesty; and it is but fair to him now to say explicitly that he would have been incapable of taking advantage of his present large allowance of familiarity to make love to the younger of his handsome cousins. Felix had grown up among traditions in the light of which such a proceeding looked like a grievous breach of hospitality. I have said that he was always happy, and it may be counted among the present sources of his happiness that he had as regards this matter of his relations with Gertrude a deliciously good conscience. His own deportment seemed to him suffused with the beauty of virtue—a form of beauty that he admired with the same vivacity with which he admired all other forms.

"I think that if you marry," said Mr. Wentworth presently, "it will conduce to your happiness."

"*Sicurissimo!*" Felix exclaimed; and then, arresting his brush, he looked at his uncle with a smile. "There is something I feel tempted to say to you. May I risk it?"

Mr. Wentworth drew himself up a little. "I am very safe; I don't repeat things." But he hoped Felix would not risk too much.

Felix was laughing at his answer.

"It's odd to hear you telling me how to be happy. I don't think you know yourself, dear uncle. Now, does that sound brutal?"

The old man was silent a moment, and then, with a dry dignity that suddenly touched his nephew: "We may sometimes point out a road we are unable to follow."

"Ah, don't tell me you have had any sorrows," Felix rejoined. "I didn't suppose it, and I didn't mean to allude to them. I simply meant that you all don't amuse yourselves."

"Amuse ourselves? We are not children."

"Precisely not! You have reached the proper age. I was saying that the other day to Gertrude," Felix added. "I hope it was not indiscreet."

"If it was," said Mr. Wentworth, with a keener irony than Felix would have thought him capable of, "it was but your way of amusing yourself. I am afraid you have never had a trouble."

"Oh, yes, I have!" Felix declared, with some spirit; "before I knew better. But you don't catch me at it again."

Mr. Wentworth maintained for a while a silence more expressive than a deep-drawn sigh. "You have no children," he said at last.

"Don't tell me," Felix exclaimed, "that your charming young people are a source of grief to you!"

"I don't speak of Charlotte." And then, after a pause, Mr. Wentworth continued, "I don't speak of Gertrude. But I feel considerable anxiety about Clifford. I will tell you another time."

The next time he gave Felix a sitting his nephew reminded him that he had taken him into his confidence. "How is Clifford to-day?" Felix asked. "He has always seemed to me a young man of remarkable discretion. Indeed, he is only too discreet; he seems on his guard against me—as if he thought me rather light company. The other day he told his sister—Gertrude repeated it to me—that I was always laughing at him. If I laugh it is simply from the impulse to try and inspire him with confidence. That is the only way I have."

"Clifford's situation is no laughing matter," said Mr. Wentworth. "It is very peculiar, as I suppose you have guessed."

"Ah, you mean his love affair with his cousin?"

Mr. Wentworth stared, blushing a little. "I mean his absence from college. He has been suspended. We have decided not to speak of it unless we are asked."

"Suspended?" Felix repeated.

"He has been requested by the Harvard authorities to absent himself for six months. Meanwhile he is studying with Mr. Brand. We think Mr. Brand will help him; at least we hope so."

"What befell him at college?" Felix asked. "He was too fond of pleasure? Mr. Brand certainly will not teach him any of those secrets!"

"He was too fond of something of which he should not have been fond. I suppose it is considered a pleasure."

Felix gave his light laugh. "My dear uncle, is there any doubt about its being a pleasure? *C'est de son âge*, as they say in France."

"I should have said rather it was a vice of later life—of disappointed old age."

Felix glanced at his uncle, with his lifted eyebrows, and then, "Of what are you speaking?" he demanded, smiling.

"Of the situation in which Clifford was found."

"Ah, he was found—he was caught?"

"Necessarily, he was caught. He couldn't walk; he staggered."

"Oh," said Felix, "he drinks! I rather suspected that, from something I observed the first day I came here. I quite agree with you that it is a low taste. It's not a vice for a gentleman. He ought to give it up."

"We hope for a good deal from Mr. Brand's influence," Mr. Wentworth went on. "He has talked to him from the first. And he never touches anything himself."

"I will talk to him—I will talk to him!" Felix declared, gayly.

"What will you say to him?" asked his uncle, with some apprehension.

Felix for some moments answered nothing. "Do you mean to marry him to his cousin?" he asked at last.

"Marry him?" echoed Mr. Wentworth. "I shouldn't think his cousin would want to marry him."

"You have no understanding, then, with Mrs. Acton?"

Mr. Wentworth stared, almost blankly. "I have never discussed such subjects with her."

"I should think it might be time," said Felix. "Lizzie Acton is admirably pretty, and if Clifford is dangerous . . ."

"They are not engaged," said Mr. Wentworth. "I have no reason to suppose they are engaged."

"*Par exemple!*" cried Felix. "A clandestine engagement? Trust me. Clifford, as I say, is a charming boy. He is incapable of that. Lizzie Acton, then, would not be jealous of another woman."

"I certainly hope not," said the old man, with a vague sense of jealousy being an even lower vice than a love of liquor.

"The best thing for Clifford, then," Felix propounded, "is to become interested in some clever, charming woman." And he paused in his painting, and, with his elbows on his knees, looked with bright communicativeness at his uncle. "You see, I believe greatly in the influence of women. Living with women helps to make a man a gentleman. It is very true Clifford has his sisters, who are so charming. But there should be a different sentiment in play from the fraternal, you know. He has Lizzie Acton; but she, perhaps, is rather immature."

"I suspect Lizzie has talked to him, reasoned with him," said Mr. Wentworth.

"On the impropriety of getting tipsy—on the beauty of temperance? That is dreary work for a pretty young girl. No," Felix continued; "Clifford ought to frequent some agreeable woman, who, without ever mentioning such unsavory subjects, would give him a sense of its being very ridiculous to be fuddled. If he could fall in love with her a little, so much the better. The thing would operate as a cure."

"Well, now, what lady should you suggest?" asked Mr. Wentworth.

"There is a clever woman under your hand. My sister."

"Your sister—under my hand?" Mr. Wentworth repeated.

"Say a word to Clifford. Tell him to be bold. He is well disposed already; he has invited her two or three times to drive. But I don't think he comes to see her. Give him a hint to come—to come often. He will sit there of an afternoon, and they will talk. It will do him good."

Mr. Wentworth meditated. "You think she will exercise a helpful influence?"

"She will exercise a civilizing—I may call it a sobering—influence. A charming, clever, witty woman always does—especially if she is a little of a coquette. My dear uncle, the society of such women has been half my education. If Clifford is suspended, as you say, from college, let Eugenia be his preceptess."

Mr. Wentworth continued thoughtful. "You think Eugenia is a coquette?" he asked.

"What pretty woman is not?" Felix demanded in turn. But this, for Mr. Wentworth, could at the best have been no answer, for he did not think his niece pretty. "With Clifford," the young man pursued, "Eugenia will simply be enough of a coquette to be a little ironical. That's what he needs. So you recommend him to be nice with her, you know. The suggestion will come best from you."

"Do I understand," asked the old man, "that I am to suggest to my son to make a—a profession of—of affection to Madame Münster?"

"Yes, yes—a profession!" cried Felix sympathetically.

"But, as I understand it, Madame Münster is a married woman."

"Ah," said Felix, smiling, "of course she can't marry him. But she will do what she can."

Mr. Wentworth sat for some time with his eyes on the floor; at last he got up. "I don't think," he said, "that I can undertake to recommend my son any such course." And without meeting Felix's surprised glance he broke off his sitting, which was not resumed for a fortnight.

Felix was very fond of the little lake which occupied so many of Mr. Wentworth's numerous acres, and of a remarkable pine grove which lay upon the further side of it, planted upon a steep embankment and hanuted by the summer breeze. The murmur of the air in the far off tree-tops had a strange distinctness; it was almost articulate. One afternoon the young man came out of his painting-room and passed the open door of Eugenia's little salon. Within, in the cool dimness, he saw his sister, dressed in white, buried in her arm-chair, and holding to her face an immense bouquet. Opposite to her sat Clifford Wentworth, twirling his hat. He had evidently just presented the bouquet to the Baroness, whose fine eyes, as she glanced at him over the big roses and geraniums, wore a conversational smile. Felix, standing on the threshold of the cottage, hesitated for a moment as to whether he should retrace his steps and enter the parlor. Then he went his way and passed into Mr. Wentworth's garden. That civilizing process to which he had suggested that Clifford should be subjected appeared to have come on of itself. Felix was very sure, at least, that Mr. Wentworth had not adopted his ingenious device for stimulating the young man's æsthetic consciousness. "Doubtless he supposes," he said to himself, after the conversation that has been narrated, "that I desire, out of fraternal benevolence, to procure for Eugenia the amusement of a flirtation— or, as he probably calls it, an intrigue—with the too susceptible Clifford. It must be admitted—and I have noticed it before—that nothing exceeds the license occasionally taken by the imagination of very rigid people." Felix, on his own side, had of course said nothing to Clifford; but he had observed to Eugenia that Mr. Wentworth was much mortified at his son's low tastes. "We ought to do something to help them, after all their kindness to us," he had added. "Encourage Clifford to come and see you, and inspire him with a taste for conversation. That will supplant the other, which only comes from his puerility, from his not taking his position in the world—that of a rich young man of ancient stock—seriously enough. Make him a little more serious. Even if he makes love to you it is no great matter."

"I am to offer myself as a superior form of intoxication—a sub-

stitute for a brandy bottle, eh?" asked the Baroness. "Truly, in this
country one comes to strange uses."

But she had not positively declined to undertake Clifford's higher
education, and Felix, who had not thought of the matter again,
being haunted with visions of more personal profit, now reflected
that the work of redemption had fairly begun. The idea in prospect
had seemed of the happiest, but in operation it made him a trifle
uneasy. "What if Eugenia—what if Eugenia"—he asked himself
softly; the question dying away in his sense of Eugenia's unde-
termined capacity. But before Felix had time either to accept or to
reject its admonition, even in this vague form, he saw Robert Acton
turn out of Mr. Wentworth's inclosure, by a distant gate, and
come toward the cottage in the orchard. Acton had evidently
walked from his own house along a shady by-way and was intending
to pay a visit to Madame Münster. Felix watched him a moment; then
he turned away. Acton could be left to play the part of Providence
and interrupt—if interruption were needed—Clifford's entanglement
with Eugenia.

Felix passed through the garden toward the house and toward
a postern gate which opened upon a path leading across the fields,
beside a little wood, to the lake. He stopped and looked up at
the house; his eyes rested more particularly upon a certain open
window, on the shady side. Presently Gertrude appeared there,
looking out into the summer light. He took off his hat to her and
bade her good-day; he remarked that he was going to row across
the pond, and begged that she would do him the honor to accompany him. She looked at him a moment; then, without saying anything, she turned away. But she soon reappeared below in one of
those quaint and charming Leghorn hats, tied with white satin bows,
that were worn at that period; she also carried a green parasol. She
went with him to the edge of the lake, where a couple of boats were
always moored; they got into one of them, and Felix, with gentle
strokes, propelled it to the opposite shore. The day was the perfection of summer weather; the little lake was the color of sunshine;
the plash of the oars was the only sound, and they found themselves
listening to it. They disembarked, and, by a winding path, ascended
the pine-crested mound which overlooked the water, whose white
expanse glittered between the trees. The place was delightfully cool,
and had the added charm that—in the softly sounding pine boughs—
you seemed to hear the coolness as well as feel it. Felix and Gertrude
sat down on the rust-colored carpet of pine-needles and talked of

many things. Felix spoke at last, in the course of talk, of his going away; it was the first time he had alluded to it.

"You are going away?" said Gertrude, looking at him.

"Some day—when the leaves begin to fall. You know I can't stay forever."

Gertrude transferred her eyes to the outer prospect, and then, after a pause, she said, "I shall never see you again."

"Why not?" asked Felix. "We shall probably both survive my departure."

But Gertrude only repeated, "I shall never see you again. I shall never hear of you," she went on. "I shall know nothing about you. I knew nothing about you before, and it will be the same again."

"I knew nothing about you then, unfortunately," said Felix. "But now I shall write to you."

"Don't write to me. I shall not answer you," Gertrude declared.

"I should of course burn your letters," said Felix.

Gertrude looked at him again. "Burn my letters? You sometimes say strange things."

"They are not strange in themselves," the young man answered. "They are only strange as said to you. You will come to Europe."

"With whom shall I come?" She asked this question simply; she was very much in earnest. Felix was interested in her earnestness; for some moments he hesitated. "You can't tell me that," she pursued. "You can't say that I shall go with my father and my sister; you don't believe that."

"I shall keep your letters," said Felix, presently, for all answer.

"I never write. I don't know how to write." Gertrude, for some time, said nothing more; and her companion, as he looked at her, wished it had not been "disloyal" to make love to the daughter of an old gentleman who had offered one hospitality. The afternoon waned; the shadows stretched themselves; and the light grew deeper in the western sky. Two persons appeared on the opposite side of the lake, coming from the house and crossing the meadow. "It is Charlotte and Mr. Brand," said Gertrude. "They are coming over here." But Charlotte and Mr. Brand only came down to the edge of the water, and stood there, looking across; they made no motion to enter the boat that Felix had felt at the mooring-place. Felix waved his hat to them; it was too far to call. They made no visible response, and they presently turned away and walked along the shore.

"Mr. Brand is not demonstrative," said Felix. "He is never demonstrative to me. He sits silent, with his chin in his hand, looking at me. Sometimes he looks away. Your father tells me he is so eloquent; and I should like to hear him talk. He looks like such a noble young man. But with me he will never talk. And yet I am so fond of listening to brilliant imagery!"

"He is very eloquent," said Gertrude; "but he has no brilliant imagery. I have heard him talk a great deal. I knew that when they saw us they would not come over here."

"Ah, he is making *la cour*, as they say, to your sister? They desire to be alone?"

"No," said Gertrude, gravely, "they have no such reason as that for being alone."

"But why doesn't he make *la cour* to Charlotte?" Felix inquired. "She is so pretty, so gentle, so good."

Gertrude glanced at him, and then she looked at the distantly-seen couple they were discussing. Mr. Brand and Charlotte were walking side by side. They might have been a pair of lovers, and yet they might not. "They think I should not be here," said Gertrude.

"With me? I thought you didn't have those ideas."

"You don't understand. There are a great many things you don't understand."

"I understand my stupidity. But why, then, do not Charlotte and Mr. Brand, who, as an elder sister and a clergyman, are free to walk about together, come over and make me wiser by breaking up the unlawful interview into which I have lured you?"

"That is the last thing they would do," said Gertrude.

Felix stared at her a moment, with his lifted eyebrows. "*Je n'y comprends rien!*" he exclaimed; then his eyes followed for a while the retreating figures of this critical pair. "You may say what you please," he declared; "it is evident to me that your sister is not indifferent to her clever companion. It is agreeable to her to be walking there with him. I can see that from here." And in the excitement of observation Felix rose to his feet.

Gertrude rose also, but she made no attempt to emulate her companion's discovery; she looked rather in another direction. Felix's words had struck her; but a certain delicacy checked her. "She is certainly not indifferent to Mr. Brand; she has the highest opinion of him."

"One can see it—one can see it," said Felix, in a tone of amused contemplation, with his head on one side. Gertrude turned her back to the opposite shore; it was disagreeable to her to look, but she hoped Felix would say something more. "Ah, they have wandered away into the wood," he added.

Gertrude turned round again. "She is *not* in love with him," she said; it seemed her duty to say that.

"Then he is in love with her; or if he is not, he ought to be. She is such a perfect little woman of her kind. She reminds me of a pair of old-fashioned silver sugar-tongs; you know I am very fond of sugar. And she is very nice with Mr. Brand; I have noticed that; very gentle and gracious."

Gertrude reflected a moment. Then she took a great resolution. "She wants him to marry me," she said. "Of course she is nice."

Felix's eyebrows rose higher than ever. "To marry you! Ah, ah, this is interesting. And you think one must be very nice with a man to induce him to do that?"

Gertrude had turned a little pale, but she went on, "Mr. Brand wants it himself."

Felix folded his arms and stood looking at her. "I see—I see," he said quickly. "Why did you never tell me this before?"

"It is disagreeable to me to speak of it even now. I wished simply to explain to you about Charlotte."

"You don't wish to marry Mr. Brand, then?"

"No," said Gertrude, gravely.

"And does your father wish it?"

"Very much."

"And you don't like him—you have refused him?"

"I don't wish to marry him."

"Your father and sister think you ought to, eh?"

"It is a long story," said Gertrude. "They think there are good reasons. I can't explain it. They think I have obligations, and that I have encouraged him."

Felix smiled at her, as if she had been telling him an amusing story about some one else. "I can't tell you how this interests me," he said. "Now you don't recognize these reasons—these obligations?"

"I am not sure; it is not easy." And she picked up her parasol and turned away, as if to descend the slope.

"Tell me this," Felix went on, going with her: "are you likely to give up—to let them persuade you?"

Gertrude looked at him with the serious face that she had constantly worn, in opposition to his almost eager smile. "I shall never marry Mr. Brand," she said.

"I see!" Felix rejoined. And they slowly descended the hill together, saying nothing till they reached the margin of the pond. "It is your own affair," he then resumed; "but do you know, I am not altogether glad? If it were settled that you were to marry Mr. Brand I should take a certain comfort in the arrangement. I should feel more free. I have no right to make love to you myself, eh?" And he paused, lightly pressing his argument upon her.

"None whatever," replied Gertrude quickly—too quickly.

"Your father would never hear of it; I haven't a penny. Mr. Brand, of course, has property of his own, eh?"

"I believe he has some property; but that has nothing to do with it."

"With you, of course not; but with your father and sister it must have. So, as I say, if this were settled, I should feel more at liberty."

"More at liberty?" Gertrude repeated. "Please unfasten the boat."

Felix untwisted the rope and stood holding it. "I should be able to say things to you that I can't give myself the pleasure of saying now," he went on. "I could tell you how much I admire you, without seeming to pretend to that which I have no right to pretend to. I should make violent love to you," he added, laughing, "if I thought you were so placed as not to be offended by it."

"You mean if I were engaged to another man? That is strange reasoning!" Gertrude exclaimed.

"In that case you would not take me seriously."

"I take every one seriously," said Gertrude. And without his help she stepped lightly into the boat.

Felix took up the oars and sent it forward. "Ah, this is what you have been thinking about? It seemed to me you had something on your mind. I wish very much," he added, "that you would tell me some of these so-called reasons—these obligations."

"They are not real reasons—good reasons," said Gertrude, looking at the pink and yellow gleams in the water.

"I can understand that! Because a handsome girl has had a spark of coquetry, that is no reason."

"If you mean me, it's not that. I have not done that."

"It is something that troubles you, at any rate," said Felix.

"Not so much as it used to," Gertrude rejoined.

He looked at her, smiling always. "That is not saying much, eh?" But she only rested her eyes, very gravely, on the lighted water. She seemed to him to be trying to hide the signs of the trouble of which she had just told him. Felix felt, at all times, much the same impulse to dissipate visible melancholy that a good housewife feels to brush away dust. There was something he wished to brush away now; suddenly he stopped rowing and poised his oars. "Why should Mr. Brand have addressed himself to you, and not to your sister?" he asked. "I am sure she would listen to him."

Gertrude, in her family, was thought capable of a good deal of levity; but her levity had never gone so far as this. It moved her greatly, however, to hear Felix say that he was sure of something; so that, raising her eyes toward him, she tried intently, for some moments, to conjure up this wonderful image of a love-affair between her own sister and her own suitor. We know that Gertrude had an imaginative mind; so that it is not impossible that this effort should have been partially successful. But she only murmured, "Ah, Felix! ah, Felix!"

"Why shouldn't they marry? Try and make them marry!" cried Felix.

"Try and make them?"

"Turn the tables on them. Then they will leave you alone. I will help you as far as I can."

Gertrude's heart began to beat; she was greatly excited; she had never had anything so interesting proposed to her before. Felix had begun to row again, and he now sent the boat home with long strokes. "I believe she does care for him!" said Gertrude, after they had disembarked.

"Of course she does, and we will marry them off. It will make them happy; it will make every one happy. We shall have a wedding and I will write an epithalamium."

"It seems as if it would make me happy," said Gertrude.

"To get rid of Mr. Brand, eh? To recover your liberty?"

Gertrude walked on. "To see my sister married to so good a man."

Felix gave his light laugh. "You always put things on those grounds; you will never say anything for yourself. You are all so afraid, here, of being selfish. I don't think you know how," he went on. "Let me show you! It will make me happy for myself, and for just the reverse of what I told you a while ago. After that, when I make love to you, you will have to think I mean it."

"I shall never think you mean anything," said Gertrude. "You are too fantastic."

"Ah," cried Felix, "that's a license to say everything! Gertrude, I adore you!"

CHAPTER VIII

CHARLOTTE AND Mr. Brand had not returned when they reached the house; but the Baroness had come to tea, and Robert Acton also, who now regularly asked for a place at this generous repast or made his appearance later in the evening. Clifford Wentworth, with his juvenile growl, remarked upon it.

"You are always coming to tea nowadays, Robert," he said. "I should think you had drunk enough tea in China."

"Since when is Mr. Acton more frequent?" asked the Baroness.

"Since you came," said Clifford. "It seems as if you were a kind of attraction."

"I suppose I am a curiosity," said the Baroness. "Give me time and I will make you a salon."

"It would fall to pieces after you go!" exclaimed Acton.

"Don't talk about her going, in that familiar way," Clifford said. "It makes me feel gloomy."

Mr. Wentworth glanced at his son, and taking note of his words, wondered if Felix had been teaching him, according to the programme he had sketched out, to make love to the wife of a German prince.

Charlotte came in late with Mr. Brand; but Gertrude, to whom, at least, Felix had taught something, looked in vain, in her face, for the traces of a guilty passion. Mr. Brand sat down by Gertrude, and she presently asked him why they had not crossed the pond to join Felix and herself.

"It is cruel of you to ask me that," he answered, very softly. He had a large morsel of cake before him; but he fingered it without eating it. "I sometimes think you are growing cruel," he added.

Gertrude said nothing; she was afraid to speak. There was a kind of rage in her heart; she felt as if she could easily persuade herself that she was persecuted. She said to herself that it was quite right that she should not allow him to make her believe she was wrong. She thought of what Felix had said to her; she wished indeed Mr. Brand would marry Charlotte. She looked away from him and spoke no more. Mr. Brand ended by eating his cake, while Felix sat opposite, describing to Mr. Wentworth the students' duels at Heidelberg. After tea they all dispersed themselves, as usual, upon the piazza and in the garden; and Mr. Brand drew near to Gertrude again.

"I didn't come to you this afternoon because you were not alone," he began; "because you were with a newer friend."

"Felix? He is an old friend by this time."

Mr. Brand looked at the ground for some moments. "I thought I was prepared to hear you speak in that way," he resumed. "But I find it very painful."

"I don't see what else I can say," said Gertrude.

Mr. Brand walked beside her for a while in silence; Gertrude wished he would go away. "He is certainly very accomplished. But I think I ought to advise you."

"To advise me?"

"I think I know your nature."

"I think you don't," said Gertrude, with a soft laugh.

"You make yourself out worse than you are—to please him," Mr. Brand said, gently.

"Worse—to please him? What do you mean?" asked Gertrude, stopping.

Mr. Brand stopped also, and with the same soft straightforwardness, "He doesn't care for the things you care for—the great questions of life."

Gertrude, with her eyes on his, shook her head. "I don't care for the great questions of life. They are much beyond me."

"There was a time when you didn't say that," said Mr. Brand.

"Oh," rejoined Gertrude, "I think you made me talk a great deal of nonsense. And it depends," she added, "upon what you call the great questions of life. There are some things I care for."

"Are they the things you talk about with your cousin?"

"You should not say things to me against my cousin, Mr. Brand," said Gertrude. "That is dishonorable."

He listened to this respectfully; then he answered, with a little vibration of the voice, "I should be very sorry to do anything dishonorable. But I don't see why it is dishonorable to say that your cousin is frivolous."

"Go and say it to himself!"

"I think he would admit it," said Mr. Brand. "That is the tone he would take. He would not be ashamed of it."

"Then I am not ashamed of it!" Gertrude declared. "That is probably what I like him for. I am frivolous myself."

"You are trying, as I said just now, to lower yourself."

"I am trying for once to be natural!" cried Gertrude passionately. "I have been pretending, all my life; I have been dishonest; it is

you that have made me so!" Mr. Brand stood gazing at her, and
she went on, "Why shouldn't I be frivolous, if I want? One has a
right to be frivolous, if it's one's nature. No, I don't care for the
great questions. I care for pleasure—for amusement. Perhaps I am
fond of wicked things; it is very possible!"

Mr. Brand remained staring; he as even a little pale, as if he had
been frightened. "I don't think you know what you are saying!" he
exclaimed.

"Perhaps not. Perhaps I am talking nonsense. But it is only with
you that I talk nonsense. I never do so with my cousin."

"I will speak to you again, when you are less excited," said Mr.
Brand.

"I am always excited when you speak to me. I must tell you
that—even if it prevents you altogether, in future. Your speaking
to me irritates me. With my cousin it is very different. That seems
quiet and natural."

He looked at her, and then he looked away, with a kind of helpless distress, at the dusky garden and the faint summer stars. After
which, suddenly turning back, "Gertrude, Gertrude!" he softly
groaned. "Am I really losing you?"

She was touched—she was pained; but it had already occurred to
her that she might do something better than say so. It would not
have alleviated her companion's distress to perceive, just then,
whence she had sympathetically borrowed this ingenuity. "I am
not sorry for you," Gertrude said; "for in paying so much attention
to me you are following a shadow—you are wasting something
precious. There is something else you might have that you don't
look at—something better than I am. That is a reality!" And then,
with intention, she looked at him and tried to smile a little. He
thought this smile of hers very strange; but she turned away and
left him.

She wandered about alone in the garden wondering what Mr.
Brand would make of her words, which it had been a singular
pleasure for her to utter. Shortly after, passing in front of the house,
she saw at a distance two persons standing near the garden gate.
It was Mr. Brand going away and bidding good-night to Charlotte, who had walked down with him from the house. Gertrude
saw that the parting was prolonged. Then she turned her back upon
it. She had not gone very far, however, when she heard her sister
slowly following her. She neither turned round nor waited for her;
she knew what Charlotte was going to say. Charlotte, who at last

overtook her, in fact presently began; she had passed her arm into Gertrude's.

"Will you listen to me, dear, if I say something very particular?"

"I know what you are going to say," said Gertrude. "Mr. Brand feels very badly."

"Oh, Gertrude, how can you treat him so?" Charlotte demanded. And as her sister made no answer she added, "After all he has done for you!"

"What has he done for me?"

"I wonder you can ask, Gertrude. He has helped you so. You told me so yourself, a great many times. You told me that he helped you to struggle with your—your peculiarities. You told me that he had taught you how to govern your temper."

For a moment Gertrude said nothing. Then, "Was my temper very bad?" she asked.

"I am not accusing you, Gertrude," said Charlotte.

"What are you doing, then?" her sister demanded, with a short laugh.

"I am pleading for Mr. Brand—reminding you of all you owe him."

"I have given it all back," said Gertrude, still with her little laugh. "He can take back the virtue he imparted! I want to be wicked again."

Her sister made her stop in the path, and fixed upon her, in the darkness, a sweet, reproachful gaze. "If you talk this way I shall almost believe it. Think of all we owe Mr. Brand. Think of how he has always expected something of you. Think how much he has been to us. Think of his beautiful influence upon Clifford."

"He is very good," said Gertrude, looking at her sister. "I know he is very good. But he shouldn't speak against Felix."

"Felix is good," Charlotte answered, softly but promptly. "Felix is very wonderful. Only he is so different. Mr. Brand is much nearer to us. I should never think of going to Felix with a trouble —with a question. Mr. Brand is much more to us, Gertrude."

"He is very—very good," Gertrude repeated. "He is more to you; yes, much more. Charlotte," she added suddenly, "you are in love with him!"

"Oh, Gertrude!" cried poor Charlotte; and her sister saw her blushing in the darkness.

Gertrude put her arm round her. "I wish he would marry you!" she went on.

Charlotte shook herself free. "You must not say such things!" she exclaimed, beneath her breath.

"You like him more than you say, and he likes you more than he knows."

"This is very cruel of you!" Charlotte Wentworth murmured.

But if it was cruel Gertrude continued pitiless. "Not if it's true," she answered. "I wish he would marry you."

"Please don't say that."

"I mean to tell him so!" said Gertrude.

"Oh, Gertrude, Gertrude!" her sister almost moaned.

"Yes, if he speaks to me again about myself, I will say, 'Why don't you marry Charlotte? She's a thousand times better than I.' "

"You *are* wicked; you *are* changed!" cried her sister.

"If you don't like it you can prevent it," said Gertrude. "You can prevent it by keeping him from speaking to me?" And with this she walked away, very conscious of what she had done; measuring it and finding a certain joy and a quickened sense of freedom in it.

Mr. Wentworth was rather wide of the mark in suspecting that Clifford had begun to pay unscrupulous compliments to his brilliant cousin; for the young man had really more scruples than he received credit for in his family. He had a certain transparent shamefacedness which was in itself a proof that he was not at his ease in dissipation. His collegiate peccadilloes had aroused a domestic murmur as disagreeable to the young man as the creaking of his boots would have been to a house-breaker. Only, as the house-breaker would have simplified matters by removing his *chaussures*, it had seemed to Clifford that the shortest cut to comfortable relations with people—relations which should make him cease to think that when they spoke to him they meant something improving—was to renounce all ambition toward a nefarious development. And, in fact, Clifford's ambition took the most commendable form. He thought of himself in the future as the well-known and much-liked Mr. Wentworth, of Boston, who should, in the natural course of prosperity, have married his pretty cousin, Lizzie Acton; should live in a wide-fronted house, in view of the Common; and should drive, behind a light wagon, over the damp autumn roads, a pair by beautifully matched sorrel horses. Clifford's vision of the coming years was very simple; its most definite features were this element of familiar matrimony and the duplication of his resources for trotting. He had not yet asked his cousin to marry him; but he meant to do so as soon as he had taken his degree. Lizzie was serenely conscious of his intention, and she had made up her mind that he would improve. Her brother, who was very fond of this light, quick, competent little Lizzie, saw on his side no reason to interpose. It seemed to him a graceful social law that Clifford and his sister should become engaged; he himself was not engaged, but every one else, fortunately, was not such a fool as he. He was fond of Clifford, as well, and had his own way—of which it must be confessed he was a little ashamed—of looking at those aberrations which had led to the young man's compulsory retirement from the neighboring seat of learning. Acton had seen the world, as he said to himself; he had been to China and had knocked about among men. He had learned the essential difference between a nice young fellow and a mean young fellow, and was satisfied that there was no harm in Clifford. He believed—although it must be added that he had not quite the courage to declare it—in the doctrine of wild oats, and thought it a useful preventive of superfluous fears. If Mr. Wentworth and Charlotte and Mr. Brand would only apply it in Clifford's case, they would be happier; and Acton thought it a pity they should be happier. They took the boy's misdemeanors too much to heart; they talked to him too solemnly; they frightened and bewildered him. Of course there was the great standard of morality, which forbade that a man should get tipsy, play at billiards for money, or cultivate his sensual consciousness; but what fear was there that poor Clifford was going to run a tilt at any great standard? It had, however, never occurred to Acton to dedicate the Baroness Münster to the redemption of a refractory collegian. The instrument, here, would have seemed to him quite too complex for the operation. Felix, on the other hand, had spoken in obedience to the belief that the more charming a woman is the more numerous, literally, are her definite social uses.

Eugenia herself, as we know, had plenty of leisure to enumerate her uses. As I have had the honor of intimating, she had come four thousand miles to seek her fortune; and it is not to be supposed that after this great effort she could neglect any apparent aid to advancement. It is my misfortune that in attempting to describe in a short compass the deportment of this remarkable woman I am obliged to express things rather brutally. I feel this to be the case, for instance, when I say that she had primarily detected such an aid to advancement in the person of Robert Acton, but that she had afterwards remembered that a prudent archer has always a second bowstring. Eugenia was a woman of finely-mingled motive, and her intentions were never sensibly gross. She had a sort of æsthetic ideal for Clifford which seemed to her a disinterested reason for taking him in hand. It was very well for a fresh-colored young gentleman to be ingenuous; but Clifford, really, was crude. With such a pretty face he ought to have prettier manners. She would teach him that, with a beautiful name, the expectation of a large property, and, as they said in Europe, a social position, an only son should know how to carry himself.

Once Clifford had begun to come and see her by himself and for himself, he came very often. He hardly knew why he should come; he saw her almost every evening at his father's house; he had nothing particular to say to her. She was not a young girl, and fellows of his age called only upon young girls. He exaggerated her age; she seemed to him an old woman; it was happy that the Baroness, with all her intelligence, was incapable of guessing this. But gradually it struck Clifford that visiting old women might be, if not a natural, at least, as they say of some articles of diet, an acquired taste. The Baroness was certainly a very amusing old woman; she talked to him as no lady—and indeed no gentleman— had ever talked to him before.

"You should go to Europe and make the tour," she said to him one afternoon. "Of course, on leaving college you will go."

"I don't want to go," Clifford declared. "I know some fellows who have been to Europe. They say you can have better fun here."

"That depends. It depends upon your idea of fun. Your friends probably were not introduced."

"Introduced?" Clifford demanded.

"They had no opportunity of going into society; they formed no *relations*." This was one of a certain number of words that the Baroness often pronounced in the French manner.

"They went to a ball, in Paris; I know that," said Clifford.

"Ah, there are balls and balls; especially in Paris. No, you must go, you know; it is not a thing from which you can dispense yourself. You need it."

"Oh, I'm very well," said Clifford. "I'm not sick."

"I don't mean for your health, my poor child. I mean for your manners."

"I haven't got any manners!" growled Clifford.

"Precisely. You don't mind my assenting to that, eh?" asked the Baroness with a smile. "You must go to Europe and get a few. You can get them better there. It is a pity you might not have come

while I was living in—in Germany. I would have introduced you;
I had a charming little circle. You would perhaps have been rather
young; but the younger one begins, I think, the better. Now, at any
rate, you have no time to lose, and when I return you must immediately come to me."

All this, to Clifford's apprehension, was a great mixture—his beginning young, Eugenia's return to Europe, his being introduced
to her charming little circle. What was he to begin, and what was
her little circle? His ideas about her marriage had a good deal of
vagueness; but they were in so far definite as that he felt it to be
a matter not to be freely mentioned. He sat and looked all round
the room; he supposed she was alluding in some way to her marriage.

"Oh, I don't want to go to Germany," he said; it seemed to him
the most convenient thing to say.

She looked at him a while, smiling with her lips, but not with
her eyes.

"You have scruples?" she asked.

"Scruples?" said Clifford.

"You young people, here, are very singular; one doesn't know
where to expect you. When you are extremely improper you are
so terribly proper. I dare say you think that, owing to my irregular
marriage, I live with loose people. You were never more mistaken.
I have been all the more particular."

"Oh, no," said Clifford, honestly distressed. "I never thought such
a thing as that."

"Are you very sure? I am convinced that your father does, and
your sisters. They say to each other that here I am on my good
behavior but that over there—married by the left hand—I associate
with light woman."

"Oh, no," cried Clifford, energetically, "they don't say such
things as that to each other!"

"If they think them they had better say them," the Baroness
rejoined. "Then they can be contradicted. Please contradict that
whenever you hear it, and don't be afraid of coming to see me
on account of the company I keep. I have the honor of knowing
more distinguished men, my poor child, than you are likely to see
in a life-time. I see very few women; but those are women of rank.
So, my dear young Puritan, you needn't be afraid. I am not in the
least one of those who think that the society of women who have
lost their place in the *vrai monde* is necessary to form a young man.

I have never taken that tone. I have kept my place myself, and I think we are a much better school than the others. Trust me, Clifford, and I will prove that to you," the Baroness continued, while she made the agreeable reflection that she could not, at least, be accused of perverting her young kinsman. "So if you ever fall among thieves don't go about saying I sent you to them."

Clifford thought it so comical that he should know—in spite of her figurative language—what she meant, and that she should mean what he knew, that he could hardly help laughing a little, although he tried hard. "Oh, no! oh, no!" he murmured.

"Laugh out, laugh out, if I amuse you!" cried the Baroness. "I am here for that!" And Clifford thought her a very amusing person indeed. "But remember," she said on this occasion, "that you are coming—next year—to pay me a visit over there."

About a week afterwards she said to him, pointblank, "Are you seriously making love to your little cousin?"

"Seriously making love"—these words, on Madame Münster's lips, had to Clifford's sense a portentous and embarrassing sound; he hesitated about assenting, lest he should commit himself to more than he understood. "Well, I shouldn't say it if I was!" he exclaimed.

"Why wouldn't you say it?" the Baroness demanded. "Those things ought to be known."

"I don't care whether it is known or not," Clifford rejoined. "But I don't want people looking at me."

"A young man of your importance ought to learn to bear observation—to carry himself as if he were quite indifferent to it. I won't say, exactly, unconscious," the Baroness explained. "No, he must seem to know he is observed, and to think it natural he should be; but he must appear perfectly used to it. Now you haven't that, Clifford; you haven't that at all. You must have that, you know. Don't tell me you are not a young man of importance," Eugenia added. "Don't say anything so flat as that."

"Oh, no, you don't catch me saying that!" cried Clifford.

"Yes, you must come to Germany," Madame Münster continued. "I will show you how people can be talked about, and yet not seem to know it. You will be talked about, of course, with me; it will be said you are my lover. I will show you how little one may mind that—how little I shall mind it."

Clifford sat staring, blushing and laughing. "I shall mind it a good deal!" he declared.

"Ah, not too much, you know; that would be uncivil. But I give you leave to mind it a little; especially if you have a passion for Miss Acton. *Voyons;* as regards that, you either have or you have not. It is very simple to say it."

"I don't see why you want to know," said Clifford.

"You ought to want me to know. If one is arranging a marriage, one tells one's friends."

"Oh, I'm not arranging anything," said Clifford.

"You don't intend to marry your cousin?"

"Well, I expect I shall do as I choose!"

The Baroness leaned her head upon the back of her chair and closed her eyes, as if she were tired. Then opening them again, "Your cousin is very charming!" she said.

"She is the prettiest girl in this place," Clifford rejoined.

"'In this place' is saying little; she would be charming anywhere. I am afraid you are entangled."

"Oh, no, I'm not entangled."

"Are you engaged? At your age that is the same thing."

Clifford looked at the Baroness with some audacity. "Will you tell no one?"

"If it's as sacred as that—no."

"Well, then—we are not!" said Clifford.

"That's the great secret—that you are not, eh?" asked the Baroness, with a quick laugh. "I am very glad to hear it. You are altogether too young. A young man in your position must choose and compare; he must see the world first. Depend upon it," she added, "you should not settle that matter before you have come abroad and paid me that visit. There are several things I should like to call your attention to first."

"Well, I am rather afraid of that visit," said Clifford. "It seems to me it will be rather like going to school again."

The Baroness looked at him a moment.

"My dear child," she said, "there is no agreeable man who has not, at some moment, been to school to a clever woman—probably a little older than himself. And you must be thankful when you get your instructions gratis. With me you would get it gratis."

The next day Clifford told Lizzie Acton that the Baroness thought her the most charming girl she had ever seen.

Lizzie shook her head. "No, she doesn't!" she said.

"Do you think everything she says," asked Clifford, "is to be taken the opposite way?"

"I think that is!" said Lizzie.

Clifford was going to remark that in this case the Baroness must desire greatly to bring about a marriage between Mr. Clifford Wentworth and Miss Elizabeth Acton; but he resolved, on the whole, to suppress this observation.

CHAPTER IX

IT SEEMED to Robert Acton, after Eugenia had come to his house, that something had passed between them which made them a good deal more intimate. It was hard to say exactly what, except her telling him that she had taken her resolution with regard to the Prince Adolf; for Madame Münster's visit had made no difference in their relations. He came to see her very often; but he had come to see her very often before. It was agreeable to him to find himself in her little drawing-room; but this was not a new discovery. There was a change, however, in this sense: that if the Baroness had been a great deal in Acton's thoughts before, she was now never out of them. From the first she had been personally fascinating; but the fascination now had become intellectual as well. He was constantly pondering her words and motions; they were as interesting as the factors in an algebraic problem. This is saying a good deal; for Acton was extremely fond of mathematics. He asked himself whether it could be that he was in love with her, and then hoped he was not; hoped it not so much for his own sake as for that of the amatory passion itself. If this was love, love had been overrated. Love was a poetic impulse, and his own state of feeling with regard to the Baroness was largely characterized by that eminently prosaic sentiment—curiosity. It was true, as Acton with his quietly cogitative habit observed to himself, that curiosity, pushed to a given point, might become a romantic passion; and he certainly thought enough about this charming woman to make him restless and even a little melancholy. It puzzled and vexed him at times to feel that he was not more ardent. He was not in the least bent upon remaining a bachelor. In his younger years he had been—or he had tried to be—of the opinion that it would be a good deal "jollier" not to marry, and he had flattered himself that his single condition was something of a citadel. It was a citadel, at all events, of which he had long since leveled the outworks. He had removed the guns from the ramparts; he had lowered the draw-bridge across the moat. The draw-bridge had swayed lightly under Madame Münster's step;

why should he not cause it to be raised again, so that she might be kept prisoner? He had an idea that she would become—in time at least, and on learning the conveniences of the place for making a lady comfortable—a tolerably patient captive. But the draw-bridge was never raised, and Acton's brilliant visitor was as free to depart as she had been to come. It was part of his curiosity to know why the deuce so susceptible a man was *not* in love with so charming a woman. If her various graces were, as I have said, the factors in an algebraic problem, the answer to this question was the indispensable unknown quantity. The pursuit of the unknown quantity was extremely absorbing; for the present it taxed all Acton's faculties.

Toward the middle of August he was obliged to leave home for some days; an old friend, with whom he had been associated in China, had begged him to come to Newport, where he lay extremely ill. His friend got better, and at the end of a week Acton was released. I use the word "released" advisedly; for in spite of his attachment to his Chinese comrade he had been but a half-hearted visitor. He felt as if he had been called away from the theatre during the progress of a remarkably interesting drama. The curtain was up all this time, and he was losing the fourth act; that fourth act which would have been so essential to a just appreciation of the fifth. In other words, he was thinking about the Baroness, who, seen at this distance, seemed a truly brilliant figure. He saw at Newport a great many pretty women, who certainly were figures as brilliant as beautiful light dresses could make them; but though they talked a great deal—and the Baronesses's strong point was perhaps also her conversation—Madame Münster appeared to lose nothing by the comparison. He wished she had come to Newport too. Would it not be possible to make up, as they said, a party for visiting the famous watering-place and invite Eugenia to join? It was true that the complete satisfaction would be to spend a fortnight at Newport with Eugenia alone. It would be a great pleasure to see her, in society, carry everything before her, as he was sure she would do. When Acton caught himself thinking these thoughts he began to walk up and down, with his hands in his pockets, frowning a little and looking at the floor. What did it prove—for it certainly proved something—this lively disposition to be "off" somewhere with Madame Münster, away from all the rest of them? Such a vision, certainly, seemed a refined implication of matrimony, after the Baroness should have formally got rid of her informal husband. At any rate, Acton, with his characteristic discretion, forbore to give expression to whatever else it might imply, and the narrator of these incidents is not obliged to be more definite.

He returned home rapidly, and, arriving in the afternoon, lost as little time as possible in joining the familiar circle at Mr. Wentworth's. On reaching the house, however, he found the piazzas empty. The doors and windows were open, and their emptiness was made clear by the shafts of lamp-light from the parlors. Entering the house, he found Mr. Wentworth sitting alone in one of these apartments, engaged in the perusal of the "North American Review." After they had exchanged greetings and his cousin had made discreet inquiry about his journey, Acton asked what had become of Mr. Wentworth's companions.

"They are scattered about, amusing themselves as usual," said the old man. "I saw Charlotte, a short time since, seated, with Mr. Brand, upon the piazza. They were conversing with their customary animation. I suppose they have joined her sister, who, for the hundredth time, was doing the honors of the garden to her foreign cousin."

"I suppose you mean Felix," said Acton. And on Mr. Wentworth's assenting, he said, "And the others?"

"Your sister has not come this evening. You must have seen her at home," and Mr. Wentworth.

"Yes. I proposed to her to come. She declined."

"Lizzie, I suppose, was expecting a visitor," said the old man, with a kind of solemn slyness.

"If she was expecting Clifford, he had not turned up."

Mr. Wentworth, at this intelligence, closed the "North American Review" and remarked that he had understood Clifford to say that he was going to see his cousin. Privately, he reflected that if Lizzie Acton had had no news of his son, Clifford must have gone to Boston for the evening: an unnatural course of a summer night, especially when accompanied with disingenuous representations.

"You must remember that he has two cousins," said Acton, laughing. And then, coming to the point, "If Lizzie is not here," he added, "neither apparently is the Baroness."

Mr. Wentworth stared a moment, and remembered that queer proposition of Felix's. For a moment he did not know whether it was not to be wished that Clifford, after all, might have gone to Boston. "The Baroness has not honored us tonight," he said. "She has not come over for three days."

"Is she ill?" Acton asked.

"No; I have been to see her."

"What is the matter with her?"

"Well," said Mr. Wentworth, "I infer she has tired of us."

Acton pretended to sit down, but he was restless; he found it impossible to talk with Mr. Wentworth. At the end of ten minutes he took up his hat and said that he thought he would "go off." It was very late; it was ten o'clock.

His quiet-faced kinsman looked at him a moment. "Are you going home?" he asked.

Acton hesitated, and then answered that he had proposed to go over and take a look at the Baroness.

"Well, *you* are honest, at least," said Mr. Wentworth, sadly.

"So are you, if you come to that?" cried Acton, laughing. "Why shouldn't I be honest?"

The old man opened the "North American" again, and read a few lines. "If we have ever had any virtue among us, we had better keep hold of it now," he said. He was not quoting.

"We have a Baroness among us," said Acton. "That's what we must keep hold of!" He was too impatient to see Madame Münster again to wonder what Mr. Wentworth was talking about. Nevertheless, after he had passed out of the house and traversed the garden and the little piece of road that separated him from Eugenia's provisional residence, he stopped a moment outside. He stood in her little garden; the long window of her parlor was open, and he could see the white curtains, with the lamp-light shining through them, swaying softly to and fro in the warm night wind. There was a sort of excitement in the idea of seeing Madame Münster again; he became aware that his heart was beating rather faster than usual. It was this that made him stop, with a half-amused surprise. But in a moment he went along the piazza, and, approaching the open window, tapped upon its lintel with his stick. He could see the Baroness within; she was standing in the middle of the room. She came to the window and pulled aside the curtain; then she stood looking at him a moment. She was not smiling; she seemed serious.

"*Mais entrez donc!*" she said at last. Acton passed in across the window-sill; he wondered, for an instant, what was the matter with her. But the next moment she had begun to smile and had put out her hand. "Better late than never," he said. "It is very kind of you to come at this hour."

"I have just returned from my journey," said Acton.

"Ah, very kind, very kind," she repeated, looking about her where to sit.

"I went first to the other house," Acton continued. "I expected to find you there."

She had sunk into her usual chair; but she got up again, and began to move about the room. Acton had laid down his hat and stick; he was looking at her, conscious that there was in fact a great charm in seeing her again. "I don't know whether I ought to tell you to sit down," she said. "It is too late to begin a visit."

"It's too early to end one," Acton declared "and we needn't mind the beginning.

She looked at him again, and, after a moment, dropped once more into her low chair, while he took a place near her. "We are in the middle, then?" she asked. "Was that where we were when you went away? No, I haven't been to the other house."

"Not yesterday, nor the day before, eh?"

"I don't know how many days it is."

"You are tired of it," said Acton.

She leaned back in her chair; her arms were folded. "That is a terrible accusation, but I have not the courage to defend myself."

"I am not attacking you," said Acton. "I expected something of this kind."

"It's a proof of extreme intelligence. I hope you enjoyed your journey."

"Not at all," Acton declared. "I would much rather have been here with you."

"Now you *are* attacking me," said the Baroness. "You are contrasting my inconstancy with your own fidelity."

"I confess I never get tired of people I like."

"Ah, you are not a poor wicked foreign woman, with irritable nerves and a sophisticated mind!"

"Something has happened to you since I went away," said Acton, changing his place.

"Your going away—that is what has happened to me."

"Do you mean to say that you have missed me?" he asked.

"If I had meant to say it, it would not be worth your making a note of. I am very dishonest and my compliments are worthless."

Acton was silent for some moments. "You have broken down," he said at last.

Madame Münster left her chair, and began to move about.

"Only for a moment. I shall pull myself together again."

"You had better not take it too hard. If you are bored, you needn't be afraid to say so—to me at least."

"You shouldn't say such things as that," the Baroness answered. "You should encourage me."

"I admire your patience; that is encouraging."

"You shouldn't even say that. When you talk of my patience you are disloyal to your own people. Patience implies suffering; and what have I had to suffer?"

"Oh, not hunger, not unkindness, certainly," said Acton, laughing. "Nevertheless, we all admire your patience."

"You all detest me!" cried the Baroness, with a sudden vehemence, turning her back toward him.

"You make it hard," said Acton, getting up, "for a man to say something tender to you." This evening there was something particularly striking and touching about her; an unwonted softness and a look of suppressed emotion. He felt himself suddenly appreciating the fact that she had behaved very well. She had come to this quiet corner of the world under the weight of a cruel indignity, and she had been so gracefully, modestly thankful for the rest she found there. She had joined that simple circle over the way; she had mingled in its plain, provincial talk, she had shared its meagre and savorless pleasures. She had set herself a task, and she had rigidly performed it. She had conformed to the angular conditions of New England life, and she had had the tact and pluck to carry it off as if she liked them. Acton felt a more downright need than he had ever felt before to tell her that he admired her and that she struck him as a very superior woman. All along, hitherto, he had been on his guard with her; he had been cautious, observant, suspicious. But now a certain light tumult in his blood seemed to tell him that a finer degree of confidence in this charming woman would be its own reward. "We don't detest you," he went on. "I don't know what you mean. At any rate, I speak for myself; I don't know anything about the others. Very likely, you detest them for the dull life they make you lead. Really, it would give me a sort of pleasure to hear you say so."

Eugenia had been looking at the door on the other side of the room; now she slowly turned her eyes toward Robert Acton. "What can be the motive," she asked, "of a man like you—an honest man, a *galant homme*—in saying so base a thing as that?"

"Does it sound very base?" asked Acton, candidly. "Suppose it does, and I thank you for telling me so. Of course, I don't mean it literally."

The Baroness stood looking at him. "How do you mean it?" she asked.

This question was difficult to answer, and Acton, feeling the least bit foolish, walked to the open window and looked out. He stood there, thinking a moment, and then he turned back. "You know that document that you were to send to Germany," he said. "You called it your 'reunuciation.' Did you ever send it?"

Madame Münster's eyes expanded; she looked very grave. "What a singular answer to my question!"

"Oh, it isn't an answer," said Acton. "I have wished to ask you, many times. I thought it probable you would tell me yourself. The question, on my part, seems abrupt now; but it would be abrupt at any time."

The Baroness was silent a moment; and then, "I think I have told you too much!" she said.

This declaration appeared to Acton to have a certain force; he had indeed a sense of asking more of her than he offered her. He returned to the window, and watched, for a moment, a little star that twinkled through the lattice of the piazza. There were at any rate offers enough he could make; perhaps he had hitherto not been sufficiently explicit in doing so. "I wish you would ask something of me," he presently said. "Is there nothing I can do for you? If you can't stand this dull life any more, let me amuse you!"

The Baroness had sunk once more into a chair, and she had taken up a fan which she held, with both hands, to her mouth. Over the top of the fan her eyes were fixed on him. "You are very strange to-night," she said, with a little laugh.

"I will do anything in the world," he rejoined, standing in front of her. "Shouldn't you like to travel about and see something of the country? Won't you go to Niagara? You ought to see Niagara, you know."

"With you, do you mean?"

"I should be delighted to take you."

"You alone?"

Acton looked at her, smiling, and yet with a serious air. "Well, yes; we might go alone," he said.

"If you were not what you are," she answered, "I should feel insulted."

"How do you mean—what I am?"

"If you were one of the gentlemen I have been used to all of my life. If you were not a queer Bostonian."

"If the gentlemen you have been used to have taught you to expect insults," said Acton, "I am glad I am what I am. You had much better come to Niagara."

"If you wish to 'amuse' me," the Baroness declared, "you need go to no further expense. You amuse me very effectually."

He sat down opposite to her; she still held her fan up to her face, with her eyes only showing above it. There was a moment's silence, and then he said, returning to his former question, "Have you sent that document to Germany?"

Again there was a moment's silence. The expressive eyes of Madame Münster seemed, however, half to break it.

"I will tell you—at Niagara!" she said.

She had hardly spoken when the door at the further end of the room opened—the door upon which, some minutes previous, Eugenia had fixed her gaze. Clifford Wentworth stood there, blushing and looking rather awkward. The Baroness rose, quickly, and Acton, more slowly, did the same. Clifford gave him no greeting; he was looking at Eugenia.

"Ah, you were here?" exclaimed Acton.

"He was in Felix's studio," said Madame Münster. "He wanted to see his sketches."

Clifford looked at Robert Acton, but said nothing; he only fanned himself with his hat. "You chose a bad moment," said Acton; "you hadn't much light."

"I hadn't any!" said Clifford, laughing.

"Your candle went out?" Eugenia asked. "You should have come back here and lighted it again."

Clifford looked at her a moment. "So I have—come back. But I have left the candle!"

Eugenia turned away. "You are very stupid, my poor boy. You had better go home."

"Haven't you a word to throw to a man when he has safely returned from a dangerous journey?" Acton asked.

"How do you do?" said Clifford. "I thought—I thought you were" —and he paused, looking at the Baroness again.

"You thought I was at Newport, eh? So I was—this morning."

"Good night, clever child!" said Madame Münster, over her shoulder.

Clifford stared at her—not at all like a clever child; and then, with one of his little facetious growls, took his departure.

"What is the matter with him?" asked Acton, when he was gone. "He seemed rather in a muddle."

Eugenia, who was near the window, glanced out, listening a moment. "The matter—the matter"—she answered. "But you don't say such things here."

"If you mean that he had been drinking a little, you can say that."

"He doesn't drink any more. I have cured him. And in return—he's in love with me."

It was Acton's turn to stare. He instantly thought of his sister; but he said nothing about her. He began to laugh. "I don't wonder at his passion! But I wonder at his forsaking your society for that of your brother's paint-brushes."

Eugenia was silent a little. "He had not been in the studio. I invented that at the moment."

"Invented it? For what purpose?"

"He has an idea of being romantic. He has adopted the habit of coming to see me at midnight—passing only through the orchard and through Felix's painting-room, which has a door opening that way. It seems to amuse him," added Eugenia, with a little laugh.

Acton felt more surprise than he confessed to, for this was a new view of Clifford, whose irregularities had hitherto been quite without the romantic element. He tried to laugh again, but he felt rather too serious, and after a moment's hesitation his seriousness explained itself. "I hope you don't encourage him," he said. "He must not be inconstant to poor Lizzie."

"To your sister?"

"You know they are decidedly intimate," said Acton.

"Ah," cried Eugenia, smiling, "has she—has she—"

"I don't know," Acton interrupted, "what she has. But I always supposed that Clifford had a desire to make himself agreeable to her."

"Ah, par exemple!" the Baroness went on. "The little monster! The next time he becomes sentimental I will him tell that he ought to be ashamed of himself."

Acton was silent a moment. "You had better say nothing about it."

"I had told him as much already, on general grounds," said the Baroness. "But in this country, you know, the relations of young people are so extraordinary that one is quite at sea. They are not engaged when you would quite say they ought to be. Take Charlotte Wentworth, for instance, and that young ecclesiastic. If I were her father I should insist upon his marrying her; but it appears to be thought there is no urgency. On the other hand, you suddenly learn that a boy of twenty and a little girl who is still with her governess—your sister has no governess? Well, then, who is never away from her mamma—a young couple, in short, between whom you have noticed nothing beyond an exchange of the childish pleasantries characteristic of their age, are on the point of setting up as man and wife." The Baroness spoke with a certain exaggerated volubility which was in contrast with the languid grace that had characterized her manner before Clifford made his appearance. It seemed to Acton that there was a spark of irritation in her eye—a note of irony (as when she spoke of Lizzie being never away from her mother) in her voice. If Madame Münster was irritated, Robert Acton was vaguely mystified; she began to move about the room again, and he looked at her without saying anything. Presently she took out her watch, and, glancing at it, declared that it was three o'clock in the morning and that he must go.

"I have not been here an hour," he said, "and they are still sitting up at the other house. You can see the lights. Your brother has not come in."

"Oh, at the other house," cried Eugenia, "they are terrible people! I don't know what they may do over there. I am a quiet little hum-drum woman; I have rigid rules and I keep them. One of them is not to have visitors in the small hours—especially clever men like you. So good night!"

Decidedly, the Baroness was incisive; and though Acton bade her good night and departed, he was still a good deal mystified.

The next day Clifford Wentworth came to see Lizzie, and Acton, who was at home and saw him pass through the garden, took note of the circumstance. He had a natural desire to make it tally with Madame Münster's account of Clifford's disaffection; but his ingen-uity, finding itself unequal to the task, resolved at last to ask help of the young man's candor. He waited till he saw him going away, and then he went out and overtook him in the grounds.

"I wish very much you would answer me a question," Acton said. "What were you doing, last night, at Madame Münster's?"

Clifford began to laugh and to blush, by no means like a young man with a romantic secret. "What did she tell you?" he asked.

"That is exactly what I don't want to say."

"Well, I want to tell you the same," said Clifford; "and unless I know it perhaps I can't."

They had stopped in a garden path; Acton looked hard at his

rosy young kinsman. "She said she couldn't fancy what had got into you, you appeared to have taken a violent dislike to her."

Clifford stared, looking a little alarmed. "Oh, come," he growled, "you don't mean that!"

"And that when—for common civility's sake—you came occasionally to the house you left her alone and spent your time in Felix's studio, under pretext of looking at his sketches."

"Oh, come!" growled Clifford, again.

"Did you ever know me to tell an untruth?"

"Yes, lots of them!" said Clifford, seeing an opening, out of the discussion, for his sarcastic powers. "Well," he presently added, "I thought you were my father."

"You knew some one was there?"

"We heard you coming in."

Acton meditated. "You had been with the Baroness, then?"

"I was in the parlor. We heard your step outside. I thought it was my father."

"And on that," asked Acton, "you ran away?"

"She told me to go—to go out by the studio."

Acton meditated more intensely; if there had been a chair at hand he would have sat down. "Why should she wish you not to meet your father?"

"Well," said Clifford, "father doesn't like to see me there."

Acton looked askance at his companion and forbore to make any comment upon this assertion. "Has he said so," he asked, "to the Baroness?"

"Well, I hope not," said Clifford. "He hasn't said so—in so many words—to me. But I know it worries him; and I want to stop worrying him. The Baroness knows it, and she wants me to stop, too."

"To stop coming to see her?"

"I don't know about that; but to stop worrying father. Eugenia knows everything," Clifford added, with an air of knowingness of his own.

"Ah," said Acton, interrogatively, "Eugenia knows everything?"

"She knew it was not father coming in."

"Then why did you go?"

Clifford blushed and laughed afresh. "Well, I was afraid it was. And besides, she told me to go, at any rate."

"Did she think it was I?" Acton asked.

"She didn't say so."

Again Robert Acton reflected. "But you didn't go," he presently said; "you came back."

"I couldn't get out of the studio," Clifford rejoined. "The door was locked, and Felix has nailed some planks across the lower half of the confounded windows to make the light come in from above. So they were no use. I waited there a good while, and then, suddenly, I felt ashamed. I didn't want to be hiding away from my own father. I couldn't stand it any longer. I bolted out, and when I found it was you I was a little flurried. But Eugenia carried it off, didn't she?" Clifford added, in the tone of a young humorist whose perception had not been permanently clouded by the sense of his own discomfort.

"Beautifully!" said Acton. "Especially," he continued, "when one remembers that you were very imprudent and that she must have been a good deal annoyed."

"Oh," cried Clifford, with the indifference of a young man who feels that however he may have failed of felicity in behavior he is extremely just in his impressions, "Eugenia doesn't care for anything!"

Acton hesitated a moment. "Thank you for telling me this," he said at last. And then, laying his hand on Clifford's shoulder, he added, "Tell me one thing more: are you by chance a little in love with the Baroness?"

"No, sir!" said Clifford, almost shaking off his hand.

CHAPTER X

THE FIRST Sunday that followed Robert Acton's return from Newport witnessed a change in the brilliant weather that had long prevailed. The rain began to fall and the day was cold and dreary. Mr. Wentworth and his daughters put on overshoes and went to church, and Felix Young, without overshoes, went also, holding an umbrella over Gertrude. It is to be feared that, in the whole observance, this was the privilege he most highly valued. The Baroness remained at home; she was in neither a cheerful nor a devotional mood. She had, however, never been, during her residence in the United States, what is called a regular attendant at divine service; and on this particular Sunday morning of which I began with speaking she stood at the window of her little drawing-room, watching the long arm of a rose-tree that was attached to her piazza, but a portion of which had disengaged itself, sway to and fro, shake and gesticulate, against the dusky drizzle of the sky. Every now and then, in a gust of wind, the rose-tree scattered a shower of water-drops against the window-pane; it appeared to have a kind of human movement—a menacing, warning intention. The room was very cold; Madame Münster put on a shawl and walked about. Then she determined to have some fire; and summoning her ancient negress, the contrast of whose polished ebony and whose crimson turban had been at first a source of satisfaction to her, she made arrangements for the production of a crackling flame. This old woman's name was Azarina. The Baroness had begun by thinking that there would be a savory wildness in her talk, and, for amusement, she had encouraged her to chatter. But Azarina was dry and prim; her conversation was anything but African; she reminded Eugenia of the tiresome old ladies she met in society. She knew, however, how to make a fire; so that after she had laid the logs, Eugenia, who was terribly bored, found a quarter of an hour's entertainment in sitting and watching them blaze and sputter. She had thought it very likely Robert Acton would come and see her; she had not met him since that infelicitous evening. But the morning waned without his coming; several times she thought she heard his steps on the piazza; but it was only a window-shutter shaking in a rain-gust. The Baroness, since the beginning of that episode in her career of which a slight sketch has been attempted in these pages, had had many moments of irritation. But to-day her irritation had a peculiar keenness; it appeared to feed upon itself. It urged her to do something; but it suggested no particularly profitable line of action. If she could have done something at the moment, on the spot, she would have stepped upon a European steamer and turned her back, with a kind of rapture, upon that profoundly mortifying failure, her visit to her American relations. It is not exactly apparent why she should have termed this enterprise a failure, inasmuch as she had been treated with the highest distinction for which allowance had been made in American institutions. Her irritation came, at bottom, from the sense, which, always present, had suddenly grown acute, that the social soil on this big, vague continent was somehow not adapted for growing those plants whose fragrance she especially inclined to inhale and by which she liked to see herself surrounded—a species of vegetation for which she carried a collection of seedlings, as we may say, in her pocket. She found her chief happiness in the sense of exerting a certain power and making a certain impression; and now she felt the annoyance of a rather wearied swimmer who, on nearing shore, to land, finds a smooth straight wall of rock when he had counted upon a clean firm beach. Her power in the American air, seemed to have lost its prehensile attributes; the smooth wall of rock was insurmountable. "Surely *je n'en suis pas là*," she said to herself, "that I let it make me uncomfortable that a Mr. Robert Acton shouldn't honor me with a visit!" Yet she was vexed that he had not come; and she was vexed at her vexation.

Her brother, at least, came in, stamping in the hall and shaking the wet from his coat. In a moment he entered the room, with a glow in his cheek and half-a-dozen rain-drops glistening on his mustache. "Ah, you have a fire," he said.

"*Les beaux jours sont passés*," replied the Baroness.

"Never, never! They have only begun," Felix declared, planting himself before the hearth. He turned his back to the fire, placed his hands behind him, extended his legs and looked away through the window with an expression of face which seemed to denote the perception of rose-color even in the tints of a wet Sunday.

His sister, from her chair, looked up at him, watching him; and what she saw in his face was not grateful to her present mood. She was puzzled by many things, but her brother's disposition was a frequent source of wonder to her. I say frequent and not constant, for there were long periods during which she gave her attention to other problems. Sometimes she had said to herself that his happy temper, his eternal gayety, was an affection, a *pose;* but she was vaguely conscious that during the present summer he had been a highly successful comedian. They had never yet had an explanation; she had not known the need of one. Felix was presumably following the bent of his disinterested genius, and she felt that she had no advice to give him that he would understand. With this, there was always a certain element of comfort about Felix—the assurance that he would not interfere. He was very delicate, this pure-minded Felix; in effect, he was her brother, and Madame Münster felt that there was a great propriety, every way, in that. It is true that Felix was delicate; he was not fond of explanations with his sister; this was one of the very few things in the world about which he was uncomfortable. But now he was not thinking of anything uncomfortable.

"Dear brother," said Eugenia at last, "do stop making *les yeux doux* at the rain."

"With pleasure. I will make them at you!" answered Felix.

"How much longer," asked Eugenia, in a moment, "do you propose to remain in this lovely spot?"

Felix stared. "Do you want to go away—already?"

"'Already' is delicious. I am not so happy as you."

Felix dropped into a chair, looking at the fire. "The fact is I *am* happy," he said in his light, clear tone.

"And do you propose to spend your life in making love to Gertrude Wentworth?"

"Yes!" said Felix, smiling sidewise at his sister.

The Baroness returned his glance, much more gravely; and then, "Do you like her?" she asked.

"Don't you?" Felix demanded.

The Baroness was silent a moment. "I will answer you in the words of the gentleman who was asked if he liked music: '*Je ne la crains pas!*'"

"She admires you immensely," said Felix.

"I don't care for that. Other women should not admire one."

"They should dislike you?"

Again Madame Münster hesitated. "They should hate me! It's a measure of the time I have been losing here that they don't."

"No time is lost in which one has been happy!" said Felix, with a bright sententiousness which may well have been a little irritating.

"And in which," rejoined his sister, with a harsher laugh, "one has secured the affections of a young lady with a fortune!"

Felix explained, very candidly and seriously. "I have secured Gertrude's affection, but I am by no means sure that I have secured her fortune. That may come—or it may not."

"Ah, well, it *may!* That's the great point."

"It depends upon her father. He doesn't smile upon our union. You know he wants her to marry Mr. Brand."

"I know nothing about it!" cried the Baroness. "Please to put on a log." Felix complied with her request and sat watching the quickening of the flame. Presently his sister added, "And you propose to elope with mademoiselle?"

"By no means. I don't wish to do anything that's disagreeable to Mr. Wentworth. He has been far too kind to us."

"But you must choose between pleasing yourself and pleasing him."

"I want to please every one!" exclaimed Felix, joyously. "I have a good conscience. I made up my mind at the outset that it was not my place to make love to Gertrude."

"So, to simplify matters, she made love to you!"

Felix looked at his sister with sudden gravity. "You say you are not afraid of her," he said. "But perhaps you ought to be—a little. She's a very clever person."

"I begin to see it!" cried the Baroness. Her brother, making no rejoinder, leaned back in his chair, and there was a long silence. At last, with an altered accent, Madame Münster put another question. "You expect, at any rate, to marry?"

"I shall be greatly disappointed if we don't."

"A disappointment or two will do you good!" the Baroness declared. "And, afterwards, do you mean to turn American?"

"It seems to me I am a very good American already. But we shall go to Europe. Gertrude wants extremely to see the world."

"Ah, like me, when I came here!" said the Baroness, with a little laugh.

"No, not like you," Felix rejoined, looking at his sister with a certain gentle seriousness. While he looked at her she rose from her chair, and he also got up. "Gertrude is not at all like you," he went on; "but in her own way she is almost as clever." He paused a moment; his soul was full of an agreeable feeling and of a lively disposition to express it. His sister, to his spiritual vision, was always like the lunar disk when only a part of it is lighted. The shadow on this bright surface seemed to him to expand and to contract; but whatever its proportions, he always appreciated the moonlight. He looked at the Baroness, and then he kissed her. "I am very much in love with Gertrude," he said. Eugenia turned away and walked about the room, and Felix continued. "She is very interesting, and very different from what she seems. She has never had a chance. She is very brilliant. We will go to Europe and amuse ourselves."

The Baroness had gone to the window, where she stood looking out. The day was drearier than ever; the rain was doggedly falling. "Yes, to amuse yourselves," she said at last, "you had decidedly better go to Europe!" Then she turned round, looking at her brother. A chair stood near her; she leaned her hands upon the back of it. "Don't you think it is very good of me," she asked, "to come all this way with you simply to see you properly married—if properly it is?"

"Oh, it will be properly!" cried Felix, with light eagerness.

The Baroness gave a little laugh. "You are thinking only of yourself, and you don't answer my question. While you are amusing yourself—with the brilliant Gertrude—what shall I be doing?"

"*Vous serez de la partie!*" cried Felix.

"Thank you: I should spoil it." The Baroness dropped her eyes for some moments. "Do you propose, however, to leave me here?" she inquired.

Felix smiled at her. "My dearest sister, where you are concerned I never propose. I execute your commands."

"I believe," said Eugenia, slowly, "that you are the most heartless person living. Don't you see that I am in trouble?"

"I saw that you were not cheerful, and I gave you some good news."

"Well, let me give you some news," said the Baroness. "You probably will not have discovered it for yourself. Robert Acton wants to marry me."

"No, I had not discovered that. But I quite understand it. Why does it make you unhappy?"

"Because I can't decide."

"Accept him, accept him!" cried Felix, joyously. "He is the best fellow in the world."

"He is immensely in love with me," said the Baroness.

"And he has a large fortune. Permit me in turn to remind you of that."

"Oh, I am perfectly aware of it," said Eugenia. "That's a great item in his favor. I am terribly candid." And she left her place and came nearer her brother, looking at him hard. He was turning over several things; she was wondering in what manner he really understood her.

There were several ways of understanding her: there was what she said, and there was what she meant, and there was something, between the two, that was neither. It is probable that, in the last analysis, what she meant was that Felix should spare her the necessity of stating the case more exactly and should hold himself commissioned to assist her by all honorable means to marry the best fellow in the world. But in all this it was never discovered what Felix understood.

"Once you have your liberty, what are your objections?" he asked.

"Well, I don't particularly like him.

"Oh, try a little."

"I am trying now," said Eugenia. "I should succeed better if he didn't live here. I could never live here."

"Make him go to Europe," Felix suggested.

"Ah, there you speak of happiness based upon violent effort," the Baroness rejoined. "That is not what I am looking for. He would never live in Europe."

"He would live anywhere, with you!" said Felix, gallantly.

His sister looked at him still, with a ray of penetration in her charming eyes; then she turned away again. "You see, at all events," she presently went on, "that if it had been said of me that I had come over here to seek my fortune it would have to be added that I have found it!"

"Don't leave it lying!" urged Felix, with smiling solemnity.

"I am much obliged to you for your interest," his sister declared, after a moment. "But promise me one thing: *pas de zèle!* If Mr. Acton should ask you to plead his cause, excuse yourself."

"I shall certainly have the excuse," said Felix, "that I have a cause of my own to plead."

"If he should talk of me—favorably," Eugenia continued, "warn him against dangerous illusions. I detest importunities; I want to decide at my leisure, with my eyes open."

"I shall be discreet," said Felix, "except to you. To you I will say, Accept him outright."

She had advanced to the open door-way, and she stood looking at him. "I will go and dress and think of it," she said; and he heard her moving slowly to her apartments.

Late in the afternoon the rain stopped, and just afterwards there was a great flaming, flickering, trickling sunset. Felix sat in his painting-room and did some work; but at last, as the light, which had not been brilliant, began to fade, he laid down his brushes and came out to the little piazza of the cottage. Here he walked up and down for some time, looking at the splendid blaze of the western sky and saying, as he had often said before, that this was certainly the country of sunsets. There was something in these glorious deeps of fire that quickened his imagination; he always found images and promises in the western sky. He thought of a good many things—of roaming about the world with Gertrude Wentworth; he seemed to see their possible adventures, in a glowing frieze, between the cloud-bars; then of what Eugenia had just been telling him. He wished very much that Madame Münster would make a comfortable and honorable marriage. Presently, as the sunset expanded and deepened, the fancy took him of making a note of so magnificent a piece of coloring. He returned to his studio and fetched out a small panel, with his palette and brushes, and, placing the panel against a window-sill, he began to daub with great gusto. While he was so occupied he saw Mr. Brand, in the distance, slowly come down from Mr. Wentworth's house, nursing a large folded umbrella. He walked with a joyless, meditative tread, and his eyes were bent upon the ground. Felix poised his brush for a moment, watching him; then, by a sudden impulse, as he drew nearer, advanced to the garden-gate and signaled to him—the palette and bunch of brushes contributing to this effect.

Mr. Brand stopped and started; then he appeared to decide to accept Felix's invitation. He came out of Mr. Wentworth's gate and passed along the road; after which he entered the little garden of the cottage. Felix had gone back to his sunset; but he made his visitor welcome while he rapidly brushed it in.

"I wanted so much to speak to you that I thought I would call you," he said, in the friendliest tone. "All the more that you have been to see me so little. You have come to see my sister; I know that. But you haven't come to see me—the celebrated artist. Artists are very sensitive, you know; they notice those things." And Felix turned round, smiling, with a brush in his mouth.

Mr. Brand stood there with a certain blank, candid majesty, pulling together the large flaps of his umbrella. "Why should I come to see you?" he asked. "I know nothing of Art."

"It would sound very conceited, I suppose," said Felix, "if I were to say that it would be a good little chance for you to learn something. You would ask me why you should learn; and I should have no answer to that. I suppose a minister has no need for Art, eh?"

"He had need for good temper, sir," said Mr. Brand, with decision.

Felix jumped up, with his palette on his thumb and a movement of the liveliest deprecation. "That's because I keep you standing there while I splash my red paint! I beg a thousand pardons! You see what bad manners Art gives a man; and how right you are to let it alone. I didn't mean you should stand, either. The piazza, as you see, is ornamented with rustic chairs; though indeed I ought to warn you that they have nails in the wrong places. I was just making a note of that sunset. I never saw such a blaze of different reds. It looks as if the Celestial City were in flames, eh? If that were really the case I suppose it would be the business of you theologians to put out the fire. Fancy me—an ungodly artist—quietly sitting down to paint it!"

Mr. Brand had always credited Felix Young with a certain impudence, but it appeared to him that on this occasion his impudence was so great as to make a special explanation—or even an apology—necessary. And the impression, it must be added, was sufficiently natural. Felix had at all times a brilliant assurance of manner which was simply the vehicle of his good spirits and his good will; but at present he had a special design, and as he would have admitted that the design was audacious, so he was conscious of having summoned all the arts of conversation to his aid. But he was so far from desiring to offend his visitor that he was rapidly asking himself what personal compliment he could pay the young clergyman that would gratify him most. If he could think of it, he was prepared to pay it down. "Have you been preaching one of your beautiful sermons to-day?" he suddenly asked, laying down his palette. This was not what Felix had been trying to think of, but it was a tolerable stop-gap.

Mr. Brand frowned—as much as a man can frown who has very fair, soft eyebrows, and, beneath them, very gentle, tranquil eyes. "No, I have not preached any sermon to-day. Did you bring me over here for the purpose of making that inquiry?"

Felix saw that he was irritated, and he regretted it immensely; but he had no fear of not being, in the end, agreeable to Mr. Brand. He looked at him, smiling and laying his hand on his arm. "No, no, not for that—not for that. I wanted to ask you something; I wanted to tell you something. I am sure it will interest you very much. Only—as it is something rather private—we had better come into my little studio. I have a western window; we can still see the sunset. *Andiamo!*" And he gave a little pat to his companion's arm.

He led the way in; Mr. Brand stiffly and softly followed. The twilight had thickened in the little studio; but the wall opposite the western window was covered with a deep pink flush. There were a great many sketches and half-finished canvasses suspended in this rosy glow, and the corners of the room were vague and dusky. Felix begged Mr. Brand to sit down; then glancing round him, "By Jove, how pretty it looks!" he cried. But Mr. Brand would not sit down; he went and leaned against the window; he wondered what Felix wanted of him. In the shadow, on the darker parts of the wall, he saw the gleam of three or four pictures that looked fantastic and surprising. They seemed to represent naked figures. Felix stood there, with his head a little bent and his eyes fixed upon his visitor, smiling intensely, pulling his mustache. Mr. Brand felt vaguely uneasy. "It is very delicate—what I want to say," Felix began. "But I have been thinking of it for some time."

"Please to say it as quickly as possible," said Mr. Brand.

"It's because you are a clergyman, you know," Felix went on. "I don't think I should venture to say it to a common man."

Mr. Brand was silent a moment. "If it is a question of yielding to a weakness, of resenting an injury, I am afraid I am a very common man."

"My dearest friend," cried Felix, "this is not an injury; it's a benefit—a great service! You will like it extremely. Only it's so delicate!" And, in the dim light, he continued to smile intensely. "You know I take a great interest in my cousins—in Charlotte and Gertrude Wentworth. That's very evident from my having traveled some five thousand miles to see them." Mr. Brand said nothing and Felix proceeded. "Coming into their society as a perfect stranger I received of course a great many new impressions, and my impressions had a great freshness, a great keenness. Do you know what I mean?"

"I am not sure that I do; but I should like you to continue."

"I think my impressions have always a good deal of freshness," said Mr. Brand's entertainer; "but on this occasion it was perhaps particularly natural that—coming in, as I say, from outside—I should be struck with things that passed unnoticed among yourselves. And then I had my sister to help me; and she is simply the most observant woman in the world."

"I am not surprised," said Mr. Brand, "that in our little circle two intelligent persons should have found food for observation. I am sure that, of late, I have found it myself!"

"Ah, but I shall surprise you yet!" cried Felix, laughing. "Both my sister and I took a great fancy to my cousin Charlotte."

"Your cousin Charlotte?" repeated Mr. Brand.

"We fell in love with her from the first!"

"You fell in love with Charlotte?" Mr. Brand murmured.

"*Dame!*" exclaimed Felix, "she's a very charming person; and Eugenia was especially smitten." Mr. Brand stood staring, and he pursued, "Affection, you know, opens one's eyes, and we noticed something. Charlotte is not happy! Charlotte is in love." And Felix, drawing nearer, laid his hand again upon his companion's arm.

There was something akin to an acknowledgment of fascination in the way Mr. Brand looked at him; but the young clergyman retained as yet quite enough self-possession to be able to say, with a good deal of solemnity, "She is not in love with you."

Felix gave a light laugh, and rejoined with the alacrity of a maritime adventurer who feels a puff of wind in his sail. "Ah, no; if she were in love with me I should know it! I am not so blind as you."

"As I?"

"My dear sir, you are stone blind. Poor Charlotte is dead in love with *you!*"

Mr. Brand said nothing for a moment; he breathed a little heavily. "Is that what you wanted to say to me?" he asked.

"I have wanted to say it these three weeks. Because of late she has been worse. I told you," added Felix, "it was very delicate."

"Well, sir"—Mr. Brand began; "well, sir"—

"I was sure you didn't know it," Felix continued. "But don't you see—as soon as I mention it—how everything is explained?" Mr. Brand answered nothing; he looked for a chair and softly sat down. Felix could see that he was blushing; he had looked straight at his host hitherto, but now he looked away. The foremost effect of what he had heard had been a sort of irritation of his modesty. "Of course," said Felix, "I suggest nothing; it would be very presumptuous in me to advise you. But I think there is no doubt about the fact."

Mr. Brand looked hard at the floor for some moments; he was oppressed with a mixture of sensations. Felix, standing there, was very sure that one of them was profound surprise. The innocent young man had been completely unsuspicious of poor Charlotte's hidden flame. This gave Felix great hope; he was sure that Mr. Brand would be flattered. Felix thought him very transparent, and indeed he was so; he could neither simulate nor dissimulate. "I scarcely know what to make of this," he said at last, without looking up; and Felix was struck with the fact that he offered no protest or contradiction. Evidently Felix had kindled a train of memories—a retrospective illumination. It was making, to Mr. Brand's astonished eyes, a very pretty blaze; his second emotion had been a gratification of vanity.

"Thank me for telling you," Felix rejoined. "It's a good thing to know."

"I am not sure of that," said Mr. Brand.

"Ah, don't let her languish!" Felix murmured, lightly and softly.

"You *do* advise me, then?" And Mr. Brand looked up.

"I congratulate you!" said Felix, smiling. He had thought at first his visitor was simply appealing; but he saw he was a little ironical.

"It is in your interest; you have interfered with me," the young clergyman went on.

Felix still stood and smiled. The little room had grown darker, and the crimson glow had faded; but Mr. Brand could see the brilliant expression of his face. "I won't pretend not to know what you mean," said Felix at last. "But I have not really interfered with you. Of what you had to lose—with another person—you have lost nothing. And think what you have gained!"

"It seems to me I am the proper judge, on each side," Mr. Brand declared. He got up, holding the brim of his hat against his mouth and staring at Felix through the dusk.

"You have lost an illusion!" said Felix.

"What do you call an illusion?"

"The belief that you really know—that you have ever really known—Gertrude Wentworth. Depend upon that," pursued Felix. "I don't know her yet; but I have no illusions; I don't pretend to."

Mr. Brand kept gazing, over his hat. "She has always been a lucid, limpid nature," he said, solemnly.

"She has always been a dormant nature. She was waiting for a touchstone. But now she is beginning to awaken."

"Don't praise her to me!" said Mr. Brand, with a little quaver in his voice. "If you have the advantage of me that is not generous."

"My dear sir, I am melting with generosity!" exclaimed Felix. "And I am not praising my cousin. I am simply attempting a scientific definition of her. She doesn't care for abstractions. Now I think the contrary is what you have always fancied—is the bias on which you have been building. She is extremely preoccupied with the concrete. I care for the concrete, too. But Gertrude is stronger than I; she whirls me along!"

Mr. Brand looked for a moment into the crown of his hat. "It's a most interesting nature."

"So it is," said Felix. "But it pulls—it pulls—like a runaway horse. Now I like the feeling of a runaway horse; and if I am thrown out of the vehicle it is no great matter. But if *you* should be thrown, Mr. Bland"—and Felix paused a moment—"another person also would suffer from the accident."

"What other person?"

"Charlotte Wentworth!"

Mr. Brand looked at Felix for a moment sidewise, mistrustfully; then his eyes slowly wandered over the ceiling. Felix was sure he was secretly struck with the romance of the situation. "I think this is none of our business," the young minister murmured.

"None of mine, perhaps; but surely yours!"

Mr. Brand lingered still, looking at the ceiling; there was evidently something he wanted to say. "What do you mean by Miss Gertrude being strong?" he asked abruptly.

"Well," said Felix meditatively, "I mean that she has had a great deal of self-possession. She was waiting—for years; even when she seemed, perhaps, to be living in the present. She knew how to wait; she had a purpose. That's what I mean by her being strong."

"But what do you mean by her purpose?"

"Well—the purpose to see the world!"

Mr. Brand eyed his strange informant askance again; but he said nothing. At last he turned away, as if to take leave. He seemed bewildered, however; for instead of going to the door he moved toward the opposite corner of the room. Felix stood and watched him for a moment—almost groping about in the dusk; then he led him to the door, with a tender, almost fraternal movement. "Is that all you have to say?" asked Mr. Brand.

"Yes, it's all—but it will bear a good deal of thinking of."

Felix went with him to the garden-gate, and watched him slowly walk away into the thickening twilight with a relaxed rigidity that tried to rectify itself. "He is offended, excited, bewildered, perplexed—and enchanted!" Felix said to himself. "That's a capital mixture."

CHAPTER XI

SINCE THAT visit paid by the Baroness Münster to Mrs. Acton, of which some account was given at an earlier stage of this narrative, the intercourse between these two ladies had been neither frequent nor intimate. It was not that Mrs. Acton had failed to appreciate Madame Münster's charms; on the contrary, her perception of the graces of manner and conversation of her brilliant visitor had been only too acute. Mrs. Acton was, as they said in Boston, very "intense," and her impressions were apt to be too many for her. The state of her health required the restriction of emotion; and this is why, receiving, as she sat in her eternal arm-chair, very few visitors, even of the soberest local type, she had been obliged to limit the number of her interviews with a lady whose costume and manner recalled to her imagination—Mrs. Acton's imagination was a marvel—all that she had ever read of the most stirring historical periods. But she had sent the Baroness a great many quaintly-worded messages and a great many nosegays from her garden and baskets of beautiful fruit. Felix had eaten the fruit, and the Baroness had arranged the flowers and returned the baskets and the messages. On the day that followed that rainy Sunday of which mention has been made, Eugenia determined to go and pay the beneficent invalid a *"visite d'adieux;"* so it was that, to herself, she qualified her enterprise. It may be noted that neither on the Sunday evening nor on the Monday morning had she received that expected visit from Robert Acton. To his own consciousness, evidently he was "keeping away;" and as the Baroness, on her side, was keeping away from her uncle's, whither, for several days, Felix had been the unembarrassed bearer of apologies and regrets for absence, chance had not taken the cards from the hands of design. Mr. Wentworth and his daughters had respected Eugenia's seclusion; certain intervals of mysterious retirement appeared to them, vaguely, a natural part of the graceful, rhythmic movement of so remarkable a life. Gertrude especially held these periods in honor; she wondered what Madame Münster did at such times, but she would not have permitted herself to inquire too curiously.

The long rain had freshened the air, and twelve hours' brilliant sunshine had dried the roads; so that the Baroness, in the late afternoon, proposing to walk to Mrs. Acton's, exposed herself to no great discomfort. As with her charming undulating step she moved along the clean, grassy margin of the road, beneath the thickly-hanging boughs of the orchards, through the quiet of the hour and place and the rich maturity of the summer, she was even conscious of a sort of luxurious melancholy. The Baroness had the amiable weakness of attaching herself to places—even when she had begun with a little aversion; and now, with the prospect of departure, she felt tenderly toward this well-wooded corner of the Western world, where the sunsets were so beautiful and one's ambitions were so pure. Mrs. Acton was able to receive her; but on entering this lady's large, freshly-scented room the Baroness saw that she was looking very ill. She was wonderfully white and transparent, and, in her flowered arm-chair, she made no attempt to move. But she flushed a little—like a young girl, the Baroness thought—and she rested her clear, smiling eyes upon those of her visitor. Her voice was low and monotonous, like a voice that had never expressed any human passions.

"I have come to bid you good-by," said Eugenia. "I shall soon be going away."

"When are you going away?"

"Very soon—any day."

"I am very sorry," said Mrs. Acton. "I hoped you would stay —always."

"Always?" Eugenia demanded.

"Well, I mean a long time," said Mrs. Acton, in her sweet, feeble tone. "They tell me you are so comfortable—that you have got such a beautiful little house."

Eugenia stared—that is, she smiled; she thought of her poor little *chalet* and she wondered whether her hostess were jesting. "Yes, my house is exquisite," she said; "though not to be compared to yours."

"And my son is so fond of going to see you," Mrs. Acton added. "I am afraid my son will miss you."

"Ah, dear madame," said Eugenia, with a little laugh, "I can't stay in America for your son!"

"Don't you like America?"

The Baroness looked at the front of her dress. "If I liked it—that would not be staying for your son!"

Mrs. Acton gazed at her with her grave, tender eyes, as if she had not quite understood. The Baroness at last found something irritating in the sweet, soft stare of her hostess; and if one were not bound to be merciful to great invalids she would almost have taken the liberty of pronouncing her, mentally, a fool. "I am afraid, then, I shall never see you again," said Mrs. Acton. "You know I am dying."

"Ah, dear madame," murmured Eugenia.

"I want to leave my children cheerful and happy. My daughter will probably marry her cousin."

"Two such interesting young people," said the Baroness, vaguely. She was not thinking of Clifford Wentworth.

"I feel so tranquil about my end," Mrs. Acton went on. "It is coming so easily, so surely." And she paused, with her mild gaze always on Eugenia's.

The Baroness hated to be reminded of death; but even in its imminence, so far as Mrs. Acton was concerned, she preserved her good manners. "Ah, madame, you are too charming an invalid," she rejoined.

But the delicacy of this rejoinder was apparently lost upon her hostess, who went on in her low, reasonable voice. "I want to leave my children bright and comfortable. You seem to me all so happy here—just as you are. So I wish you could stay. It would be so pleasant for Robert."

Eugenia wondered what she meant by its being pleasant for Robert; but she felt that she would never know what such a woman as

that meant. She got up; she was afraid Mrs. Acton would tell her
again that she was dying. "Good-bye, dear madame," she said. "I
must remember that your strength is precious."

Mrs. Acton took her hand and held it a moment. "Well, you *have*
been happy here, haven't you? And you like us all, don't you? I
wish you would stay," she added, "in your beautiful little house."

She had told Eugenia that her waiting-woman would be in the
hall, to show her down-stairs; but the large landing outside her door
was empty, and Eugenia stood there looking about. She felt irritated;
the dying lady had not "*la main heureuse.*" She passed slowly down-
stairs, still looking about. The broad staircase made a great bend, and
in the angle was a high window, looking westward, with a deep
bench, covered with a row of flowering plants in curious old pots of
blue china-ware. The yellow afternoon light came in through the
flowers and flickered a little on the white wainscots. Eugenia paused
a moment; the house was perfectly still, save for the ticking somewhere, of a great clock. The lower hall stretched away at the foot
of the stairs, half covered over with a large Oriental rug. Eugenia
lingered a little, noticing a great many things. "*Comme c'est bien!*"
she said to herself; such a large, solid, irreproachable basis of
existence the place seemed to her to indicate. And then she reflected
that Mrs. Acton was soon to withdraw from it. The reflection
accompanied her the rest of the way down-stairs, where she paused
again, making more observations. The hall was extremely broad,
and on either side of the front door was a wide, deeply-set window,
which threw the shadows of everything back into the house. There
were high-backed chairs along the wall and big Eastern vases upon
tables, and, on either side, a large cabinet with a glass front and
little curiosities within, dimly gleaming. The doors were open—into
the darkened parlor, the library, the dining-room. All these rooms
seemed empty. Eugenia passed along, and stopped a moment on the
threshold of each. "*Comme c'est bien!*" she murmured again; she
had thought of just such a house as this when she decided to come
to America. She opened the front door for herself—her light tread
had summoned none of the servants—and on the threshold she gave a
last look. Outside, she was still in the humor for curious contemplation; so instead of going directly down the little drive, to the
gate, she wandered away towards the garden, which lay to the
right of the house. She had not gone many yards over the grass
before she paused quickly; she perceived a gentleman stretched
upon the level verdure, beneath a tree. He had not heard her coming,

and he lay motionless, flat on his back, with his hands clasped under his head, staring up at the sky; so that the Baroness was able to reflect, at her leisure, upon the question of his identity. It was that of a person who had lately been much in her thoughts; but her first impulse, nevertheless, was to turn away; the last thing she desired was to have the air of coming in quest of Robert Acton. The gentleman on the grass, however, gave her no time to decide; he could not long remain unconscious of so agreeable a presence. He rolled back his eyes, stared, gave an exclamation, and then jumped up. He stood an instant, looking at her.

"Excuse my ridiculous position," he said.

"I have just now no sense of the ridiculous. But, in case you have, don't imagine I came to see you."

"Take care," rejoined Acton, "how you put it into my head! I was thinking of you."

"The occupation of extreme leisure!" said the Baroness. "To think of a woman when you are in that position is no compliment."

"I didn't say I was thinking well!" Acton affirmed, smiling.

She looked at him, and then she turned away. "Though I didn't come to see you," she said, "remember at least that I am within your gates."

"I am delighted—I am honored! Won't you come into the house?"

"I have just come out of it. I have been calling upon your mother. I have been bidding her farewell."

"Farewell?" Acton demanded.

"I am going away," said the Baroness. And she turned away again, as if to illustrate her meaning.

"When are you going?" asked Acton, standing a moment in his place. But the Baroness made no answer, and he followed her.

"I came this way to look at your garden," she said, walking back to the gate, over the grass. "But I must go."

"Let me at least go with you." He went with her, and they said nothing till they reached the gate. It was open, and they looked down the road which was darkened over with long bosky shadows. "Must you go straight home?" Acton asked.

But she made no answer. She said, after a moment, "Why have you not been to see me?" He said nothing, and then she went on, "Why don't you answer me?"

"I am trying to invent an answer," Acton confessed.

"Have you none ready?"

"None that I can tell you," he said. "But let me walk with you now."

"You may do as you like."

She moved slowly along the road, and Acton went with her. Presently he said, "If I had done as I liked I would have come to see you several times."

"Is that invented?" asked Eugenia.

"No, that is natural. I stayed away because—"

"Ah, here comes the reason, then?"

"Because I wanted to think about you."

"Because you wanted to lie down!" said the Baroness. "I have seen you lie down—almost—in my drawing-room."

Acton stopped in the road, with a movement which seemed to beg her to linger a little. She paused, and he looked at her awhile; he thought her very charming. "You are jesting," he said; "but if you are really going away it is very serious."

"If I stay," and she gave a little laugh, "it is more serious still!"

"When shall you go?"

"As soon as possible."

"And why?"

"Why should I stay?"

"Because we all admire you so."

"That is not a reason. I am admired also in Europe." And she began to walk homeward again.

"What could I say to keep you?" asked Acton. He wanted to keep her, and it was a fact that he had been thinking of her for a week. He was in love with her now; he was conscious of that, or he thought he was; and the only question with him was whether he could trust her.

"What you can say to keep me?" she repeated. "As I want very much to go it is not in my interest to tell you. Besides, I can't imagine."

He went on with her in silence; he was much more affected by what she had told him than appeared. Ever since that evening of his return from Newport her image had had a terrible power to trouble him. What Clifford Wentworth had told him—that had affected him, too, in an adverse sense; but it had not liberated him from the discomfort of a charm of which his intelligence was impatient. "She is not honest, she is not honest," he kept murmuring to himself. That is what he had been saying to the summer sky, ten minutes before. Unfortunately, he was unable to say it finally, definitively; and now that he was near her it seemed to matter wonderfully little. "She is a woman who will lie," he had said to himself. Now, as he went along, he reminded himself of this observation; but it failed to frighten him as it had done before. He almost wished he could make her lie and then convict her of it, so that he might see how he should like that. He kept thinking of this as he walked by her side, while she moved forward with her light, graceful dignity. He had sat with her before; he had driven with her; but he had never walked with her.

"By Jove, how *comme il faut* she is!" he said, as he observed her sidewise. When they reached the cottage in the orchard she passed into the gate without asking him to follow; but she turned round, as he stood there, to bid him good-night.

"I asked you a question the other night which you never answered," he said. "Have you sent off that document—liberating yourself?"

She hesitated for a single moment—very naturally. Then, "Yes," she said, simply.

He turned away; he wondered whether that would do for his lie. But he saw her again that evening, for the Baroness reappeared at her uncle's. He had little talk with her, however; two gentlemen had driven out from Boston, in a buggy, to call upon Mr. Wentworth and his daughters, and Madame Münster was an object of absorbing interest to both of the visitors. One of them, indeed, said nothing to her; he only sat and watched with intense gravity, and leaned forward solemnly, presenting his ear (a very large one), as if he were deaf, whenever she dropped an observation. He had evidently been impressed with the idea of her misfortunes and reverses; he never smiled. His companion adopted a lighter, easier style; sat as near as possible to Madame Münster; attempted to draw her out, and proposed every few moments a new topic of conversation. Eugenia was less vividly responsive than usual and had less to say than, from her brilliant reputation, her interlocutor expected, upon the relative merits of European and American institutions; but she was inaccessible to Robert Acton, who roamed about the piazza with his hands in his pockets, listening for the grating sound of the buggy from Boston, as it should be brought round to the side-door. But he listened in vain, and at last he lost patience. His sister came to him and begged him to take her home, and he presently went off with her. Eugenia observed him leaving the house with Lizzie; in her present mood the fact seemed a contribution to her irritated conviction that he had several precious qualities. "Even that *mal-élevée* little girl," she reflected, "makes him do what she wishes."

She had been sitting just within one of the long windows that opened upon the piazza; but very soon after Acton had gone away she got up abruptly, just when the talkative gentleman from Boston was asking her what she thought of the "moral tone" of that city. On the piazza she encountered Clifford Wentworth, coming round from the other side of the house. She stopped him; she told him she wished to speak to him.

"Why didn't you go home with your cousin?" she asked.

Clifford stared. "Why, Robert has taken her," he said.

"Exactly so. But you don't usually leave that to him."

"Oh," said Clifford, "I want to see those fellows start off. They don't know how to drive."

"It is not, then, that you have quarreled with your cousin?"

Clifford reflected a moment, and then with a simplicity which had, for the Baroness, a singularly baffling quality, "Oh, no; we have made up!" he said.

She looked at him for some moments; but Clifford had begun to be afraid of the Baroness's looks, and he endeavored, now, to shift himself out of their range. "Why do you never come to see me any more?" she asked. "Have I displeased you?"

"Displeased me? Well, I guess not!" said Clifford, with a laugh.

"Why haven't you come, then?"

"Well, because I am afraid of getting shut up in that back room."

Eugenia kept looking at him. "I should think you would like that."

"Like it!" cried Clifford.

"I should, if I were a young man calling upon a charming woman."

"A charming woman isn't much use to me when I am shut up in that back room!"

"I am afraid I am not of much use to you anywhere!" said Madame Münster. "And yet you know how I have offered to be."

"Well," observed Clifford, by way of response, "there comes the buggy."

"Never mind the buggy. Do you know I am going away?"

"Do you mean now?"

"I mean in a few days. I leave this place."

"You are going back to Europe?"

"To Europe, where you are to come and see me."

"Oh, yes, I'll come out there," said Clifford.

"But before that," Eugenia declared, "you must come and see me here."

"Well, I shall keep clear of that back room!" rejoined her simple young kinsman.

The Baroness was silent a moment. "Yes, you must come frankly —boldly. That will be very much better. I see that now."

"I see it!" said Clifford. And then, in an instant, "What's the matter with that buggy?" His practiced ear had apparently detected an unnatural creak in the wheels of the light vehicle which had been brought to the portico, and he hurried away to investigate so grave an anomaly.

The Baroness walked homeward, alone, in the starlight, asking herself a question. Was she to have gained nothing—was she to have gained nothing?

Gertrude Wentworth had held a silent place in the little circle gathered about the two gentlemen from Boston. She was not interested in the visitors; she was watching Madame Münster, as she constantly watched her. She knew that Eugenia also was not interested—that she was bored; and Gertrude was absorbed in study of the problem how, in spite of her indifference and her absent attention, she managed to have such a charming manner. That was the manner Gertrude would have liked to have; she determined to cultivate it, and she wished that—to give her the charm—she might in future very often be bored. While she was engaged in these researches, Felix Young was looking for Charlotte, to whom he had something to say. For some time, now, he had had something to say to Charlotte, and this evening his sense of the propriety of holding some special conversation with her had reached the motive-point—resolved itself into acute and delightful desire. He wandered through the empty rooms on the large ground-floor of the house, and found her at last in a small apartment denominated, for reasons not immediately apparent, Mr. Wentworth's "office": an extremely neat and well-dusted room, with an array of law-books, in time-darkened sheep-skin, on one of the walls; a large map of the United States on the other, flanked on either side by an old steel engraving of one of Raphael's Madonnas; and on the third several glass cases containing specimens of butterflies and beetles. Charlotte was sitting by a lamp, embroidering a slipper. Felix did not ask for whom the slipper was destined; he saw it was very large.

He moved a chair toward her and sat down, smiling as usual,

but, at first, not speaking. She watched him, with her needle poised, and with a certain shy, fluttered look which she always wore when he approached her. There was something in Felix's manner that quickened her modesty, her self-consciousness; if absolute choice had been given her she would have preferred never to find herself alone with him; and in fact, though she thought him a most brilliant, distinguished, and well-meaning person, she had exercised a much larger amount of tremulous tact than he had ever suspected, to circumvent the accident of *tête-à-tête*. Poor Charlotte could have given no account of the matter that would not have seemed unjust both to herself and to her foreign kinsman; she could only have said—or rather, she would never have said it—that she did not like so much gentleman's society at once. She was not reassured, accordingly, when he began, emphasizing his words with a kind of admiring radiance, "My dear cousin, I am enchanted at finding you alone."

"I am very often alone," Charlotte observed. Then she quickly added, "I don't mean I am lonely!"

"So clever a woman as you is never lonely," said Felix. "You have company in your beautiful work." And he glanced at the big slipper.

"I like to work," declared Charlotte, simply.

"So do I!" said her companion. "And I like to idle too. But it is not to idle that I have come in search of you. I want to tell you something very particular."

"Well," murmured Charlotte; "of course, if you must—"

"My dear cousin," said Felix, "it's nothing that a young lady may not listen to. At least I suppose it isn't. But *voyons;* you shall judge. I am terribly in love."

"Well, Felix," began Miss Wentworth, gravely. But her very gravity appeared to check the development of her phrase.

"I am in love with your sister; but in love, Charlotte—in love!" the young man pursued. Charlotte had laid her work in her lap; her hands were tightly folded on top of it; she was staring at the carpet. "In short, I'm in love, dear lady," said Felix. "Now I want you to help me."

"To help you?" asked Charlotte, with a tremor.

"I don't mean with Gertrude; she and I have a perfect understanding; and oh, how well she understands one! I mean with your father and with the world in general, including Mr. Brand."

"Poor Mr. Brand!" said Charlotte, slowly, but with a simplicity

which made it evident to Felix that the young minister had not
repeated to Miss Wentworth the talk that had lately occurred between them.

"Ah, now, don't say 'poor' Mr. Brand! I don't pity Mr. Brand
at all. But I pity your father a little, and I don't want to displease
him. Therefore, you see, I want you to plead for me. You don't
think me very shabby, eh?"

"Shabby?" exclaimed Charlotte softly, for whom Felix represented the most polished and iridescent qualities of mankind.

"I don't mean in my appearance," rejoined Felix, laughing; for
Charlotte was looking at his boots. "I mean in my conduct. You
don't think it's an abuse of hospitality?"

"To—to care for Gertrude?" asked Charlotte.

"To have really expressed one's self. Because I *have* expressed
myself, Charlotte; I must tell you the whole truth—I have! Of
course I want to marry her—and here is the difficulty. I held off
as long as I could; but she is such a terribly fascinating person!
She's a strange creature, Charlotte; I don't believe you really know
her." Charlotte took up her tapestry again, and again she laid it
down. "I know your father has had higher views," Felix continued;
"and I think you have shared them. You have wanted to marry her
to Mr. Brand."

"Oh, no," said Charlotte, very earnestly. "Mr. Brand has always
admired her. But we did not want anything of that kind."

Felix stared. "Surely, marriage was what you proposed."

"Yes; but we didn't wish to force her."

"*A la bonne heure!* That's very unsafe you know. With these
arranged marriages there is often the deuce to pay."

"Oh, Felix," said Charlotte, "we didn't want to 'arrange.' "

"I am delighted to hear that. Because in such cases—even when
the woman is a thoroughly good creature—she can't help looking
for a compensation. A charming fellow comes along—and *voilá!*"
Charlotte sat mutely staring at the floor, and Felix presently added,
"Do go on with your slipper, I like to see you work."

Charlotte took up her variegated canvas, and began to draw
vague blue stitches in a big round rose. "If Gertrude is so—so
strange," she said, "why do you want to marry her?"

"Ah, that's it, dear Charlotte! I like strange women; I always
have liked them. Ask Eugenia! And Gertrude is wonderful; she
says the most beautiful things!"

Charlotte looked at him, almost for the first time, as if her meaning required to be severely pointed. "You have a great influence over her."

"Yes—and no!" said Felix. "I had at first, I think; but now it is six of one and half-a-dozen of the other; it is reciprocal. She affects me strongly—for she is so strong. I don't believe you know her; it's a beautiful nature."

"Oh, yes, Felix; I have always thought Gertrude's nature beautiful."

"Well, if you think so now," cried the young man, "wait and see! She's a folded flower. Let me pluck her from the parent tree and you will see her expand. I'm sure you will enjoy it."

"I don't understand you," murmured Charlotte. "I *can't*, Felix."

"Well, you can understand this—that I beg you to say a good word for me to your father. He regards me, I naturally believe, as a very light fellow, a Bohemian, an irregular character. Tell him I am not all this; if I ever was, I have forgotten it. I am fond of pleasure—yes; but of innocent pleasure. Pain is all one; but in pleasure, you know, there are tremendous distinctions. Say to him that Gertrude is a folded flower and that I am a serious man!"

Charlotte got up from her chair slowly rolling up her work. "We know you are very kind to every one, Felix," she said. "But we are extremely sorry for Mr. Brand."

"Of course you are—you especially! Because," added Felix hastily, "you are a woman. But I don't pity him. It ought to be enough for any man that you take an interest in him."

"It is not enough for Mr. Brand," said Charlotte, simply. And she stood there a moment, as if waiting conscientiously for anything more than Felix might have to say.

"Mr. Brand is not so keen about his marriage as he was," he presently said. "He is afraid of your sister. He begins to think she is wicked."

Charlotte looked at him now with beautiful, appealing eyes—eyes into which he saw the tears rising. "Oh, Felix, Felix," she cried, "what have you done to her?"

"I think she was asleep; I have waked her up!"

But Charlotte, apparently, was really crying; she walked straight out of the room. And Felix, standing there and meditating, had the apparent brutality to take satisfaction in her tears.

Late that night Gertrude, silent and serious, came to him in the garden; it was a kind of appointment. Gertrude seemed to like appointments. She plucked a handful of heliotrope and stuck it into the front of her dress, but she said nothing. They walked together along one of the paths, and Felix looked at the great, square, hospitable house, massing itself vaguely in the starlight, with all its windows darkened.

"I have a little of a bad conscience," he said. "I oughtn't to meet you this way till I have got your father's consent."

Gertrude looked at him for some time. "I don't understand you."

"You very often say that," he said. "Considering how little we understand each other, it is a wonder how well we get on!"

"We have done nothing but meet since you came here—but meet alone. The first time I ever saw you we were alone," Gertrude went on. "What is the difference now? Is it because it is at night?"

"The difference, Gertrude," said Felix, stopping in the path, "the difference is that I love you more—more than before!" And then they stood there, talking, in the warm stillness and in front of the closed dark house. "I have been talking to Charlotte—been trying to bespeak her interest with your father. She has a kind of sublime perversity; was ever a woman so bent upon cutting off her own head?"

"You are too careful," said Gertrude; "you are too diplomatic."

"Well," cried the young man, "I didn't come here to make any one unhappy!"

Gertrude looked round her awhile in the odorous darkness. "I will do anything you please," she said.

"For instance?" asked Felix, smiling.

"I will go away. I will do anything you please."

Felix looked at her in solemn admiration. "Yes, we will go away," he said. "But we will make peace first."

Gertrude looked about her again, and then she broke out, passionately, "Why do they try to make one feel guilty? Why do they make it so difficult? Why can't they understand?"

"I will make them understand!" said Felix. He drew her hand into his arm, and they wandered about in the garden, talking, for an hour.

CHAPTER XII

FELIX ALLOWED Charlotte time to plead his cause; and then, on the thrid day, he sought an interview with his uncle. It was in the morning; Mr. Wentworth was in his office; and, on going in, Felix found that Charlotte was at that moment in conference with her father.

She had, in fact, been constantly near him since her interview with Felix; she had made up her mind that it was her duty to repeat very literally her cousin's passionate plea. She had accordingly followed Mr. Wentworth about like a shadow, in order to find him at hand when she should have mustered sufficient composure to speak. For poor Charlotte, in this matter, naturally lacked composure; especially when she meditated upon some of Felix's intimations. It was not cheerful work, at the best, to keep giving small hammer-taps to the coffin in which one had laid away, for burial, the poor little unacknowledged offspring of one's own misbehaving heart; and the occupation was not rendered more agreeable by the fact that the ghost of one's stifled dream had been summoned from the shades by the strange, bold words of a talkative young foreigner. What had Felix meant by saying that Mr. Brand was not so keen? To herself her sister's justly depressed suitor had shown no sign of faltering. Charlotte trembled all over when she allowed herself to believe for an instant now and then that, privately, Mr. Brand might have faltered; and as it seemed to give more force to Felix's words to repeat them to her father, she was waiting until she should have taught herself to be very calm. But she had now begun to tell Mr. Wentworth that she was extremely anxious. She was proceeding to develop this idea, to enumerate the objects of her anxiety, when Felix came in.

Mr. Wentworth sat there, with his legs crossed, lifting his dry, pure countenance from the Boston "Advertiser." Felix entered smiling, as if he had something particular to say, and his uncle looked at him as if he both expected and deprecated this event. Felix vividly expressing himself had come to be a formidable figure to his uncle, who had not yet arrived at definite views as to a proper tone. For the first time in his life, as I have said, Mr. Wentworth shirked a responsibility; he earnestly desired that it might not be laid upon him to determine how his nephew's lighter propositions should be treated. He lived under an apprehension that Felix might yet beguile him into assent to doubtful inductions, and his conscience instructed him that the best form of vigilance was the avoidance of discussion. He hoped that the pleasant episode of his nephew's visit would pass away without a further lapse of consistency.

Felix looked at Charlotte with an air of understanding, and then at Mr. Wentworth, and then at Charlotte again. Mr. Wentworth bent his refined eyebrows upon his nephew and stroked down the first page of the "Advertiser." "I ought to have brought a bouquet," said Felix, laughing. "In France they always do."

"We are not in France," observed Mr. Wentworth, gravely, while Charlotte earnestly gazed at him.

"No, luckily, we are not in France, where I am afraid I should have a harder time of it. My dear Charlotte, have you rendered me that delightful service?" And Felix bent toward her as if some one had been presenting him.

Charlotte looked at him with almost frightened eyes; and Mr. Wentworth thought this might be the beginning of a discussion. "What is the bouquet for?" he inquired, by way of turning it off.

Felix gazed at him, smiling. "*Pour la demande!*" And then, drawing up a chair, he seated himself, hat in hand, with a kind of conscious solemnity.

Presently he turned to Charlotte again. "My good Charlotte, my admirable Charlotte," he murmured, "you have not played me false—you have not sided against me?"

Charlotte got up, trembling extremely, though imperceptibly. "You must speak to my father yourself," she said. "I think you are clever enough."

But Felix, rising too, begged her to remain. "I can speak better to an audience!" he declared.

"I hope it is nothing disagreeable," said Mr. Wentworth.

"It's something delightful, for me!" And Felix, laying down his hat, clasped his hands a little between his knees. "My dear uncle," he said, "I desire, very earnestly, to marry your daughter Gertrude." Charlotte sank slowly into her chair again, and Mr. Wentworth sat staring, with a light in his face that might have been flashed back from an iceberg. He stared and stared; he said nothing. Felix fell back, with his hands still clasped. "Ah—you don't like it. I was afraid!" He blushed deeply, and Charlotte noticed it—remarking to herself that it was the first time she had ever seen him blush. She began to blush herself and to reflect that he might be much in love.

"This is very abrupt," said Mr. Wentworth, at last.

"Have you never suspected it, dear uncle?" Felix inquired. "Well, that proves how discreet I have been. Yes, I thought you wouldn't like it."

"It is very serious, Felix," said Mr. Wentworth.

"You think it's an abuse of hospitality!" exclaimed Felix, smiling again.

"Of hospitality?—an abuse?" his uncle repeated very slowly,

"That is what Felix said to me," said Charlotte, conscientiously.

"Of course you think so; don't defend yourself!" Felix pursued. "It *is* an abuse, obviously; the most I can claim is that it is perhaps a pardonable one. I simply fell head over heels in love; one can hardly help that. Though you are Gertrude's progenitor I don't believe you know how attractive she is. Dear uncle, she contains the elements of a singularly—I may say a strangely—charming woman!"

"She has always been to me an object of extreme concern," said Mr. Wentworth. "We have always desired her happiness."

"Well, here it is!" Felix declared. "I will make her happy. She believes it, too. Now hadn't you noticed that?"

"I had noticed that she was much changed," Mr. Wentworth declared, in a tone whose unexpressive, unimpassioned quality appeared to Felix to reveal a profundity of opposition. "It may be that she is only becoming what you call a charming woman."

"Gertrude, at heart, is so earnest, so true," said Charlotte, very softly, fastening her eyes upon her father.

"I delight to hear you praise her!" cried Felix.

"She has a very peculiar temperament," said Mr. Wentworth.

"Eh, even that is praise!" Felix rejoined. "I know I am not the man you might have looked for. I have no position and no fortune; I can give Gertrude no place in the world. A place in the world—that's what she ought to have; that would bring her out."

"A place to do her duty!" remarked Mr. Wentworth.

"Ah, how charmingly she does it—her duty!" Felix exclaimed, with a radiant face. "What an exquisite conception she has of it! But she comes honestly by that, dear uncle." Mr. Wentworth and Charlotte both looked at him as if they were watching a greyhound doubling. "Of course with me she will hide her light under a bushel," he continued; "I being the bushel! Now I know you like me—you have certainly proved it. But you think I am frivolous and penniless and shabby! Granted—granted—a thousand times granted. I have been a loose fish—a fiddler, a painter, an actor. But there is this to be said: In the first place, I fancy you exaggerate; you lend me qualities I haven't had. I have been a Bohemian—yes; but in Bohemia I always passed for a gentleman. I wish you could see some of my old *camarades*—they would tell you! It was the liberty I liked, but not the opportunities! My sins were all peccadilloes; I always respected my neighbor's property—my neighbor's wife. Do you see, dear uncle?" Mr. Wentworth ought to have seen; his cold blue eyes were intently fixed. "And ,then, *c'est fini!* It's all over. *Je me range.* I have settled down to a jog-trot. I find I can earn my living—a very fair one—by going about the world and painting bad portraits. It's not a glorious profession, but it is a perfectly respectable one. You won't deny that, eh? Going about the world, I say? I must not deny that, for that I am afraid I shall always do—in quest of agreeable sitters. When I say agreeable, I mean susceptible of delicate flattery and prompt of payment. Gertrude declares she is willing to share my wanderings and help to pose my models. She even thinks it will be charming; and that brings me to my third point. Gertrude likes me. Encourage her a little and she will tell you so."

Felix's tongue obviously moved much faster than the imagination of his auditors; his eloquence, like the rocking of a boat in a deep, smooth lake, made long eddies of silence. And he seemed to be pleading and chattering still, with his brightly eager smile, his uplifted eyebrows, his expressive mouth, after he had ceased speaking, and while, with his glance quickly turning from the father to the daughter, he sat waiting for the effect of his appeal. "It is not your want of means," said Mr. Wentworth, after a period of severe reticence.

"Now it's delightful of you to say that! Only don't say it's my want of character. Because I have a character—I assure you I have; a small one, a little slip of a thing; but still something tangible."

"Ought you not to tell Felix that it is Mr. Brand, father?" Charlotte asked, with infinite mildness.

"It is not only Mr. Brand," Mr. Wentworth solemnly declared. And he looked at his knee for a long time. "It is difficult to explain," he said. He wished, evidently, to be very just. "It rests on moral grounds, as Mr. Brand says. It is the question whether it is the best thing for Gertrude."

"What is better—what is better, dear uncle?" Felix rejoined urgently, rising in his urgency and standing before Mr. Wentworth. His uncle had been looking at his knee; but when Felix moved he transferred his gaze to the handle of the door which faced him. "It is usually a fairly good thing for a girl to marry the man she loves!" cried Felix.

While he spoke, Mr. Wentworth saw the handle of the door begin to turn; the door opened and remained slightly ajar, until Felix had delivered himself of the cheerful axiom just quoted. Then it opened altogether and Gertrude stood there. She looked excited;

there was a spark in her sweet, dull eyes. She came in slowly, but with an air of resolution, and, closing the door softly, looked round at the three persons present. Felix went to her with tender gallantry, holding out his hand, and Charlotte made a place for her on the sofa. But Gertrude put her hands behind her and made no motion to sit down.

"We are talking of you!" said Felix.

"I know it," she answered. "That's why I came." And she fastened her eyes on her father, who returned her gaze very fixedly. In his own cold blue eyes there was a kind of pleading, reasoning light.

"It is better you should be present," said Mr. Wentworth. "We are discussing your future."

"Why discuss it?" asked Gertrude. "Leave it to me."

"That is, to me!" cried Felix.

"I leave it, in the last resort, to a greater wisdom than ours," said the old man.

Felix rubbed his forehead gently. "But *en attendant* the last resort, your father lacks confidence," he said to Gertrude.

"Haven't you confidence in Felix?" Gertrude was frowning; there was something about her that her father and Charlotte had never seen. Charlotte got up and came to her, as if to put her arm round her; but suddenly, she seemed afraid to touch her.

Mr. Wentworth, however, was not afraid. "I have had more confidence in Felix than in you," he said.

"Yes, you have never had confidence in me—never, never! I don't know why."

"Oh sister, sister!" murmured Charlotte.

"You have always needed advice," Mr. Wentworth declared. "You have had a difficult temperament."

"Why do you call it difficult? It might have been easy, if you had allowed it. You wouldn't let me be natural. I don't know what you wanted to make of me. Mr. Brand was the worst."

Charlotte at last took hold of her sister. "He cares so much for you," she almost whispered.

Gertrude looked at her intently an instant; then kissed her. "No, he does not," she said.

"I have never seen you so passionate," observed Mr. Wentworth, with an air of indignation mitigated by high principles.

"I am sorry if I offend you," said Gertrude.

"You offend me, but I don't think you are sorry."

"Yes, father, she is sorry," said Charlotte.

"I would even go further, dear uncle," Felix interposed. "I would question whether she really offends you. How can she offend you?"

To this Mr. Wentworth made no immediate answer. Then, in a moment, "She has not profited as we hoped."

"Profited? Ah *voilà!*" Felix exclaimed.

Gertrude was very pale; she stood looking down. "I have told Felix I would go away with him," she presently said.

"Ah, you have said some admirable things!" cried the young man.

"Go away, sister?" asked Charlotte.

"Away—away; to some strange country."

"That is to frighten you," said Felix, smiling at Charlotte.

"To—what do you call it?" asked Gertrude, turning an instant to Felix. "To Bohemia."

"Do you propose to dispense with preliminaries?" asked Mr. Wentworth, getting up.

"Dear uncle, *vous plaisantez!*" cried Felix. "It seems to me that these are preliminaries."

Gertrude turned to her father. "I *have* profited," he said. "You wanted to form my character. Well, my character is formed—for my age. I know what I want; I have chosen. I am determined to marry this gentleman."

"You had better consent, sir," said Felix very gently.

"Yes, sir, you had better consent," added a very different voice.

Charlotte gave a little jump, and the others turned to the direction from which it had come. It was the voice of Mr. Brand, who had stepped through the long window which stood open to the piazza. He stood patting his forehead with his pocket-handkerchief; he was very much flushed; his face wore a singular expression.

"Yes, sir, you had better consent," Mr. Brand repeated, coming forward. "I know what Miss Gertrude means."

"My dear friend!" murmured Felix, laying his hand caressingly on the young minister's arm.

Mr. Brand looked at him; then at Mr. Wentworth; lastly at Gertrude. He did not look at Charlotte. But Charlotte's earnest eyes were fastened to his own countenance; they were asking an immense question of it. The answer to this question could not come all at once; but some of the elements of it were there. It was one of the elements of it that Mr. Brand was very red, that he held his head very high, that he had a bright, excited eye and an air of embarrassed boldness—the air of a man who has taken a resolve, in the execution of which he apprehends the failure, not of his moral, but of his personal, resources. Charlotte thought he looked very grand; and it is incontestable that Mr. Brand felt very grand. This, in fact, was the grandest moment of his life; and it was natural that such a moment should contain opportunities of awkwardness for a large, stout, modest young man.

"Come in, sir," said Mr. Wentworth, with an angular wave of his hand. "It is very proper that you should be present."

"I know what you are talking about," Mr. Brand rejoined. "I heard what your nephew said."

"And he heard what you said!" exclaimed Felix, patting him again on the arm.

"I am not sure that I understood," said Mr. Wentworth, who had angularity in his voice as well as in his gestures.

Gertrude had been looking hard at her former suitor. She had been puzzled, like her sister; but her imagination moved more quickly than Charlotte's. "Mr. Brand asked you to let Felix take me away," she said to her father.

The young minister gave her a strange look. "It is not because I don't want to see you any more," he declared, in a tone intended as it were for publicity.

"I shouldn't think you would want to see me any more," Gertrude answered, gently.

Mr. Wentworth stood staring. "Isn't this rather a change, sir?" he inquired.

"Yes, sir." And Mr. Brand looked anywhere; only still not at Charlotte. "Yes, sir," he repeated. And he held his handkerchief a few moments to his lips.

"Where are our moral grounds?" demanded Mr. Wentworth, who had always thought Mr. Brand would be just the thing for a younger daughter with a peculiar temperament.

"It is sometimes very moral to change, you know," suggested Felix.

Charlotte had softly left her sister's side. She had edged gently toward her father, and now her hand found its way into his arm. Mr. Wentworth had folded up the "Advertiser" into a surprisingly small compass, and, holding the roll with one hand, he earnestly clasped it with the other. Mr. Brand was looking at him; and yet, though Charlotte was so near, his eyes failed to meet her own. Gertrude watched her sister.

"It is better not to speak of change," said Mr. Brand. "In one sense there is no change. There was something I desired—something I asked of you; I desire something still—I ask it of you." And he paused a moment; Mr. Wentworth looked bewildered. "I should like, in my ministerial capacity, to unite this young couple."

Gertrude, watching her sister, saw Charlotte flushing intensely, and Mr. Wentworth felt her pressing upon his arm. "Heavenly Powers!" murmured Mr. Wentworth. And it was the nearest approach to profanity he had ever made.

"That is very nice; that is very handsome!" Felix exclaimed.

"I don't understand," said Mr. Wentworth; though it was plain that every one else did.

"That is very beautiful, Mr. Brand," said Gertrude, emulating Felix.

"I should like to marry you. It will give me great pleasure."

"As Gertrude says, it's a beautiful idea," said Felix.

Felix was smiling, but Mr. Brand was not even trying to. He himself treated his proposition very seriously. "I have thought of it, and I should like to do it," he affirmed.

Charlotte, meanwhile, was staring with expanded eyes. Her imagination, as I have said, was not so rapid as her sister's, but now it had taken several little jumps. "Father," she murmured, "consent!"

Mr. Brand heard her; he looked away. Mr. Wentworth, evidently, had no imagination at all. "I have always thought," he began, slowly, "that Gertrude's character required a special line of development."

"Father," repeated Charlotte, "*consent*."

Then, at last, Mr. Brand looked at her. Her father felt her leaning more heavily upon his folded arm than she had ever done before; and this, with a certain sweet faintness in her voice, made him wonder what was the matter. He looked down at her and saw the encounter of her gaze with the young theologian's; but even this told him nothing, and he continued to be bewildered. Nevertheless, "I consent," he said at last, "since Mr. Brand recommends it."

"I should like to perform the ceremony very soon," observed Mr. Brand, with a sort of solemn simplicity.

"Come, come, that's charming!" cried Felix, profanely.

Mr. Wentworth sank into his chair. "Doubtless, when you understand it," he said, with a certain judicial asperity.

Gertrude went to her sister and led her away, and Felix having

passed his arm into Mr. Brand's and stepped out of the long window
with him, the old man was left sitting there in unillumined perplexity.

Felix did no work that day. In the afternoon, with Gertrude, he
got into one of the boats and floated about with idly-dipping oars.
They talked a good deal of Mr. Brand—though not exclusively.

"That was a fine stroke," said Felix. "It was really heroic."

Gertrude sat musing, with her eyes upon the ripples. "That was
what he wanted to be; he wanted to do something fine."

"He won't be comfortable till he has married us," said Felix. "So
much the better."

"He wanted to be magnanimous; he wanted to have a fine moral
pleasure. I know him so well," Gertrude went on. Felix looked at
her; she spoke slowly, gazing at the clear water. "He thought of
it a great deal, night and day. He thought it would be beautiful.
At last he made up his mind that it was his duty, his duty to do
just that—nothing less than that. He felt exalted; he felt sublime.
That's how he likes to feel. It is better for him than if I had listened to him."

"It's better for me," smiled Felix. "But do you know, as regards
the sacrifices, that I don't believe he admired you when this decision
was taken quite so much as he had done a fortnight before?"

"He never admired me. He admires Charlotte; he pitied me.
I know him so well."

"Well, then, he didn't pity you so much."

Gertrude looked at Felix a little, smiling. "You shouldn't permit
yourself," she said, "to diminish the splendor of his action. He
admires Charlotte," she repeated.

"That's capital!" said Felix laughingly, and dipping his oars. "I
cannot say exactly to which member of Gertrude's phrase he alluded; but he dipped his oars again, and they kept floating about.

Neither Felix nor his sister, on that day, was present at Mr. Wentworth's at the evening repast. The two occupants of the chalet
dined together, and the young man informed his companion that
his marriage was now an assured fact. Eugenia congratulated him,
and replied that if he were as reasonable a husband as he had been,
on the whole, a brother, his wife would have nothing to complain
of.

Felix looked at her a moment, smiling. "I hope," he said, "not
to be thrown back on my reason."

"It is very true," Eugenia rejoined, "that one's reason is dismally flat. It's a bed with the mattress removed."

But the brother and sister, later in the evening, crossed over to the larger house, the Baroness desiring to compliment her prospective sister-in-law. They found the usual circle upon the piazza, with the exception of Clifford Wentworth and Lizzie Acton; and as every one stood up as usual to welcome the Baroness, Eugenia had an admiring audience for her compliment to Gertrude.

Robert Acton stood on the edge of the piazza, leaning against one of the white columns, so that he found himself next to Eugenia while she acquitted herself of a neat little discourse of congratulation.

"I shall be so glad to know you better," she said; "I have seen so much less of you than I should have liked. Naturally; now I see the reason why! You will love me a little, won't you? I think I may say I gain on being known." And terminating these observations with the softest cadence of her voice, the Baroness imprinted a sort of grand official kiss upon Gertrude's forehead.

Increased familiarity had not, to Gertrude's imagination, diminished the mysterious impressiveness of Eugenia's personality, and she felt flattered and transported by this little ceremony. Robert Acton also seemed to admire it, as he admired so many of the gracious manifestations of Madame Münster's wit.

They had the privilege of making him restless, and on this occasion he walked away, suddenly, with his hands in his pockets, and then came back and leaned against his column. Eugenia was now complimenting her uncle upon his daughter's engagement, and Mr. Wentworth was listening with his usual plain yet refined politeness. It is to be supposed that by this time his perception of the mutual relations of the young people who surrounded him had become more acute; but he still took the matter very seriously, and he was not at all exhilarated.

"Felix will make her a good husband," said Eugenia. "He will be a charming companion; he has a great quality—indestructible gayety."

"You think that's a great quality?" asked the old man.

Eugenia meditated, with her eyes upon his. "You think one gets tired of it, eh?"

"I don't know that I am prepared to say that," said Mr. Wentworth.

"Well, we will say, then, that it is tiresome for others but delightful for one's self. A woman's husband, you know, is supposed to be her second self; so that, for Felix and Gertrude, gayety will be a common property."

"Gertrude was always very gay," said Mr. Wentworth. He was trying to follow this argument.

Robert Acton took his hands out of his pockets and came a little nearer to the Baroness. "You say you gain by being known," he said. "One certainly gains by knowing you."

"What have *you* gained?" asked Eugenia.

"An immense amount of wisdom."

"That's a questionable advantage for a man who was already so wise!"

Acton shook his head. "No, I was a great fool before I knew you!"

"And being a fool you made my acquaintance? You are very complimentary."

"Let me keep it up," said Acton, laughing. "I hope, for our pleasure, that your brother's marriage will detain you."

"Why should I stop for my brother's marriage when I would not stop for my own?" asked the Baroness.

"Why shouldn't you stop in either case, now that, as you say, you have dissolved that mechanical tie that bound you to Europe?"

The Baroness looked at him a moment. "As I say? You look as if you doubted it."

"Ah," said Acton, returning her glance, "that is a remnant of my old folly! We have other attractions," he added. "We are to have another marriage."

But she seemed not to hear him; she was looking at him still. "My word was never doubted before," she said.

"We are to have another marriage," Acton repeated, smiling.

Then she appeared to understand. "Another marriage?" And she looked at the others. Felix was chattering to Gertrude; Charlotte, at a distance, was watching them; and Mr. Brand, in quite another quarter, was turning his back to them, and, with his hands under his coat-tails and his large head on one side, was looking at the small, tender crescent of a young moon. "It ought to be Mr. Brand and Charlotte," said Eugenia, "but it doesn't look like it."

"There," Acton answered, "you must judge just now by contraries. There is more than there looks to be. I expect that combination one of these days; but that is not what I meant."

"Well," said the Baroness, "I never guess my own lovers; so I can't guess other people's."

Acton gave a loud laugh, and he was about to add a rejoinder when Mr. Wentworth approached his niece. "You will be interested to hear," the old man said, with a momentary aspiration toward jocosity, "of another matrimonial venture in our little circle."

"I was just telling the Baroness," Acton observed.

"Mr. Acton was apparently about to announce his own engagement," said Eugenia.

Mr. Wentworth's jocosity increased. "It is not exactly that; but it is in the family. Clifford, hearing this morning that Mr. Brand had expressed a desire to tie the nuptial knot for his sister, took it into his head to arrange that, while his hand was in, our good friend should perform a like ceremony for himself and Lizzie Acton."

The Baroness threw back her head and smiled at her uncle; then turning, with an intenser radiance, to Robert Acton, "I am certainly very stupid not to have thought of that," she said. Acton looked down at his boots, as if he thought he had perhaps reached the limits of legitimate experimentation, and for a moment Eugenia said nothing more. It had been, in fact, a sharp knock, and she needed to recover herself. This was done, however, promptly enough. "Where are the young people?" she asked.

"They are spending the evening with my mother."

"Is not the thing very sudden?"

Acton looked up. "Extremely sudden. There had been a tacit understanding; but within a day or two Clifford appears to have received some mysterious impulse to precipitate the affair."

"The impulse," said the Baroness, "was the charms of your very pretty sister."

"But my sister's charms were an old story; he had always known her." Acton had begun to experiment again.

Here, however, it was evident the Baroness would not help him. "Ah, one can't say! Clifford is very young; but he is a nice boy."

"He's a likeable sort of boy, and he will be a rich man." This was Acton's last experiment. Madame Münster turned away.

She made but a short visit and Felix took her home. In her little drawing-room she went almost straight to the mirror over the chimney-piece, and, with a candle uplifted, stood looking into it. "I shall not wait for your marriage," she said to her brother. "Tomorrow my maid shall pack up."

"My dear sister," Felix exclaimed, "we are to be married immediately! Mr. Brand is too uncomfortable."

But Eugenia, turning and still holding her candle aloft, only looked about the little sitting-room at her gimcracks and curtains and cushions. "My maid shall pack up," she repeated. "*Bonté divine*, what rubbish! I feel like a strolling actress; these are my 'properties.'"

"Is the play over, Eugenia?" asked Felix.

She gave him a sharp glance. "I have spoken my **part**."

"With great applause!" said her brother.

"Oh, applause—applause!" she murmured. And she gathered up two or three of her dispersed draperies. She glanced at the beautiful brocade, and then, "I don't see how I can have endured it!" she said.

"Endure it a little longer. Come to my wedding."

"Thank you; that's your affair. My affairs are elsewhere."

"Where are you going?"

"To Germany—by the first ship."

"You have decided not to marry Mr. Acton?"

"I have refused him," said Eugenia.

Her brother looked at her in silence. "I am sorry," he rejoined at last. "But I was very discreet, as you asked me to be. I said nothing."

"Please continue, then, not to allude to the matter," said Eugenia.

Felix inclined himself gravely. "You shall be obeyed. But your position in Germany?" he pursued.

"Please to make no observations upon it."

"I was only going to say that I supposed it was altered."

"You are mistaken."

"But I thought you had signed—"

"I have not signed!" said the Baroness.

Felix urged her no further, and it was arranged that he should immediately assist her to embark.

Mr. Brand was indeed, it appeared, very impatient to consummate his sacrifice and deliver the nuptial benediction which would set it off so handsomely; but Eugenia's impatience to withdraw from a country in which she had not found the fortune she had come to seek was even less to be mistaken. It is true she had not made any very various exertion; but she appeared to feel justified in generalizing—in deciding that the conditions of action on this provincial continent were not favorable to really superior women. The elder world was, after all, their natural field. The unembarrassed directness with which she proceeded to apply these intelligent conclusions appeared to the little circle of spectators who have figured in our narrative but the supreme exhibition of a character to which the experience of life had imparted an inimitable pliancy. It had a distinct effect upon Robert Acton, who, for the two days preceding her departure, was a very restless and irritated mortal. She passed her last evening at her uncle's, where she had never been more charming; and in parting with Clifford Wentworth's affianced bride she drew from her own finger a curious old ring and presented it to her with the prettiest speech and kiss. Gertrude, who as an affianced bride was also indebted to her gracious bounty, admired this little incident extremely, and Robert Acton almost wondered whether it did not give him the right, as Lizzie's brother and guardian, to offer in return a handsome present to the Baroness. It would have made him extremely happy to be able to offer a handsome present to the Baroness; but he abstained from this expression of his sentiments, and they were in consequence, at the very last, by so much the less comfortable. It was almost at the very last that he saw her—late the night before she went to Boston to embark.

"For myself, I wish you might have stayed," he said. "But not for your own sake."

"I don't make so many differences," said the Baroness. "I am simply sorry to be going."

"That's a much deeper difference than mine," Acton declared; "for you mean you are simply glad!'

Felix parted with her on the deck of the ship. "We shall often meet over there," he said.

"I don't know," she answered. "Europe seems to me much larger than America."

Mr. Brand, of course, in the days that immediately followed, was not the only impatient spirit; but it may be said that of all the young spirits interested in the event none rose more eagerly to the level of the occasion. Gertrude left her father's house with Felix Young; they were imperturbably happy and they went far away. Clifford and his young wife sought their felicity in a narrower circle, and the latter's influence upon her husband was such as to justify, strikingly, that theory of the elevating effect of easy intercourse with clever women which Felix had propounded to Mr. Wentworth. Gertrude was for a good while a distant figure, but she came back when Charlotte married Mr. Brand. She was present at the wedding feast, where Felix's gayety confessed to no change.

Then she disappeared, and the echo of a gayety of her own,
mingled with that of her husband, often came back to the home of
her earlier years. Mr. Wentworth at last found himself listening for
it; and Robert Acton, after his mother's death, married a particularly
nice young girl.

DAISY MILLER

Part I

At the little town of Vevey, in Switzerland, there is a particularly comfortable hotel. There are, indeed, many hotels; for the entertainment of tourists is the business of the place, which, as many travellers will remember, is seated upon the edge of a remarkably blue lake—a lake that it behooves every tourist to visit. The shore of the lake presents an unbroken array of establishments of this order, of every category, from the "grand hotel" of the newest fashion, with a chalk-white front, a hundred balconies, and a dozen flags flying from its roof, to the little Swiss *pension* of an elder day, with its name inscribed in German-looking lettering upon a pink or yellow wall, and an awkward summer-house in the angle of the garden. One of the hotels at Vevey, however, is famous, even classical, being distinguished from many of its upstart neighbors by an air both of luxury and of maturity. In this region, in the month of June, American travellers are extremely numerous; it may be said, indeed, that Vevey assumes at this period some of the characteristics of an American watering-place. There are sights and sounds which evoke a vision, an echo, of Newport and Saratoga. There is a flitting hither and thither of "stylish" young girls, a rustling of muslin flounces, a rattle of dance-music in the morning hours, a sound of high-pitched voices at all times. You receive an impression of these things at the excellent inn of the Trois Couronnes, and are transported in fancy to the Ocean House or to Congress Hall. But at the Trois Couronnes, it must be added, there are other features that are much at variance with these suggestions; neat German waiters, who look like secretaries of legation; Russian princesses sitting in the garden; little Polish boys walking about, held by the hand, with their governors; a view of the sunny crest of the Dent du Midi and the picturesque towers of the Castle of Chillon.

I hardly know whether it was the analogies or the differences that were uppermost in the mind of a young American, who, two or three years ago, sat in the garden of the Trois Couronnes, looking about him, rather idly, at some of the graceful objects I have mentioned. It was a beautiful summer morning, and in whatever fashion the young American looked at things they must have seemed to him charming. He had come from Geneva the day before by

the little steamer to see his aunt, who was staying at the hotel—
Geneva having been for a long time his place of residence. But his
aunt had a headache—his aunt had almost always a headache—and
now she was shut up in her room, smelling camphor, so that he was
at liberty to wander about. He was some seven-and-twenty years
of age. When his friends spoke of him, they usually said that he
was at Geneva "studying"; when his enemies spoke of him, they
said—but, after all, he has no enemies; he was an extremely amiable
fellow, and universally liked. What I should say is, simply, that
when certain persons spoke of him they affirmed that the reason
of his spending so much time at Geneva was that he was extremely
devoted to a lady who lived there—a foreign lady—a person older
than himself. Very few Americans—indeed I think none—had ever
seen this lady, about whom there were some singular stories. But
Winterbourne had an old attachment for the little metropolis of
Calvinism; he had been put to school there as a boy, and he had
afterwards gone to college there—circumstances which had led to
his forming a great many youthful friendships. Many of these he
had kept, and they were a source of great satisfaction to him.

After knocking at his aunt's door, and learning that she was
indisposed, he had taken a walk about the town, and then he had
come in to his breakfast. He had now finished his breakfast; but he
was drinking a small cup of coffee, which had been served to him
on a little table in the garden by one of the waiters who looked like
an attaché. At last he finished his coffee and lit a cigarette. Presently
a small boy came walking along the path—an urchin of nine or ten.
The child, who was diminutive for his years, had an aged expression
of countenance: a pale complexion, and sharp little features. He was
dressed in knickerbockers, with red stockings, which displayed his
poor little spindle-shanks; he also wore a brilliant red cravat. He
carried in his hand a long alpenstock, the sharp point of which he
thrust into everything that he approached—the flower-beds, the
garden-benches, the trains of the ladies' dresses. In front of Winterbourne he paused, looking at him with a pair of bright, penetrating
little eyes.

"Will you give me a lump of sugar?" he asked, in a sharp, hard
little voice—a voice immature, and yet, somehow, not young.

Winterbourne glanced at the small table near him, on which his
coffee-service rested, and saw that several morsels of sugar remained.
"Yes, you may take one," he answered; "but I don't think sugar is
good for little boys."

This little boy stepped forward and carefully selected three of the coveted fragments, two of which he buried in the pocket of his knickerbockers, depositing the other as promptly in another place. He poked his alpenstock, lance-fashion, into Winterbourne's bench, and tried to crack the lump of sugar with his teeth.

"Oh, blazes; it's har-r-d!" he exclaimed, pronouncing the adjective in a peculiar manner.

Winterbourne had immediately perceived that he might have the honor of claiming him as a fellow-countryman. "Take care you don't hurt your teeth," he said, paternally.

"I haven't got any teeth to hurt. They have all come out. I have only got seven teeth. My mother counted them last night, and one came out right afterwards. She said she'd slap me if any more came out. I can't help it. It's this old Europe. It's the climate that makes them come out. In America they didn't come out. It's these hotels."

Winterbourne was much amused. "If you eat three lumps of sugar, your mother will certainly slap you," he said.

"She's got to give me some candy, then," rejoined his young interlocutor. "I can't get any candy here—any American candy. American candy's the best candy."

"And are American little boys the best little boys?" asked Winterbourne.

"I don't know. I'm an American boy," said the child.

"I see you are one of the best!" laughed Winterbourne.

"Are you an American man?" pursued this vivacious infant. And then, on Winterbourne's affirmative reply—"American men are the best!" he declared.

His companion thanked him for the compliment; and the child, who had now got astride of his alpenstock, stood looking about him, while he attacked a second lump of sugar. Winterbourne wondered if he himself had been like this in his infancy, for he had been brought to Europe at about this age.

"Here comes my sister!" cried the child, in a moment. "She's an American girl."

Winterbourne looked along the path and saw a beautiful young lady advancing. "American girls are the best girls!" he said, cheerfully, to his young companion.

"My sister ain't the best!" the child declared. "She's always blowing at me."

"I imagine that is your fault, not hers," said Winterbourne. The young lady meanwhile had drawn near. She was dressed in white muslin, with a hundred frills and flounces, and knots of pale-colored ribbon. She was bareheaded; but she balanced in her hand a large parasol, with a deep border of embroidery; and she was strikingly, admirably pretty. "How pretty they are!" thought Winterbourne, straightening himself in his seat, as if he were prepared to rise.

The young lady paused in front of his bench, near the parapet of the garden, which overlooked the lake. The little boy had now converted his alpenstock into a vaulting-pole, by the aid of which he was springing about in the gravel, and kicking it up a little.

"Randolph," said the young lady, "what *are* you doing?"

"I'm going up the Alps," replied Randolph. "This is the way!" And he gave another little jump, scattering the pebbles about Winterbourne's ears.

"That's the way they come down," said Winterbourne.

"He's an American man!" cried Randolph, in his little hard voice.

The young lady gave no heed to this announcement, but looked straight at her brother. "Well, I guess you had better be quiet," she simply observed.

It seemed to Winterbourne that he had been in a manner presented. He got up and stepped slowly towards the young girl, throwing away his cigarette. "This little boy and I have made acquaintance," he said, with great civility. In Geneva, as he had been perfectly aware, a young man was not at liberty to speak to a young unmarried lady except under certain rarely occurring conditions; but here at Vevey, what conditions could be better than these? —a pretty American girl coming and standing in front of you in a garden. This pretty American girl, however, on hearing Winterbourne's observation, simply glanced at him; she then turned her head and looked over the parapet, at the lake and the opposite mountains. He wondered whether he had gone too far; but he decided that he must advance farther, rather than retreat. While he was thinking of something else to say, the young lady turned to the little boy again.

"I should like to know where you got that pole?" she said.

"I bought it," responded Randolph.

"You don't mean to say you're going to take it to Italy?"

"Yes, I am going to take it to Italy," the child declared.

The young girl glanced over the front of her dress, and smoothed out a knot or two of ribbon. Then she rested her eyes upon the prospect again. "Well, I guess you had better leave it somewhere," she said, after a moment.

"Are you going to Italy?" Winterbourne inquired, in a tone of great respect.

The young lady glanced at him again. "Yes, sir," she replied. And she said nothing more.

"Are you—a—going over the Simplon?" Winterbourne pursued, a little embarrassed.

"I don't know," she said. "I suppose it's some mountain. Randolph, what mountain are we going over?"

"Going where?" the child demanded.

"To Italy," Winterbourne explained.

"I don't know," said Randolph. "I don't want to go to Italy. I want to go to America."

"Oh, Italy is a beautiful place!" rejoined the young man.

"Can you get candy there?" Randolph loudly inquired.

"I hope not," said his sister. "I guess you have had enough candy, and mother thinks so, too."

"I haven't had any for ever so long—for a hundred weeks!" cried the boy, still jumping about.

The young lady inspected her flounces and smoothed her ribbons again, and Winterbourne presently risked an observation upon the beauty of the view. He was ceasing to be embarrassed, for he had begun to perceive that she was not in the least embarrassed herself. There had not been the slightest alteration in her charming complexion; she was evidently neither offended nor fluttered. If she looked another way when he spoke to her, and seemed not particularly to hear him, this was simply her habit, her manner. Yet, as he talked a little more, and pointed out some of the objects of interest in the view, with which she appeared quite unacquainted, she gradually gave him more of the benefit of her glance; and then he saw that this glance was perfectly direct and unshrinking. It was not, however, what would have been called an immodest glance, for the young girl's eyes were singularly honest and fresh. They were wonderfully pretty eyes; and, indeed, Winterbourne had not seen for a long time anything prettier than his fair countrywoman's various features—her complexion, her nose, her ears, her teeth. He had a great relish for feminine beauty; he was addicted to observing and analyzing it; and as regards this young lady's face he made several observations. It was not at all insipid, but it was not exactly expressive; and though it was eminently delicate, Winterbourne mentally accused it—very forgivingly—of a want of finish. He thought it very possible that Master Randolph's sister was a coquette; he was sure she had a spirit of her own; but in her bright, sweet, superficial little visage there was no mockery, no irony. Before long it became obvious that she was much disposed towards conversation. She told him that they were going to Rome for the winter—she and her mother and Randolph. She asked him if he was a "real American"; she shouldn't have taken him for one; he seemed more like a German—this was said after a little hesitation—especially when he spoke. Winterbourne, laughing, answered that he had met Germans who spoke like Americans; but that he had not, so far as he remembered, met an American who spoke like a German. Then he asked her if she should not be more comfortable in sitting upon the bench which he had just quitted. She answered that she liked standing up and walking about; but she presently sat down. She told him she was from New York State—"if you know where that is." Winterbourne learned more about her by catching hold of her small, slippery brother, and making him stand a few minutes by his side.

"Tell me your name, my boy," he said.

"Randolph C. Miller," said the boy, sharply. "And I'll tell you her name;" and he levelled his alpenstock at his sister.

"You had better wait till you are asked!" said this young lady, calmly.

"I should like very much to know your name," said Winterbourne.

"Her name is Daisy Miller!" cried the child. "But that isn't her real name; that isn't her name on her cards."

"It's a pity you haven't got one of my cards!" said Miss Miller.

"Her real name is Annie P. Miller," the boy went on.

"Ask him his name," said his sister, indicating Winterbourne.

But on this point Randolph seemed perfectly indifferent; he continued to supply information in regard to his own family. "My father's name is Ezra B. Miller," he announced. "My father ain't in Europe; my father's in a better place than Europe."

Winterbourne imagined for a moment that this was the manner in which the child had been taught to intimate that Mr. Miller had been removed to the sphere of celestial rewards. But Randolph immediately added, "My father's in Schenectady. He's got a big business. My father's rich, you bet!"

"Well!" ejaculated Miss Miller, lowering her parasol and look-ing at the embroidered border. Winterbourne presently released the child, who departed, dragging his alpenstock along the path. "He doesn't like Europe," said the young girl. "He wants to go back."

"To Schenectady, you mean?"

"Yes; he wants to go right home. He hasn't got any boys here. There is one boy here, but he always goes round with a teacher; they won't let him play."

"And your brother hasn't any teacher?" Winterbourne inquired.

"Mother thought of getting him one to travel round with us. There was a lady told her of a very good teacher; an American lady—perhaps you know her—Mrs. Sanders. I think she came from Boston. She told her of this teacher, and we thought of getting him to travel round with us. But Randolph said he didn't want a teacher travelling round with us. He said he wouldn't have lessons when he was in the cars. And we *are* in the cars about half the time. There was an English lady we met in the cars—I think her name was Miss Featherstone; perhaps you know her. She wanted to know why I didn't give Randolph lessons—give him 'instructions,' she called it. I guess he could give me more instructions than I could give him. He's very smart."

"Yes," said Winterbourne; "he seems very smart."

"Mother's going to get a teacher for him as soon as we get to Italy. Can you get good teachers in Italy?"

"Very good, I should think," said Winterbourne.

"Or else she's going to find some school. He ought to learn some more. He's only nine. He's going to college." And in this way Miss Miller continued to converse upon the affairs of her family, and upon other topics. She sat there with her extremely pretty hands, ornamented with very brilliant rings, folded in her lap, and with her pretty eyes now resting upon those of Winterbourne, now wander-ing over the garden, the people who passed by, and the beautiful view. She talked to Winterbourne as if she had known him a long time. He found it very pleasant. It was many years since he had heard a young girl talk so much. It might have been said of this unknown young lady, who had come and sat down beside him upon a bench, that she chattered. She was very quiet; she sat in a charming, tranquil attitude, but her lips and her eyes were constantly moving. She had a soft, slender, agreeable voice, and her tone was decidedly sociable. She gave Winterbourne a history of her movements and intentions, and those of her mother and brother, in Europe, and enumerated, in particular, the various hotels at which they had stopped. "That English lady in the cars," she said—"Miss Feather-stone—asked me if we didn't all live in hotels in America. I told her I had never been in so many hotels in my life as since I came to Europe. I have never seen so many—it's nothing but hotels." But Miss Miller did not make this remark with a querulous accent; she appeared to be in the best humor with everything. She declared that the hotels were very good, when once you got used to their ways, and that Europe was perfectly sweet. She was not disappointed—not a bit. Perhaps it was because she had heard so much about it before. She had ever so many intimate friends that had been there ever so many times. And then she had had ever so many dresses and things from Paris. Whenever she put on a Paris dress she felt as if she were in Europe.

"It was a kind of a wishing-cap," said Winterbourne.

"Yes," said Miss Miller, without examining this analogy; "it always made me wish I was here. But I needn't have done that for dresses. I am sure they send all the pretty ones to America; you see the most frightful things here. The only thing I don't like," she proceeded, "is the society. There isn't any society; or, if there is, I don't know where it keeps itself. Do you? I suppose there is some society somewhere, but I haven't seen anything of it. I'm very fond of society, and I have always had a great deal of it. I don't mean only in Schenectady, but in New York. I used to go to New York every winter. In New York I had lots of society. Last winter I had seventeen dinners given me; and three of them were by gentlemen," added Daisy Miller. "I have more friends in New York than in Schenectady—more gentleman friends; and more young lady friends, too," she resumed in a moment. She paused again for an instant; she was looking at Winterbourne with all her prettiness in her lively eyes, and in her light, slightly monotonous smile. "I have always had," she said, "a great deal of gentlemen's society."

Poor Winterbourne was amused, perplexed, and decidedly charmed. He had never yet heard a young girl express herself in just this fashion—never, at least, save in cases where to say such things seemed a kind of demonstrative evidence of a certain laxity of deport-ment. And yet was he to accuse Miss Daisy Miller of actual or po-tential *inconduite*, as they said at Geneva? He felt that he had lived at Geneva so long that he had lost a good deal; he had become dis-habituated to the American tone. Never, indeed, since he had grown old enough to appreciate things had he encountered a young American girl of so pronounced a type as this. Certainly she was very charming, but how deucedly sociable! Was she simply a pretty girl from New York State? were they all like that, the pretty girls who had a good deal of gentlemen's society? Or was she also a designing, an audacious, an unscrupulous young person? Winterbourne had lost his instinct in this matter, and his reason could not help him. Miss Daisy Miller looked extremely innocent. Some people had told him that, after all, American girls were exceedingly innocent; and others had told him that, after all, they were not. He was inclined to think Miss Daisy Miller was a flirt—a pretty American flirt. He had never, as yet, had any relations with young ladies of this category. He had known, here in Europe, two or three women —persons older than Miss Daisy Miller, and provided, for respectability's sake, with husbands—who were great coquettes—dangerous, terrible women, with whom one's relations were liable to take a serious turn. But this young girl was not a coquette in that sense; she was very unsophisticated; she was only a pretty American flirt. Winterbourne was almost grateful for having found the formula that applied to Miss Daisy Miller. He leaned back in his seat; he remarked to himself that she had the most charming nose he had ever seen; he wondered what were the regular conditions and limitations of one's intercourse with a pretty American flirt. It presently became apparent that he was on the way to learn.

"Have you been to that old castle?" asked the young girl, pointing with her parasol to the far-gleaming walls of the Château de Chillon.

"Yes, formerly, more than once," said Winterbourne. "You too, I suppose, have seen it?"

"No; we haven't been there. I want to go there dreadfully. Of course I mean to go there. I wouldn't go away from here without having seen that old castle."

"It's a very pretty excursion," said Winterbourne, "and very easy to make. You can drive or go by the little steamer."

"You can go in the cars," said Miss Miller.

"Yes; you can go in the cars," Winterbourne assented.

"Our courier says they take you right up to the castle," the young girl continued. "We were going last week; but my mother gave out. She suffers dreadfully from dyspepsia. She said she couldn't go. Randolph wouldn't go, either; he says he doesn't think much of old castles. But I guess we'll go this week, if we can get Randolph."

"Your brother is not interested in ancient monuments?" Winterbourne inquired, smiling.

"He says he don't care much about old castles. He's only nine. He wants to stay at the hotel. Mother's afraid to leave him alone, and the courier won't stay with him; so we haven't been to many places. But it will be too bad if we don't go up there." And Miss Miller pointed again at the Château de Chillon.

"I should think it might be arranged," said Winterbourne. "Couldn't you get some one to stay for the afternoon with Randolph?"

Miss Miller looked at him a moment, and then very placidly, "I wish *you* would stay with him!" she said.

Winterbourne hesitated a moment. "I should much rather go to Chillon with you."

"With me?" asked the young girl, with the same placidity.

She didn't rise, blushing, as a young girl at Geneva would have done; and yet Winterbourne, conscious that he had been very bold, thought it possible that she was offended. "With your mother," he answered, very respectfully.

But it seemed that both his audacity and his respect were lost upon Miss Daisy Miller. "I guess my mother won't go, after all," she said. "She don't like to ride around in the afternoon. But did you really mean what you said just now, that you would like to go up there?"

"Most earnestly," Winterbourne declared.

"Then we may arrange it. If mother will stay with Randolph, I guess Eugenio will."

"Eugenio?" the young man inquired.

"Eugenio's our courier. He doesn't like to stay with Randolph; he's the most fastidious man I ever saw. But he's a splendid courier. I guess he'll stay at home with Randolph if mother does, and then we can go to the castle."

Winterbourne reflected for an instant as lucidly as possible—"we" could only mean Miss Daisy Miller and himself. This programme seemed almost too agreeable for credence; he felt as if he ought to kiss the young lady's hand. Possibly he would have done so, and quite spoiled the project; but at this moment another person, presumably Eugenio, appeared. A tall, handsome man, with superb whiskers, wearing a velvet morning-coat and a brilliant watch-chain, approached Miss Miller, looking sharply at her companion. "Oh, Eugenio!" said Miss Miller, with the friendliest accent.

Eugenio had looked at Winterbourne from head to foot; he now bowed gravely to the young lady. "I have the honor to inform mademoiselle that luncheon is upon the table."

Miss Miller rose. "See here, Eugenio!" she said; "I'm going to that old castle, anyway."

"To the Château de Chillon, mademoiselle?" the courier inquired. "Mademoiselle has made arrangements?" he added, in a tone which struck Winterbourne as very impertinent.

Eugenio's tone apparently threw, even to Miss Miller's own apprehension, a slightly ironical light upon the young girl's situation. She turned to Winterbourne, blushing a little—a very little. "You won't back out?" she said.

"I shall not be happy till we go!" he protested.

"And you are staying in this hotel?" she went on. "And you are really an American?"

The courier stood looking at Winterbourne offensively. The young man, at least, thought his manner of looking an offence to Miss Miller; it conveyed an imputation that she "picked up" acquaintances. "I shall have the honor of presenting to you a person who will tell you all about me," he said, smiling, and referring to his aunt.

"Oh, well, we'll go some day," said Miss Miller. And she gave him a smile and turned away. She put up her parasol and walked back to the inn beside Eugenio. Winterbourne stood looking after her; and as she moved away, drawing her muslin furbelows over the gravel, said to himself that she had the *tournure* of a princess.

He had, however, engaged to do more than proved feasible, in promising to present his aunt, Mrs. Costello, to Miss Daisy Miller. As soon as the former lady had got better of her headache he waited upon her in her apartment; and, after the proper inquiries in regard to her health, he asked her if she had observed in the hotel an American family—a mamma, a daughter, and a little boy.

"And a courier?" said Mrs. Costello. "Oh yes, I have observed them. Seen them—heard them—and kept out of their way." Mrs. Costello was a widow with a fortune; a person of much distinction, who frequently intimated that, if she were not so dreadfully liable to sick-headaches, she would probably have left a deeper impress upon her time. She had a long, pale face, a high nose, and a great deal of very striking white hair, which she work in large puffs and *rouleaux* over the top of her head. She had two sons married in New York, and another who was now in Europe. This young man was amusing himself at Hombourg; and, though he was on his travels, was rarely perceived to visit any particular city at the moment selected by his mother for her own appearance there. Her nephew, who had come up to Vevey expressly to see her, was therefore more attentive than those who, as she said, were nearer to her. He had imbibed at Geneva the idea that one must always be attentive to one's aunt. Mrs. Costello had not seen him for many years, and she was greatly pleased with him, manifesting her approbation by initiating him into many of the secrets of that social sway which, as she gave him to understand, she exerted in the American capital. She admitted that she was very exclusive; but, if he were acquainted with New York, he would see that one had to be. And her picture of the minutely hierarchical constitution of the society of that city, which she presented to him in many different lights, was, to Winterbourne's imagination, almost oppressively striking.

He immediately perceived, from her tone, that Miss Daisy Miller's place in the social scale was low. "I am afraid you don't approve of them," he said.

"They are very common," Mrs. Costello declared. "They are the sort of Americans that one does one's duty by not—not accepting."

"Ah, you don't accept them?" said the young man.

"I can't, my dear Frederick. I would if I could, but I can't."

"The young girl is very pretty," said Winterbourne, in a moment.

"Of course she's pretty. But she is very common."

"I see what you mean, of course," said Winterbourne, after another pause.

"She has that charming look that they all have," his aunt resumed. "I can't think where they pick it up; and she dresses in perfection —no, you don't know how well she dresses. I can't think where they get their taste."

"But, my dear aunt, she is not, after all, a Comanche savage."

"She is a young lady," said Mrs. Costello, "who has an intimacy with her mamma's courier."

"An intimacy with the courier?" the young man demanded.

"Oh, the mother is just as bad! They treat the courier like a familiar friend—like a gentleman. I shouldn't wonder if he dines with them. Very likely they have never seen a man with such good manners, such fine clothes, so like a gentleman. He probably corresponds to the young lady's idea of a count. He sits with them in the garden in the evening. I think he smokes."

Winterbourne listened with interest to these disclosures; they helped him to make up his mind about Miss Daisy. Evidently she was rather wild.

"Well," he said, "I am not a courier, and yet she was very charming to me."

"You had better have said at first," said Mrs. Costello, with dignity, "that you had made her acquaintance."

"We simply met in the garden, and we talked a bit."

"*Tout bonnement!* And pray what did you say?"

"I said I should take the liberty of introducing her to my admirable aunt."

"I am much obliged to you."

"It was to guarantee my respectability," said Winterbourne.

"And pray who is to guarantee hers?"

"Ah, you are cruel," said the young man. "She's a very nice young girl."

"You don't say that as if you believed it," Mrs Costello observed.

"She is completely uncultivated," Winterbourne went on. "But she is wonderfully pretty, and, in short, she is very nice. To prove that I believe it, I am going to take her to the Château de Chillon."

"You two are going off there together? I should say it proved just the contrary. How long had you known her, may I ask, when this interesting project was formed? You haven't been twenty-four hours in the house."

"I had known her half an hour!" said Winterbourne, smiling.

"Dear me!" cried Mrs. Costello. "What a dreadful girl!"

Her nephew was silent for some moments. "You really think, then," he began, earnestly, and with a desire for trustworthy information—"you really think that——" But he paused again.

"Think what, sir?" said his aunt.

"That she is the sort of young lady who expects a man, sooner or later, to carry her off?"

"I haven't the least idea what such young ladies expect a man to do. But I really think that you had better not meddle with little American girls that are uncultivated, as you call them. You have lived too long out of the country. You will be sure to make some great mistake. You are too innocent."

"My dear aunt, I am not so innocent," said Winterbourne, smiling and curling his mustache.

"You are too guilty, then!"

Winterbourne continued to curl his mustache, meditatively. "You won't let the poor girl know you, then?" he asked at last.

"Is it literally true that she is going to the Château de Chillon with you?"

"I think that she fully intends it."

"Then, my dear Frederick," said Mrs. Costello, "I must decline the honor of her acquaintance, I am an old woman, but I am not too old, thank Heaven, to be shocked!"

"But don't they all do these things—the young girls in America?" Winterbourne inquired.

Mrs. Costello stared a moment. "I should like to see my granddaughters do them!" she declared, grimly.

This seemed to throw some light upon the matter, for Winterbourne remembered to have heard that his pretty cousins in New York were "tremendous flirts." If, therefore, Miss Daisy Miller exceeded the liberal margin allowed to these young ladies, it was probable that anything might be expected of her. Winterbourne was impatient to see her again, and he was vexed with himself that, by instinct, he should not appreciate her justly.

Though he was impatient to see her, he hardly knew what he should say to her about his aunt's refusal to become acquainted with her; but he discovered, promptly enough, that with Miss Daisy Miller there was no great need of walking on tiptoe. He found her that evening in the garden, wandering about in the warm starlight like an indolent sylph, and swinging to and fro the largest fan he had ever beheld. It was ten o'clock. He had dined with his aunt, had been sitting with her since dinner, and had just taken leave of her till the morrow. Miss Daisy Miller seemed very glad to see him; she declared it was the longest evening she had ever passed.

"Have you been all alone?" he asked.

"I have been walking round with mother. But mother gets tired walking round," she answered.

"Has she gone to bed?"

"No; she doesn't like to go to bed," said the young girl. "She doesn't sleep—not three hours. She says she doesn't know how she lives. She's dreadfully nervous. I guess she sleeps more than she thinks. She's gone somewhere after Randolph; she wants to try to get him to go to bed. He doesn't like to go to bed."

"Let us hope she will persuade him," observed Winterbourne.

"She will talk to him all she can; but he doesn't like her to talk to him," said Miss Daisy, opening her fan. "She's going to try to get Eugenio to talk to him. But he isn't afraid of Eugenio. Eugenio's a splendid courier, but he can't make much impression on Randolph!

I don't believe he'll go to bed before eleven." It appeared that Randolph's vigil was in fact triumphantly prolonged, for Winterbourne strolled about with the young girl for some time without meeting her mother. "I have been looking round for that lady you want to introduce me to," his companion resumed. "She's your aunt." Then, on Winterbourne's admitting the fact, and expressing some curiosity as to how she had learned it, she said she had heard all about Mrs. Costello from the chambermaid. She was very quiet, and very *comme if faut;* she wore white puffs; she spoke to no one, and she never dined at the *table d'hôte.* Every two days she had a headache. "I think that's a lovely description, headache and all!" said Miss Daisy, chattering along in her thin, gay voice. "I want to know her ever so much. I know just what *your* aunt would be; I know I should like her. She would be very exclusive. I like a lady to be exclusive; I'm dying to be exclusive myself. Well, we *are* exclusive, mother and I. We don't speak to every one—or they don't speak to us. I suppose it's about the same thing. Anyway, I shall be ever so glad to know your aunt."

Winterbourne was embarrassed. "She would be most happy," he said; "but I am afraid those headaches will interfere."

The young girl looked at him through the dusk. "But I suppose she doesn't have a headache every day," she said, sympathetically.

Winterbourne was silent a moment. "She tells me she does," he answered at last, not knowing what to say.

Miss Daisy Miller stopped, and stood looking at him. Her prettiness was still visible in the darkness; she was opening and closing her enormous fan. "She doesn't want to know me!" she said, suddenly. "Why don't you say so? You needn't be afraid. I'm not afraid!" And she gave a little laugh.

Winterbourne fancied there was a tremor in her voice; he was touched, shocked, mortified by it. "My dear young lady," he protested, "she knows no one. It's her wretched health."

The young girl walked on a few steps, laughing still. "You needn't be afraid," she repeated. "Why should she want to know me?" Then she paused again; she was close to the parapet of the garden, and in front of her was the starlit lake. There was a vague sheen upon its surface, and in the distance were dimly-seen mountain forms. Daisy Miller looked out upon the mysterious prospect, and then she gave another little laugh. "Gracious! she *is* exclusive!" she said. Winterbourne wondered whether she was seriously wounded, and for a moment almost wished that her sense of injury might be such as to make it becoming in him to attempt to reassure and comfort her. He had a pleasant sense that she would be very approachable for consolatory purposes. He felt then, for the instant, quiet ready to sacrifice his aunt, conversationally; to admit that she was a proud, rude woman, and to declare that they needn't mind her. But before he had time to commit himself to this perilous mixture of gallantry and impiety, the young lady, resuming her walk, gave an exclamation in quite another tone. "Well, here's mother! I guess she hasn't got Randolph to go to bed." The figure of a lady appeared, at a distance, very indistinct in the darkness, and advancing with a slow and wavering movement. Suddenly it seemed to pause.

"Are you sure it is your mother? Can you distinguish her in this thick dusk?" Winterbourne asked.

"Well!" cried Miss Daisy Miller, with a laugh; "I guess I know my own mother. And when she has got on my shawl, too! She is always wearing my things."

The lady in question, ceasing to advancing, hovered vaguely about the spot at which she had checked her steps.

"I am afraid your mother doesn't see you," said Winterbourne. "Or perhaps," he added, thinking, with Miss Miller, the joke permissible—"perhaps she feels guilty about your shawl!"

"Oh, it's a fearful old thing!" the young girl replied, serenely. "I told her she could wear it. She won't come here, because she sees you."

"Ah, then," said Winterbourne, "I had better leave you."

"Oh no; come on!" urged Miss Daisy Miller.

"I'm afraid your mother doesn't approve of my walking with you."

Miss Miller gave him a serious glance. "It isn't for me; it's for you —that is, it's for *her*. Well, I don't know who it's for! But mother doesn't like any of my gentlemen friends. She's right down timid. She always makes a fuss if I introduce a gentleman. But I *do* introduce them—almost always. If I didn't introduce my gentlemen friends to mother," the young girl added, in her little soft, flat monotone, "I shouldn't think it was natural."

"To introduce me," said Winterbourne, "you must know my name." And he proceeded to pronounce it to her.

"Oh dear, I can't say all that!" said his companion, with a laugh. But by this time they had come up to Mrs. Miller, who, as they drew near, walked to the parapet of the garden and leaned upon it, looking intently at the lake, and turning her back to them.

"Mother!" said the young girl, in a tone of decision. Upon this the elder lady turned round. "Mr. Winterbourne," said Miss Daisy Miller, introducing the young man very frankly and prettily. "Common," she was, as Mrs. Costello had pronounced her; yet it was a wonder to Winterbourne that, with her commonness, she had a singularly delicate grace.

Her mother was a small, spare, light person with a wandering eye, a very exiguous nose, and a large forehead, decorated with a certain amount of thin, much-frizzled hair. Like her daughter, Mrs. Miller was dressed with extreme elegance; she had enormous diamonds in her ears. So far as Winterbourne could observe, she gave him no greeting—she certainly was not looking at him. Daisy was near her, pulling her shawl straight. "What are you doing, poking round here?" this young lady inquired, but by no means with that harshness of accent which her choice of words may imply.

"I don't know," said her mother, turning towards the lake again.

"I shouldn't think you'd want that shawl!" Daisy exclaimed.

"Well, I do!' her mother answered, with a little laugh.

"Did you get Randolph to go to bed?" asked the young girl.

"No; I couldn't induce him," said Mrs. Miller, very gently. "He wants to talk to the waiter. He likes to talk to that waiter."

"I was telling Mr. Winterbourne," the young girl went on; and to the young man's ear her tone might have indicated that she had been uttering his name all her life.

"Oh yes!" said Winterbourne; "I have the pleasure of knowing your son."

Randolph's mamma was silent; she turned her attention to the lake. But at last she spoke. "Well, I don't see how he lives!"

"Anyhow, it isn't so bad as it was at Dover," said Daisy Miller.

"And what occurred at Dover?" Winterbourne asked.

"He wouldn't go to bed at all. I guess he sat up all night in the public parlor. He wasn't in bed at twelve o'clock; I know that."

"It was half-past twelve," declared Mrs. Miller, with mild emphasis.

"Does he sleep much during the day?" Winterbourne demanded.

"I guess he doesn't sleep much," Daisy rejoined.

"I wish he would!" said her mother. "It seems as if he couldn't."

"I think he's real tiresome," Daisy pursued.

Then for some moments there was silence. "Well, Daisy Miller," said the elder lady, presently, "I shouldn't think you'd want to talk against your own brother!"

"Well, he *is* tiresome, mother," said Daisy, quite without the asperity of a retort.

"He's only nine," urged Mrs. Miller.

"Well, he wouldn't go to that castle," said the young girl. "I'm going there with Mr. Winterbourne."

To this announcement, very placidly made, Daisy's mamma offered no response. Winterbourne took for granted that she deeply disapproved of the projected excursion; but he said to himself that she was a simple, easily-managed person, and that a few deferential protestations would take the edge from her displeasure. "Yes," he began; "your daughter has kindly allowed me the honor of being her guide."

Mrs. Miller's wandering eyes attached themselves, with a sort of appealing air, to Daisy, who, however, strolled a few steps farther, gently humming to herself. "I presume you will go in the cars," said her mother.

"Yes, or in the boat," said Winterbourne.

"Well, of course, I don't know," Mrs. Miller rejoined. "I have never been to that castle."

"It is a pity you shouldn't go," said Winterbourne, beginning to feel reassured as to her opposition. And yet he was quite prepared to find that, as a matter of course, she meant to accompany her daughter.

"We've been thinking ever so much about going," she pursued; "but it seems as if we couldn't. Of course Daisy, she wants to go round. But there's a lady here—I don't know her name—she says she shouldn't think we'd want to go to see castles *here;* she should think we'd want to wait till we got to Italy. It seems as if there would be so many there," continued Mrs. Miller, with an air of increasing confidence. "Of course we only want to see the principal ones. We visited several in England," she presently added.

"Ah, yes! in England there are beautiful castles," said Winterbourne. "But Chillon, here, is very well worth seeing."

"Well, if Daisy feels up to it——" said Mrs. Miller, in a tone impregnated with a sense of the magnitude of the enterprise. "It seems as if there was nothing she wouldn't undertake."

"Oh, I think she'll enjoy it!" Winterbourne declared. And he desired more and more to make it a certainty that he was to have the privilege of a tête-à-tête with the young lady, who was still strolling along in front of them, softly vocalizing. "You are not disposed, madam," he inquired, "to undertake it yourself?"

Daisy's mother looked at him an instant askance, and then walked forward in silence. Then—"I guess she had better go alone," she said, simply. Winterbourne observed to himself that this was a very different type of maternity from that of the vigilant matrons who massed themselves in the forefront of social intercourse in the dark old city at the other end of the lake. But his meditations were interrupted by hearing his name very distinctly pronounced by Mrs. Miller's unprotected daughter.

"Mr. Winterbourne!" murmured Daisy.

"Mademoiselle!" said the young man.

"Don't you want to take me out in a boat?"

"At present!" he asked.

"Of course!' said Daisy.

"Well, Annie Miller!" exclaimed her mother.

"I beg you, madam, to let her go," said Winterbourne, ardently; for he had never yet enjoyed the sensation of guiding through the summer starlight a skiff freighted with a fresh and beautiful young girl.

"I shouldn't think she'd want to," said her mother. "I should think she'd rather go indoors."

"I'm sure Mr. Winterbourne wants to take me," Daisy declared. "He's so awfully devoted!"

"I will row you over to Chillon in the starlight."

"I don't believe it!" said Daisy.

"Well!" ejaculated the elder lady again.

"You haven't spoken to me for half an hour," her daughter went on.

"I have been having some very pleasant conversation with your mother," said Winterbourne.

"Well, I want you to take me out in a boat!" Daisy repeated. They had all stopped, and she had turned round and was looking at Winterbourne. Her face wore a charming smile, her pretty eyes were gleaming, she was swinging her great fan about. "No; it's impossible to be prettier than that," thought Winterbourne.

"There are half a dozen boats moored at that landing-place," he said, pointing to certain steps which descended from the garden to the lake. "If you will do me the honor to accept my arm, we will go and select one of them."

Daisy stood there smiling; she threw back her head and gave a little light laugh. "I like a gentleman to be formal!" she declared.

"I assure you it's a formal offer."

"I was bound I would make you say something." Daisy went on.

"You see, it's not very difficult," said Winterbourne. "But I am afraid you are chaffing me."

"I think not, sir," remarked Mrs. Miller, very gently.

"Do, then, let me give you a row," he said to the young girl.

"It's quite lovely, the way you say that!" cried Daisy.

"It will be still more lovely to do it."

"Yes, it would be lovely!" said Daisy. But she made no movement to accompany him; she only stood there laughing.

"I should think you had better find out what time it is," interposed her mother.

"It is eleven o'clock, madam," said a voice, with a foreign accent, out of the neighboring darkness; and Winterbourne, turning, perceived the florid personage who was in attendance upon the two ladies. He had apparently just approached.

"Oh, Eugenio," said Daisy, "I am going out in a boat!"

Eugenio bowed. "At eleven o'clock, mademoiselle?"

"I am going with Mr. Winterbourne—this very minute."

"Do tell her she can't" said Mrs. Miller to the courier.

"I think you had better not go out in a boat, mademoiselle," Eugenio declared.

Winterbourne wished to Heaven this pretty girl were not so familiar with her courier; but he said nothing.

"I suppose you don't think it's proper!" Daisy exclaimed. "Eugenio doesn't think anything's proper."

"I am at your service," said Winterbourne.

"Does mademoiselle propose to go alone?" asked Eugenio of Mrs. Miller.

"Oh, no; with this gentleman!" answered Daisy's mamma.

The courier looked for a moment at Winterbourne—the latter thought he was smiling—and then, solemnly, with a bow, "As mademoiselle pleases!" he said.

"Oh, I hoped you would make a fuss!" said Daisy. "I don't care to go now."

"I myself shall make a fuss if you don't go," said Winterbourne.

"That's all I want—a little fuss!" And the young girl began to laugh again.

"Mr. Randolph has gone to bed!" the courier announced, frigidly.

"Oh, Daisy; now we can go!" said Mrs. Miller.

Daisy turned away from Winterbourne, looking at him, smiling, and fanning herself. "Good-night," she said; "I hope you are disappointed, or disgusted, or something!"

He looked at her, taking the hand she offered him. "I am puzzled," he answered.

"Well, I hope it won't keep you awake!" she said, very smartly; and, under the escort of the privileged Eugenio, the two ladies passed towards the house.

Winterbourne stood looking after them; he was indeed puzzled. He lingered beside the lake for a quarter of an hour, turning over the mystery of the young girl's sudden familiarities and caprices. But the only very definite conclusion he came to was that he should enjoy deucedly "going off" with her somewhere.

Two days afterwards he went off with her to the Castle of Chillon. He waited for her in the large hall of the hotel, where the couriers, the servants, the foreign tourists, were lounging about and staring. It was not the place he should have chosen, but she had appointed it. She came tripping downstairs, buttoning her long gloves, squeezing her folded parasol against her pretty figure, dressed in the perfection of a soberly elegant travelling costume. Winterbourne was a man of imagination and, as our ancestors used to say, sensibility; as he looked at her dress and—one the great staircase—her little rapid, confiding step, he felt as if there were something romantic going forward. He could have believed he was going to elope with her. He passed out with her among all the idle people that were assembled there; they were all looking at her very hard; she had begun to chatter as soon as she joined him. Winterbourne's preference had been that they should be conveyed to Chillon in a carriage; but she expressed a lively wish to go in the little steamer; she declared that she had a passion for steamboats. There was always such a lovely breeze upon the water, and you saw such lots of people. The sail was not long, but Winterbourne's companion found time to say a great many things. To the young man himself their little excursion was so much of an escapade—an adventure—that, even allowing for her habitual sense of freedom, he had some expectation of seeing her regard it in the same way. But it must be confessed that, in this particular, he was disappointed. Daisy Miller was extremely animated, she was in charming spirits; but she was apparently not at all excited; she was not fluttered; she avoided neither his eyes nor those of any one else; she blushed neither when she looked at him nor when she felt that people were looking at her. People continued to look at her a great deal, and Winterbourne took much satisfaction in his pretty companion's distinguished air. He had been a little afraid that she would talk loud, laugh overmuch, and even, perhaps, desire to move about the boat a good deal. But he quite forgot his fears; he sat smiling, with his eyes upon her face, while, without moving from her place, she delivered herself of a great number of original reflections. It was the most charming garrulity he had ever heard. He had assented to the idea that she was "common"; but was she so, after all, or was he simply getting used to her commonness? Her conversation was chiefly of what metaphysicians term the objective cast; but every now and then it took a subjective turn.

"What on *earth* are you so grave about?" she suddenly demanded, fixing her agreeable eyes upon Winterbourne's.

"Am I grave?" he asked. "I had an idea I was grinning from ear to ear."

"You look as if you were taking me to a funeral. If that's a grin, your ears are very near together."

"Should you like me to dance a hornpipe on the deck?"

"Pray do, and I'll carry round your hat. It will pay the expenses of our journey."

"I never was better pleased in my life," murmured Winterbourne.

She looked at him a moment, and then burst into a little laugh. "I like to make you say those things! You're a queer mixture!"

In the castle, after they had landed, the subjective element decidedly prevailed. Daisy tripped about the vaulted chambers, rustled her skirts in the corkscrew staircases, flirted back with a pretty little cry and a shudder from the edge of the *oubliettes*, and turned a singularly well-shaped ear to everything that Winterbourne told her about the place. But he saw that she cared very little for feudal antiquities, and that the dusky traditions of Chillon made but a slight impression upon her. They had the good-fortune to have been able to walk without other companionship than that of the custodian; and Winterbourne arranged with this functionary that they should not be hurried—that they should linger and pause wherever they chose. The custodian interpreted the bargain generously—Winterbourne, on his side, had been generous—and ended by leaving them quite to themselves. Miss Miller's observations were not remarkable for logical consistency; for anything she wanted to say she was sure to find a pretext. She found a great many pretexts in the rugged embrasures of Chillon for asking Winterbourne sudden questions about himself—his family, his previous history, his tastes, his habits, his intentions—and for supplying information upon corresponding points in her own personality. Of her own tastes, habits, and intentions Miss Miller was prepared to give the most definite, and, indeed, the most favorable account.

"Well, I hope you know enough!" she said to her companion, after he had told her the history of the unhappy Bonnivard. "I never saw a man who knew so much!" The history of Bonnivard had evidently, as they say, gone into one ear and out of the other. But Daisy went on to say that she wished Winterbourne would travel with them, and "go round" with them; they might know something, in that case. "Don't you want to come and teach Randolph?" she asked. Winterbourne said that nothing could possibly please him so much, but that he had unfortunately other occupations. "Other occupations? I don't believe it!" said Miss Daisy. "What do you mean? You are not in business." The young man admitted that he was not in business; but he had engagements which, even within a day or two, would force him to go back to Geneva. "Oh, brother!" she said; "I don't believe it!" and she began to talk about something else. But a few moments later, when he was pointing out to her the pretty design of an antique fireplace, she broke out irrelevantly, "You don't mean to say you are going back to Geneva?"

"It is a melancholy fact that I shall have to return to-morrow."

"Well, Mr. Winterbourne," said Daisy, "I think you're horrid!"

"Oh, don't say such dreadful things!" said Winterbourne—"just at the last!"

"The last!" cried the young girl; "I call it the first. I have half a mind to leave you here and go straight back to the hotel alone." And for the next ten minutes she did nothing but call him horrid. Poor Winterbourne was fairly bewildered; no young lady had as yet done him the honor to be so agitated by the announcement of his movements. His companion, after this, ceased to pay any attention to the curiosities of Chillon or the beauties of the lake; she opened fire upon the mysterious charmer of Geneva, whom she appeared to have instantly taken for granted that he was hurrying back to see. How did Miss Daisy Miller know that there was a charmer in Geneva? Winterbourne, who denied the existence of such a person, was quite unable to discover; and he was divided between amazement at the rapidity of her induction and amusement at the frankness of her *persiflage*. She seemed to him, in all this, an extraordinary mixture of innocence and crudity. "Does she never allow you more than three days at a time?" asked Daisy, ironically. "Doesn't she give you a vacation in summer? There is no one so hard worked but they can get leave to go off somewhere at this season. I suppose, if you stay another day, she'll come after you in the boat. Do wait over till Friday, and I will go down to the landing to see her arrive!" Winterbourne began to think he had been wrong to feel disappointed in the temper in which the young lady had embarked. If he had missed the personal accent, the personal accent was now making its appearance. It sounded very distinctly, at last, in her telling him she would stop "teasing" him if he would promise her solemnly to come down to Rome in the winter.

"That's not a difficult promise to make," said Winterbourne. "My aunt has taken an apartment in Rome for the winter, and has already asked me to come and see her."

"I don't want you to come for your aunt," said Daisy; "I want you to come for me." And this was the only allusion that the young man was ever to hear her make to his invidious kinswoman. He declared that, at any rate, he would certainly come. After this Daisy stopped teasing. Winterbourne took a carriage, and they drove back to Vevey in the dusk. The young girl was very quiet.

In the evening Winterbourne mentioned to Mrs. Costello that he had spent the afternoon at Chillon with Miss Daisy Miller.

"The Americans—of the courier?" asked this lady.

"Ah, happily," said Winterbourne, "the courier stayed at home."

"She went with you all alone?"

"All alone."

Mrs. Costello sniffed a little at her smelling-bottle. "And that," she exclaimed, "is the young person whom you wanted me to know!"

PART II

ROME

WINTERBOURNE, WHO had returned to Geneva the day after his excursion to Chillon, went to Rome towards the end of January. His aunt had been established there for several weeks, and he had received a couple of letters from her. "Those people you were so devoted to last summer at Vevey have turned up here, courier and all," she wrote. "They seem to have made several acquaintances, but the courier continues to be the most *intime*. The young lady, however, is also very intimate with some third-rate Italians, with whom she rackets about in a way that makes much talk. Bring me that pretty novel of Cherbuliez's—*Paule Méré*—and don't come later than the 23d."

In the natural course of events, Winterbourne, on arriving in Rome, would presently have ascertained Mrs. Miller's address at the American banker's, and have gone to pay his compliments to Miss Daisy. "After what happened at Vevey, I think I may certainly call upon them," he said to Mrs. Costello.

"If, after what happens—at Vevey and everywhere—you desire to keep up the acquaintance, you are very welcome. Of course a man may know every one. Men are welcome to the privilege!"

"Pray what is it that happens—here, for instance?" Winterbourne demanded.

"The girl goes about alone with her foreigners. As to what happens further, you must apply elsewhere for information. She has picked up half a dozen of the regular Roman fortune-hunters, and she takes them about to people's houses. When she comes to a party she brings with her a gentleman with a good deal of manner and a wonderful mustache."

"And where is the mother?"

"I haven't the least idea. They are very dreadful people."

Winterbourne meditated a moment. "They are very ignorant—very innocent only. Depend upon it they are not bad."

"They are hopelessly vulgar," said Mrs. Costello. "Whether or no being hopelessly vulgar is being 'bad' is a question for the metaphysicians. They are bad enough to dislike, at any rate; and for this short life that is quite enough."

The news that Daisy Miller was surrounded by half a dozen wonderful mustaches checked Winterbourne's impulse to go straightaway to see her. He had, perhaps, not definitely flattered himself that he had made an ineffaceable impression upon her heart, but he was annoyed at hearing of a state of affairs so little in harmony with an image that had lately flitted in and out of his meditations; the image of a very pretty girl looking out of an old Roman window and asking herself urgently when Mr. Winterbourne would arrive. If, however, he determined to wait a little before reminding Miss Miller of his claims to her consideration, he went very soon to call upon two or three other friends. One of these friends was an American lady who had spent several winters at Geneva, where she had placed her children at school. She was a very accomplished woman, and she lived in the Via Gregoriana. Winterbourne found her in a little crimson drawing-room on a third floor; the room was filled with southern sunshine. He had not been there ten minutes when the servant came in, announcing "Madame Mila!" This announcement was presently followed by the entrance of little Randolph Miller, who stopped in the middle of the room and stood staring at Winterbourne. An instant later his pretty sister crossed the threshold; and then, after a considerable interval, Mrs. Miller slowly advanced.

"I know you!" said Randolph.

"I'm sure you know a great many things," exclaimed Winterbourne, taking him by the hand. "How is your education coming on?"

Daisy was exchanging greetings very prettily with her hostess; but when she heard Winterbourne's voice she quickly turned her head. "Well, I declare!" she said.

"I told you I should come, you know," Winterbourne rejoined, smiling.

"Well, I didn't believe it," said Miss Daisy.

"I am much obliged to you," laughed the young man.

"You might have come to see me!" said Daisy.

"I arrived only yesterday."

"I don't believe that!" the young girl declared.

Winterbourne turned with a protesting smile to her mother; but this lady evaded his glance, and, seating herself, fixed her eyes upon her son. "We've got a bigger place than this," said Randolph. "It's all gold on the walls."

Mrs. Miller turned uneasily in her chair. "I told you if I were going to bring you, you would say something!" she murmured.

"I told *you!*" Randolph exclaimed. "I tell *you*, sir!" he added, jocosely, giving Winterbourne a thump on the knee. "It *is* bigger, too!"

Daisy had entered upon a lively conversation with her hostess, and Winterbourne judged it becoming to address a few words to her mother. "I hope you have been well since we parted at Vevey," he said.

Mrs. Miller now certainly looked at him—at his chin. "Not very well, sir," she answered.

"She's got the dyspepsia," said Randolph. "I've got it, too. Father's got it. I've got it most!"

This announcement, instead of embarrassing Mrs. Miller, seemed to relieve her. "I suffer from the liver," she said. "I think it's this climate; it's less bracing than Schenectady, especially in the winter season. I don't know whether you know we reside at Schenectady. I was saying to Daisy that I certainly hadn't found any one like Dr. Davis, and I didn't believe I should. Oh, at Schenectady he stands first; they think everything of him. He has so much to do, and yet there was nothing he wouldn't do for me. He said he never saw anything like my dyspepsia, but he was bound to cure it. I'm sure there was nothing he wouldn't try. He was just going to try something new when we came off. Mr. Miller wanted Daisy to see Europe for herself. But I wrote to Mr. Miller that it seems as if I couldn't get on without Dr. Davis. At Schenectady he stands at the very top; and there's a great deal of sickness there, too. It affects my sleep."

Winterbourne had a good deal of pathological gossip with Dr. Davis's patient, during which Daisy chattered unremittingly to her own companion. The young man asked Mrs. Miller how she was pleased with Rome. "Well, I must say I am disappointed," she answered. "We had heard so much about it; I suppose we had heard too much. But we couldn't help that. We had been led to expect something different."

"Ah, wait a little, and you will become very fond of it," said Winterbourne.

"I hate it worse and worse every day!" cried Randolph.

"You are like the infant Hannibal," said Winterbourne.

"No, I ain't!" Randolph declared, at a venture.

"You are not much like an infant," said his mother. "But we have seen places," she resumed, "that I should put a long way before Rome." And in reply to Winterbourne's interrogation, "There's Zürich," she concluded, "I think Zürich is lovely; and we hadn't heard half so much about it."

"The best place we've seen is the City of Richmond!" said Randolph.

"He means the ship," his mother explained. "We crossed in that ship. Randolph had a good time on the *City of Richmond*."

"It's the best place I've seen," the child repeated. "Only it was turned the wrong way."

"Well, we've got to turn the right way some time," said Mrs. Miller, with a little laugh. Winterbourne expressed the hope that her daughter at least found some gratification in Rome, and she declared that Daisy was quite carried away. It's on account of the society—the society's splendid. She goes round everywhere; she has made a great number of acquaintances. Of course she goes round more than I do. I must say they have been very sociable; they have taken her right in. And then she knows a great many gentlemen. Oh, she think's there's nothing like Rome. Of course, it's a great deal pleasanter for a young lady if she knows plenty of gentlemen."

By this time Daisy had turned her attention again to Winterbourne. "I've been telling Mrs. Walker how mean you were!" the young girl announced.

"And what is the evidence you have offered?" asked Winterbourne, rather annoyed at Miss Miller's want of appreciation of the zeal of an admirer who on his way down to Rome had stopped neither at Bologna nor at Florence, simply because of a certain sentimental impatience. He remembered that a cynical compatriot had once told him that American women—the pretty ones, and this gave a largeness to the axiom—were at once the most exacting in the world and the least endowed with a sense of indebtedness.

"Why, you were awfully mean at Vevey," said Daisy. "You wouldn't do anything. You wouldn't stay there when I asked you."

"My dearest young lady," cried Winterbourne, with eloquence, "have I come all the way to Rome to encounter your reproaches?"

"Just hear him say that!" said Daisy to her hostess, giving a twist to a bow on this lady's dress. "Did you ever hear anything so quaint?"

"So quaint, my dear?" murmured Mrs. Walker, in a tone of a partisan of Winterbourne.

"Well, I don't know," said Daisy, fingering Mrs. Walker's ribbons. "Mrs. Walker, I want to tell you something."

"Mother-r," interposed Randolph, with his rough ends to his words, "I tell you you've got to go. Eugenio 'll raise—something!"

"I'm not afraid of Eugenio," said Daisy, with a toss of her head. "Look here, Mrs. Walker," she went on, "you know I'm coming to your party."

"I am delighted to hear it."

"I've got a lovely dress!"

"I am very sure of that."

"But I want to ask a favor—permission to bring a friend."

"I shall be happy to see any of your friends," said Mrs. Walker, turning with a smile to Mrs. Miller.

"Oh, they are not my friends," answered Daisy's mamma, smiling shyly, in her own fashion. "I never spoke to them."

"It's an intimate friend of mine—Mr. Giovanelli," said Daisy, without a tremor in her clear little voice, or a shadow on her brilliant little face.

Mrs. Walker was silent a moment; she gave a rapid glance at Winterbourne. "I shall be glad to see Mr. Giovanelli," she then said.

"He's an Italian," Daisy pursued, with the prettiest serenity. "He's a great friend of mine; he's the handsomest man in the world—except Mr. Winterbourne! He knows plenty of Italians, but he wants to know some Americans. He thinks ever so much of Americans. He's tremendously clever. He's perfectly lovely!"

It was settled that this brilliant personage should be brought to Mrs. Walker's party, and then Mrs. Miller prepared to take her leave. "I guess we'll go back to the hotel," she said.

"You may go back to the hotel, mother, but I'm going to take a walk," said Daisy.

"She's going to walk with Mr. Giovanelli," Randolph proclaimed.

"I am going to the Pincio," said Daisy, smiling.

"Alone, my dear—at this hour?" Mrs. Walker asked. The afternoon was drawing to a close—it was the hour for the throng of carriages and of contemplative pedestrians. "I don't think it's safe, my dear," said Mrs. Walker.

"Neither do I," subjoined Mrs. Miller. "You'll get the fever, as sure as you live. Remember what Dr. Davis told you!"

"Give her some medicine before she goes," said Randolph.

The company had risen to its feet; Daisy, still showing her pretty teeth, bent over and kissed her hostess. "Mrs. Walker, you are perfect," she said. "I'm not going alone; I am going to meet a friend."

"Your friend won't keep you from getting the fever," Mrs. Miller observed.

"Is it Mr. Giovanelli?" asked the hostess.

Winterbourne was watching the young girl; at his question his attention quickened. She stood there smiling and smoothing her bonnet ribbons; she glanced at Winterbourne. Then, while she glanced and smiled, she answered, without a shade of hesitation, "Mr. Giovanelli—the beautiful Giovanelli."

"My dear young friend," said Mrs. Walker, taking her hand, pleadingly, "don't walk off to the Pincio at this unhealthy hour to meet a beautiful Italian."

"Well, he speaks English," said Mrs. Miller.

"Gracious me!" Daisy exclaimed, "I don't want to do anything improper. There's an easy way to settle it." She continued to glance at Winterbourne. "The Pincio is only a hundred yards distant; and

if Mr. Winterbourne were as polite as he pretends, he would offer
to walk with me!"

Winterbourne's politeness hastened to affirm itself, and the young
girl gave him gracious leave to accompany her. They passed
down-stairs before her mother, and at the door Winterbourne perceived Mrs. Miller's carriage drawn up, with the ornamental courier,
whose acquaintance he had made at Vevey, seated within. "Good-
bye, Eugenio!" cried Daisy; "I'm going to take a walk." The distance from the Via Gregoriana to the beautiful garden at the other
end of the Pincian Hill is, in fact, rapidly traversed. As the day was
splendid, however, and the concourse of vehicles, walkers, and
loungers numerous, the young Americans found their progress much
delayed. This fact was highly agreeable to Winterbourne, in spite
of his consciousness of his singular situation. The slow-moving, idly-
gazing Roman crowd bestowed much attention upon the extremely
pretty young foreign lady who was passing through it upon his arm;
and he wondered what on earth had been in Daisy's mind when she
proposed to expose herself, unattended, to its appreciation. His own
mission, to her sense, apparently, was to consign her to the hands
of Mr. Giovanelli; but Winterbourne, at once annoyed and gratified, resolved that he would do no such thing.

"Why haven't you been to see me?" asked Daisy. "You can't get
out of that."

"I have had the honor of telling you that I have only just stepped
out of the train."

"You must have stayed in the train a good while after it stopped!"
cried the young girl, with her little laugh. "I suppose you were
asleep. You have had time to go to see Mrs. Walker."

"I knew Mrs. Walker——" Winterbourne began to explain.

"I know where you knew her. You knew her at Geneva. She
told me so. Well, you knew me at Vevey. That's just as good. So
you ought to have come." She asked him no other question than
this; she began to prattle about her own affairs. "We've got splendid
rooms at the hotel; Eugenio says they're the best rooms in Rome. We
are going to stay all winter, if we don't die of the fever; and I guess
we'll stay then. It's a great deal nicer than I thought; I thought it
would be fearfully quiet; I was sure it would be awfully poky. I
was sure we should be going round all the time with one of those
dreadful old men that explain about the pictures and things. But
we only had about a week of that, and now I'm enjoying myself.
I know ever so many people, and they are all so charming. The

society's extremely select. There are all kinds—English and Germans and Italians. I think I like the English best. I like their style of conversation. But there are some lovely Americans. I never saw anything so hospitable. There's something or other every day. There's not much dancing; but I must say I never thought dancing was everything. I was always fond of conversation. I guess I shall have plenty at Mrs. Walker's, her rooms are so small." When they had passed the gate of the Pincian Gardens, Miss Miller began to wonder where Mr. Giovanelli might be. "We had better go straight to that place in front," she said, "where you look at the view."

"I certainly shall not help you to find him," Winterbourne declared.

"They I shall find him without you," said Miss Daisy.

"You certainly won't leave me!" cried Winterbourne.

She burst into her little laugh. "Are you afraid you'll get lost—or run over? But there's Giovanelli, leaning against that tree. He's staring at the women in the carriages; did you ever see anything so cool?"

Winterbourne perceived at some distance a little man standing with folded arms nursing his cane. He had a handsome face, an artfully poised hat, a glass in one eye, and a nosegay in his buttonhole. Winterbourne looked at him a moment, and then said, "Do you mean to speak to that man?"

"Do I mean to speak to him? Why, you don't suppose I mean to communicate by signs?"

"Pray understand, then," said Winterbourne, "that I intend to remain with you."

Daisy stopped and looked at him, without a sign of troubled consciousness in her face; with nothing but the presence of her charming eyes and her happy dimples. "Well, she's a cool one!" thought the young man.

"I don't like the way you say that," said Daisy. "It's too imperious."

"I beg your pardon if I say it wrong. The main point is to give you an idea of my meaning."

The young girl looked at him more gravely, but with eyes that were prettier than ever. "I have never allowed a gentleman to dictate to me, or to interfere with anything I do."

"I think you have made a mistake," said Winterbourne. "You should sometimes listen to a gentleman—the right one."

Daisy began to laugh again. "I do nothing but listen to gentlemen!" she exclaimed. "Tell me if Mr. Giovanelli is the right one."

The gentleman with the nosegay in his bosom had now perceived our two friends, and was approaching the young girl with obsequious rapidity. He bowed to Winterbourne as well as to the latter's companion; he had a brilliant smile, an intelligent eye; Winterbourne thought him not a bad-looking fellow. But he nevertheless said to Daisy, "No, he's not the right one."

Daisy evidently had a natural talent for performing introductions; she mentioned the name of each of her companions to the other. She strolled along with one of them on each side of her; Mr. Giovanelli, who spoke English very cleverly—Winterbourne afterwards learned that he had practised the idiom upon a great many American heiresses—addressed to her a great deal of very polite nonsense; he was extremely urbane, and the young American, who said nothing, reflected upon that profundity of Italian cleverness which enables people to appear more gracious in proportion as they are more acutely disappointed. Giovanelli, of course, had counted upon something more intimate; he had not bargained for a party of three. But he kept his temper in a manner which suggested far-stretching intentions. Winterbourne flattered himself that he had taken his measure. "He is not a gentleman," said the young American; "he is only a clever imitation of one. He is a music-master, or a penny-a-liner, or a third-rate artist. D—n his good looks!" Mr. Giovanelli had certainly a very pretty face; but Winterbourne felt a superior indignation at his own lovely fellow-country woman's not knowing the difference between a spurious gentleman and a real one. Giovanelli chattered and jested, and made himself wonderfully agreeable. It was true that, if he was an imitation, the imitation was brilliant. "Nevertheless," Winterbourne said to himself, "a nice girl ought to know!" And then he came back to the question whether this was, in fact, a nice girl. Would a nice girl, even allowing for her being a little American flirt, make a rendezvous with a presumably low-lived foreigner? The rendezvous in this case, indeed, had been in broad daylight, and in the most crowded corner of Rome; but was it not impossible to regard the choice of these circumstances as a proof of extreme cynicism? Singular though it may seem, Winterbourne was vexed that the young girl, in joining her *amoroso*, should not appear more impatient of his inclination. It was impossible to regard her as a perfectly well-conducted young lady; she was wanting in a certain indispensable delicacy. It would therefore simplify matters greatly to be able to treat her as the object of one of those sentiments which are called by romancers "lawless passions." That she should seem to wish to get rid of him would help him to think more lightly of her, and to be able to think more lightly of her would make her much less perplexing. But Daisy, on this occasion, continued to present herself as an inscrutable combination of audacity and innocence.

She had been walking some quarter of an hour, attended by her two cavaliers, and responding in a tone of very childish gayety, as it seemed to Winterbourne, to the pretty speeches of Mr. Giovanelli, when a carriage that had detached itself from the revolving train drew up beside the path. At the same moment Winterbourne perceived that his friend Mrs. Walker—the lady whose house he had lately left—was seated in the vehicle, and was beckoning to him. Leaving Miss Miller's side, he hastened to obey her summons. Mrs. Walker was flushed; she wore an excited air. "It is really too dreadful," she said. "That girl must not do this sort of thing. She must not walk here with you two men. Fifty people have noticed her."

Winterbourne raised his eyebrows. "I think it's a pity to make too much fuss about it."

"It's a pity to let the girl ruin herself!"

"She is very innocent," said Winterbourne.

"She's very crazy!" cried Mrs. Walker. "Did you ever see anything so imbecile as her mother? After you had all left me just now I could not sit still for thinking of it. It seemed too pitiful not even to attempt to save her. I ordered the carriage and put on my bonnet, and came here as quickly as possible. Thank Heaven I have found you!"

"What do you propose to do with us?" asked Winterbourne, smiling.

"To ask her to get in, to drive her about here for half an hour, so that the world may see that she is not running absolutely wild, and then to take her safely home."

"I don't think it's a very happy thought," said Winterbourne; "but you can try."

Mrs. Walker tried. The young man went in pursuit of Miss Miller, who had simply nodded and smiled at his interlocutor in the carriage, and had gone her way with her companion. Daisy, on learning that Mrs. Walker wished to speak to her, retraced her steps with a perfect good grace and with Mr. Giovanelli at her side. She declared that she was delighted to have a chance to present this gentleman to Mrs. Walker. She immediately achieved the introduction, and declared that she had never in her life seen anything so lovely as Mrs. Walker's carriage-rug.

"I am glad you admire it," said this lady, smiling sweetly. "Will you get in and let me put it over you?"

"Oh no, thank you," said Daisy. "I shall admire it much more as I see you driving round with it."

"Do you get in and drive with me!" said Mrs. Walker.

"That would be charming, but it's so enchanting just as I am" and Daisy gave a brilliant glance at the gentlemen on either side of her.

"It may be enchanting, dear child, but it is not the custom here," urged Mrs. Walker, leaning forward in her victoria, with her hands devoutly clasped.

"Well, it ought to be, then!" said Daisy. "If I didn't walk I should expire."

"You should walk with your mother, dear," cried the lady from Geneva, losing patience.

"With my mother, dear!" exclaimed the young girl. Winterbourne saw that she scented interference. "My mother never walked ten steps in her life. And then, you know," she added, with a laugh, "I am more than five years old."

"You are old enough to be more reasonable. You are old enough, dear Miss Miller, to be talked about."

Daisy looked at Mrs. Walker, smiling intensely. "Talked about? What do you mean?"

"Come into my carriage, and I will tell you."

Daisy turned her quickened glance again from one of the gentlemen beside her to the other. Mr. Giovanelli was bowing to and fro, rubbing down his gloves and laughing very agreeably; Winterbourne thought it a most unpleasant scene. "I don't think I want to know what you mean," said Daisy, presently. "I don't think I should like it."

Winterbourne wished that Mrs. Walker would tuck in her carriage-rug and drive away; but this lady did not enjoy being defied, as she afterwards told him. "Should you prefer being thought a very reckless girl?" she demanded.

"Gracious?" exclaimed Daisy. She looked again at Mr. Giovanelli, then she turned to Winterbourne. There was a little pink flush in her cheek; she was tremendously pretty. "Does Mr. Winterbourne think," she added slowly, smiling, throwing back her head and glancing at him from head to foot, "that, to save my reputation, I ought to get into the carriage?"

Winterbourne colored; for an instant he hesitated greatly. It seemed so strange to hear her speak that way of her "reputation." But he himself, in fact, must speak in accordance with gallantry. The finest gallantry here was simply to tell her the truth, and the truth for Winterbourne—as the few indications I have been able to give have made him known to the reader—was that Daisy Miller should take Mrs. Walker's advice. He looked at her exquisite prettiness, and then said, very gently, "I think you should get into the carriage."

Daisy gave a violent laugh. "I never heard anything so stiff! If this is improper, Mrs. Walker," she pursued, "then I am all improper, and you must give me up. Good-bye; I hope you'll have a lovely ride!" and, with Mr. Giovanelli, who made a triumphantly obsequious salute, she turned away.

Mrs. Walker sat looking after her, and there were tears in Mrs. Walker's eyes. "Get in here, sir," she said to Winterbourne, indicating the place beside her. The young man answered that he felt bound to accompany Miss Miller; whereupon Mrs. Walker declared that if he refused her this favor she would never speak to him again. She was evidently in earnest. Winterbourne overtook Daisy and her companion, and, offering the young girl his hand, told her that Mrs. Walker had made an imperious claim upon his society. He expected that in answer she would say something rather free, something to commit herself still further to that "recklessness" from which Mrs. Walker had so charitably endeavored to dissuade her. But she only shook his hand, hardly looking at him; while Mr. Giovanelli bade him farewell with a too emphatic flourish of the hat.

Winterbourne was not in the best possible humor as he took his seat in Mrs. Walker's victoria. "That was not clever of you," he said, candidly, while the vehicle mingled again with the throng of carriages.

"In such a case," his companion answered, "I don't wish to be clever; I wish to be *earnest!*"

"Well, your earnestness has only offended her and put her off."

"It has happened very well," said Mrs. Walker. "If she is so perfectly determined to compromise herself, the sooner one knows it the better; one can act accordingly."

"I suspect she meant no harm," Winterbourne rejoined.

"So I thought a month ago. But she has been going too far."

"What has she been doing?"

"Everything that is not done here. Flirting with any man she could pick up; sitting in corners with mysterious Italians; dancing all the evening with the same partners; receiving visits at eleven o'clock at night. Her mother goes away when visitors come."

"But her brother," said Winterbourne, laughing, "sits up till midnight."

"He must be edified by what he sees. I'm told that at their hotel every one is talking about her, and that a smile goes round among all the servants when a gentleman comes and asks for Miss Miller."

"The servants be hanged!" said Winterbourne, angrily. "The poor girl's only fault," he presently added, "is that she is very uncultivated."

"She is naturally indelicate," Mrs. Walker declared. "Take that example this morning. How long had you known her at Vevey?"

"A couple of days."

"Fancy, then, her making it a personal matter that you should have left the place!"

Winterbourne was silent for some moments; then he said, "I suspect, Mrs. Walker, that you and I have lived too long at Geneva!" And he added a request that she should inform him with what particular design she had made him enter her carriage.

"I wished to beg you to cease your relations with Miss Miller—not to flirt with her—to give her no further opportunity to expose herself—to let her alone, in short."

"I'm afraid I can't do that," said Winterbourne. "I like her extremely."

"All the more reason that you shouldn't help her to make a scandal."

"There shall be nothing scandalous in my attentions to her."

"There certainly will be in the way she takes them. But I have said what I had on my conscience," Mrs. Walker pursued. "If you wish to rejoin the young lady I will put you down. Here, by-the-way, you have a chance."

The carriage was traversing that part of the Pincian Garden that overhangs the wall of Rome and overlooks the beautiful Villa Borghese. It is bordered by a large parapet, near which there are several seats. One of the seats at a distance was occupied by a gentleman and a lady, towards whom Mrs. Walker gave a toss of her head. At the same moment these persons rose and walked towards the parapet. Winterbourne had asked the coachman to stop; he now descended from the carriage. His companion looked at him a moment in silence; then, while he raised his hat, she drove majestically away. Winterbourne stood there; he had turned his eyes towards Daisy and her cavalier. They evidently saw no one; they were too deeply occupied with each other. When they reached the low garden-wall they stood a moment looking off at the great flat-topped pine-clusters of the Villa Borghese; then Giovanelli seated himself familiarly upon the broad ledge of the wall. The western sun in the opposite sky sent out a brilliant shaft through a couple of cloud-bars, whereupon Daisy's companion took her parasol out of her hands and opened it. She came a little nearer, and he held the parasol over her; then, still holding it, he let it rest upon her shoulder, so that both of their heads were hidden from Winterbourne. This young man lingered a moment, then he began to walk. But he walked—not towards the couple with the parasol— towards the residence of his aunt, Mrs. Costello.

He flattered himself on the following day that there was no smiling among the servants when he, at least, asked for Mrs. Miller at her hotel. This lady and her daughter, however, were not at home; and on the next day after, repeating his visit, Winterbourne again had the misfortune not to find them. Mrs. Walker's party took place on the evening of the third day, and, in spite of the frigidity of his last interview with the hostess, Winterbourne was among the guests. Mrs. Walker was one of those American ladies who, while residing abroad, make a point, in their own phrase, of studying European society; and she had on this occasion collected several specimens of her diversely-born fellow-mortals to serve, as it were, as text-books. When Winterbourne arrived, Daisy Miller was not there, but in a few moments he saw her mother come in alone, very shyly and ruefully. Mrs. Miller's hair above her exposed-looking temples was more frizzled than ever. As she approached Mrs. Walker, Winterbourne also drew near.

"You see I've come all alone," said poor Mrs. Miller. "I'm so frightened I don't know what to do. It's the first time I've ever been to a party alone, especially in this country. I wanted to bring Randolph, or Eugenio, or some one, but Daisy just pushed me off by myself. I ain't used to going round alone."

"And does not your daughter intend to favor us with her society?" demanded Mrs. Walker, impressively.

"Well, Daisy's all dressed," said Mrs. Miller, with that accent of the dispassionate, if not of the philosophic, historian with which she always recorded the current incidents of her daughter's career. "She got dressed on purpose before dinner. But she's got a friend of hers there; that gentleman—the Italian—that she wanted to bring. They've got going at the piano; it seems as if they couldn't leave off. Mr. Giovanelli sings splendidly. But I guess they'll come before very long," concluded Mrs. Miller, hopefully.

"I'm sorry she should come in that way," said Mrs. Walker.

"Well, I told her that there was no use in her getting dressed before dinner if she was going to wait three hours," responded Daisy's mamma. "I didn't see the use of her putting on such a dress as that to sit round with Mr. Giovanelli."

"This is most horrible!" said Mrs. Walker, turning away and addressing herself to Winterbourne. "*Elle s'affiche.* It's her revenge for my having ventured to remonstrate with her. When she comes I shall not speak to her."

Daisy came after eleven o'clock; but she was not, on such an occasion, a young lady to wait to be spoken to. She rustled forward in radiant loveliness, smiling and chattering, carrying a large bouquet, and attended by Mr. Giovanelli. Every one stopped talking, and turned and looked at her. She came straight to Mrs. Walker. "I'm afraid you thought I never was coming, so I sent mother off to tell you. I wanted to make Mr. Giovanelli practise some things before he came; you know he sings beautifully, and I want you to ask him to sing. This is Mr. Giovanelli; you know I introduced him to you; he's got the most lovely voice, and he knows the most charming set of songs. I made him go over them this evening on purpose; we had the greatest time at the hotel." Of all this Daisy delivered herself with the sweetest, brightest audibleness, looking now at her hostess and now round the room, while she gave a series of little pats round her shoulders to the edges of her dress. "Is there any one I know?" she asked.

"I think every one knows you!" said Mrs. Walker, pregnantly, and she gave a very cursory greeting to Mr. Giovanelli. This gentleman bore himself gallantly. He smiled and bowed, and showed his white teeth; he curled his mustaches and rolled his eyes, and performed all the proper functions of a handsome Italian at an evening party. He sang very prettily half a dozen songs, though Mrs. Walker afterwards declared that she had been quite unable to find out who asked him. It was apparently not Daisy who had given him his orders. Daisy sat at a distance from the piano; and though she had publicly, as it were, professed a high admiration for his singing, talked, not inaudibly, while it was going on.

"It's a pity these rooms are so small; we can't dance," she said to Winterbourne, as if she had seen him five minutes before.

"I am not sorry we can't dance," Winterbourne answered; "I don't dance."

"Of course you don't dance; you're too stiff," said Miss Daisy. "I hope you enjoyed your drive with Mrs. Walker!"

"No, I didn't enjoy it; I preferred walking with you."

"We paired off; that was much better," said Daisy. "But did you ever hear anything so cool as Mrs. Walker's wanting me to get into her carriage and drop poor Mr. Giovanelli, and under the pretext that it was proper? People have different ideas! It would have been most unkind; he had been talking about that walk for ten days."

"He should not have talked about it at all," said Winterbourne; "he would never have proposed to a young lady of this country to walk about the streets with him."

"About the streets?" cried Daisy, with her pretty stare. "Where, then, would he have proposed to her to walk? The Pincio is not the streets, either; and I, thank goodness, am not a young lady of this country. The young ladies of this country have a dreadfully poky time of it, so far as I can learn; I don't see why I should change my habits for *them*."

"I am afraid your habits are those of a flirt," said Winterbourne, gravely.

"Of course they are," she cried, giving him her little smiling stare again. "I'm a fearful, frightful flirt! Did you ever hear of a nice girl that was not? But I suppose you will tell me now that I am not a nice girl."

"You're a very nice girl; but I wish you would flirt with me, and me only," said Winterbourne.

"Ah! thank you—thank you very much; you are the last man I should think of flirting with. As I have had the pleasure of informing you, you are too stiff."

"You say that too often," said Winterbourne.

Daisy gave a delighted laugh. "If I could have the sweet hope of making you angry, I should say it again."

"Don't do that; when I am angry I'm stiffer than ever. But if you won't flirt with me, do cease, at least, to flirt with your friend at the piano; they don't understand that sort of thing here."

"I thought they understood nothing else!" exclaimed Daisy.

"Not in young unmarried women."

"It seems to me much more proper in young unmarried women than in old married ones," Daisy declared.

"Well," said Winterbourne, "when you deal with natives you must go by the custom of the place. Flirting is a purely American custom; it doesn't exist here. So when you show yourself in public with Mr. Giovanelli, and without your mother——"

"Gracious! poor mother!" interposed Daisy.

"Though you may be flirting, Mr. Giovanelli is not; he means something else."

"He isn't preaching, at any rate," said Daisy, with vivacity. "And if you want very much to know, we are neither of us flirting; we are too good friends for that; we are very intimate friends."

"Ah!" rejoined Winterbourne, "if you are in love with each other, it is another affair."

She had allowed him up to this point to talk so frankly that he had no expectation of shocking her by this ejaculation; but she immediately got up, blushing visibly, and leaving him to exclaim mentally that little American flirts were the queerest creatures in the world. "Mr. Giovanelli, at least," she said, giving her interlocutor a single glance, "never says such very disagreeable things to me."

Winterbourne was bewildered; he stood staring. Mr. Giovanelli had finished singing. He left the piano and came over to Daisy. "Won't you come into the other room and have some tea?" he asked, bending before her with his ornamental smile.

Daisy turned to Winterbourne, beginning to smile again. He was still more perplexed, for this inconsequent smile made nothing clear, though it seemed to prove, indeed, that she had a sweetness and softness that reverted instinctively to the pardon of offences. "It has never occurred to Mr. Winterbourne to offer me any tea," she said, with her little tormenting manner.

"I have offered you advice," Winterbourne rejoined.

"I prefer weak tea!" cried Daisy, and she went off with the brilliant Giovanelli. She sat with him in the adjoining room, in the embrasure of the window, for the rest of the evening. There was an interesting performance at the piano, but neither of these young people gave heed to it. When Daisy came to take leave of Mrs. Walker, this lady conscientiously repaired the weakness of which she had been guilty at the moment of the young girl's arrival. She turned her back straight upon Miss Miller, and left her to depart with what grace she might. Winterbourne was standing near the door; he saw it all. Daisy turned very pale, and looked at her mother; but Mrs. Miller was humbly unconscious of any violation of the usual social forms. She appeared, indeed, to have felt an incongruous impulse to draw attention to her own striking observance of them. "Good-night, Mrs. Walker," she said; "we've had a beautiful evening. You see, if I let Daisy come to parties without me, I don't want her to go away without me." Daisy turned away, looking with a pale, grave face at the circle near the door; Winterbourne saw that, for the first moment, she was too much shocked and puzzled even for indignation. He on his side was greatly touched.

"That was very cruel," he said to Mrs. Walker.

"She never enters my drawing-room again!" replied his hostess.

Since Winterbourne was not to meet her in Mrs. Walker's drawing-room, he went as often as possible to Mrs. Miller's hotel. The ladies were rarely at home; but when he found them the devoted Giovanelli was always present. Very often the brilliant little Roman was in the drawing-room with Daisy alone, Mrs. Miller being apparently constantly of the opinion that discretion is the better part of surveillance. Winterbourne noted, at first with surprise, that Daisy on these occasions was never embarrassed or annoyed by his own entrance; but he very presently began to feel that she had no more surprises for him; the unexpected in her behavior was the only thing to expect. She showed no displeasure at her tête-à-tête with Giovanelli being interrupted, she could chatter as freshly and freely with two gentlemen as with one; there was always, in her conversation, the same odd mixture of audacity and puerility. Winterbourne remarked to himself that if she was seriously interested in Giovanelli, it was very singular that she should not take more trouble to preserve the sanctity of their interviews; and he liked her the more for her innocent-looking indifference and her apparently inexhaustible good-humor. He could hardly have said why, but she seemed to him a girl who would never be jealous. At the risk of exciting a somewhat derisive smile on the reader's part, I may affirm that with regard to the women who had hitherto interested him, it very often seemed to Winterbourne among the possibilities that, given certain contingencies, he should be afraid—literally afraid—of these ladies; he had a pleasant sense that he should never be afraid of Daisy Miller. It must be added that this sentiment was not altogether flattering to Daisy; it was part of his conviction, or rather of his apprehension, that she would prove a very light young person.

But she was evidently very much interested in Giovanelli. She looked at him whenever he spoke; she was perpetually telling him to do this and to do that; she was constantly "chaffing" and abusing him. She appeared completely to have forgotten that Winterbourne had said anything to displease her at Mrs. Walker's little party. One Sunday afternoon, having gone to St. Peter's with his aunt, Winterbourne perceived Daisy strolling about the great church in company with the inevitable Giovanelli. Presently he pointed out the young girl and her cavalier to Mrs. Costello. This lady looked at them a moment through her eye-glass, and then she said,

"That's what makes you so pensive in these days, eh?"

"I had not the least idea I was pensive," said the young man.

"You are very much preoccupied; you are thinking of something."

"And what is it," he asked, "that you accuse me of thinking of?"

"Of that young lady's—Miss Baker's, Miss Chandler's—what's her name?—Miss Miller's intrigue with that little barber's block."

"Do you call it an intrigue," Winterbourne asked—"an affair that goes on with such peculiar publicity?"

"That's their folly," said Mrs. Costello; "it's not their merit."

"No," rejoined Winterbourne, with something of that pensiveness to which his aunt had alluded. "I don't believe that there is anything to be called an intrigue."

"I have heard a dozen people speak of it; they say she is quite carried away by him."

"They are certainly very intimate," said Winterbourne.

Mrs. Costello inspected the young couple again with her optical instrument. "He is very handsome. One easily sees how it is. She thinks him the most elegant man in the world—the finest gentleman. She has never seen anything like him; he is better, even, than the courier. It was the courier, probably, who introduced him; and if he succeeds in marrying the young lady, the courier will come in for a magnificent commission."

"I don't believe she thinks of marrying him," said Winterbourne, "and I don't believe he hopes to marry her."

"You may be very sure she thinks of nothing. She goes on from day to day, from hour to hour, as they did in the Golden Age. I can imagine nothing more vulgar. And at the same time," added Mrs. Costello, "depend upon it that she may tell you any moment that she is 'engaged.'"

"I think that is more than Giovanelli expects," said Winterbourne.

"Who is Giovanelli?"

"The little Italian. I have asked questions about him, and learned something. He is apparently a perfectly respectable little man. I believe he is, in a small way, a *cavaliere avvocato*. But he doesn't move in what are called the first circles. I think it is really not absolutely impossible that the courier introduced him. He is evidently immensely charmed with Miss Miller. If she thinks him the finest gentleman in the world, he, on his side, has never found himself in personal contact with such splendor, such opulence, such expensiveness, as this young lady's. And then she must seem to him wonderfully pretty and interesting. I rather doubt that he dreams of marrying her. That must appear to him too impossible a piece of luck. He has nothing but his handsome face to offer, and there is a substantial Mr. Miller in that mysterious land of dollars. Giovanelli knows that he hasn't a title to offer. If he were only a count or a *marchese!* He must wonder at his luck, at the way they have taken him up."

"He accounts for it by his handsome face, and thinks Miss Miller a young lady *qui se passe ses fantaisies!*" said Mrs. Costello.

"It is very true," Winterbourne pursued, "that Daisy and her mamma have not yet risen to that stage of—what shall I call it?—of culture, at which the idea of catching a count or a *marchese* begins. I believe that they are intellectually incapable of that conception."

"Ah! but the *avvocato* can't believe it," said Mrs. Costello.

Of the observation excited by Daisy's "intrigue," Winterbourne gathered that day at St. Peter's sufficent evidence. A dozen of the American colonists in Rome came to talk with Mrs. Costello, who sat on a little portable stool at the base of one of the great pilasters. The vesper service was going forward in splendid chants and organ-tones in the adjacent choir, and meanwhile, between Mrs. Costello and her friends, there was a great deal said about poor little Miss Miller's going really "too far." Winterbourne was not pleased with what he heard; but when, coming out upon the great steps of the church, he saw Daisy, who had emerged before him, get into an open cab with her accomplice and roll away through the cynical streets of Rome, he could not deny to himself that she was going very far indeed. He felt very sorry for her—not exactly that he believed that she had completely lost her head, but because it was painful to hear so much that was pretty and undefended and natural assigned to a vulgar place among the categories of disorder. He made an attempt after this to give a hint to Mrs. Miller. He met one day in the Corso a friend, a tourist like himself, who had just come out of the Doria Palace, where he had been walking through the beautiful gallery. His friend talked for a moment about the superb portrait of Innocent X., by Velasquez, which hangs in one of the cabinets of the palace, and then said, "And in the same cabinet, by-the-way, I had the pleasure of contemplating a picture of a different kind—that pretty American girl whom you pointed out to me last week." In answer to Winterbourne's inquiries, his friend narrated that the pretty American girl—prettier than ever —was seated with a companion in the secluded nook in which the great papal portrait was enshrined.

"Who was her companion?" asked Winterbourne.

"A little Italian with a bouquet in his button-hole. The girl is delightfully pretty; but I thought I understood from you the other day that she was a young lady *du meilleur monde.*"

"So she is!" answered Winterbourne; and having assured himself that his informant had seen Daisy and her companion but five minutes before, he jumped into a cab and went to call on Mrs. Miller. She was at home; but she apologized to him for receiving him in Daisy's absence.

"She's gone out somewhere with Mr. Giovanelli," said Mrs. Miller. "She's always going round with Mr. Giovanelli."

"I have noticed that they are very intimate," Winterbourne observed.

"Oh, it seems as if they couldn't live without each other!" said Mrs. Miller. "Well, he's a real gentleman, anyhow. I keep telling Daisy she's engaged!"

"And what does Daisy say?"

"Oh, she says she isn't engaged. But she might as well be!" this impartial parent resumed; "she goes on as if she was. But I've made Mr. Giovanelli promise to tell me, if *she* doesn't. I should want to write to Mr. Miller about it—shouldn't you?"

Winterbourne replied that he certainly should; and the state of mind of Daisy's mamma struck him as so unprecedented in the annals of parental vigilance that he gave up as utterly irrelevant the attempt to place her upon her guard.

After this Daisy was never at home, and Winterbourne ceased to meet her at the houses of their common acquaintances, because, as he perceived, these shrewd people had quite made up their minds that she was going too far. They ceased to invite her; and they intimated that they desired to express to observant Europeans the great truth that, though Miss Daisy Miller was a young American lady, her behavior was not representative—was regarded by her compatriots as abnormal. Winterbourne wondered how she felt about all the cold shoulders that were turned towards her, and sometimes it annoyed him to suspect that she did not feel at all. He said to himself that she was too light and childish, too uncultivated and unreasoning, too provincial, to have reflected upon her ostracism, or even to have perceived it. Then at other moments he believed that she carried about in her elegant and irresponsible little organism a defiant, passionate, perfectly observant consciousness of the impression she produced. He asked himself whether Daisy's defiance came from the consciousness of innocence, or from her being, essentially, a young person of the reckless class. It must be admitted that holding one's self to a belief in Daisy's "innocence" came to seem to Winterbourne more and more a matter of finespun gallantry. As I have already had occasion to relate, he was angry at finding himself reduced to chopping logic about this young lady; he was vexed at his want of instinctive certitude as to how far her eccentricities were generic, national, and how far they were personal. From either view of them he had somehow missed her, and now it was too late. She was "carried away" by Mr. Giovanelli.

A few days after his brief interview with her mother, he encountered her in that beautiful abode of flowering desolation known as the Palace of the Cæsars. The early Roman spring had filled the air with bloom and perfume, and the rugged surface of the Palatine was muffled with tender verdure. Daisy was strolling along the top of one of those great mounds of ruin that are embanked with mossy marble and paved with monumental inscriptions. It seemed to him that Rome had never been so lovely as just then. He stood looking off at the enchanting harmony of line and color that remotely encircles the city, inhaling the softly humid odors, and feeling the freshness of the year and the antiquity of the place reaffirms themselves in mysterious interfusion. It seemed to him, also, that Daisy had never looked so pretty; but this had been an observation of his whenever he met her. Giovanelli was at her side, and Giovanelli, too, wore an aspect of even unwonted brilliancy.

"Well," said Daisy, "I should think you would be lonesome!"

"Lonesome?" asked Winterbourne.

"You are always going round by yourself. Can't you get any one to walk with you?"

"I am not so fortunate," said Winterbourne, "as your companion."

Giovanelli, from the first, had treated Winterbourne with distinguished politeness. He listened with a deferential air to his remarks; he laughed punctiliously at his pleasantries; he seemed disposed to testify to his belief that Winterbourne was a superior young man. He carried himself in no degree like a jealous wooer; he had obviously a great deal of tact; he had no objection to your expecting a little humility of him. It even seemed to Winterbourne at times that Giovanelli would find a certain mental relief in being able to have a private understanding with him—to say to him, as an intelligent man, that, bless you, *he* knew how extraordinary was this young lady, and didn't flatter himself with delusive—or, at least, *too* delusive—hopes of matrimony and dollars. On this occasion he strolled away from his companion to pluck a sprig of almond-blossom, which he carefully arranged in his button-hole.

"I know why you say that," said Daisy, watching Giovanelli. "Because you think I go round too much with *him*." And she nodded at her attendant.

"Every one thinks so—if you care to know," said Winterbourne.

"Of course I care to know!" Daisy exclaimed, seriously. "But I don't believe it. They are only pretending to be shocked. They don't really care a straw what I do. Besides, I don't go round so much."

"I think you will find they do care. They will show it disagreeably."

Daisy looked at him a moment. "How disagreeably?"

"Haven't you noticed anything?" Winterbourne asked.

"I have noticed you. But I noticed you were as stiff as an umbrella the first time I saw you."

"You will find I am not so stiff as several others," said Winterbourne, smiling.

"How shall I find it?"

"By going to see the others."

"What will they do to me?"

"They will give you the cold shoulder. Do you know what that means?"

Daisy was looking at him intently; she began to color.

"Do you mean as Mrs. Walker did the other night?"

"Exactly!" said Winterbourne.

She looked away at Giovanelli, who was decorating himself with his almond-blossom. Then, looking back at Winterbourne, "I shouldn't think you would let people be so unkind!" she said.

"How can I help it?" he said.

"I should think you would say something."

"I did say something," and he paused a moment. "I say that your mother tells me that she believes you are engaged."

"Well, she does," said Daisy, very simply.

Winterbourne began to laugh. "And does Randolph believe it?" he asked.

"I guess Randolph doesn't believe anything," said Daisy. Randolph's scepticism excited Winterbourne to further hilarity, and he observed that Giovanelli was coming back to them. Daisy, observing it too, addressed herself again to her countryman. "Since you have mentioned it," she said, "I *am* engaged." . . . Winterbourne looked at her; he had stopped laughing. "You don't believe it!" she added.

He was silent a moment; and then, "Yes, I believe it," he said.

"Oh, no, you don't!" she answered. "Well, then—I am not!"

The young girl and her cicerone were on their way to the gate of the enclosure, so that Winterbourne, who had but lately entered, presently took leave of them. A week afterwards he went to dine at a beautiful villa on the Cælian Hill, and, on arriving, dismissed his hired vehicle. The evening was charming, and he promised himself the satisfaction of walking home beneath the Arch of Constantine and past the vaguely-lighter monuments of the Forum. There was a waning moon in the sky, and her radiance was not brilliant, but she was veiled in a thin cloud-curtain which seemed to diffuse and equalize it. When, on his return from the villa (it was eleven o'clock), Winterbourne approached the dusky circle of the Colosseum, it occurred to him, as a lover of the picturesque, that the interior, in the pale moonshine, would be well worth a glance. He turned aside and walked to one of the empty arches, near which, as he observed, an open carriage—one of the little Roman street-cabs—was stationed. Then he passed in, among the cavernous shadows of the great structure, and emerged upon the clear and silent arena. The place had never seemed to him more impressive. One-half of the gigantic circus was in deep shade, the other was sleeping in the luminous dusk. As he stood there he began to murmur Byron's famous lines, out of "Manfred"; but before he had finished his quotation he remembered that if nocturnal meditations in the Colosseum are recommended by the poets, they are deprecated by the doctors. The historic atmosphere was there, certainly; but the historic atmosphere, scientifically considered, was no better than a villainous miasma. Winterbourne walked to the middle of the arena, to take a more general glance, intending thereafter to make a hasty retreat. The great cross in the centre was covered with shadow; it was only as he drew near it that he made it out distinctly. Then he saw that two persons were stationed upon the low steps which formed its base. One of these was a woman, seated; her companion was standing in front of her.

Presently the sound of the woman's voice came to him distinctly in the warm night air. "Well, he looks at us as one of the old lions or tigers may have looked at the Christian martyrs!" These were the words he heard, in the familiar accent of Miss Daisy Miller.

"Let us hope he is not very hungry," responded the ingenious Giovanelli. "He will have to take me first; you will serve for dessert!"

Winterbourne stopped, with a sort of horror, and, it must be added, with a sort of relief. It was as if a sudden illumination had been flashed upon the ambiguity of Daisy's behavior, and the riddle had become easy to read. She was a young lady whom a gentleman need no longer be at pains to respect. He stood there looking at her—looking at her companion, and not reflecting that though he saw them vaguely, he himself must have been more brightly visible. He felt angry with himself that he had bothered so much about the right way of regarding Miss Daisy Miller. Then, as he was going to advance again, he checked himself; not from the fear that he was doing her injustice, but from the sense of the danger of appearing unbecomingly exhilarated by this sudden revulsion from cautious criticism. He turned away towards the entrance of the place, but, as he did so, he heard Daisy speak again.

"Why, it was Mr. Winterbourne! He saw me, and he cuts me!"

What a clever little reprobate she was, and how smartly she played at injured innocence! But he wouldn't cut her. Winterbourne came forward again, and went towards the great cross. Daisy had got up; Giovanelli lifted his hat. Winterbourne had now begun to think simply of the craziness, from a sanitary point of view, of a delicate young girl lounging away the evening in this nest of malaria. What if she *were* a clever little reprobate? that was no reason for her dying of the *perniciosa*. "How long have you been here?" he asked, almost brutally.

Daisy, lovely in the flattering moonlight, looked at him a moment. Then—"All the evening," she answered, gently. . . . "I never saw anything so pretty."

"I am afraid," said Winterbourne, "that you will not think Roman fever very pretty. This is the way people catch it. I wonder," he added, turning to Giovanelli, "that you, a native Roman, should countenance such a terrible indiscretion."

Ah," said the handsome native, "for myself I am not afraid."

"Neither am I—for you! I am speaking for this young lady."

Giovanelli lifted his well-shaped eyebrows and showed his brilliant teeth. But he took Winterbourne's rebuke with docility. "I told the signorina it was a grave indiscretion; but when was the signorina ever prudent?"

"I never was sick, and I don't mean to be!" the signorina declared. "I don't look like much, but I'm healthy! I was bound to see the Colosseum by moonlight; I shouldn't have wanted to go home without that; and we have had the most beautiful time, haven't we, Mr. Giovanelli? If there has been any danger, Eugenio can give me some pills. He has got some splendid pills."

"I should advise you," said Winterbourne, "to drive home as fast as possible and take one!"

"What you say is very wise," Giovanelli rejoined. "I will go and make sure the carriage is at hand." And he went forward rapidly.

Daisy followed with Winterbourne. He kept looking at her; she seemed not in the least embarrassed. Winterbourne said nothing; Daisy chattered about the beauty of the place. "Well, I *have* seen the Colosseum by moonlight!" she exclaimed. "That's one good thing." Then, noticing Winterbourne's silence, she asked him why he didn't speak. He made no answer, he only began to laugh. They passed under one of the dark archways; Giovanelli was in front with the carriage. Here Daisy stopped a moment, looking at the young American. "*Did* you believe I was engaged the other day?" she asked.

"It doesn't matter what I believed the other day," said Winterbourne, still laughing.

"Well, what do you believe now?"

"I believe that it makes very little difference whether you are engaged or not!"

He felt the young girl's pretty eyes fixed upon him through the thick gloom of the archway; she was apparently going to answer. But Giovanelli hurried her forward. "Quick! quick!" he said; "if we get in by midnight we are quite safe."

Daisy took her seat in the carriage, and the fortunate Italian placed himself beside her. "Don't forget Eugenio's pills!" said Winterbourne, as he lifted his hat.

"I don't care," said Daisy, in a little strange tone, "whether I have Roman fever or not!" Upon this the cab-driver cracked his whip, and they rolled away over the desultory patches of the antique pavement.

Winterbourne, to do him justice, as it were, mentioned to no one that he had encountered Miss Miller, at midnight, in the Colosseum with a gentleman, but nevertheless, a couple of days later, the fact of her having been there under these circumstances was known to every member of the little American circle, and commented accordingly. Winterbourne reflected that they had of course known it at the hotel, and that, after Daisy's return, there had been an exchange of remarks between the porter and the cab-driver. But the young man was conscious, at the same moment, that it had ceased to be a matter of serious regret to him that the little American flirt should be "talked about" by low-minded menials. These people, a day or two later, had serious information to give: the little American flirt was alarmingly ill. Winterbourne, when the rumor came to him, immediately went to the hotel for more news. He found that two or three charitable friends had preceded him, and that they were being entertained in Mrs. Miller's salon by Randolph.

"It's going round at night," said Randolph—"that's what made her sick. She's always going round at night. I shouldn't think she'd want to, it's so plaguy dark. You can't see anything here at night, except when there's a moon! In America there's always a moon!" Mrs. Miller was invisible; she was now, at least, giving her daughter the advantage of her society. It was evident that Daisy was dangerously ill.

Winterbourne went often to ask for news of her, and once he saw Mrs. Miller, who, though deeply alarmed, was, rather to his surprise, perfectly composed, and, as it appeared, a most efficient and judicious nurse. She talked a good deal about Dr. Davis, but Winterbourne paid her the compliment of saying to himself that she was not, after all, such a monstrous goose. "Daisy spoke of you the other day," she said to him. "Half the time she doesn't know what she's saying, but that time I think she did. She gave me a message. She told me to tell you—she told me to tell you that she never was engaged to that handsome Italian. I am sure I am very glad. Mr. Giovanelli hasn't been near us since she was taken ill. I thought he was so much of a gentleman; but I don't call that very polite! A lady told me that he was afraid I was angry with him for taking Daisy round at night. Well, so I am; but I suppose he knows

I'm a lady. I would scorn to scold him. Anyway, she says she's not engaged. I don't know why she wanted you to know; but she said to me three times, 'Mind you tell Mr. Winterbourne.' And then she told me to ask if you remembered the time you went to that castle in Switzerland. But I said I wouldn't give any such messages as that. Only, if she is not engaged, I'm sure I'm glad to know it."

But, as Winterbourne had said, it mattered very little. A week after this the poor girl died; it had been a terrible case of the fever. Daisy's grave was in the little Protestant cemetery, in an angle of the wall of imperial Rome, beneath the cypresses and the thick spring-flowers. Winterbourne stood there beside it, with a number of other mourners—a number larger than the scandal excited by the young lady's career would have led you to expect. Near him stood Giovanelli, who came nearer still before Winterbourne turned away. Giovanelli was very pale; on this occasion he had no flower in his button-hole; he seemed to wish to say something. At last he said, "She was the most beautiful young lady I ever saw, and the most amiable;" and then he added in a moment, "and she was the most innocent."

Winterbourne looked at him, and presently repeated his words, "And the most innocent?"

"The most innocent!"

Winterbourne felt sore and angry. "Why the devil," he asked, "did you take her to that fatal place?"

Mr. Giovanelli's urbanity was apparently imperturbable. He looked on the ground a moment, and then he said, "For myself I had no fear; and she wanted to go."

"That was no reason!" Winterbourne declared.

The subtle Roman again dropped his eyes. "If she had lived, I should have got nothing. She would never have married me, I am sure."

"She would never have married you?"

"For a moment I hoped so. But no, I am sure."

Winterbourne listened to him: he stood staring at the raw protuberance among the April daisies. When he turned away again, Mr. Giovanelli with his light, slow step, had retired.

Winterbourne almost immediately left Rome; but the following summer he again met his aunt, Mrs. Costello, at Vevey. Mrs. Costello was fond of Vevey. In the interval Winterbourne had often thought of Daisy Miller and her mystifying manners. One day he spoke of her to his aunt—said it was on his conscience that he had done her injustice.

"I am sure I don't know," said Mrs. Costello. "How did your injustice affect her?"

"She sent me a message before her death which I didn't understand at the time; but I have understood it since. She would have appreciated one's esteem."

"Is that a modest way," asked Mrs. Costello, "of saying that she would have reciprocated one's affection?"

Winterbourne offered no answer to this question; but he presently said, "You were right in that remark that you made last summer. I was booked to make a mistake. I have lived too long in foreign parts."

Nevertheless, he went back to live at Geneva, whence there continue to come the most contradictory accounts of his motives of sojourn: a report that he is "studying" hard—an intimation that he is much interested in a very clever foreign lady.

AN INTERNATIONAL EPISODE

FOUR YEARS ago—in 1874—two young Englishmen had occasion to go to the United States. They crossed the ocean at midsummer, and, arriving in New York on the first day of August, were much struck with the fervid temperature of that city. Disembarking upon the wharf, they climbed into one of those huge high-hung coaches which convey passengers to the hotels, and, with a great deal of bouncing and bumping, took their course through Broadway. The midsummer aspect of New York is not, perhaps, the most favorable one; still, it is not without its picturesque and even brilliant side. Nothing could well resemble less a typical English street than the interminable avenue, rich in incongruities, through which our two travellers advanced—looking out on each side of them at the comfortable animation of the sidewalks, the high-colored, heterogeneous architecture, the huge, white marble façades glittering in the strong, crude light, and bedizened with gilded lettering, the multifarious awnings, banners, and streamers, the extraordinary number of omnibuses, horse-cars, and other democratic vehicles, the venders of cooling fluids, the white trousers and big straw-hats of the policemen, the tripping gait of the modish young persons on the pavement, the general brightness, newness, juvenility, both of people and things. The young men had exchanged few observations; but in crossing Union Square, in front of the monument ot Washington —in the very shadow, indeed, projected by the image of the *pater patriæ*—one of them remarked to the other, "It seems a rum-looking place."

"Ah, very odd, very odd," said the other, who was the clever man of the two.

"Pity it's so beastly hot," resumed the first speaker, after a pause.

"You know we are in a low latitude," said his friend.

"I dare say," remarked the other.

"I wonder," said the second speaker, presently, "if they can give one a bath?"

"I dare say not," rejoined the other.

"Oh, I say!" cried his comrade.

This animated discussion was checked by their arrival at the hotel,

which had been recommended to them by an American gentleman whose acquaintance they made—with whom, indeed, they
became very intimate—on the steamer, and who had proposed to
accompany them to the inn and introduce them, in a friendly way,
to the proprietor. This plan, however, had been defeated by their
friend's finding that his "partner" was awaiting him on the wharf,
and that his commercial associate desired him instantly to come
and give his attention to certain telegrams received from St. Louis.
But the two Englishmen, with nothing but their national prestige
and personal graces to recommend them, were very well received
at the hotel, which had an air of capacious hospitality. They found
that a bath was not unattainable, and were indeed struck with the
facilities for prolonged and reiterated immersion with which their
apartment was supplied. After bathing a good deal—more, indeed,
than they had ever done before on a single occasion—they made
their way into the dining-room of the hotel, which was a spacious
restaurant, with a fountain in the middle, a great many tall plants
in ornamental tubs, and an array of French waiters. The first dinner
on land after a sea-voyage is, under any circumstances, a delightful
occasion, and there was something particularly agreeable in the circumstances in which our young Englishmen found themselves. They
were extremely good-natured young men; they were more observant than they appeared; in a sort of inarticulate, accidentally
dissimulative fashion, they were highly appreciative. This was, perhaps, especially the case with the elder, who was also, as I have said,
the man of talent. They sat down at a little table, which was a very
different affair from the great clattering seesaw in the saloon of the
steamer. The wide doors and windows of the restaurants stood open,
beneath large awnings, to a wide pavement, where there were other
plants in tubs and rows of spreading trees, and beyond which there
was a large, shady square, without any palings, and with marble-
paved walks. And above the vivid verdure rose other façades of
white marble and of pale chocolate-colored stone, squaring themselves against the deep blue sky. Here, outside, in the light and the
shade and the heat, there was a great tinkling of the bells of innumerable street-cars, and a constant strolling and shuffling and rustling of many pedestrians, a large proportion of whom were young
women in Pompadour-looking dresses. Within, the place was cool
and vaguely lighted, with the plash of water, the odor of flowers,
and the flitting of French waiters, as I have said, upon soundless
carpets.

"It's rather like Paris, you know," said the younger of our two travellers.

"It's like Paris—only more so," his companion rejoined.

"I suppose it's the French waiters," said the first speaker. "Why don't they have French waiters in London?"

"Fancy a French waiter at a club," said his friend.

The young Englishman stared a little, as if he could not fancy it. "In Paris I'm very apt to dine at a place where there's an English waiter. Don't you know what's-his-name's, close to the thingum-bob? They always set an English waiter at me. I suppose they think I can't speak French."

"Well, you can't." And the elder of the young Englishmen unfolded his napkin.

His companion took no notice whatever of this declaration. "I say," he resumed, in a moment, "we must learn to speak American. I suppose we must take lessons."

"I can't understand them," said the clever man.

"What the deuce is *he* saying?" asked his comrade, appealing from the French waiter.

"He is recommending some soft-shell crabs," said the clever man.

And so, in desultory observation of the idiosyncrasies of the new society in which they found themselves, the young Englishmen proceeded to dine—going in largely, as the phrase is, for cooling draughts and dishes, of which their attendant offered them a very long list. After dinner they went out and slowly walked about the neighboring streets. The early dusk of waning summer was coming on, but the heat was still very great. The pavements were hot even to the stout boot soles of the British travellers, and the trees along the curbstone emitted strange exotic odors. The young men wandered through the adjoining square—that queer place without palings, and with marble walks arranged in black and white lozenges. There were a great many benches, crowded with shabby-looking people, and the travellers remarked, very justly, that it was not much like Belgrave Square. On one side was an enormous hotel, lifting up into the hot darkness an immense array of open, brightly lighted windows. At the base of this populous structure was an eternal jangle of horse-cars, and all round it, in the upper dusk, was a sinister hum of mosquitoes. The ground-floor of the hotel seemed to be a huge transparent cage, flinging a wide glare of gaslight into the street, of which it formed a sort of public adjunct, absorbing and emitting the passers-by promiscuously. The young Englishmen went in with every one else, from curiosity, and saw a couple of hundred men sitting on divans along a great marble-paved corridor, with their legs stretched out, together with several dozen more standing in a *queue*, as at the ticket-office of a railway station, before a brilliantly illuminated counter of vast extent. These latter persons, who carried portmanteaus in their hand, had a dejected, exhausted look; their garments were not very fresh, and they seemed to be rendering some mysterious tribute to a magnificent young man with a waxed mustache, and a shirt-front adorned with diamond buttons, who every now and then dropped an absent glance over their multitudinous patience. They were American citizens doing homage to a hotel clerk.

"I'm glad he didn't tell us to go there," said one of our Englishmen, alluding to their friend on the steamer, who had told them so many things. They walked up Fifth Avenue, where, for instance, he had told them that all the first families lived. But the first families were out of town, and our young travellers had only the satisfaction of seeing some of the second—or, perhaps, even the third—taking the evening air upon balconies and high flights of door-steps, in the streets which radiate from the more ornamental thoroughfare. They went a little way down one of these side streets, and they saw young ladies in white dresses—charming-looking persons—seated in graceful attitudes on the chocolate-colored steps. In one or two places these young ladies were conversing across the street with other young ladies seated in similar postures and costumes in front of the opposite houses, and in the warm night air their colloquial tones sounded strange in the ears of the young Englishmen. One of our friends, nevertheless—the younger one—intimated that he felt a disposition to interrupt a few of these soft familiarities; but his companion observed, pertinently enough, that he had better be careful. "We must not begin with making mistakes," said his companion.

"But he told us, you know—he told us," urged the young man. alluding again to the friend on the steamer.

"Never mind what he told us!" answered his comrade, who, if he had greater talents, was also apparently more of a moralist.

By bedtime—in their impatience to taste of a terrestrial couch again, our seafarers went to bed early—it was still insufferably hot, and the buzz of the mosquitoes at the open windows might have passed for an audible crepitation of the temperature. "We can't stand this, you know," the young Englishmen said to each other; and they tossed about all night more boisterously than they had tossed upon the Atlantic billows. On the morrow their first thought was that they would re-embark that day for England; and then it occurred to them that they might find an asylum nearer at hand. The cave of Eolus became their ideal of comfort, and they wondered where the Americans went when they wished to cool off. They had not the least idea, and they determined to apply for information to Mr. J. L. Westgate. This was the name inscribed in a bold hand on the back of a letter carefully preserved in the pocketbook of our junior traveller. Beneath the address, in the left-hand corner of the envelope, were the words, "Introducing Lord Lambeth and Percy Beaumont, Esq." The letter had been given to the two Englishmen by a good friend of theirs in London, who had been in America two years previously, and had singled out Mr. J. L. Westgate from the many friends he had left there as the consignee, as it were, of his compatriots. "He is a capital fellow," the Englishman in London had said, "and he has got an awfully pretty wife. He's tremendously hospitable—he will do everything in the world for you; and as he knows every one over there, it is quite needless I should give you any other introduction. He will make you see every one; trust to him for putting you into circulation. He has got a tremendously pretty wife." It was natural that in the hour of tribulation Lord Lambeth and Mr. Percy Beaumont should have bethought themselves of a gentleman whose attractions had been thus vividly depicted—all the more so that he lived in Fifth Avenue, and that Fifth Avenue, as they had ascertained the night before, was contiguous to their hotel. "Ten to one he'll be out of town," said Percy Beaumont; "but we can at least find out where he has gone, and we can immediately start in pursuit. He can't possibly have gone to a hotter place, you know."

"Oh, there's only one hotter place," said Lord Lambeth, "and I hope he hasn't gone there."

They strolled along the shady side of the street to the number indicated upon the precious letter. The house presented an imposing chocolate-colored expanse, relieved by facings and window cornices of florid sculpture, and by a couple of dusty rosetrees which clambered over the balconies and the portico. This last-mentioned feature was approached by a monumental flight of steps.

"Rather better than a London house," said Lord Lambeth, looking down from this altitude, after they had rung the bell.

"It depends upon what London house you mean," replied his companion. "You have a tremendous chance to get wet between the house door and your carriage."

"Well," said Lord Lambeth, glancing at the burning heavens, "I 'guess' it doesn't rain so much here!"

The door was opened by a long negro in a white jacket, who grinned familiarly when Lord Lambeth asked for Mr. Westgate.

"He ain't at home, sah; he's down-town at his o'fice."

"Oh, at his office?" said the visitor. "And when will he be at home?"

"Well, sah, when he goes out dis way in de mo'ning, he ain't liable to come home all day."

This was discouraging; but the address of Mr. Westgate's office was freely imparted by the intelligent black, and was taken down by Percy Beaumont in his pocket-book. The two gentlemen then returned, languidly, to their hotel, and sent for a hackney-coach, and in this commodious vehicle they rolled comfortably down-town. They measured the whole length of Broadway again, and found it a path of fire; and then, deflecting to the left, they were deposited by their conductor before a fresh, light, ornamental struc-ture, ten stories high, in a street crowded with keen-faced, light-limbed young men, who were running about very quickly, and stopping each other eagerly at corners and in doorways. Passing into this brilliant building, they were introduced by one of the keen-faced young men—he was a charming fellow, in wonderful cream-colored garments and a hat with a blue ribbon, who had evi-dently perceived them to be aliens and helpless—to a very snug hydraulic elevator, in which they took their place with many other persons, and which, shooting upward in its vertical socket, presently projected them into the seventh horizontal compartment of the edifice. Here, after brief delay, they found themselves face to face with the friend of their friend in London. His office was composed of several different rooms, and they waited very silently in one of them after they had sent in their letter and their cards. The letter was not one which it would take Mr. Westgate very long to read, but he came out to speak to them more instantly than they could have expected; he had evidently jumped up from his work. He was a tall, lean personage, and was dressed all in fresh white linen; he had a thin, sharp, familiar face, with an expression that was at one and the same time sociable and business-like, a quick, intelligent eye, and a large brown mustache, which concealed his mouth and made his chin beneath it look small. Lord Lambeth thought he looked tremendously clever.

"How do you do, Lord Lambeth—how do you do, sir?" he said, holding the open letter in his hand. "I'm very glad to see you; I hope you're very well. You had better come in here; I think it's cooler," and he led the way into another room, where there were law-books and papers, and windows wide open beneath striped awning. Just opposite one of the windows, on a line with his eyes, Lord Lambeth observed the weather-vane of a church steeple. The uproar of the street sounded infinitely far below, and Lord Lambeth felt very high in the air. "I say it's cooler," pursued their host, "but everything is relative. How do you stand the heat?"

"I can't say we like it," said Lord Lambeth; "but Beaumont likes it better than I."

"Well, it won't last," Mr. Westgate very cheerfully declared; "nothing unpleasant lasts over here. It was very hot when Captain Littledale was here; he did nothing but drink sherry-cobblers. He expresses some doubt in his letter whether I will remember him —as if I didn't remember making six sherry-cobblers for him one day in about twenty minutes. I hope you left him well, two years having elapsed since then."

"Oh, yes, he's all right," said Lord Lambeth.

"I am always very glad to see your countrymen," Mr. Westgate pursued. "I thought it would be time some of you should be coming along. A friend of mine was saying to me only a day or two ago, 'It's time for the watermelons and the Englishmen.'"

"The Englishmen and the watermelons just now are about the same thing," Percy Beaumont said, wiping his dripping forehead.

"Ah, well, we'll put you on ice, as we do the melons. You must go down to Newport."

"We'll go anywhere," said Lord Lambeth.

"Yes, you want to go to Newport; that's what you want to do," Mr. Westgate affirmed. "But let's see—when did you get here?"

"Only yesterday," said Percy Beaumont.

"Ah, yes, by the *Russia*. Where are you staying?"

"At the Hanover, I think they call it."

"Pretty comfortable?" inquired Mr. Westgate.

"It seems a capital place, but I can't say we like the gnats," said Lord Lambeth.

Mr. Westgate stared and laughed. "Oh no, of course you don't like gnats. We shall expect you to like a good many things over here, but we sha'n't insist upon your liking the gnats; though certainly you'll admit that, as gnats, they are fine, eh? But you oughtn't to remain in the city."

"So we think," said Lord Lambeth. "If you would kindly suggest something——"

"Suggest something, my dear sir?" and Mr. Westgate looked at him, narrowing his eyelids. "Open your mouth and shut your eyes! Leave it to me, and I'll put you through. It's a matter of national pride with me that all Englishmen should have a good time; and as I have had considerable practice, I have learned to minister to their wants. I find they generally want the right thing. So just please to consider yourselves my property; and if any one should try to appropriate you, please to say, 'Hands off; too late for the market.' But let's see," continued the American, in his slow, humorous voice, with a distinctness of utterance which appeared to his visitors to be a part of a humorous intention—a strangely leisurely speculative voice for a man evidently so busy and, as they felt, so professional—"let's see; are you going to make something of a stay, Lord Lambeth?"

"Oh, dear no," said the young Englishman; "my cousin was coming over on some business, so I just came across, at an hour's notice, for the lark."

"Is it your first visit to the United States?"

"Oh dear yes."

"I was obliged to come on some business," said Percy Beaumont, "and I brought Lambeth along."

"And *you* have been here before, sir?"

"Never—never."

"I thought, from your referring to business——" said Mr. Westgate.

"Oh, you see I'm by way of being a barrister," Percy Beaumont answered. "I know some people that think of bringing a suit against one of your railways, and they asked me to come over and take measures accordingly."

Mr. Westgate gave one of his slow, keen looks again. "What's your railroad?" he asked.

"The Tennessee Central."

The American tilted back his chair a little, and poised it an instant. "Well, I'm sorry you want to attack one of our institutions," he said, smiling. "But I guess you had better enjoy yourself *first!*"

"I'm certainly rather afraid I can't work in this weather," the young barrister confessed.

"Leave that to the natives," said Mr. Westgate. "Leave the Tennessee Central to me, Mr. Beaumont. Some day we'll talk it over, and I guess I can make it square. But I didn't know you Englishmen ever did any work, in the upper classes."

"Oh, we do a lot of work; don't we, Lambeth?" asked Percy Beaumont.

"I must certainly be at home by the 19th of September," said the younger Englishman, irrelevantly but gently.

"For the shooting, eh? or is it the hunting, or the fishing?" inquired his entertainer.

"Oh, I must be in Scotland," said Lord Lambeth, blushing a little.

"Well, then," rejoined Mr. Westgate, "you had better amuse yourself first, also. You must go down and see Mrs. Westgate."

"We should be so happy, if you would kindly tell us the train," said Percy Beaumont.

"It isn't a train—it's a boat."

"Oh, I see. And what is the name of—a—the—a—town?"

"It isn't a town," said Mr. Westgate, laughing. "It's a—well, what shall I call it? It's a watering-place. In short, it's Newport. You'll see what it is. It's cool; that's the principal thing. You will greatly oblige me by going down there and putting yourself into the hands of Mrs. Westgate. It isn't perhaps for me to say it, but you couldn't be in better hands. Also in those of her sister, who is staying with her. She is very fond of Englishmen. She thinks there is nothing like them."

"Mrs. Westgate or—a—her sister?" asked Percy Beaumont, modestly, yet in the tone of an inquiring traveller.

"Oh, I mean my wife," said Mr. Westgate. "I don't suppose my sister-in-law knows much about them. She has always led a very quiet life; she has lived in Boston."

Percy Beaumont listened with interest. "That, I believe," he said, "is the most—a—intellectual town?"

"I believe it is very intellectual. I don't go there much," responded his host.

"I say, we ought to go there," said Lord Lambeth to his companion.

"Oh, Lord Lambeth, wait till the great heat is over," Mr. Westgate interposed. "Boston in this weather would be very trying; it's not the temperature for intellectual exertion. At Boston, you know, you have to pass an examination at the city limits; and when you come away they give you a kind of degree."

Lord Lambeth stared, blushing a little; and Percy Beaumont stared a little also—but only with his fine natural complexion—glancing aside after a moment to see that his companion was not looking too credulous, for he had heard a great deal of American humor. "I dare say it is very jolly," said the younger gentleman.

"I dare say it is," said Mr. Westgate. "Only I must impress upon you that at present—to-morrow morning, at an early hour—you will be expected at Newport. We have a house there; half the people of New York go there for the summer. I am not sure that at this very moment my wife can take you in; she has got a lot of people staying with her; I don't know who they all are; only she may have no room. But you can begin with the hotel, and meanwhile you can live at my house. In that way—simply sleeping at the hotel —you will find it tolerable. For the rest, you must make yourself at home at my place. You mustn't be shy, you know; if you are only here for a month, that will be a great waste of time. Mrs. Westgate won't neglect you, and you had better not try to resist her. I know something about that. I expect you'll find some pretty girls on the premises. I shall write to my wife by this afternoon's mail, and to-morrow morning she and Miss Alden will look out for you. Just walk right in and make yourself comfortable. Your steamer leaves from this part of the city, and I will immediately send out and get you a cabin. Then, at half-past four o'clock, just call for me here, and I will go with you and put you on board. It's a big boat; you might get lost. A few days hence, at the end of the week, I will come down to Newport, and see how you are getting on."

The two young Englishmen inaugurated the policy of not resisting Mrs. Westgate by submitting, with great docility and thankfulness, to her husband. He was evidently a very good fellow, and he made an impression upon his visitors; his hospitality seemed to recommend itself consciously—with a friendly wink, as it were—as if it hinted, judiciously, that you could not possibly make a better bargain. Lord Lambeth and his cousin left their entertainer to his labors and returned to their hotel, where they spent three or four hours in their respective shower-baths. Percy Beaumont had suggested that they ought to see something of the town; but "Oh, d—n the town!" his noble kinsman had rejoined. They returned to Mr. Westgate's office in a carriage, with their luggage, very punctually; but it must be reluctantly recorded that, this time, he kept them waiting so long that they felt themselves missing the steamer, and were deterred only by an amiable modesty from dispensing with his attendance, and starting on a hasty scramble to the wharf. But when at last he appeared, and the carriage plunged into the purlieus of Broadway, they jolted to such good purpose that they reached the huge white vessel while the bell for departure was still ringing, and the absorption of passengers still active. It was indeed, as Mr. Westgate had said, a big boat, and his leadership in the innumerable and interminable corridors and cabins, with which he seemed perfectly acquainted, and of which any one and every one appeared to have the entrée, was very grateful to the slightly bewildered voyagers. He showed them their state-room—a spacious apartment, embellished with gas-lamps, mirrors *en pied*, and sculptured furniture—and then, long after they had been intimately convinced that the steamer was in motion and launched upon the unknown stream that they were about to navigate, he bade them a sociable farewell.

"Well, good-bye, Lord Lambeth," he said; "good-bye, Mr. Percy Beaumont. I hope you'll have a good time. Just let them do what they want with you. I'll come down by-and-by and look after you."

The young Englishmen emerged from their cabin and amused themselves with wandering about the immense labyrinthine steamer, which struck them as an extraordinary mixture of a ship and a hotel. It was densely crowded with passengers, the larger number of whom appeared to be ladies and very young children; and in the big saloons, ornamented in white and gold, which followed each other in surprising succession, beneath the swinging gaslight, and among the small side passages where the negro domestics of both sexes assembled with an air of philosophic leisure, every one was moving to and fro and exchanging loud and familiar observations. Eventually, at the instance of a discriminating black, our young men went and had some "supper" in a wonderful place arranged like a theatre, where, in a gilded gallery, upon which little boxes appeared to open, a large orchestra was playing operatic selections, and, below, people were handing about bills of fare, as if they had been programmes. All this was sufficiently curious; but the agreeable thing, later, was to sit out on one of the great white decks of the steamer, in the warm, breezy darkness, and, in the vague starlight, to make out the line of low, mysterious coast. The young Englishmen tried American cigars—those of Mr. Westgate—and talked together as they usually talked, with many odd silences, lapses of logic, and incongruities of transition, like people who have grown old together, and learned to supply each other's missing phrases; or, more specially, like people thoroughly conscious of a common point of view, so that a style of conversation superficially lacking in finish might suffice for reference to a fund of associations in the light of which everything was all right.

"We really seem to be going out to sea," Percy Beaumont observed. "Upon my word, we are going back to England. He has shipped us off again. I call that 'real mean.'"

"I suppose it's all right," said Lord Lambeth. "I want to see those pretty girls at Newport. You know he told us the place was an island; and aren't all islands in the sea?"

"Well," resumed the elder traveller after a while, "if his house is as good as his cigars, we shall do very well indeed."

"He seems a very good fellow," said Lord Lambeth, as if this idea just occurred to him.

"I say, we had better remain at the inn," rejoined his companion, presently. "I don't think I like the way he spoke of his house. I don't like stopping in the house with such a tremendous lot of women."

"Oh, I don't mind," said Lord Lambeth. And then they smoked a while in silence. "Fancy his thinking we do no work in England!" the young man resumed.

"I dare say he didn't really think so," said Percy Beaumont.

"Well I guess they don't know much about England over here!" declared Lord Lambeth, humorously. And then there was another long pause. "He was devilish civil," observed the young nobleman.

"Nothing, certainly, could have been more civil," rejoined his companion.

"Littledale said his wife was great fun," said Lord Lambeth.

"Whose wife—Littledale's?"

"This American's—Mrs. Westgate. What's his name? J. L."

Beaumont was silent a moment. "What was fun to Littledale," he said at last, rather sententiously, "may be death to us."

"What do you mean by that?" asked his kinsman. "I am as good a man as Littledale."

"My dear boy, I hope you won't begin to flirt," said Percy Beaumont.

"I don't care. I dare say I sha'n't begin."

"With a married woman, if she's bent upon it, it's all very well," Beaumont expounded. "But our friend mentioned a young lady—a sister, a sister-in-law. For God's sake, don't get entangled with her!"

"How do you mean entangled?"

"Depend upon it she will try to hook you."

"Oh, bother!" said Lord Lambeth.

"American girls are very clever," urged his companion.

"So much the better," the young man declared.

"I fancy they are always up to some game of that sort," Beaumont continued.

"They can't be worse than they are in England," said Lord Lambeth, judicially.

"Ah, but in England," replied Beaumont, "you have got your natural protectors. You have got your mother and sisters."

"My mother and sisters——" began the young nobleman, with a certain energy. But he stopped in time, puffing at his cigar.

"Your mother spoke to me about it, with tears in her eyes," said Percy Beaumont. "She said she felt very nervous. I promised to keep you out of mischief."

"You had better take care of yourself," said the object of maternal and ducal solicitude.

"Ah," rejoined the young barrister, "I haven't the expectation of a hundred thousand a year, not to mention other attractions."

"Well," said Lord Lambeth, "don't cry out before you're hurt!"

It was certainly very much cooler at Newport, where our travellers found themselves assigned to a couple of diminutive bedrooms in a far-away angle of an immense hotel. They had gone ashore in the early summer twilight, and had very promptly put themselves to bed; thanks to which circumstance, and to their having, during the previous hours in their commodious cabin slept the sleep of youth and health, they began to feel, towards eleven o'clock, very alert and inquisitive. They looked out of their windows across a row of small green fields, bordered with low stone walls of rude construction, and saw a deep blue ocean lying beneath a deep blue sky, and flecked now and then with scintillating patches of foam. A strong, fresh breeze came in through the curtainless casements, and prompted our young men to observe generally that it didn't seem half a bad climate. They made other observations after they had emerged from their rooms in pursuit of breakfast—a meal of which they partook in a huge bare hall, where a hundred negroes in white jackets were shuffling about upon an uncarpeted floor; where the flies were superabundant, and the tables and dishes covered over with a strange, voluminous integument of coarse blue gauze; and where several little boys and girls, who had risen late, were seated in fastidious solitude at the morning repast. These young persons had not the morning paper before them, but they were engaged in languid perusal of the bill of fare.

The latter document was a great puzzle to our friends, who, on reflecting that its bewildering categories had relation to breakfast alone, had an uneasy prevision of an encyclopædic dinner list. They found a great deal of enterainment at the hotel, an enormous wooden structure, for the erection of which it seemed to them that the virgin forests of the West must have been terribly deflowered. It was perforated from end to end with immense bare corridors, through which a strong draught was blowing—bearing along wonderful figures of ladies in white morning-dresses and clouds of valenciennes lace, who seemed to float down the long vistas with expanded furbelows like angels spreading their wings. In front was a gigantic veranda, upon which an army might have encamped—a vast wooden terrace, with a roof as lofty as the nave of a cathedral. Here our young Englishmen enjoyed, as they supposed, a glimpse of American society, which was distributed over the measureless expanse in a variety of sedentary attitudes, and appeared to consist largely of pretty young girls, dressed as if for a *fête champêtre*, swaying to and fro in rocking chairs, fanning themselves with large straw fans, and enjoying an enviable exemption from social cares. Lord Lambeth had a theory, which it might be interesting to trace to its origin, that it would be not only agreeable, but easily possible, to enter into relations with one of these young ladies; and his companion (as he had done a couple of days before) found occasion to check the young nobleman's colloquial impulses.

"You had better take care," said Percy Beaumont, "or you will have an offended father or brother pulling out a bowie-knife."

"I assure you it is all right," Lord Lambeth replied. "You know the Americans come to these big hotels to make acquaintances."

"I know nothing about it, and neither do you," said his kinsman, who, like a clever man, had begun to perceive that the observation of American society demanded a readjustment of one's standard.

"Hang it, then, let's find out!" cried Lord Lambeth, with some impatience. "You know I don't want to miss anything."

"We will find out," said Percy Beaumont, very reasonably. "We will go and see Mrs. Westgate, and make all the proper inquiries."

And so the two inquiring Englishmen, who had this lady's address inscribed in her husband's hand upon a card, descended from the veranda of the big hotel and took their way, according to direction, along a large, straight road, past a series of fresh-looking villas embosomed in shrubs and flowers, and enclosed in an ingenious variety of wooden palings. The morning was brilliant and cool, the villas were smart and snug, and the walk of the young travellers was very entertaining. Everything looked as if it had received a coat of fresh paint the day before—the red roofs, the green shutters, the clean, bright browns and buffs of the house fronts. The flower beds on the little lawns seemed to sparkle in the radiant air, and the gravel in the short carriage sweeps to flash and twinkle. Along the road came a hundred little basket-phaetons, in which, almost always, a couple of ladies were sitting—ladies in white dresses and long white gloves, holding the reins and looking at the two Englishmen—whose nationality was not elusive—through thick blue veils tied tightly about their faces, as if to guard their complexions. At last the young men came within sight of the sea again, and then, having interrogated a gardener over the paling of a villa, they turned into an open gate. Here they found themselves face to face with the ocean and with a very picturesque structure, resembling a magnified chalet, which was perched upon a green embankment just above it. The house had a veranda of extraordinary width all around it, and a great many doors and windows standing open to the veranda. These various apertures had, in common, such an accessible, hospitable air, such a breezy flutter within of light curtains, such expansive thresholds and reassuring interiors, that our friends hardly knew which was the regular entrance, and, after hesitating a moment, presented themselves at one of the windows. The room within was dark, but in a moment a graceful figure vaguely shaped itself in the rich-looking gloom, and a lady came to meet them. Then they saw that she had been seated at a table writing, and that she had heard them and had got up. She stepped out into the light; she wore a frank, charming smile, with which she held out her hand to Percy Beaumont.

"Oh, you must be Lord Lambeth and Mr. Beaumont," she said. "I have heard from my husband that you would come. I am extremely glad to see you." And she shook hands with each of her visitors. Her visitors were a little shy, but they had very good manners; they responded with smiles and exclamations, and they apologized for not knowing the front door. The lady rejoined, with vivacity, that when she wanted to see people very much she did not insist upon these distinctions, and that Mr. Westgate had written to her of his English friends in terms that made her really anxious. "He said you were so terribly prostrated," said Mrs. West-gate.

"Oh, you mean by the heat?" replied Percy Beaumont. "We were rather knocked up, but we feel wonderfully better. We had such a jolly—a—voyage down here. It's so very good of you to mind."

"Yes, it's so very kind of you," murmured Lord Lambeth.

Mrs. Westgate stood smiling; she was extremely pretty. "Well, I did mind," she said; "and I thought of sending for you this morning to the Ocean House. I am very glad you are better, and I am charmed you have arrived. You must come round to the other side of the piazza." And she led the way, with a light, smooth step, looking back at the young men and smiling.

The other side of the piazza was, as Lord Lambeth presently re-marked, a very jolly place. It was of the most liberal proportions, and with its awnings, its fanciful chairs, its cushions and rugs, its view of the ocean, close at hand, tumbling along the base of the low cliffs whose level tops intervened in lawn-like smoothness, it formed a charming complement to the drawing-room. As such it was in course of use at the present moment; it was occupied by a social circle. There were several ladies and two or three gentlemen, to whom Mrs. Westgate proceeded to introduce the distinguished strangers. She mentioned a great many names very freely and dis-tinctly; the young Englishmen, shuffling about and bowing, were rather bewildered. But at last they were provided with chairs—low, wicker chairs, gilded, and tied with a great many ribbons—and one of the ladies (a very young person, with a little snub-nose and several dimples) offered Percy Beaumont a fan. The fan was also adorned with pink love-knots; but Percy Beaumont declined it, although he was very hot. Presently, however, it became cooler; the breeze from the sea was delicious, the view was charming, and the people sitting there looked exceedingly fresh and comfortable. Several of the ladies seemed to be young girls, and the gentlemen were slim, fair youths, such as our friends had seen the day before in New York. The ladies were working upon bands of tapestry, and one of the young men had an open book in his lap. Beaumont afterwards learned from one of the ladies that this young man had been reading aloud; that he was from Boston, and was very fond of reading aloud. Beaumont said it was a great pity that they had interrupted him; he should like so much (from all he had heard) to hear a Bostonian read. Couldn't the young man be induced to go on?

"Oh no," said his informant, very freely; "he wouldn't be able to get the young ladies to attend to him now."

There was something very friendly, Beaumont perceived, in the attitude of the company; they looked at the young Englishmen with an air of animated sympathy and interest; they smiled, brightly and unanimously, at everything either of the visitors said. Lord Lambeth and his companion felt that they were being made very welcome. Mrs. Westgate seated herself between them, and, talking a great deal to each, they had occasion to observe that she was as pretty as their friend Littledale had promised. She was thirty years old, with the eyes and the smile of a girl of seventeen, and she was extremely light and graceful—elegant, exquisite. Mrs. Westgate was extremely spontaneous. She was very frank and demonstrative, and appeared always—while she looked at you delightedly with her beautiful young eyes—to be making sudden confessions and concessions after momentary hesitations.

"We shall expect to see a great deal of you," she said to Lord Lambeth, with a kind of joyous earnestness. "We are very fond of Englishmen here—that is, there are a great many we have been fond of. After a day or two you must come and stay with us; we hope you will stay a long time. Newport's a very nice place when you come really to know it—when you know plenty of people. Of course you and Mr. Beaumont will have no difficulty about that. Englishmen are very well received here; there are almost always two or three of them about. I think they always like it, and I must say I should think they would. They receive ever so much attention. I must say I think they sometimes get spoiled; but I am sure you and Mr. Beaumont are proof against that.

"My husband tells me you are a friend of Captain Littledale. He was such a charming man: he made himself most agreeable here, and I am sure I wonder he didn't stay. It couldn't have been pleasanter for him in his own country, though, I suppose, it is very pleasant in England—for English people. I don't know myself; I have been there very little. I have been a great deal abroad, but I am always on the Continent. I must say I am extremely fond of Paris; you know we Americans always are; we go there when we die. Did you ever hear that before? That was said by a great wit—I mean the good Americans; but we are all good; you'll see that for yourself.

"All I know of England is London, and all I know of London is that place on that little corner, you know, where you buy jackets—jackets with that coarse braid and those big buttons. They make very good jackets in London; I will do you the justice to say that. And some people like the hats; but about the hats I was always a heretic; I always got my hats in Paris. You can't wear an English hat—at least, I never could—unless you dress your hair *à l'Anglaise;* and I must say that is a talent I never possessed. In Paris they will make things to suit your peculiarities; but in England I think you like much more to have—how shall I say it?—one thing for everybody. I mean as regards dress. I don't know about other things; but I have always supposed that in other things everything was different. I mean according to the people—according to the classes, and all that. I am afraid you will think that I don't take a very favorable view; but you know you can't take a very favorable view in Dover Street in the month of November. That has always been my fate.

"Do you know Jones's Hotel, in Dover Street? That's all I know of England. Of course every one admits that the English hotels are your weak point. There was always the most frightful fog; I couldn't see to try my things on. When I got over to America—into the light—I usually found they were twice too big. The next time I mean to go in the season; I think I shall go next year. I want very much to take my sister; she has never been to England. I don't know whether you know what I mean by saying that the Englishmen who come here sometimes get spoiled. I mean that they take things as a matter of course—things that are done for them. Now, naturally, they are only a matter of course when the Englishmen are very nice. But, of course, they are almost always very nice. Of course this isn't nearly such an interesting country as England; there are not nearly so many things to see, and we haven't your country life. I have never seen anything of your country life; when I am in Europe I am always on the Continent. But I have heard a great deal about it; I know that when you are among yourselves in the country you have the most beautiful time. Of course we have nothing of that sort; we have nothing on that scale.

"I don't apologize, Lord Lambeth; some Americans are always apologizing; you must have noticed that. We have the reputation of always boasting and bragging and waving the American flag; but I must say that what strikes me is that we are perpetually making excuses and trying to smooth things over. The American flag has quite gone out of fashion; it's very carefully folded up like an old table-cloth. Why should we apologize? The English never apologize —do they? No; I must say I never apologize. You must take us as we come—with all our imperfections on our heads. Of course we haven't your country life, and your old ruins, and your great estates, and your leisure class, and all that. But if we haven't, I should think you might find it a pleasant change—I think any country is pleasant where they have pleasant manners.

"Captain Littledale told me he had never seen such pleasant manners as at Newport, and he had been a great deal in European society. Hadn't he been in the diplomatic service? He told me the dream of his life was to get appointed to a diplomatic post at Washington. But he doesn't seem to have succeeded. I suppose that in England promotion—and all that sort of thing—is fearfully slow. With us, you know, it's a great deal too fast. You see, I admit our drawbacks. But I must confess I think Newport is an ideal place. I don't know anything like it anywhere. Captain Littledale told me he didn't know anything like it anywhere. It's entirely different from most watering-places; it's a most charming life. I must say I think that when one goes to a foreign country one ought to enjoy the differences. Of course there are differences, otherwise what did one come abroad for? Look for your pleasure in the differences, Lord Lambeth; that's the way to do it; and then I am sure you will find American society—at least, Newport society—most charming and interesting. I wish very much my husband were here; but he's dreadfully confined to New York. I suppose you think that is very strange—for a gentleman. But you see we haven't any leisure class."

Mrs. Westgate's discourse, delivered in a soft, sweet voice, flowed on like a miniature torrent, and was interrupted by a hundred little smiles, glances, and gestures, which might have figured the irregularities and obstructions of such a stream. Lord Lambeth listened to her with, it must be confessed, a rather ineffectual attention, although he indulged in a good many little murmurs and ejaculations of assent and deprecation. He had no great faculty for apprehending generalizations. There were some three or four indeed which, in the play of his own intelligence, he had originated, and which had seemed convenient at the moment; but at the present time he could hardly have been said to follow Mrs. Westgate as she darted gracefully about in the sea of speculation. Fortunately, she asked for no special rejoinder, for she looked about at the rest of the company as well, and smiled at Percy Beaumont, on the other side of her, as if he, too, must understand her and agree with her. He was rather more successful than his companion; for besides being, as we know, cleverer, his attention was not vaguely distracted by close scrutiny to a remarkably interesting young girl with dark hair and blue eyes. This was the case with Lord Lambeth, to whom it occurred after a while that the young girl with blue eyes and dark hair was the pretty sister of whom Mrs. Westgate had spoken. She presently turned to him with a remark which established her identity.

"It's a great pity you couldn't have brought my brother-in-law with you. It's a great shame he should be in New York in these days."

"Oh yes! it's so very hot," said Lord Lambeth.

"It must be dreadful," said the young girl.

"I dare say he is very busy," Lord Lambeth observed.

"The gentlemen in America work too much," the young girl went on.

"Oh, do they? I dare say they like it," said her interlocutor.

"I don't like it. One never sees them."

"Don't you, really?" asked Lord Lambeth. "I shouldn't have fancied that."

"Have you come to study American manners?" asked the young girl.

"Oh, I don't know. I just came over for a lark. I haven't got long." Here there was a pause, and Lord Lambeth began again. "But Mr. Westgate will come down here, will he not?"

"I certainly hope he will. He must help to entertain you and Mr. Beaumont."

Lord Lambeth looked at her a little with his handsome brown eyes. "Do you suppose he would have come down with us if we had urged him?"

Mr. Westgate's sister-in-law was silent a moment, and then, "I dare say he would," she answered.

"Really!" said the young Englishman. "He was immensely civil to Beaumont and me," he added.

"He is a dear, good fellow," the young lady rejoined, "and he is a perfect husband. But all Americans are that," she continued, smiling.

"Really!" Lord Lambeth exclaimed again, and wondered whether all American ladies had such a passion for generalizing as these two.

He sat there a good while: there was a great deal of talk; it was all very friendly and lively and jolly. Every one present, sooner or later, said something to him, and seemed to make a particular point of addressing him by name. Two or three other persons came in, and there was a shifting of seats and changing of places; the gentlemen all entered into intimate conversation with the two Englishmen, made them urgent offers of hospitality, and hoped they might frequently be of service to them. They were afraid Lord Lambeth and Mr. Beaumont were not very comfortable at their hotel; that it was not, as one of them said, "so private as those dear little English inns of yours." This last gentleman went on to say that unfortunately, as yet, perhaps, privacy was not quite so easily obtained in America as might be desired; still, he continued, you could generally get it by paying for it; in fact, you could get everything in America nowadays by paying for it. American life was certainly growing a great deal more private; it was growing very much like England. Everything at Newport, for instance, was thoroughly private; Lord Lambeth would probably be struck with that. It was also represented to the strangers that it mattered very little whether their hotel was agreeable, as every one would want them to make visits; they would stay with other people, and, in any case, they would be a great deal at Mrs. Westgate's. They would find that very charming; it was the pleasantest house in Newport. It was a pity Mr. Westgate was always away; he was a man of the highest ability—very acute, very acute. He worked like a horse, and he left his wife—well, to do about as she liked. He liked her to enjoy herself, as she seemed to know how. She was extremely brilliant, and a splendid talker. Some people preferred her sister; but Miss Alden was very different; she was in a different style altogether. Some people even thought her prettier, and, certainly, she was not so sharp. She was more in the Boston style; she had lived a great deal in Boston, and she was very highly educated. Boston girls, it was propounded, were more like English young ladies.

Lord Lambeth had presently a chance to test the truth of this proposition, for on the company rising in compliance with a suggestion from their hostess that they should walk down to the rocks and look at the sea, the young Englishman again found himself, as they strolled across the grass, in proximity to Mrs. Westgate's sister. Though she was but a girl of twenty, she appeared to feel the obligation to exert an active hospitality; and this was, perhaps, the more to be noticed as she seemed by nature a reserved and retiring person, and had little of her sister's fraternizing quality. She was perhaps, rather too thin, and she was a little pale; but as she moved slowly over the grass, with her arms hanging at her sides, looking gravely for a moment at the sea and then brightly, for all her gravity, at him, Lord Lambeth thought her at least as pretty as Mrs. Westgate, and reflected that if this was the Boston style the Boston style was very charming. He thought she looked very clever; he could imagine that she was highly educated; but at the same time she seemed gentle and graceful. For all her cleverness, however, he felt that she had to think a little what to say; she didn't say the first thing that came into her head; he had come from a different part of the world and from a different society, and she was trying to adapt her conversation. The others were scattering themselves near the rocks; Mrs. Westgate had charge of Percy Beaumont.

"Very jolly place, isn't it?" said Lord Lambeth. "It's a very jolly place to sit."

"Very charming," said the young girl. "I often sit here; there are all kinds of cosey corners—as if they had been made on purpose."

"Ah, I suppose you have had some of them made," said the young man.

Miss Alden looked at him a moment. "Oh no, we have had nothing made. It's pure nature."

"I should think you would have a few little benches—rustic seats, and that sort of thing. It might be so jolly to sit here, you know," Lord Lambeth went on.

"I am afraid we haven't so many of those things as you," said the young girl, thoughtfully.

"I dare say you go in for pure nature, as you were saying. Nature over here must be so grand, you know." And Lord Lambeth looked about him.

The little coast-line hereabouts was very pretty, but it was not at all grand, and Miss Alden appeared to rise to a perception of this fact. "I am afraid it seems to you very rough," she said. "It's not like the coast scenery in Kingsley's novels."

"Ah, the novels always overdo it, you know," Lord Lambeth rejoined. "You must not go by the novels."

They were wandering about a little on the rocks, and they stopped and looked down into a narrow chasm where the rising tide made a curious bellowing sound. It was loud enough to prevent their hearing each other, and they stood there for some moments in silence. The young girl looked at her companion, observing him attentively, but covertly, as women, even when very young, know how to do. Lord Lambeth repaid observation; tall, straight, and strong, he was handsome as certain young Englishmen, and certain young Englishmn almost alone, are handsome, with a perfect finish of feature and a look of intellectual repose and gentle good-temper which seemed somehow to be consequent upon his well-cut nose and chin. And to speak of Lord Lambeth's expression of intellectual repose is not simply a civil way of saying that he looked stupid. He was evidently not a young man of an irritable imagination; he was not, as he would himself have said, tremendously clever; but though there was a kind of appealing dulness in his eye, he looked thoroughly reasonable and competent, and his appearance proclaimed that to be a nobleman, an athlete, and an excellent fellow was a sufficiently brilliant combination of qualities. The young girl beside him, it may be attested without further delay, thought him the handsomest young man she had ever seen; and Bessie Alden's imagination, unlike that of her companion, was irritable. He, however, was also making up his mind that she was uncommonly pretty.

"I dare say it's very gay here—that you have lots of balls and parties," he said; for, if he was not tremendously clever, he rather prided himself on having, with women, a sufficiency of conversation.

"Oh yes, there is a great deal going on," Bessie Alden replied. "There are not so many balls, but there are a good many other things. You will see for yourself; we live rather in the midst of it."

"It's very kind of you to say that. But I thought you Americans were always dancing."

"I suppose we dance a good deal; but I have never seen much of it. We don't do it much, at any rate, in summer. And I am sure," said Bessie Alden. "that we don't have so many balls as you have in England."

"Really!" exclaimed Lord Lambeth. "Ah, in England it all depends, you know."

"You will not think much of our gayeties," said the young girl, looking at him with a little mixture of interrogation and decision which was peculiar to her. The interrogation seemed earnest and the decision seemed arch; but the mixture, at any rate, was charming. "Those things, with us, are much less splendid than in England."

"I fancy that you don't mean that," said Lord Lambeth, laughing.

"I assure you I mean everything I say," the young girl declared. "Certainly, from what I have read about English society, it is very different."

"Ah well, you know," said her companion, "those things are often described by fellows who know nothing about them. You mustn't mind what you read."

"Oh, I *shall* mind what I read!" Bessie Alden rejoined. "When I read Thackeray and George Eliot, how can I help minding them?"

"Ah, well, Thackeray and George Eliot," said the young nobleman; "I haven't read much of them."

"Don't you suppose they know about society?" asked Bessie
Alden.

"Oh, I dare say they know; they were so clever. But these fashionable novels," said Lord Lambeth, "they are awful rot, you know."

His companion looked at him a moment with her dark blue eyes,
and then she looked down in the chasm where the water was tumbling about. "Do you mean Mrs. Gore, for instance?" she said,
presently, raising her eyes.

"I am afraid I haven't read that, either," was the young man's
rejoinder, laughing a little and blushing. "I am afraid you'll think
I am not very intellectual."

"Reading Mrs. Gore is no proof of intellect. But I like reading
everything about English life—even poor books. I am so curious
about it."

"Aren't ladies always curious?" asked the young man, jestingly.

But Bessie Alden appeared to desire to answer his question
seriously. "I don't think so—I don't think we are enough so—that
we care about many things. So it's all the more of a compliment,"
she added, "that I should want to know so much about England."

The logic here seemed a little close; but Lord Lambeth, made
conscious of a compliment, found his natural modesty just at hand.
"I am sure you know a great deal more than I do."

"I really think I know a great deal—for a person who has never
been there."

"Have you really never been there?" cried Lord Lambeth.
"Fancy!"

"Never—except in imagination," said the young girl.

"Fancy!" repeated her companion. "But I dare say you'll go soon,
won't you?"

"It's the dream of my life!" said Bessie Alden, smiling.

"But your sister seems to know a tremendous lot about London,"
Lord Lambeth went on.

The young girl was silent a moment. "My sister and I are two
very different persons," she presently said. "She has been a great
deal in Europe. She has been in England several times. She has known
a great many English people."

"But you must have known some, too," said Lord Lambeth.

"I don't think that I have ever spoken to one before. You are the first Englishman that—to my knowledge—I have ever talked with."

Bessie Alden made this statement with a certain gravity—almost, as it seemed to Lord Lambeth, an impressiveness. Attempts at impressiveness always made him feel awkward, and he now began to laugh and swing his stick. "Ah, you would have been sure to know!" he said. And then he added, after an instant, "I'm sorry I am not a better specimen."

The young girl looked away; but she smiled, laying aside her impressiveness. "You must remember that you are only a beginning," she said. Then she retraced her steps, leading the way back to the lawn, where they saw Mrs. Westgate come towards them with Percy Beaumont still at her side. "Perhaps I shall go to England next year," Miss Alden continued; "I want to, immensely. My sister is going to Europe, and she has asked me to go with her. If we go, I shall make her stay as long as possible in London."

"Ah, you must come in July," said Lord Lambeth. "That's the time when there is most going on."

"I don't think I can wait till July," the young girl rejoined. "By the first of May I shall be very impatient." They had gone farther, and Mrs. Westgate and her companion were near them. "Kitty," said Miss Alden, "I have given out that we are going to London next May. So please to conduct yourself accordingly."

Pearcy Beaumont wore a somewhat animated—even a slightly irritated—air. He was by no means so handsome a man as his cousin, although in his cousin's absence he might have passed for a striking specimen of the tall, muscular, fair-bearded, clear-eyed Englishman. Just now Beaumont's clear eyes, which were small and of a pale gray color, had a rather troubled light, and, after glancing at Bessie Alden while she spoke, he rested them upon his kinsman. Mrs. Westgate meanwhile, with her superfluously pretty gaze, looked at every one alike.

"You had better wait till the time comes," she said to her sister. "Perhaps next May you won't care so much about London. Mr. Beaumont and I," she went on, smiling at her companion, "have had a tremendous discussion. We don't agree about anything. It's perfectly delightful."

"Oh, I say, Percy!" exclaimed Lord Lambeth

"I disagree," said Beaumont, stroking down his back hair, "even to the point of not thinking it delightful."

"Oh, I say!" cried Lord Lambeth again.

"I don't see anything delightful in my disagreeing with Mrs. Westgate," said Percy Beaumont.

"Well, I do!" Mrs. Westgate declared; and she turned to her sister. "You know you have to go to town. The phaeton is there. You had better take Lord Lambeth."

At this point Percy Beaumont certainly looked straight at his kinsman; he tried to catch his eye. But Lord Lambeth would not look at him; his own eyes were better occupied. "I shall be very happy," cried Bessie Alden. "I am only going to some shops. But I will drive you about and show you the place."

"An American woman who respects herself," said Mrs. Westgate, turning to Beaumont with her bright expository air, "must buy something every day of her life. If she cannot do it herself, she must send out some member of her family for the purpose. So Bessie goes forth to fulfil my mission."

The young girl had walked away, with Lord Lambeth by her side, to whom she was talking still; and Percy Beaumont watched them as they passed towards the house. "She fulfils her own mission," he presently said; "that of being a very attractive young lady."

"I don't know that I should say very attractive," Mrs. Westgate rejoined. "She is not so much that as she is charming, when you really know her. She is very shy."

"Oh, indeed!" said Percy Beaumont.

"Extremely shy," Mrs. Westgate repeated. "But she is a dear, good girl; she is a charming species of a girl. She is not in the least a flirt; that isn't at all her line; she doesn't know the alphabet of that sort of thing. She is very simple, very serious. She has lived a great deal in Boston, with another sister of mine—the eldest of us—who married a Bostonian. She is very cultivated—not at all like me; I am not in the least cultivated. She has studied immensely and read everything; she is what they call in Boston 'thoughtful.'"

"A rum sort of girl for Lambeth to get hold of!" his lordship's kinsman privately reflected.

"I really believe," Mrs. Westgate continued, "that the most charming girl in the world is a Boston superstructure upon a New York *fonds;* or perhaps a New York superstructure upon a Boston *fonds.* At any rate, it's the mixture," said Mrs. Westgate, who continued to give Percy Beaumont a great deal of information.

Lord Lambeth got into a little basket phaeton with Bessie Alden, and she drove him down the long avenue, whose extent he had measured on foot a couple of hours before, into the ancient town, as it was called in that part of the world, of Newport. The ancient town was a curious affair—a collection of fresh-looking little wooden houses, painted white, scattered over a hill-side and clustered about a long, straight street, paved with enormous cobble-stones. There were plenty of shops, a large proportion of which appeared to be those of fruit venders, with piles of huge watermelons and pumpkins stacked in front of them; and, drawn up before the shops, or bumping about on the cobble-stones, were innumerable other basket-phaetons freighted with ladies of high fashion, who greeted each other from vehicle to vehicle, and conversed on the edge of the pavement in a manner that struck Lord Lambeth as demonstrative, with a great many "Oh, my dears," and little, quick exclamations and caresses. His companion went into seventeen shops—he amused himself with counting them—and accumulated at the bottom of the phaeton a pile of bundles that hardly left the young Englishman a place for his feet. As she had no groom nor footman, he sat in the phaeton to hold the ponies, where, although he was not a particularly acute observer, he saw much to entertain him—especially the ladies just mentioned, who wandered up and down with the appearance of a kind of aimless intentness, as if they were looking for something to buy, and who, tripping in and out of their vehicles, displayed remarkably pretty feet. It all seemed to Lord Lambeth very odd and bright and gay. Of course, before they got back to the villa, he had had a great deal of desultory conversation with Bessie Alden.

The young Englishmen spent the whole of that day and the whole of many successive days in what the French call the *intimité* of their new friends. They agreed that it was extremely jolly, that they had never known anything more agreeable. It is not proposed to narrate minutely the incidents of their sojourn on this charming shore; though if it were convenient I might present a record of impressions none the less delectable that they were not exhaustively analyzed. Many of them still linger in the minds of our travellers, attended by a train of harmonious images—images of brilliant mornings on lawns and piazzas that overlooked the sea; of innumerable pretty girls; of infinite lounging and talking and laughing and flirting and lunching and dining; of universal friendliness and frankness; of occasions on which they knew every one and everything, and had an extraordinary sense of ease; of drives and rides in the late afternoon over gleaming beaches, on long sea-roads beneath a sky lighted up by marvellous sunsets; of suppers, on the return, informal, irregular, agreeable; of evenings at open windows or on the perpetual verandas.

in the summer starlight, above the warm Atlantic. The young Englishmen were introduced to everybody, entertained by everybody, intimate with everybody. At the end of three days they had removed their luggage from the hotel, and gone to stay with Mrs. Westgate—a step to which Percy Beaumont at first offered some conscientious opposition. I call his opposition conscientious, because it was founded upon some talk that he had had, on the second day, with Bessie Alden. He had indeed had a good deal of talk with her, for she was not literally always in conversation with Lord Lambeth. He had meditated upon Mrs. Westgate's account of her sister, and he discovered for himself that the young lady was clever, and appeared to have read a great deal. She seemed very nice, though he could not make out that, as Mrs. Westgate had said, she was shy. If she was shy, she carried it off very well.

"Mr. Beaumont," she had said, "please tell me something about Lord Lambeth's family. How would you say it in England—his position?"

"His position?" Percy Beaumont repeated.

"His rank, or whatever you call it. Unfortunately, we haven't got a 'peerage,' like the people in Thackeray."

"That's a great pity," said Beaumont. "You would find it all set forth there so much better than I can do it."

"He is a peer, then?"

"Oh yes, he is a peer."

"And has he any other title than Lord Lambeth?"

"His title is the Marquis of Lambeth," said Beaumont; and then he was silent. Bessie Alden appeared to be looking at him with interest. "He is the son of the Duke of Bayswater," he added, presently.

"The eldest son?"

"The only son."

"And are his parents living?"

"Oh yes; if his father were not living he would be a duke."

"So that when his father dies," pursued Bessie Alden, with more simplicity than might have been expected in a clever girl, "he will become Duke of Bayswater?"

"Of course," said Percy Beaumont. "But his father is in excellent health."

"And his mother?"

Beaumont smiled a little. "The duchess is uncommonly robust."

"And has he any sisters?"

"Yes, there are two."

"And what are they called?"

"One of them is married. She is the Countess of Pimlico."

"And the other?"

"The other is unmarried; she is plain Lady Julia."

Bessie Alden looked at him a moment. "Is she very plain?"

Beaumont began to laugh again. "You would not find her so handsome as her brother," he said; and it was after this that he attempted to dissuade the heir of the Duke of Bayswater from accepting Mrs. Westgate's invitation. "Depend upon it," he said, "that girl means to try for you."

"It seems to me you are doing your best to make a fool of me," the modest young nobleman answered.

"She has been asking me," said Beaumont, "all about your people and your possessions."

"I am sure it is very good of her!" Lord Lambeth rejoined.

"Well, then," observed his companion, "if you go, you go with your eyes open."

"D—n my eyes!" exclaimed Lord Lambeth. "If one is to be a dozen times a day at the house, it is a great deal more convenient to sleep there. I am sick of travelling up and down this beastly avenue."

Since he had determined to go, Percy Beaumont would, of course, have been very sorry to allow him to go alone; he was a man of conscience, and he remembered his promise to the duchess. It was obviously the memory of this promise that made him say to his companion a couple of days later that he rather wondered he should be so fond of that girl.

"In the first place, how do you know how fond I am of her?" asked Lord Lambeth. "And, in the second place, why shouldn't I be fond of her?"

"I shouldn't think she would be in your line."

"What do you call my 'line?' You don't set her down as 'fast?' "

"Exactly so. Mrs. Westgate tells me that there is no such thing as the 'fast girl' in America; that it's an English invention, and that the term has no meaning here."

"All the better. It's an animal I detest."

"You prefer a blue-stocking."

"Is that what you call Miss Alden?"

"Her sister tells me," said Percy Beaumont, "that she is tremendously literary."

"I don't know anything about that. She is certainly very clever."

"Well," said Beaumont, "I should have supposed you would have found that sort of thing awfully slow."

"In point of fact," Lord Lambeth rejoined, "I find it uncommonly lively."

After this Percy Beaumont held his tongue; but on August 10th he wrote to the Duchess of Bayswater. He was, as I have said, a man of conscience, and he had a strong, incorruptible sense of the proprieties of life. His kinsman, meanwhile, was having a great deal of talk with Bessie Alden—on the red sea-rocks beyond the lawn; in the course of long island rides, with a slow return in the glowing twilight; on the deep veranda late in the evening. Lord Lambeth, who had stayed at many houses, had never stayed at a house in which it was possible for a young man to converse so frequently with a young lady. This young lady no longer applied to Percy Beaumont for information concerning his lordship. She addressed herself directly to the young nobleman. She asked him a great many questions, some of which bored him a little; for he took no pleasure in talking about himself.

"Lord Lambeth," said Bessie Alden, "are you a hereditary legislator?"

"Oh, I say!" cried Lord Lambeth, "don't make me call myself such names as that."

"But you are a member of Parliament," said the young girl.

"I don't like the sound of that either."

"Don't you sit in the House of Lords?" Bessie Alden went on.

"Very seldom," said Lord Lambeth.

"Is it an important position?" she asked.

"Oh dear no," said Lord Lambeth.

"I should think it would be very grand," said Bessie Alden, "to possess, simply by an accident of birth, the right to make laws for a great nation."

"Ah, but one doesn't make laws. It's a great humbug."

"I don't believe that," the young girl declared. "It must be a great privilege, and I should think that if one thought of it in the right way—from a high point of view—it would be very inspiring."

"The less one thinks of it the better," Lord Lambeth affirmed.

"I think it's tremendous," said Bessie Alden; and on another occasion she asked him if he had any tenantry. Hereupon it was that, as I have said, he was a little bored.

"Do you want to buy up their leases?" he asked.

"Well, have you got any livings?" she demanded.

"Oh, I say!" he cried. "Have you got a clergyman that is looking out?" But she made him tell her that he had a castle; he confessed to but one. It was the place in which he had been born and brought up, and, as he had an old-time liking for it, he was beguiled into describing it a little, and saying it was really very jolly. Bessie Alden listened with great interest, and declared that she would give the world to see such a place. Whereupon—"It would be awfully kind of you to come and stay there," said Lord Lambeth. He took a vague satisfaction in the circumstance that Percy Beaumont had not heard him make the remark I have just recorded.

Mr. Westgate all this time had not, as they said at Newport, "come on." His wife more than once announced that she expected him on the morrow; but on the morrow she wandered about a little, with a telegram in her jewelled fingers, declaring it was very tiresome that his business detained him in New York; that he could only hope the Englishmen were having a good time. "I must say," said Mrs. Westgate, "that it is no thanks to him if you are." And she went on to explain, while she continued that slow-paced promenade which enabled her well-adjusted skirts to display themselves so advantageously, that unfortunately in America there was no leisure class. It was Lord Lambeth's theory, freely propounded when the young men were together, that Percy Beaumont was having a very good time with Mrs. Westgate, and that, under the pretext of meeting for the purpose of animated discussion, they were indulging in practices that imparted a shade of hypocrisy to the lady's regret for her husband's absence.

"I assure you we are always discussing and differing," said Percy Beaumont. "She is awfully argumentative. American ladies certainly don't mind contradicting you. Upon my word, I don't think I was ever treated so by a woman before. She's so devilish positive."

Mrs. Westgate's positive quality, however, evidently had its attractions, for Beaumont was constantly at his hostess's side. He detached himself one day to the extent of going to New York to talk over the Tennessee Central with Mr. Westgate; but he was absent only forty-eight hours, during which, with Mr. Westgate's assistance, he completely settled this piece of business. "They certainly do things quickly in New York," he observed to his cousin; and he added that Mr. Westgate had seemed very uneasy lest his wife should miss her visitor—he had been in such an awful hurry to send him back to her. "I'm afraid you'll never come up to an American husband, if that's what the wives expect," he said to Lord Lambeth.

Mrs. Westgate, however, was not to enjoy much longer the entertainment with which an indulgent husband had desired to keep her provided. On August 21st Lord Lambeth received a telegram from his mother, requesting him to return immediately to England; his father had been taken ill, and it was his filial duty to come to him.

The young Englishman was visibly annoyed. "What the deuce does it mean?" he asked of his kinsman. "What am I to do?"

Percy Beaumont was annoyed as well; he had deemed it his duty, as I have narrated, to write to the duchess, but he had not expected that this distinguished woman would act so promptly upon his hint. "It means," he said, "that your father is laid up. I don't suppose it's anything serious; but you have no option. Take the first steamer; but don't be alarmed."

Lord Lambeth made his farewells; but the few last words that he exchanged with Bessie Alden are the only ones that have a place in our record. "Of course I needn't assure you," he said, "that if you should come to England next year, I expect to be the first person that you inform of it."

Bessie Alden looked at him a little and she smiled. "Oh, if we come to London," she answered, "I should think you would hear of it."

Percy Beaumont returned with his cousin, and his sense of duty compelled him, one windless afternoon, in mid-Atlantic, to say to Lord Lambeth that he suspected that the duchess's telegram was in part the result of something he himself had written to her. "I wrote to her—as I explicitly notified you I had promised to do—that you were extremely interested in a little American girl."

Lord Lambeth was extremely angry, and he indulged for some moments in the simple language of indignation. But I have said that he was a reasonable young man, and I can give no better proof of it than the fact that he remarked to his companion at the end of half an hour, "You were quite right, after all. I am very much interested in her. Only, to be fair," he added, "you should have told my mother also that she is not—seriously—interested in me."

Percy Beaumont gave a little laugh. "There is nothing so charming as modesty in a young man in your position. That speech is a capital proof that you are sweet on her."

"She is not interested—she is not!" Lord Lambeth repeated.

"My dear fellow," said his companion, "you are very far gone."

PART II

In point of fact, as Percy Beaumont would have said, Mrs. Westgate disembarked on May 18th on the British coast. She was accompanied by her sister, but she was not attended by another member of her family. To the deprivation of her husband's society Mrs. Westgate was, however, habituated; she had made half a dozen journeys to Europe without him, and she now accounted for his absence, to interrogative friends on this side of the Atlantic, by allusion to the regrettable but conspicuous fact that in America there was no leisure class. The two ladies came up to London and alighted at Jones's Hotel, where Mrs. Westgate, who had made on former occasions the most agreeable impression at this establishment, received an obsequious greeting. Bessie Alden had felt much excited about coming to England; she had expected the "associations" would be very charming, that it would be an infinite pleasure to rest her eyes upon the things she had read about in the poets and historians. She was very fond of the poets and historians, of the picturesque, of the past, of retrospect, of mementos and reverberations of greatness; so that on coming into the great English world, where strangeness and familiarity would go hand in hand, she was prepared for a multitude of fresh emotions. They began very promptly—these tender, fluttering sensations; they began with the sight of the beautiful English landscape, whose dark richness was quickened and brightened by the season; with the carpeted fields and flowing hedge-rows, as she looked at them from the window of the train; with the spires of the rural churches peeping above the rook-haunted tree-tops; with the oak-studded parks, the ancient homes, the cloudy light, the speech, the manners, the thousand differences. Mrs. Westgate's impressions had, of course, much less novelty and keenness, and she gave but a wandering attention to her sister's ejaculations and rhapsodies.

"You know my enjoyment of England is not so intellectual as Bessie's," she said to several of her friends in the course of her visit to this country. "And yet if it is not intellectual, I can't say it is physical. I don't think I can quite say what it is—my enjoyment of England." When once it was settled that the two ladies should come abroad and should spend a few weeks in England on their way to the Continent, they of course exchanged a good many allusions to their London acquaintance.

"It will certainly be much nicer having friends there," Bessie Alden had said one day, as she sat on the sunny deck of the steamer at her sister's feet, on a large blue rug.

"Whom do you mean by friends?" Mrs. Westgate asked.

"All those English gentlemen whom you have known and entertained. Captain Littledale, for instance. And Lord Lambeth and Mr. Beaumont," added Bessie Alden.

"Do you expect them to give us a very grand reception?"

Bessie reflected a moment; she was addicted, as we know, to reflection. "Well, yes."

"My poor, sweet child!" murmured her sister.

"What have I said that is so silly?" asked Bessie.

"You are a little too simple; just a little. It is very becoming, but it pleases people at your expense."

"I am certainly too simple to understand you," said Bessie.

"Shall I tell you a story?" asked her sister.

"If you would be so good. That is what they do to amuse simple people."

Mrs. Westgate consulted her memory, while her companion sat gazing at the shining sea. "Did you ever hear of the Duke of Green-Erin?"

"I think not," said Bessie.

"Well, it's no matter," her sister went on.

"It's a proof of my simplicity."

"My story is meant to illustrate that of some other people," said Mrs. Westgate. "The Duke of Green-Erin is what they call in England a great swell, and some five years ago he came to America. He spent most of his time in New York, and in New York he spent his days and his nights at the Butterworths'. You have heard, at least, of the Butterworths. *Bien.* They did everything in the world for him—they turned themselves inside out. They gave him a dozen dinner-parties and balls, and were the means of his being invited to fifty more. At first he used to come into Mrs. Butterworth's box at the opera in a tweed travelling suit; but some one stopped that. At any rate, he had a beautiful time, and they parted the best friends in the world. Two years elapse, and the Butterworths come abroad and go to London. The first thing they see in all the papers—in England those things are in the most prominent place—is that the Duke of Green-Erin has arrived in town for the season. They wait a little, and then Mr. Butterworth—as polite as ever—goes and leaves a card. They wait a little more; the visit is not returned; they wait three weeks—*silence de mort*—the duke gives no sign. The Butterworths see a lot of other people, put down the Duke of Green-Erin as a rude, ungrateful man, and forget all about him. One fine day they go to the Ascot races, and there they meet him face to face. He stares a moment, and then comes up to Butterworth, taking something from his pocket-book—something which proves to be a banknote. 'I'm glad to see you, Mr. Butterworth,' he says, 'so that I can pay you that £10 I lost to you in New York. I saw the other day you remembered our bet; here are the £10, Mr. Butterworth. Good-bye, Mr. Butterworth.' And off he goes, and that's the last they see of the Duke of Green-Erin."

"Is that your story?" asked Bessie Alden.

"Don't you think it's interesting?" her sister replied.

"I don't believe it."

"Ah," cried Mrs. Westgate, "you are not so simple, after all! Believe it or not, as you please; there is no smoke without fire."

"Is that the way," asked Bessie, after a moment, "that you expect your friends to treat you?"

"I defy them to treat me very ill, because I shall not give them the opportunity. With the best will in the world, in that case they can't be very offensive."

Bessie Alden was silent a moment. "I don't see what makes you talk that way," she said. "The English are a great people."

"Exactly; and that is just the way they have grown great—by dropping you when you have ceased to be useful. People say they are not clever; but I think they are very clever."

"You know you have liked them—all the Englishmen you have seen," said Bessie.

"They have liked me," her sister rejoined; "it would be more correct to say that. And, of course, one likes that."

Bessie Alden resumed for some moments her studies in sea-green. "Well," she said, "whether they like me or not, I mean to like them. And, happily," she added, "Lord Lambeth does not owe me £10."

During the first few days after their arrival at Jones's Hotel our charming Americans were much occupied with what they would have called looking about them. They found occasion to make a large number of purchases, and their opportunities for conversation were such only as were offered by the deferential London shopmen. Bessie Alden, even in driving from the station, took an immense fancy to the British metropolis, and at the risk of exhibiting her as a young woman of vulgar tastes, it must be recorded that for a considerable period she desired no higher pleasure than to drive about the crowded streets in a hansom cab. To her attentive eyes they were full of a strange, picturesque life, and it is at least beneath the dignity of our historic muse to enumerate the trivial objects and incidents which this simple young lady from Boston found so entertaining. It may be freely mentioned, however, that whenever, after a round of visits in Bond Street and Regent Street, she was about to return with her sister to Jones's Hotel, she made an earnest request that they should be driven home by way of Westminster Abbey. She had begun by asking whether it would not be possible to take in the Tower on the way to their lodgings; but it happened that at a more primitive stage of her culture Mrs. Westgate had paid a visit to this venerable monument, which she spoke of ever afterwards vaguely as a dreadful disappointment; so that she expressed the liveliest disapproval of any attempt to combine historical researches with the purchase of hair-brushes and notepaper. The most she would consent to do in this line was to spend half an hour at Madame Tussaud's, where she saw several dusty wax effigies of members of the royal family. She told Bessie that if she wished to go to the Tower she must get some one else to take her. Bessie expressed hereupon an earnest disposition to go alone; but upon this proposal as well, Mrs. Westgate sprinkled cold water.

"Remember," she said, "that you are not in your innocent little Boston. It is not a question of walking up and down Beacon Street." Then she went on to explain that there were two classes of American girls in Europe—those that walked about alone and those that did not. "You happen to belong, my dear," she said to her sister, "to the class that does not."

"It is only," answered Bessie, laughing, "because you happen to prevent me." And she devoted much private meditation to this question of effecting a visit to the Tower of London.

Suddenly it seemed as if the problem might be solved; the two ladies at Jones's Hotel received a visit from Willie Woodley. Such was the social appelation of a young American who had sailed from New York a few days after their own departure, and who, having the privilege of intimacy with them in that city, had lost no time, on his arrival in London, in coming to pay them his respects. He had, in fact, gone to see them directly after going to see his tailor, than which there can be no greater exhibition of promptitude on the part of a young American who had just alighted at the Charing Cross Hotel. He was a slim, pale youth, of the most amiable disposition, famous for the skill with which he led the "German" in New York. Indeed, by the young ladies who habitually figured in this Terpsichorean revel he was believed to be "the best dancer in the world;" it was in these terms that he was always spoken of, and that his identity was indicated. He was the gentlest, softest young man it was possible to meet; he was beautifully dressed—"in the English style"—and he knew an immense deal about London. He had been at Newport during the previous summer, at the time of our young Englishmen's visit, and he took extreme pleasure in the society of Bessie Alden, whom he always adressed as "Miss Bessie." She immediately arranged with him, in the presence of her sister, that he should conduct her to the scene of Anne Boleyn's execution.

"You may do as you please," said Mrs. Westgate. "Only—if you desire the information—it is not the custom here for young ladies to knock about London with young men."

"Miss Bessie has waltzed with me so often," observed Willie Woodley; "she can surely go out with me in a hansom!"

"I consider waltzing," said Mrs. Westgate, "the most innocent pleasure of our time."

"It's a compliment to our time!" exclaimed the young man, with a little laugh in spite of himself.

"I don't see why I should regard what is done here," said Bessie Alden. "Why should I suffer the restrictions of a society of which I enjoy none of the privileges?"

"That's very good—very good," murmured Willie Woodley.

"Oh, go to the Tower, and feel the axe, if you like," said Mrs. Westgate. "I consent to your going with Mr. Woodley; but I should not let you go with an Englishman."

"Miss Bessie wouldn't care to go with an Englishman!" Mr. Woodley declared, with a faint asperity that was, perhaps, not unnatural in a young man, who, dressing in the manner that I have indicated, and knowing a great deal, as I have said, about London, saw no reason for drawing these sharp distinctions. He agreed upon a day with Miss Bessie—a day of that same week.

An ingenious mind might, perhaps, trace a connection between the young girl's allusion to her destitution of social privileges and a question she asked on the morrow, as she sat with her sister at lunch.

"Don't you mean to write to—to any one?" said Bessie.

"I wrote this morning to Captain Littledale," Mrs. Westgate replied.

"But Mr. Woodley said that Captain Littledale had gone to India."

"He said he thought he had heard so; he knew nothing about it."

For a moment Bessie Alden said nothing more; then, at last, "And don't you intend to write to—to Mr. Beaumont?" she inquired.

"You mean to Lord Lambeth," said her sister.

"I said Mr. Beaumont, because he was so good a friend of yours."

Mrs. Westgate looked at the young girl with sisterly candor. "I don't care two straws for Mr. Beaumont."

"You were certainly very nice to him."

"I am nice to every one," said Mrs. Westgate, simply.

"To every one but me," rejoined Bessie, smiling.

Her sister continued to look at her; then, at last, "Are you in love with Lord Lambeth?" she asked.

The young girl stared a moment, and the question was apparently too humorous even to make her blush. "Not that I know of," she answered.

"Because, if you are," Mrs. Westgate went on, "I shall certainly not send for him."

"That proves what I said," declared Bessie, smiling—"that you are not nice to me."

"It would be a poor service, my dear child," said her sister.

"In what sense? There is nothing against Lord Lambeth that I know of."

Mrs. Westgate was silent a moment. "You *are* in love with him then?"

Bessie stared again; but this time she blushed a little. "Ah! if you won't be serious," she answered, "we will not mention him again."

For some moments Lord Lambeth was not mentioned again, and it was Mrs. Westgate who, at the end of this period, reverted to him. "Of course I will let him know we are here, because I think he would be hurt—justly enough—if we should go away without seeing him. It is fair to give him a chance to come and thank me for the kindness we showed him. But I don't want to seem eager."

"Neither do I," said Bessie, with a little laugh.

"Though I confess," added her sister, "that I am curious to see how he will behave."

"He behaved very well at Newport."

"Newport is not London. At Newport he could do as he liked; but here it is another affair. He has to have an eye to consequences."

"If he had more freedom, then, at Newport," argued Bessie, "it is the more to his credit that he behaved well; and if he has to be so careful here, it is possible he will behave even better. "

"Better—better," repeated her sister. "My dear child, what is your point of view?"

"How do you mean—my point of view?"

"Don't you care for Lord Lambeth—a little?"

This time Bessie Alden was displeased; she slowly got up from the table, turning her face away from her sister. "You will oblige me by not talking so," she said.

Mrs. Westgate sat watching her for some moments as she moved slowly about the room and went and stood at the window. "I will write to him this afternoon," she said at last.

"Do as you please!" Bessie answered; and presently she turned round. "I am not afraid to say that I like Lord Lambeth. I like him very much."

"He is not clever," Mrs. Westgate declared.

"Well, there have been clever people whom I have disliked," said Bessie Alden; "so that I suppose I may like a stupid one. Besides, Lord Lambeth is not stupid."

"Not so stupid as he looks!" exclaimed her sister, smiling.

"If I were in love with Lord Lambeth, as you said just now, it would be bad policy on your part to abuse him."

"My dear child, don't give me lessons in policy!" cried Mrs. Westgate. "The policy I mean to follow is very deep."

The young girl began to walk about the room again; then she stopped before her sister. "I have never heard in the course of five minutes," she said, "so many hints and innuendoes. I wish you would tell me in plain English what you mean."

"I mean that you may be much annoyed."

"That is still only a hint," said Bessie.

Her sister looked at her, hesitating an instant. "It will be said of you that you have come after Lord Lambeth—that you followed him."

Bessie Alden threw back her pretty head like a startled hind, and a look flashed into her face that made Mrs. Westgate rise from her chair. "Who says such things as that?" she demanded.

"People here."

"I don't believe it," said Bessie.

"You have a very convenient faculty of doubt. But my policy will be, as I say, very deep. I shall leave you to find out this kind of thing for yourself."

Bessie fixed her eyes upon her sister, and Mrs. Westgate thought for a moment there were tears in them. "Do they talk that way here?" she asked.

"You will see, I shall leave you alone."

"Don't leave me alone," said Bessie Alden. "Take me away."

"No; I want to see what you make of it," her sister continued.

"I don't understand."

"You will understand after Lord Lambeth has come," said Mrs. Westgate, with a little laugh.

The two ladies had arranged that on this afternoon Willie Woodley should go with them to Hyde Park, where Bessie Alden expected to derive much entertainment from sitting on a little green chair, under the great trees, beside Rotten Row. The want of a suitable escort had hitherto rendered this pleasure inaccessible, but no escort now, for such an expedition, could have been more suitable than their devoted young countryman, whose mission in life, it might almost be said, was to find chairs for ladies, and who appeared on the stroke of half past five with a white camellia in his buttonhole.

"I have written to Lord Lambeth, my dear," said Mrs. Westgate to her sister, on coming into the room where Bessie Alden, drawing on her long gray gloves, was entertaining their visitor.

Bessie said nothing, but Willie Woodley exclaimed that his lordship was in town; he had seen his name in the *Morning Post*.

"Do you read the *Morning Post?*" asked Mrs. Westgate.

"Oh yes; it's great fun," Willie Woodley affirmed.

"I want so to see it," said Bessie; "there is so much about it in Thackeray."

"I will send it to you every morning," said Willie Woodley.

He found them what Bessie Alden thought excellent places, under the great trees, beside the famous avenue whose humors had been made familiar to the young girl's childhood by the pictures in *Punch*. The day was bright and warm, and the crowd of riders and spectators, and the great procession of carriages, were proportionately dense and brilliant. The scene bore the stamp of the London Season at its height, and Bessie Alden found more entertainment in it than she was able to express to her companions. She sat silent, under her parasol, and her imagination, according to its wont, let itself loose into the great changing assemblage of striking and suggestive figures. They stirred up a host of old impressions and preconceptions, and she found herself fitting a history to this person and a theory to that, and making a place for them all in her little private museum of types. But if she said little, her sister on one side and Willie Woodley on the other expressed themselves in lively alternation.

"Look at that green dress with blue flounces," said Mrs. Westgate. "*Quelle toilette!*"

"That's the Marquis of Blackborough," said the young man—"the one in the white coat. I heard him speak the other night in the House of Lords; it was something about ramrods; he called them *wamwods*. He's an awful swell."

"Did you ever see anything like the way they are pinned back?" Mrs. Westgate resumed. "They never know where to stop."

"They do nothing but stop," said Willie Woodley. "It prevents them from walking. Here comes a great celebrity, Lady Beatrice Bellevue. She's awfully fast; see what little steps she takes."

"Well, my dear," Mrs. Westgate pursued, "I hope you are getting some ideas for your *couturiére?*"

"I am getting plenty of ideas," said Bessie, "but I don't know that my *couturiére* would appreciate them."

Willie Woodley presently perceived a friend on horseback, who drove up beside the barrier of the Row and beckoned to him. He went forward, and the crowd of pedestrians closed about him, so that for some ten minutes he was hidden from sight. At last he reappeared, bringing a gentleman with him—a gentleman whom Bessie at first supposed to be his friend dismounted. But at a second glance she found herself looking at Lord Lambeth, who was shaking hands with her sister.

"I found him over there," said Willie Woodley, "and I told him you were here."

And then Lord Lambeth, touching his hat a little, shook hands with Bessie. "Fancy your being here!" he said. He was blushing and smiling; he looked very handsome, and he had a kind of splendor that he had not had in America. Bessie Alden's imagination, as we know, was just then in exercise; so that the tall young Englishman, as he stood there looking down at her, had the benefit of it. "He is handsomer and more splendid than anything I have ever seen," she said to herself. And then she remembered that he was a marquis, and she thought he looked like a marquis.

"I say, you know," he cried, "you ought to have let a man know you were here!"

"I wrote to you an hour ago," said Mrs. Westgate.

"Doesn't all the world know it?" asked Bessie, smiling.

"I assure you I didn't know it!" cried Lord Lambeth. "Upon my honor, I hadn't heard of it. Ask Woodley, now; had I, Woodley?"

"Well, I think you are rather a humbug," said Willie Woodley.

"You don't believe that—do you, Miss Alden?" asked his lordship. "You don't believe I'm a humbug, eh?"

"No," said Bessie, "I don't."

"You are too tall to stand up, Lord Lambeth," Mrs. Westgate observed. "You are only tolerable when you sit down. Be so good as to get a chair."

He found a chair and placed it sidewise, close to the two ladies. "If I hadn't met Woodley I should never have found you," he went on. "Should I, Woodley?"

"Well, I guess not," said the young American.

"Not even with my letter?" asked Mrs. Westgate.

"Ah, well, I haven't got your letter yet; I suppose I shall get it this evening. It was awfully kind of you to write."

"So I said to Bessie," observed Mrs. Westgate.

"Did she say so, Miss Alden?" Lord Lambeth inquired. "I dare say you have been here a month."

"We have been here three," said Mrs. Westgate.

"Have you been here three months?" the young man asked again of Bessie.

"It seems a long time," Bessie answered.

"I say, after that you had better not call me a humbug!" cried Lord Lambeth. "I have only been in town three weeks; but you must have been hiding away; I haven't seen you anywhere."

"Where should you have seen us—where should we have gone?" asked Mrs. Westgate.

"You should have gone to Hurlingham," said Woodley.

"No; let Lord Lambeth tell us," Mrs. Westgate insisted.

"There are plenty of places to go to," said Lord Lambeth; "each one stupider than the other. I mean people's houses; they send you cards."

"No one has sent us cards," said Bessie.

"We are very quiet," her sister declared. "We are here as travellers."

"We have been to Madame Tussaud's," Bessie pursued.

"Oh, I say!" cried Lord Lambeth.

"We thought we should find your image there," said Mrs. Westgate—"yours and Mr. Beaumont's."

"In the Chamber of Horrors?" laughed the young man.

"It did duty very well for a party," said Mrs. Westgate. "All the women were *décolletées*, and many of the figures looked as if they could speak if they tried."

"Upon my word," Lord Lambeth rejoined, "you see people at London parties that look as if they couldn't speak if they tried."

"Do you think Mr. Woodley could find us Mr. Beaumont?" asked Mrs. Westgate.

Lord Lambeth stared and looked round him. "I dare say he could. Beaumont often comes here. Don't you think you could find him, Woodley? Make a dive into the crowd."

"Thank you; I have had enough diving," said Willie Woodley. "I will wait till Mr. Beaumont comes to the surface."

"I will bring him to see you," said Lord Lambeth; "where are you staying?"

"You will find the address in my letter—Jones's Hotel."

"Oh, one of those places just out of Piccadilly? Beastly hole, isn't it?" Lord Lambeth inquired.

"I believe it's the best hotel in London," said Mrs. Westgate.

"But they give you awful rubbish to eat, don't they?" his lordship went on.

"Yes," said Mrs. Westgate.

"I always feel so sorry for the people that come up to town and go to live in those places," continued the young man. "They eat nothing but filth."

"Oh, I say!" cried Willie Woodley.

"Well, how do you like London, Miss Alden?" Lord Lambeth asked, unperturbed by this ejaculation.

"I think it's grand," said Bessie Alden.

"My sister likes it, in spite of the 'filth!' " Mrs. Westgate exclaimed.

"I hope you are going to stay a long time."

"As long as I can," said Bessie.

"And where is Mr. Westgate?" asked Lord Lambeth of this gentleman's wife.

"He's where he always is—in that tiresome New York."

"He must be tremendously clever," said the young man.

"I suppose he is," said Mrs. Westgate.

Lord Lambeth sat for nearly an hour with his American friends; but it is not our purpose to relate their conversation in full. He addressed a great many remarks to Bessie Alden, and finally turned towards her altogether, while Willie Woodley entertained Mrs. Westgate. Bessie herself said very little; she was on her guard, thinking of what her sister had said to her at lunch. Little by little, however, she interested herself in Lord Lambeth again, as she had done at Newport; only it seemed to her that here he might become more interesting. He would be an unconscious part of the antiquity, the impressiveness, the picturesqueness, of England; and poor Bessie Alden, like many a Yankee maiden, was terribly at the mercy of picturesqueness.

"I have often wished I were at Newport again," said the young man. "Those days I spent at your sister's were awfully jolly."

"We enjoyed them very much; I hope your father is better."

"Oh dear, yes. When I got to England he was out grouse-shooting. It was what you call in America a gigantic fraud. My mother had got nervous. My three weeks at Newport seemed like a happy dream."

"America certainly is very different from England," said Bessie.

"I hope you like England better, eh?" Lord Lambeth rejoined, almost persuasively.

"No Englishman can ask that seriously of a person of another country."

Her companion looked at her for a moment. You mean it's a matter of course?"

"If I were English," said Bessie, "it would certainly seem to me a matter of course that every one should be a good patriot."

"Oh dear, yes, patriotism is everything," said Lord Lambeth, not quite following, but very contented. "Now, what are you going to do here?"

"On Thursday I am going to the Tower."

"The Tower?"

"The Tower of London. Did you never hear of it?"

"Oh yes, I have been there," said Lord Lambeth. "I was taken there by my governess when I was six years old. It's a rum idea, your going there."

"Do give me a few more rum ideas," said Bessie. "I want to see everything of that sort. I am going to Hampton Court, and to Windsor, and to the Dulwich Gallery."

Lord Lambeth seemed greatly amused. "I wonder you don't go to the Rosherville Gardens."

"Are they interesting?" asked Bessie.

"Oh, wonderful!"

"Are they very old? That's all I care for," said Bessie.

"They are tremendously old; they are falling to ruins."

"I think there is nothing so charming as an old ruinous garden," said the young girl. "We must certainly go there."

Lord Lambeth broke out into merriment. "I say, Woodley," he cried, "here's Miss Alden wants to go to the Rosherville Gardens!"

Willie Woodley looked a little blank; he was caught in the fact of ignorance of an apparently conspicuous feature of London life. But in a moment he turned it off. "Very well," he said, "I'll write for a permit."

Lord Lambeth's exhilaration increased. "Gad, I believe you Americans would go anywhere!" he cried.

"We wish to go to Parliament," said Bessie. "That's one of the first things."

"Oh, it would bore you to death!" cried the young man.

"We wish to hear you speak."

"I never speak—except to young ladies," said Lord Lambeth, smiling.

Bessie Alden looked at him a while, smiling, too, in the shadow of her parasol. "You are very strange," she murmured. "I don't think I approve of you."

"Ah, now, don't be severe, Miss Alden," said Lord Lambeth, smiling still more. "Please don't be severe. I want you to like me—awfully."

"To like you awfully?" You must not laugh at me, then, when I make mistakes. I consider it my right, as a free-born American, to make as many mistakes as I choose."

"Upon my word I didn't laugh at you," said Lord Lambeth.

"And not only that," Bessie went on; "but I hold that all my mistakes shall be set down to my credit. You must think the better of me for them."

"I can't think better of you than I do," the young man declared.

Bessie Alden looked at him a moment. "You certainly speak very well to young ladies. But why don't you address the House?—isn't that what they call it?"

"Because I have nothing to say," said Lord Lambeth.

"Haven't you a great position?" asked Bessie Alden.

He looked a moment at the back of his glove. "I'll set that down," he said, "as one of your mistakes to your credit." And as if he disliked talking about his position, he changed the subject. "I wish you would let me go with you to the Tower, and to Hampton Court, and to all those other places."

"We shall be most happy," said Bessie.

"And of course I shall be delighted to show you the House of Lords—some day that suits you. There are a lot of things I want to do for you. I want to make you have a good time. And I should like very much to present some of my friends to you, if it wouldn't bore you. Then it would be awfully kind of you to come down to Branches."

"We are much obliged to you, Lord Lambeth," said Bessie. "What is Branches?"

"It's a house in the country. I think you might like it."

Willie Woodley and Mrs. Westgate at this moment were sitting in silence, and the young man's ear caught these last words of Lord Lambeth's. "He's inviting Miss Bessie to one of his castles," he murmured to his companion.

Mrs. Westgate, foreseeing what she mentally called "complications," immediately got up; and the two ladies, taking leave of Lord Lambeth, returned, under Mr. Woodley's conduct, to Jones's Hotel.

Lord Lambeth came to see them on the morrow, bringing Percy Beaumont with him—the latter having instantly declared his intention of neglecting none of the usual offices of civility. This declaration, however, when his kinsman informed him of the advent of their American friends, had been preceded by another remark.

"Here they are, then, and you are in for it."

"What am I in for?" demanded Lord Lambeth.

"I will let your mother give it a name. With all respect to whom," added Percy Beaumont, "I must decline on this occasion to do any more police duty. Her Grace must look after you yourself."

"I will give her a chance," said her Grace's son, a trifle grimly. "I shall make her go and see them."

"She won't do it, my boy."

"We'll see if she doesn't," said Lord Lambeth.

But if Percy Beaumont took a sombre view of the arrival of the two ladies at Jones's Hotel, he was sufficiently a man of the world to offer them a smiling countenance. He fell into animated conversation—conversation, at least, that was animated on her side—with Mrs. Westgate, while his companion made himself agreeable to the young lady. Mrs. Westgate began confessing and protesting, declaring and expounding.

"I must say London is a great deal brighter and prettier just now than when I was here last—in the month of November. There is evidently a great deal going on, and you seem to have a good many flowers. I have no doubt it is very charming for all you people, and that you amuse yourselves immensely. It is very good of you to let Bessie and me come and sit and look at you. I suppose you think I am satirical, but I must confess that that's the feeling I have in London."

"I am afraid I don't quite understand to what feeling you allude," said Percy Beaumont.

"The feeling that it's all very well for you English people. Everything is beautifully arranged for you."

"It seems to me it is very well for some Americans, sometimes," rejoined Beaumont.

"For some of them, yes—if they like to be patronized. But I must say I don't like to be patronized. I may be very eccentric and undisciplined and outrageous, but I confess I never was fond of patronage. I like to associate with people on the same terms as I do in my own country; that's a peculiar taste that I have. But here people seem to expect something else—Heaven knows what! I am afraid you will think I am very ungrateful, for I certainly have received a great deal of attention. The last time I was here, a lady sent me a message that I was at liberty to come and see her."

"Dear me! I hope you didn't go," observed Percy Beaumont.

"You are deliciously naïve, I must say that for you!" Mrs. Westgate exclaimed. "It must be a great advantage to you here in London. I suppose if I myself had a little more naïvete, I should enjoy it more. I should be content to sit on a chair in the park, and see the people pass, and be told that this is the Duchess of Suffolk, and that is the Lord Chamberlain, and that I must be thankful for the privilege of beholding them. I dare say it is very wicked and critical of me to ask for anything else. But I was always critical, and I freely confess to the sin of being fastidious. I am told there is some remarkably superior second-rate society provided here for strangers. Merci! I don't want any superior second-rate society. I want the society that I have been accustomed to."

"I hope you don't call Lambeth and me second-rate," Beaumont interposed.

"Oh, I am accustomed to you," said Mrs. Westgate. "Do you know that you English sometimes make the most wonderful speeches? The first time I came to London I went out to dine— as I told you, I have received a great deal of attention. After dinner, in the drawing-room I had some conversation with an old lady; I assure you I had. I forget what we talked about, but she presently said, in allusion to something we were discussing, 'Oh, you know, the aristocracy do so-and-so; but in one's own class of life it is very different.' In one's own class of life! What is a poor unprotected American woman to do in a country where she is liable to have that sort of thing said to her?"

"You seem to get hold of some very queer old ladies; I compliment you on your acquaintance!" Percy Beaumont exclaimed. "If you are trying to bring me to admit that London is an odious place, you'll not succeed. I'm extremely fond of it, and I think it the jolliest place in the world."

"*Pour vous autres*. I never said the contrary," Mrs. Westgate retorted. I make use of this expression, because both interlocutors had begun to raise their voices. Percy Beaumont naturally did not like to hear his country abused, and Mrs. Westgate, no less naturally, did not like a stubborn debater.

"Hallo!" said Lord Lambeth; "what are they up to now?" And he came away from the window, where he had been standing with Bessie Alden.

"I quite agree with a very clever countrywoman of mine," Mrs. Westgate continued, with charming ardor, though with imperfect relevancy. She smiled at the two gentlemen for a moment with terrible brightness, as if to toss at their feet—upon their native heath —the gauntlet of defiance. "For me there are only two social positions worth speaking of—that of an American lady, and that of the Emperor of Russia."

"And what do you do with the American gentlemen?" asked Lord Lambeth.

"She leaves them in America!" said Percy Beaumont.

On the departure of their visitors, Bessie Alden told her sister that Lord Lambeth would come the next day, to go with them to the Tower, and that he had kindly offered to bring his "trap," and drive them thither.

Mrs. Westgate listened in silence to this communication, and for some time afterwards she said nothing. But at last: "If you had not requested me the other day not to mention it," she began, "there is something I should venture to ask you." Bessie frowned a little; her dark blue eyes were more dark than blue. But her sister went on. "As it is, I will take the risk. You are not in love with Lord Lambeth: I believe it, perfectly. Very good. But is there, by chance, any danger of your becoming so? It's a very simple question; don't take offence. I have a particular reason," said Mrs. Westgate, "for wanting to know."

Bessie Alden for some moments said nothing; she only looked displeased. "No; there is no danger," she answered at last, curtly.

"Then I should like to frighten them," declared Mrs. Westgate, clasping her jewelled hands.

"To frighten whom?"

"All these people; Lord Lambeth's family and friends."

"How should you frighten them?" asked the young girl.

"It wouldn't be I—it would be you. It would frighten them to think that you should absorb his lordship's young affections."

Bessie Alden, with her clear eyes still overshadowed by her dark brows, continued to interrogate. "Why should that frighten them?"

Mrs. Westgate poised her answer with a smile before delivering it. "Because they think you are not good enough. You are a charming girl, beautiful and amiable, intelligent and clever, and as *bien-élevée* as it is possible to be; but you are not a fit match for Lord Lambeth."

Bessie Alden was decidedly disgusted. "Where do you get such extraordinary ideas?" she asked. "You have said some such strange things lately. My dear Kitty, where do you collect them?"

Kitty was evidently enamoured of her idea. "Yes, it would put them on pins and needles, and it wouldn't hurt you. Mr. Beaumont is already most uneasy; I could soon see that."

The young girl meditated a moment. "Do you mean that they spy upon him—that they interfere with him?"

"I don't know what power they have to interfere, but I know that a British mamma may worry her son's life out."

It has been intimated that, as regards certain disagreeable things, Bessie Alden had a fund of scepticism. She abstained on the present occasion from expressing disbelief, for she wished not to irritate her sister. But she said to herself that Kitty had been misinformed —that this was a traveller's tale. Though she was a girl of lively imagination, there could in the nature of things be, to her sense, no reality in the idea of her belonging to vulgar category. What she said aloud was, "I must say that in that case I am very sorry for Lord Lambeth."

Mrs. Westgate, more and more exhilarated by her scheme, was smiling at her again. "If I could only believe it was safe!" she exclaimed. "When you begin to pity him, I, on my side, am afraid."

"Afraid of what?"

"Of your pitying him too much."

Bessie Alden turned away impatiently; but at the end of a minute she turned back. "What if I should pity him too much?" she asked.

Mrs. Westgate hereupon turned away, but after a moment's reflection she also faced her sister again. "It would come, after all, to the same thing," she said.

Lord Lambeth came the next day with his trap, and the two ladies, attended by Willie Woodley, placed themselves under his guidance, and were conveyed eastward, through some of the dusker portions of the metropolis, to the great turreted donjon which overlooks the London shipping. They all descended from their vehicle and entered the famous enclosure; and they secured the services of a venerable beef-eater, who, though there were many other claimants for legendary information, made a fine exclusive party of them, and marched them through the courts and corridors, through armories and prisons. He delivered his usual peripatetic discourse, and they stopped and stared, and peeped and stooped, according to the official admonitions. Bessie Alden asked the old man in the crimson doublet a great many questions; she thought it a most fascinating place. Lord Lambeth was in high good-humor; he was constantly laughing; he enjoyed what he would have called the lark. Willie Woodley kept looking at the ceilings and tapping the walls with the knuckle of a pearl-gray glove; and Mrs. Westgate, asking at frequent intervals to be allowed to sit down and wait till they came back, was as frequently informed that they would never come back. To a great many of Bessie's questions—chiefly on collateral points of English history—the ancient warder was naturally unable to reply; whereupon she always appealed to Lord Lambeth. But his lordship was very ignorant. He declared that he knew nothing about that sort of thing, and he seemed greatly diverted at being treated as an authority.

"You can't expect every one to know as much as you," he said.

"I should expect you to know a great deal more," declared Bessie Alden.

"Women always know more than men about names and dates, and that sort of thing," Lord Lambeth rejoined. "There was Lady Jane Grey we have just been hearing about, who went in for Latin and Greek, and all the learning of her age."

"*You* have no right to be ignorant, at all events," said Bessie.

"Why haven't I as good a right as any one else?"

"Because you have lived in the midst of all these things."

"What things do you mean? Axes, and blocks, and thumb-screws?"

"All these historical things. You belong to a historical family."

"Bessie is really too historical," said Mrs. Westgate, catching a word of this dialogue.

"Yes, you are too historical," said Lord Lambeth, laughing, but thankful for a formula. "Upon my honor, you are too historical!"

He went with the ladies a couple of days later to Hampton Court, Willie Woodley being also of the party. The afternoon was charming, the famous horse-chestnuts were in blossom, and Lord Lambeth, who quite entered into the spirit of the cockney excursionist, declared that it was a jolly old place. Bessie Alden was in ecstasies; she went about murmuring and exclaiming.

"It's too lovely," said the young girl; "it's too enchanting; it's too exactly what it ought to be!"

At Hampton Court the little flocks of visitors are not provided with an official bell-wether, but are left to browse at discretion upon the local antiquities. It happened in this manner that, in default of another informant, Bessie Alden, who on doubtful questions was able to suggest a great many alternatives, found herself again applying for intellectual assistance to Lord Lambeth. But he again assured her that he was utterly helpless in such matters—that his education had been sadly neglected.

"And I am sorry it makes you unhappy," he added, in a moment.

"You are very disappointing, Lord Lambeth," she said.

"Ah, now, don't say that!" he cried. "That's the worst thing you could possibly say."

"No," she rejoined, "it is not so bad as to say that I had expected nothing of you."

"I don't know. Give me a notion of the sort of thing you expected."

"Well," said Bessie Alden, "that you would be more what I should like to be—what I should try to be—in your place."

"Ah, my place!" exclaimed Lord Lambeth. "You are always talking about my place!"

The young girl looked at him; he thought she colored a little; and for a moment she made no rejoinder.

"Does it strike you that I am always talking about your place?" she asked.

"I am sure you do it a great honor," he said, fearing he had been uncivil.

"I have often thought about it," she went on, after a moment. "I have often thought about your being a hereditary legislator. A hereditary legislator ought to know a great many things."

"Not if he doesn't legislate."

"But you do legislate; it's absurd your saying you don't. You are very much looked up to here—I am assured of that."

"I don't know that I ever noticed it."

"It is because you are used to it, then. You ought to fill the place."

"How do you mean to fill it?" asked Lord Lambeth.

"You ought to be very clever and brilliant, and to know almost everything."

Lord Lambeth looked at her a moment. "Shall I tell you something?" he asked. "A young man in my position, as you call it——"

"I didn't invent the term," interposed Bessie Alden. "I have seen it in a great many books."

"Hang it! you are always at your books. A fellow in my position, then, does very well whatever he does. That's about what I mean to say."

"Well, if your own people are content with you," said Bessie Alden, laughing, "it is not for me to complain. But I shall always think that, properly, you should have been a great mind—a great character."

"Ah, that's very theoretic," Lord Lambeth declared. "Depend upon it, that's a Yankee prejudice."

"Happy the country," said Bessie Alden, "where even people's prejudices are so elevated!"

"Well, after all," observed Lord Lambeth, "I don't know that I am such a fool as you are trying to make me out."

"I said nothing so rude as that; but I must repeat that you are disappointing."

"My dear Miss Alden," exclaimed the young man, "I am the best fellow in the world!"

"Ah, if it were not for that!" said Bessie Alden, with a smile.

Mrs. Westgate had a good many more friends in London than she pretended, and before long she had renewed acquaintance with most of them. Their hospitality was extreme, so that, one thing leading to another, she began, as the phrase is, to go out. Bessie Alden, in this way, saw something of what she found it a great satisfaction to call to herself English society. She went to balls and danced, she went to dinners and talked, she went to concerts and listened (at concerts Bessie always listened), she went to exhibitions and wondered. Her enjoyment was keen and her curiosity insatiable, and, grateful in general for all her opportunities, she especially prized the privilege of meeting certain celebrated persons—authors and artists, philosophers and statesmen—of whose renown she had been a humble and distant beholder, and who now, as a part of the habitual furniture of London drawing-rooms, struck her as stars fallen from the firmament and become palpable—revealing also sometimes, on contact, qualities not to have been predicted of sidereal bodies.

Bessie, who knew so many of her contemporaries by reputation, had a good many personal disappointments; but, on the other hand, she had innumerable satisfactions and enthusiasms, and she communicated the emotions of either class to a dear friend of her own sex in Boston, with whom she was in voluminous correspondence. Some of her reflections, indeed, she attempted to impart to Lord Lambeth, who came almost every day to Jones's Hotel, and whom Mrs. Westgate admitted to be really devoted. Captain Littledale, it appeared, had gone to India; and of several others of Mrs. Westgate's ex-pensioners—gentlemen who, as she said, had made, in New York, a clubhouse of her drawing-room—no tidings were to be obtained; but Lord Lambeth was certainly attentive enough to make up for the accidental absences, the short memories, all the other irregularities, of every one else. He drove them in the park, he took them to visit private collections of pictures, and, having a house of his own, invited them to dinner. Mrs. Westgate, following the fashion of many of her compatriots, caused herself and her sister to be presented at the English court by her diplomatic representative—for it was in this manner that she alluded to the American minister to England, inquiring what on earth he was put there for, if not to make the proper arrangements for one's going to a Drawing-room.

Lord Lambeth declared that he hated Drawing-rooms, but he participated in the ceremony on the day on which the two ladies at Jones's Hotel repaired to Buckingham Palace in a remarkable coach which his lordship had sent to fetch them. He had a gorgeous uniform, and Bessie Alden was particularly struck with his appearance, especially when on her asking him—rather foolishly, as she felt—if he were a loyal subject, he replied that he was a loyal subject to *her*. This declaration was emphasized by his dancing with her at a royal ball to which the two ladies afterwards went, and was not impaired by the fact that she thought he danced very ill. He seemed to her wonderfully kind; she asked herself, with growing vivacity, why he should be so kind. It was his disposition—that seemed the natural answer. She had told her sister that she liked him very much, and now that she liked him more she wondered why. She liked him for his disposition; to this question as well that seemed the natural answer. When once the impressions of London life began to crowd thickly upon her she completely forgot her sister's warning about the cynicism of public opinion. It had given her great pain at the moment, but there was no particular reason why she should remember it; it corresponded too little with any sensible reality; and it was disagreeable to Bessie to remember disagreeable things. So she was not haunted with the sense of a vulgar imputation. She was not in love with Lord Lambeth—she assured herself of that.

It will immediately be observed that when such assurances become necessary the state of a young lady's affections is already ambiguous; and, indeed, Bessie Alden made no attempt to dissimulate —to herself, of course—a certain tenderness that she felt for the young nobleman. She said to herself that she liked the type to which he belonged—the simple, candid, manly, healthy English temperament. She spoke to herself of him as women speak of young men they like—alluded to his bravery (which she had never in the least seen tested), to his honesty and gentlemanliness, and was not silent upon the subject of his good looks. She was perfectly conscious, moreover, that she liked to think of his more adventitious merits; that her imagination was excited and gratified by the sight of a handsome young man endowed with such large opportunities— opportunities she hardly knew for what, but, as she supposed, for doing great things—for setting an example, for exerting an influence, for conferring happiness, for encouraging the arts. She had a kind of ideal of conduct for a young man who should find himself in this magnificent position, and she tried to adapt it to Lord Lambeth's deportment, as you might attempt to fit a silhouette in cut paper upon a shadow projected upon a wall.

But Bessie Alden's silhouette refused to coincide with his lordship's image, and this want of harmony sometimes vexed her more than she thought reasonable. When he was absent it was, of course, less striking; then he seemed to her a sufficiently graceful combination of high responsibilities and amiable qualities. But when he sat there within sight, laughing and talking with his customary good-humor and simplicity, she measured it more accurately, and she felt acutely that if Lord Lambeth's position was heroic, there was but little of the hero in the young man himself. Then her imagination wandered away from him—very far away; for it was an incontestable fact that at such moments he seemed distinctly dull. I am afraid that while Bessie's imagination was thus invidiously roaming, she cannot have been herself a very lively companion; but it may well have been that these occasional fits of indifference seemed to Lord Lambeth a part of the young girl's personal charm. It had been a part of this charm from the first that he felt that she judged him and measured him more freely and irresponsibly—more at her ease and her leisure, as it were—than several young ladies with whom he had been, on the whole, about as intimate. To feel this, and yet to feel that she also liked him, was very agreeable to Lord Lambeth. He fancied he had compassed that gratification so desirable to young men of title and fortune—being liked for himself. It is true that a cynical counsellor might have whispered to him, "Liked for yourself? Yes; but not so very much!" He had, at any rate, the constant hope of being liked more.

It may seem, perhaps, a trifle singular—but it is nevertheless true—that Bessie Alden, when he struck her as dull, devoted some time, on grounds of conscience, to trying to like him more. I say on grounds of conscience, because she felt that he had been extremely "nice" to her sister, and because she reflected that it was no more than fair that she should think as well of him as he thought of her. This effort was possibly sometimes not so successful as it might have been, for the result of it was occasionally a vague irritation, which expressed itself in hostile criticism of several British institutions. Bessie Alden went to some entertainments at which she met Lord Lambeth; but she went to others at which his lordship was neither actually nor potentially present; and it was chiefly on these latter occasions that she encountered those literary and artistic celebrities of whom mention has been made. After a while she reduced the matter to a principle. If Lord Lambeth should appear anywhere, it was a symbol that there would be no poets and philosophers; and in consequence—for it was almost a strict consequence—she used to enumerate to the young man these objects of her admiration.

"You seem to be awfully fond of those sort of people," said Lord Lambeth one day, as if the idea had just occurred to him.

"They are the people in England I am most curious to see," Bessie Alden replied.

"I suppose that's because you have read so much," said Lord Lambeth, gallantly.

"I have not read so much. It is because we think so much of them at home."

"Oh, I see," observed the young nobleman. "In Boston."

"Not only in Boston; everywhere," said Bessie. "We hold them in great honor; they go to the best dinner-parties."

"I dare say you are right. I can't say I know many of them."

"It's a pity you don't," Bessie Alden declared. "It would do you good."

"I dare say it would," said Lord Lambeth, very humbly. "But I must say I don't like the looks of some of them."

"Neither do I—of some of them. But there are all kinds, and many of them are charming."

"I have talked with two or three of them," the young man went on, "and I thought they had a kind of fawning manner."

"Why should they fawn?" Bessie Alden demanded.

"I'm sure I don't know. Why, indeed?"

"Perhaps you only thought so," said Bessie.

"Well, of course," rejoined her companion, "that's a kind of thing that can't be proved."

"In America they don't fawn," said Bessie.

"Ah, well, then, they must be better company."

Bessie was silent a moment. "That is one of the things I don't like about England," she said—"your keeping the distinguished people apart."

"How do you mean apart?"

"Why, letting them come only to certain places. You never see them."

Lord Lambeth looked at her a moment. "What people do you mean?"

"The eminent people—the authors and artists—the clever people."

"Oh, there are other eminent people besides those," said Lord Lambeth.

"Well, you certainly keep them apart," repeated the young girl.

"And there are other clever people," added Lord Lambeth, simply.

Bessie Alden looked at him, and she gave a light laugh. "Not many," she said.

On another occasion—just after a dinner-party—she told him that there was something else in England she did not like.

"Oh, I say!" he cried, "haven't you abused us enough?"

"I have never abused you at all," said Bessie; "but I don't like your *precedence*."

"It isn't my precedence!" Lord Lambeth declared, laughing.

"Yes, it is yours—just exactly yours; and I think it's odious," said Bessie.

"I never saw such a young lady for discussing things! Has some one had the impudence to go before you?" asked his lordship.

"It is not the going before me that I object to," said Bessie; "it is their thinking that they have a right to do it—*a right that I recognize.*"

"I never saw such a young lady as you are for not 'recognizing.' I have no doubt the thing is *beastly*, but it saves a lot of trouble."

"It makes a lot of trouble. It's horrid," said Bessie.

"But how would you have the first people go?" asked Lord Lambeth. "They can't go last."

"Whom do you mean by the first people?"

"Ah, if you mean to question first principles!" said Lord Lambeth.

"If those are your first principles, no wonder some of your arrangements are horrid," observed Bessie Alden, with a very pretty ferocity. "I am a young girl, so of course I go last; but imagine what Kitty must feel on being informed that she is not at liberty to budge until certain other ladies have passed out."

"Oh, I say she is not 'informed'!" cried Lord Lambeth. "No one would do such a thing as that."

"She is made to feel it," the young girl insisted—"as if they were afraid she would make a rush for the door. No; you have a lovely country," said Bessie Alden, "but your precedence is horrid."

"I certainly shouldn't think your sister would like it," rejoined Lord Lambeth, with even exaggerated gravity. But Bessie Alden could induce him to enter no formal protest against this repulsive custom, which he seemed to think an extreme convenience.

Percy Beaumont all this time had been a very much less frequent visitor at Jones's Hotel than his noble kinsman; he had, in fact, called but twice upon the two American ladies. Lord Lambeth, who often saw him, reproached him with his neglect, and declared that, although Mrs. Westgate had said nothing about it, he was sure that she was secretly wounded by it. "She suffers too much to speak," said Lord Lambeth.

"That's all gammon," said Percy Beaumont; "there's a limit to what people can suffer!" And, though sending no apologies to Jones's Hotel, he undertook, in a manner, to explain his absence. "You are always there," he said, "and that's reason enough for my not going."

"I don't see why. There is enough for both of us."

"I don't care to be a witness of your—your reckless passion," said Percy Beaumont.

Lord Lambeth looked at him with a cold eye, and for a moment said nothing. "It's not so obvious as you might suppose," he rejoined, dryly, "considering what a demonstrative beggar I am."

"I don't want to know anything about it—nothing whatever," said Beaumont. "Your mother asks me every time she sees me whether I believe you are really lost—and Lady Pimlico does the same. I prefer to be able to answer that I know nothing about it— that I never go there. I stay away for consistency's sake. As I said the other day, they must look after you themselves."

"You are devilish considerate," said Lord Lambeth. "They never question me."

"They are afraid of you. They are afraid of irritating you and making you worse. So they go to work very cautiously, and, some- where or other, they get their information. They know a great deal about you. They know that you have been with those ladies to the dome of St. Paul's and—where was the other place?—to the Thames Tunnel."

If all their knowledge is as accurate as that, it must be very valuable," said Lord Lambeth.

"Well, at any rate, they know that you have been visiting the 'sights of the metropolis.' They think—very naturally, as it seems to me—that when you take to visiting the sights of the metropolis with a little American girl, there is serious cause for alarm." Lord Lam- beth responded to this intimation by scornful laughter, and his companion continued, after a pause: "I said just now I didn't want to know anything about the affair; but I will confess that I am curious to learn whether you propose to marry Miss Bessie Alden."

On this point Lord Lambeth gave his interlocutor no immediate satisfaction; he was musing, with a frown. "By Jove," he said, "they go rather too far! They *shall* find me dangerous—I promise them."

Percy Beaumont began to laugh. "You don't redeem your prom- ises. You said the other day you would make your mother call."

Lord Lambeth continued to meditate. "I asked her to call," he said, simply.

"And she declined?"

"Yes; but she shall do it yet."

"Upon my word," said Percy Beaumont, "if she gets much more frightened I believe she will." Lord Lambeth looked at him, and he went on. "She will go to the girl herself."

"How do you mean she will go to her?

"She will beg her off, or she will bribe her. She will take strong measures."

Lord Lambeth turned away in silence, and his companion watched him take twenty steps and then slowly return. "I have invited Mrs. Westgate and Miss Alden to Branches," he said, "and this evening I shall name a day."

"And shall you invite your mother and your sisters to meet them?"

"Explicitly!"

"That will set the duchess off," said Percy Beaumont. "I suspect she will come."

"She may do as she pleases."

Beaumont looked at Lord Lambeth. "You do really propose to marry the little sister, then?"

"I like the way you talk about it!" cried the young man. "She won't gobble me down; don't be afraid."

"She won't leave you on your knees," said Percy Beaumont. "What *is* the inducement?"

"You talk about proposing: wait till I *have* proposed," Lord Lambeth went on.

"That's right, my dear fellow; think about it," said Percy Beaumont.

"She's a charming girl," pursued his lordship.

"Of course she's a charming girl. I don't know a girl more charming, intrinsically. But there are other charming girls nearer home."

"I like her spirit," observed Lord Lambeth, almost as if he were trying to torment his cousin.

"What's the peculiarity of her spirit?"

"She's not afraid, and she says things out, and she thinks herself as good as any one. She is the only girl I have ever seen that was not dying to marry me."

"How do you know that, if you haven't asked her?"

"I don't know how; but I know it."

"I am sure she asked me questions enough about your property and your titles," said Beaumont.

"She has asked me questions, too; no end of them," Lord Lambeth admitted. "But she asked for information, don't you know."

"Information? Aye, I'll warrant she wanted it. Depend upon it that she is dying to marry you just as much and just as little as all the rest of them."

"I shouldn't like her to refuse me—I shouldn't like that."

"If the thing would be so disagreeable, then, both to you and to her, in Heaven's name leave it alone," said Percy Beaumont.

Mrs. Westgate, on her side, had plenty to say to her sister about the rarity of Mr. Beaumont's visits and the non-appearance of the Duchess of Bayswater. She professed, however, to derive more satisfaction from this latter circumstance than she could have done from the most lavish attentions on the part of this great lady. "It is most marked," she said—"most marked. It is a delicious proof that we have made them miserable. The day we dined with Lord Lambeth I was really sorry for the poor fellow." It will have been gathered that the entertainment offered by Lord Lambeth to his American friends·had not been graced by the presence of his anxious mother. He had invited several choice spirits to meet them; but the ladies of his immediate family were to Mrs. Westgate's sense—a sense possibly morbidly acute—conspicuous by their absence.

"I don't want to express myself in a manner that you dislike," said Bessie Alden; "but I don't know why you should have so many theories about Lord Lambeth's poor mother. You know a great many young men in New York without knowing their mothers."

Mrs. Westgate looked at her sister, and then turned away. "My dear Bessie, you are superb!" she said.

"One thing is certain," the young girl continued. "If I believed I were a cause of annoyance—however unwitting—to Lord Lambeth's family, I should insist——"

"Insist upon my leaving England," said Mrs. Westgate.

"No, not that. I want to go to the National Gallery again; I want to see Stratford-on-Avon and Canterbury Cathedral. But I should insist upon his coming to see us no more."

"That would be very modest and very pretty of you; but you wouldn't do it now."

"Why do you say 'now'?" asked Bessie Alden. "Have I ceased to be modest?"

"You care for him too much. A month ago, when you said you didn't, I believe it was quite true. But at present, my dear child," said Mrs. Westgate, "you wouldn't find it quite so simple a matter never to see Lord Lambeth again. I have seen it coming on."

"You are mistaken," said Bessie. "You don't understand."

"My dear child, don't be perverse," rejoined her sister.

"I know him better, certainly, if you mean that," said Bessie. "And I like him very much. But I don't like him enough to make trouble for him with his family. However, I don't believe in that."

"I like the way you say 'however,'" Mrs. Westgate exclaimed. "Come; you would not marry him?"

"Oh no," said the young girl.

Mrs. Westgate for a moment seemed vexed. "Why not, pray?" she demanded.

"Because I don't care to," said Bessie Alden.

The morning after Lord Lambeth had had, with Percy Beaumont, that exchange of ideas which has just been narrated. the ladies at Jones's Hotel received from his lordship a written invitation to pay their projected visit to Branches Castle on the following Tuesday. "I think I have made up a very pleasant party," the young nobleman said. "Several people whom you know, and my mother and sisters, who have so long been regrettably prevented from making your acquaintance." Bessie Alden lost no time in calling her sister's attention to the injustice she had done the Duchess of Bayswater, whose hostility was now proved to be a vain illusion.

"Wait till you see if she comes," said Mrs. Westgate. "And if she is to meet us at her son's house, the obligation was all the greater for her to call upon us."

Bessie had not to wait long, and it appeared that Lord Lambeth's mother now accepted Mrs. Westgate's view of her duties. On the morrow, early in the afternoon, two cards were brought to the apartment of the American ladies—one of them bearing the name of the Duchess of Bayswater, and the other that of the Countess of Pimlico. Mrs. Westgate glanced at the clock. "It is not yet four," she said; "they have come early; they wish to see us. We will receive them." And she gave orders that her visitors should be admitted. A few moments later they were introduced, and there was a solemn exchange of amenities. The duchess was a large lady, with a fine fresh color; the Countess of Pimlico was very pretty and elegant.

The duchess looked about her as she sat down—looked not especially at Mrs. Westgate. "I dare say my son has told you that I have been wanting to come and see you," she observed.

"You are very kind," said Mrs. Westgate, vaguely—her conscience not allowing her to assent to this proposition—and, indeed, not permitting her to enunciate her own with any appreciable emphasis.

"He says you were so kind to him in America," said the duchess.

"We are very glad," Mrs. Westgate replied, "to have been able to make him a little more—a little less—a little more comfortable."

"I think that he stayed at your house," remarked the Duchess of Bayswater, looking at Bessie Alden.

"A very short time," said Mrs. Westgate.

"Oh!" said the duchess; and she continued to look at Bessie, who was engaged in conversation with her daughter.

"Do you like London," Lady Pimlico had asked of Bessie, after looking at her a good deal—at her face and her hands, her dress and her hair.

"Very much indeed," said Bessie.

"Do you like this hotel?"

"It is very comfortable," said Bessie.

"Do you like stopping at hotels?" inquired Lady Pimlico, after a pause.

"I am very fond of travelling," Bessie answered, "and I suppose hotels are a necessary part of it. But they are not the part I am fondest of."

"Oh, I hate travelling," said the Countess of Pimlico, and transferred her attention to Mrs. Westgate.

"My son tells me you are going to Branches," the duchess said, presently.

"Lord Lambeth has been so good as to ask us," said Mrs. Westgate, who perceived that her visitor had now begun to look at her, and who had her customary happy consciousness of a distinguished appearance. The only mitigation of her felicity on this point was that, having inspected her visitor's own costume, she said to herself, "She won't know how well I am dressed!"

"He has asked me to go, but I am not sure I shall be able," murmured the duchess.

"He had offered us the p— the prospect of meeting you," said Mrs. Westgate.

"I hate the country at this season," responded the duchess.

Mrs. Westgate gave a little shrug. "I think it is pleasanter than London."

But the duchess's eyes were absent again; she was looking fixedly at Bessie. In a moment she slowly rose, walked to a chair that stood empty at the young girl's right hand, and silently seated herself. As she was a majestic, voluminous woman, this little transaction had, inevitably, an air of somewhat impressive attention. It diffused a certain awkwardness, which Lady Pimlico, as a sympathetic daughter, perhaps desired to rectify in turning to Mrs. Westgate.

"I dare say you go out a great deal," she observed.

"No, very little. We are strangers, and we didn't come here for society."

"I see," said Lady Pimlico. "It's rather nice in town just now."

"It's charming," said Mrs. Westgate. "But we only go to see a few people—whom we like."

"Of course one can't like every one," said Lady Pimlico.

"It depends upon one's society," Mrs. Westgate rejoined.

The duchess meanwhile had addressed herself to Bessie. "My son tells me the young ladies in America are so clever."

"I am glad they made so good an impression on him," said Bessie, smiling.

The duchess was not smiling; her large, fresh face was very tranquil. "He is very susceptible," she said. "He thinks every one clever, and sometimes they are."

"Sometimes," Bessie assented, smiling still.

The duchess looked at her a little, and then went on: "Lambeth is very susceptible, but he is very volatile, too."

"Volatile?" asked Bessie.

"He is very inconstant. It won't do to depend on him."

"Ah," said Bessie, "I don't recognize that description. We have depended on him greatly—my sister and I—and he has never disappointed us."

"He will disappoint you yet," said the duchess.

Bessie gave a little laugh, as if she were amused at the duchess's persistency. "I suppose it will depend on what we expect of him."

"The less you expect the better," Lord Lambeth's mother declared.

"Well," said Bessie, "we expect nothing unreasonable."

The duchess for a moment was silent, though she appeared to have more to say. "Lambeth says he has seen so much of you," she presently began.

"He has been to see us very often; he has been very kind," said Bessie Alden.

"I dare say you are used to that. I am told there is a great deal of that in America."

"A great deal of kindness?" the young girl inquired, smiling.

"Is that what you call it? I know you have different expressions."

"We certainly don't always understand each other," said Mrs. Westgate, the termination of whose interview with Lady Pimlico allowed her to give attention to their elder visitor.

"I am speaking of the young men calling so much upon the young ladies," the duchess explained.

"But surely in England," said Mrs. Westgate, "the young ladies don't call upon the young men?"

"Some of them do—almost!" Lady Pimlico declared. "When the young men are a great *parti*."

"Bessie, you must make a note of that," said Mrs. Westgate. "My sister," she added, "is a model traveller. She writes down all the curious facts she hears in a little book she keeps for the purpose."

The duchess was a little flushed; she looked all about the room, while her daughter turned to Bessie. "My brother told us you were wonderfully clever," said Lady Pimlico.

"He should have said my sister," Bessie answered—"when she says such things as that."

"Shall you be long at Branches?" the duchess asked, abruptly, of the young girl.

"Lord Lambeth has asked us for three days," said Bessie.

"I shall go," the duchess declared, "and my daughter, too."

"That will be charming!" Bessie rejoined.

"Delightful!" exclaimed Mrs. Westgate.

"I shall expect to see a great deal of you," the duchess continued. "When I go to Branches I monopolize my son's guests."

"They must be most happy," said Mrs. Westgate, very graciously.

"I want immensely to see it—to see the castle," said Bessie to the duchess. "I have never seen one—in England, at least; and you know we have none in America."

"Ah, you are fond of castles?" inquired her Grace.

"Immensely!" replied the young girl. "It has been the dream of my life to live in one."

The duchess looked at her a moment, as if she hardly knew how to take this assurance, which, from her Grace's point of view, was either very artless or very audacious. "Well," she said, rising, "I will show you Branches myself." And upon this the two great ladies took their departure.

"What did they mean by it?" asked Mrs. Westgate, when they were gone.

"They meant to be polite," said Bessie, "because we are going to meet them."

"It is too late to be polite," Mrs. Westgate replied, almost grimly. "They meant to overawe us by their fine manners and their grandeur, and to make you *lâcher prise*."

"*Lâcher prise*? What strange things you say!" murmured Bessie Alden.

"They meant to snub us, so that we shouldn't dare to go to Branches," Mrs. Westgate continued.

"On the contrary," said Bessie, "the duchess offered to show me the place herself."

"Yes, you may depend upon it she won't let you out of her sight. She will show you the place from morning till night."

"You have a theory for everything," said Bessie.

"And you apparently have none for anything."

"I saw no attempt to 'overawe' us," said the young girl. "Their manners were not fine."

"They were not even good!" Mrs. Westgate declared.

Bessie was silent for a while, but in a few moments she observed that she had a very good theory. "They came to look at me," she said, as if this had been a very ingenious hypothesis. Mrs. Westgate did it justice; she greeted it with a smile, and pronounced it most brilliant, while, in reality, she felt that the young girl's scepticism, or her charity, or, as she had sometimes called it appropriately, her idealism, was proof against irony. Bessie, however, remained meditative all the rest of the day and well on into the morrow.

On the morrow, before lunch, Mrs. Westgate had occasion to go out for an hour, and left her sister writing a letter. When she came back she met Lord Lambeth at the door of the hotel, coming away. She thought he looked slightly embarrassed; he was certainly very grave. "I am sorry to have missed you. Won't you come back?" she asked.

"No," said the young man, "I can't. I have seen your sister. I can never come back." Then he looked at her a moment, and took her hand. "Goodbye, Mrs. Westgate," he said. "You have been very kind to me." And with what she thought a strange, sad look in his handsome young face, he turned away.

She went in, and she found Bessie still writing her letter—that is, Mrs. Westgate perceived she was sitting at the table with the pen in her hand and not writing. "Lord Lambeth has been here," said the elder lady at last.

Then Bessie got up and showed her a pale, serious face. She bent this face upon her sister for some time, confessing silently and a little pleading. "I told him," she said at last, "that we could not go to Branches."

Mrs. Westgate displayed just a spark of irritation. "He might have waited," she said, with a smile, "till one had seen the castle." Later, an hour afterwards, she said, "Dear Bessie, I wish you might have accepted him."

"I couldn't," said Bessie, gently.

"He is an excellent fellow," said Mrs. Westgate.

"I couldn't," Bessie repeated.

"If it is only," her sister added, "because those women will think that they succeeded—that they paralyzed us!"

Bessie Alden turned away; but presently she added, "They were interesting; I should have liked to see them again."

"So should I!" cried Mrs. Westgate, significantly.

"And I should have liked to see the castle," said Bessie. "But now we must leave England," she added.

Her sister looked at her. "You will not wait·to go to the National Gallery?"

"Not now."

"Nor to Canterbury Cathedral?"

Bessie reflected a moment. "We can stop there on our way to Paris," she said.

Lord Lambeth did not tell Percy Beaumont that the contingency he was not prepared at all to like had occurred; but Percy Beaumont, on hearing that the two ladies had left London, wondered with some intensity what had happened—wondered, that is, until the Duchess of Bayswater came a little to his assistance. The two ladies went to Paris, and Mrs. Westgate beguiled the journey to that city by repeating several times: "That's what I regret; they will think they petrified us." But Bessie Alden seemed to regret nothing.